Penthouse
Uncensored VII

Other Books in the Series

The Editors of Penthouse

Penthouse Uncensored VII

Erotica Unbound

GRAND CENTRAL
PUBLISHING

NEW YORK   BOSTON

Grand Central Publishing
Hachette Book Group
1290 Avenue of the Americas
New York, NY 10104

www.HachetteBookGroup.com

First Edition: July 2010

Grand Central Publishing is a division of Hachette Book Group, Inc.
The Grand Central Publishing name and logo is a trademark of Hachette Book Group, Inc.

ISBN: 978-0-446-55748-1

Library of Congress Control Number: 2009942015

Contents

CONTENTS

Part One

Letters to
Penthouse VIII

Clusterfucks I

WIFE TAKES THE BAIT ON FISHING TRIP

*L*ike many men who have been married for a while, my marriage had become sexually stale. My wife, Cindy, wasn't the problem. She has kept herself in great shape. Her five-foot frame is one hundred five pounds, and her 34C-22-36 figure complements a pretty face and natural red hair. Several times I have mentioned swinging with another couple, but Cindy always got angry. I just dropped the subject and kept my fantasies to myself.

A few weeks before the end of the summer, Cindy and I went to a national forest near our home to enjoy a few days of camping and swimming. My job allows me to get away during the middle of the week, but I'm still on call via a pager. In the middle of the week we had our choice of prime camp sites and we selected a shaded one by the lakeshore. It was like having the park all to ourselves. Later that day we were disappointed when a large R.V. drove by just as Cindy was coming back from a swim. I saw the man driving checking her out. He then pulled into the site next to ours.

Cindy was ready to move camp to another site, but I talked her out of it by reminding her of the hassle of breaking camp and setting up again. While we were talking we noticed four men get out of the R.V. One was a young black man, who was about twenty years younger than the rest of the group.

Later that afternoon the men came over and introduced themselves. They were on a fishing trip and all worked for the same firm. Jim, the young black guy, was a college student working as an intern. Chris and Joe were both engineers, slightly overweight and middle-age. Kevin was tall, thickly built, with a coarse, aggressive personality. He was a production manager.

It was obvious their main reason for coming over was to get a closer look at my wife. Cindy surprised me by enjoying the attention of these men, flirting and returning their jokes. After a few beers the guys left to try to get some fishing in before nightfall. Chris came back over later and invited us to dinner.

The R.V. was a big one with all the comforts of home. While the steaks were grilled we drank red wine and let Kevin give us a tour of the motor home. I noticed a VCR in a large entertainment center and jokingly asked Kevin if he had any porno movies. He opened a cabinet door and pulled out a couple of tapes. "Like this?" he asked.

Everyone had been drinking so it didn't take much convincing to get Cindy to agree to watch at least a little of a movie. We all settled in with another drink as Jim turned down the lights. Cindy and I sat down on a low-backed couch. Chris sat down next to my wife and Kevin started the movie. It was clear to me that there was a lot of sexual tension in the room as the movie started.

The movie was a hot one: a blonde giving head to some guy built like a small horse. As the movie continued Cindy cuddled up to me and started to nibble on my ear and neck. This show of affection before these men surprised me, but also made me proud. I noticed that when the guys weren't watching the film, they were eyeing my wife's shapely, tanned legs and round, firm breasts.

About this time the blonde in the movie was taking on two men at once. She was on her hands and knees, fucking one guy and blowing another, all the while imploring the men like a wanton slut to fill her up. I sensed Cindy was thrilled by the action because she was squirming and fidgeting in her seat.

Kevin noticed this, too, and wasn't shy about cutting to the chase and breaking the ice. He looked over and asked Cindy if what she was watching looked good.

"Oh shut up Kevin," she said, but she never took her eyes off the screen. I knew then that it was now or never. I reached back and cycled my pager so it would go off.

"Well shit," I said, as the movie was shut off and the lights came back on. "I have to go into work," I told them. "Go ahead and watch the rest of the movie. I should be back in a couple of hours, max."

"Oh, all right. As long as the guys promise to behave themselves," Cindy said with a smile. Of course they were quick with their assurances that she had nothing to worry about. As I left I pushed the curtain on the door window back so there was a gap big enough to scope the action from outside. I gave Cindy a kiss and drove down the access road to an unused site about a quarter mile away. On the short walk back, my hard-on was pushing against my pants.

When I got to the R.V. I was happy to see that there was enough light on inside to see easily. The opening allowed me to see most of the living area. The movie was still on, but Joe had taken my place on the couch beside Cindy. The mood, I noticed, appeared a little cheerier, owing to the consumption of drinks while I was gone. The real clincher, however, was the location of Chris's hand. It was on Cindy's leg, stroking the top of her tan thigh with soft but deliberate caresses. When Joe scooted closer to her, Cindy sat up and downed Chris's glass of scotch in one gulp. I knew then that the dam of sexual frustration was about to break.

Everyone was watching her as she leaned back on the couch and put both arms out. Chris moved his hand inside the leg opening of her shorts. Slowly moving his hand under the loose-fitting cloth, he began to rub my wife's pussy through her panties.

"You're very juicy tonight," I heard him mutter into Cindy's ear. Joe turned and kissed Cindy's long, smooth neck as he moved his hand up and under her sweatshirt to knead her full round tits. Cindy sat up a little so Joe could pull her shirt up and over her head. He gave her other tit a nice squeeze as he placed the shirt next to her on the couch.

I was going nuts, breathing in shallow gasps and massaging my cock as this tense action unfolded. Nobody was saying anything, which gave it kind of a dramatic intensity. Cindy was doing most of the expressing, and it was all in her body language. Her eyes were almost closed to tiny slits as she pressed their heads against her heaving chest, allowing them access to her ripe melons. Their hands were in her panties. They were finger-fucking her tight twat at the same time they kissed her tits. Her eyes closed as she blanked out in sexual euphoria, giving in to the temptation of servicing a whole group of men. I loved what I was seeing.

Both Kevin and Jim had been raptly watching the show on the couch, and now Kevin got up to move the coffee table out of the way. He got down on the floor and spread my lovely wife's knees apart, exposing her panty-clad muff to the whole room. Kissing and nibbling the inside of her thighs, he reached up and pulled her shorts and panties down with the help of the other two men. As he eased the panties off her feet, Kevin took her foot and sucked on her toes.

This was too much for me, watching my beautiful naked wife about to fuck four strange men. I pulled out my cock and shot the night's first load of come into the bushes. When I looked back Kevin had his head between Cindy's legs, where he was licking and sucking away on her sweet, red-trimmed, pussy.

Chris and Joe continued to suck her tits. Jim now got into the act and moved around behind the couch. Looking down at my wife's face, he pulled down his zipper and pulled out his hard, seven-inch cock and pointed it right at her pouting lips.

Cindy gazed at his black pole as it oozed pre-come. Jim caught it with his finger and spread it over the helmet of his cock, as if he were dipping an ice cream cone in a rich topping. Cindy stared into Jim's face and, with a wicked smile, opened her mouth to accept the phallic treat.

Jim slipped his cock past her red lips and shoved it deep into her mouth. Moving his hot ebony meat in and out over my wife's pink, wet tongue was an extremely erotic sight. It really got to me and it must have done it for him, too. Jim grabbed the back of her head and thrust his dick deep into her throat until her chin was pressed against his balls. She was gagging slightly, but still sucking on him hard enough that I could plainly see the bulge of his cockhead against her cheek, sawing in and out.

Chris and Joe sat on the coffee table watching and toying with their meaty packages. Cindy sucked hard on Jim's pole, while Kevin licked her inflamed cunt. It was totally depraved, I thought, when Cindy grabbed her hot tits and squeezed and pinched her taut nipples.

Kevin got up and turned her around so she was leaning against the back of the couch. Her knees were spread on the edge of the seat. Kevin pulled down his pants and shorts, exposing his thick, hard cock. He eased it up and down Cindy's slit and between her titillating ass-cheeks.

Cindy moaned, still gurgling with a mouthful of Jim's dick. She wiggled her hot cunt back toward Kevin's probing cock. He got the head in the opening of Cindy's pussy, and held back until she was positioned as far back as she could while still keeping Jim's cock in her mouth. Kevin roughly jammed his cock to the hilt. He let it rest there for several seconds before he began to quickly stroke her. Kevin was banging Cindy so hard that Jim had to pull out of her mouth. He stood back, joining Chris and Joe in watching the free sex show.

By now, Cindy was concentrating on Kevin's dick, which was hammering her hungry cunt. Kevin grabbed her hips and stroked so hard and deep that all she could do was grunt and moan on each thrust. Finally, he came, filling her love-hole with his come and leaving Cindy wanting more. Kevin let his cock shrink out of Cindy's red-hot pussy. When he pulled out I could see their combined juices flowing down her thighs.

The other three men had been busy talking among themselves while removing their clothes. They moved the coffee table against the wall and had Cindy move to the center of the room. Chris stood behind her and reached around to cup her tits in the palm of his hands. Jim laid down on the floor and Chris guided her over to him. She leaned over Jim and placed her knees on either side of his body.

Her alabaster skin and red muff made his skin seem even darker as she reached back and placed the head of his throbbing cock against her pussy lips. The other men didn't want to miss this sight and gathered around to watch as she slowly lowered her well-lubed twat onto his pole. She sat there for a few seconds and slowly started to bob up and down.

Jim's black cock was slick and shining with my wife's love-juice as she repeatedly impaled herself on him. Chris came up and gently pushed her down so her tits jiggled over Jim's chest. Jim reached up and pinched and rubbed one while lifting his head up and taking the nipple of the other into his mouth.

Chris spread Cindy's ass-cheeks apart and slowly worked his finger deep into her ass. Cindy has never let me fuck her there, so I watched with another hard-on as Chris sawed two fingers in and out of her hole. Chris moved closer and put the head of his dick on Cindy's ass, then pushed past her sphincter and plunged into her ass.

Cindy was now in a state of passion I had never dreamed she was capable of. She tossed her head from side to side as she was being sandwiched between the salt-and-pepper team. Joe moved around and put his cock before her face. Jim and Cindy came at the same time, but Cindy continued to work on the other two men, humping back against Chris's rod and bobbing her lips on Joe's.

Joe pulled back and shot his come all over Cindy's tits, laughing and telling the others he had always wanted to do that. Cindy reached up and licked the wet cock like a lollipop until it was clean. Chris was hammering into Cindy's ass, which caused her to collapse against Jim. A few minutes later Joe filled her ass with his come, and Jim fucked her cunt.

I left then and went back to the car. Later that night when I got back to camp Cindy was already in the tent. She was almost asleep and I asked her if she had been bored without me. She laughed lightly and said she had a good time playing cards. The guys had entertained her. It's been a few months now and we are going to Jamaica for the holidays. Hopefully I'll have another reason to write later.—*R.K., Sausalito, California* ⊶▩

SOME PARTIES YOU NEVER FORGET

*L*et me tell you about a party that my husband, Gary, and I went to about five years ago. On the day of the party, Gary and I had a leisurely Saturday morning together. I woke him up by sucking his beautiful cock to life. He reciprocated by licking my nipples and clit until I screamed with joy. Most of the morning was spent making love. In spite of all of the hot action with Gary, I was still very horny.

The party was at the home of Brenda, one of my close friends from work. Most of those invited were coworkers, so I anticipated a relatively sedate party. I made it a point not to seduce or be seduced by anyone from work, feeling that I should keep my wild side separate from these people.

Because we were both horny, Gary was able to convince me to wear a backless summer dress. I was braless, wearing only bikini panties, thigh hose and garter belt. The fabric was sheer enough that my nipples and areolae were visible. The thought of showing off my big breasts excited me. I figured that Gary and I would park on the way home for some heavy necking and a little oral sex. The outfit was too sexy for my work image. They only saw me in conservative suits and dresses.

When we arrived, I could tell that several of the men appreciated this new look. After two or three drinks, I relaxed and enjoyed all of the attention I was getting. Most of those at the party were married couples, but there were a few who didn't bring their spouses. One who came alone was Dave, Brenda's new boss. She had told me how hot he made her just working together. I knew that she would love to have him make a move on her.

He was in his forties, at least fifteen years older than Brenda and me. Dave was tall, athletic and had great blue eyes. In spite of his quiet, mature manner, I found myself getting turned on when he talked to me at the office. I loved the way he looked at me.

Brenda had a very revealing dress on, cut low between her breasts, barely concealing her nipples. It also was slit on the side showing her leg to mid-thigh. The green dress was a dramatic contrast to her white skin and beautiful red hair. Looking at this outfit, I wondered if she had known that Dave's wife wouldn't be there. They stood in a corner talking, very close to one another. Dave's eyes roamed over her exposed cleavage. It made me hot to watch them, but I was concerned that Brenda's husband, Jerry, might become upset. I decided to find him and keep him away from Brenda and Dave.

As I looked for Jerry in the crowd, I saw Gary dancing with Tina, one of my friends who was there alone. She didn't get enough attention from her husband and always wanted to hear about my sex life. I knew that Gary turned her on. Maybe I should let him seduce her tonight, I thought. As horny as she was, I knew that he would drive her crazy. He would love to put his tongue in her sweet little pussy.

She held his face in her hands as they danced, staring into his blue eyes. One of Gary's hands was slowly caressing her ass, cupping her cheeks. I knew that he would go much further if Tina let him. Either way, Gary would be extra hot for my pussy when we got home. Thinking about this, I smiled.

Looking around the room again, I spotted Jerry. He was a handsome man, with blond hair, full beard and moustache. He was talking to Doug, a sexy black man who had worked with me for the past year and lived next door to Brenda and Jerry. Doug also played on the company's coed softball team with me and loved to flirt and tease when his wife was not around. She was out of town on business, so I knew Doug would be in good form tonight.

They both smiled at me as I approached. "That's a very sexy dress,

Pam. I've never seen you in anything more becoming." Jerry said. Doug didn't say a word, but his eyes were glued to my breasts. His stare caused my nipples to grow hot and hard.

"Thank you. It's nice of you to notice," I responded. "Since you're so sweet, would you like to dance? It looks like I've lost Gary."

Jerry didn't answer, but took my hand and led me to a corner of the room. He pulled me against him as we began to dance. His hands explored the bare flesh of my back as we moved with the music. The feel of him against me made me hot. I knew I would have to be careful and control my emotions.

Luckily the next song was a fast rock number. Doug appeared and led me back to dance with him. As I moved to the music, my breasts moved wildly against the fabric of my dress. Doug smiled as he watched my breasts, a wicked grin covering his face.

I found myself getting horny. It was exciting to display my sexy side to my coworkers. Shaking my tits even more, I began to move my ass under the short skirt, turning to make sure that Doug had a good view of both. My feelings were getting out of hand, but I really didn't want to misbehave in front of these people from work. The impact of my behavior on the other men was predictable. I was a popular dance partner for the next three hours. I did not miss a fast or slow dance. Many different hands caressed my back and ass as I danced with the men. But I liked dancing with Jerry and Doug the best. It was their flirting and touching that turned me on.

At about one-thirty the crowd began to thin out. As a slow number began, Doug appeared and pulled me to him, pressing my breasts against his muscular body. While we danced, he talked softly in my ear, telling me how beautiful my breasts looked in the soft dress.

"Honey, you always look great, but your breasts are fantastic without a bra. I can tell that you love showing them off. You need to let me see them. I'll bet you have never had them licked by a black man. I know how hot I would make you if my beautiful black skin touched those sexy white titties. I'll bet you love to have your titties fucked. You need to have my big, black cock rubbing on your nipples and squirting all over you. I'll bet your pussy is wet just thinking about it."

He was right. My panties were soaked.

As he talked his hands caressed my ass. He reached under the hem of my dress and his long fingers stroked the crack of my ass. His fingertips traced the lips of my pussy through the soft lace. His talk and touch made me even wetter. Before he could do more, a rock number began, saving me from my sexy thoughts. My body shook to the music. Dave and Brenda were dancing near me. As she danced, the slit in her dress would open to reveal glimpses of her panties and stocking tops. Dave's eyes were glued to her body as she moved.

I decided to distract him before Jerry noticed the sexual tension between them. I danced very close to them, then turned quickly to rub my braless breasts against Dave's arm. As he turned and reached for me to apologize, I moved again so that his hand ran across both of my breasts, touching my erect nipples. This produced a reaction in me that I had not anticipated. My pussy was on fire, needing a mouth or cock to make love to it.

Dave laughed, saying he was sorry, but his face was flushed and he watched me until the song ended. Brenda headed toward the bathroom, as a slow dance began. Dave came toward me and took my hand, leading me back to dance. He pulled me tightly against his body, with his hands on my hips as we moved to the music.

"I really wasn't sorry that happened," he said, grinning. "Judging from how your breasts felt, you weren't either. I've always loved looking at your beautiful face, but I never knew what a fantastic body you were hiding under your suits at work. Or how much you liked to play and show off. I noticed that nobody could keep their hands off of your cute fanny, and I am jealous. But I think they were missing the two best parts. Your husband shouldn't let you go out like this. I won't be able to concentrate anymore at work when you are around."

As he spoke, he moved his hands to my back, running them over the bare flesh. His arms were so long that they easily wrapped around me. He ran his fingers under the fabric of my dress, stroking the sides of my breasts, almost reaching the nipples. My body responded to his touch. I wanted more. I needed for him to play with my nipples. Closing my eyes, I imagined the feel of his face against my thighs, his mouth kissing my pussy.

Almost involuntarily, I brushed my leg between his, feeling his hard cock on my thigh. He took my hand and put it between us, on his cock. It was hot and very big. As he held my hand there, I traced my fingers over the head. Moving my fingers over his bulge, I could feel the wetness of his pre-come through his slacks. I raised my wet fingertips to my lips and licked them, looking into his eyes.

"Something on my fingers sure tastes good," I said, smiling at him. Before we could go further, Brenda came back to take Dave away. I hadn't seen Gary for over an hour when he appeared to dance a slow number with me.

"It looks like you're having a good time," he said.

"I saw the big boss trying to get into your panties." As he talked, he leaned forward to kiss me, frenching me with passion. Watching me with Dave had made him hot too.

I asked, "Do you want to watch him suck my nipples? Or would you like to see him eat my pussy?" I could tell that this talk was turning Gary on. And me too. Until now, Gary had only had me tell him about my experiences with other men. Maybe it was time to let him watch, I knew that it would turn me on to perform for him, and I was sure it would make him hot too.

Heated up from these thoughts, I headed for the restroom with Gary when the music stopped. Looking in the mirror, my nipples were still hard and clearly visible through the fabric of my dress. Standing behind me, Gary squeezed them with his fingers, causing me to shudder. Turning me around, he kneeled and slid my panties down my thighs. Leaning forward, he put his mouth on my cunt, licking the swollen lips.

"You're sure wet. Did someone already play with this sweet pussy?" he asked.

"Not yet. Eat my pussy now. Make me come," I begged. It only took a minute for Gary to send me over the edge. As my body relaxed, I had to taste Gary's cock. Pushing him against the sink, I undid his belt and zipper to reveal his meat.

"Do you want to watch me with Dave later tonight? He has me so turned on that I have to fuck him." I said, licking the head of Gary's cock. Undoing my dress to expose my breasts, I asked, "Do you think he will like these?"

"You will drive him crazy with that body. You know I want to see you with him. How can you fix it so that I can watch?" he asked.

"Don't worry. I'll find a way," I responded. "You play with Tina to stay horny. Drive her home. I know that she wants to suck you off.

And you'll love to touch her little titties. Just be home before two-thirty. I'll find a way to get Dave away from Brenda long enough for him to take me home. Once we're in the house, he won't be able to resist my goodies."

With that, I worked on Gary's cock until he filled my mouth with his come. Standing, we kissed tenderly and Gary went back to the party as I fixed my dress. Opening the bathroom door, I looked into Jerry's smiling face.

"I brought you a tequila shooter. I think you will like it," he said. He took my hand and led me into a room away from the party. He then took the glass and raised it to his lips, taking a large swig. Lowering the glass, he put his hand behind my head and pulled my mouth to his.

Surprised, I felt his tongue go between my teeth, then tasted the tequila. Swallowing, I said, "That was nice, but you are very naughty. We are both married and we can't do this."

Ignoring me, he raised the glass again, taking another mouthful. Again he pulled my face to his in a kiss. This time my lips opened and I ran my tongue into his mouth, drinking in the booze. I wanted Dave, but Jerry was making my pussy hot now. My panties were drenched again.

I knew that I was losing the battle to control my emotions. I also knew what to say to make Jerry try harder. "We have to stop now, Jerry. I'm only human and you're turning me on. Brenda is my good friend. We can't do this."

With that, he pulled me to him as his beard rubbed my face. Automatically, my arms wrapped around his neck, pulling him to me as my mouth opened to accept his tongue. I loved the feel of his hands as they caressed my naked back.

"Don't worry about Brenda. She told me earlier what she had planned. It was no accident that her boss showed up without his wife." As Jerry kissed me again, I felt hands cup and caress my ass. Turning, I saw Doug. He put his hands on my face and kissed me, running his thick tongue into my mouth. My battle to maintain my work image was quickly being lost.

"Relax and enjoy, Pam. You obviously need more loving than Gary can give you. You need to try two men at once and let yourself go. See how hot we can make you," Doug said, reaching under my dress to run his long fingers over my pussy again. My panties were getting wetter as he rubbed my clit. I pulled his face to my mouth, opening my lips to suck in his tongue. Gently, he slid his fingers under the leg of my panties to touch my pussy lips.

"I knew you were wet," he said as his fingers stroked my pussy.

"Come with us for a minute and we'll show you something that will really make you hot," Jerry said. With that, they led me out a back door and around the side of the house. Jerry motioned for me to be quiet as we neared his bedroom window. A soft light came through the louvers and I could hear Brenda's voice. "Oh yes, Dave, tell me, please."

"You've made me hot since my first day in the office. When I saw you leaning over a file cabinet, showing those beautiful legs, I wanted them wrapped around my neck so I could lick your sweet pussy. I wanted you to take my cock and suck it until my come shot all over you."

As Dave talked, I saw him unzip Brenda's dress, easing the fabric down her arms to expose her bra. Brenda then took a step back, pushing her dress over her hips. As it fell to the floor, I noticed that her panties were around her knees, leaving the beautiful red hair on her pussy exposed to view. Dave had been busy even before we got to the window. Brenda reached to put her panties and dress on a chair, followed by her bra. She then stood to proudly display her body, clad only in hose and garter belt. Dave quickly leaned down to lick her nipples.

"Please let me see your cock. I've wanted it for two months. I'll take it in my mouth and suck it until you come. I'm so glad you came to my party," Brenda said.

Dave pulled his shirt over his head. He then reached to undo his belt, stepping out of his pants and shoes. Standing in briefs, he said, "You come take these off, Brenda. Then we will 69 until we both come."

Kneeling, she pulled his briefs off. His cock stood out, about seven inches long and incredibly thick. While Brenda licked Dave's cock, I felt Doug and Jerry's hands undo my dress, letting it fall to expose my naked breasts. Their hands worked on the hot flesh of my breasts as I watched Brenda and Dave fall to the bed in a hot 69. Dave was working his tongue in and out of her pussy as she bucked on the bed.

I was definitely hot. I was somewhat surprised that Jerry seemed to be turned on by his wife fucking other men, but also glad. As we watched, Brenda got on her knees while Dave fucked her from behind. Watching him pull her nipples while they fucked made me need a cock. It had been a long time since I had made love to two men at once. But I wanted Jerry and Doug now. Turning, I kissed Doug and then Jerry. Then I pulled a mouth to each of my breasts. They licked and sucked them until I could not stand it. Taking my hands, they led me to Doug's house, not bothering to cover my naked tits. Fortunately, no one saw me in my partially clothed state as we left the party.

We went in to the master bedroom and Jerry removed my dress. He sat me on the king-size bed and began to lick my cunt through my panties. I could not believe how good his hairy face felt against my thighs. He pulled my panties off and ran his tongue over my clit, back and forth until I was bouncing on the bed in anticipation. I reached to take off my garter belt, but Doug stopped me.

"You look fantastic like that," he said. Doug had taken his clothes off and climbed on the bed to lick my breasts while Jerry ate my cunt. His body was gorgeous, with large muscular shoulders and chest. His small hips set off a long, very thick cock. I laid back on the bed to touch his tool while Jerry's mouth devoured me. The black cock looked beautiful in contrast with my white skin. My body shook in a climax as soon as I put Doug's cock in my mouth. I continued to lick and suck, needing to taste his come.

Just as Doug was about to climax, Jerry pulled me to my feet and kissed me. The taste of my juices on his beard was great. I needed a cock in me now. "Suck my cock, Pam. I need that," Jerry said. "Show me what a hot woman you are."

I sat back on the bed and pulled his belt and pants off to see his bikini underwear. Pulling them down, I looked at his beautiful cock, devouring it with my wet lips. I wanted to suck him more, but I wanted Doug's thick muscle in me too. While I continued my blow-job on Jerry, I got on my knees with my ass high in the air, toward Doug. He quickly went to work on my pussy with his tongue. With one hand, I reached back for Doug's cock, pulling it toward my hot cunt. He pushed the fat head into me, stretching me. Finally, he pushed it all into me, taking my breath away with its size.

I was on fire, working my pussy on Doug while I ate Jerry's cock. Jerry was also driving me crazy, playing with my breasts and nipples. I had almost forgotten how fantastic it could be with more than one man.

Watching Brenda must have turned Jerry on too much, because he quickly squirted his come into my mouth. I licked the head clean, smiling up at him. Then I concentrated all my energy on Doug, working my hips and ass against his cock. He did not last long, filling my pussy with his come. I was not done. I wanted more fucking and more cock in my mouth. "Please fuck me now, Jerry. I need to feel you inside me."

He sat on a chair and pulled me on his lap, my back against him as he put his cock into me. Doug stood in front of me, offering me his thick tool while he pinched my swollen nipples. I was crazy with lust. For over forty-five minutes, the three of us made love in every possible position. Both men were worn out, but I was getting even hotter from this activity, unable to get enough. Kissing Jerry and Doug, I dressed and headed back to the party.

I saw Dave as I entered the house. He and another man were talking with Brenda. Her hair was combed, but her dress was wrinkled and her face was still flushed. Her neckline gaped, exposing most of her breasts, including her areolae. She had obviously not bothered to put her bra back on. Both men seemed to like the view, and Brenda did not try to conceal her nipples.

Doug and Jerry had not returned. Only one couple besides Brenda's group remained. Trying to sport an innocent look, I walked over to Brenda and asked if she knew where Gary was. She told me that Tina had asked for a ride home and that Gary had looked for me to go with him to drive her home. "He asked me to have Jerry take you," she said.

"I don't see Jerry now," I responded. "Dave, would you drop me off on your way home?"

"I'll be glad to. Let me get my things in the kitchen," he said, walking with Brenda to the other room. Not wanting him to have too much time alone with Brenda, I waited only five minutes before I went to the kitchen. To let them know I was coming, I made plenty of noise as I entered. Hearing me, they broke a passionate kiss. As Dave pulled back, both of Brenda's breasts were totally exposed. I smiled to myself as Brenda turned her back to fix her dress. Dave would still be very horny, I thought.

Sitting in Dave's big Lincoln, I decided that he would have to initiate any sexual activity. I made sure that my dress did not even reveal too much of my legs. In a couple of minutes, we were parked in front of my neighbor's house.

"It looks like your husband is not home," he said. "Let me check the house for you."

"I'll be okay, but I would appreciate it if you would come in until I'm sure that the house is safe."

Dave came in with me and I asked him to sit in the living room while I went upstairs. He asked if he could fix us a drink, and I told him that would be nice. I told him to open some champagne for us. Gary was hiding in a bedroom adjoining the master bath. He kissed me passionately, telling me what a sexy woman I was. He then whispered to me to play the answering machine when I went downstairs.

Dave was waiting for me with my champagne when I returned. He handed it to me and we raised our glasses in a gesture, as if to toast each other. "I love this stuff but it makes me silly," I said as I drank the glass dry. He was quick to refill it.

I went to the answering machine and pressed playback. Gary had left a message saying that he had had too much to drink and was resting on Tina's couch until he sobered up. Dave seemed very happy to hear this. "I'm glad that I have some time to talk to you. You don't need to be afraid of me," he said. "I don't bite. Not too hard anyway," he said grinning. "Come sit by me, please."

"I don't think that would be too smart," I answered. "After all, we're both married. You had me so turned on earlier that I don't think I can trust either one of us. Besides, I noticed that you and Brenda were heavily involved tonight. You were playing with her breasts in the kitchen. Watching that just made me hornier. Judging from tonight, you know too much about making young women like Brenda and me hot."

Dave seemed to love what I said. He walked over and refilled my glass. Setting his glass on the table, he put his arms around me, pulling my body against him. Then he raised my glass to my lips until I drank all of it. Hoping to work on his ego, I said, "You have to go now. We can't do this. I love my husband and I don't need to get involved. Also, I don't want to interfere with you and Brenda. Please leave now."

Dave ignored what I said and pressed his lips to mine. I kept my lips closed so he could not get his tongue in my mouth. I knew this would make him try harder. Two more times he kissed me, but I kept his tongue out. This was not easy because I was getting hot. But I wanted to make him work to get into my panties. Pushing away, I turned my back to him. He then wrapped his arms around my waist from behind me, kissing my neck and licking my shoulders. Then his hands began to work on my breasts, pinching my nipples through the fabric of my dress. I moaned as he worked his hands under my top to touch my naked flesh.

"Please stop, Dave. You need to leave now. You're making me too hot and Gary isn't even home to take care of me. It isn't fair to do this to me. I can't take any more."

This was what Dave had wanted to hear. As he kissed me again, I opened my mouth to let him know I was at the edge. His tongue worked against mine as he undid the top of my dress to reveal my breasts. He took each nipple into my mouth, expertly using his tongue and lips to arouse them further. I held his head as he worked on my breasts. I had to admit that he was very talented.

His hands pulled my zipper down and he removed my dress. I stood back to let him look at me, clad only in bikinis, garter belt, hose and shoes. "You bastard! You don't play fair," I said. "Don't stop now. You can't leave me this hot. I need you." Taking his hand, I led him to the couch, which was in full view for Gary.

He pulled off my panties and began to lick my thighs, above the tops of my hose. He then started talking to me, telling me how beautiful my blonde pussy looked, what incredible breasts and nipples I had. He told me he couldn't believe how wet my pussy was as he slid his tongue into me. He didn't know that I was full of come from two other men. He knew things to say that drove me wild as he ate me. I had an incredible orgasm.

Even I was surprised that he brought me off before I saw or touched his cock. I could wait no longer. I had him stand as I took off his pants and underwear. I was excited. His cock was even longer and thicker than it had looked while he was with Brenda. Maybe I turned him on even more. I got on my knees so he could fuck me from behind. As wet and turned-on as I was, his cock seemed to stretch my cunt even further. I started to talk to him, telling him what a fantastic lover he was and how I loved his fat cock. Listening to me, he worked on my clit and nipples while we fucked again taking me over the edge.

Knowing that Gary was watching and listening to all of this was almost too much to stand. Dave's sexual imagination was unbelievable. We did things that I had never done before. He told me sexy things constantly, keeping the intensity very high. I liked sexy talk, but he took it to new levels. Several times he had me suck him to orgasm, but each time he squirted his come over my breasts, having me rub the jism into my skin. Never believe that people over forty have lost their sexual prowess.

It was after four in the morning when he left. He made me promise that I would let him fuck me whenever we could get away. That was a promise that I would be happy to keep over and over again. Gary was so hot from watching that we made love and talked until nine that morning. Gary fell asleep, exhausted. But I was so turned on from fucking four men that I couldn't sleep. All I could think about was more sex. After hiding my sexy body and my horniness from all of my coworkers for over a year, I had totally blown my quiet, proper image in one night. I had flaunted my body in front of all of the men at the party. But you know what, it really didn't matter. Neither work or softball would ever be the same. So much for a quiet party with my coworkers.—*P.D., Savannah, Georgia* ⊶▪

COUNTRY COUPLE GETS PLENTY TO EAT AT END-OF-SUMMER BARBECUE

*M*y girlfriend and I, like many people, I believe, enjoy your magazine, but we didn't believe all of the experiences we read about. Having discovered that we could have just as much fun as your other readers, we decided to write in and once and for all put that idea to rest. I also want to dispel the myth that living in a small town has to be boring.

My name is Leo. I'm twenty-five, and my girlfriend is twenty-one. I met Barbara when she started working at the one and only diner we have in town. We hit it off right away. She was new in town, and soon we were going everywhere together. Our sex life started off awkward and slow, because I suffered from the misconception that Barbara was a little bit of a prude. But over time I discovered that she enjoyed X-rated movies and *Penthouse* as much as I did, and discussing these things has opened up our relationship.

Barbara is a looker by any standards, and when I say I am the luckiest son of a bitch I know, I mean it! She's all of five foot two, with a small but nicely toned chest, and the rest of her is as close to perfect as a girl could hope to get. She has long brown hair that she wears in what she calls an Egyptian style. She's just plain beautiful. And, as it turns out, that sweet smile hides the fact that she's a slut.

After a few months, Barbara and I had developed a unique sexual relationship. We talked about sharing our sex with others, and I soon realized that nothing excited me more than the idea of seeing her use her cocksucking skills on a bunch of men. I also wanted to watch her lick another girl's pussy, but didn't know if she would be willing to go that far. But last weekend, as we enjoyed the last hurrah of summer, all hell broke loose. We had a big barbecue planned, and there ended up being a lot of hot meat.

One of my closest friends in the world is a girl named Wendy. We grew up together, and all through school we were the best of friends. Wendy has blonde hair and, although she's a bit average in looks, she's got a killer body. Wendy and I used to fuck quite a bit. Giving up sex with each other hadn't destroyed our friendship. I had informed her of my relationship with Barbara and my fantasies about where it might go. After a lot of bullshit and teasing, I got Wendy to agree to aid me in my efforts. The one thing she was not interested in was having Barbara lick her pussy, because she wasn't sure if she could go through with it, and didn't want an embarrassing situation. Wendy and Barbara weren't great friends at that point.

On the day of the pig roast, Barbara wore a tight pair of cutoffs and a little tank top, with no panties or bra. Wendy looked good too, in button shorts and a cowboy shirt. I began to think that maybe she might have thought a little more about Barbara, because she was openly flirting with her. After lots of beer and food and horse-shoes, when the party was winding down, I asked Barbara if she was ready for something really wild. She gave me a huge, wet kiss, and I explained what I had in mind. Barb went off to get ready.

Next I looked around and saw what I had expected—a bunch of my single buddies standing around the keg. I walked them down to the basement of my house, and there was Barbara, on the couch, naked. The guys looked at me with a variety of expressions. Stunned, I would say, was the look of choice. It was a tense moment, so I decided to break the ice. I pulled my shorts to one side, exposing my dick.

Barbara came over and began licking my balls and sucking me to a hard-on. I looked at my old buddies and told them to have at it. Barbara's looks and sexy body were all the convincing the old farm boys needed. Soon I was sitting on the couch, stroking my meat, while Barbara stuffed dick after dick into her mouth.

There were five nude guys gathered around when the show began. I suspected that some of these dudes had never had pussy in their life. The scene laid out before me was awesome. My little honey was being ravished by cock after cock, her cunt dripping as tongues and fingers played with her wetness. I watched her suck four cocks in a row, each one filling her mouth with sperm and semen, each load eagerly swallowed by my beautiful slut. Her pussy was dripping with come. There was one guy left to go, Rick, and I told him to fuck her in the ass, something I hadn't done yet myself.

To my amazement, Barbara got into the doggie position without a blink, her perfect ass waving in the air. With the other guys cheering him on, Rick spit into her ass and then slowly penetrated her tight, brown hole. Barbara closed her eyes and buried her face in my lap. She squealed and moaned, and Rick looked like he'd died and gone to heaven. I told him to give it to her good, that she'd been waiting a long time for this.

Barbara looked up and said to Rick, while looking at me, "Ram it! Let me really feel you pumping!" I was delighted. She took his cock like a champ and soon he was pounding her ass.

That's when I heard the cellar door open and shut once more. I watched a sexy pair of legs walk down the steps. It was Wendy. She peeked down, and her mouth opened in disbelief, but I could tell she was horny as hell, and maybe even envious of Barbara. I kissed Wendy and pulled off her T-shirt. About four other guys helped her out of her bra. She knelt down beside Rick and watched close up as he whaled away at Barbara's ass. Wendy seemed mesmerized. A couple of the other guys waved their cocks in Wendy's face. She looked at them, then began to suck.

All of a sudden, Rick pulled out and offered Wendy his cock. Barbara turned around, gave Wendy a wicked smile, and stuffed Rick's dick into her mouth. Wendy joined in, and they took turns polishing his knob. When they started running their lips up the two sides of his dick at the same time, Rick couldn't make it last, and blasted his load. They struggled to see who could get more of his come into her mouth. I about knocked over two buddies just to get a good look at their tongues as they played with each other and swallowed Rick's huge load.

Wendy came and sat beside me, not sure where the party would be going next. Some of the guys went up to get more beer, and Barbara crawled over to me and began to suck my cock. Sitting beside me, Wendy watched her. I played with her tits and Barbara's hair. Barbara looked up at Wendy and told her there was plenty if she wanted to share. Wendy got down on her knees beside Barbara, and the two girls traded spit and my cock back and forth until it became too much. I shot my wad into Wendy's mouth. Barbara stuck her tongue into Wendy's mouth to get her share of my come. I didn't think it could get any better.

I looked around. Only a couple of guys were still in the cellar, and they looked pretty worn out. But Barbara wasn't finished yet. She took Wendy by the hand and laid her down on the carpet. She straddled Wendy on all fours and looked into her eyes, then kissed her, feeling her tits. Barbara had Wendy completely worked up, and I knew Wendy was hot enough to want what was coming.

I got down beside them, and watched Barbara sucking Wendy's tits. She slowly licked her way down Wendy's stomach to where her shorts began. Barbara began to unbutton Wendy's shorts, licking the skin beneath each button until she arrived at her panties. She pulled off her shorts, revealing a large wet spot in Wendy's panties. Barbara smiled, and eagerly slid Wendy's cotton panties off. Wendy's pussy and her pubic hair were soaked. Barbara began to feel the folds of her cunt and finger her. Barbara looked at me and licked her fingers. Then she got right down and began to lick Wendy's legs all around her cunt. Finally, she began to gently lick Wendy's folds. Wendy moaned and spread her legs. I got as close as I could as Barbara began to get braver, really starting to tongue the goo out of Wendy's hole, sticking her tongue in deep and wiggling it around.

It wasn't long before Wendy was ready to gush. I thought Barbara might pull away from her when she climaxed, but she didn't, she continued to tongue and suck her hole. Wendy arched her back and grabbed Barbara's hair. Barbara sucked and licked all the cream that Wendy could offer, I was so proud of her, and I could see that she loved the taste of pussy.

Wendy looked down, a gaze of pure animal lust in her eyes, and ordered Barbara to sit on her face. Barbara quickly obliged, and went totally wild as Wendy buried her mouth as far as she could in Barbara's wet cunt. Barbara wantonly wiggled her hips, whooping and hollering as she crashed through an amazing orgasm. After that they kissed and fondled each other gently until they calmed down.

Since then, Wendy has offered her pussy up any time Barbara wants to eat it. In return, she has gotten into eating Barbara as well.

Life in the city? Who needs it? My country girl is all the fun I need.—*L.Z., Bareback, Georgia*

SKIING GIVES WAY TO SURFING AND DIVING ON MORE INTIMATE WATERS

*L*ike a lot of couples, my wife and I had long discussed inviting a person or persons into bed with us to share the delights of the body. We were both enthusiastic. The only problem was how to make it happen in such a way that everyone involved would be comfortable with the situation and fully enjoy themselves.

We've shared many fantasies in the bedroom, and I noticed Patty became much more aroused when I described a situation involving her and more than one other man. At such times she would become so wet and tasty that she would come almost instantly, and it would be over almost before it really got going.

One day, when we were out waterskiing at our favorite lake, our friend Kirk and his wife Terri, along with a friend of theirs named Greg, dropped by to picnic and water-ski. Terri is a tall lady, with

Long legs and nice curves, but had always seemed to me to be the type who would just lie there, or maybe if you're lucky she might moan a little. Kirk is involved in a lot of sports and keeps himself in pretty good shape. Greg had skied occasionally with us in the past, and I had always noticed women staring at his crotch, because it looked like he had a whole salami in his bathing suit. Patty and I had sometimes discussed what was in there, and she'd said she'd like to find out sometime. I told her that if the opportunity came she should take it.

On this particular day, everyone had skied except the two women, who had not brought their bathing suits with them. That wasn't really a problem, as both had skied with just their panties and bra on under the wet suit before. Terri went first. When she came back aboard and peeled off the wet suit, all our eyes followed her legs up to her sopping wet crotch. Her heavy bush was clearly visible. We could all read her lips, and she knew it. She slowly climbed the rest of the way into the boat, and bent over to pick up a towel. We got a delectable rear view. All the men were in a state of high arousal.

When Patty came back aboard after skiing, Greg helped her remove the wet suit. As it slid down past her hips, her panties went with it. There was a frozen moment, until Patty said it would be easier to towel off that way. A smile crossed her face as she finished removing the wet suit and panties, reached back, unsnapped her bra and dropped it at Greg's feet. The look on his face was indescribable as his eyes perused my wife's beautiful body. Terri thought that Patty had a good idea, and she too quickly removed her bra and panties. A pregnant silence ensued, as we feasted our eyes on the two women's glorious nudity. Then Patty cleared her throat and said, "Okay, Greg, now show me yours." She reached over and stroked the salami that was poking a hole in his swimsuit. The next moment she removed his swimsuit, and out popped a monster cock, of a size most men can only dream of having.

Terri said, "Well, what's wrong with you other two? Let's see yours." She was talking more to me, of course, as she knew exactly what was under Kirk's swimsuit. After I had removed my suit, I looked over at Greg and my wife, who had been joined by Kirk, leaving Terri and her long legs all to me.

My wife sat in front of Greg and started licking her way up to his enormous organ. Kirk's hand was between her legs, and she was moving her hips in passionate circles.

Terri was watching all this. She apparently wanted Greg more than me, but I was available and Greg wasn't. I decided to make her forget what she was missing. When I reached for her bush, I found her cunt dripping wet from watching the other three. Terri seemed to be enjoying my attention, and I encouraged her to bend over and take my penis in her mouth in such a way that we could both continue watching the threesome while getting off.

Patty had Kirk's penis (which was pretty impressive in its own right) in one hand and Tom's in her mouth, although it was so big she couldn't fit all that much of it. Terri was so hot from watching that she took her mouth off my cock and told me she had to get off. She pushed my head down toward her crotch, and pulled my face hard against her. She verbally guided my tongue to her most sensitive spots. I shot my tongue in, up and around. Then she raised her legs and moved my head down to her anus, saying, "Push your tongue in hard," which I very willingly did. At the same time I slid two fingers into her huge box. Her juices were dripping down to my tongue, and the combined odor and taste had me so worked up I was delirious.

Excited beyond belief, Terri pulled me up, looked at the size of my erection and guided me into her waiting box. That feeling was incredible. She devoured me like I wasn't even there. The hot, slick, soft, squeezing length of her cunt did its work quickly, and I blasted her with a load of sperm.

At the same time that I was shooting my load into Terri I heard a moan behind us. When I looked over, Kirk was penetrating Patty with his fat cock. She had her legs spread to allow him access, all the while hanging onto Greg's penis so it wouldn't get away. Kirk started pumping his fat dick into Patty, and she was moaning like I'd never heard before. It didn't take Kirk long to fill Patty with his juice. As he pulled out, some of it ran down her lips, which I found wrenchingly sexy.

Patty pulled Greg over between her legs, saying she was ready for him. She guided the head of his dick into her. He entered her slowly, sinking all nine or ten inches until he hit bottom. She was screaming and urging him on, shouting, "Screw me! Screw me hard, but screw me slowly." For a couple of minutes we watched him slowly stroke in and out, while Patty moaned and shuddered in ecstasy. Then she said, "Now, let it all go! Fuck me fast and fill me with your juice!" Greg started ramming it in hard and fast, and Patty screamed at him, "Yes, yes! More, more!" When it seemed that he couldn't move any faster, she screamed, "Oh, Jesus, you're making me come! Harder, harder. That's it!" Greg had to be nearing orgasm himself. His thrusts increased in urgency, then finally he shuddered all over and emptied his load into Patty. He had a lot, and she groaned and panted every time his penis convulsed. He was still pumping when his sperm started oozing out around his penis, although I don't know how it found room to get out.

When Greg pulled that monster of his out, Patty just lay there, her legs splayed apart. Her beautiful pussy lips were saturated with her own juice and overflowing with the sperm of two men. I dove in like a virgin getting his first piece of tail. The taste and sensation were incredible as I licked and sucked on her box.

Meanwhile, Kirk was hard again and had started sliding it into Terri, who had been pretty well ignored for the last several minutes. Her eyes were on Greg's crotch, and she beckoned him over to her, so she could stroke his meat and suck it back to life. It didn't take Kirk long to come again and, even as he was pulling his dripping penis out, Terri was guiding Greg's in. She gasped as he entered her, and began to growl as they hammered at each other. She has a large vagina compared to Patty, but when Greg stroked in you could see from the look in her eyes that it was all she could take.

Kirk could have Terri any time, so he returned his attention to Patty, who saw him coming and said she would like me to lick and eat her while Kirk was fucking her. She sat on him with her back to his face, so I could lick her clit while she stroked his meat. I almost came spontaneously from the kinky excitement of licking Kirk's shaft as Patty rode up and down on him. Patty turned and sat on Kirk, facing him. I drove my tongue into her anus and she moaned, "Yes, darling, yes. That's perfect. Don't stop." Once she rode too high and his penis popped out. In the passion of the moment I gave it a suck before putting it back in.

Greg and Terri were still going at it, and Kirk and Patty were beginning to build to a frenzy. I was hard as a rock, but had nowhere to plug my penis.

Terri had been watching what I had done to Patty while Kirk was in her, and motioned that she wanted me to do the same for her. She bent over so that Greg was entering her from behind. I dove for her clit, and watched closely as every part of her expanded when Greg reentered. She was in a frenzy, stroking the back of my head and encouraging me as Greg stroked into her pussy. With every stroke from Greg, the whole area around her mound rose and fell in a frenzied, uncontrollable rhythm. I hung with her as best I could until Greg let go, and I was rewarded with the excess of both their juices, churned together in a delightful mixture.

After that we all lay around in the boat, naked and exhausted. When we got home that night we discussed the day and agreed that it had been the best sex any of us had ever had, and that we would like it to happen again. No doubt it will.—*A.L., Fort Myers, Florida*

True Romance

A SOLDIER'S RETURN PROVES WELL
WORTH WAITING FOR

*M*y lover's overseas military duty is almost over. It has been a long six months. The slightest thought of him brings a smile from deep within. I can hear his soft voice whispering in my ear and it fills me with excitement. I imagine his touch, so gentle, and it warms my entire body. Knowing today is the day our eyes will meet again, I dress myself in something comfortable, yet soft and sexy, just for him.

At work, anxiously waiting for him to arrive, I turn around just in time to see him walk in. I lose my train of thought as we embrace. I can feel myself getting excited as he holds me in his arms. After he greets everyone, we leave.

Arriving at his place, he makes himself comfortable as I freshen up. I slowly enter the bedroom. The lights are low, the music soft. Standing at the foot of his bed, I slowly remove my dress, dropping it to the floor. I drop to my knees and crawl toward him. Kneeling between his legs, my hands begin to caress him.

Passionately massaging his strong legs and thighs, feeling the warmth of his body, my hands roam freely. Gently rubbing his crotch, I feel the hardness of his cock through his shorts. Feeling his excitement build, I slowly remove his pants, exposing his big, hard cock. Using my tongue, lips and hands on him, I begin to lick and suck his big cock, taking it into my mouth. He spreads his legs to give me more room.

My juices start flowing, as again and again he fills my mouth and throat with his hard, hot cock. My body tingles from the sensation of his hands, so soft and warm, caressing my breasts, my body. My legs spread as I feel his fingers slip inside my hot pussy, making me squirm with every thrust.

My excitement increasing even more, the anticipation of feeling his hard cock deep inside me is overwhelming. I lie back on the bed next to him, my back against his chest. I feel the hardness of his cock against my ass and his warm hands touching me. I get on all fours and stick my ass in the air. At last his cock penetrates my wet pussy.

His hands on my hips, he starts pumping me as fast as he can. My pussy juices flow, my muscles grip him, and before we even settle into a steady rhythm, I come. My juices gush all over his balls, while his fingers play with my ass, heightening my excitement even further. After I come he continues to fuck me, deeper and deeper. As I grow juicier, he pumps harder, deeper, our bodies moving together in perfect rhythm. I start playing with my clit, my body shaking with each stroke as he pushes his cock deeper into my hole, until my body is seized with one orgasm after another. Finally, his cock pulsing, I feel him shoot his load of come deep inside me.

He continues pumping until his cock softens, and, as he pulls out, a flood of juices run over my pussy and down my legs. Lying there in complete exhaustion, our bodies tingling from head to toe, we drift off to sleep together in each other's arms.—*M.S., Rochester, New York* ⚬┼▪

HE GETS OFF ON HER RANDY BEDTIME STORIES

*O*ne night a couple of weeks ago, lying in bed while my husband tenderly played with my clit and sucked on my tits, he asked me if anyone had ever made a pass at me when I was out dancing with my friend Theresa. You see, when we first got married, my husband was still in graduate school, working toward his doctorate, and he spent every spare minute studying and cramming for exams. Rather than sit home bored, I would go out dancing with my best friend.

Well, to answer my husband's question, I told him about a man I had met who was in town on business. I told him how we had danced together a couple of times, how we had rubbed up against each other, and how he tried to feel me up.

On hearing this, my husband became extremely aroused—his dick seemed to grow another two inches. He quickly mounted me and we had one of the best fucks we'd had in a long time. Since then, he's often asked me to tell him the story again. Whenever I do, we fuck with wild abandon. However, I've never told him the whole story and I think he suspects as much. Our tenth anniversary is approaching and I asked him what he wanted. He said he wanted to hear the whole story of what happened that long-ago night. Well, honey, happy anniversary. Here it is.

I danced with Tim a couple of times that night and I enjoyed teasing him by pressing up against the bulge in his pants. I knew he was getting turned on by that and by the sensation of my rather large tits pressing into his chest. After one slow song ended, the band went into a hot, fast number and we stayed on the dance floor bumping and grinding away.

By the time the number ended, we were both soaked with sweat and out of breath. The alcohol we had consumed didn't help either. Tim suggested that we take a walk outside to cool off.

We went out the side door of the club, which opened onto a darkened quadrangle of shops. It was after midnight and we found ourselves completely alone. To tell the truth, I kind of suspected what would happen next.

Tim encircled me with his arms from behind, pressing the bulge in his trousers into the crack of my ass. He kissed my neck, then slowly ran his tongue up and down the side of my neck, sending shivers through me. I closed my eyes and moaned softly as his obviously talented mouth continued on its path up and down the side of my throat.

My eyes still closed, I felt his hands move from my waist to the front of my blouse, which he slowly began to unbutton, kissing and licking my neck all the while.

I knew I should stop him, but it felt so good! Almost of its own volition, my hand found its way to the lump in his trousers. Even through the fabric, I could feel the heat being generated by what felt like a massive prick.

After Tim had unbuttoned my blouse, he cupped both of my bra-clad tits and gently squeezed them, sending yet another shiver through me. He then slid his hand around to my back, deftly unhooked my bra and lifted it up, baring my tits to the cool evening air. Tim then took both my naked tits in his large, warm hands, and slowly squeezed and massaged them, lightly rubbing and tugging on my tender, swollen, fully erect nipples.

Still holding me from behind, he let go of one of my tits and, with his free hand, lifted the hem of my skirt. He slid his questing fingers between my thighs and directly to my pussy. I parted my legs to give him better access. The feelings that rippled through me as he massaged my hot, wet cunt were indescribable.

While Tim manipulated my drenched pussy with one hand, playing with my tits with the other, all the while kissing me up and down my neck, I kept right on rubbing his cock through his pants. It wasn't long before I decided that this just wasn't enough. I turned in his arms and kissed him deeply.

There I was, married just about a year, standing in the dark outside of a nightclub, my blouse open, my bra hanging loose, my breasts exposed, kissing the hell out of a stranger while he played with my pussy and tits and I stroked his cock! At this point though, I was too far gone to care. Still kissing him, I reached down and unzipped his pants, sticking my hand in to touch his cock.

I pulled his underwear aside and, with my thumb and two fingers, started to caress and stroke his dick, causing him to shudder. He again lifted my dress and, this time, reached into the top of my panties and slid his hand straight down to my hot, throbbing cunt.

As we kissed again, he slipped a finger inside my pussy, causing me to moan loudly. Breaking the kiss, Tim leaned down and started sucking on my tits, first taking one nipple into his warm, moist mouth, circling it with his tongue, then gently sucking on it, before turning his attention to my other tit.

Tim kept right on finger-fucking me as his thumb played with my clit. I could feel my resolve weakening by the moment, and I knew that if I didn't do something to defuse him soon, his cock was going to wind up buried in me to the hilt, marriage or no marriage. I decided the only way to stop him from coming in my cunt was for him to come in my mouth.

My decision made, I freed his cock from his pants and continued to stroke it, feeling it throb in my hand. Dislodging his fingers from my pussy, I quickly glanced around and, seeing no one, crouched and slid Tim's thick penis in my mouth. I didn't know what was more erotic—sucking a cock outside a busy nightclub, with the possibility of being seen by anybody walking nearby, or sucking a cock that didn't belong to my husband!

Anyway, I eagerly took Tim in my mouth, feeling his cock slide all the way to the back of my throat, before I pulled it out and began to lick and suck it like it was a big lollipop.

Taking him in my mouth again, I deep-throated him, sliding my lips down the length of his shaft to his pubic hair, my nose bumping against his zipper. Tim held my head in his hands as his hips started to buck, and I knew it wouldn't be long before he came. Tim thrust in and out, furiously fucking my mouth.

With one last thrust, Tim erupted, spurting his warm and slightly salty come in my mouth. I swallowed it and proceeded to lick his dick clean, then stood up to kiss him, letting him sample the taste of his come still lingering in my mouth. As he stood there swaying, overcome by the force of his orgasm, I hurriedly fastened my bra and buttoned my blouse.

Just as I finished, he asked me to go back to his hotel room with him so he could repay the blowjob by fucking me. I regretfully told him that I couldn't, and that we shouldn't have even done what we did. He pulled me close, reached under my dress again and, placing the palm of his hand between my legs and pressing my aching mound, told me that he knew I was hot and that he knew a good way to cool me off.

I was wavering, torn between a desire not to cheat on my husband and a desire to feel a strange cock in my cunt, when my girlfriend, who had been looking for me, found us. With that, I told him I had to leave.

I dropped my friend off at her apartment and, from there home, I kept one hand on the wheel and the other between my legs, frantically rubbing my inflamed pussy. My husband was sound asleep but awoke rather abruptly when I grabbed his cock and started sucking it like there was no tomorrow. When he was both fully awake and fully erect, I climbed on top of him and buried his cock in my oozing snatch. With my hands on his shoulders, I bounced up and down on his shaft. He sucked my tits as we fucked, which I love him to do when he's inside me.

Finally I couldn't stand any more and I erupted in a long, violent orgasm just as he, too, came, mingling his come with my cunt juice, soaking the sheets.

After I collapsed on top of him, he asked me what, or who, had gotten me so worked up. I told him that it was just a cute guy I had seen at the club!

If giving him only some of the details led to such wild fucking,

I wonder what this letter will do! Maybe I ought to tell him about the time the neighbor downstairs made a pass at me!—*Name and address withheld*

JUST PLAIN FOLKS ENJOYING OUTSTANDING FUCKS

*T*his is not one of those letters where everybody looks like a model, but it did happen and we both enjoyed our time together.

I was just coming in the front door from the worst day in my life. Everything that could go wrong had, and the phone was ringing off its hook.

"Barry, I want you to come down here and fuck me!" she said when I picked up the phone. An obscene phone call, I thought, just the ending I needed to an already perfectly lousy day.

"Barry, I'm horny and need to be serviced," she continued. "Since we used to talk all the time, I thought of you as a possibility."

Over the next fifteen minutes, I gradually realized that the woman at the other end of the phone line was Jo. We had worked for the same company for years. I was a branch manager and Jo worked in the head office. We had spent lots of company time talking on the phone about our lives, our problems and, when we thought of it, company business.

We made a date for dinner and a movie the next night, even though I'd never actually met her and had no idea what she looked like. Jo hung up, saying, "It will be nice to finally meet you. But you're staying all night so remember to bring some protection."

Dinner and the new Stallone movie were great! My date was not a Penthouse Pet. She was a mature woman with a great personality and great boobs. But, then, I'm not Fabio, so we suited each other.

When we got back to Jo's place, we sat and talked for a while before heading off to bed. When we did, we didn't tear off each other's clothes. Instead, we were more like a long-married couple. After quietly undressing ourselves, she helped me put on a condom. We got into bed and snuggled with each other. We knew that the first time was important, and we wanted it to go right.

I started kissing Jo while my free hand explored her breasts and her hardening nipples. With our bodies pressed together, one of her hands wandered over my back while the other moved up my leg until she held my hardening cock.

My mouth moved from hers to kiss her eyes, then to her ears and gradually down her neck to her breasts. My tongue circled first one breast and then the other, working my way to her large, nipples. Jo's breasts were too large to be just a mouthful, but none of the excess went to waste. I played with her other breast while one hand moved down to her pubic hair. I gently stroked it and then slid farther down so my hand could run up and down the inside of her legs. I almost touched her slit but didn't. Jo's fingers were driving me crazy, playing with my nuts while squeezing my cock.

I started nibbling gently on her erect nipples and rubbing them between my finger and thumb. Jo raised her knees and spread them apart. My hand moved higher on her legs until I felt the heat and moisture of her cunt on my thumb. I ran my fingers up and down her slit several times and she squeezed my cock hard in response. "Play with me. Make me come," Jo whispered. I spread her cunt lips, slipped a finger into the wet hole and then moved my moistened finger to diddle her clit. Jo came for the first time that night.

"I want your cock in me now. I need to feel you shoving your prick in my cunt. I need to be fucked!" Jo almost shouted, as she tried to pull my cock to her hole, I let her lead the way. She wasn't the only one who needed to fuck. Jo was so wet I slid the first inch or so in easily. After I backed out a little to ensure that I didn't hurt her and that all of me was wet, I slid back in a little farther. I kept going farther and farther into her tight hole.

"Oh, you feel so good. I feel like a virgin on her first night. I don't care if I can't walk tomorrow, I want all of you now," Jo said as her hands pulled at my ass to get more of me.

"I'm trying to go slow, so you'll only walk bowlegged tomorrow."

"I don't care, I want all of your cock. Go faster, faster! Fuck me harder! I want to feel all of you inside me!"

When my whole cock was in her and I could rub against her clit, I began to move faster. Then I stopped moving and let Jo do all the work. I wanted her to come without me orgasming, so I could last the night.

"It feels so good. Don't stop! Keep fucking me. I need you to fuck me," Jo said, moving wildly up and down. I barely held on while Jo's hips bucked as she came. Her contractions squeezed my cock so much I almost came too.

Jo laughed as she squeezed her pussy around my prick. I slowly began to slide my cock in and out, and I felt Jo start lifting her hips to match me stroke for stroke.

Within minutes we were going full tilt as we tried to get my cock as deep into Jo as possible. My pubic bone rubbed her clit whenever I drove my cock deep into her pussy. We carried on until I thought one of us would have a heart attack, but what a way to go!

"I'm going to come! Come with me, baby," she cried, as I felt her cunt start contracting. "We'll need a rest after this, so don't hold back, come with me!"

"I'm coming too!" I yelled as I felt my balls tighten, and I shot spurt after spurt of come.

We held each other until we cooled down and could think straight again. Jo got a wet cloth and wiped off our sweat-covered bodies and our come-soaked genitals.

After carefully taking off my rubber, she cleaned my cock last. She kept running her hands along it and playing with my balls. Her manual resuscitation became oral when my cock showed some signs of life. "I like to suck cock," Jo announced before taking my shaft into her mouth. She sucked like a woman just off a desert island.

It became mutual when I slipped my head between her legs for a 69. You'd have thought I hadn't eaten for a month the way my tongue dove into her cunt. I stopped every few strokes to suck up her juices, and then ran my tongue up and down her slit. I paused at her clit, which I gently stimulated and sucked. Her asshole received an occasional lick and visits from my fingers. Jo seemed to like that, as it made her suck extra hard and moan. When I finally shoved two fingers into her pussy while licking her clit, Jo came again and again until she collapsed.

Next, after another rest, Jo insisted I had to lie perfectly still while she did whatever she wanted. Leaning over my head, she started by rubbing her breasts and nipples all over my body. It took willpower to remain still as Jo rubbed them over my face, eyes and lips. Jo gradually worked her tits down to my cock, rubbing all of me with them as she moved. When all I could see and smell was pussy, Jo began rubbing her nipples all over my prick and balls.

Jo then showed me an oral way to put on a rubber. Within moments my cock was at full attention. She continued to play with it, alternately rubbing my cock between her breasts and sucking on it, until she felt I was ready to come. Jo sat up, turned around and carefully lowered herself onto my cock.

As she raised and lowered herself, I slid my fingers between our bodies and gently played with her clit. Jo came almost immediately and collapsed on top of me.

I got up and positioned Jo facedown on the bed with her pussy at the edge, fully exposed between her widely spread legs. I asked, "Which hole do you want me to fuck? Your cunt or your asshole?"

"I want your cock in my pussy until I can't come anymore, then you can use my asshole if you have any cock left."

I couldn't let that dare go by, so I started driving my cock into her pussy as fast and hard as I could. I slid two fingers around front to collect her juices and then rubbed the fingers into her asshole, first one finger, then both. I slid my other hand back to her clit and gently squeezed it, and continued pumping until she came, gripping the sheets and screaming.

We crawled into bed and fell asleep with my cock locked between her thighs and a breast in each of my hands.

I later awoke from a sexy dream of fucking a Penthouse Pet to find I really *was* fucking. I was madly fucking in my dreams and fucking Jo in reality. "Didn't you get enough?" Jo asked sleepily as I came. She soon followed.

The next morning came all too soon and we both had to drag our tails to work, but with that just-fucked look on our happy faces. I never hang up on an obscene phone call now, and gladly invite Jo over for many weekends.—*B.O., Milwaukee, Wisconsin*

THE LOVE MACHINE UPSTAIRS GOT
THEIR MOTORS RUNNING

I enjoy camping with my wife and kids, but after a week in a tent at Yellowstone all four of us wanted to sleep in a real bed. We drove into a nearby town in the early afternoon and found a motel with a pool. We all were a little edgy after having shared close quarters for so long, so we decided to get the kids a room that adjoined ours. That way they could each have their own bed, and my wife and I could have some much-needed privacy.

After we had settled in, the kids headed straight for the pool, which could be seen from our first-floor window. The water looked inviting but Trudy and I desperately wanted to shower first. Trudy must have seen me watching appreciatively as she removed her blouse, because she slowed down her actions and made a dramatic show of it. Then she untied her ponytail and threw her head back, running her fingers through her hair.

I stepped behind her, unhooked her bra and slid it off her lightly freckled shoulders. I cupped and lifted a full breast with one hand while I pulled back her long brown hair with the other so I could kiss her behind the ear where it arouses her the most. She leaned her head back, closed her eyes and smiled contentedly, a sure sign that she's enjoying my sexual attention. I gently released her breast and slid my hand down her soft, flat belly and into her panties. She turned, kissed me on the mouth and said she wanted to shower so she'd smell nice and clean for me. She then ran her tongue around her lips and gave me a playful wink as she disappeared into the bathroom.

We normally have an active sex life, but spending seven days in a tent with our kids had put a damper on our libidos. When Trudy emerged, I greeted her in the nude with a kiss and proceeded to nibble her ears and neck. She caressed my cock for about five seconds. Then she told me I needed a shower worse than she did and pushed me into the bathroom. When I finished my shower and stepped out of the bathroom, I saw that she and her bathing suit were gone.

Knowing how much she likes to tease me, I put on my own suit and joined the family at the pool. The kids were swimming in the shallow end with others their own age. I jumped in next to Trudy and stayed in the water until my cock returned to its dormant state and everybody started getting hungry.

After we came back from dinner, the kids stretched out in front of the TV in their room and I went out for some wine coolers. When I returned, Trudy was propped up in bed watching TV, wearing my favorite short silky nightie and looking flushed and excited. I could smell one of my favorite perfumes, one that I hadn't even known she had packed for the trip. She hopped out of bed, turned down the TV and told me to listen. I heard a familiar steady squeaking sound coming from the room above us. Suddenly I knew why she was in such a state! Whoever had the room upstairs was really going at it!

I knew the kids wouldn't be going to bed for almost an hour, and since they might barge in at any time we had to keep ourselves under control until they were asleep. Believe me, after what had transpired earlier in the afternoon, I knew it was going to be tough! But I also knew that the delayed gratification might take our sex to that deeper, almost spiritual, level we sometimes reach after a romantic evening alone.

I changed into some comfortable shorts, put two of the wine coolers on ice and joined her on the bed with two open bottles. We cuddled with my arm around her shoulders while her fingernails traced designs on my inner thigh. After a while we made some romantic small talk about how lucky we were to have each other. Trudy sighed softly and moved her hand up my leg to tease my balls through my shorts. We kissed deeply, and then I put my own hand to work pleasing her. I love the feel of her full breasts through the silk of her nightie. As I tweaked her hardened nipples, she moaned and squirmed in pleasure.

Thankfully it was soon time to kiss the kids good night and put them to bed. Since the bulge in my shorts would have raised embarrassing questions, Trudy did the honors while I pulled down the spread, dimmed the lights and turned off the TV. To my surprise, I could hear that they were still going at it upstairs! When Trudy returned I told her to listen. Her eyes widened and her jaw dropped when she realized the couple upstairs had been going at it for over an hour. That did it! Nothing could keep us apart any longer.

Trudy pulled her nightie over her head as I took off my shorts. Her arms went around my neck and her tongue went crazy in my mouth as my hands traveled down her back and squeezed her buttocks. My cock pressed against the warm softness of her heaving belly, leaving hot sticky trails on her smooth-skin. Still standing up, she locked her hands behind my neck and brought first one leg and then the other up and around my back. She gyrated her pelvis as we endeavored to get her dripping pussy positioned above my thrusting rod. I soon felt the familiar wet softness surround the tip of my cock, and Trudy cried out in pleasure as I lowered her the rest of the way. I turned us so her back was to the bed and then fell forward, never leaving that wonderful pussy. We tried to take it slow but I was too far gone. I came mere seconds later, shooting semen into the farthest recesses of her body.

I lay on top of her for a minute, still panting. Then I gently withdrew and lay down next to her. She hadn't had an orgasm yet, but we both knew I would be hard again in a few minutes.

Kneeling on the bed, she began to administer a lip massage to my flaccid penis. I told her I wanted to reciprocate, so she stretched out next to me on her side and resumed work on my now-stiffening cock. I lifted her legs at the knees, spread her labia with my fingers and licked her protruding love-button, making her moan with delight.

My cock was now fully recuperated, and she let go of it to concentrate on her own pleasure. She placed her hand firmly behind my head and began arching her hips toward my face. I put two fingers deep into her pussy and began massaging her G-spot. She lay back on the bed and cried out as she experienced the first of many orgasms.

Finally she pulled me up, got on her knees and rested her head upon a pillow. I got on my knees behind her, taking hold of her hips as she reached between her legs to guide my organ to its favorite place once again. I began pumping into her, slowly at first, then harder and faster as we found our rhythm. After we both came, I collapsed on top of her.

As we lay together catching our breath, I couldn't believe my ears. I could still hear the squeaking sound coming through the ceiling!

In the morning, as we loaded the car, I kept an eye on the room above us to see if I could catch a glimpse of the love machine that had been operating up there. I didn't see any activity, so I decided to investigate more closely. Trying to look casual, I strolled across the second-floor landing. The curtains to the room were closed tight, but when I stopped I could hear the squeaking again—only I suddenly realized it wasn't coming from the room after all! Standing there was an old ice machine whose compressor was apparently about to give out. Trudy and I had a good laugh over that one!—*E.H., San Diego, California* ⚬━▪

A WEEKEND GETAWAY LEADS TO
ALFRESCO SEX AND INDOOR SPORTS

*R*ecently my friend Judy and I spent a long weekend at my country home. Judy and I have been lovers for eight years. Even though we live in different parts of the country, fate seems to keep bringing us together to fuck. Judy is one of the most passionate women I have ever had the good fortune to make love to.

We left my apartment in the city on a beautiful October morning and headed to my home in the mountains. During the drive the sexual tension increased until I thought that I'd have to pull over and fuck her right there in my Blazer. Judy kept turning all my words into sexual innuendos. I, in turn, reminded her that I had been cooped up working for nearly two months and didn't need to beat around the bush about my intentions: I wanted to spend the entire weekend fucking her silly.

When I said that she gave me a sexy smile, licked her lips and told me to speed up. Well, not being the kind of guy to disappoint a lady, I put the pedal to the metal.

One of the nice things about fucking someone you know is that there is seldom any letdown. We had barely carried in our bags before we were locked in a deep, passionate kiss. We each knew that the other had been without sex for some time and that therefore this first round would burn hot and fast.

My hands began to roam up her sides. With my right thumb I slowly caressed her nipple through her blouse and bra. She shuddered, and I felt her nipple begin to harden. With that encouragement I moved both hands over her breasts. She broke the kiss long enough to smile at me and ask if I was ready for what was to come. I smiled a wicked little smile and told her to try me on for size.

Judy asked me what I needed. All I could answer was, "You." She gave me a passionate kiss. Her mouth opened and she gently sucked my lips. She then darted her tongue into my mouth. While our tongues sparred, she began to unbutton my shirt. Not to be outdone, my hands began roaming over her body, touching all of the secret places that only lovers know.

Judy is a petite woman. She's five feet two inches tall and has a slender build. She has perfect breasts—round, firm and fully packed. They are just a little large for her frame and are topped with delicious strawberry nipples. Her breasts are linked directly to her pussy, and massaging her breasts makes her twat hot.

As I rubbed her breasts through her clothes, Judy rubbed her body up and down mine. All the while we never broke our liplock. I pulled her blouse loose and ran my hands up to her bra-covered breasts. She moaned and drove her tongue deep into my throat. I unhooked her bra and freed her tits. Her nipples stiffened in the cool air.

At this point it was a race to see who could get undressed first. Judy was first under the covers and I rewarded her by slowly taking her left breast into my mouth. When I ran my tongue around her nipple, she rolled on top of me, but I wasn't ready to fuck.

I pulled her hips forward so that her pussy was touching my nose. She thrust her hips toward me as I stuck out my tongue. She tasted great. Judy grabbed the headboard and began to fuck my face. I tugged on her clit with my lips and caressed it with the tip of my tongue, which caused Judy to come all over my face.

At this point she said something about giving me a reward for the licking she had just received. As she started to kiss her way down to my dick, I stopped her and said, "Save that for later. Let's fuck now." She slid her pussy up my body until my dick was against her slit. Then she gently rocked back and forth, making my seven inches hard as a rock.

She raised herself and slowly slid her tight, wet pussy down onto my dick. The feeling of a hot pussy wrapped around me is one of the reasons I am glad to be a man. Judy was filled with dick and I was surrounded by warm velvet. She rode my dick like a cowgirl and I met her every stroke with a thrust of my hips.

When she tired, we rolled over and I lifted her legs over my shoulders. I knew I wouldn't last much longer. My dick seemed to grow bigger and thicker, and I yelled out that I was about to come. Judy cried out that she was coming too. With that, I felt all the muscles in my abdomen and legs contract as I expelled a series of hot blasts of come deep inside Judy's spasming pussy. Judy let out a primal scream as she thrashed back and forth.

After a few minutes we regained our composure. I commented

that this had been a good start but said that I couldn't wait for the real fun and games to begin. We both laughed at that, not realizing how true that statement was to be.

That evening we drove to town for a great steak dinner. Little did I know that dessert was going to blow my mind. When we got back to the house, we looked up and saw the stars. They were so clear and bright! They never look like that in the city. I came up behind Judy, wrapped my arms around her slender waist and rested my chin on her head as we admired the view. While observing the celestial bodies, I began to move my hands over Judy's body. She shivered when my hands covered her breasts and she reached behind her to find my dick growing rapidly in my jeans. I turned her to face me. We kissed passionately, our tongues dancing inside each other's mouth as our hands roamed over one another.

Making a mutual unspoken decision to make love under the stars, we quickly undressed each other. It was a marvelous sensation to feel the cool mountain air against our hot bodies. Judy's hands burned a path to my dick as my hands caressed her body. Soon two of my fingers were buried in her pussy. As she danced on my fingers, my other hand played with her nipples, which had hardened in the night air.

I picked her up and carried her to the other side of the car so that we would be shielded in the event that a car came down the country lane that ran in front of the house. Judy bent over the hood and I stood behind her with my dick poised to penetrate her hot pussy. It was a strange and wonderful sensation to fuck outside. As my dick slid into Judy's pussy, it was enveloped by that warm, wet sensation that men love. Each time I pulled out, the air cooled off my dick, providing a real head rush. While fucking this way I was also able to watch cars on a main road a half mile away. It was a sensory delight.

After about ten minutes of fucking Judy doggie-style, she turned around, dropped to her knees and proceeded to suck my cock. It is always great to get a blowjob outdoors. Something about Judy's mouth around my dick, her hand caressing my balls and the billions of stars overhead was very erotic. But I felt selfish about her doing all the work, so I threw my jacket on the ground, laid Judy down on it and poised to fuck her hard and fast.

I lifted her legs over my shoulders and penetrated her as deeply as my dick would go. When I do this it allows me to roll my pelvis against her and thus stimulate her clit. It only took a few rolls of my hips for Judy to have her first orgasm. I slowed my pace for a moment so that she could catch her breath. We continued to fuck this way for several more minutes and Judy had two more intense orgasms. I was still recovering from the intense fuck we had had earlier that afternoon so I wasn't able to come again, but this enabled me to concentrate on giving Judy pleasure.

Afterward we gathered our clothes, which were strewn around the yard, and walked naked into the house for a glass of wine and a respite. We sat on the couch naked, chuckling about fucking outside like a couple of teenagers. I went and got a cigar for a rare evening smoke. I lit the cigar and held Judy in my arms as she slowly began playing with my dick.

While I was smoking the cigar, Judy transformed my dick into steel. Without saying a word she knelt on the floor and began to suck my cock. It was the most sensual experience I've ever had. Finally I put out the cigar and told Judy that it was now her turn to receive. Hand in hand, we walked to the bedroom.

Judy stretched out on the bed and purred that she wanted to be fucked. I told her to just lay back and enjoy herself. I started by kissing my way to her pussy. I began to explore its shape with the tip of my tongue. Judy began to squirm when I stuck my tongue into her slit and slowly moved it up to her clit. Then I moved back down to the entrance of her pussy and slowly inserted my tongue into her hot hole. I tongue-fucked her for a few minutes until she began rolling around the bed. Next I dragged my tongue up to her clit and lightly moved the tip around the base of her pearl of pleasure.

I sucked lightly on her clit while I flicked the end of it with the tip of my tongue. That was all it took for her to go over the top and experience the first of several orgasms. After allowing her to recuperate, I began gently sucking her clit again and was soon rewarded with her second orgasm. At this point she was ready to fuck.

I moved up her body and positioned my dick at the entrance to her pussy. She arched her back, inviting me to penetrate her. But I wanted her to enjoy the sensation of my hard member slowly piercing her pussy. I wanted her to feel her pussy expand around the head of my dick and then slowly envelop the shaft. It was important to me that she feel each ridge and bump on my dick as it made its way into the depths of her pussy.

Slowly, slowly I pushed my engorged member into her depths. Then I waited as she luxuriated in the flood of sensations. When she opened her eyes and smiled, I began to slowly fuck her with long, deep strokes. She responded with another orgasm.

We rolled over and she began to ride my dick as if it were a wild stallion. As she bounced up and down and rubbed her clit against my pelvis, she kept telling me how much she liked to fuck me. I asked her if she would like me to penetrate even deeper. She smiled and said, "Sure." So, with her still on top, I pulled her legs onto my shoulders and she sank even deeper onto my dick.

Though this position got my dick deep in her pussy, it made it somewhat difficult to move. I suggested that Judy turn around and face my feet so she'd have greater mobility. Judy likes new ways to fuck, so she quickly assumed this new position. She could move more easily this way and we both enjoyed the sensations as my dick penetrated her pussy from a whole new angle.

While we were fucking this way I had a terrific view of Judy's pink, puckered asshole. I knew from past experience that Judy had never developed a taste for anal play, so I decided to go slowly. I positioned a finger so that it grazed her asshole every time she rocked back toward me. At first she was a bit surprised. She seemed on the verge of asking me to remove my finger until I told her in a firm, husky voice that she should enjoy the new experience. I continued to play with her back door as we continued to fuck.

When Judy got tired we repositioned ourselves so that I was fucking her doggie-style. This is a position she likes when she is really hot, and I had never seen her this hot before. I moved my dick in and out in long, measured strokes so that we could establish a rhythm. At this point we had been fucking for about an hour, and I could feel that I would soon come.

As I fucked Judy from behind, I continued to play with her ass. Slowly I inserted a finger up to the first knuckle. Judy was skeptical but I was gentle, and soon she began to feel pleasurable sensations welling up from both her pussy and her ass. I pushed my finger in deeper and soon I could feel my dick through her pussy wall. I asked Judy what she wanted. She turned her head and said that I already knew what she wanted. I asked her if she was sure. She said that until now she had never trusted anyone to fuck her in the ass and reminded me to be gentle.

The fact that she had enough faith in me to let me fuck her virgin ass both flattered and aroused me. I began to slowly massage her anus. Then I worked two fingers into her up to my knuckles. She was enjoying the sensation, so I put lubricant on my dick and very slowly entered her ass. I wanted to go slow and gentle so that Judy wouldn't feel any pain. After I had my dick deep in her ass, I stopped moving so that she could get accustomed to the feeling. I asked her if everything was all right. She said she was fine. Then she rocked back onto my dick, and I started fucking her ass in earnest. Judy had never been as vocal as she was then. She squealed in pleasure and asked me to keep fucking her ass.

Soon the cumulative excitement of the evening and the delicious novelty of fucking Judy's tight ass became too much for me. I could feel my abdominal muscles begin to contract. This was going to be one big fucking orgasm. I told Judy that I was about to come and she said she was too. It felt like molten lava when the come came out of the end of my dick. I bellowed like a wild bull and Judy screamed as she had her own orgasm. I continued to pump her ass, shooting wad after wad into the depths of her bowels.

We collapsed on the bed with my dick still buried deep in her ass. I tried to pull out but Judy wanted me to stay in her ass. She said it felt too good to lose. After a few minutes we disentangled and collapsed into an exhausted sleep.—*R.G., New York, New York*

Someone's Watching

GOLFING BUDDIES BALL CLUB SECRETARY IN HEAD PRO'S INNER SANCTUM

During the first six years of our marriage, I tried talking to my wife about things like swapping, or possibly engaging in a three-way, but Amanda never had the nerve to do anything. However, shortly after I got her a job, as the director's secretary at the country club where I'm the physical training instructor, she had an adventure I'd like to share.

It all started one morning when Amanda was in my office, which is next to the men's locker room. Right in the middle of our conversation, I noticed her staring out the door with her mouth hanging open, her eyes bulging. Out in the hallway, two of the members, who are always playing stupid macho games, were standing stark naked, arguing over which one of them had the biggest dick. Amanda couldn't take her eyes off them, and I couldn't blame her; even hanging limp, it was obvious that both these guys had huge cocks. I waited a minute, but when they didn't go back into the locker room I yelled, "Gentlemen please, there's a lady present." They stopped horsing around but made no effort to cover themselves. Instead, when they saw Amanda's expression, they just stood there letting her have a good, long look. It had such an effect on her, I wondered if Amanda could be tempted to experiment with someone who was really hung.

The director goes home at two o'clock, leaving Amanda alone on the second floor until five. If I'm not busy, I go up and visit with her when no one's around. A little after three o'clock, I was approaching her office when I heard voices. Not wanting to disturb her, if whatever she was doing was important, I crept forward and peeked around the corner. As soon as I saw Butch and David, the same two men from that morning, I knew what they were up to. My only problem with it was, when I'd talked to Amanda about a threesome, I'd assumed I'd be one of the three.

The two men had come to Amanda on the pretext of checking their memberships. While she was going through their files, David said, "We're sorry about what happened earlier. Did we embarrass you?"

Amanda gave them a sheepish smile and replied, "A little."

Butch then asked, "Since you had the opportunity to check us out, which one of us do you think has the biggest cock?" I was shocked by my conservative wife's boldness; without looking up from the file she was holding, she meekly answered, "Before I can make a definite statement, I'd have to see them again, up close and hard."

In an instant, the two men were out of their clothes and around the desk, with both their dicks being stroked to erection by my sexy wife. They were so similar, it took Amanda a while to choose, but when she picked Butch, he yelled, "Yes, and to the victor go the spoils. I get to go first."

He quickly spun Amanda around, bent her over the desk, pulled her slacks and panties down and moved in to fuck her from behind.

Right then I nearly panicked. Even though I had encouraged this, and even though I was standing there watching it happen, I suddenly wasn't sure if I wanted another man screwing my wife. Well, it was too late. Amanda had a look of pure ecstasy on her face as Butch pushed his thick, ten-inch pleasure stick inside her, stretching and filling her vagina like I'll never be able to. His equipment was so much larger than she was accustomed to, he had to go slow. But he eventually got it all the way in.

It must have felt wonderful, because Amanda climaxed after just a few full strokes. She bit her lower lip and pumped her ass backward to make sure she was getting everything Butch could offer. Feeling Amanda's pussy contracting must have been too much for Butch because, unfortunately, Butch quickly blew his load. Amanda's disappointment (and Butch's embarrassment) caused him to leave without saying another word.

Meanwhile, David went to Amanda and repositioned her so that she was lying longways atop the desk, on her back. I watched with fascination as my wife spread her legs and guided the second stranger's erection to her love-hole. With one slow but steady push, he sank his big shaft all the way inside, once again filling Amanda's pussy to the brim. Then, as he began pumping into her, she sighed with joy, wrapped her legs around his hips, and humped her pelvis to meet his every thrust.

He had her hold the edge of the desk, to prevent her from sliding. This freed his hands to unbutton her blouse and open the front hook of her 34C bra. He then squeezed her titties and pinched her nipples while he plunged in and out of her love-nest. David turned out to be a much better lover than Butch, giving Amanda three good orgasms before he climaxed. Then, as his cock exploded inside her, she had one more superstrong orgasm. They were really slamming into each other, all squishy and hot.

When they were finished, they went to the director's private bathroom. Amanda stopped at the door, saying, "I have to use the toilet." What she wanted was for David to wait while she went, because she's very shy about anyone seeing her going.

When Amanda returned, she licked David's dick and balls, and when he started getting hard again, she took his cock into her mouth and sucked him back to full erection. This really knocked me for a loop, since Amanda always insisted that oral sex is dirty and didn't want anything to do with it. Yet there she was, lovingly slurping away on David's big, fat boner, giving him her first blowjob.

I think she would have continued until he came down her throat, but a phone call interrupted them. While Amanda sat on the director's chair talking on the phone, David crawled under the desk and buried his face between her thighs. It was kind of funny watching my wife trying to carry on a conversation while her new friend was licking her slit and nibbling her clit. By the time the call ended, Amanda's legs were spread wide open, hanging over the chair's armrests, and her free hand was pushing on the back of David's head. Shortly after she hung up, she began jerking and letting out a series of short, raspy sighs as David brought her to another tremendous climax.

After her orgasm subsided, Amanda sat David down and mounted him right there behind the director's desk. Unfortunately, their location greatly limited my view. I could see Amanda from the chest up, as she rocked back and forth, humping David's big dick. And I saw her placing his hands on her breasts, but the real action, down below, eluded me.

Then, when David stood up and laid my wife back on the floor,

I had to be content with the sounds of my wife's moans and that unique sloshing noise that only a well-fucked pussy makes. I think David gave Amanda four more strong orgasms, as once again he proved to be a very apt lover. He lasted a good twenty minutes before shooting his second load deep inside her.

After that, Amanda was really cute when she took hold of David's spent cock and led him back to the bathroom, where this time she insisted that they bathe each other. The two of them then jumped into the shower together where, incredibly, David got another erection and fucked Amanda again, filling her full of his seed for the third time.

After that day, Amanda was very receptive to the idea of a repeat liaison with the two men. But unfortunately we haven't seen either of them since they found out she's my wife.—*T.O.*, *Gainesville, Florida*

HOW ARE YOU GOING TO KNOW WHAT YOUR WIFE WANTS IF YOU DON'T ASK HER?

I never thought I'd be writing our experiences to *Penthouse Letters*. I have enjoyed reading *Penthouse Letters* for years, but that's precisely why I've never written in, because I've never experienced anything like what I read in your magazine.

It happened like this: The air-conditioning system at work broke down. It was hot, humid and claustrophobic, so I decided to go home early. I told my secretary to forward any important phone calls to me at home.

Well, the phone was ringing as I entered the house. I thought, Not already. I put my briefcase down and answered the phone—just seconds after my wife had evidently answered it upstairs.

Before I could say hello, I realized a conversation was already beginning. I heard a man's voice identifying himself as Stan. This Stan, who was a stranger to me, was evidently very intimate with my wife. He was telling Cheryl, my wife, that he wanted to bring a friend of his over on Wednesday. He said he'd bragged to his friend about how sexy, talented and enthusiastic Cheryl was. He interrupted his train of thought to ask if Cheryl was playing with her clit.

"Of course I am, you silly man. Didn't I tell you that I finger myself every time we talk on the phone? I get turned on just by the sound of your voice."

It sounded like bad phone sex.

Stan went on, saying that he'd told George that when Cheryl gave him a blowjob, she'd not only blow his cock, she'd blow his mind! "So when I bring him over, I want you to really gobble his dick like he's never had it before."

I was astounded, to say the least.

Cheryl then asked what he looked like. Stan said he had sandy-colored hair and a good build—they knew each other from the gym. He also said that he knew Cheryl liked her lovers to be well hung, and he didn't think she'd be disappointed with George.

Stan wanted to know if one o'clock Wednesday afternoon would be okay. Cheryl said it would. Stan then said he'd still be by for their regular fun and games on Friday. He said that yet another guy, Nick, would also be along on Friday, but that he was really pissed that he couldn't get off work on Wednesday. Stan said, "We could have really given you a good workout if all three of us could have made it. Maybe some other time. How would that suit you?"

"You know I'm always open to new experiences, Stan-the-Man."

I hung up confused, angry, intrigued and uncertain. But one thing was sure—I had an aching hard-on.

Now, Cheryl and I have shared a lot of fantasies and viewed a lot of erotic videotapes. We especially dig threesomes, and I've always told Cheryl that I'd like to see her take on two guys like in the movies. She was always turned-on by the fantasies, but she would never commit to actually trying one.

From the sound of this phone call, however, she had suddenly taken on a second personality. The prim and proper housewife had given way to a new personality—a liberated, free-loving, open-to-anything (or anyone) sexpot.

When Cheryl came downstairs, I decided not to say anything. I decided to let circumstances follow their own path, but I took my lunch hour Wednesday a little late so that I'd be able to observe my wife's "friends" arrive at the appointed hour. I recognized Stan. He was a fellow who worked at the garage where we get our cars fixed. He had dark, wavy hair, a perpetual five-o'clock shadow, a dark complexion and a great build. The other guy I'd never seen before, as far as I could tell. I watched them enter the house, and I wanted desperately to observe whatever was going to happen, but I had to get back to work. Visions kept forming in my mind of Cheryl servicing these two hot studs. I realized I wasn't angry or even jealous, really. I was excited, and I couldn't get rid of my rock-hard cock.

I made a point on Thursday of stopping for gas at the garage on the way home from work. When I saw that Stan was working, I decided to get a quick oil change as well.

Stan was seated in the office. His broad shoulders and muscled chest tapered to a narrow waist. His hefty thighs were spread wide—I imagined how he would look naked, seated like that with my wife kneeling between his thighs, sucking his cock—which I was sure she had done. More than once.

I stuck my head in his door. "How you doing, Stan?"

He was cool as a cucumber. "I'm great, Joe. How's that sexy wife of yours. Haven't seen her in here in a while."

"She's fine, Stan. She's fine."

The next day, Friday, I went by our house to see if Stan would show with Nick. As it happened, Stan's car was already there, as was another. I wasn't pissed that the three of them were having a wild time. I wanted to be there with them.

I suddenly remembered that there had been a recent change in our sex life. I recalled that Cheryl was much more randy lately, and that she seemed to enjoy sucking my cock more and longer than she used to. So I related this increased interest in sex to what she was learning from these guys, her lovers.

I decided I would quietly enter the house, just to see how things were transpiring, and leave undetected, if possible, without having interrupted things.

I successfully entered and heard Stan yelling, "Fuck her, Nick, fuck her hard. Oh shit, I think she's going to suck my nuts right through my cock. Go, Cheryl. Yeah, baby, suck my cock, sweet thing. Oh, God, I'm coming, I'm coming."

Then there was a silence. Finally Stan said, "Eat it all! Oh God, yes. You are the one."

I walked up to our bedroom and peeked in through the crack in the door. There was my loving wife, lying back on the bed naked, a white man's dick in her mouth and a black man's dick between her spread legs.

Just as I looked in, Stan was pulling his spent dick out of Cheryl's mouth and Nick was speeding up his humping motion.

Cheryl lifted up her legs so that the backs of them were flush against Nick's dark chest. Nick started reaming my wife like I've seen nowhere else before, not on videotape, not in real life. I started sweating just watching.

When Cheryl started yelling that she was going to come. Stan started nibbling on her engorged nipples. This really set her off, and as her pussy started contracting around Nick's dick, Nick started shooting into Cheryl's cunt. Their natural rhythm was incredible and they came simultaneously for close to five minutes.

I decided to hightail it out of there before I was discovered. I was glad I finally knew what the deal was.

That night I told my wife that I'd seen her that afternoon. I told her that I'd forgotten some papers and had to come home to get them at lunchtime. Cheryl looked like a doe caught by a pair of headlights, but I assured her that I wasn't angry. I just wanted her to be honest with me and keep me informed of her activities. I said, "You know we used to fantasize with that black rubber dildo. I'd fuck you with that rubber dick and you'd suck my cock and we'd pretend to be having a threesome." I felt responsible for pushing the idea, and I wanted to let Cheryl know that it was all right with me.

I asked her how she had gotten it started. She explained that it began when her car had needed work. She took it to the garage, and Stan offered to drive her home, saying he'd bring her car to her when it was repaired.

When he drove her home, Cheryl invited him in for a cup of coffee. Stan started putting the make on her, but nothing actually happened. When he brought her car back, however, Cheryl had just gotten out of the shower and was wearing only a dressing gown. When she tried to write out the check, her left breast popped free. She apologized.

Stan said "Don't apologize. It's beautiful, and I bet you have another just like it." He got behind her, kissed her on the back of the neck and reached his right hand around her and into her gown to grab hold of a tit. From then on, she became putty in his hands, and before he left she sucked him off and got him hard again so he could fuck her.

They started seeing each other regularly. Stan used to quiz her a lot about what she and I did in bed. She'd even gotten out the black dildo and had Stan use it on her as I did. He told her he had something better. He said, "Why pretend we're having a threesome when we can have the real thing?" and that's how he introduced Nick to the equation.

The next date she had with Stan was at his place. He got her all naked and hot and ready to be fucked, and then he asked if she would like a big black dick to fuck her while she sucked his cock. She agreed and he called Nick in. He was already stripped, and he came in sporting the biggest, blackest, thickest cock she'd ever seen. She let Stan's cock drop out of her mouth in amazement as Nick got on the bed between her legs and rubbed his big purple head all over her cunt lips. Then he gently eased into her and stuffed her cunt with more cock than she had ever imagined. She said she thought she'd go out of her mind with ecstasy as Stan fucked her mouth and Nick reamed her deeper and wider than she'd ever been reamed.—*Name and address withheld*

BASS PLAYER STOPS PLAYING SECOND FIDDLE AND SCREWS LEAD SINGER'S WIFE

*M*y wife hadn't been on a lot of dates before I met her—she's too damn shy. She hasn't really turned into a party animal since we've been married, either. 'Bout the only socializing she does is when she helps me out with the band I play in—on the few gigs we get.

She's known the bass player for years, and she really loves talking to him. Sometimes Kelly cooks dinner for the band, and on those occasions she and Paul will talk for hours. After dinner, Paul would sit on the couch across from Kelly and completely monopolize her time.

One night I noticed him playing with his crotch, and I wondered why. I looked over at my wife, and there was Kelly, sitting with her legs just slightly open. Kelly's white lace panties were showing, and you could see just a few light brown hairs curling around from behind her panties. I'd never known my wife to be an exhibitionist, and I wondered if she knew what she was doing.

Every time Paul came over, he would sit across from Kelly and look her over. If she crossed her legs, or got up, or sat down, he would quickly look over.

Another night Kelly became a little drunk and Paul got bold and just stared at her pantied crotch all night long. Later that night, after everyone had gone, I talked to Kelly and asked if she knew what she was doing. Having had too much to drink, she admitted that she was fond of Paul and she didn't care if he was sneaking a peek. She said that it was kind of exciting, the idea that Paul would want to see her. I suggested she should go the whole nine yards and wear a nightie next time he's around. She looked at me with those chestnut eyes and said she could never do such a thing. She didn't mind flirting, but that was as far as she could go.

After that night, however, she became more adventurous, leaving her shirt halfway unbuttoned, wearing see-through panties. I must admit, I was starting to feel sorry for poor Paul. He would leave horny, and I would get the best sex of my life.

One night we were watching *Mary Poppins* on TV. Kelly was wearing a dark blue negligee. We had been drinking wine, and right when Kelly went to get another bottle from the kitchen, I heard the doorbell ring and went to answer the door. There I found a very sad-looking Paul. He had just broken up with his girlfriend and needed a shoulder to cry on.

Kelly came back with more wine, poured Paul a glass and we all settled down to watch the rest of the movie. I'll be damned if Paul wasn't constantly looking at Kelly throughout the whole goddamned movie. Kelly was getting tipsy (it doesn't take much) and with every commercial seemed to slide closer to Paul. Before long, she had her head in his lap and he was playing with her hair. She would giggle and purr each time he tickled her ear, and Paul started looking down the length of her body. When he got to her toes, he looked up and saw me looking at him. He knew he was caught, and he stammered something about how pretty Kelly's lacy nightie was.

I sarcastically told him he should see her underwear. Kelly got up at that moment to get another glass of wine, and Paul remarked that he could see plenty. When Kelly sat back down, she said, "If you show me yours, I'll show you mine."

"How far do you want to go?" Paul asked.

"Well, let's just start with the undies. Are you game, honey?" she asked me.

"You guys are on your own," I said. "You don't need my approval."

"All right Paul," Kelly said. "You first."

"You come uncover whatever you want to see," Paul intoned.

Kelly slowly undid Paul's shirt and pulled it open. Giggling, she pinched his nipples and then rubbed her hands over his hairy chest. Then she licked her finger and attacked his belly button. Paul jumped at having a wet finger stuck in his belly button, but Kelly was not deterred. She reached down and started unbuttoning his fly.

When she got them all the way open, there was this huge bulge of dick and balls encased in tightie-whitie Calvins.

"Holy shit," my wife said in genuine surprise. When she realized that she'd said it out loud, she covered her blushing face and ran into the kitchen.

"C'mon, honey," I yelled into the kitchen, "a deal's a deal."

She came sheepishly back into the TV room but soon broke into a shit-eating grin.

"All right, Paul, what do you want to see?"

"Whatever you want to show me, Kelly."

She stood in front of my band mate, and I watched as Kelly's eyes grew bigger and bigger. Paul took each of Kelly's hands and pulled her toward him. I could not believe the look of lust in this man's eyes. He untied the bow at the front of my wife's nightie and gasped as the thing fell open. Kelly was wearing panties, but she wasn't wearing a bra, and Paul looked like he was trying to stare at everything all at once.

"Man, Kelly," Paul gasped, "you're tits aren't particularly big, but they're the most perfectly shaped tits I've ever laid eyes on."

Turning to me with a salacious smile on his face, he said, "Damn, Ned, now I know why you're always late for our jam sessions. You been bonin' this fine piece of meat all day long."

"Watch it, Paul," I solemnly said. "That's my wife standing naked in front of you."

We all laughed, and in his mirth. Paul took the opportunity to slide his hand up the back of Kelly's leg and grab ahold of her ass. "Jesus, Kelly, I never realized you were so sexy," Paul said. Kelly, who had suddenly become very nervous, stammered a thank-you and quickly grabbed her wine glass.

As she drank, the room became very quiet. We went back to watching the movie, and Paul continued to look Kelly over. After a while, Kelly's wine glass was empty again, and she got up and walked over to Paul, where the wine bottle was. When she started to go back to her chair, Paul asked her to put her head back in his lap.

"Oh, what the fuck," Kelly said. Once her head was in his lap, it was my turn to feel that lovely butt. From my end of the couch, I slid my hand up Kelly's taut legs and firmly grabbed a cheek. Paul's right, I have to admit it: she's a fine piece of meat.

Toward the end of the movie, when I knew that Paul was catching a buzz himself, I slid Kelly's panties away from her crotch and stared down at her twat. I could clearly see her pussy lips—they had started to glisten with her juices. Paul started to play with her hair again, and Kelly started to purr just like before. Then Paul bent over and kissed her ear, whispering how great she looked. Kelly smiled and stated that she was really very plain.

Paul started to laugh and asked if she could feel anything getting hard in his pants. I had failed to notice her hand under her head. She very quietly said yes, and she did not remove her hand.

Paul started to get very interested in Kelly's back. He started to rub her neck and lower back and Kelly mentioned how great it felt. He asked if she would like a back rub.

"Only if you stay right where you are," was her answer.

"You mean my hand?" Paul asked.

"That's right."

Paul started rubbing Kelly's back through her nightie, and with each stroke, more and more of her back became visible. Paul was acting like he was watching the movie, but most of the time his eyes were glued to Kelly's great ass.

I said to myself, Oh, what the hell, and proceeded to pull Kelly's panties off. Kelly's pussy lips were bright pink, and juices were starting to run into the couch.

Paul kissed Kelly's neck and asked her if she would like to undo his pants. All Kelly could say was yes. Paul stopped rubbing her back, and she sat up and threw her nightie to the floor. Paul quickly started unbuttoning his pants, and Kelly said, "Wait a minute, That's my job."

When Kelly saw Paul's underwear-clad package again, all she could say was, "Oh, Paul." She slowly started to play with Paul's dick and Paul started to rub Kelly's ass, then lightly scratching her back all the way up the back of her neck.

He kissed her again and asked if she wanted to see his cock. Kelly said nothing and Paul said, "I'll take that as a yes."

Kelly still did not say anything, and so Paul decided to wait, turning his attention instead to Kelly's hot torso. Paul looked over my wife's body, touching her very softly and telling her how soft her skin was. I got on the floor behind Kelly and started to tickle her ass, running my fingers over her pussy lips.

Judging from the wetness of it, I could tell that Kelly's pussy was ready to be fucked, and my cock just ached to do that. I had been playing with Kelly's pussy for so long that I did not notice Paul starting to moan. I looked at Paul's crotch, and there was my wife's little hand, slowly rubbing his cock up and down. I hadn't even seen her pull his underwear down!

Paul quickly pulled his pants off, and Kelly's full attention was on his cock. She started to cup his balls and then kissed each one. Then she licked them and rolled her face into his crotch. I couldn't believe my eyes when I saw my wife sit all the way up and then slowly lower her head to Paul's pole, sucking him all the way into her mouth. Paul started to moan, begging Kelly not to stop before he came.

All of a sudden we had gone from light petting to serious love-making. Kelly pulled her mouth away and blew on Paul's wet cock before engulfing the thing again. My wife is kind of small, and it was so sexy watching her dainty little head being skull-dragged by Paul's huge dick. She was huffing and puffing but she was not giving up.

After about twenty minutes of this, I watched as Paul's toes started to go straight, then limp, then straight again. Then a look of absolute pleasure crossed Paul's face as he started to pump his hips. I guess my wife figured she didn't have anywhere else to put his come, so she decided to put it in her stomach. Kelly started to giggle as Paul continued to pump come into her mouth. As he started to relax, he looked down and could only see her back and butt. He slowly rubbed her and told her how great she was. He was trying to see her pussy as I fingered and licked her pink hole.

Even after he was soft, Kelly continued to play with Paul's cock. She told him how beautiful it was, and with that Paul started to get hard again.

All this time I continued to finger my wife, and I could tell it would only be a matter of minutes before she came. Presently, Kelly started to moan, and I continued to work on her pussy. Her butt started to go up and down on my hand. All of a sudden Kelly turned around and said she didn't want Paul to see her come.

"Honey, he just shot his wad down your throat. I think you guys are beyond the coy stage."

With that she let go, vigorously humping up and down on my hand. I was working my two big fingers all the way in to her cervix, and when my entire hand was wet I slipped my thumb up her tight asshole. She really started going crazy, crying out the high-pitched scream she emits every time she comes.

"See, goddamn it, I don't want Paul to hear how silly I sound when I come." To muffle her cries, she stuck Paul's cock back in her mouth. I had two fingers up her dripping twat and my thumb up her ass: I felt like we were connected.

Then, about five minutes later, I watched her legs straighten and, popping Paul's cock out of her mouth, she slammed her ass down on my hand and started coming, screaming out loud like a madwoman.

When she was done, she hid her face in Paul's lap and said how embarrassed she was. Paul was lightly playing with her hair and said how sexy it was to see her come. Kelly asked for a glass of wine, and Paul refilled her glass, handing it to her.

After one sip, Kelly announced that she had to pee. She jumped up and ran for the bathroom. Paul followed her pussy lips all the way. After Kelly left, Paul apologized, but I would hear none of it.

Suddenly realizing that I was the only one who was dressed, I stripped, and when I saw my cock and how hard it was. I brought it to Paul's attention and said, "Judging from the size of this thing, do you think I mind?"

"Man, I've been wanting to see your wife in the buff ever since I met her. She's incredible, Ned."

"Don't I know it, Paul."

Kelly came back in time to hear the last of our conversation. Seeing her bush for the first time, Paul had to catch his breath.

"I wish I could have some of that," Paul said, and Kelly just walked right up to Paul and straddled his lap.

Paul's cock was so hard, the head was purple. It was just grazing her pubic hair, and he grabbed hold of her ass and started to pull her closer to him. All she could say was, "Paul, I can't stop you," and with that she closed her eyes and he kissed her. I watched as she took hold of his cock, lifted herself up and put it into her. She opened her eyes and whispered into his ear, "Fuck me, please."

Paul slowly started to push his cock in, and with each push, Kelly would gasp. Kelly started to move up and down, and Paul started to push it deeper. They both started to moan, and soon Paul was seriously banging his cock into her. He slowly turned her so that she was lying down and he was on top. Kelly wrapped her legs around him and begged him to go faster. She started to cry and laugh at the same time, saying how great it felt. I could tell she was coming when she spread her legs and hands, then pushed her groin into him and grabbed his ass. Then he started to come into her. With each spurt, he moaned aloud. They were truly bumping uglies, slapping into each other's sweaty body.

Finally, he let out a shriek and collapsed onto Kelly's chest.

Kelly looked at my pole sticking up and said, "You poor dear, you need some help." With that she pushed Paul onto the floor, got on all fours and put that beautiful butt in the air. I could see Paul's come on her pussy, and it felt really weird as I slid my cock into her. I started to fuck her and Paul just watched her breasts swinging.

"I didn't think anything would be hotter than fucking you," Paul said, "but watching Ned fuck you like that is so incredibly hot..."

As soon as he said that, she seemed to change and started to come one more time. I could hardly contain myself. I could feel the pressure in my balls and Kelly knew I was ready to come. As she reached under to play with my balls, Paul stood up and positioned himself before my wife's face. She opened her mouth to take Paul's cock one more time. When I started to come, Kelly was so taken with Paul's cock that she leaned forward and my dick popped out. I grabbed my cock and jerked off all over Kelly's ass.

Right about the same time, Paul started coming again, and when

Kelly could take no more in her mouth, she pulled her mouth away and took a couple of last squirts in her face before collapsing onto the couch.

Paul looked at me and said, "I guess we burned her out." Kelly could not move. She had her finger on her clit and all she could do was moan. Paul looked at me, and asked if he could look at her pussy, as he'd really never gotten a good look at it. I turned Kelly over and Paul sat at my end of the sofa. He very gently opened Kelly's legs and pulled her pubic hair back. He separated her lips, bent over and softly kissed her pink hole.

Then Paul said he'd better be going, he had to be at work at six in the morning. Just before he walked out the door, he went back to Kelly, and I heard him say, "I've always loved you, and I will always be jealous of Ned."

He touched her right breast, kissed her lightly on the head and said good night.—*N.H., Barnwell, South Carolina* ⊙┼▪

HUBBY HIRES AN ITALIAN STALLION TO GIVE WIFEY THE RIDE OF HER LIFE

*M*ichelle and I have been married for ten years. We have a good marriage because we are always very understanding of each other. Michelle was a virgin before our honeymoon and, up until recently, I was the only man she had ever known sexually.

For quite some time I fantasized about Michelle in the hands of other men. Her conservative style always made me reluctant to ask her what she thought of this fantasy. One morning, I told her that I had dreamt she was having an affair with her favorite soap star—a tall, dark Italian stud. She didn't say much, but I could tell by the took on her face that she wished it were true.

Michelle has a good body for a thirty-year-old. She stands five feet two inches tall, has medium-sized tits, shapely legs and a nice, round ass. Her curly reddish-brown hair and deep blue eyes are eye-catching, and so is her soft smile and graceful body. She has creamy skin and powder-pink nipples atop firm, perky tits. Working out daily has kept her in top form.

I am a very wealthy, thirty-two-year-old businessman. I am five feet eleven inches tall and of average build. I travel quite a bit and my schedule changes constantly, often on very short notice. Unfortunately, my business causes me to neglect Michelle. It also causes some erection problems when we make love. Even when erect, my penis is only five inches long. I've always thought Michelle needed more than I can give. Several times I have hinted at this—telling her how I've heard women love big, thick cocks. She always blushes and compliments the things I can do with my own apparatus. I wonder if my hints have made her think I'm insecure.

Anyway, I thought of a way to find out if she could use something more. I had to create a situation behind her back because she is much too shy to help in the planning. I remembered the son of one of my clients who lives a hundred miles away. Tom is unemployed, twenty-one years old and looks a great deal like my wife's television idol. I knew he would catch Michelle's eye with his six-foot frame, dark complexion, thick black hair and self-assured style. I hired Tom for a few days to do yard work on the back acres of our country estate. Since Tom lives so far away, I invited him to stay with us until completing the job.

The first morning, Michelle cooked breakfast for us. As we ate, I noticed Michelle furtively inspecting Tom from head to toe. He was wearing a T-shirt, shorts, and old sneakers. She was pretty slick about her inspection, but I could tell she had noticed the magnificent bulge in the young stud's shorts.

After we were through eating, I helped Tom get started on the landscaping project. That evening Tom and I showered while Michelle started dinner. I went to the master bathroom and Tom went to the shower in the guest room. I hurried, hopping in and out of the shower. As I dried off I noticed, through the partially open door, that Michelle was standing in the doorway of Tom's room. She could see him, but he couldn't see her. She stood watching him dry himself for a few minutes before she walked back into the kitchen.

When Tom and I came to dinner, he was wearing nothing but a blue pair of loose-fitting satin shorts that magnified the heft and length of his large penis. I could tell that he was having an effect on Michelle, even though she was trying hard not to look at him. She had a worried look on her face, as though she were having troubled thoughts.

As we ate, music became the topic of conversation and it became apparent that Michelle and Tom had quite a few tastes in common. As they were reminiscing about some old favorites, Michelle started loosening up. She got up to refill Tom's glass, brought it back and sat down in the chair beside him. I caught her looking Tom over more openly. There was a look in her eye that I had never seen before. As they got deeper into a discussion of early punk bands, I excused myself.

I left the room, but instead of going into my office, I crept around to the backyard and hunched down next to the glass patio door. I could barely see them but, as I had hoped, Michelle soon led Tom into the den and put some music on the stereo. I had a completely unobstructed view.

They started to dance very innocently, holding hands only. Then, about halfway through the song, Tom put his hands around Michelle's waist and she put hers around his neck. Michelle had the look of a woman who needed attention. She stared up into Tom's eyes as they swayed slowly across the floor, and his hands began to rub and caress her ass. She let him pull her against his hard body. Suddenly, the song ended and Michelle seemed to snap out of a trance. She rushed to the kitchen to clean up. I passed the kitchen on my way upstairs and told Michelle I would be leaving town in the morning and that I'd be gone on business for three to four days.

I left the next morning, driving to a path just down the road that led to the back of our property. I parked my car and walked back to the edge of the woods surrounding our backyard. Once there, I made myself comfortable, took out my high-powered binoculars and waited.

Tom had already started working in the yard. Towards noon, Michelle left in her car and returned about an hour later carrying a shopping bag. A little while later she came out wearing the tightest shorts I have ever seen. The shorts were shiny black vinyl and cut shorter than any she'd ever worn. She also had on a loose black blouse made entirely of lace that glided over her beautiful figure. She had come out to bring Tom a glass of water.

She handed Tom the water and bent over to inspect some of the new shrubs. Tom stared at her sassy-looking little body, and I noticed his shorts change shape as his dick rose within. It was so big, the head almost came out the top of his shorts. When Michelle turned around, she was staring right at Tom's dick.

Without a word, Tom reached out his hand and lifted her to him. Immediately they started kissing. Michelle started running her hands all over his back while he kissed her and pressed his hands against her cute little ass. She kissed his neck, sucked on his nipples and then ran her tongue all over his chest. Then she made her way down his dark body, raking her lips and tongue over his rippled abdomen and his waist as she slipped her hands into the back of his shorts to feel his butt.

She stood up and quickly unbuttoned her shorts and Tom pulled them down. He kneaded her beautiful ass while she felt up his dick and pulled his shorts completely off. They headed for the patio where Tom sat in a lounge chair. I was sure they would start fucking immediately. Instead, Michelle knelt down and started kissing Tom's enormous erection. This shocked me. Michelle has never given me head.

There she was, French-kissing the big swollen head of Tom's huge dick, causing his pre-come to glisten. She noticed it, touched the tip of her tongue to it and swirled it around, spreading pre-come all over the head of his dark red cock. Then she placed little wet, warm, sticky kisses all the way down the underside of his long, thick shaft.

I was so caught up in the action, it took me a while to notice that my own dick was harder than Chinese arithmetic. I watched as Michelle licked up and down Tom's massive shaft and washed his balls with her tongue. She worked her tongue back up to the head and sucked it inside her mouth. As she sucked, she moved her lips up and down very slowly.

Damn, she looked sexy, wearing nothing but that tight shirt, her long hair loose and tangled, her hands clutching the boy's thighs, her lips puckered up—kissing, sucking and licking that dick with a lustful look on her face!

She cupped one hand under his balls and started running the tips of her fingers across his sac. Meanwhile, she was still sucking his big dick, pulling on the head with her lips on every stroke. Her slim fingers caressing his balls and her hot, pink lips pulling on his peter were starting to get to him. I noticed his scrotum starting to draw up. It was for resolution this good that I shelled out over two grand for these binoculars.

Anyway, Michelle quit sucking and started licking again. She stiffened her tongue, pressing it against the side of his hard, swollen dick. Her tongue was so stiff and his dick was so hard that when her tongue touched it, it bobbed around, slipping away from her tongue and rubbing against her face. Tom's face was blood red and he started coming in jets, straight into the air! Michelle licked and fondled his cockhead as he came, catching a good deal of his come with her tongue and mouth. The rest splattered onto the patio.

Michelle licked her lips clean and sucked the last of the come off the end of Tom's cock. It was still hard as a rock. She stood and peeled off her skirt and climbed onto his lap, sliding her hot little pussy down over his dick. Michelle has the tightest pussy I've ever touched. Even though she and Tom were both wet and well-lubed, she still had to squirm to get his big dick all the way inside her.

Tom put his large, calloused hands on my wife's beautiful creamy ass and started squeezing and rubbing her sexy cheeks. She swayed slowly back and forth, impaling herself ever deeper on his hard dick. Michelle's creamy skin contrasted beautifully with Tom's dark skin. I watched her ass moving back and forth on his thighs, her tits with those hard pink nipples pressing into his huge hairy chest, her serious face kissing his neck and, most impressively, Tom's massive dick pumping in and out of her tight pink tunnel.

I thought it was all I could stand, but as I watched, things just kept getting better. Tom was thrusting and pumping while Michelle went into a fucking frenzy. The look on her face was something between pleasure and awe. Her hands and forearms flailed helplessly in the air as she was overtaken by the orgasm of her life. She was coming so feverishly that she tried to say something but couldn't. I thought they were going to stop, but they just slowed down a little and kept fucking.

When Michelle regained control, they established a slow, steady rhythm to their fucking. Michelle swiveled her hips around and around, bringing her gorgeous ass up high every time she rotated to the top. Tom's dick would almost pop out with every swivel. The head would slowly appear and poke at her tight opening before slipping back in.

One time, when his dick slipped out of her, she reached back and guided it back in with her sexy little hand. When it went in this time, it went all the way to the hilt, and Michelle gasped loudly. They both started thrusting and pumping at a faster pace, moaning and breathing heavily. He was pushing and pulling that whole nine inches of thick, hard dick in and out of my wife as she moaned loudly with pleasure. I couldn't believe I was standing in the bushes watching my horny little honey humping her heart out—fucking another man silly.

Suddenly Michelle leaned her head back, arched her back, stiffened her midsection and started jerking her pussy back and forth over Tom's dick. She started screaming as she came, her face turning red and tears of passion rolling down her flushed cheeks. Tom started coming inside my wife, moaning and gasping for breath as his scrotum tightened like wet leather in hot sunshine. They climaxed together and they weren't alone. I came in my pants and nothing had even touched my dick.

Later that night, while Tom and Michelle bathed and ate, I crept up to the house and set up my post outside the guest bedroom window. After dinner and drinks. Michelle led Tom to the guest room and dimmed the lights. He lay down on the bed on his back. She left and returned a few minutes later wearing a new negligee made of some see-through white fabric.

As I watched from the window, I found Michelle's bright red pubic hair and erect nipples startling under the translucent material. I couldn't take it anymore. I sneaked into the house for a better vantage point. I hid in the dim light behind my bedroom door, which was just across from the guest room.

Now I could hear them as well as see them. As Michelle climbed on top of Tom, I noticed she wasn't wearing panties. She sat on his stomach, and Tom reached up and started rubbing her beautiful tits. Michelle started grinding her pussy into his hairy chest. She carefully placed her wet pussy right on top of one of his stiff little nipples and pressed and rubbed against it. Watching her beautiful white flesh mash against Tom's tan muscles was arousing as hell!

She touched his large, hard dick and brushed her hand provocatively all over his balls and dick. Then she leaned over and started massaging his neck and caressing his chest. Tom reached up, tore the flimsy gown from her body and pulled her to him. She sucked his nipples awhile, then moved backwards, raking her tits across his chest and stomach before stopping at his dick. She rubbed both tits over his dick and balls. Then she took one tit and mashed it nipple-first into the top of his dick, causing pre-come to soak her nipple. Finally she put his dick between her tits and played with it. After a few minutes, she sat back on his chest and started humping with her ass again. I could hear her moan as she ground her cunt into his chest.

Tom grabbed her by her butt and pulled her hot pussy up to his face. He licked and kissed for a while, then started tongue-fucking her. It only took about a minute before she started coming. He rubbed his face back and forth against her pussy, really turning her on. He kissed her stomach and waist then concentrated once again on her hot cunt. This time he sucked. He was trying to suck her clit up into his mouth when Michelle started coming again. She bucked wildly while he fucked her with his tongue.

Tired of foreplay, Tom mounted Michelle, putting his monster cock inside her and pounding her pussy with everything he had. Michelle was whining with ecstasy. His balls bounced off her pussy every time he entered her. Tom was fucking so hard, the bed started shaking back and forth. All of a sudden Tom's muscles flexed. He withdrew his excited, reddish-purple cock and aimed it right at Michelle's tits. His come was under so much pressure it sprayed warm jets of semen all over her belly up to her chin.

That was the last round I witnessed. I tended to my business and gave them the next two days alone.

I still get a hard-on every time I think of Michelle putting Tom's big, tan dick in her mouth or in her tight pussy. I almost come thinking about how their bodies looked together—his hard, dark muscles mashing and pressing against her sweet, pink, tits and white body.

Despite all the lovemaking, Tom got through with the yard work. Now, every time I see him he asks me if I need help. I tell him not to worry. I'm saving all the chores for him since I know he can get the job done. Michelle seems happier than ever; but I know she's going to want some more of Tom before the leaves need raking.—*N.A., Chesapeake, Virginia* ⚬╍▪

THREE CARPENTERS NAIL COWORKER'S WIFE AND FIND SHE NEEDS GALVANIZING

I work for a large construction company, and I sometimes travel far away from home. Sometimes I'm on the road for weeks at a time.

There's one town about an hour away that I work in so often that I've got a regular setup. I share a room in a cheap boarding house with three other guys—all of whom happen to be black (except for me, of course). We've developed a pretty good friendship, these guys and me, and we often talk about fucking.

Now, James, Angus and Willie like to tease me about them wanting to fuck a white woman. They make no pretense at modesty, walking from the shower and bathroom completely naked, their long cocks hanging down. They say things like "Hey, could your wife take one this big?" and "Why don't you bring your wife up and let us stretch her pussy."

I always tell them they couldn't handle it. Anyway, they sure weren't going to get the chance to fuck her, if I had anything to do with it. I wasn't going to let her anywhere near those horny characters.

Well, as it turns out, I didn't have too much to do with it.

I usually phone my wife two or three times a week. When I told her about all of the teasing I had been getting from my roommates, about their wanting to fuck her, my wife got a devious tone in her voice. Alicia said that since they had never seen her, maybe she could come up Friday evening and stay the weekend. She would let them pick her up and we would pretend we didn't know each other. I told her about a bar we hang out at in the evening. We decided that she should go straight to the bar before we got off work and act like she was looking to pick somebody up.

When the day rolled around, it had been a particularly rough workday. I teased my friends back, saying that even if they could get some white pussy, they would be too tired to fuck it. This brought a lot of laughter.

"Oh, yes, white boy, you just watch and see how we stretch that white pussy."

I just nodded my head.

When we got to the bar, Alicia was already flirting with the bartender. She was really dressed up and perfectly manicured. Her pretty auburn hair had been styled, and she wore a very expensive, form-fitting, strapless black dress. The back was very low cut. When I saw her white panties just showing through the black dress, I knew that she was wearing her crotchless panties. Nylon stockings and black spike heels completed her outfit.

She made it appear that she was there just to be picked up. Angus was the first to notice her. He stated that he was going to fuck that rich white bitch. I egged them on, telling them, "She wouldn't even give you guys a chance to smell her pussy, much less fuck it."

Alicia looked our way and eyed Angus up and down. She turned on her stool and, as she parted her legs, the tight dress slid up her thighs, exposing her panties and her swollen cunt lips.

Angus said, "I know she wants my black dick. Hell, I'm going to fuck that white pussy."

I said I'd have to see it to believe it, and then I lied and said I was tired and that I was going back to the house. I knew it wouldn't be long before I was going to see what I had wanted to see for a long time: my beautiful Alicia getting gang-banged.

It was a couple of hours before I heard them coming down the hall. Alicia was giggling, and I took that as a good sign. When she's high on the booze, her pussy gets really hot. The door opened and I saw that James was carrying Alicia in his arms. The four of them swept right past me and headed for the bedroom. Alicia was giggling uncontrollably.

"Okay, baby," I heard James saying from the bedroom, "let's see those white titties." When I peeked my head in, I saw James unzipping her dress and pulling it down to her waist. Her perfectly rounded tits were revealed to him in all of their glory. The nipples looked like cherries, and Alicia moaned as James's black hands squeezed and tweaked them. James said, "I'm going to come on your titties." Alicia laughed and said, "Man, you been reading my mail. I love that."

All three took off their clothes and showed Alicia their hard cocks. Alicia said, "Oh, yes, fuck me. I want to feel your cocks inside of me."

James pulled off Alicia's crotchless panties and tossed them on the floor. He looked at Angus and said, "I'll get her pussy, you get her ass."

James lay back on the bed and Alicia straddled him. She sat straight down on his big cock. I know she was hot as a motherfucker, because his cock shot right up into her. Then she leaned forward and Angus spread her ass-cheeks, pushing two fingers into her puckered asshole.

Alicia moaned and pushed back, saying, "Oh, yes, fuck my tight ass. I want it up my ass. Show me how good you can fuck. Are you as good as you say you are?"

Angus pushed his dick all the way up her ass. Alicia moaned as two big, black cocks fucked her ass and pussy furiously. It looked like they couldn't be fucking her harder, but she kept crying out for more. Then Alicia cried out she was coming.

James laughed and said, "Come on my black dick. Let me feel your come."

Alicia screamed out, "Here it comes, baby."

Her pussy must have started doing some serious contractions, because James started busting his load inside of her.

In all the commotion, Angus's snake had slipped out of Alicia's ass. When she pulled up off of James, Angus grabbed her hips and thrust his dick into her come-filled pussy.

He was pounding like a madman, and he started coming almost immediately.

"Shoot it all over my back," Alicia cried, as Angus slipped out and started spewing wildly all over my wife's gorgeous back.

When Angus was finished blowing his wad, Alicia laughed and asked, "Who's next?" Willie offered her his cock. Alicia licked up and down his long, black shaft, sucking one of his balls into her mouth, then working back up to the large, velvety head. She sucked and jacked his cock at the same time.

When Alicia felt Willie's dick starting to erupt, she slipped his cock from her mouth and aimed it at her tits. She jerked him the rest of the way off, and he shot what must have been a half a pint onto her alabaster tits.

Alicia then lay on her back, her legs spread wide, her auburn pussy hair still smeared with come.

"Well, I thought you guys wanted to fuck. I'm waiting."

They each took turns fucking Alicia, and Alicia kept telling them she wanted more. Finally, they said they were all fucked out.

I mentioned the fact that I hadn't had my turn.

Alicia said, "Well, they sure can't satisfy me. Maybe you can."

I fucked Alicia three times while the others watched. Finally, Alicia said she had to stop for a while. I guess her pussy was a little sore from all of that good fucking.

We all fell asleep utterly exhausted. I woke up much later to the squeaking sound of a bed and Alicia's moans of passion. I looked and saw James's big black cock pumping in and out of Alicia's hot pussy. I just shook my head and continued to watch.

Alicia spent the weekend fucking and sucking. You should have seen the surprised looks on my colleagues' faces on Monday morning when Alicia hugged and kissed me and said, "Darling, do you want me to come up next weekend? This has been fun."

So I said, "Gentlemen, would you like for my wife to return next weekend?"

I swear to God, all three of those black guys turned white as a sheet.—*Name and address withheld* ⚬━▪

WHY NOT GIVE A LITTLE NOOKY TO HELP YOUR HUSBAND'S CAUSE?

*M*y wife and I have been married for almost fifteen years. Over the past seven years, Louise has screwed numerous men with my full knowledge and approval. She has settled down a little, but there was a time when she was screwing at least five guys a week. Although there is one aspect of this situation that bothers me, I am happy to have such a promiscuous wife. These extramarital relationships have transformed her from a straight-laced puritan into a wanton and completely uninhibited lover.

Although my wife would indulge in some heavy petting after we got engaged, she refused to let me screw her until our wedding night and continued to be very straight-laced after we were married. Most people who know Louise think that she would be the last woman in the world to be promiscuous. She plays the organ during church services and helps teach a children's Sunday school class. Although she favors sexy lingerie, she usually dresses quite conservatively, unless we are out on the part of town where people do not know us.

The stage for my wife's first affair was set when the company I work for got bought out and we became worried that I might be laid off. Louise reluctantly agreed that since our two oldest kids were in school, it would be okay for her to get a job, even though the baby was still in diapers. This would give us something to fall back on until I found a new position if I got laid off. She ended up getting work as a receptionist and secretary for a commercial real estate broker.

Soon after she started, however, Louise got upset and wanted to quit when her new boss requested that she wear more revealing clothes to the office. I've always been proud of her 36DD-26-38 figure and frustrated by her refusal to dress provocatively, so I insisted that she not quit and abide by her boss's dress code. Although she was uncomfortable with her new wardrobe at first, my wife soon relaxed and even admitted that she enjoyed the lustful looks she got from men. She also started to be a little more amorous with me.

Things got even more interesting when the holding corporation sent out one of their vice presidents to evaluate my office. It was understood that he would decide who would get laid off and would also pick the new division manager. Although I was young, I had done some excellent work and felt that I deserved the manager's position. The vice president was obviously a ladies' man and shamelessly flirted with the more attractive women at the office.

I was flattered by the interest he showed in the pictures of my wife that I keep on my desk. When he invited everyone to a banquet, I decided that it might help my chances if I could get Louise to flaunt her charms or even come on to him a bit. When I explained the situation to her, she agreed to do it. She even let me buy her a very low-cut evening gown and a sexy set of matching bra, panties, garter belt and stockings for the occasion. My mother had come to visit and she offered to watch the kids so that we could spend a romantic night at the hotel together. Although my wife was a little nervous about the banquet, she seemed to be looking forward to it. On the drive to the hotel, she told me she was feeling amorous and would be willing to help me out in any way she could.

As fate would have it, the vice president's suite was right next to ours, and there was even a set of connecting doors between the rooms. We ran into him in the hall as we were checking in. Alan obviously was attracted to my wife in her alluring evening gown, and she seemed to be taken by his rugged good looks and tall, heavily muscled body. He had a liter of rum and some mixers, which he shared with us in our room. As we drank and talked, Louise put the finishing touches on her hair and makeup while I got my camcorder set up so I could film the banquet.

Although he had to mingle with the other employees, Alan spent a lot of time at our table. He eventually asked my wife to dance with him, and of course I encouraged her to accept. The band favored slow songs, so he held her close as they danced.

The lighting was low, but I could tell that he was exploiting the opportunity to caress Louise's rear and fondle her breasts. I didn't think my wife was up to it, but she welcomed his roaming hands and let him do as he wished. It was like a parallel universe.

When I danced with my wife afterwards, she apologized to me for allowing my boss to take such liberties with her. She explained that while she felt like she was being somewhat unfaithful to me, she didn't want to pass up the chance to get crazy. I assured her that she hadn't done anything wrong, because letting another man feel her up wasn't the same as letting him screw her. When Louise mentioned that she could feel my erect dick pressed against her belly, I admitted that watching them had turned me on. She giggled and asked me if she had my permission to indulge in a little heavy petting with him as long as she didn't let things go too far. I encouraged her to do so.

Alan treated us to a continuous stream of free drinks during the evening, and Louise and I both got quite drunk. Alan and I took turns dancing with her, and we were both kissing her and reaching into her dress to fondle her breasts.

I eventually lost track of them and finally found them making out in a dark, secluded alcove. Alan was sitting on a couch and my wife was standing in front of him with the top of her evening gown pulled down to her waist. The scene was very exciting for me, and since my wife had assured me she wouldn't go too far, I didn't interrupt them. I took cover behind a potted tree where I could watch and tape the action on my camcorder without being noticed.

After engaging in some deep kissing, Louise stopped to take off her bra, then leaned forward to offer her bare breasts to him. Alan began to vigorously fondle, kiss, lick and suck on them. As he was feasting on Louise's tits, Alan slowly slid her dress over her hips and down her legs, leaving her naked except for her garter belt, stockings and skimpy panties.

After a few minutes, my wife knelt in front of Alan and pulled his pants down to release an impressive penis. I was a little jealous when she started to rub the head of his dick in her ample cleavage. She's seldom been willing to do that for me. Louise was obviously pleased with how big Alan's erection got as it reached its full glory, and I found the sight a little daunting. I have always known that at a little less than five inches long and barely four inches in circumference when fully erect, my penis is a lot smaller than average. Alan's dick appeared to be at least ten inches long and must have been as thick as my forearm!

After rubbing his tool in her cleavage for a while longer, my wife got up and sat on his lap, facing him so that his penis was pressed against her pubic mound. As he kissed and sucked on her breasts, she began to rub her pussy against the massive head. The flimsy material of my wife's G-string panties stretched enough that she was able to work an inch or two of the shaft into her slit. He kept encouraging her to take him in deeper and was soon getting frustrated because she either couldn't or wouldn't. He finally grabbed the waistband of her panties and pulled until it broke, then tossed them aside. Louise laughed out loud, saying, "Well, I never thought I'd be doing this."

Alan laughed as he held her in place with a firm grip on her hips, then pulled her toward him until his dick was pressed against her pussy again.

My wife giggled and told him that she wasn't sure she could trust herself, and then she allowed him to penetrate her a little farther. I was a little jealous that Louise was agreeing to go on. Although she had often gotten us both off by rubbing her pussy against my penis while we were engaged, she had always insisted on leaving her panties on to act as a chastity belt. As my wife rubbed herself against Alan's big dick, he used his hold on her hips to coax her into taking him even deeper.

I wasn't worried at first, but as I watched my wife gradually impale herself on Alan's massive pole, I realized that she might go all the way with him. I was trying to think of a way to stop them without creating a scene when she had an orgasm. This made her come to her senses a bit, and she told Alan they had to stop. He started to get upset with her for teasing him, but calmed down when she explained that she wasn't using any birth control and was afraid he would get her pregnant. He asked Louise if she would get him off by giving him a blowjob. Although my wife has always enjoyed having me eat her pussy, she has never been willing to try sucking cock—until now! I was surprised and jealous when she eagerly agreed to suck Alan off.

My wife got off of Alan's lap and knelt in front of him. She explained that she had never done this before, even for her husband, and asked him to coach her. My boss had her start by kissing and licking the head of his dick. Louise was tentative at first, but she soon relaxed and kissed her way down the shaft and playfully sucked on his tennis ball-sized testicles. He finally had her try taking his dick in her mouth. She giggled as she sucked on the head, then gradually worked her lips down the shaft. As hard as my wife tried, she couldn't get more than about half of Alan's big dick in her mouth. She was startled when he started to come, but she kept on bobbing up and down, eventually swallowing his entire load. She told him how good his come tasted as she licked his dick and balls clean for him.

As they started to get dressed, my boss asked Louise if he could keep her bra and panties as a souvenir. She was a little embarrassed about being naked under her low-cut gown, but she agreed and put her dress on while he pocketed her underwear. Alan told her that since she had given him such a great blowjob, her husband's job was secure. He went on to tell her that I was qualified to be the division manager and that he couldn't wait to be my colleague. He then asked her if she would come to his room later and let him screw her. I was surprised to hear my wife tell him that she would think about it.

I waited until they left before I came out of my hiding place. Watching my wife give my boss a blowjob had been just as exciting as I imagined it would be. Although I was relieved that she hadn't risked getting pregnant by letting him screw her, I was surprised to find that I was disappointed too. When I got to our table, Alan and Louise were having another round of drinks and had ordered two for me.

I asked my wife to dance with me again. I reached into her dress to fondle her naked breasts, then teased her by asking her what had happened to her bra. At first my wife tried to lie by telling me that she had taken it off because one of the straps had broken, but she finally confessed everything when I told her I had seen them in the alcove. I assured her that I wasn't angry with her because she hadn't cheated on me by going all the way with him. She was so relieved to hear this that she gave me a deep kiss. I felt myself getting an erection when I realized that I was tasting Alan's semen in my wife's mouth. She felt it too and asked me if it had turned me on to watch her suck my boss's cock. I reluctantly admitted that it had, and I asked her if she would be willing to give me a blowjob too. I was disappointed when she explained that she didn't feel embarrassed about sucking Alan's cock because she didn't care if he thought she was a slut, but she didn't want to give me a blowjob because she wanted me to respect her!

As we continued to dance, Louise reached down to fondle my erect penis through my pants and asked me what I thought of my boss—she wanted to know if I thought he was good-looking. I said I thought it was great, and then asked her what she thought about him. She explained that while she wouldn't break her marriage vows by screwing Alan behind my back, it wouldn't be adultery if I gave her permission to do it.

I asked my wife if she wanted to fuck him because he was my boss or if she just wanted to have Alan's big dick all the way in her pussy. She reluctantly confessed that lust was her main motive. I admitted that the idea of her screwing my boss turned me on, but I was worried that she might get pregnant and asked her if she would be willing to let him use a condom. I wasn't surprised when she refused this request because of her religious beliefs against using artificial birth control. Louise assured me that it would be safe enough because Alan's semen probably wouldn't have much sperm left in it after she sucked him off. She went on to say that while she would enjoy feeling Alan's big dick pumping his semen into her pussy, she would be willing to ask him to pull out before he came in her the way I did when we didn't want her to get pregnant. While I was sure that my boss wouldn't be as careful as I was, I had to admit that the idea of my wife screwing him without any protection turned me on. I told her that she could do as she wished with Alan, but she ought to give me a blowjob if he came in her. My wife eagerly agreed to this.

I had another drink with Alan and Louise and we talked for a while. After about a half hour, I told them I was really drunk and should go to bed before I passed out. I urged Louise to stay and have some more fun. The booze was really starting to hit me by the time I got to our room, so I got undressed and got in bed. I dozed off but woke up when I heard my wife and Alan in his room about an hour later. I pretended that I was still asleep when she opened the connecting door to check on me. Satisfied that I was out cold, she went back to Alan's room and didn't even bother to close the door. I waited a bit, then grabbed my camcorder and went to the door to tape the action.

Louise was obviously very drunk and was having trouble getting her evening gown unzipped. She giggled when Alan literally tore the expensive dress off of her and tossed it in the corner. They got on the bed and made out for a while. Alan's dick was soon hard and my wife spread her legs for him, asking him to put it in her. He started to put a condom on, but she pulled it off and told him she didn't want him to use one because she was a devout Catholic and wanted him to screw her without any protection. She went on to warn him that it was the fertile part of her cycle and he should pull out before he came in her unless he wanted to get her pregnant. Alan rubbed the head of his dick against my wife's pussy as he told her that he was willing to take his chances, and then he asked her if she would be upset if he shot his sperm in her. I felt like I had been rocketed to the moon when she told him he could do whatever he wanted. Then she guided his dick to her pussy.

I watched as my boss began to gradually work his big dick into my wife's slit. Although I knew he intended to come in her, I was so turned on that I couldn't interrupt them. When he was finally all the way in, he asked Louise how his meat felt inside her compared to her husband's. It was a little humiliating to hear my wife reply that he felt wonderful compared to my husband's pathetic little prick. Alan started to screw Louise with long, slow strokes, and she was soon on the verge of an orgasm. He was an expert lover and held her on the edge until she was pleading with him to let her come. He laughed and told her she should tell him when to squirt his semen into her. My wife didn't even hesitate. She yelled, "Please, Alan, come in my pussy. God forgive me, but I love being fucked by your big dick so much that I don't care if I cuckold my husband. Please shoot your sperm into my cunt and make me come." It turned me on to hear my formerly prim and proper wife using such vulgar language.

I was enthralled as I watched Alan start to screw my wife again. She soon had her first orgasm and she was so turned on that her nipples were nearly an inch long. Alan grabbed Louise's breasts and held on to them as if they were the handlebars on a motorcycle that he was riding. He squeezed my wife's big tits so gently that I wondered why he wasn't a masseur. But she smiled and smiled as he pummeled her pussy with his tool. She was moaning in pleasure as she had one orgasm after another. My wife was screaming in ecstasy as she begged Alan to keep fucking her with his big dick and to shoot his sperm into her.

When Alan finally told Louise he was ready to come, she wrapped her legs around his hips and pulled him deep inside her. My wife had an incredibly intense orgasm when she felt his big dick finally pumping his semen into her womb. I could tell by the look of ecstasy on Alan's face that she was using her powerful pussy muscles to squeeze every last drop of semen out of his penis. His enormous balls produced such a large volume of come that my wife's pussy was literally running over. The sight was so exciting that I felt my cock spasming as I shot my own meager load into the wall.

After a short rest, Alan's big dick was hard again and my wife asked him to screw her a second time. Although Louise had always insisted that we do it in the missionary position, she let my boss use every position imaginable. My wife kept telling him how much she loved his giant cock and begged him to pump more of his sperm into her cunt. When he was finally finished with her, she lay on the bed with her knees up to help his dick reach deeper into her vagina. He eventually had to tell her to go back to her husband.

Louise was surprised and embarrassed to find that I was awake when she came into our room. I hugged her and kissed her, telling her that I was glad she had enjoyed herself. I then dipped my fingers into my wife's semen-soaked pussy and told her that she owed me a blowjob. She was worried that I was angry with her for begging Alan to come in her, but I assured her that I wasn't. I even admitted that I had gotten so turned on when he shot his first load of semen into her that I came too! We started making love and my wife had me lay back on the bed so that she could give me a blowjob. As she sucked my cock, she said it was nice that I was so much smaller than Alan because she could easily fit me all the way in her mouth. When I came, she was able to swallow my load without spilling a drop.

My wife wasn't finished with me yet. She positioned herself so that her freshly fucked pussy was right over my face, then told me that if I didn't want Alan to get her pregnant, I should try to suck his semen out of her. She laughed as she lowered her pelvis onto my face and I eagerly started to lick her pussy. She was so loose that my tongue slid effortlessly into her. The aroma and flavor were pungent but not unpleasant, and I ate her with more relish than I had in years.

When my wife noticed that my dick was starting to get hard, she asked me if it turned me on to eat another man's semen out of her pussy. I had to confess that it did. She laughed as she told me she was glad that I liked having a wanton wife because now that she had screwed Alan, she would never be satisfied with my little dick again. Louise was far more responsive than usual and had several orgasms within a few minutes before she was satisfied and lowered herself onto my cock. She teased me by telling me that she could barely feel my little dick and asked me if I was sure that I was in yet. I had to admit that Alan's enormous penis had stretched her out so much that I felt lost inside of her. I've always been a bit of a quick comer, but I lasted much longer than usual and was able to bring my wife to a mild orgasm. I didn't say anything to warn her, but she knew when I was about to come and raised herself off my dick so that my sperm sprayed into her blonde pubic hair.

My wife became extremely promiscuous after her tryst with Alan. The only thing that bothered me about it is that she refused to use any protection with her lovers. If it was the fertile part of her cycle, she would suck them off before she screwed them and ask them to pull out before they came in her, but many of the guys didn't do that. Whenever this happened, Louise would have me suck their sperm out of her pussy before she got pregnant. She would also reward me for my indulgence by giving me a blowjob whenever she had been with another man.

Many people who read this letter will wonder if my wife ever got pregnant from her dalliances with these other men. She has given birth to three babies since she started having affairs. I am certain that I am not the father of two of these kids and have doubts about the paternity of the third. While it bothers me to be cuckolded, I consider it to be a small price to pay to have a wife who is truly uninhibited when she has sex with me.—*Name and address withheld* ○┼▪

"WHAT THE FUCK, GUS, MY WIFE WANTS TO FUCK YOU"

*M*y wife Marjorie is a beautiful, wonderful curvaceous, sexy brunette. Although she appears and acts pretty conservative, she definitely has an adventurous nature. Her specialty is staging little surprises for me. At her urging, I'd like to share with you one of her all-time best!

There was nothing particularly special about the day. I mean, it was Friday, and that's always special in its own way, but it wasn't Christmas or anything. I was expecting the usual evening at home with the kids. Maybe a few margaritas. Maybe, if everything worked out just right, one of my wife Marjorie's awesome blowjobs. Just a typical Friday.

The evening before, Marjorie had asked me what I thought about rearranging the seats in our new minivan. She suggested removing the middle seat, saying that she felt having the extra area between the back seat and the front seats would make the van feel roomier. I agreed and went out to set it up. We both liked the change and decided to leave it that way for a while.

So anyway, after work, Marjorie asked if I felt like going to have a few drinks. I said, "Sure!" assuming that she had made some sort of arrangements for someone to watch the kids for a few hours. She suggested a hotel bar in the downtown area.

We sat and drank for a while, slowly unwinding from the day's work. After our third scotch and water, the waitress came over and asked if we needed another. Marjorie told her that I was driving, but that she would have another. I objected, but Marjorie insisted. When her drink arrived, I reached for a sip, but she quickly brushed my hand away, again reminding me that I had to drive. At this point I began to pout.

She allowed me to pout for a while, then casually mentioned that she had arranged a night out for us and that we had a room in the hotel for the night. As it sank in, I said, "You bitch! I don't have to drive anywhere!" and again reached for her drink. She brushed my hand away, informing me that I would indeed be driving. As I sat wondering what was going on, she ordered yet another drink.

I sat silently as she slowly, deliberately sipped away at her fifth scotch and water. When she finished, she ordered a soft drink for me. She leaned over to me and said, "You sit here and drink your Coke like a good boy. I'll be back in a minute." I was beginning to get pretty curious and more than a little excited. I was tempted to order a drink while she was gone, but opted to do exactly as I was told.

Marjorie returned after about twenty minutes. She'd obviously been up to the room. Instead of the conservative business attire she was wearing when she'd left, she was dressed down, wearing a long blue sweater and a pair of black stretch pants. She had pulled her hair back and, quite frankly, looked gorgeous. "Let's go for a drive," she said.

We walked over to the parking garage. She unlocked the sliding door and scooted to the middle of the back seat. Noticing the puzzled expression on my face, she nonchalantly said, "I feel like being chauffeured."

"Yes, ma'am, where to?" I asked.

"Oh, I'd just kind of like to tour the downtown area," she said.

As we drove out of the garage, I adjusted the rearview mirror. With the seat moved back, I could see just about her whole body. I was really beginning to wonder what she was up to. I tried to catch her eyes to see if I could read anything, but she made a point of remaining oblivious to me.

After I'd driven for about three minutes, I saw her reach into her purse and pull out a small brown glass bottle, a little mirror, and a straw.

"Hey!" I said.

"Can't a girl have some privacy around here?" she quickly replied.

I watched as she finished off two lines and put everything away. I continued driving the dark, almost empty streets of downtown, wondering what she had planned. I noticed movement in the mirror and looked, just in time to see her pulling off the black stretch pants. She folded them up neatly and placed them under the seat. Then, gazing out the side window like she was really interested in something out there, she slipped her hand underneath the bottom of her sweater and began rubbing between her legs. This was getting serious!

Little by little, the sweater worked its way upward, and I could now see her fingers as they made circular motions on her beautifully trimmed pussy. I was beginning to have an extremely hard time concentrating on the road. Other things were getting pretty hard too.

She reached into her purse, removing her favorite vibrator. Before long, as I watched squirming in the front seat, she was working the full length of her toy in and out of her very wet pussy. Things were getting damn warm and I was beginning to think about finding my way back to the hotel room, when suddenly she said, "Turn left here."

Still working the vibrator, she continued giving directions until we were parked directly in front of a downtown bar we frequent.

"Why don't you go in and see if Gus is ready for his break," she said.

Gus! I could feel my heart pounding with excitement. I had played in a rock band with Gus for many years, but had pretty much lost track of him until he suddenly resurfaced as a bartender at this joint. Gus and I had shared more than a few sexual exploits in those wild rock and roll days. He was good-looking, charismatic—and sported one of the biggest, thickest cocks I've ever seen. It was a pretty deadly combination and, as you might imagine, he was always quite popular with the ladies. I had only recently introduced him to Marjorie but had talked to her about him many times. For some reason, even before he showed back up, I had often fantasized about watching him slam his oversize cock into my wife's beautiful little pussy. Running back into him and actually introducing him to Marjorie had only served to fan this fire. After we'd seen him at the bar, I brought his name up a couple of times when Marjorie and I were having sex to see if there was any interest. It seemed to make her hot, but despite my constant urging, she'd always been pretty cool to the idea of having sex with another man.

"Uhhh, what if he's not here?" I stammered.

"Oh, he's here. I've already talked to him," she replied. I should have known. I went into the bar and returned with Gus in tow. I took my place at the wheel and he slipped into the back seat of the van beside my very sexy, very hot wife. Obviously, he knew the plan.

While I was in the bar, she had pulled her sweater back down over her naked thighs and put her vibrator away. She handed Gus her little mirror with a long line of coke on it, then looked up at me and said, "Dave, a tour of the city, please." As I pulled away from the curb, Gus wasted no time in snorting the coke she had given him. "Does Dave get any of this?" he inquired.

"Dave will get his later," she replied, winking.

I drove the streets of our fair city, watching in the rearview mirror as she began kissing Gus's ear. I saw her take his hands and guide them underneath her sweater. A moan of approval escaped his lips as he began exploring her nakedness.

Eagerly returning her kisses, he slowly worked the sweater up over her hips. I couldn't have asked for a better view. In the mirror I watched his fingers gently trace small circles between Marjorie's open legs, then disappear into her wetness. She thrust her tongue deep into Gus's mouth and began moaning as she moved her hips in unison with the motion of his probing fingers.

Fortunately, the streets were pretty empty and driving wasn't requiring a lot of my attention. I heard the sound of pants unsnapping and a zipper going down. I heard Marjorie gasp, "My goodness, Gus!" and I glanced up to the mirror just in time to see Gus's thick, nine-inch cock literally spring from the confines of his tight jeans. "Home of the Whopper!" Marjorie giddily exclaimed as she slowly worked her hand up and down the length of his shaft.

I had just pulled up to an intersection when I heard Marjorie whisper, "Ummmm, this definitely looks good enough to eat." By the time I pulled away and reestablished my view in the mirror, her head was bobbing up and down in Gus's lap. Every now and then, as we passed under a streetlight, I could see his fat cock sliding in and out of her sweet lips. She was giving him her best. Slurping, sucking and moaning sounds filled the inside of the van like the sound track of a porno movie.

When she finally came up for air, Gus scooted off the seat, kneeling on the floorboard. He gently pushed Marjorie's legs open wide and eagerly dived face-first into her beautifully trimmed cunt. Her eyes slowly closed as her body began to writhe and jerk to the sensation of Gus's talented tongue dancing around on her pussy lips and clit.

Marjorie loves to have her pussy eaten, but suddenly she pulled Gus's head from between her thighs and slid off the seat onto the floorboard, exclaiming, "I've got to get some of that big thing inside me!"

I could no longer see the two of them in the mirror. I took a quick glance back and saw her pull a thick quilt from under the seat and begin spreading it out on the floorboard. It wasn't long before she was spreading something else out in the floorboard.

Although I couldn't see, the sounds that were now coming from directly behind me were unmistakable. A very loud, very deep, "Ohh, Gaawwwd!" announced that Gus's big dick had definitely found its way inside her. Gus, the consummate lover, patiently worked his massive cock into my wife's accommodating pussy, filling her as she'd never been filled before, her stream of constant guttural, cat-like moans attesting to Gus's skill as a master cocksman. My own dick strained against the fabric of my jeans as my ultimate fantasy, the scene I'd envisioned so many times, played out just behind me.

I was tempted to stop the van and jump into the back with them—to see the lusty look of pleasure on Marjorie's beautiful face, to get down between her legs and witness her pussy being stretched to its limits, to smell the smell of their mingling scents and to taste the taste of their combined juices. But I knew that wasn't part of Marjorie's plan, so I contentedly continued my role as chauffeur.

The van shook as I drove the dark streets. Unintelligible, animal-like grunts and groans of fucking accompanied by the rhythmic slapping of thighs against thighs, balls against ass, drowned out the sounds of the city. Sweet musky sex smells began to fill the air as the two of them went at each other with all the lustful fury of a first-time fuck.

I knew Marjorie had come several times, but it was hard to tell when one orgasm ended and the next began. She just didn't seem to be able to get enough of Gus's artful fucking. I didn't think it was possible, but the distinctive sound of Gus's balls slapping against Marjorie's ass signaled that she was taking in every inch of his awesome manhood. I couldn't continue. I pulled the van into a deserted parking lot and turned to watch the unstoppable action. The van rocked violently back and forth as Gus pounded Marjorie to yet another powerful orgasm. It was a long, loud come. He plunged his dick deep into her and held it there to delight in the gripping massage of her contracting pussy muscles. Then, as soon as it appeared that the waves of her orgasm had subsided, he continued his relentless, expert pumping. His grunting sex sounds deepened and intensified as he suddenly cried out and lunged deeply into her. His buttocks began to shiver and his cock jerked as his pace slowed and he emptied his balls into my little wife's sucking, begging pussy. Marjorie, her strength gone, just lay there, moaning, quivering, barely able to fuck back, as he totally flooded her insides with his hot, sticky come.

The squishy, smacking sounds began to slow and cease. The van was quiet, except for some gentle, after-sex kissing and cooing.

I started the van and pulled out of the parking lot. I saw a flame and smelled pot. Marjorie and Gus lay softly chatting, playfully touching, as they enjoyed a joint and the afterglow.

Eventually, we made our way back to the bar. Gus and Marjorie exchanged a lingering kiss. Then Gus waved good-bye to me and was gone.

As I pulled the van away from the curb, I looked up in the mirror to find Marjorie's big, brown half-closed eyes staring back at me. Her sweater was again pulled up above her waist and her legs were spread wide. Maintaining eye contact, she made a big show of slowly swiping her fingers through the come leaking from her freshly fucked pussy, then bringing them to her lips, painstakingly licking the sticky liquid from each individual finger.

"Did you enjoy that as much as I did?" she asked coyly.

"I think you know the answer to that!" I replied.

"Mmmm, I should have tried some of that a long time ago," she teased. "Maybe, if you're good, I'll let you join us next time."

"That would be great," I said. "If you think you could handle it."

"Oh, I can handle it, Honey," she replied. "Just get me back to the hotel and I'll prove it to you."

I floored it!—*H.S., Little Rock, Arkansas*

Girl Meets Girl

A MASSAGE IS JUST THE THING TO GET THOSE SAPPHIC FIRES FLAMING

*B*eing a senior executive in an international accounting firm, I have little time for a social life, let alone sex. As a matter of fact, the most exercise I get is a steady workout in hotel exercise rooms. It was stressful, to say the least, and I guess it must have shown, because one day a friend of mine suggested that I get a total body massage to relieve my stress.

I put it off and put it off until I was finally able to work it into my busy schedule. When the day rolled around, I arrived home just minutes before the masseuse showed up. When the doorbell rang, I opened the door to find an attractive young woman of medium height and build with soft, brown hair shimmering in the afternoon sunlight. Her eyes were warm and riveting. Strangely, I was immediately attracted to her. I reacted to her as I'd reacted only to men in the past, yet toward this woman my attraction felt very right.

When she came in, she noted the fact that I was still dressed and that our time, though not rushed, was limited. I watched as she immediately started setting up her equipment and preparing the oils and scents. I should have been getting ready, but all I could do was watch, mesmerized by the beauty of this woman's lithe body covered by a light cotton shift. I finally broke the silence by asking if she would like a glass of wine, and in the same anxious breath I asked her name. We laughed together at the awkwardness. Then she said, "Yes, and it's Alice."

Alice threw a jazz tape into my stereo system, and when she went to draw a warm bath, I turned on the speakers in the bathroom. Soon I was being led into the bathroom. Motioning in a questioning manner, she began to remove my clothes: She slowly pushed my jacket over my shoulders and placed it on a chair. Gently she turned me to face the full-length mirror and, standing behind me, she reached around and began to slowly rub my breasts through my blouse, searching out each button and carefully and deliberately unbuttoning me top to tail. My heart began to race and my breathing became deeper and shorter as a warm glow began to sweep over my entire body. Soon I began to tingle all over, and then I felt the juices flowing in my pussy.

Alice further heightened my excitement by rubbing my thighs and fondling my buttocks as she unzipped and removed my skirt. Not letting it fall to the floor, she gently pushed it down to my ankles and guided my shoe-encased feet out of the gathered material.

Alice stepped back from me and removed her cotton shift. I watched, a voyeur from my position in front of the mirror, and I gasped at the beauty being revealed before me. Alice was wearing a pair of white silk exercise shorts and a thin, white cotton tank top which left little to the imagination. Her breasts were firm and round, with the darkest areolae I have ever seen, easily visible through the material. Her nipples jutted out at least three quarters of an inch.

Obviously noticing my interest in her body, Alice whispered that my strong nipples were pushing out of my bra and that maybe they would like to be released. Before I could answer, she unfastened my bra and slipped her smooth fingers over my shoulders, pushing the straps forward, letting the material fall free of my aching orbs. Alice reached under my arms and gathered my breasts into her strong hands. She fondled them with the gentlest of touches, paying particular attention to my sensitive nipples. As she continued her ministrations, I began to moan and feel the waves of pleasure surround me even more—I felt an intense orgasm building deep within my body.

Not wishing me to reach that ultimate point of pleasure so quickly, Alice moved her hands slowly down my stomach and penetrated the waistband of my pantyhose with two of her fingers. Then, ever so slowly and gently, her hands moved down my legs, pushing my pantyhose down to my ankles. Removing my shoes, Alice pushed the bunched up nylon off my feet. With her soft, pert lips she began to kiss my toes, then she slowly worked her way up my legs to the lacy softness of my panties to begin the process all over again.

Alice's applied magic, through the sensitivity of her mouth, sent my senses into orbit. As she neared my rounded butt-cheeks, I fought the urge to reach around and guide her head into my crack. My mind was filled with images of past experiences of rear entry, but the desire was heightened by a wanton desire to be taken by another woman. Alice continued to massage my ass with her lips and tongue as she slowly moved her soft hands gently around my hips to my love-mound.

As she touched my pussy, I exploded into an intense orgasm. Weak-kneed and wobbly, I almost fell over but for Alice's steadying arms. She said softly to relax and allow myself to be swept away. As my breathing subsided, I realized that I had my eyes clamped shut and that I was clutching Alice's hand to my pussy. Alice hugged me and gently reassured me that I was in good hands.

Easing me into the tub, Alice began the most sensuous massage I have ever felt—from a man or a woman. Using the loofah sponge to heighten my sensitivity, she tweaked my nipples to near orgasmic levels and rubbed my pussy with wanton abandon. Paying particular attention to my clit, she repeatedly brought me to the edge of orgasmic release, just to let me slide back again. The feeling she gave me was filled with waves of pleasure that took over my body and were so intense that I nearly passed out. In fact, all I really remember is Alice's sweet, soft voice whispering the question of whether I wanted more in the tub or did I need something else? I couldn't imagine what else there could be, but I was so totally captivated and relaxed that I said I was game for anything she had in mind.

Helping me out of the tub, Alice led me to the massage table. Pouring warm oil all over my back, butt and legs, Alice systematically massaged and rubbed each inch of my skin, releasing the last vestiges of tension in each muscle. Working up my legs, my anticipation grew as she neared my butt, only to be disappointed by her avoidance. She did the same starting from my neck down. This time I found myself unconsciously humping the table. Alice sarcastically asked if I had a problem.

To this I responded, "I want more, I want to feel you. I need you to touch me!" I surprised myself. I'm usually a demure person when it comes to sex.

Alice asked me to be specific: "What do you need? What do you want to feel? Where do you want me to touch you?"

I could only respond with, "My butt."

Alice poured more oil down the crack of my ass and ever so slowly began kneading my ass-cheeks. I responded by humping in time with the rhythm of her motions.

It was then that I realized that if I wanted something, I would either have to ask for it specifically or take more control of the situation. But I was hopelessly lost under the control of Alice's magical fingers. All I could do was roll over as Alice moved to the head of the table. A bit surprised, Alice asked, "What's this? Do you want something else?"

I said yes, in a deep, throaty voice, and added, "Concentrate on my tits and pussy!" Alice responded immediately by placing her fingers on my pussy mound and working them aggressively into my soaked love-hole, saying, "Now, there is the real woman I've been searching for."

Becoming more bold, I reached behind my head and began to slowly rub up and down the backs of Alice's legs and ass. Responding to her moans, I began to slowly remove her silky shorts. Alice was totally nude in seconds and inches from my head. I asked that she spend time on my tits and nipples, and Alice serviced them as only a woman can. Alice asked if I wanted them kissed and sucked, and I surprised myself by saying, "Yes. Oh, please, yes!" As she was sucking and rubbing, I became more involved: "Rub my pussy, finger-fuck me until I come. Alice, don't stop this time. Fuck me, make me come." Fingering me hard, harder than I have ever done for myself, but gently and knowingly as only a woman can, Alice brought me to an intense orgasm that had me shaking for what seemed like hours. As my spasms subsided, Alice gently rubbed my pussy and kissed my mouth.

I'd never kissed a woman before, and I'd always thought it would be strange, but at that moment I wanted and got the deepest, wettest, longest and most sensual kiss of my life. Alice captured my mind with it. I still can't imagine how long it was before Alice, panting sensuously, said that it was time to wrap things up. She had enjoyed herself so much, however, that she offered me a special treat, if I had the time.

Nodding approvingly, I let her take control again as she moved to the other end of the table. Again, she began a slow, deliberate lip and tongue massage of my feet, legs and pussy. When her hot tongue reached the inside folds of my pussy, Alice lit my fire and quickly brought me to the boiling point of orgasm. I was out of control, screaming, "Yes, suck my pussy, you're making me come, fuck me with your tongue, yes, I'm coming, coming..."

Bidding Alice good-bye at the door was much like seeing your best friend leaving you. Tenderly I kissed her lips, tasting my pussy juices for the first time in my life.—*T.L., Fairfax, Virginia*

STRANGE INTERLUDE LEADS TO A ROOM OF THEIR OWN

*F*or my birthday a few months ago, a friend of mine gave me two tickets to see a Broadway show. Naturally, my husband and I were excited to be going the minute we received the tickets. The night before the show, however, my husband came home from work and said he had a very important business meeting the next day and wouldn't be able to go. I was upset at first, but then I decided to call my friend Darlene (who had given me the tickets) to see if she would be able to go with me. She said she didn't have any plans and would be happy to come along.

The following morning I picked Darlene up at her house and we drove to the train station. The conversation on the way into the city was about our husbands. Darlene explained to me that she doesn't enjoy having sex with her husband anymore.

"I'm tired of him humping me and then falling asleep. It seems like it's usually over in five minutes or less," Darlene said. "Is your husband good in bed?"

"He's okay, but I would prefer more foreplay," I said.

As the conversation continued, Darlene looked at me all of a sudden and said, "I've always wanted to see what it would be like to make love to a woman." When she said this, she gently slid her hand up my thigh and squeezed my hand. My heart beat a little faster as she looked into my eyes. I have always had feelings for Darlene, but because we were both married, I never pursued anything.

She held me for a little while and then eventually let go. We didn't say anything more until we arrived at Grand Central. When we stood up to get off the train, we faced each other and she moved her body close to me. So close, in fact, that I could feel her hard nipples press against mine through our clothes. I had to resist the urge to kiss her since people were all around us.

We finally made it out of the station and started walking toward Broadway. After we walked for ten minutes, Darlene announced that she had to go to the bathroom. Since I've been to the city many times before, I suggested we stop at a hotel. They never know if you're a guest or not. When we reached the bathroom, Darlene grabbed my hand and we both went into the handicapped stall.

"What are you doing?" I asked. "Someone will catch us, crazy!" As I said this, I just kept smiling because the only thing I wanted to do was kiss her.

"I'm not doing anything," Darlene said as she pushed her body up against me.

Darlene moved her face right up to mine and said, "Now I got you right where I want you." She licked my lips gently before she softly kissed them. Next thing I knew, she was unbuttoning my shirt as we kept on kissing. I could feel my pussy getting wet just from her kissing me, so I couldn't imagine how wet it would be if we started doing anything else.

When my shirt was all the way undone, and my bra as well, Darlene pulled away from our kiss and looked into my eyes. She brought her index finger up to her mouth and licked it with the tip of her tongue. Then she moved her hand down to one of my hard nipples and started to circle the areola with her wet finger. Darlene did the same thing with her other hand to my other nipple. My knees were about to buckle.

Darlene kissed me gently on the lips one more time and moved her head down toward where her hands were. I looked down to see Darlene push my breasts together with her hands as her head moved back and forth, the tip of her tongue gently flicking one nipple and then the other. I didn't think my nipples could get any harder, but I was wrong. Each time her tongue touched one, it seemed to get a tiny bit harder.

I could feel my pussy throbbing, and I knew I was going to explode soon. I was moaning so loud, I thought for sure we would be arrested. As Darlene's tongue massaged my nipples, her hands were massaging the under parts of my breasts, squeezing them lightly and lifting them up at the same time. It felt so wonderful that I didn't want her to stop. I grabbed her head and pulled her closer to my chest. She was making me crazy.

As I grabbed Darlene's head, she reached under my skirt and moved my panties to the side. Her middle finger moved into my slit.

"You are so wet," Darlene said. "You must like what I've been doing so far."

All I could do was moan louder. Darlene pushed her finger gently into my soaking wet hole and then slid it almost all the way out.

"Do you want me to put it back in?" Darlene asked.

"Oh, yes! Please don't stop. You're going to make me explode," I said.

"Then tell me what you want," Darlene said.

"I want you to put your finger in my pussy and make me come," I said.

Darlene slid her finger into my hole again and just twisted it around really slow. That was when I lost it and started coming all over her hand. I could feel my pussy contracting around her finger, and I didn't ever want her to remove it.

As my breathing returned to normal, we heard someone enter the stall next to us. That's when I suggested to Darlene that we get a room.

"What about the play?" Darlene asked.

"Who cares," I said. "I want to make love to you for the rest of the day."

When we checked in and got up to the room, we ordered a bottle of champagne. It didn't take us long to pick up where we'd left off.

After the champagne was delivered, I popped the cork and poured two glasses. I turned to Darlene, who was standing by the bed watching me. We didn't say a word, we just gazed into each other's eyes. I could feel my body tingle as we stepped toward each other and kissed. We started taking off each other's clothes as we kissed. I laid Darlene down on the bed and positioned myself on top of her.

"Now I have you right where I want you," I said to her.

"Prove it," Darlene said, kissing me again. I moved my face away and reached for a glass of champagne. I took a sip of it and put the tip of my finger into the glass. With my wet finger, I traced around her nipples with the cold champagne. I could feel her nipples getting hard from my touch.

"I love that. I love when you touch my nipples," Darlene moaned. When both her nipples were rock-hard, I lifted myself up so my breasts were above hers. I lowered myself slowly so that the tip of her nipples touched mine. I moved my body up and down so that just our nipples rubbed against each other. As Darlene moaned louder, I moved a little faster. Then I repositioned my body so that my nipples rubbed against Darlene's stomach. My tongue started going to work on her nipples, licking and flicking the tips of them.

"Oh, yeah, suck my nipples! Suck on them. I love it!" Darlene moaned.

So I started sucking on her nipples. They were rock-hard in my mouth. As I sucked each one, I continued to flick the tip with my tongue.

Darlene was going wild. Her hips were moving against my body, so I reached down and felt her pussy lips with my finger. She was soaked! I pushed my finger gently into her hole and pulled it out. I stopped sucking on her nipples for a minute so I could circle her nipples again with my finger. I spread her pussy juice all around each nipple and then looked into her eyes. I put my finger into my mouth and sucked the rest of the juice off. After I pulled my finger out of my mouth, I started sucking her sweet nectar from her nipples.

"Oh, my God, you're making me crazy," Darlene said. She was moaning so loud that I thought I would have an orgasm just listening to her.

While I was still sucking on Darlene's nipples, I moved my hand back down toward her pussy. My body was on top of hers, so it was easy to slip my finger back into her juicy hole. As I did this, I stopped sucking her nipples and moved up to kiss Darlene on the lips. Darlene reached down with her right hand and I felt her finger slide into my pussy.

"Oh, my God, you're so wet!" Darlene said.

This seemed to arouse her even more. We both moved our fingers in and out of each other's pussy with the same rhythm.

"Oh, yeah," I said. "You're going to make me come!"

We moved our bodies against each other as our fingers moved slowly in and out of our slippery pussies.

When I felt Darlene's pussy start to contract around my finger, I slowly pushed it in as far as I could. She went crazy. You should have heard her scream. Right about the same time, I exploded, and I could feel my own contractions pulling Darlene's finger in and out of me!

Our orgasms were so similar, it was hard to tell who was who. Needless to say, we never made it to the show. But we do go to New York City a whole lot more often.—*L.S., Mamaroneck, New York* ⊶◪

ROOMMATES FIND SOMETHING ELSE
THEY HAVE IN COMMON

I have a story to tell you, and I'm actually kind of excited that I really have the nerve to write it down.

I have been reading *Penthouse Letters* since I first found a copy in a friend of mine's dad's room one night during a sleepover. I'm twenty-two now, and I read it every time I get drunk enough to go buy one. I may be an anomaly among women, but I must admit that after reading the letters and looking at the pictorials (especially the multigirl ones) I masturbate fiercely. When I see three girls going at it, it really puts me over the edge. Keep 'em coming! (No pun intended.)

I am at work right now, but in my office things are slow so I decided to relate this story.

I live in a small-town suburb of Philadelphia where you don't expect much to happen, and not much does. My name is Jenny and I have shoulder-length brown hair, a rather skinny body—but decent enough to look at, I guess—and since high school I have generally been regarded as preppy.

I rent a part of a house with my best friend Samantha. She is really pretty, half-Spanish with long, curly, jet black hair. Her face, with its dark eyes, looks like a model's. She comes from a wealthy family, and her stepdad owns the house we live in.

Samantha always had it all, and every girl in school envied her, even her friends, even me. I come from a small and not so well-to-do family. I couldn't go to college, and since Samantha didn't even want to go to college, we ended up moving in together.

Sexually, Samantha is pretty much a whore. I don't mean anything bad by this, it's just that she has to have sex all the time. I, on the other hand, have only recently found out what an actual hard cock looks like. I've always been shy, and I guess I still am, and yet I've always had a secret sex life in my mind that would rival anyone's.

I was always fascinated with Samantha and her attitude, and she has helped me enjoy sex. It started out as a game. Samantha has always had a maid, and when we moved in together I found out that without domestic help, she's a slob. The good thing is that I don't mind doing housework, and it's a pretty good tradeoff, when you get down to it. I mean, I pay next to nothing in rent, we don't have to pay the utilities, and we've got all the best appliances, a killer sound system—home entertainment center, as Samantha calls it—and a computer apiece, with all the latest software and access to the Internet.

Anyway, one day, when I was doing the dishes, Samantha came up behind me just out of the shower and hugged me. I could feel her boobs rubbing against my back as she kissed me on the cheek good morning. This wasn't too unusual—we always walk around topless. I giggled and turned around, only to find that Samantha was buck naked. I ran my eyes over her perfect body—it was the first time I'd really seen her completely naked.

I couldn't help but stare at her shaved pussy. I blushed and she laughed. "I think that somewhere, deep down inside, you're thinking about what it would be like to be a man right now," she said to me.

She laughed, but I felt a little self-conscious. And do you know why? Because it was true! I wasn't just admiring her body objectively; I was admiring her sexually.

I asked her what she wanted me to do. She suggested I massage her entire body, and then she just walked back into the bedroom. I didn't know if she was serious, and I finished the dishes and walked into her room expecting to see her dressed and giggling like usual—she's such a kidder. But she wasn't kidding, and she was lying on her back on the bed.

I didn't say anything. I didn't know what to say or do, really.

"Go get your lotion. It smells so good," she said. I felt a shiver of apprehension and sexual excitement at the prospect of feeling her naked body. I was still a virgin, and she looked so calm and reassuring. I went to my room and found my lotion, my hands shaking and mouth dry as I returned. She was sitting up.

She somehow knew I needed to be prodded a little to open up, and I was playing like a lost puppy into her hands. She was so beautiful that at that moment I would have done anything for her; I did actually, and I still do. I love her so much.

But anyway, she smiled and said, "You don't have to, Jenny, if you don't want to. I'll understand if you're not into it. We can forget it all."

"Not into what?" I asked, even though I knew damn well.

"You know, get sexual."

I told her I wanted to and that she was just the person I wanted to do it with my first time. She asked me what I was willing to do with her, and I felt an electric shock enter my slit when I said, "Anything."

I went to shut the door, I guess as a habit, and when I turned back around Samantha was rubbing her pussy. I just stared in fascination. She knew she had me. I silently and slowly undressed, embarrassed because my pussy wasn't shaved. But I'm not a hairy person, so I tried to calm my nerves by thinking that it wasn't too bad—like that really mattered.

Samantha smiled at me and looked at my pussy. Then she took my breath away when she reached out and fingered my pussy lips. I was so wet I thought I would faint. She picked up the lotion that had fallen to the floor, then tossed it aside.

"Together we have enough of our own lotion, Jenny," she said. She then stood up and, with the swiftest, smoothest steps, walked up to me and put her tongue in my mouth. I felt the first stirrings of orgasm as she kept rubbing my pussy. I could feel her saliva dripping into my open mouth, and I sucked it in and drank it like a hungry wolf.

Samantha pushed my head to her boobs and I suckled and kissed each one. She started screaming like mad, and finally she yelled out, "I can't take it any longer!"

She bent her head down to my nipples and started feverishly licking and nibbling them. My knees started to go weak, and she must have sensed this, for she immediately told me to lie back on the bed. I did, and she then got on top of me and pressed her body against mine. After kissing my mouth and my neck, she went back to work on my modest boobs as her fingers slipped into my now soaking pussy. Eventually she licked and kissed down my stomach, and I can't describe the anticipation that I felt when she began to lick all around my pussy.

Finally, she spread my pussy and then looked up at me. "What would you like me to do? Would you like me to take my time, or do you want me to give you the most incredible orgasm you have or ever will experience?"

I must have zoned for a moment, because I didn't really hear her question.

"Jenny?" she asked.

"What?" I answered.

"What would you like?" and then she repeated her question.

I giggled, and then we both broke up laughing.

"Do me," I said, and for the next ten minutes I really zoned out. I've never done drugs, but I felt the way you must feel when you're high. She knew exactly where everything was (which I guess is pretty obvious). She licked my inner thighs all over, and then she started fucking me with her tongue, darting over and around my clitoris. And when I started heaving, she stayed right with me until the very end.

I was looking at her while she continued to lick me, and all I wanted to do was lick her pussy. It was, like, the most important thing in the world to me then. Samantha's face was so wet with my come that when she kissed me I could taste myself. I had tasted myself before, because I like licking my fingers clean after a masturbation session. But this time it was so awesome, tasting me in her mouth.

Samantha got up and went over to her little couch next to her bed and sat down. I waited until everything calmed down a little and then looked over. She had a dildo in her pussy really deep, and I watched amazed and subdued. Then she reached to her side, grabbed a smaller dildo and stuck it up her ass. Good God, I would never have dreamed that this kind of stuff could be arousing. It was a very educational day for me.

All I could do was watch, so horny I didn't know what to think or do. She suddenly pulled out the front dildo and tossed it to me on the bed.

"Lick it and tell me if you like it."

Oh, I liked it very much, and I told her so.

"Why don't you come over and lap my pussy like I did yours."

I smiled and looked at her pretty face. She spread her wet pussy lips really wide. I still couldn't think of anything to say. I looked at the dildo in my hand. It was glistening and slimy. I did love how she seduced me, and I loved being sexual with her.

She was opening me up and making me feel like a vixen. I wanted to be hers, even though I really didn't think of myself as a homosexual. I don't think of it that way, really—it's just sex. Once I tasted the goo on the dildo, I knew I was hooked.

Samantha leaned back on the couch and spread her legs. I could see the wetness in her pussy and knew I would eat it. I sexily crawled off the bed and across the floor to her waiting hole. She caressed my hair and then arched her back, pushing her pussy out to me. I didn't even touch it; I stayed on all fours and began to lick all around it. I wasn't apprehensive, anymore. I was just into it, and I wanted to work her up like she did me.

I began licking her smooth pussy and then, as I got more into the groove—literally—her taste and smell subdued me and I lapped away like a kitten, pushing my tongue as far into her warm and salty hole as I could. As soon as Samantha began to moan a little, I sucked her whole pink pussy into my mouth.

Soon I felt Samantha's hands on my head as she gently pushed me back onto the floor, sitting on my face.

I could taste her and feel the wetness on my face. She squealed and continued to grind her pussy on my chin. That's when she really came, and I was almost smothered with her pussy. I swallowed eagerly every drop of cream as if my life depended on it.

I'd never thought about sex with a girl before that morning, but I suggest trying it because it is like nothing you'll ever experience. I am happily sexually active with Allen (my man), but he doesn't know that his fun with me is due to Samantha's fun with me.—*J.A., King of Prussia, Pennsylvania*

THE ONLY THING BETTER THAN A TONGUE IN YOUR PUSSY? THREE TONGUES

I recently went on an all-girl vacation to an island, with three buddies. Tracey is my closest friend, and we were joined by two girls, Giselle and Dierdre, that Tracey works with. Dierdre and I are married, and Giselle and Tracey are single. We are all in our late twenties and attractive.

Of course, on the flight down Giselle and Tracey were talking about meeting some guys at the resort. Dierdre and I, being married, kept quiet, but I was thinking that a little sexual encounter would be fun. I've had a few affairs that my husband has no idea about.

The four of us spent the first day on the beach, just relaxing. All of us except Dierdre were wearing thong bikinis that left little to the imagination. Dierdre wore a one-piece. We were approached by a lot of guys, but nothing really interested us.

After dinner, with nothing promising, we decided to go back to our villa and just hang out with each other. Tracey ordered a few bottles of champagne. We all had a few drinks, and I was getting to know the other girls better, when Tracey suggested we each tell a secret about our sex life. Tracey volunteered me to go first. Dierdre didn't think our game was a good idea, but I started anyway.

I told them that my boss Eliot is very good-looking. When he was away on a recent sales trip, I got a frantic call that he had left some important files in his office. He wanted me to get the next flight out and bring him his work. He said he'd need my help all week, and that I should plan on staying.

I'd never gone on a sales trip before, and getting away sounded interesting. I called my husband, told him about the emergency, and got the next flight. I got there in the late afternoon, and was met by Eliot at the hotel. He decided that his customers Tom and Earl would meet us there to finish the contract. I checked into my room, then went to Eliot's suite. Tom and Earl were already there.

We finished our work around eight p.m., and I got up to leave. Earl, who was really hung, suggested that I stay for a drink and some coffee. Tom, also very handsome, sat next to me on the couch and, after a drink, placed his hand on my thigh while we talked. Eliot was soon on my other side. As Tom went to kiss me, I could feel Eliot's hand on my other thigh. I was incredibly horny, and offered no resistance to his kiss.

Before I knew it, my dress was up around my waist and both men were rubbing my pussy through my panties. Earl came around the back of the couch, pushed my dress down off my shoulders and took my bra off. Tom now had his hand in my panties and began to remove them. They then removed my dress, so all I had on was stockings and pearls. I was sitting, totally nude, with my legs spread wide open for three studs.

Eliot told me he'd always wanted to fuck me, and that I was about to be completely and thoroughly fucked. They brought me close to orgasm several times, playing with my pussy and tits for an hour while they remained clothed. When Earl asked me if I was ready for three cocks, all I could mutter was, "My pussy is ready."

Eliot began to remove his clothes first. When he took his underwear off, he had the biggest, fattest cock I'd ever seen. Eliot began to eat my pussy out, as Tom and Earl also stripped. Eliot got up, and Tom put the head of his cock just inside my pussy. Eliot put his cock in my mouth. I held Earl's organ in my hand. Earl and Tom each took turns fucking me as I sucked on Eliot's enormous cock. I had several orgasms.

Eliot finally withdrew from my mouth and began to penetrate my already well-fucked cunt hole. I could feel every inch sliding in. When he got all the way in, he withdrew, then slammed back into my pussy, and set me off on the most intense orgasms I'd ever had. I was writhing and bucking in a frenzy. Eliot completely filled my pussy with each thrust. I was in heaven when he finally filled my hole with cream.

I fucked and sucked the three guys all night, in every position we could think of. My favorite was when I was on top of Eliot, with my back turned to him. I humped his huge cock while Earl and Tom took turns filling my mouth. On Tuesday morning we quickly finished up our work and had an orgy that lasted until Friday morning, when I went home. Eliot was right when he said I would be thoroughly fucked.

When I finished my story, Giselle asked me if I still fuck Eliot. I told them he knows my pussy is his anytime he wants it. I turned to Tracey and said, "Now it's your turn."

To be brief, Tracey told us she loves to be facedown on the bed while her boyfriends fuck her ass. I could feel my panties soak when she told us she has huge orgasms when her lover comes in her ass. I could see Dierdre, who was really shy, blushing from all our sex talk.

Tracey told Giselle it was her turn. Giselle began by telling us she'd been to bed with other women. She had been sleeping regularly with a girl from work, and her boyfriend didn't know it. She went on to tell us that only another woman knows how to eat pussy, and the best is the feeling of your tongue in another girl's pussy when she is coming. The first time she had sex with a woman, an older woman seduced her. In their many love sessions, the woman had taught her how to make love to another woman's pussy. While she said she loves her boyfriend's cock in her cunt, her orgasms are much longer and more intense with women.

I was getting hot as she gave us all the details of how her older woman had used vibrators and dildos on her. I had often fantasized about having sex with women.

Tracey told Dierdre it was her turn. Dierdre very nervously told us she'd only had two lovers, and that she was true to her husband. We asked her if she'd ever had an orgasm, and she said, "I think so." She told us she had a "regular" sex life, that she sometimes gave her husband blowjobs but he never came in her mouth. She also said they have sex about once a week.

I asked her if she ever fantasized. She admitted that she had found other women attractive, and wondered what it would be like to be with another woman. I was sitting closest to Dierdre who, while shy, was the prettiest and had the best figure of the four of us.

I leaned over to kiss her, and found no resistance. This was the first time either of us had ever kissed a woman passionately. In no time, Dierdre and I were embracing and I was removing her panties. With her panties off, I spread her legs wide open and had my first taste of pussy. Giselle and Tracey were now alongside Dierdre, rubbing her tits and kissing her all over. Giselle was telling her how sexy she was. I had my tongue deep in her pussy. We were all working on a different part of Dierdre when I sensed she was about to explode in orgasm. She started bucking and moaning uncontrollably. I kept my mouth firmly planted on her soaked little slit as she came.

When things calmed down a bit, Dierdre realized that that had been her first real orgasm. We all decided that we should forget about men for the week, and have our own private orgy, with Dierdre being our little slut. While we all had sex with each other, we paid special attention to Dierdre's pussy, making sure she had as many orgasms as she could stand. We sucked each other's pussies out constantly. Several times Giselle, Tracey and I ate Dierdre's pussy out at the same time. I got really turned on when Dierdre was thrashing around in orgasm, with my tongue stuffed up her pussy.

By the end of the week, Dierdre was also an expert at eating our pussies to orgasm. When we got home, we never repeated our experience together, but at least we all have another story to tell if the situation arises.—*N.D., La Crosse, Wisconsin* ⚬─▪

SOMETIMES THE BEST OPPORTUNITIES ARE THE ONES THAT FIND YOU

*M*y husband John and I have fantasized about another woman joining us in a fantastic lovemaking session. We really enjoy the thought of another woman eating me, followed by my getting to delve into the unknown by eating her lovely pussy. We have become quite aroused thinking of different women in the role of "the other woman."

Although we tried to figure a way to get a women to join us, the chance never arose.

Then, while on a business trip together in Virginia, we met a beautiful lawyer. She was five feet eight inches tall, around a hundred thirty-five pounds and in her mid-forties. When I was first introduced to Abigail, I immediately felt a rush of heat throughout my body.

All the next day my husband John, Abigail and a few other associates were in meetings. John called at noon, to let me know they were going to be through around four-thirty, and that they wanted me to join them at an exclusive restaurant. When I asked John what I should wear, he handed the phone to Abigail. She asked me if I had a short, dressy dress and stockings. When I told her I did, she said that would do fine. We discussed the restaurant a little, Abby saying that if I really wanted to enjoy myself I shouldn't wear panties. When I laughed, she said she wouldn't either! I was really wet when I hung up the phone.

That evening was great. The sexual teasing between Abigail and me was outrageous. I wasn't sure, and I didn't care, who noticed it. When my husband and I got up to dance, he told me he had noticed it, and was extremely turned on. Then he danced with Abigail. She was a great flirt, and I could tell they were talking about me by the way they kept glancing my way. When they came back to the table, Abigail excused herself, leaving John and me alone.

John told me that Abigail had made a proposition. She wanted to make love to me, and have John videotape it. She would keep a copy for herself and give us a copy. I couldn't believe it. We both laughed. After all our efforts to find someone, a woman had walked up and propositioned us! John told me that Abigail had gone back to her hotel room, and he showed me a key. I laughed and said, "Let's go!"

I was nervous when we arrived at the hotel room. When John opened the door, Abigail met us in a short, silky nightgown. She gave one to me to put on. Then she handed John a pair of silk boxers, telling him he wouldn't be as restricted in them.

After we were all changed, she invited us into the living room of the suite. She opened some champagne. John and I told her about our fantasies about another woman.

After drinking the first bottle of champagne, we all seemed to be relaxing. We talked about all kinds of things. It felt like we had known each other for a long time.

Then Abigail asked us to come into the bedroom. She had a camera on a tripod. She showed John how it worked, and how to take it off to get in close if he wished. While they talked techniques, I sat on the bed. Abigail asked me to lie back so she could show John how to focus. She asked me to lift my gown up and show her my pussy. When I did as I was told, she complimented me on my blonde bush.

The next thing I knew she was beside me. She kissed me and started rubbing my breasts. The heat started rising. I completely forgot about John and the camera.

Abigail seemed to kiss and suck every inch of my body, and I was climaxing almost constantly. My head felt like it was floating. I've never felt so wonderful in my life. Abigail was very adept at eating pussy, her tongue licking and flicking, in, out and then around my clit. When she stuck her tongue deep into me, it felt so very thick that I came in a few seconds.

Abigail left me lying on the bed enjoying the wonderful, tingling aftermath of her attentions, as she helped John change the tape. After that she finally removed her gown, and I saw her dark bush glistening. I wanted to taste it.

Abigail pulled me onto the bed. John grabbed the camera. Abigail and I shared a long, deep, sweet kiss. I could feel her need rising, along with my want. I kissed her full, large breasts. I was enjoying the role reversal. I kissed down her firm stomach, anticipating what was to come!

When I got to her dark cunt it was dripping, and her moans were long and low. My first taste was delicious, and I immediately started licking and sucking. I kept up as best I could, with her hips thrusting against my face. When I found her deep hole with my tongue, her shrieks told me her climax had hit. When I tasted that thicker fluid, I truly found heaven. I loved eating pussy. I was hooked.

We opened a fresh bottle of champagne, and watched the tape we had made. Abigail gave us our copy. She told us we could have the room, that she had a business meeting early, and left. John and I laughed, drank champagne, watched the tape again and made love many times.

The next morning she left a note that just said "Thanks!" What a climactic way to end the day.—*N.T., Chicago, Illinois* ○┼▪

YOU'RE NEVER TOO OLD TO LEARN
WHAT YOU'VE BEEN MISSING

*W*e are a couple in our early sixties. I'm no Adonis, but I'm certainly not bad to look at.

My wife Annie is five foot three, and weighs a hundred and thirty pounds. She has exceptional boobs: large, firm and quite heavy, though there is no sag to them. Her tits are so erect and shapely that she would look beautiful if she dressed without a bra. Her areolae are brown, with small nipples. She has a tight little snatch, set off by a pretty brown bush.

We were both sexually inexperienced when we got married. As a teenager, the only fuck I managed was really not a success. Before we got together, my wife had never even had her pussy touched, let alone fucked. Maybe some guy touched her tits, but I'm sure no one ever saw them bare. I now regret the lack of experience, both hers and mine.

Our sex life has deteriorated lately. It seems as though we only fuck on rare occasions. In our early years we were quite active in bed. It was simple, straight fucking, with no variations in positions, but we both loved it. I would have liked oral sex, but the one time we tried was not a success. She sucked my cock, and it felt so good that I lost control and shot into her mouth. She didn't like that at all, and that was the end of that. I have tried to eat her pussy quite a few times, but she always made me stop after just a few licks. I have suggested that we go outside our marriage for extra sex, but she has nixed that idea. I questioned her about the possibility of my going pussy-hunting. She said it wouldn't bother her at all, but she didn't want to know about it. I've been propositioned several times, by guys wanting to get into her pants and also by couples wanting to swing. I have had to sorrowfully decline.

I retired two years ago, and we moved into a nice house in this community. One of the first friends that Annie made was a woman, a few years older than us, named Rose. She was quite pleasant and, although I didn't see much of her, I thought she was a good friend for Annie. I didn't quite understand her marital status, and my wife didn't want to pry. She had a grown daughter, but we didn't know if she was a widow, divorced or even an unmarried mother. After a while, I got the feeling that she was paying attention to Annie in a special way. It made no difference to me if she was a lesbian, and my wife seemed to be too innocent to notice, so I just let things ride.

About a month ago I decided to bring things to a head. I informed Annie that I thought that Rose was hot for her body. Annie acted like she didn't know what I meant. I asked my wife to find out why Rose was acting like that. Annie asked me what she should do. I suggested that instead of greeting her with a little peck on the cheek she should move to Rose's lips, holding the kiss firmly for a little. Also, she might try a firm hug, not just a quick arm clasp. If Rose had ulterior motives, these advances would encourage her to become more intimate. Annie said she didn't believe I knew what I was talking about. I had started the ball rolling so I just held my peace.

One afternoon last week, Annie returned home after having been to tea with Rose. Her face appeared somewhat flushed as she moved over to where I was sitting. She whispered into my ear, "Feel my pussy!" Her language never, ever gets dirty, so I was surprised to hear her come out with the word pussy. I lifted up her skirt. I was astonished not to see any panties. Her snatch was glistening with love juice, and was dripping wet. I inserted first one finger, then two, into her twat. I rubbed them around the walls of her canal, then brought them to my nose. The faintly fishy smell informed me that this was cunt juice, not come from a cock.

Annie's slippery pussy turned me on, and my prick was hard and throbbing. I took off her skirt and unbuttoned her blouse. She wasn't wearing her bra either. I pulled her over to the sofa, laid her down and spread her legs apart. I tore off my pants and shorts, plunged my dick into her slippery slit all the way up to my balls and fucked her as hard as I could. I was so excited that I could not tell if she had come or not, but I sure did. I pulled out my limp cock and held Annie tightly in my arms.

"Would you tell me what happened to get you like this?" I demanded.

Annie said, "It's a long story. I don't want to talk about it now."

"But I want to know. It looks like you've had a very nice experience," I told her. "Please tell me!"

She hesitated for a little while. Then she said that Rose and she had sex together on three occasions, the latest that afternoon. Then she told me, "After I recover a little, I'll tell you how it all happened."

After we ate supper she started her explanation. When I had told her Rose might be romantically interested in her, she had considered the idea absurd. But then she reflected that it might be possible. With that in mind, she followed the advice I had given her. The kiss on the lips was the beginning of a whole new relationship.

The day of the first kiss ended at Rose's house. Annie was getting ready to go home after lunch. Rose said she needn't rush off, and asked her to sit on the couch and talk a little. Soon Annie felt Rose's hand creeping up her thigh. She stiffened, but didn't try to prevent it. The hand moved higher, gently rubbing the crotch of her panties. Rose was breathing noticeably faster. Annie didn't know what to do, so she simply opened her legs and permitted Rose to continue. Her finger slipped into my wife's panties and stroked the lips of her pussy. After just a little of this ministration, Annie trembled and had an orgasm. Rose kissed her and said she hoped Annie liked it. My wife regained her composure, said good-bye, and came home.

About a week later the second episode took place. Again, Annie was saying good-bye in Rose's living room. They were sitting on the sofa this time too. Once more, Rose's hand started on its little trip. Annie thought she knew what to expect this time, but she got a surprise. Rose was not content with merely stroking my wife's twat. She began tugging at Annie's panties. My wife lifted her hips slightly, and Rose pulled them down and completely off. Then she knelt on the floor and buried her face in my wife's cunt hair. Rose's tongue thrust and probed rapidly. Her lips enveloped those of my wife's twat. Annie was shivering and gasping with delight. Some of her cunt juice was escaping from Rose's mouth. Annie then orgasmed, with a shuddering explosion. Annie picked up her panties, said good-bye and almost ran to her car.

The third occasion again was in Rose's house. Annie went to pick her up to go to a women's club meeting. Rose greeted Annie with a lingering kiss on the lips. Then she asked Annie if she'd enjoyed the last time that they saw each other. My wife stammered and stuttered, finally admitting that she had. Rose asked if she would like to do it again. Without waiting for an answer, she informed Annie that she had just called and told the women's club that neither of them would attend the meeting.

She took Annie by the hand and walked her toward the bedroom. Then she wrapped her arms around my wife and gave her a passionate kiss. Her hands dropped lower, to massage my wife's ass. Annie was getting hot by then. She entered into the spirit and rubbed Rose's ass-cheeks. They then broke the embrace and slowly started to disrobe each other. Their panties were the last to go. Annie was a little embarrassed to be bare-assed, but Rose did not give her time to consider it. They fell onto the bed, with Rose's head at Annie's crotch. Rose tongue-fucked her until Annie was almost ready to shoot.

Then she rose up, gave Annie a long, hard kiss and informed her that it was time for Annie to start sucking Rose's pussy. Annie complained that she didn't know how, but Rose explained that she should just give what she enjoyed receiving from Rose's tongue and lips. My wife went to work, trying to do the same as Rose had done to her. Annie did real well, because it didn't take long for Rose to explode. They rested a few minutes, then Rose returned to Annie's twat. They continued their lovemaking until both of them had two satisfying orgasms. Annie then came home and showed me her dripping pussy.

Annie was terrified that I would be angry with her for having sex with someone other than me, and that I would think she was a lesbian because she did it with another woman. I comforted her, saying that I was actually a little jealous that she had managed to have sex when I had not. The truth of the matter was that I privately believed that this was the start of a new sex experience for me as well as for her. I told her that a sexual experience with another woman in no way made her a lesbian. It was just a release, and I knew she still loved me. I asked her what she would think if I had sex with another man. She thought a minute and then said that she wouldn't mind if I really wanted to do it and if it made me feel good. I told her that if she wanted to do it again with Rose, it would be perfectly all right with me and I would be happy to encourage her.

A few days later, Annie informed me that Rose was coming to pick her up, and that they were going out to lunch. This was the opportunity I had been waiting for. When Rose rang the doorbell, I managed to be there before Annie. I opened the door and greeted her with a friendly kiss on the cheek. I said, "I want to thank you for being such a good friend to Annie."

I could see that both Rose and Annie were embarrassed. I told Rose that Annie had told me what they had done together lately. I said, "I really appreciate your initiating my wife into these pleasures. Annie told me she enjoyed it very much. I don't know how I can express my appreciation."

Then I embraced Rose and gave her a big kiss. She appeared discomfited by the hug I was giving her. I took her by the hand and led her toward the bedroom. I had previously stripped the bedspread and blankets from the bed and now it only had the sheet, and was ready for action. I put my lips to hers and sat her on the edge of the bed, my right hand straying from her back to cup her breast.

"I don't think I like this," Rose said. "I only do this with girls! I don't like men!" I was ready to stop when she said that, but she voluntarily put her lips back on mine. My hand wandered down from her boobs to rub her stomach and navel. Annie was standing there with her mouth hanging open. I pulled Rose's skirt down and dropped my hands to her firm thighs, then inched my fingers inside her panties. She said, "I hate to fuck. I only like girls," but again, when I took my hand away she moved it back to her opening. I was surprised that my finger was moist. Despite what she had been saying, I could tell she was getting pleasure from my finger. I kept fingering her, but now started stroking the lips of her cunt. Her cunt hair was a curly blonde thatch.

By this time, she had stopped complaining. She was moving her hips very slightly from side to side, and occasionally would lift her ass a little. I inserted my index finger into her twat and began finger-fucking her. I didn't really know what I was doing, since I had never done any finger-fucking before, let alone the cunt lapping that I was intending to do. My fingers were now slippery with her juice, so I knew I wasn't doing too badly.

I replaced my finger with my tongue, licking the lips of her twat. After a couple of minutes, I pushed my tongue into her slot as far as I could and began to tongue-fuck her. After several insertions and withdrawals of my tongue, I felt her hands firmly hold and push my head into her snatch.

Annie then got into the act, believing that I was getting ready to fuck Rose. She pulled off my shoes and socks, and tugged at my pants, I had managed to unbutton my shirt and unzip my trousers, but I had not been able to undress any further because I was so busy with Rose. I was elated that Annie was being so understanding. I lifted up a little, and she was able to get my pants off, then my shorts. Rose observed what Annie had done, and she asked Annie to take off her clothes and join us on the bed.

I then began to alternately suck on Rose's cunt with as much suction as I could manage, and then to blow into it with quick little puffs. Her hips were moving in little jerks. I could hear her mumbling, "I like it, I like it. More, more!" She began to quiver, then tremble, and then her orgasm exploded. The muscles in her cunt walls squeezed my tongue, then relaxed, then squeezed again. I was satisfied that I had been able to give her a satisfying orgasm.

By now, Annie was nude and had joined us on the bed. I lay between the two ladies, one of Annie's melons in one hand, and one of Rose's in the other. Rose had stopped panting and seemed to be coming back down to earth from her eruptive orgasm.

Rose lifted herself up on one elbow, looked at me, looked at Annie, and announced, "John, I want you to fuck Annie! Then I will eat out her pussy and eat your come. Let's get her ready for your prick. I'll work on her cunt while you suck and massage her titties."

This seemed like a splendid idea to me. My dick had gotten hard while I was burying my tongue in Rose's snatch. My cock had not stopped throbbing, and it was still stiff. I asked Annie if she liked Rose's suggestion. "It sounds good to me," my wife replied.

Both of us bent over Annie and started working with our tongues. In just a few moments, Annie was quivering and moaning. Rose put her tongue back in her mouth after licking her lips. I gave each little nipple a final kiss. Rose said, "Her pussy's ready! You can stick your prick in her cunt now and give her a good fucking. I can't wait until you shoot so I can taste all the love juice."

Rose spread Annie's legs a little more, and I climbed on top of her. Rose reached in to grasp my cock and steer it into my wife's twat. One hard thrust and I slapped my balls up against her ass. I felt my cockhead pulsing, and I knew that I was going to shoot before I had really given Annie a good fucking. But I didn't care. I knew that Rose was ready and waiting to finish her off. I paused at the end of a stroke that completely buried my prick inside her cunt. I shot out one, then another, load of sperm. I relished the sensation, then withdrew my shrinking rod.

Rose grasped my shoulder with one hand and my hip with the other. She rolled me off my wife and plunged between her legs for the feast that she had been anticipating. Rose was so eager that she was making slurping sounds as she sucked my come out of my wife's pussy. Then she started to clean out the inside with her tongue. Annie lay there, twitching and gasping for breath. She gave a final hard shudder, lifted her ass, and her orgasm nearly bucked Rose off her.

After we had recovered somewhat from our strenuous exertions, Annie said, "It's my turn, now, Johnny. You do it to Rose, and I'll finish it off."

"Get me ready," I said. They both got down, and one rubbed my cock while the other cupped my nuts. It was only seconds before I was hard again. I jumped on top of Rose, and Annie put both hands on my ass-cheeks, ready to push when I shoved my dick into Rose. I plunged in and started a rhythmic fucking. It only took a few minutes for me to shoot. Rose said, "That was the first fuck I've had for years and years. It wasn't bad at all. I guess I've been missing more than I thought."

I rolled off of Rose, and my wife took over. I was kind of surprised at the way she went after Rose's cunt. After all, this was only her second time eating pussy. She sucked and tongued her vigorously, and it wasn't long before Rose orgasmed.

After we rested awhile, it was Annie's turn to get fucked and then sucked. I had slowed down considerably and gave her a long, leisurely session of fucking. This time she had orgasms both while being fucked and sucked.

Our afternoon matinee ended with Annie eating Rose after I gave her my last drop of white cream. We tallied up the score of orgasms. Four for me—two in each pussy. Three for Rose—my cunt-lapping, and two sucks by Annie. Annie also had three—two sucks and a fuck. We all agreed that us old folks still had enough piss and vinegar to enjoy this kind of fucking as much as the younger generation.

I'm sure that there will be more situations where the three of us share cocks and cunts.—*J.P., Salem, Oregon*

Gang Bangs

SERVICING THE TROOPS TO KEEP UP MORALE

*T*he experience I'm about to relate happened to my wife and me several years ago. I was a lieutenant in the army, and we had just gotten married. Alanna, my bride, was a petite, twenty-year-old honey with blonde hair and a body what wouldn't quit—and still won't!

It was Saturday night and we had gone out to dinner at a nice restaurant in the country. Alanna looked particularly sexy that evening in a clingy knit dress that hugged every curve of her luscious body. Beneath it she wore matching beige undergarments, complete with garter belt and stockings.

One the way back to post, I decided to fuck my sexy little wife under the stars. I pulled my car off the road and drove to a secluded area overlooking a large lake. As we kissed, my hands roamed over her body. I caressed her tits with one hand while the other was up under her dress exploring her dripping pussy.

The car was small, and the gearshift kept getting in the way, so I got out and went around to the passenger side. Opening the door, I took Alanna by the hand and helped her out. We stood and kissed for a moment, then I told her to turn around and hold onto the door. She bent over and grabbed the door, placing her head partly through the open window. I raised her dress, pulled the crotch of her panties to one side and shoved my rock-hard dick into her slippery cunt.

Alanna let out a groan as my dick slid firmly up the heavenly space between her smooth thighs. I began rocking in and out of her, and she bit the back of her hand and pushed back at me, urging me to fuck her harder. I started pumping into her with long, firm strokes, and she was really moaning. I pushed her dress up higher and higher until it was up around her neck. She pulled it over her head and tossed it into the car. Next, I unhooked her bra. Her 34C tits bounced free and began swaying to the rhythm of the fucking she was getting.

Not wanting to come too soon, I pulled out, turned my lovely wife around and gently pushed her to her knees. She knew what to do and hungrily took my cock into her mouth, sucking for all she was worth. I held her head and pumped my cock into her warm mouth. After a few minutes, I pulled her back up and removed her panties. Now she was standing under the starry sky clad only in her garter belt, stockings and high heels.

I took her around to the front of the car and lifted her onto the hood. Holding her legs up over my shoulders, I pushed into her cunt again and began fucking her as hard as I could. Holding on to her luscious ass-cheeks, I pulled her cunt up to meet each powerful thrust of my cock. With each stroke, her cunt made a loud sucking noise. Soon, Alanna began moaning as an intense orgasm swept over her. Unable to hold back any longer, I increased my pace and shot a huge load in her pussy.

I still had my dick buried deep in Alanna's cunt when, suddenly, a bright light hit us. Alanna jumped down and got behind me, trying to hide her nudity. It was an MP sedan. Alanna was frightened that we would be arrested and that all our friends would find out. I told her we were in big trouble, and maybe we could talk our way out of it.

The sedan pulled closer and two burly, young MPs got out. They were trying to act official, but they were clearly having a hard time keeping their eyes off of my sexy wife. From the bulges in their trousers, I knew they liked what they saw. They told my wife to step out from behind me and, after some hesitation, she did. Then they asked me to come over to them.

When I got to them and the light was out of my eyes, I realized that I knew them!

"Shit, lieutenant, we didn't realize it was you. What you doin'?"

I guess he was joking, because I think it was fairly obvious what I was doing. Still, I played along.

"I'm doing some top secret investigations. Can I enlist you men for some help?"

My wife and I had often talked about a gang bang, and here it was happening without any planning at all.

We went over to the car and one MP stayed outside while the

other got in the back seat with Alanna. I couldn't hear what he was saying, but the next thing I knew Alanna had her legs up on the front seat and the MP was between them, banging away at her. He was really fucking her good, because Alanna was moaning loudly and her stocking-clad toes were curling up, a sure sign that she was enjoying herself.

After the first MP fucked her, he got out of the car and brought Alanna with him. He gave my young wife to the second MP, who reached between her legs with both hands and lifted Alanna up in the air. She grabbed him around his neck and looked straight into his eyes as he lowered her onto his huge, meaty cock. With my wife holding on for dear life, the second guy fucked her with such intensity I thought she was going to pass out. Alanna was screaming for more and, when the guy came, his load immediately began dribbling out of Alanna's gaping love-hole.

After the second MP had finished, they "let us go." We departed so fast that I left Alanna's panties on the ground and she didn't even bother putting her dress back on. When we got home, gobs of thick come were still dripping from her freshly fucked pussy. As soon as we got inside, Alanna was all over me and we fucked till dawn!

About a week later, Alanna called me at work. She told me that her two MP friends had just paid her a visit, to return her panties. She said they stripped her naked and fucked her doggie-style for over two hours. She said she came several times and her pussy was sore. She added, "Hurry home, 'cause I'm one horny bitch!"

We were reassigned about a month later and left that post forever. But in those last few weeks, Alanna became a good friend of the MPs. They visited her almost daily. On our last weekend on post, they took Alanna to their barracks for a farewell party where she took on all comers, sucking and fucking from Saturday night till early Monday morning. When I got her back, she smelled of booze, sweat and sex, and her pussy and asshole were flaccid and oozing come.

We've had a couple of threesomes since those days, and we've gone to a few swingers' parties, but nothing beats the memory of that night and the time Alanna "serviced the troops."—*Name and address withheld*

SERVICING THE TEAM TO KEEP
THOSE BATTERS UP

*M*y wife Maureen and I are regular readers of *Penthouse Letters,* and we both enjoy the Gang Bangs the best. We have had a few group gropes over the years and, to my surprise, I most enjoy seeing my wife pleased by two cocks—as does she.

Maureen is in her mid-twenties, has long blonde hair, a wonderfully small, tight figure, great tits—and she's an avid semen connoisseur. In all the orgies we've had, Maureen always comes two or three times before insisting that she take care of the rest of us. The first time, I was a little hesitant about my wife swallowing another man's come, but in the heat of the moment I'll let anything happen as long as I get off.

During a recent threesome with Brad, a friend of ours from the local college, Maureen suddenly mentioned that she was very satisfied, but something was missing. I asked her what she meant, and she looked at Brad and me with a smile on her come-coated face and replied, "More guys!"

We didn't do anything about it that night, but a few days later, Brad and I decided to throw a little party for his school's baseball team. I told Maureen that I had a surprise for her the night of the get-together, but she had no idea what was in store for her. All that I said was that she would have to do a little entertaining that night. "I would love to," she replied.

At about six o'clock, the guys started showing up at our house. Each one had been told to bring some booze and an open mind. Maureen answered the door and introduced herself to the guys, giving each a kiss on the lips.

After all seventeen players had arrived, Maureen served appetizers in her skimpy French maid outfit that barely covers her tits and ass. She accentuated her long legs in fishnet stockings. The booze flowed freely and it wasn't long before everyone was feeling good, including my wife. It was at this point that Brad and I decided to get things started.

We made up a little drinking game in which there was a bucket full of pieces of paper with the letters B, P, A and O printed on them.

Before each could draw from the bucket, he had to first down a glass of beer, wine or a shot of the hard stuff. The bucket moved around the living room, and each time it came to Maureen, she would drink but would receive no ticket. She was becoming suspicious of this game but played along willingly.

After the first round, I told the guys to save their valuable coupons, which they could redeem later. After four rounds, I told the crowd that each ticket had significance and, with Maureen's permission, each would be fulfilled. I asked my wife to come to the center of the room and then proceeded to say that anyone with a P ticket could fuck Maureen's pussy, an A ticket could fuck her ass, a B ticket could receive a blowjob and an O could not touch her but only jack off. Anyone having a combination of letters could do what each letter entitled them to do. The only catch was that nobody could come until I said so.

I'd loaded the bucket mostly with Os, and it turned out that six guys couldn't touch her at all.

We all took off our clothes, and soon my wife was surrounded by seventeen hard cocks, each guy taking his turn as his ticket dictated. Maureen looked so happy.

I got the video camera to catch some of this once-in-a-lifetime experience on film, and when I returned, I was surprised to find my wife in a most overwhelming position. As I looked through the camera she was straddling one guy and riding him hard while alternating between sucking two well-hung studs in front of her and jacking off two others, one on each side of her. She was soon anally penetrated by one of the largest shanks I have ever seen. It must have been ten inches long and as big around as a large cucumber.

So there I was, taping my wife simultaneously servicing six studs from the local college baseball team as the rest were yanking their puds as they waited for their turn at my petite wife. She, meanwhile, seemed to have turned into a dick-hungry slut who couldn't get enough cock in her. I got a good close-up of what still seems physically impossible.

None of the guys came, however, and after an hour and a half of group fucking, the entire team was lined up against the wall pulling their hard dicks. My wife was going up and down the line giving each dick a few minutes of attention before moving to the next. When she got to the end of the line, I gave her a glass and told her that she could now suck the men to the point just short of coming, at which time they could jack off in the glass.

With a smile on her face, she started to suck the first dick, and because he had been so close before, he quickly unleashed a giant load of cream right into her mouth and on her chin.

She licked the last of the come from the guy's rod and then went happily to the next dick. As this guy started to arch his back and moan, she stopped sucking and placed the glass over the tip of his cock, milking his cock for every last drop of spunk. She licked the second man's dick clean of come and moved to the next.

My wife continued down the line working the well-hung studs with her mouth as she stroked the next guy in line. She continued to suck off each guy with slutlike enthusiasm, having them pull out and either shoot their loads on her face on in the glass. She was being my dream whore, and I was capturing it all on film.

After the seventh or eighth guy, she would move to the next guy in line and within seconds he would come on her waiting face. It was a come depository assembly line, and the guys were enjoying it almost as much as my wife.

The last guy in line was a well-hung man with a horselike dick. When she got to him, she put his meat well down her tiny throat and stroked the exposed six inches that she couldn't swallow with two-handed enthusiasm.

When he was close to coming, he told her to sit back and open wide. His first two shots went well over her head, but they were followed by eight to ten more streams of thick semen that completely covered her already sticky face.

Seeing the woman of my dreams drain the semen from seventeen hard dicks was more that I could handle. I handed the camera to the big-dicked man and told him not to miss a thing. I laid Maureen down and began to fuck her yearning vagina. Before I came, I pulled out and asked her where she wanted my load.

"On my face," she replied, as I sent what seemed to be a gallon of come showering over her pretty face. As she lay there in exhaustion, sucking my limp cock, I picked up the twelve ounces of collected come and slowly poured it in her mouth, which she swallowed one gulp at a time.

The day after the party we watched the tape several times, fucking all the while.—*L.M.*, *Fayetteville, Arkansas* ⦿┼▪

SWINGING BOATERS HEAT THINGS UP, BUT IT'S NOT CABIN FEVER

*M*ia and I have been married for five years. We enjoy your magazine, especially the letters about threesomes and crowds.

We were reading a letter about a threesome one night when we were both naked in bed. My cock was up and hard, and Mia's nipples were like two hard pebbles.

"How would you like to add another guy or girl to our lovemaking and have a threesome," I asked.

Mia said, "I'd rather add a couple. That way we'd both get to fuck a new person."

A week later I stopped in an adult-book store and picked up a local swingers magazine. That night, while lying in bed, I handed it to Mia and said, "See if you can find a couple we might like to get together with."

Mia said, "You're really serious about this, aren't you." Mia went through the magazine a few times and finally said, "How about this couple."

The ad showed a man and a woman in swimsuits and read "Late twenties new to swinging would like to meet same. Must be discreet."

We sent a letter off the following day and waited for an answer. A few weeks later we received a reply saying they would like to meet us. They named a hotel lounge where we could meet and gave a phone number.

Friday night arrived and off we went. Mia was dressed to kill in her favorite minidress.

When we got to the lounge, we sat at the bar and ordered drinks. After a few minutes a man walked up and asked, "Are you Bob and Mia?"

I said, "Yes, are you Broderick?"

He said, "Yes, we're sitting over at a table. Bring your drinks and join us."

Broderick introduced us to Heather, an exceptionally nice-looking brunette. We hit it off real good. After about an hour, Broderick said, "Why don't you two talk it over while me and Heather hit the johns."

I asked Mia, "What do you think." She said, "Okay with me, if you want to."

When Broderick and Heather came back we said, "Let's do it."

Broderick gave us the name of a marina and said he would see us there around ten the next morning.

He had an awesome boat with plenty of sleeping room, if you know what I mean. We went about six miles offshore and dropped anchor. The ocean was flat. The girls had on bikinis and were enjoying the sun.

Broderick said, "Let's go down in the cabin and have a few drinks."

I sat with Mia on one bed and Broderick sat on the other with Heather. We were new at this, so I took Broderick's lead when he took off Heather's top and started playing with her tits. I did the same with Mia. After a few minutes Heather came over and sat next to me, telling Mia to go over with Broderick.

Heather's hand went to my cock as I sucked on her tits. She said, "Let's get these off," and knelt on the floor pulling off my trunks. I glanced over at Mia right as she was doing the same for Broderick. His cock sprang free. Christ, it was big. I had to be all of eight inches and big around as a Coke bottle.

My attention was soon on my own cock as Heather took it in her hot mouth. I heard Broderick say, "Oh, yeah, suck it, suck it."

I felt that tingling sensation in my balls and knew I would be coming soon. I wanted my cock in Heather's cunt when I came, so I sat her on the bed and started eating her pussy. She was very verbal, just like her husband, and started screaming, "Oh, fuck, baby, eat me, eat me, make me come." Man, she tasted sweet.

When I heard Mia moaning, I looked over to see that Broderick was eating her cunt. It was like making out in front of a mirror. Meanwhile, Heather's ass came off the bed and her hands held my head on her cunt. She screamed, "Oh, fuck, I'm coming."

Her juices started flowing from her cunt. I tongue-fucked her till she relaxed. "God, that was good," she said. "This is so fucking awesome."

My cock was throbbing as I knelt between Heather's legs. She put the head in her hole and put her legs around my ass as I slammed all six inches into her cunt. She screamed, "Oh, yes, baby, fuck me good."

Her cunt muscles tightened around my cock as I fucked in and out of her wet hole. I heard Mia whimper, "Easy, easy," and so I glanced over at her and Broderick. He had her legs bent back with her knees smashing into her tits. Her cunt lips were spread wide and his monster dick reamed in and out of her like a pile driver.

She moaned as inch after inch disappeared in her cunt. Her cunt was soon mashed up to his balls. She wrapped her legs around his ass and said, "Don't move. Let me get used to your big cock." Her legs soon pulled on his ass and he started fucking her nice and slow.

I glanced over at Mia so many times because this was a first for us, and I was as excited to see that big cock fucking her cunt as I was to have my own cock in some strange pussy.

Heather's cunt muscles were milking my cock, and I was soon shooting hot come in her cunt. We lay back and watched as Mia and Broderick continued to go at it. He lasted much longer than I did. Mia finally moaned, "Fuck me hard with that big cock. I'm coming." Her legs tightened around his ass and his cock was soon coated with her cunt cream. He screamed, "Oh, fuck, here it comes."

His ass muscles tightened as he shot his hot sperm in her cunt. A river of come was soon funneling down the crack of her ass.

Both girls went to the head to clean up while Broderick made us more drinks. We sat around the cabin naked, Mia and Broderick on one bed, Heather and me on the other. Presently, Broderick started kissing Mia. His hands went from her tits to her pussy. His cock was rock-hard as Mia jerked up and down on it. I followed his lead and started finger-fucking Heather. Broderick laid Mia back and straddled her chest, fucking her tits. Her legs were spread as his hand rubbed her cunt.

Heather then slipped off the bed and knelt between Mia's legs. She pushed Broderick's hand away and started eating my wife's pussy.

Mia moaned. "Oh, yes, honey, eat me." She thought it was me eating her cunt.

Heather was waving her ass at me, so I knelt behind her and slid my cock up her cunt. Mia soon started moaning, humping her cunt at Heather's mouth. Heather feasted on her cunt juice.

Broderick said, "Oh, fuck, here it comes. Suck it, suck it."

Hearing this, my cock started unloading hot come in Heather's cunt. Broderick rolled off Mia and lay back on the bed. My cock was still spewing wildly in Heather's cunt, and when I was spent, I pulled out and sat back on the bed.

Mia's eyes were closed, and Heather was still feasting on her cunt. Mia's hands went down to Heather's head, and when she felt the long hair her eyes sprung open. This was the first time a woman had ever gone down on her. She just moaned, "Oh, yes, yes, eat me, girlfriend." Her ass came off the bed as she fucked her cunt at Heather's mouth.

Her orgasms came crashing down and she came for nearly five minutes. My wife unleashes a torrent of juices, and Heather was good to lap it all up.

When the girls were done, Broderick suggested we all go up on deck and get some sun. We grabbed our drinks and off we went. We were naked, but there were no boats in sight. Broderick said, "Why don't you put some oil on Heather and I'll do Mia." We spent a lot of time rubbing oil on the girls' tits, and their nipples were soon stone-hard. They were lying side by side. Mia's cunt lips were swollen and her clit poked out about a quarter of an inch.

After about an hour, Mia said, "I've had enough sun, I'm going down below." Broderick said, "Me too," and off they went.

The cabin windows were open, and I watched as Mia lay back on the bed. Broderick knelt between her legs and started eating her pussy. I heard her saying how good his tongue felt. I was sitting Indian style on the deck and Heather maneuvered around till her head was between my legs. She started sucking my cock.

My wife gives great head, but I have to say, Heather has some kind of technique that she ought to have patented. I don't know exactly what she was doing, but my dick practically mushroomed up into her mouth. I felt like the head of my dick was banging against the back of her skull. The more she sucked, the harder I got, but it wasn't like blue balls or anything. It was only like I had a huge cock all of a sudden.

I didn't want her to stop, and I was in luck. Judging from the sound of her moans, she was enjoying this every bit as much as I was.

From the sound of it, Broderick was doing a good job on Mia's pussy. She kept moaning, "Oh, oh, God, I'm there."

I looked back into the cabin to see Mia's legs wrapped around Broderick's back. She started to shake, and I knew she was about to come again. Her ass arched off the bed and she flooded his mouth with her cunt cream.

When Bob sat up on the bed, his cock looked even bigger than it had before. He told Mia to sit on it. She straddled his hips and put the head in her swollen cunt. I watched as inch after inch disappeared in her cunt. She kept moaning, "Oh, God, you're big." She leaned over and he started sucking on her tits. His cock was slick with her cunt cream as it reamed in and out of her cunt. After a few minutes Mia moaned, "I'm there again. Fuck me hard with that big cock."

Broderick stood up and turned my wife over the bed. Slamming her from behind, he gave me a perfect view of his monster dick flying in and out of my wife's steaming gash. I felt like I was watching a porn flick. Hell, I felt like I was *living* a porn flick.

All of a sudden, Broderick moaned, "I'm coming." Frothy cream soon coated his cock as their combined juices ran out Mia's cunt. Seeing this, my cock swelled and I shot my own cock cream down Heather's throat.

Heather and I went down to the cabin and we all got dressed. We had been anchored for about five hours. Broderick said, "Well, guys, it's time we went in. I think we had one great adventure. We'll have to get together again soon."

We all had one last drink to toast the afternoon and then headed back to port.

On the way home, Mia and I talked about our first swinging session. Mia said she enjoyed herself but that her cunt was a little tender from Broderick's big cock.

If you've never had a swinging session, you don't know what you're missing. Even if your sex life is the greatest you can imagine, fucking someone else's wife while he fucks yours is like moving into the stratosphere.—*B.V., West Palm Beach, Florida* ○—▪

HEAVYWEIGHT CHAMP GIVES GROUPIE KNOCKOUT HUMP

I have always been a confident guy, full of arrogance and fury. From childhood I have known that I am destined to be the world boxing champion in my weight class. Accordingly, several months ago I joined a gym that is well known for producing champions.

I spent my first day at the gym sparring, shadowboxing and working out with the other fighters on various pieces of high- and low-tech equipment.

A week later the guys introduced me to a boxing groupie named Wanda. Wanda is a sexy blonde fox if ever there was a sexy blonde fox. She really has a big thing for boxers, I was told, and just about any fighter who wants to fuck her is welcomed with open arms—and legs.

As a matter of course I tired to seduce Wanda but to my dismay she rejected every one of my advances. She wouldn't give herself a chance to find out that, while I may not be as handsome a hunk as some of the other guys, I do have one asset that few men can match: a ten-inch cock. Wanda would have all the prick her hands, mouth and cunt could handle if only she tried me out. But as week after uneventful week rolled by I began to think I would never get my chance with Wanda.

One month after I joined, the gym held a Golden Gloves tournament. I fought hard in my match and quickly knocked out my opponent. After the match I rushed into the locker room to shower and change before heading out to celebrate.

To my astonishment, Wanda suddenly strolled into the locker room. She matter-of-factly checked out the naked boxers with unmistakable lust in her eyes. I didn't know what to make of it. I was shocked and visibly aroused by her boldness.

When Wanda caught sight of my jumbo tube steak, her mouth dropped open and her eyes widened. Now was my moment, it appeared. With a visible effort, Wanda finally managed to tear her eyes away from my cock and balls and address the roomful of fighters.

"Hey! It's time for my workout, boys!" she announced loudly as she started taking off her clothes. "I need a big prick and I need it now." While the guys gathered all around her, Wanda hopped onto the massage table and peeled off her few remaining garments. Now she was altogether naked—stripped for action.

"Who do you want, Wanda?" one of the boxers called out in the crowd.

"Whoever has the biggest dick!" she shouted with no hesitation, and pointed a steady finger directly at me. A bunch of fellows pushed me in her direction. She anticipated the move and lay back with her legs spread wide to receive my tallywhacker.

Wanda screamed with joy as I plunged my hambone into her steamy cunt. To my surprise, she was able to take it almost all the way in on the first stroke—something no other woman had ever done before! I marveled at her sexual talents and abilities, and I blew my wad in a very short time.

Wanda, bless her heart, was insatiable. She fucked several more boxers and also delighted some do-it-yourselfers who stood around and jerked off as they watched the sex show. She was a happy camper, ravishing, energized and eager for more.

Sitting up on the massage table, she spoke to me in a sexy, sultry voice. "I still haven't come yet," she cooed. "Would you be a dear and eat me out?" Her sopping cunt was dripping with sperm; but the guys urged me on and, next thing I knew, I was down on my knees facing her wet, sloppy cunt.

I tenderly tongued her swollen clit before I started work on her pussy. Soon I was sucking on her labia and slurping up the orgasmic mixture overflowing from her well-fucked cunt. She shrieked and writhed as she came, drenching my face with a mixture of sex juices.

Then I realized all at once that all my fellow boxers had been standing close by, taking in this cunt-lapping show and enjoying the spectacle!

I had eaten their come right out of this gorgeous babe and they were pleased as Punch about it. "How did I taste?" one of them shouted.

"I hope you didn't spoil your appetite for dinner," another called. Others laughed and chimed in with clever comments of their own. I was humiliated and I was feeling betrayed and uneasy.

Fortunately the guys were too good-natured to let me suffer long. While chuckling and patting me on the back, they explained that the entire orgy had been a setup. It was their way of initiating new boxers into their exclusive circle.

I am now officially on the team and I'm looking forward to setting up the next cocky kid who wants to join. Meanwhile, Wanda and I have become lovers. She is truly the undisputed mistress of boxing.—*W.S., Brooklyn, New York* ○⊢▪

SHE DOESN'T MIND BREAKING AND ENTERING—BUT BE SURE TO ENTER HER

*A*s soon as the new *Penthouse Letters* arrives in the mail, my husband and I take time out to read it aloud to each other. The exciting and diverse letters have inspired us to reveal our kinkiest desires, as well as to try out some things we might never have thought of on our own.

Recently we enjoyed an exciting erotic experience which we would like to share with your readers.

Dan and I are in our mid-thirties. We both take good care of ourselves and retain attractive youthful appearances. I'm proud of my figure and enjoy a bit of playful exhibitionism and friendly flirtation when Dan and I go nightclubbing on weekends.

I have extremely long legs and my shapely hips are accentuated by a wasp-waist. When we go dancing I like to wear short skirts and tight-fitting tops. Dan always gets a big kick out of the amount of male attention I attract on the dance floor, as well as in any bar.

This adventure began as a typical night out for us. I dressed in an obscenely short red dress and matching red high-heeled shoes. Dan and I then drove to one of our favorite hangouts. After picking up a pitcher at the bar, we chose a table near the dance floor.

Three men were seated at the table next to ours. Even though all three were good-looking guys in their mid-twenties, they were having absolutely no luck with the ladies. Nearly all the women in the bar that night were already accompanied by men of their own.

I was pleased to see that all three of the guys kept glancing in my direction. I flirted right back at them. They seemed to appreciate my deliberately provocative body language. I made certain to show them as much leg and thigh as I could manage. And I can manage a lot.

When Dan went to buy another pitcher the best-looking of the three asked me to dance. He told me his name was Ned and that he and his friends—Robert and Nathan—were in town to visit a friend in the hospital. We danced to several numbers together, including a very slow number throughout which I clung tightly to Ned. I relished the feeling of his strong hands on my buttocks and of his hard cock pressing against my pussy.

When Dan returned, we all introduced ourselves. As the night wore on, I made it my business to dance with—and dance close to—each of the three young hunks.

Sometime after midnight, Dan and I decided it was time to go home. Before we got to the car, our three new acquaintances rushed out and invited us to finish the party in their motel room. I thought it was a great idea, but before I could open my mouth, Dan declined the invitation. This annoyed me but I consoled myself by slipping Ned a card behind Dan's back with my name and address printed on it. Then I hopped into the car and forgot all about it.

I was so tired and light-headed when we got home that I promised Dan that if he let me sleep, I would spend all of Sunday in bed with him, doing some fancy fucking and sucking. He readily agreed to that proposition. I slipped hastily into my lacy black nightgown, collapsed into bed and instantly fell asleep.

I couldn't have been asleep for more than an hour before I was awakened. There was a strange hand on my shoulder. I opened my eyes sleepily and saw an unfamiliar figure beside the bed. I thought of shaking Dan awake, but then I realized that it was Ned. My confusion turned to lust, and I decided to let sleeping husbands lie—at least for the time being.

I had often fantasized about having more than one man make love to me at the same time, but I still hadn't had the guts to share this fantasy with Dan. I silently swore to tell him everything the very next day, but for the moment I had urgent needs that could neither be dismissed nor delayed.

Dan continued to snore softly. He was sound asleep. Motioning to Ned to be quiet, I eased myself from the bed. We then tiptoed out of the bedroom, carefully pulling the door shut behind us.

To my delight I found Ned's friends sitting on the living-room couch. They were waiting impatiently for me.

Ned eased my nightie off, and seated me between Robert and Nathan. Then he described quite graphically the wild and pleasurable things they intended to do for me and how much I was going to enjoy it.

Suddenly three pairs of hands were crawling up my legs, caressing my breasts and fondling my pussy. I squirmed with excitement. Ned kissed my lips, neck and shoulders while Robert sucked hard on my nipples. Nathan paused just long enough to rip off his clothing. He then knelt between my legs and plunged his snakelike tongue deep into my moistening pussy. I gasped and ground my grotto into his face. It was wonderful to be cosseted by so many tongues and hands.

Ned stripped and waved his enormously swollen red prick in my face. I was delighted. I placed my lips around its well-shaped head and sucked the entire length deep into my enthusiastic mouth.

Robert was the last to undress. He had a muscular physique and a long, thick cock to match. Seizing his rigid pole, I gave him my best handjob while Ned filled my mouth with rich creamy come.

After all this foreplay, I felt it was time for some serious sex. I lay back on the couch and spread my legs. Nathan immediately fell on top of me. As he penetrated my snapping pussy with his thick prick, I wrapped my legs around his waist and pulled his lovely whang in as deep as I could manage.

While Nathan plunged his prick in and out of my sopping love-box, Robert pushed his boner between my lips and fucked my mouth. While this delightful activity was taking place, I reached out and grabbed hold of Ned's cock and balls. I stroked skillfully until Ned's warm jism showered upon me. Less than ten seconds later Nathan stiffened and spurted a load of hot jism deep inside of me. At the same time, Robert fed me another generous serving of thick, salty come.

Now it was my turn. Bucking and moaning, I writhed in the throes of a powerful orgasm. The boys beamed and Ned assured me that the fun had only just begun.

He insisted that it was now his turn to get his wand inside of me. He let me suck on that magnificent pole of his until it was rigid again. Then, as his friends stood by watching, he gently pulled me down to the carpet and asked me to get down on all fours.

Kneeling behind me, Ned penetrated my pussy, sinking the entire length of his shaft into my hungry honey-pot with one forceful push. It was fortunate that my pussy was so well-lubricated because I had never had a cock that size before. And frankly, I felt my pussy was fortunate to have that experience.

Ned grabbed my hips and pumped me harder and faster with every stroke as I panted and bounced my ass against him. Robert and Nathan cheered us on. Each orgasm I had seemed more euphoric than the last. I had never come so many times. When Ned finally filled me with his come, I nearly collapsed with exhaustion. Fortunately my three ardent lovers showed no signs at all of tiring.

By the time Ned filled me with his seed the other two were ready to go again. Nathan's cock entered my mouth while Robert eased his handsome prick into my hot, wet cunt. Robert lifted my legs over his shoulders and fucked me more ferociously than anyone ever had before.

Suddenly I realized that there were now four men in the room. Even though I'd done my best to be quiet, my moans and yelps had awakened Dan, and he'd crept into the room to find out what was going on.

I almost panicked. But I saw lust rather than anger etched in my husband's face. Also, a sizable bulge was tenting out his pajamas and he was grinning from ear to ear.

The boys looked a little sheepish but Dan quickly put their fears to rest by thanking them for making me so happy and for putting on such a great show.

"Now it's time for the grand finale," Dan said, and he motioned to me to approach him. I quickly unfastened his pajamas and sucked his erect prick—a good-sized one—into my mouth. There I was, kneeling in front of my husband and sucking him off while three strangers stared as their come ran plentifully down the insides of my thighs.

Dan came very quickly and after a few drinks and a lot of friendly chatter our three new friends departed. Dan and I collapsed into bed, exhausted. After several hours of sleep, we woke up and made love as we had planned. I was still horny, remembering the night's exploits and adventures. We spent most of the day together in bed, storing up more exciting memories for a rainy day.—*C.K., Rapid City, South Dakota*

REBECCA'S FANTASY COMES TRUE
IN LIVING COLOR

I have been married to Rebecca for three years. She is a gorgeous, blue-eyed, five-foot-two-inch blonde bombshell blessed with full

36C breasts and an absolutely fabulous ass. Surprisingly, in spite of her great beauty, Rebecca had hardly had any sexual experience prior to our marriage—only straight sex with two different guys.

After we were married, I took it upon myself to educate her. We began experimenting with sex toys, exhibitionism and group sex.

More important, however, we learned to trust one another enough to openly discuss our fantasies and to work together to fulfill as many of them as possible. Recently we had the opportunity to fulfill one of Rebecca's favorite fantasies. I'm writing to share this experience with your readers.

It all started when we decided to spend a long weekend at the seashore. While we lounged on the beach sunning ourselves, a group of muscular and agile young, black men started playing touch football about a hundred yards away from us.

I soon became aware that Rebecca couldn't keep her eyes off the players. We discussed this, and she confessed that she had always fantasized about fucking a black guy with a really huge prick.

I could tell from the look in her eyes and from the way she kept squirming that she was getting really hot. I told Rebecca that this was a fantasy we simply had to fulfill. She agreed, gratefully, and I immediately began planning a way to turn her fantasy into reality. My only condition was that she must allow me to watch her being pleasured by her new black stud and lover.

The next day, Rebecca headed for the beach wearing her skimpiest bikini. I followed at a distance, careful not to be seen with her. Rebecca quickly found two black guys who were to her liking. Both were in their mid-twenties and in great physical condition. One of them was about six feet tall and quite muscular. The other was slim, and sinewy, at least six-foot-four. Rebecca spread her towel on the sand next to the two studs and sat down facing them.

As she pulled off her T-shirt and started making small talk, I could see she had their rapt attention.

The taller of the two was wearing a Speedo suit that clearly outlined his sizable cock. As he chatted with Rebecca and checked out her magnificent body, his prick grew noticeably larger.

After a while, Rebecca undid her top and lay down on her stomach. As she continued her conversation with her two new acquaintances, she would occasionally prop herself up, and while pretending to cover her titties, she managed to give both studs tantalizing views of those milk-white mammaries.

The more muscular of the two men gracefully agreed when she asked him to rub sunscreen on her shapely back. When he started rubbing it in, I really became aroused. I watched mesmerized as his muscular black hands roamed freely over her pale flesh. As he massaged her beautifully rounded buttocks, Rebecca parted her legs ever so slightly. This allowed him to stroke her pussy through the thin fabric of her suit.

At this point, Rebecca caught my eye and signaled that she was about to make her move. Wrapping a towel around my waist to cover the growing bulge in my briefs, I dashed back to the hotel to get ready. When I got to our room I opened the blinds and hid on the balcony where I would have a perfect view of the bed.

Rebecca soon returned with her two new friends in tow. As soon as she closed the door, she turned to the muscular one (whose name, I later learned, is Warren) and kissed him passionately. Meanwhile, the tall, thin guy (whose name is Albert) cupped her ass with one hand and fingered her pussy with the other, closing his eyes as he enjoyed the ecstasy of the sensation. Rebecca reached out, grabbed Albert's cock and continued playing tongue hockey with Warren. When Warren pulled off her T-shirt and fondled her breasts, I saw Rebecca stiffen and heard her cry out. Thus she announced her first orgasm of the day.

When her knees stopped trembling, Rebecca kicked off her sandals, stripped off her panties and jumped onto the bed. There she lay spread-eagle. She beckoned her Nubian studs to join her and she didn't have to invite them twice! Both men were out of their trunks and on the bed before I could even blink.

From my vantage point I could see the three of them clearly. Albert snuggled between Rebecca's legs and started devouring her pussy while Warren brandished his stiff cock in her avidly attentive face. Rebecca grabbed Warren's massive balls with one hand and the base of his cock with the other. She then hungrily licked and kissed his love-stick. I wouldn't have thought it possible, but that blacksnake seemed to grow even longer and thicker.

Under Rebecca's tender ministrations, Warren's cock rapidly grew to its full size—and what a size it was! It must have been at least eleven inches long and as wide as a Coke bottle. In spite of her best efforts, Rebecca could barely get the head of the monster into her mouth. She had to settle for licking her way up and down the length of its shaft.

Meanwhile, Albert was busy sliding his long fingers in and out of Rebecca's warm, wet pussy and licking her engorged clitoris. As another orgasm surged through her body, Rebecca thrust her hips forward so her pussy would meet Albert's tongue. She stared wildly at Warren and gasped, "Fuck me now! Fuck me with that big black prick!"

Eager to comply, Warren changed positions with Albert and slowly pushed his prodigious prong into her tight, wet pussy. Inch by inch Warren's ebony shaft vanished within the soft pink folds of Rebecca's pussy. As the final inch of his cock disappeared within her, Rebecca arched her back and exploded in yet another orgasm.

As she cried out with pleasure, Albert took the opportunity to slip his cock into her open mouth. Albert's prick was almost as long as Warren's but not quite as thick. Rebecca didn't have much trouble sucking it all the way into her mouth. As Warren plunged his huge, throbbing cock in and out of my wife's pussy, Albert pumped his prong in and out of her mouth. He was bewitched at the sight of her swallowing and gobbling on his huge prick. Albert babbled on about how much he liked fucking white pussy and how good his black cock looked buried in her glowing white face.

In the meantime, Warren had grabbed Rebecca by the ankles, lifted her legs into the air and gone into overdrive. As he pounded her with his huge dick, Rebecca achieved orgasm after orgasm. I could hear her moaning deliriously as her petite body quivered and shook between her two black lovers.

All this hot and heavy action was really getting to me. The spectacle of my wife taking on two huge black cocks at the same time was more than I could bear. I pushed my swimming trunks down around my knees and began jerking off furiously.

When Warren emitted a groan and shot his load deep into Rebecca's pussy, I shot my load onto the floor with a whimper.

By the time I looked up again, Warren had moved aside and Albert had taken his place between Rebecca's legs. His cock slid easily into her well-stretched cunt and he was soon fucking away.

Rebecca was in another world. She kept telling him to fuck her with his "beautiful black cock" and she climaxed in one orgasm after another. Warren lay beside Rebecca and played with her tits. To reciprocate the kind attention she grabbed his cock and gently and lovingly jacked him off.

Just then, Albert pulled his johnson out of Rebecca's cunt and shot a huge load all over her belly. All three of them rubbed the jism all over her heaving bosom.

Rebecca's expert handjob soon had Warren ready for some more fucking. Circling her slim waist with a muscular arm, he flipped Rebecca over and mounted her doggie-style. As Warren gave her throbbing pussy another workout, Rebecca sucked Albert's monster back to life.

Rebecca surrendered herself completely to the situation: sucking, kissing and licking Albert's cock with wild abandon. This went on for at least half an hour. I never saw Rebecca so sexually alive. She came so many times that by the end of the session she quivered and wept.

Finally Albert couldn't stop himself. He exploded into Rebecca's mouth. She tried to swallow it all but some of his come dribbled down her chin.

Warren, still pumping in and out of Rebecca's sloshing love-box, raised his head and said he was ready for a ride on the Hershey highway.

Albert dashed to the bathroom and returned with a bottle of lotion. He handed the bottle to Warren who carefully lubricated Rebecca's bung-hole while still plumbing her pussy. He then stuck two fingers covered with lotion into Rebecca's puckered little asshole. This gave her still another shuddering orgasm. He plunged his fingers in and out of her anus while continuing to work her pussy with his tireless dick. Finally, he pulled out of her cunt and started trying to insinuate his prick into her asshole.

At first he had a hard time getting the monster into her pink, tight rectum. I began to think he would never succeed. But with infinite patience, Rebecca's skillful new lover slowly worked his way in.

Before I knew it, he was fucking her ass with gusto. His balls slapped against her pussy-lips as he rammed his ebony pole all the way up her ass. Rebecca braced herself and thrust her hips back against him, meeting his every thrust. Warren quickened his pace, let out a bellow and filled her asshole with his load.

When he finally pulled his shrinking cock out of her ass, Rebecca rolled over with a huge smile on her face. She ran her hands over her two lovers and thanked them for the greatest fuck of her life. They got up and dressed.

Before they left, Rebecca kissed each of them and told them she wanted to see them again—and soon. She gave them our phone number and begged them to come back and visit.

As soon as they were gone I came in off the balcony. Still smiling, Rebecca told me that she wanted me to fuck her. It was one of the best sessions of our lives.

All this happened over a month ago but we still get excited thinking about it. Last night Warren called Rebecca. He told her he was coming to town and that he and a few of his friends wanted to get together with her. Needless to say, we can hardly wait.—*M.L., Spokane, Washington*

Boy Meets Boy

A ROUTINE WORKOUT LEADS TO A
RADICAL CHANGE OF ROUTINE

A few months ago I had my one and only sexual encounter with another man, and I'm beginning to realize that it has changed my life forever. I find myself thinking about this guy almost all the time.

I'm pretty much an average guy, forty-nine years old, been married twice. I have been a school teacher for twenty-five years. There are two things about me that people tend to notice and remember. First, I'm a bodybuilder, and I get a lot of comments about my body. Second, I have a large dick. My cock seems to draw as much attention from the guys in the shower room as it has from my two wives and the one woman that I've had an affair with. My dick is fairly long, but I think it's the thickness that makes it so exceptional. My second wife and the lady I had the affair with called my cock "Mighty Dog." A couple of guys that I work out with at the gym nicknamed me "Wonder Boy," so you get the picture: I have a larger than average penis. Angela (she was the school teacher that I had the affair with) kept K-Y jelly in her night stand the whole time we were seeing each other.

Anyway, I was at the gym very late one night about five months ago when this big hunk of a guy walked in and started working out. We were the only two people there, so we spoke and made small talk while we were working out. After a while I started to get this embarrassed feeling, and soon I realized it was because I was staring at this guy's body. He must have been about six foot seven or six foot eight, and he must have weighed at least two hundred and seventy-five pounds. To put it plainly, he was beautiful. I know that I have never seen such a perfect man in my life, and I'm around a lot of very well-built guys all the time.

I finished my workout and hit the showers. I had just lathered up my whole body when in walks this guy. I must have gasped as I first saw this giant's cock, because he looked right at me and smiled as he walked by me. He stopped at a shower just across from me and turned the water on very hot. He turned and asked me if he could borrow my soap, and when I nodded yes, he walked by me very close and took the soap out of the soap dish on the wall behind me. As he turned to go back to his shower, he let his meat loaf brush against my ass and upper thigh. My normal reaction would be to punch him right then, but to tell the truth, I guess I realized that I was aroused by it.

He was facing me as he started soaping his very large and hairy chest. Then he went on to his cock and balls. He was making small talk as he did this, and I can't even remember what he said or if I answered him. All I can remember is staring at what must have been the world's biggest prick, and I am not excepting my own.

He continued to make small talk as he slowly soaped his cock. He said that he was from another part of the state and that he stopped here to work out a couple of times a year. He started talking about how horny he was. He had been on the road all week and hadn't seen his girlfriend in ten days. I was just listening and watching him wash his huge cock when I realized he was starting to get hard. I was getting really turned on by the thought of seeing him hard.

He asked if I would mind washing his back, and he held out the bar of soap to me. I moved forward and took the soap with no hesitation. Mr. Wonderful turned toward the shower wall and placed his hands high and wide against the tiles. I started washing his back slowly, and I kept thinking that I should stop because I'm not gay and I had never touched another man in this way before.

He turned suddenly and faced me. My knees almost buckled when I saw that his cock was rock-hard and standing straight up. Once again, he smiled at me and asked if I would like to wash his chest. I felt weak and didn't say a word as I started washing his chest, and for the first time I believe I knew what was going to happen. I stopped trying not to look at his cock and just stared at it as I washed his chest. He then took hold of my wrist with his huge hands and, looking right into my eyes, pushed my hands down onto his cock.

I didn't resist. I started soaping a cock that felt as big as my arm, and for the first time started wondering what it would be like to have a man's cock in my mouth. I didn't have to wonder long, because things happened very fast after that. He put his long arms around me and pulled me hard up against him. His cock was pressing against my stomach, and I can't began to tell you how large and hot it felt between us.

After a minute, we backed away slightly and I stared at his cock as I fondled it. I thought that I would explode with excitement because I knew for sure that I was going to suck him right then. I held on to his cock with both hands as he pushed me down to my knees. I was scared and not sure what to do first. I held my face against the side of his cock and again thought how hard and hot it felt. I started sucking him slowly and he then put his hand behind my head as he started to fuck my mouth. This lasted only a few more seconds, when he started to come into my mouth. I started swallowing as fast as I could, but it's very hard to do with your mouth open that wide. I started choking and he pulled his cock out of my mouth and shot huge globs of come on my face and chest.

I was still on my knees and swallowing come when I reached down and started pounding my own cock. I came in about five seconds. I shot my load onto the shower floor between his legs. It felt so good.

I felt slightly embarrassed as he helped me up and I walked back to my shower. I started washing the come off my face. I was facing the showerhead, so I was startled when he put his arms around me from behind and hugged me firmly. I could feel his cock lying between the cheeks of my ass as he held me very tight and whispered in my ear, "Thanks, that was great, and I wish that I had time to fuck your ass." He slapped me on the ass as he walked away from me and said over his shoulder, "I hope I see you on my next trip."

I waited for a while before I left the shower. I wasn't sure that I wanted to face him. By the time I went into the locker room, he was gone.

For the first couple of months after this happened, I was pretty much in a state of denial. I tried not to think about it, and I screwed my wife harder than I had screwed her in years. I guess I wanted to reassert my manhood. Well, I have finally given up trying not to think about Mr. Wonderful. Even if I never see him again, I don't ever want to forget what we had. And I've even started dreaming up scenarios in which we see each other again. This is one of my dreams: I'm going to invite him to spend a weekend at my house. My place is great for lovemaking. I have a huge shower with a large seat in it and, of course, there's also a hot tub. I have several large mirrors in the bedroom that always make for great viewing. When I get Mr. Wonderful in my house, I'm going to do a lot of the things that my lover used to do to me. I'll wash him slowly in the shower and then I'll dry him as I admire his body. I'll ask him to lie on the bed while I massage him and make loving comments about his muscles. And I definitely want to rub his cock with oil while I kiss it gently.

I'm sure by now both of our cocks will be rock-hard, and when I lie down beside him, our cocks will rub against each other while he puts his arms around me and holds me very close. I then want to feel his huge cock resting against my stomach. I want to feel it gently throbbing as he holds me.

My dream then calls for him to kiss me over and over and to push his tongue deep into my throat as he starts to grind his cock against me. I'll then start kissing and licking his body as I slip down under the sheets to position my mouth in front of his cock. I start licking and sucking him, and I know that he'll hold the back of my head as he starts fucking my mouth like he did in the shower. This time I'll be ready for him, because I have been practicing with a huge dildo that I bought. I can put most of it in my mouth, and I'm able to put the whole thing up my ass. When he comes this time, I'm not going to miss a drop, and I hope he pushes his dick into my mouth so far that it slides down my throat. I can't wait.

Most of all, I want Mr. Wonderful to fuck my ass from the missionary position. I want to feel his body all over me as he drills my ass. My lover used to kiss my neck and lick my ears as she would keep repeating, "Fuck me, fuck me harder. Please, fuck me." I want to do the same thing to Mr. Wonderful, and I hope his nipples are as sensitive as mine, because I want to pinch them and lick them as he fucks my ass very hard. I want it all, I want all of his cock in me.

After I have cleaned him and rubbed him awhile longer, I can fall asleep in his arms with his cock lying between my legs. I want so much for him to kiss my neck and ears as we fall off to sleep.

I plan to wake up first so I can slip under the covers and wake him by slowly licking and sucking his beautiful cock until he gives me one more load of his hot come. When he is finished throbbing, I will slip up beside him and he will kiss me so that he can share the taste of his gorgeous cock as we hold each other for a while before he leaves.

I have given up trying to convince myself that I'm not gay, and now all I can think about is Mr. Wonderful coming back to town.

If he reads this, I hope he gets superhorny and plans a trip my way.—*Name and address withheld* ⊶▪

FRIENDS DON'T LET FRIENDS WASTE SPUNK

*S*ince this isn't the kind of story you can share at work, I thought it might be fun to share it with your readers.

Last spring, three of my buddies and I took a weekend fishing vacation. On Friday, we said good-bye to our wives and headed up north to Glenn's cottage to catch a few bass. After a six-hour car trip, we were all pretty tired and hungry. So Martin and I carried in the bags and gear, while Owen fired up the grill and Glenn checked out his boat.

After grilling a few steaks and drinking some beer, we all went out on the lake and spent a few hours hoping for fish. While we waited for a bite, Martin told us some wild stories about fucking his wife with, as he described it, his "incredibly huge" cock. He said his orgasms were so enormous, they'd always have to change the sheets, and the mattress would be soaked. This brought out bursts of laughter from Owen, Glenn and myself. After a time, Owen caught an eighteen-inch bass. Martin caught a fourteen-incher and I caught a snapping turtle, earning the biggest applause.

Around midnight, we got back to the cottage and sat around the living room talking. That's when Glenn sprang two surprises on us: He pulled out a box of fine cigars and produced a selection of porno tapes. We sat through the first tape laughing, smoking and drinking, just like a small bachelor party.

As Glenn put in the second tape, Owen started complaining, saying that he didn't like getting so turned on with his wife nowhere around.

"Looks like you'll be stroking the pickle tonight," Martin said, slapping Owen on the shoulder.

"Yeah, unless you can get one of us to stroke it for you," I added.

"Oh, man," Glenn said, "that'd be hilarious. We should all play a round of poker and the loser has to stroke off Owen."

Martin jumped in, "Why stop there? Why should the other two be left out?" Now, normally this idea might have been quickly dismissed, but with four close friends and a lot of beer and a porno tape...

So Glenn dealt out the cards and said we would play one hand and the loser would have to jerk off the winners.

"Well, if we're going this far," Martin said, "let's double the stakes so I can get a blowjob out of the deal."

"You may be giving the blowjob," I said. This was followed by a round of laughter, and the bet was on. I have to say that my cock was pretty damn hard from all this talk, and I was excited about the prospect of getting a blowjob from one of my good buddies. With my five cards in hand, I put on my best poker face. In a matter of minutes, the hand was done...and I'd lost!

The next thing I knew, my three good buddies were sitting bare-ass naked on the couch. There was a lot of chuckling going on as they cued up a new tape. As the movie started, they all looked at me to see if I was going to weasel out of the bet. Being a man of my word, I knelt down on the floor in front of Glenn and took a long look at his cock. It was about five inches long and covered in a bush of pubic hair. To say the least, I was nervous about blowing my friends. But as the tape got kicking, I could see three eager smiles and three hardening cocks. They weren't letting me out of this.

So as Glenn puffed on his fresh cigar, I leaned forward and began stroking his cock. As I grew comfortable with his rod in my hand, I leaned forward, opened my mouth and began smoking his bone. The uneasiness left me immediately. The feel of his rigid tool in my mouth was exhilarating! As my head bobbed forward, I took in deep breaths of the wonderful aroma coming from his crotch. It made my own cock hard with enjoyment.

Each bob of my head made me happier that I'd lost the game. Glenn soon stopped watching the film, closing his eyes and enjoying my work. His moans and body rhythm told me I was handling this like a pro. As his hips moved with my bobbing head, I reached up and ran my fingers through that wonderful pubic hair. Glenn put down his cigar and placed his hands on the back of my head, urging me on. Holding his balls tight in my hands, I gave a nice tug and Glenn blew a hot load into my waiting mouth.

I felt quite good after my first blowjob, and I was eager to try again. Martin and Owen were quite pleased to see this, as I saw each of them holding their cocks, ready to be the next recipient. I decided to go with Owen's smaller cock, since Martin wields a long, nine-inch pecker with an enormous set of balls. I started to believe all of his stories were true. He was going to be a challenge.

As the movie continued, I opened my greedy mouth and took in Owen's scrawny rod. His cock fit so nicely that I began running my tongue around it as if it were a Popsicle. It wasn't long before Owen followed Glenn's example and forgot all about the movie. I was having so much fun sucking his cock. It felt incredible to please my friends like this. Now I realize why my wife loves sucking my cock so much!

Owen swung his legs up over my shoulders and wrapped them around my head. Beads of sweat were dripping from Owen's bald head, and I could tell by his increased moans that the end was near. After a few seconds, Owen let loose a tremendous orgasm, dropping his beer in the process! It was hard to believe that his small dick carried so much jam. Half of his load flew out of the sides of my mouth and dripped onto his thighs. Gulping down as much of his juice as I could, I found myself sliding his spent cock across my face until I was covered with his load. With a happy sigh of relief, Owen thanked me and got up to clean off.

Even with two satisfied customers, I knew my real work was still ahead of me. Drinking down the remainder of Owen's beer, I took a long look at Martin's enormous cock. It must have been seven inches hanging limp! And as I moved toward it, it began to stiffen. I grabbed that incredible rock-hard bone and readied myself. Martin sucked on his cigar and, with a smile, said, "Now, suck me like a good bitch, Howard."

He need not have worried. I was just hitting my stride. I started slowly tonguing his balls, making him anticipate my warm mouth around his huge organ. Lifting his balls, I licked my tongue around the perimeter of his cock. Finally, my warm lips locked around the luscious bone. Martin's cock was so big, it took me a long time before my throat accepted the whole shaft. I must have slurped on that cock for half an hour! Owen and Glenn had completely forgotten about the video. They just stared at me in amazement, jerking their recharged rods.

Martin was just a cool customer, smiling as he smoked his cigar and talked with them. He didn't moan, and I couldn't figure out why he wasn't enjoying himself—I sure was! Finally, as Martin finished his smoke, his balls gave a shutter and his cock blasted me with a gallon of burning juice. There was no way possible I could have been prepared for that load!

I swallowed as much of his wad as I could, but I looked down and Martin's legs were drenched with come. I knew what was coming next.

"Well, Howard, looks like you'll have to try again," Martin said with a chuckle. Owen and Glenn each cracked up, and I started laughing through my sloppy wet mouth as I licked his legs clean. Now I realized why Martin hadn't enjoyed my blowjob—he expected a second one. I didn't complain. In fact, this turned me on. The thought of engaging his bone again made my cock squirt out its own ample load. Knowing this situation might never happen again, I was fully prepared to let his second load slip so I could go for a three-peat.

Owen and Glenn said good night as Martin stretched back on the vacant couch and lead my face back to his ready member. As I resumed my cocksucking, Martin helped himself to another cigar and a couple of brews. I could tell by the look in his eye that he was planning on being up for a while. I must have spent half the night working that cock, and I loved every minute of it. Martin never failed to fill my mouth with his scorching loads. By the end of the night, I was drunk with his come.

On Sunday, our trip ended and we headed back home. Everyone agreed we'd have to come back again. And I'm sure we'll find our way back to the poker table. I think I'll ask my wife for a few pointers on cocksucking, because next time I plan on losing on purpose.—*H.L., Sterling Heights, Michigan* ⚬╾▪

NUPTIALS PROMISE BRAND-NEW BOND FOR THESE MEMBERS OF THE WEDDING

I had driven most of Friday afternoon to attend the wedding of my closest college friend, Mark. He and Margaret were to be married the next afternoon. Mark had made reservations for me to share a room with Brian, a cousin of Margaret's, who had just returned from a two-year stay in Europe.

I checked into the motel and went to the room. Clothes were strewn over the two double beds. I unpacked and showered.

As I was drying off, I heard the door open. I wrapped a towel around my waist and walked out to meet my roommate.

"Vernon, I'm Brian. Mark told me all about you. Glad to meet you." We shook hands.

Brian was very handsome. Only his slightly hawkish nose kept him from looking pretty. He wore only a brief bikini that hardly covered his cock and balls. I couldn't help but admire his well-proportioned body. He was tall, about six foot two, lean and muscular, though not overly.

"We'd better hurry if we're going to make it to the party on time. I stayed too long in the pool," he said. I couldn't help but notice that he was staring at me as I dressed.

We drove to the party in separate cars. Much later that evening, Brian told me that he was leaving and asked that I give him an hour head start. I saw him go out with one of the brides-maids. With his looks and obvious sex appeal, he probably could have gotten any girl there.

My date was more cute that good-looking. We danced for another hour before I drove her home.

There wasn't any action in the motel lounge, so I went on up to the room. The drapes were drawn and the room was dark.

Immediately, I saw that Brian was fucking the girl he had left with. They were illuminated only by the light from the bathroom. Her legs were wrapped round his waist as he pounded her. Brian glanced at me and kept on screwing. I waited outside until I saw them leave. Then I went in, undressed and crawled naked into bed. I did not awake when Brian returned.

I woke up late in the morning with my usual erection in hand. I lay quietly for a while, then opened my eyes. Brian was propped up in his bed watching me slowly stroke myself.

"Good morning, Vernon," he chuckled. "What are you going to do with that big hard-on? It would be a pity to waste it."

"Just try to piss it away, I suppose. I don't have any use for it. Sorry I walked in on you last night."

"That's okay. I thought it was funny." His eyes were glued to my extended prick as I walked across the room.

It was about noon and we were due at a brunch. The affair, which was over by two that afternoon, was uneventful, and when the girls all left to prepare for the wedding, Brian and I decided to spend the rest of the afternoon by the motel pool.

Brian laughed at me when I put on my baggy swim shorts. "American men are so modest. In Europe, they wear as little as possible, and often swim nude. The women also. Men here are even afraid to be caught looking at another guy. I like to look at sexy bodies like yours." I blushed. "Do I embarrass you? You should learn to be more open about sex."

"You sound like you're hung up on sex," I said.

"Sure, I go for whatever sex I can get," he replied.

The pool was almost deserted. We swam some laps and lay in the sun for an hour or so. All the while, I couldn't help but think about what Brian had said. It began to dawn on me that if you're on this planet for a finite period of time, there doesn't seem to be much reason not to experience all it has to offer, even if this means only checking out another guy's package every once in a while.

I rode with Brian to the wedding. It was all very nice, but I had a little too much champagne at the party afterwards. Brian suggested that he take me home before I made a fool of myself. I resisted, but he insisted. Somehow, he got me into the room still on my feet.

"Here, take these aspirin and then take a hot shower, or you'll have one hell of a hangover." Brian helped me undress and then turned on the water in the bathroom.

I must have stayed in the shower a long time, because I was actually starting to sober up. When Brian came in and got me, he was buck naked.

"Feel better, don't you? Stand still and I'll dry you off." He started with my head and worked his way down my back to my ass and legs.

"Now for the front. Turn around," he said. He carefully dried my crotch, and it felt good. I have to report that my cock started to swell.

"Look at yourself in the mirror. You're beautiful. See what's happening. You're not such a prude, after all. Let's see if it will get hard."

Brian held the base of my dick in one hand and tickled the tip with the other. I just stood there and watched my cock rise. It felt strange letting a guy fondle me like that.

"It's beautiful. Thick and growing. Come on, I'm going to put you to bed. Maybe you won't waste this one."

I sat on the side of my bed. My shaft stood straight up. Brian yanked on his own prick as he stood looking at me.

"Do you want me to bring you off?" he asked. I fell back sprawled on the bed and didn't answer.

His hands began to run lightly over my body. He pinched and sucked my nipples. My heart was pounding. I didn't know a guy could make me feel this way. He held my balls and licked my navel. It tingled all over. His lips followed his exploring fingers, and my cock leapt at his touch. It was growing bigger and bigger, feeling like it was going to burst. Brian's tongue swirled around the sensitive knob. I lifted my head and watched as his head moved up and down. Twice he took me to the brink of explosion and held me there, only to stop and start again. He was driving me crazy. I don't think I had ever been so sexually aroused.

Then Brian crawled up over me and sat lightly on my stomach, holding his long cock in front of my face.

"Go ahead, touch it. It's not going to bite you."

I'd never held another guy's dick. I jacked it with both hands. It felt different from my own, the same way his hands felt different on me. He leaned forward and brushed the head against my cheek.

"Okay, that's enough. I might cream all over your face. Unless you're ready to suck some cock."

I didn't care. I grabbed his ass-cheeks and pulled him into my mouth. I was impressed by the way his cock completely filled my mouth. I swirled my tongue on the head for a while, just as I'd experienced it with my girlfriends, and sure enough his penis started to throb.

Pulling out, he gasped, "No, I want to do you first."

I thought I was going to come right when he engulfed my cock. I started humping my hips, and he slurped with wild abandon. When I felt like I was starting to come, I yelled out, "I'm coming," just in case he didn't want to swallow. But he just kept right on sucking.

Spurt after spurt of creamy jism flooded his throat, and he sucked and slurped for more.

When I calmed down, I asked Brian if I could return the favor. When I opened my eyes, I realized I was too late. Brian was on his knees beside me, jacking off, and soon I felt warm jets of come start to tickle my tummy.—*V.J., North Myrtle Beach, South Carolina*

THE ROAD TRIP, THE MOVIE, AND
THE ROMAN-NOSED MAN

I had a hell of a row with my girlfriend the night before I left on this sales trip. There was a lot to it, but the catalyst that kicked it off was her remark that she sometimes misses her ex-husband. She said that after all, he was an interesting guy when he wasn't being nice to her. That cheesed me off real good, and I remarked that maybe that was when he was most interesting. That cheesed her off. No legs around me that night!

It was a pretty dreary plane ride the next morning, some pretty dreary driving around in a rented car with a kind of reluctant transmission and some pretty dreary stories from customers who like to make me strain harder for a reorder than I've ever strained for sexual favors. Adding to the dreariness were the hotel room where I was staying and the restaurant I chose the first night. A couple of double bourbons washed away the taste of the restaurant fare, but as I left that miserable grease trap I wondered which was worse off, my mind or my stomach.

I sometimes get mildly perverse desires when on the road; among them, all-male movies. I went to an X-rated movie theater in that city that features such movies, and when I go to see something there I always make it plain I'm interested only in what's onscreen and not in any of the live performances going on in or under the folding seats. So it seemed I'd be spending that evening just watching a movie called *Rising Star*, starring Billy Hungwell, who's a favorite with all-male audiences everywhere.

I sat in one of the back rows, on the aisle, the way I usually do. That way, I know that anyone coming along to sit beside me is probably up to something I'm not interested in and I'll tell him so. And sure enough, along came a dark figure, just when I was becoming amused at Billy's antics. Not long after this guy sat down, he put a hand against my leg, but not on my knee. I pulled the leg away. He tried again, and normally I'd be ready to murmur, "Fuck off, queer!" But I didn't, not that night. I let him keep going this time. His hand was soon on my knee, then up my thigh. By the time his hand pressed lightly against what he was looking for, I was surprised to find it was hard.

Fondling followed. I pushed the hand away but welcomed it back a couple of minutes later. I concentrated on Billy until the fondler became more interesting. I looked sideways and saw, by the light the screen reflected, a Roman-nosed face. How young, how old? I couldn't tell. The bourbon buzz and that gentle male hand, moving now to caress my tight scrotum, gave me a good feeling, but one I nevertheless felt uneasy abut.

"Unzip your fly."

It was a low but clearly audible tone, with a Continental tinge. In response, I made a grunt that was negative and unfriendly. Suddenly, Billy was no longer amusing and Roman-nose was disgusting. I lurched upward and to the left, springing into the aisle. I hurried up the aisle toward the exit, hearing somebody's high voice in the dark saying, "Another satisfied customer!"

On the street, I started roaming around, not wanting to go back to the hotel. I sat on a park bench for a few minutes, then walked around again, looking in store windows. I wasn't paying attention to what I was looking at, so I don't know whether it was a bookstore or a men's clothing store I was standing in front of when I heard that Continental voice again, this time saying, "I'm truly sorry if I've upset you." I turned to look at Roman-nose. I couldn't think of any sensible thing to say, so I hoped the guy, who was a little taller than I was and very well dressed, would keep talking.

"I saw you in the lobby of the Broadwood Hotel. I'm staying there too," he said. "I wouldn't have bothered you if I hadn't seen you later, in the theater."

"You can see real good in the dark, is that it?" I replied.

"Sometimes." He smiled, looked down, and brought his hands together in a nervous-looking gesture, in front of the place where his fine houndstooth jacket was buttoned. They were slim hands, with long fingers.

"Look, can I buy you a drink?" he asked. He looked at me sincerely and I found myself wondering just what guys like him go through. I mean, he must have had that Roman nose bent sideways a few times by those who didn't take to all his sincerity and concern.

"No," I answered. "Tell you what, if you like bourbon, knock on the door of room four-twenty in about a half hour. I'll be there." I turned and walked away quickly, making it plain we were to find our way back to the hotel separately.

I'd carried a bottle of Old Grand-Dad in my briefcase and had knocked back one shot already by the time I heard my phone ring. He was calling first, just to make sure. Why didn't he just come ahead and knock? But I told him the invitation was still open and he was soon in my room.

I offered him a hanger for that fine jacket and then a tumbler with bourbon in it. He stood in the middle of the room, looking nervous again and not interested in the glass or its contents.

"May I be frank?" he asked. "I don't think we need hesitate any longer. I'm here in the hope of giving you a blowjob."

"I don't know if I'm in the mood for one," I answered.

"It's more like you aren't quite ready for one," he countered, "not as ready as you were in the movie theater. But I can attend to that. Please, sir. You'll enjoy it."

His nervousness was replaced by a sense of authority. He put the glass on the counter by the television set, then went to the windows and pulled the shades. He came back to me and lightly put his hands on either side of my waist. What the hell, I thought, sucked off by a Continental queer. Could be worse.

After making me pry off my shoes with my feet, he dropped my trousers to the floor, then picked them up and placed them over the chair by the writing table. As he came back to me, he was loosening his tie. With that light touch again, he took my drawers and pulled them down my legs.

"You might wish to sit on the edge of the bed?" he said, as if asking me. I knew it was a strong recommendation. I sat down. "There," he said, "now you can relax."

He parted my knees, slid his hands up my thighs, and took my half-staff penis in his right hand, while his left slid beneath my balls. His thumb worked skillfully, just under the head, and built me up, giving me a good feeling. I did relax, leaning back on the bed, on my elbows. I thought of my girlfriend as his mouth enclosed the head. Then he slid up the shaft until my entire dick was in his mouth and his large, stately nose was buried in my hairy bush.

He sucked me with his eyes closed, grunting small exclamations of approval, looking like a gourmet of fellatio. Thoughts of my girl-friend faded. She wasn't doing me any good. I looked at the man's neatly combed, graying hair as it started to fall forward. Here was my girlfriend now, for tonight anyway.

I pushed my hips upward, thrusting my dick deep into his mouth. My gesture broke his rhythm, and I was amused by his annoyance. I wanted to assert a little more authority. He quickly adjusted, slip-ping his hands around my hips and taking the rhythm back. He had a smooth touch on my bare flanks and buttocks.

I brought one of my hands around to touch his face. His forehead was moist with small beads of sweat. I got the feeling this was a criti-cal moment, when I'd decide whether I wanted this blowjob to be merely an experience or an outright pleasure.

I could feel myself choosing pleasure. I was struck by the odd beauty of this sight, this dignified-looking stranger bent to what seemed to be the indignity of giving head to a total stranger. If any-one could make it look good, he could, by enjoying it thoroughly.

Then he surprised me. As if aware of my appreciation, he opened his eyes and looked upward till they met with mine. It was all I needed. I could feel the final surge coming on. He pulled on me with his mouth, sensing how close to the end I was. He pushed downward, taking in all my dick, then brought himself back. As he was ready to push forward again, I came. It was intensely good.

He moaned deeply and swallowed my rod so he could hold it deep in his mouth as long as it was hard. My come shot, then oozed out of me. He eagerly drank the drink he'd really wanted when he'd come to my room. As I became limp he gave me last licks, then arose, pull-ing a handkerchief from his pocket and pressing it to his mouth.

I lay on the bed, my legs spread and my wet, droopy genitals exposed. He might be dressed again, houndstooth jacket and all, before I got my underwear back on.

But he turned and went to the bathroom, where he turned on the light and stood before the mirror. I looked at him only briefly, then scrambled to get dressed again. I was grabbing for my pants on the chair when I heard him say, "Would you—"

"Would I what?" I asked, looking around for a shoe instead of putting my pants back on. I looked into the bathroom to see that he faced the mirror as he spoke.

"There are some who might find fault in what I've just done, or the way I did it," he said. "They might wish to show their disapproval or displeasure by—" He turned to look at me and I noticed his tie was back in place. He swept both his hands over the crown of his head, leaving his hair once again neat.

He came out of the bathroom and I went in. I hung my pants on a hook on the door and stood over the toilet bowl. I could hear him behind me, putting his jacket on and opening the door. He shut it quietly, before I was finished.

I'm in another town now. I closed a new sale today, one that should get me the best commission I've had all year. I phoned my girlfriend, and after a half hour, I felt better off than when I'd last seen her. Things are back to normal, or even better. But as I lie here on my hotel room bed, drinking the last of the bourbon I brought with me, I don't think so much about her as about him.

Never mind what might have been, I must remember what was. He went down on me. He would have done it in the dark of that smelly movie theater, just the way he actually did it in my room. His mouth offered me a better climax than I'd lately gotten from my girlfriend. Certainly better than the one I'm trying to raise with my right hand is likely to be. As I massage myself under the head with my index finger, I think about her and try to feel the stimulus. Then I think about him and the effect is improved. Just a little rub while I remember…how nice it was…nothing to feel ashamed of…just a little more…feeling better…better…better…just about…there…there…there.—*A.M., Dayton, Ohio*

ABSENCE MADE THEIR HEARTS AND OTHER PARTS GROW FONDER

I made a big discovery about Rob over brandy, and now I'm making discoveries about myself.

I arrived late in the afternoon at Rob's rustic cabin on Root Lake in the Adirondacks. It was good to see him again. We had been roommates and best friends in college.

We had a few drinks, then grilled steaks for supper. The conversation was free and easy: about the girls we had dated, the ball games, parties, our jobs and travels—the usual catching-up after not having seen each other for a long time. We were both apologetic about that. How had we let five years pass before we saw each other again?

"Jim," he asked me, "whatever happened to that good-looking girl, Lillian? You were going with her the last time I saw you in school."

"We dated a few times after graduation, but she moved up north," I told him. "I heard she got married a couple of years ago. What about you and Polly? She was cute."

"Yeah, she was," Rob replied, "but we split up and I've been, playing the field since. No one serious. I haven't dated much recently. What's your current status?"

"Well," I told him, "nobody, actually. After Lillian, I started going with a girl named Trudy. You would have liked her. Lots of fun, very good-looking. We lived together for a year but decided to split. Too much arguing, we're just different. But the sex was great. We broke up six months ago and I still miss her."

"So, there's no current pussy," he said, judging me matter-of-factly. "That's not like you. You always had somebody, after you discovered it was better than jerking off. Remember how that was about all you were good for when we were first roomies? How many times did you come in, crawl into bed and beat off, thinking I was asleep and couldn't hear you? But then you found girls were more fun. Either way, you were one horny bastard."

"Still am," I replied.

"Still jerking off, then?"

I laughed. "I'd like to go on like this, Rob," I said, "but it's been a long day of traveling. Let's have a brandy, now that you can afford the good stuff, and call it a night."

"Okay," he said. "It's in the cabinet over there. Fix me one too."

His voice was oddly tense as he said that. When I pulled out the bottle of Armagnac, a bunch of photos fell on the floor. I looked at them as I picked them up.

They shocked me. Some of the photographs were of Rob making love with other men and others were of an all male orgy. I just stood there, numbing over.

"Say something," Rob said. "Now you know. I put them there, hoping you would find them. I didn't know how to tell you."

I silently poured a couple of drinks and looked him in the eye as I handed one to him. "Are you happy?" I asked.

"Yes, as happy as I'll ever be," Rob replied. "I'm free to live as I've wanted to live for a long time. I've hidden my true sexual feelings all my life. Born this way I guess. I was a good actor. You never were suspicious, were you?"

"No, I wasn't. You're very masculine, Rob. You don't look or act gay."

"Thanks," he said, with a wry grin, "but I have to insist, Jim, that not all gays are sissy acting. We just prefer cocks to cunts. Anyway, you and I were friends before you knew, so why can't we be friends now that you know? Think about it."

We finished our drinks and went to bed.

I awoke the next morning with my usual erection and went to the bathroom. I was standing naked and shaving when Rob came in, also naked, ready for his shower. Playfully he patted me on the rear end and I snapped a towel at him.

"Let's go for a run after breakfast," he suggested.

"Sure," I replied, still trying to sort out my thoughts. Could I still feel the same friendship for Rob, or would it be different? I asked myself. Probably different, I concluded. Surely he wouldn't make a pass at me. How would I respond if he did?

We had run for a mile or so and were just working up a good sweat when a car pulled up beside us. I was introduced to Frank and Grant. Frank, the older of the two, asked us to stop by his house. "Okay," said Rob, "we'll be there in an hour or so." We ran another four miles and cooled down as we approached Frank's cabin. Rob called to them and the reply was to come out on the deck. There, the two guys were sunbathing, naked.

I tried not to act surprised. Grant got up and offered each of us a beer. Rob casually undressed and wiped off with a towel. "Come on, join us, don't be modest, Jim," said Frank.

Rob said, "Jim's not used to this, fellows. Let him take his time."

Actually, I became embarrassed about being the only one with clothes on. We talked for a while, and I thought, Why not? Nothing is going to happen. Why be modest? So I took off my shorts and lay nude in the sun with them.

As Grant served more beers he said to me, "It's a shame to cover up a tool like that. You have a beautiful body and ought to be proud to show it off." Then he proceeded to rub oil over Frank's back, arms and legs.

"Better cut that out, Grant, or you'll give me a hard-on," said Frank.

Grant laughed and replied, "It wouldn't be the first time." Frank turned over and his big cock stood straight up. "Why don't you do the front?" he asked. Grant responded by massaging him with oil from head to toe, though avoiding his dick.

I was getting a little turned on. Grant leaned over and gave Frank's cock a lick from the base to the head.

"Cut it out, Grant," said Rob. "I told you, Jim isn't used to this."

"Oh, don't worry, Rob, maybe I'll learn something," I said.

Grant laughed and said, "I'm a good teacher. Let's have some fun. Okay with you, Rob? Jim doesn't have to join us if he doesn't want to."

Frank stood and waved his semi-erect cock at Grant. "What are you going to do with this?"

"Come here and I'll drain you dry," Grant replied. He got hold of Frank's cock and pumped it up. "Feels good, doesn't it?" he said.

Frank pushed his hips forward and guided his meat to Grant's face. He opened his mouth and took in the head of Frank's penis. His hands encircled the rest of what Frank had. It didn't take much of this before Frank said that he was about to come. Grant pulled back, smiled and jacked Frank's cock until it shot off.

"I love to see him spurt," Grant said, laughing.

Rob's rod was rigid and he was stroking it slowly. My own cock was swelling.

Frank whispered something to Rob. They smiled at each other as Frank's hands began to move lightly over Rob's body. He started at his shoulders and worked his way over my friend's chest and stomach. He fondled his balls and tickled his thighs. Rob was squirming. "Come on, do it, suck my cock, I can't take any more of this."

Frank held Rob's dick and lowered his head. Before taking the cock deep in his mouth, he looked at me and smiled.

I sat up and watched. Grant walked over and stood behind me, putting his hands on my shoulders and saying, "Look at him go. Frank's a great cocksucker. Watch him take it all. Rob loves it."

Obviously he did. His legs were spread wide. Frank was sucking frantically and fondling his balls. When Frank finger-fucked him in the ass, Rob groaned and came powerfully.

Grant's hands moved over my chest. He hadn't asked permission to pinch my nipples and tickle my navel, but I was letting him do it. My cock became fully erect. The knob of Grant's dick poked my back.

Frank pulled on Rob's cock and wiped the excess juice from his own chin. Rob moaned happily.

Grant walked over and looked down at Rob. "Now it's your turn to take this," he said as he straddled Rob's chest and rubbed his thick throbbing tool on Rob's face. Rob licked at the head. Grant moved forward and sank his cock in Rob's throat. Rob held Grant's hips as he sucked. I was holding my hard dick while watching them. Grant pulled his cock out and shot globs of come all over Rob.

Frank looked at me and said, "Now it's your turn. You want it, don't you?"

I looked down at my hard cock and replied, "It looks like I want something doesn't it?"

Rob intervened. "Wait your turn, Grant. I've wanted to eat Jim's dick ever since the first time we met." He knelt between my legs. "Please, will you let me?"

I answered by pulling his head to my crotch. I leaned back and let him do things that made me feel sensations I didn't know were possible. Several times he held me on the brink, only to pause and start again. I was going wild, my body convulsing and exploding. A huge reserve of my semen burst into my old friend's mouth. He swallowed frantically, taking it in with the torrent that followed. We were both trembling violently with excitement. As we cooled down, he cupped my balls and licked my cock as if it were an ice cream cone.

We all cooled down, and the eating we did after that consisted of the excellent soup and salad that Frank and Grant prepared for lunch. While we enjoyed that and a bottle of wine, I wondered what Rob had been thinking all along. Had he arranged a confrontation, thinking I was bisexual? And was I? I had to admit I'd loved what had happened!

We were in a joking mood and once again clad in our running shorts as we bid Frank and Grant good-bye, having politely turned down their offer of a drunken ride back to Rob's cabin. Instead, we jogged there quite unsteadily.

And as we went, we talked. Our speech may have been a little slurred, but our conversation was serious. I said I respected the leap he had made into the gay world, but that I was not ready to go to such a length, even after the great time we'd just had. Fine, he said, for the moment we could leave it at that. We got back and crashed for a couple of hours.

As the afternoon waned, we fished from a small landing on the lake. In the early evening, we decided to go swimming. "Suit your-self," Rob said to me, "but I'm going bare-ass." So I went naked too. Never had I felt closer to him.

That night, we fondled each other till we boiled over, laughing with delight. He sucked me again and I liked it again. But we slept separately.

I had to leave by early afternoon, headed for a hectic workweek. I'm in the midst of it now. I'm also in the midst of wondering about myself. I'm sure there are still women to attract me (I can even think of one I might make a move on if I get the chance to see her), but I'm amazed; and not at all displeased, at the new way I now must regard my old friend.

"Don't know when I'll see you again," I said to him on the phone last night, "but let's not make it five years. That's a crime." He said he might be in town the end of next month and be able to give me a call. Good; for all I know, I may have a new girlfriend to show him then. And he'll understand perfectly.—*J.A., Buffalo, New York* ⚷ ▪

MY NEW LOVE'S MY OLD LOVE'S BROTHER

*H*ow'd I get here?

I've asked myself that question a lot of times in the last few years. I'm asking it now as I suck on Bren's penis while he sucks on mine. Speaking of blowjobs, how'd I wind up blowing on a saxophone in a band, attempting to make a living that way?

The summary question might be, why am I back on the Cape; love-locked with my old girlfriend's brother?

But this is no time for an explanation, not when I have Bren's delicious rod down my throat, my rod is down his throat, and our bodies are pressed against each other—hairy, sweaty and surging with desire. I'll have to put off the *how* and *why* questions for the time being, concentrating instead on such delights as the reddish hair on my young man's balls, the balls I cradle lovingly in my hand and stare at intensely as I'm stuffing my mouth with his hardness. I'm feeling eager about the approaching explosion, a burst of sauce to adorn and enhance the flavor of his wonderful meat; yet I'm also anxious to be there for him at that moment too, that we may at the same time taste deeply of each other.

Dierdre and I were sleeping with each other the summer I first met her brother Brendan. More politely put, we were working in a restaurant on the Cape and sharing an apartment about ten miles away. She was twenty, I was twenty-two, and we knew each other from college. After warning us that he was coming, Brendan appeared one weekend, bringing with him several friends and a couple of cars. That presented no problem to us. We were glad to let Bren and a friend of his crash at the apartment, and the rest of them had Cape connections of their own.

"We're typical for our age, we've got musical pretensions," he said of himself and his friends. His age was "nineteen in October." He talked and joked incessantly; I suggested he quit being a guitarist and try stand-up comedy. We got along terrifically. It's true he was no great guitarist, but I have to like a guy who admires my musical ability, and Bren seemed to be awestruck by the way I could play bass and piano. We did some late-night jamming at a noisy dive, in the company of a house band called Desperation, while Dierdre, facing work the next day, went back to the apartment alone. When the session broke up and we went back to the apartment in his car, Bren chattered madly as he drove, while his friend and I yawned and barely stayed awake. Between then and noon, when he and the rest of them left, I think he was awake for all but a couple of hours. I thought I was young and resilient, but seeing Bren in action made me feel old.

I saw him one other time that summer, when the season ended and Dierdre and I went to where she lived, near Worcester. Bren was in and out, forever busy with his friends, but he found the time to point me out to friends who hadn't met me yet, saying I was "a real musician, not like us, he's not just fuckin' around."

But Dierdre and I knew it was over for the two of us. I was done with

school and headed for work in Connecticut and she had her last year
of college to complete before heading for journalism school. It had
been a summer to remember, but our lives were going on separately.

The next four years frequently surprised me; but I've already indicated that. *How'd I get here?* might be the title of the story of my life.
And why did I take my love affair with music and try to turn it into
a career, the equivalent of marrying it? I never thought I'd be fool
enough to try.

But in moments of doubt, I sometimes heard an enthusiastic teenager's words and saw his bright face before me. Bren was an encouragement, though I never expected to see him again.

Perhaps I hoped, though, even while rambling from Puerto Rico to
Alaska; hoped beyond my realization that the brother of a departed
girlfriend would re-enter my life. But because I was all over the place,
I didn't think there was anything especially significant about a gig on
the Cape, beyond the job opportunity itself, though I was surprised to
reflect how much time had gone by since I was last there. I was offered
an opening, four weeks in late July and August, with the big band at
the Rushfield Inn. I was in the tenor saxophone section, though also
ready to go if anyone needed a pianist or bassist. It wasn't until my
third night there that I discovered one of the waiters was Brendan.

He lit up like a sparkler when he saw me. We just had to get together
later, he said. By the time we were free, it was past midnight. I looked
at him and a lot came back to me. He must be nearly twenty-three, I
thought, and still a take-charge guy. He proved that by telling me I
was going with him on this hot-as-hell evening for several beers and
maybe, if we got crazy enough, for a swim.

I smiled and shrugged. As it turned out, within an hour we were
parked near this dark body of water, leaning on his car and sharing
a six-pack, and talking about ourselves and Dierdre, who was still in
journalism, but also in Oregon, and married and pregnant.

"But I said I was here for a swim, didn't I, Nick?" he said, as he
walked from the car toward the water. I said it was risky in the dark,
but he only went "Ha!" and pulled his shirt off. He tossed it care-
lessly and quickly dropped his cut-off jeans. The fact that he wore
no underwear oddly stirred me, and I felt a little lift as I looked at his
buttocks and his lithe body.

"Coming?" he asked, half-turning.

"Maybe to rescue you," I said, and again he went "Ha!" as he waded in. I put my beer can on the car hood and stepped toward the shore, looking at Bren's dim form by the light of the quarter moon.

"It never gets very deep, think I'll have to sit down," he said, and did. "Come on, Nick, get naked."

Feeling silly, I stripped myself of much more clothing than Bren had worn, listening to him joke that he hoped I'd be undressed before sunrise. I waded in, fearful of the muddy, uneven floor of the pond. Bren was a few feet away, seated in shallow water.

"You've got a lot to be proud of, I can see that even in this light," he said. "I'm speaking of your instrument, music man."

"Thanks," I said, at a loss to say anything more.

"I think I could play some sweet music on it," he added. I ventured farther into the water, moving away from him a little, still feeling perplexed.

"No offense, hey?" he asked.

"No."

"No hard feelings."

I turned to face his seated form. "What's up, Bren?" I asked, immediately regretting my words.

"Well, I am," he answered, quickly coming to his feet. His erection was a silhouette that he displayed for a few seconds before he walked out of the water. I watched him look around for the shorts, shirt and shoes he had merrily abandoned a few minutes before. I then trudged out of the water to the spot where I'd neatly piled my clothes. As I put them on, I noticed him walking nude toward the car, carrying what he'd picked up.

When he got to the car, he turned and leaned on a front fender, holding his clothing over his crotch. I finished dressing and walked toward him. He had some cigarettes in the car and a lighted one glowed between his lips.

"Smoke?" he asked.

"No," I said, "I gave up smoking and don't want to get back to it, not even just a little."

"No bad habits."

"I've got a few, Bren," I said, smiling.

"And I've revealed at least one of mine."

"Talk about it, Bren. Like I said, I'm not offended."

He didn't say anything. He took a drag on the cigarette, flipped it away, and bent to put his shorts on.

"Been queer since I don't know when, Nick," he said. "You haven't seen much of me, but even with what you've seen you'll have to admit I'm not a guy who keeps much to himself. Talk about it? I could talk about it for days, I suppose, but when I feel like talking about it, I just go to P-town instead, and get it out of my system there. I talk about it by getting right to what's on my mind. Like just now. I'll rephrase what I said a few minutes ago, in the water, when I was talking so cute. I wanted to get you undressed and offer to suck you off. I didn't want to be blunt. I was even willing to talk about it, before getting down to business. But what we wound up with was an awkward moment and the usual shit about no hard feelings."

"I'm sorry—"

"Oh, nothing to be sorry about. Instead of being sorry, give me one last chance, if you can find it in your heart."

He took a stance before me in the dark and gave me a lively, smiling expression, one hand placed theatrically over his heart.

"You're positively loveable," I said, and we laughed.

"I wanna hold your wand," he sang. "No kidding. If you love me, drop your shorts. But drop your pants first."

Another hesitation, but then I said, "All right, try anything once," and pulled my pants and underwear down.

"Once?" Bren asked, laughing. "Oh, baby, once you try me, you'll never go back!" He took my joint in one hand and it started to grow. "See, I know one part of you doesn't mind this at all." With a couple of strokes of his hand, it was as tall and firm as any woman had ever made it.

Bren looked me in the eyes as he held my erection. I could see that even now he didn't wish to be too serious.

"If what I'm about to do may be displeasing to you," he said, "may I suggest you sip a beer and look at the dark treetops, the way they say our grandmothers counted the flowers on the wallpaper as our grandfathers had their way with them. May I get you a beer?"

"No thanks," I answered. "Just play that funky instrument, white boy."

He knelt in the sand. I had a moment of doubt as I thought of cops discovering us, even at this hour of the morning, but fuck it, I thought, we're damned. May I feel good first.

And I did feel good. Bren knew what he wanted—not merely a stiff dick for himself, but pleasure for the man at the other end of the blowjob. He worked up and down my shaft, and caressed my balls and my buttocks, until I was groaning and unsteady on my feet. At first I stood like a statue, but soon I came to life and caressed the back of his neck, his face, and his curly hair, wishing I could see the deep red color of that hair in the dark.

When I made a thrusting movement with my hips, Bren's hands quickly but gently touched me on either side of my crotch to stem my eagerness. He pulled back to work on my dickhead intensely, bringing the feeling to be brink of irritation, before he took the shaft in his mouth again to go into the final phase. And that straightened me up, made me quiver and utter a light cry of surprise. This was going to be something! I could feel the climactic moment building like a wave that would crash on the shore and leave us astonished by its force. I had a vision of that wave headed toward me, then looming over me, then dropping on and consuming me. When it did, I took the blow, then felt an intense delight that had the pull of an undertow. The wave-force was outgoing now, strong and riotously good. I looked down to see Bren accepting it. My jism was flowing out of me, down his throat. My guts felt spasms of pleasure. As Bren pulled away from my softening dick, to behold that which had kept him so busy, my strength at last gave out. I sank to my knees in the sand, then crashed on my back. Bren immediately embraced me, bringing the top of his head, and that dark red hair, just below my chin.

"Tell me you didn't like that, I'll call you a fuckin' liar!" he said, and squeezed me around my shoulders.

"Oh yeah, mister," I said, gasping and laughing, "it was pretty good. Pretty great, if you really want to know."

Bren wasn't surprised when I told him hours later that he wasn't my first gay encounter. But I was the surprised one to find I wanted to respond. "Let me just see what it's like," I said, proposing a blowjob.

"Nicky, Nicky, be my fuckin', ever-lovin' guest!" he said.

"I wouldn't do it with any dick but yours," I said.

"Talk like that'll get you anywhere with me, handsome," he assured me.

So I had a man in my mouth for the first time. Then came 69. Our affair was carried on discreetly—no prancing in P-town—for the rest of my gig. Just before I went away, Bren told me everything was cool, we each had our work to do. "Absence may make our hearts grow fonder for somebody nearby," he said. "So be it."

I'm a thousand miles away now, on the road again and trying to get over him.—*N.P., New York, New York* ⚬┱

WHEN SQUIRES BECOME KNIGHTS, LOVE ARISES

Owen and I were boyhood friends. We never did anything sexual with each other, but one day when we were eighteen, we went swimming in his parents' pool naked. We were at his home alone, and the people in the neighboring house were away, so we just swam naked for the fun of it. What the hell, they swim naked at the YMCA, we'd done that, with lots of other guys, but we'd never acted as if the pools at his house or mine were Y pools. Only once, anyway.

By the time we were twenty-one, we were off at different colleges. At the end of my second year, my school let out for the summer and I was due to begin a job in Alaska within ten days. Owen was going to take a summer course and work near his campus, so he invited me to come up an spend a couple of days there before I went home and then headed to Seattle and points northward. I brought my sleeping bag, assuming that Owen might have a roomie.

But the roomie had gone home. I had a bed in Owen's dorm room. I don't know why, but we seemed especially glad to see each other. I'd arrived in the late afternoon, so within a couple of hours we were drinking beer and eating bar food at his regular campus hangout.

"Do you remember that time we swam bare-ass in my pool?" he asked me.

"Shit, that's funny, Owen," I replied. "I was thinking of that on my way here."

"Really?" he asked. "You're right, that's amazing. I wonder if you were thinking what else I was thinking."

"What's that?"

"Oh, about what we might have been thinking unconsciously," he said. "I kind of remember liking the sight of you naked. I got kind of a thrill at seeing your weenie—and that was before I found out what fun I could have with my own. We had such hairless little danglers didn't we?"

I laughed. "They sure were. And I have to say I had sort of the same thoughts then, and lately I've been remembering them."

"Let me get to the point, Walt," he said. "Why don't we go back to the dorm and get naked? I'd like to see what you look like now, and maybe you'd like to see what I look like."

"Right, okay," I said, looking into his eyes. "Let's do it."

I can't get over how much our heads were in the same place, or how much that mysterious feeling we had had vanished but stayed hidden through the years before coming back to us. We left the restaurant and a few minutes later were standing before each other the way we did when we were younger. But now our nudity brought us direct, unmysterious thrills.

"It a hairy dangler these days, Owen," I said, "but it sure isn't little."

"Neither's yours," he said. He made the first move, taking my member in one hand. It swelled and lengthened in his gentle grasp. The feeling was great, but when he took his other hand and caressed my balls, it was exquisite! I wanted to take hold of his hearty rod, but I let him build mine until I thought I'd explode. Then I reached over and closed my hand around his, bringing it to full vitality.

"Let go, and I'll let go," he said to me. "And we'll have crossed swords." So we did. We brought our long warm blades together as we looked at them and then at each other. I was excited and eager as I thought of how it might feel to be entered by that Excalibur of his.

I uttered what had been in my thoughts, about how our heads were in the same place.

"Not yet, Walt," he said, smiling. "Not till we 69."

So we began by swallowing those swords. I wanted to tell Owen what a musky treat he was and I hoped I was nearly as flavorful. But we didn't need to speak to get our feelings in perfect coordination. We knew wordlessly how to bring the great moment to each other at exactly the same time. Our swords became cannons, firing blasts delightful to feel and delicious to taste. Our bodies were racked with orgasmic spasms. When we fell away, our swords and ourselves momentarily weary, we knew that a treasure that had been hidden years before was now claimed.

"Your armor shineth, my knight," I told him.

"If you mean I'm sweaty, I'm glad to agree," he said. "So are you. We need to shower."

We felt a little heady with the risk we were taking, going together only in towels to the shower room at the end of the hall. We were still a little shy under the water. I felt a great urge to soap Owen's buttocks and I don't know what he wished to do with me; but we simply showered quickly and got out. As we toweled off, I checked to see that we were still alone. We were, so I took Owen's face in my hands and kissed him. Our tongues mingled and I could feel his maleness coming to life again against my thigh, while mine stirred against his. When we wrapped towels around ourselves again, we had to wait until the bulge under each subsided, before going into the hallway.

Back in the room, I offered myself to him. My anxiety and reluctance were still strong, though, and he was having trouble getting in. But he knew just what to say.

"Mmm, Walt, your buttocks were so smooth then and so bristly now," he said. I was turned on; my sphincter relaxed and his sword went swiftly into me up to the hilt. We were on his bed and I had to stuff a corner of his pillow into my mouth to muffle my squeals of delight. I cupped both hands under my penis to catch the flood of fluid as I came, just after Owen did. When I was able to turn around, I rubbed it all over his chest and shoulders, making him shiny again. We spent a blissful interlude recovering our strength; then I became the knight, mounting my willing steed, who made whinnying sounds as we rode. As we both came, we captured the joys of ecstasy.

My heart had never felt so full of joy nor had my body ever experienced a sexual encounter so full of lust, hardness and more inches that I could count.

Owen and I were entangled and sweaty but feeling fresh from our romping of pure, unbridled sexual gratification. I reached over to see if he was real and found myself once again overcome with wanting this man.

As my hand found his manhood at half-mast he also was reaching for mine and found my throbbing, pulsing purple rod aching to be sucked once more. And he did accommodate me with his warm, wet, hot sultry mouth. I came with the mere flick of his tongue tracing my vein.

Many a joust we had for the rest of the time I was there. I had to ride away eventually, bound for other errands, but we both knew we'd be together again someday, staging another pleasure tournament.
—*W.N., Flagstaff, Arizona*

Different Strokes

WHAT'S GOOD FOR THE GOOSE IS
GOOSING THE GANDER

*I*t all started last Halloween. Lori, my girlfriend, decided that I was unsympathetic to women, and all the work she puts into being a woman. She said that for Halloween we should switch roles for a day. I agreed.

On Halloween morning I woke up to see Lori dressed in my sweats. I asked her what was going on. She replied, "Did you forget we switch roles today? I prepared a bubble bath for you. Don't worry. It will be fun."

As I got into the tub, Lori came over to me with a razor and some shaving cream. "To be a proper lady, you're going to have to shave," she said. "Don't forget to do your chest, your legs and under your arms." I did as instructed. When I was done, Lori came back and said my pubic hair would need to be trimmed also. She offered to help me, and I asked for her assistance. She proceeded to trim and shave my pubic region into a heart.

When I got out of the bath Lori dusted me with some of her powder and led me into the bedroom. She saw me becoming aroused and said, pointing to my erection, "You're going to have to get rid of that. Go into the bathroom, jerk off into this cup and bring it back to me." When I returned with the cup full of my come, Lori took it, called me a good girl and told me to get dressed and make lunch while she ran some errands. She left, so I put on some clothes and proceeded to make lunch.

After an hour, she came back carrying several bags and brought them into the apartment. "Did you make lunch?" she asked. She then told me I was improperly dressed and that she would correct that after we ate.

After lunch Lori led me back to the bedroom to show me what she had bought. She opened the bags and showed me all the makeup she had bought for me. Lori led me into the bathroom, sat me down and started my transformation. First, she plucked my eyebrows slightly to give them more of a feminine look. Then came foundation, eyeliner, four shades of eye shadow, mascara, blush and lipstick. She also applied fake fingernails. Knowing that I find redheads very attractive, Lori had bought me a wig of long, red hair. She put that on me last. Seeing myself in the mirror for the first time, I became highly aroused at what I saw—a beautiful girl looking back at me. Lori reminded me that a lady does not get erections and gave me the cup again. After I went into the bathroom and filled the cup, I returned to the bedroom.

Lori then showed me the clothes she had bought me and proceeded to help me get dressed. We started with the light-blue panties and matching bra. She filled out the bra with falsies and helped me with the blue garter belt and blue stockings. The feeling of the silk on my shaven legs gave me another erection and Lori handed me the cup again. With a laugh, she reminded me that I was a lady.

When I came back, Lori helped me into a lacy white dress and gave me a pair of shoes to put on. She then dressed herself in my clothes and asked if I was ready for the Halloween party. I wasn't too thrilled, but we went.

After we got back, I told Lori that I had a new appreciation of women and the troubles they go through. Smiling, she said, "The night is not over. Take off your dress and panties but leave on the rest of your clothes. Lie down on the bed and I'll be right back, baby." I lay down and nervously waited for her. She came back wearing a robe and said, "Since you're playing the role of the girl, I'll play the role of the man, and make a woman out of you." She opened the robe, showing me that she was wearing a strapon dildo, and asked me if I was ready.

Too late to turn back now, I thought. I told her, "I'm yours, but be gentle, I'm a virgin." Lori laughed and told me to kneel down.

"Suck my cock," she said, and put the rubber dildo in front of me. Licking the head and shaft of her cock, I made my first attempt at deep-throating her but gagged halfway down. Pulling it back, she grinned and said, "Not as easy as you thought, is it? Now lean over so I can lick your pussy." I bent over and Lori started to lick my ass. While tonguing and fingering my ass, she reached around and slowly jerked me to a climax. "Now it's time for you to lose your virginity," she told me. She slowly eased the head of the dildo into my ass. At first it was painful, but then pleasure set in. Lori then shoved her cock in up to the hilt and slowly started to fuck me. In time she started to increase the rhythm. She was moaning and grunting as if the dildo was a part of her. She continued to fuck me for what seemed like hours. When she finally pulled out of my ass she told me to kneel so she could feed me her orgasm.

After she took off the condom and cleaned the dildo I started to lick it, beginning at the head. As I was licking it, I noticed there was a small hole in the head. Lori yelled. "Suck it, don't lick it! How do you expect me to get off? Now suck me baby!"

I did as Lori said. I wrapped my mouth around her cock and started to bob up and down on her shaft. "Try to deep-throat me again," Lori said, "but go down on your exhale." Doing as she told me, I managed to deep-throat her on the third try. She giggled with delight when I succeeded.

"Faster baby, faster," she screamed. "You're one hell of a cocksucker. Are you ready for my come, baby?" Not really sure what she meant by her come, I moaned and nodded yes. "Open your mouth so I can watch you swallow," she said. "I expect you to eat every bit of it." She said that the dildo was equipped with a special feature. The balls could be filled with a fluid and squeezed to simulate a male orgasm. Kneeling and looking up at Lori with my mouth open, she laid her cock on my tongue. "I filled it with all the come you gave me today. Eat up, baby," she said, and squeezed the dildo, coming in my mouth and on my lips and face. "Lick your lips and swallow it, baby," Lori giggled. "It's an acquired taste."

I swallowed as much as I could, licking my lips and not feeling too bad, since it was my own come. Lori bent over and pinched my nipples and kissed me, saying how much she loved me. She also told me that if I ever forget how hard it is to be a woman, this night could be repeated. I hope so.—*D.L., Baltimore, Maryland*

WHEN THE TIMING'S JUST RIGHT,
FANTASIES TURN REAL

*M*y boyfriend has been gone for nearly two weeks now, on a business trip to Los Angeles. He should be home any day, but that doesn't help me now. I miss our frequent lovemaking sessions.

We both love sex and aren't afraid to show it. Even though our phone sex is great, I miss the real thing, and sometimes you just have to improvise.

I have this wonderful vibrating dildo he bought me when we went to a convention in New York City. It looks just like a real penis. It has veins and is at least eight inches long and three inches around.

I sit watching a really good fuck flick. They are getting it on so good! I put the dildo on the coffee table so that it stands straight up. I rub my hard nipples and take one in my mouth. I lick it, suck on it and then move on to the next one. I can just imagine Billy doing it instead of me.

I put a finger deep inside my cunt. Oh God, I'm so wet. Just a rub on my clit, then maybe a few more strokes, then I mount the dildo with it set on low speed. I ride it just like I would ride Billy, if only he was here. Then the door opens and he's home. I start to dismount and he says, "No. Don't. I love watching you fuck yourself on that big thing." He undresses and strokes his cock, then kisses me deeply, then kisses my neck and breasts. His hands move to my cunt and as I ride my toy, he rubs my clit and fingers deeply into my ass, spreading my juices all around, making me so wet.

He removes his finger and takes the lotion off the table and rubs it all over his cock and on my ass. I lean forward, being sure to keep my toy deep inside. He slides his hard hot cock deep in my ass. Grabbing my hips, he fucks me deep and hard until I come. He says, "It feels so good, your hot, tight ass and the vibrations from the dildo." He pinches my tits as he presses deeply and erupts into my waiting ass. It is so good to have him home. We move to the shower and on to the bedroom. The fun is just beginning. Billy lies flat on his back. I kiss him deeply, using lots of tongue, then I lick his neck. I move to each nipple, licking and nibbling. He moans, which excites me further. I feel his cock—it is hard as rock.

I make him turn on his side and I lick his butt. I move my mouth and tongue to his asshole. I love licking all around, he always moans so good. I grab his cock and give it a few strokes, all the while tonguing his hole. I put my finger in my mouth and get it slippery, then slide it into his asshole, moving it around and fucking him. I have him turn on his back while my finger is fucking him, then take his long, hard cock in my mouth, licking and sucking up and down his shaft. I let it slip out, and I lick the underside. He says, "Oh God, that feels so good, but stop, stop." I stop because I know he is about to shoot down my throat. I take my finger out of his ass. "What do you think I'm going to do to you now? I'm going to mount you and ride you till I come." I move up to him and feed him each breast in turn as I slide onto his wonderful hot cock. I ride him hard and fast. Oh God, I love the look on his face as I ride that wonderful prick! Then I lean back and rub my clit. I explode. I tell him how much I love him. I quickly move between his legs and take him in my mouth. I have a special, small dildo, which I like to lubricate and slide into his ass.

He moans and his cock expands. He can only take this for a short time and then I taste his beautiful come. I love having him shoot in my mouth. I always feel as if he's giving me a piece of himself.

We shower, then return to bed to hold each other tight. I never thought I'd find someone so sexually compatible. Lucky me.—*C.F., Des Moines, Iowa*

THEIR BATTERIES GET CHARGED WHEN SOMEONE ELSE PLUGS IN

*M*y wife and I are occasional readers of your magazine. Since we were inspired by the letters we've read, we decided to write and share our experience. Though we love each other dearly, the tedium of nine years of marriage has taken some of the sizzle out of our romance. Our sex life, though good, had become somewhat humdrum. So, after reading about the experiences of other couples, we decided to add spice to our own lives.

Jennifer is twenty-nine, very beautiful and, after two kids, has kept her dynamite 38-23-36 figure. She still turns men's heads in lust.

For my part, I've never been interested in another woman sexually since we've been married and I had no desire to try sex with anyone else. Jennifer, however, admitted to occasional feelings of lust when men hit on her and, quite frankly, I would get quite turned on thinking of her in bed with another man.

After discussing it, we decided our marriage was sound enough to try a little experimenting. We agreed Jennifer would go on a date or two, engage in extramarital sex and fill me in on the details when she came home.

I still remember that first evening. I looked at my wife in her short, tight, split-up-the-thigh, low-cut, revealing dress, her hair and makeup impeccable as usual, and her sexy spiked heels. I inhaled the fragrance of the enticing, alluring perfume she was wearing and had to restrain myself from attacking her. But I managed to control myself until Andrew—one of her coworkers, who had been quite amazed by Jennifer's sudden change of attitude toward his suggestive remarks—came to pick her up. I kept the kids in the family room, peering through the partially opened door at Andrew, staggered by the sultry seductress who greeted him when he rang the doorbell. He couldn't take his eyes off her as she got her purse. I saw Jennifer smile at him when his hand touched her sexy, shapely bottom as he escorted her out the door.

I fed the kids, put them to bed at nine and tried vainly to watch TV and read. I could not keep my mind off Jennifer and Andrew, wondering what they were doing all evening. I turned in at eleven but got no sleep. I lay there with a raging hard-on, imagining my wife naked in bed with Andrew screwing her as the hour turned to midnight, then one, then two in the morning.

By that time, I had little doubt Jennifer's evening had gone well and that Andrew was getting the best piece of ass he'd ever had in his life. I was so horny I dared not touch my throbbing cock lest I lose my ardent fervor for the erotic encounter I was anticipating when Jennifer came home and told me about her evening.

A little past two-thirty I heard the car drive up. I slipped to the darkened hallway at the end of the stairs, where a window overlooked the driveway and the front door below. A streetlight illuminated Andrew and Jennifer kissing passionately in the car.

He escorted her to the door and they kissed again, Andrew's hands raising her skirt to her hips, cupping her ass as their bodies ground together.

I went back to the bedroom, turned on the lamp and watched Jennifer's entrance. She came into our bedroom and smiled at me with a dreamy sigh as I looked her over. Her mussed hair, smeared lipstick, and rumpled dress, along with the freshly fucked look on her face left little doubt as to what had transpired, but I had to ask. "Did something happen you want to tell me about?"

Jennifer grinned. "I do if you want to hear about it." My wife then relived her evening for me, starting with dinner and drinks, their passionate kissing in the car and the ride to Andrew's apartment. All the way there, she stroked his bulging trousers while his hand rested on her inner thigh, a finger in her hot, sopping-wet hole through her crotchless panties.

Once at his place, their passion and lust was completely out of control. They frantically undressed and pawed each other. Once stripped, she told how Andrew expertly ate her out on the couch, bringing her off twice with the expert ministrations of his tongue before he carried her into his bedroom.

Incredibly turned on, I listened as Jennifer described how Andrew had mounted her, sinking what turned out to be a very large cock deep in her pussy. She came twice more before Andrew shot a gusher of his semen in her, filling her cunt with come. He then fucked her twice more—once with her on top, then doggie-style, blasting two more creamy loads of sperm into her snatch. I gazed at her, rapt. "Did all that really happen?" She grinned naughtily and took off her dress. "Exactly as I said," she told me.

Jennifer's black, lacy, crotchless panties were stained white and soaked with jism. Her dark pubic hair was wet, matted with come.

White globs of semen clung to her pussy and an oozing white river of sperm seeped down her thighs.

I could stand no more. Pulling her down on top of me, still clad in panties and heels, I impaled her sloppy pussy on my rigid cock, sinking my dick deep into my wife's come-filled hole. I ejaculated almost immediately. Jennifer's pussy overflowed, gushing her juices, mixed with Andrew's sperm and mine, all over my cock and balls. We lay there together, in love and in lust, knowing we'd added a new dimension to our relationship.

Over the next three months, we repeated this erotic experience sixteen times, with Andrew and two of her other coworkers.

We've pretty much stopped for now, but if things ever get dull again, we'll know exactly what to do.—*T.A., Bethesda, Maryland*

WAITING TO INHALE THE STAFF OF LIFE AND LOVE

*H*ere I am, just lying on the bed naked. My legs are slightly parted and I'm sort of dozing and thinking dreamily of you. I wish you were here, so you could place that hot hard dick in my mouth.

Suddenly you appear! Immediately I notice that you have a huge hard-on already. Ahh... so you've been thinking about me too, huh, lover? Well come over here and sit down on the bed. I want to talk to you.

The instant you sit down I slide my leg over your lap and start to rub against you. Ahh, the feeling of my soft skin touching your hot cock is wonderful. I reach out my hand and grab your cock. I feel the quiver your cock makes as I touch your flesh. I slowly start to stroke you. Yes lover, I have been waiting to long for you. I've been wet, and my poor pussy has been waiting for you all morning.

I climb over and sit down in your lap, facing you. You gently slide back until you are lying down on the bed. I move forward, pressing my tits against your chest as I lie on top of you. I reach for your mouth with my soft lips. Oh, my tongue finds yours and we share an electrifying kiss. My tongue meets yours as ripples of pleasure pour through my body.

I start to grind just a bit against you. My pussy is in control, not me. As my tongue continues to search your mouth I start to slowly move up and down against the shaft of your dick, making sure it is nice and hard before I take it into my mouth. Yes, you do want me to take it into my mouth, don't you? I move my head down from your face, kissing you every step of the way. As I get closer to your cock, I can feel my own excitement rising. I want to suck your cock, babe! I want you to fill my mouth with your hot, hard piece of flesh. My lips lightly touch the head of your cock softly, and then more firmly, as I take you into my mouth. Ahh, I just slide my wet mouth up and down on your cock for now, sucking lightly at first. I'm giving my mouth all of you, and then teasing myself and just letting the head of your cock in my mouth. My tongue runs circles around your head, with my lips wrapping tightly around it at times. Oh, your cock is just glistening with moisture, so slippery, so easily sliding in and out of my mouth.

I climb on top of you and put my pussy in front of your mouth. I need you to kiss it for me. I need you to lap up my juices! I need to feel your hot tongue on my clit while I suck and lick your hard cock. Yes, that's it lover, slip your tongue up inside me. Mmmmm, it feels so good I almost forget what I'm doing to you. Almost!

I take my hand and slowly, teasingly, stroke your dick as I suck on the head of your cock. I want to just slide my head all the way down. I want to take you all the way into my mouth and lick your balls when my mouth gets to the base of your dick. As I slide back up I keep my tongue nice and flat as it presses against the side of your cock. You have my cunt lips completely parted and are sliding your tongue up and down my slit. I am wriggling against your tongue. Lover, you feel so good! I move down to sit on top of you. I just have to feel your cock inside my soaking wet pussy. I move up and down so just the head enters me and then all of a sudden I just sit down on your cock.

My God! The intensity is too much. I begin to fuck you uncontrollably. I can't stop! My pussy is aching to come. I have to fuck you and fuck you hard, grinding my ass into your balls on each downstroke. I am bouncing wildly now, in a frenzy, and I'm about to come. Yesss!

You grab the base of your dick and hold it tightly. You don't want to come yet, and try to make it through the tight spasms you feel from my orgasm. You know that I'm not done with you yet!

I jump off you and place your cock back in my mouth, licking all my come juices off your dick. You are slowly pumping into my mouth, using your hand to slowly jerk off into my mouth.

I replace your hand with mine. I want to control your orgasm and you seem way too close. I suck on your dick for a few minutes more and then go back to fucking you, only letting the head of your dick into my pussy. Every now and then I just slide the whole length of you in, but not too often, because I am scared that you will come. I fuck you, ever so slowly, then move back so I can suck your dick with my wet lips and tongue and mouth. I let you pump your cock into my mouth a few times furiously, then I slow down the pace, only giving you a little. You are on the edge of coming, but not yet, not yet, lover. You have one more thing you have to do before I can let you come.

As I am sucking on your cock, you take a finger and slip it into my dripping pussy. You get it well lubricated and then insert it into my ass. This drives me wild! I start to buck against your hand, wanting more up my ass. I need you, lover! I need you to put that hot cock of yours right up my ass. I want to feel your balls slapping against my pussy as your cock is hammering in and out my tight asshole. I move around onto all fours and you press your cock up against the entrance of my ass. You know how wild I'm going to get when you drive your rod into my tight little opening. Your excitement heightens as you think about how good and hot and tight my ass is going to feel. You are ready to fuck me and start to move into my asshole. I am crazy for it. I take one hand and start to play with my clit as I back onto you, meeting your increasing thrusts. You are fucking my ass, and I am slamming into you, meeting your raging passion. Yessss! I am going to come again, a most intense orgasm. You feel this and scream out! We both come together in wild abandonment.—*S.P., Missoula, Montana* ⚬—▪

THESE BIRDS OF PLAY FLY SOUTH
TO GET THEIR KICKS

*A*fter reading your magazine for the last few months in total enjoyment, we decided to write and tell you the fun that we had on our last holiday.

First, a little bit about who we are. I'm Natalie: 36C-25-36, blonde hair, blue eyes and always ready for a lot of fun. I'm pretty successful, too, given my hot little body. Can you picture those tits on a five-four, one-hundred-and-ten pound frame?

Michael, my husband of twelve years, is slim, firm and tan at a hundred and fifty pounds. We started reading *Penthouse Letters* about four months ago and have relished every issue.

Michael has a lust for eating pussy that every woman who loves to be eaten out longs for in a partner. I'm sure you know there is nothing like being manipulated by a warm and skillful tongue. But on to our fun!

When we started planning a spring vacation on the Gulf coast, one of the main things we wanted to do was try some of the thrilling things we'd read about in your letters. We were looking forward to a lot of fun, sun and what I'll call risky sex.

The flight was a short one, but we were determined to have the fun begin the minute the vacation began—that is, the minute our everyday routine ended. I chose my traveling clothes very carefully. I decided upon a strapless dress with full skirt, for easy access. Even before everyone had boarded, Michael had one finger already working on my hot pussy. I raised my skirt to avoid any telltale wet spots. Soon (but not soon enough) the plane took off and the lights were dimmed. With two fingers in my twat and my own fingers rubbing and teasing my clit, it was almost impossible for me to remain quiet and still.

With no one the wiser to our antics, Michael pulled down the front of my dress and starting licking and sucking on my firm and full breasts. The guy in the next seat didn't seem to notice what was happening right next to him. Michael took his fingers out of my pussy and licked and sucked off all my juices, telling me how much he wanted to eat my pussy. So right there he put his head in my lap and started finger-fucking me while licking and sucking on my clit. I never thought it was possible to enjoy oneself so quietly—right there, with all our company unaware of what was happening, right under their noses, so to speak. But as I said, it was a short flight.

After finding our rental car, we went right back to making our trip a memorable one. The drive to the motel was ecstasy. After a few good licks, we were on our way again. Michael stuck his amazing finger in his mouth and then slipped it up between my legs again. Michael brought me to another wet and tasty orgasm while driving down the ocean highway. As you might have guessed, Michael's seven inches were rock-hard and ready for action. With my hand in Michael's pants and my dress around my waist, we raced to the motel.

It felt like forever getting the keys, and the minute we were in the room, I was on my knees and freeing Michael's anxious member. I sucked that thing down my throat so fast I almost choked. Poor fella, he must have been wanting to come ever since the plane took off. I hadn't swirled my tongue once around his cockhead before he was shooting his warm, tasty come down my throat. It sure got the taste of the airplane snacks out of my mouth.

Well, it was great to taste his come, but we wanted to do more exhibitionism like on the plane. So, after some good clean fun in our room, the next stop was the Jacuzzi, in hopes of finding our next audience. Our luck was good. Three guys were cooling off down by the pool. So with a quick walk around the pool just for show, I took off my robe and got in the Jacuzzi with Michael, all the while sure that my every move was watched.

After only a few minutes in the hot water, I decided to go down again on my favorite shaft, knowing there were probably three more just as hard less than fifteen feet away. But, alas, two kids came out for a late swim and we had to move our fun back up to the room. We watched the pool for a long time after that, but those kids just stayed and stayed. We went out on the landing several times, Michael in his birthday suit and me in only my little teddy. I thought at least the three grown guys who were also still out there would get a glimpse of what they were missing. When the kids finally went in, those three guys were still waiting down at the pool for our return.

So we threw our suits back on and headed out to the pool. It was after dusk now, and the only light was the light coming from the pool and the Jacuzzi. Michael jumped in and immediately took off his shorts. I sat beside him and started to stroke his fine prick. He is so big that the head poked out of the bubbling water. I leaned over and took the head in my mouth. I licked it for a while and then Michael untied the back of my bikini top. I held my breath and went all the way down on his pole.

When I came back up, he grabbed me by the waist and sat me on his lap. I could feel his throbbing shaft against my mound through my bottoms, and I knew I had to take him. I pulled his head (his real head) down to my breasts and urged him to take my huge nipples into his mouth. While he was sucking my tits, I looked around to see the three guys watching us, each of them stroking their rods through their suits. That's when I decided to really give them a show.

Reaching under the water, I slid my bikini off and started rubbing Michael's cock against my lower lips. That was all I had to do. Michael's cock shot up into my snatch without the least bit of effort on either of our parts. I started humping high and hard on my baby's tool, and immediately the three guys let up a resounding cheer.

I was coming almost immediately, and when I felt Michael's dick start to throb, in orgasm, I threw caution to the wind and started whooping and hollering.

My tits were bouncing all over the place, Michael's head was thrown back and I noticed that the three guys were suddenly quiet. After Michael loosed his load in me, I turned around to see what was up with the other guys.

Needless to say, I was very pleasantly surprised to find that all three of them had dropped their shorts and were whipping their puds. When I showed Michael what was happening, he said, "Well, let's give them something more to jack off to." With that, he lifted me up out of the water, sat me on the edge of the Jacuzzi and buried his face between my legs. As Michael sucked me to a shuddering orgasm, I watched amazed as each of those guys, their eyes glued on me, shot their wads high in the air, one after the other.

Now we're having a Jacuzzi installed by our own pool here at home. It's a strange thing some people will do to live their fantasies, but we now like to fuck in the backyard and imagine that all the world is watching. Call us crazy!—*N.M., Memphis, Tennessee* ○━▪

A SCHOOLGIRL'S PRIMER ON HOW TO DO IT RIGHT

I'm sitting here in this hotel room reading your magazine. I use it to give me ideas of things to do to the guys when I'm back at school. I've done this for quite some time: Read your magazine, try stuff out on my conquests. It is one of the best ways I know to get into the male mind and see what turns them on.

Well, since I've nothing going on right now, I thought I'd relate a couple of adventures I had during the last school year. They were definitely inspired by *Penthouse Letters.*

First, let me describe me and my roommate, Alicia. I'm tall and thin with large, firm tits. They're my most distinctive characteristic. They have dark, sensitive nipples that really contrast with the rest of my body. My bush is dark and I have full, pouting pussy lips that just love a stiff cock passing through them. Alicia is blonde, has a great set of tits that the guys love to ogle and shoot off onto, and a tight pussy that is covered with curly brown hair. Neither of us has trouble attracting guys.

Well, Alicia and I have a little friendly competition between us concerning our sexual abilities. The root of the competition is our love of dick. We are both extremely lustful. She and I have a couple of steady fellas, but they both understand (her boyfriend and mine) that we are free to do as we please, sexually. My boyfriend, Dylan, likes to watch me take on other guys, anyway, so it really isn't an issue. The four of us (including Woody, Alicia's boyfriend) have had sex together, but not an orgy. I mean, I've never had sex with Woody, and Alicia has never had sex with Dylan, we've just fucked in each other's presence.

One time, the four of us were in our apartment and Alicia and I were in a playful mood. After a little "arguing" about who could get their guy off the fastest by sucking his cock, we decided to have a contest.

When Dylan and Woody stripped, they were already sporting nice erections. Both cocks are about the same size, but when Dylan gets hard, his cock arcs upward, whereas Woody's stiffens straight out. Dylan's balls tend to be higher in his sac than Woody's too. (This actually was another of our contests, comparing our boyfriends' erect cocks. Guys love that kind of shit—they're so competitive.)

Anyway, we had them sit down in front of a TV showing erotic videos. We wanted to get the guys really hot for the contest. We watched a couple of hot scenes where the actor's cock sprays a nice load of jizz. (Guys love that too. Watching another guy lose his load on some pretty girl's face or tits is a real turn-on for a guy. Males are so visual, and I like to use it to the max.)

After a while, we knelt in front of the guys and had them stand up so that their cocks were bobbing before our eyes. The whole time there was a lot of sexual banter going on. It was a lot of fun. We each reached up and grabbed our guy's cock at the base, saying, "One, two, three, go!" We started sucking their cocks for all we were worth. I was watching Woody's prong disappear into Alicia's mouth and she watched Dylan's cock slipping in and out of mine. The deal was that we had to make our guy come first. In order to make it fair, when the guy started squirting you had to remove your mouth so you could see the jizz. Another reason for letting the come fly and not cover it up was we knew Dylan wanted to see Woody's load and Woody wanted to see Dylan's. And sure enough, the guys were watching how the other guy's cock was doing.

I could see by Woody's balls rising up in his pouch that he was getting there pretty quick. And the thing of the deal was, the better I went at Dylan's cock, the better it looked to Woody and the faster he was going to drop a nut. So I had to change tactics. I put Dylan's cockhead in my mouth and sucked and rolled all the sensitive parts with my tongue. Alicia continued to work all along Woody's cock, letting it bob and flop along her face and mouth as she tried to coax his load. Well, she looked like she was giving really good head, which is what I wanted Dylan to think as I tickled his plum. I felt Dylan start shivering and felt his balls contract. I removed my mouth and said, "Ta-da!" as Dylan shot his load in the air. When Woody saw the first stream of white goo, his cock spasmed and started squirting. Just like I knew it would. Alicia and I were both fucked good that night.

Another time, Alicia and I came up with the idea of trying to get two cocks to shoot off on each other. We thought we could do it, so one night we tried. We had a couple of our other guy friends over and Dylan. Dylan is friends with both of the guys, so he was excited, also. We started with some videos (videos: never leave home without them) and eventually we were all naked. Dylan was in the easy chair watching the action, which consisted of the guy I was with doing a good job eating my pussy and Alicia getting her tits rubbed and sucked. When the action was getting pretty hot, Alicia and I asked the guys to stand up.

We both got to our knees in front of their erections and started to give them head. Now, both these guys had long cocks, longer than either Dylan's or Woody's, which is one of the reasons we (Alicia and I) picked them. As we were sucking these big cocks, Dylan was pulling his in the easy chair.

After a short while, Alicia and I maneuvered the guys together where we could each suck the other guy's cock. Alicia would offer me her guy's cock and I'd do the same with my guy's dong. We swapped off like that for a while, the guys getting pretty close to losing it. Soon, we had their cocks inches apart, Alicia on one side and me on the other. Both guys had their pelvises thrust forward. Alicia and I started jerking on each guy's cock, trying to get the heads to touch. Eventually, we did get their cocks touching, and they formed a triangle with their cockheads forming the apex. Suddenly, Alicia's guy started to squirt, followed by my guy. That was a wonderful sight. Each guy's jizz coated the other's cock. We kept coaxing their loads and aiming them at the other's plum. When they were finished, they looked a little awkward, but extremely satisfied. I looked at Dylan and he had come running down his dick and hand. He'd obviously enjoyed it too. And I enjoyed the fucking he gave me later.

I have one more time that was outstanding in my mind. Dylan's fraternity was initiating some freshmen, and they wanted to do a little good-natured hazing. Alicia and I said count us in.

To cut to the chase, Alicia and I decided to have the pledges sit through a cocksucking lesson—nude. We picked our favorite upperclassmen with long cocks and got them in on it.

The night of the event came. Dylan had the pledges (there were four of them) in a room naked, sitting on some folding chairs, all in a line. Dylan had a chair in the corner, out of the way. You should have seen the looks on those pledges' faces when Alicia and I walked in— nude! Their eyes were darting from pussy to titties back to pussy. They were all attempting to hide their cocks, but Alicia and I soon made that impossible.

Alicia said, "Since you are soon to become members of this fraternity, we wanted to show you how your sisters will take care of your needs." I didn't have a clue what she was talking about, but it sounded good. We had one of the guys come in.

Anyway, Alicia said, "This is how we service a nice cock." I interrupted, "All you pledges, stand up." They did, but you could tell they were embarrassed. Their hard-ons were revealed to everyone in the room. Nice, young, hard cocks. Full of come. Four of them standing straight up at attention. What a sight! I told them to move their chairs a little further apart and sit down with their legs open. I wanted to judge the effect we were going to have.

Alicia moved her guy right up in front of the pledges. She squatted down in front of them, spreading her legs so the pledges could see her pussy. She was damp (as was I). She said, "These are balls."

She cupped them in her hand. "I'm going to show you the proper way to suck the jism out of them." All the pledges' cocks twitched and they shifted in their seats. Alicia said, "First, you need to prime the pump." She started to slowly jerk her guy's long cock. Her hand looked good sliding over his hard shaft. She said, "By the way, isn't this a nice specimen of a cock?" She shook it gently. "Here is the most sensitive part, the cockhead. And here is where you will soon see this guy's load shooting out." She licked his hole. She then positioned him sideways to the pledges and started to really give him head. She licked up and down his shaft and twirled her tongue around his knob. I watched the pledges and they were mesmerized.

Soon, Alicia had her guy's cock squirting long strings of sperm across the room. She stood up and kissed him and said, "Now, that was a load."

I then had my long-dicked guy come in, and I sucked him off for them, except I had him facing the pledges, so they could watch the changing expressions on his face. It made me hot thinking about the view of my bobbing head from behind. When I felt my guy's dick start to throb, I pulled away and continued to jerk his shaft. Presently, he was shooting wildly all over the place, and a little landed on the legs of a couple of the pledges.

I said, "Okay, time to become brothers!"

We told them if they failed this test, they would not be allowed to enter the group as a frat brother. We had the pledges face off. Alicia had two and I had two. We grabbed a cock in each hand and started to slowly jerk them. All the pledges were hair-trigger, so we had to be careful.

Alicia said, "In order for you to become brothers, you must perform this ritual. You and the pledge in front of you will press your cocks together. Then, my partner and I are going to jerk the both of your cocks, together, until you come. If you cannot come, or will not come, you will not be admitted." Sounded good to me.

I had my two guys and I could watch Alicia and her two guys. We were facing each other across four cocks and eight nuts. When we had them like we wanted them, we began to jerk all of their cocks at the same time. I put saliva on my hands to make the sensation slicker. It wasn't long before my pledges were both shooting off. They each had a tremendous load of come. Each guy's load landed on the other's tummy and ran down his cock and balls. I looked over at Alicia just as her guys started emptying. She cheated—she let a couple of squirts go, then she started sucking on both their knobs. She later told me she couldn't resist.

Then Alicia said, "You are now brothers." We then left and Dylan and I fucked until morning. Alicia probably did too. With Woody.
—*R.B., Statesboro, Georgia* ○┼─■

I HAD A DREAM, CRAZY DREAM.
AW, COME ON, NOW

I'm not going to tell you their names, but they have to be two of the sexiest gals I've seen in the market since I moved here, which was five years ago. When I first saw them, they were both dressed in miniskirts which did not leave much to the imagination.

They both were sporting at least 36–24–36 bodies, with long, voluptuous, tanned legs clear up to their asses. Their tits just seemed to be trying to pop right out of their tops. It was a hard-on just waiting to happen. Standing in front of the meat counter, checking out my grocery list, I tried not to look too obvious, even though it was almost impossible not to stare at both these gorgeous gals.

I guess we all had the same thoughts, because there they were, checking out the meat too. To my welcome surprise, they had turned their attentions toward me. Well, needless to say, it had been quite some time since the last time, so I had to ask, "What looks good?" and they both gave me the biggest, sexiest smile. One of them looked me over from head to toe and stopped at the middle, saying, "You're not looking bad. What are you doing for dinner?"

Little did they know about my somewhat lonely situation as of late. So the natural reply was, "Nothing I wouldn't mind sharing with the both of you."

It was confirmed. I was to bring my meat and myself to their apartment at eight. I had a feeling, a wonderful, delightful feeling.

Of course, I arrived exactly at eight. Okay, so I arrived a little early and waited outside their apartment till eight. I rang the doorbell, and before I knew it, I heard those sweet voices, "Hi, sweety, we're so glad you made it." They were definitely an eyeful, one dressed in a short, red teddy and the other dressed in a short, hot pink chemise. I was almost hard already; just following them inside. It was quite obvious that they had nothing on underneath. As they walked, the delicate fabrics clung to every curve, and my cock responded to all of them.

I could smell the bouquet of a delightful dinner cooking, and we all decided to have a cocktail before dinner. They took me into the living room, these two gorgeous, sexy females, handed me a drink— Crown Royal, of course—and got me comfortable on the couch, one on either side of me.

It was almost alarmingly uncomfortable to know that these two beauties definitely had no other clothing on whatsoever. When they crossed their legs, there was definitely nothing left to the imagination. My cock was bulging right through my jeans. I gathered they both noticed the strain on my swollen member, because they proceeded to remove every stitch of my clothing. As they did, it was not very hard to notice that both of them were shaved completely.

One said to the other, "I think he could use a shave too, don't you?" The other didn't hesitate to get a basin of hot water, shaving cream and razor.

"You lather, I'll shave."

At this point, we were all naked, and they were even more gorgeous than I could have dreamed. One started slowly applying lather all over my cock and balls. Between the warmth of the water and the application of the lather, I thought I was going to blow a load right then and there. Especially with both of these naked beauties touching me with their tits and rubbing their pussies on me. It seemed that with every stroke of the razor, the other girl would apply more lather, making my cock as hard as a rock. I was determined to hold out at least till they were done shaving me.

To watch these two beauties shaving me while staring at their baldness was simply exquisite. I wanted to lick their shaved pussies so bad I could literally taste it. After they had completely shaved my pubes, one said, "Roll over, we're not finished yet."

I couldn't believe what happened next. They spread my cheeks, lathered my ass and then shaved my asshole and ass completely clean. I mentioned, "Then I guess I'm done."

They both replied, "Not yet. The fun has just begun."

After a light dinner, we retired to the bedroom. Since we were already naked, we started right in kissing and fondling one another. Then both girls laid me back and told me to enjoy. One started at the top with her light fingers and tongue, and the other started on my inner thighs. Just watching these hairless pussies teasing me all over made my cock hard as steel, to say nothing of the exquisite feelings tingling in my balls. Then it was my turn to return the delightful fantasy. I proceeded to lick every inch of both their glistening bodies, softly running my fingers over the curves of their breasts, teasing all around their nipples while working my way down to lick and tease each pussy till it bloomed open like a rose petal. Not to let the one cool down while I was eating the other, I had my fingers inside her, tantalizing her pussy lips while I ate her friend out.

After a few minutes of this, the one I wasn't eating came around and gobbled my dick down. I knew I was going to blow a load and a half. God almighty, could this gal suck a cock. Her friend started telling me, "Come, baby, come for us."

That was all I could take. I thought my dick was exploding, and that beautiful creature licked every bit of juice from my cock while I teased her friend's clit till the cows came home.—*Name and address withheld* ⊶▪

RITES OF PASSION, RITES OF SPRING, RIGHTS OF INITIATION

Growing up together, my best friend Jamey and I shared many experiences. When we turned eighteen, these included masturbation. This slowly came to a head as the summer before college wore on. Sometimes, when I was over at Jamey's house, we would read his *Penthouse* magazine and beat off.

Since I was one of a very few guys in our group of friends who was not circumcised, I could tell that Jamey was intrigued by the appearance of my cock. Fortunately, I started developing fairly early and have nothing to be ashamed of in the size department.

Even though I looked mature, though, I was still a frustrated virgin, and I was pretty sure Jamey was too. Jamey went on to attend a university about two hundred miles away, while I went to the local community college. We saw each other several times that first year, when he came home for a weekend or when I went to visit him.

The first quarter of school was uneventful. Jamey's roommate was a senior finishing his last quarter, so they didn't have much in common and pretty much kept to themselves. The next quarter was entirely different. His new roommate was a sophomore transfer, so their ages were closer and they had more interests in common. The first time I met Perry, Jamey's new roommate, was quite memorable.

As usual when I visited, I arrived fairly late in the evening. Jamey was working at his computer and asked if I had eaten yet, to which I replied no, I hadn't. Jamey said that he had to go downstairs to get his laundry. When he got back, we could go to the pizza place down the street. After my long drive, I needed to take a major piss, so I went down the hall to the bathroom. When I got back, I sat at Jamey's computer and saw that he was working on some boring report for school. I put that aside and looked around his filed until I found a *"Penthouse"* folder. Now that's more like it!

There were literally hundreds of letters that had been scanned in and saved by subject. Then I found a "Sex" folder with lots of large files in it. Probably porn pictures downloaded from the Internet, I thought. There were some of those, but mostly they were nude pictures of Jamey and some other guy I assumed to be his new roommate. In some pictures they were together, some alone, and in various states of arousal. There were a few in which they were ejaculating.

I called up a picture of Jamey coming and left it on the screen while I paged through some of the magazines on his bed. When Jamey got back to the room I told him, "I always did like to watch you shoot your wad."

"I thought you might find those," he said as he put his laundry down and called up a picture of a guy stroking his hard-on. "That's Perry, after I told him about your foreskin. He's been eager to meet you ever since. Are you still up for pizza?"

We walked down the street to the pizza place. Along the way he told me about Perry. "I think he was testing me from the day he arrived. First he offered me use of his extensive *Penthouse* collection. After a couple of weeks, probably when he figured I didn't have a steady girlfriend, he started reading them in bed, and after we shut out the lights he would jack off. You can't be in the same room and not get turned on, so I would quietly slip my shorts down and beat off along with him.

"After a couple of nights of that, he said, 'Here's one that'll make you hard,' and he read one out loud. Then, Saturday morning, Perry finished his shower a few minutes before I did. When I got back to the room, he was sitting naked on his bed reading a *Penthouse* and playing with his cock. He said, 'This one turns me on every time,' and read a letter. I picked a magazine from his collection and sat on my bed. We took turns reading letters until we were both really hard. Perry said he couldn't let a good hard-on go to waste and started stroking away. I followed along and we both came quickly. A few days later, I was jacking off when he got home, so he stripped, sat next to me and we jerked each other off.

"Once, when we were looking at some of his magazines and jacking off, we found a couple of pictures of uncircumcised guys, and Perry said he wondered what it was like to have foreskin. He asked if I had ever played with one, and that's when I told him about you."

When we got back to the dorm, Perry was in his swimsuit and said he was going out to soak in the Jacuzzi to unwind before going to bed and asked if we wanted to join him. We agreed, though I said that I hadn't brought a swimsuit, so I'd just go in my underwear. I stripped down to my briefs, giving Perry a good view of my bulge, but no more.

We had a nice soak, and the warm water was indeed relaxing. When we got back to the room, I said I was going to take a shower to wash off the chlorine. Perry readily agreed that this was a good idea, and Jamey followed along to watch.

I peeled off my wet shorts and stood under the running water. As I soaped up my hair, I casually turned toward Perry to give him a tantalizing view of my gently swaying balls. I rinsed off my hair and continued washing, casually pulling back my foreskin to clean the head of my penis. Perry's cock stiffened a little and he turned his eyes away. A virgin, I thought.

We dried off, went back to the room and hung up the towels. As Jamey and Perry pulled back their bedcovers, I knelt down to pull my sleeping bag out of my duffel. With my back to Perry, I was giving him a nice view of my testicles, which, due to the hot shower, were dangling very low between my legs. I could see in the mirror on the wall that Perry was staring at them. When I turned to spread out the bag, he quickly looked away, but I could see that he was starting to get hard. Jamey was getting hard by watching Perry trying to hide being turned on. I pointed at Jamey and asked Perry, "Did Jamey ever tell you that we use to jack off together? He always liked to play with my foreskin. It looks like you would too." I sat up on Jamey's desk. "Come on, it's what you want, isn't it?"

He sat on the chair before me, lifted my cock and carefully examined it, gently tugging at my foreskin to expose the head, which he licked. Then he put all of it in his mouth and sucked it to its full hardness. Then he pulled it out and stroked it, playing with the foreskin some more, followed by some licking and sucking of my balls. It wasn't long before he was back to chowing on my meat. He certainly had the best lips that had ever been around my cock. He soon had me shooting my load down his throat. He swallowed most of it, with a little semen dribbling down his chin.

After that I introduced myself to my new seven-inch friend between Perry's legs and got to watch sperm shoot from Jamey's familiar penis while I squeezed his balls.

The next day we hiked up to some hot springs in the hills behind the school where we could skinny-dip and generally be naked and play with each other. Perry showed me how he got all those great pictures that I'd seen on Jamey's computer. He had both a video camera and a digital camera which we used to take pictures of us doing everything to each other.

When we got back to their room, they transferred the pictures into the computer so we could see what we'd done that day. That set us off for another night of sex.

The next morning, after we had all been drained, we went to the local nude beach to check out the scenery. After swimming around to a more secluded cove, we had another round of sex on the sand before I had to pack up and go home.

I went home with a tape full of pictures of the three of us that I can enjoy on my computer at my leisure. I visited Jamey and Perry several more times that year. And when I'm not with them in person,

I always have them on my computer. I must say, I look at them more often than I care to admit.—*Name and address withheld* ⚬┼▪

THIS WOMAN LOVES TO LET HER
HUSBAND DO HER RIGHT

I married my wife over eleven years ago. We have had our share of good and learning times, but more importantly we have endured and grown to a healthy relationship. I love my wife, but then again, who in his right mind wouldn't? Anyway, the story I am about to relate deals with the sexy style in which she pleases me.

My wife was born twenty-nine years ago in Puerto Rico, even though she looks a lot younger because of the way she takes care of herself. She's a pretty and sexy brunette. She is about five feet four, has a pair of nice tits, a large mouth and full lips which she keeps nicely shiny with red lipstick. In short, my wife is a good piece of ass. At parties and other social occasions, men always and invariably remark that I have a very pretty wife and I feel proud. Let me tell you about my favorite get-off pastime and the one thing I never get tired of.

I have my wife give me good head at least twice a week. First, she gets ready by wearing white, black or red sexy panties with a short matching top and high-heeled shoes which also match the panties. She proceeds by applying makeup to her face and the shiny red lipstick I told you about.

Sometimes, however, she dances for me to get me hot, although she enjoys dancing, anyway. Most of the time, however, I first eat her cunt real good until she comes and she's real wet. I then put her in the doggie-style position and fuck her. I may pull out of her juicy cunt and stick my cock right up her ass and fuck her ass until she's had enough. Then I ask her to turn around and suck my cock. She kneels before me on the bed and goes to work on my rod. Anyway, our bed faces large mirrors on the closet doors and I get a terrific all-angles view as she kneels and proceeds to suck my fat cock.

After all the fucking I have given her in her cunt and up her ass, my cock is oozing drops of semen which she rubs and smears around her mouth. My wife really loves to swallow come, and that makes me a very happy man. She looks beautiful as she kneels there before me, her big mouth and her lips shining with the red glossy lipstick and saliva. She's got her mouth crammed and stuffed with my fat, glistening dick that goes in and out of her mouth as I'm pumping and fucking her face. She's sucking and slurping, making mouth noises and occasionally grabbing my thick hose and jerking it into her mouth. I love dangling my dick right in front of her erotic face. I tell her, "You are my good little cocksucker." She doesn't mind when I tell her that, or when I ask her, "Lick the balls, spread your legs, get your hands and knees on the floor just like a dog, open your mouth real wide, my beautiful cocksucker, I'm gonna come deep into your mouth!"

While she's kneeling on the bed, her ass facing the mirror and her mouth stuffed with my thick raw meat, I grab and pull her black or white sexy panties right into the crack of her ass. She's wearing a sexy tank top and her high-heeled shoes. I must say, the sight of her is so erotic and lusty that it will turn on even a ninety-year-old man. Her black, coarse, long hair and her nice, big, light brown ass look great.

As I'm standing there in front of her with my big fat cock going in and out of her mouth, I feel like kneeling behind her and fucking her in the pussy or in the ass, but I know that it won't be long before I come, and I prefer to watch the come explode all in her mouth. By this time, my balls are heavy with a big load of semen and my cock's purple head is getting bigger and glistening with her saliva. Red lipstick is smeared all over my fat pole. Her lips look red and bigger from all the sucking and fucking they've been receiving. Her luscious mouth is stretched wide as I fuck and keep stroking my eight inches of swollen meat deep into the back of her throat.

I hold the back of her head with both hands as I fuck her face, increasing my humping speed. She really enjoys this, and occasionally opens her eyes and looks up at me, asking me with her eyes to pull my cock out of her mouth so she can get a better grip. I pull out and grab my fat hose and jack off just inches from her fluttering eyelids. Drops of semen are slowly seeping from the swollen purple head and I feel like I'm about to shoot, so I stick my cock back in.

She gobbles up my dick again and I proceed to fuck her beautiful, lust-filled face. Her head is bobbing back and forth, giving me a glorious blowjob like she knows how to do best. I keep looking at her beautiful, petite, brown, sexy body in the large mirrors on the closet doors. She looks pretty small next to my six-feet-two body. I wonder how many men would love to fuck my wife's sexy little body and fuck her beautiful, erotic big mouth and then come all in her mouth the way I proudly do. I'm sure the numbers are legion.

As I'm thinking about these things, my eight-inch cock pulsates and I'm ready to fill her beautiful, warm, velvety mouth with a large, hot load of white semen. She has confided to me that she gets off sucking big fat cocks and that she likes the feel of having her mouth filled with thick sperm. She loves it when I tell her that I enjoy coming all in her beautiful mouth.

She has fucked other guys before, but she prefers them big. One time, when I told her that it was okay for her to fuck other guys, she went out that night to a disco and came back hot like a bitch to tell me this story: She had a few drinks at the disco place and got picked up by this good-looking big guy who fucked the shit out of her. The guy had her suck off his big cock, and when the guy was starting to come in her mouth, she pulled his cock out and told him, "Don't come on my face, shoot the come all in my mouth like my husband does." When the guy heard this, she told me, he grabbed his big thick dick and sprayed his big wad deep down her throat. She was sucking like there was no tomorrow. She said she had to wash her face and put fresh makeup on. As she related the whole story to me, I had her kneeling on the floor with her nightdress still on, sucking my hard and swollen prick and jacking me off like a pro. This time I shot into the air and smeared the hot jism all over my washboard tummy. It gave me a warm, tingly feeling.

Another time, a few years ago, when my wife was about twenty-five years of age, she told me she went out with this guy at work that had been after her. He wanted to take her out and fuck her. So she let him. When the guy took her to his apartment and gave her some wine, he gave her a memorable fuck. This fellow had complimented her that she had a beautiful mouth and sexy, meaty lips. Anyway, the guy finally fucked her mouth, and he kept coming in little spurts of semen which he kept depositing in her open mouth and down her throat. As she was gulping the semen, she managed to pull out and told this guy, "Please keep coming in my mouth, I love it so much." She said that this guy got really excited and must have put a quart of semen in her tummy. She went crazy with ecstasy because she felt like she was doing something illicit.

Later, the lucky guy showed her a Polaroid shot he had taken of her while she was sucking his raging hard-on with a vengeance. She said that she got kind of embarrassed when she saw herself doing the deed, but the guy told her, "Nobody could recognize you and I want to keep this picture to jack off with and as a gift from you, okay?" She said okay.

When she told me this hot story, I jacked off as she was talking and held the swollen head of my cock tightly in my hand, feverishly pulling my pud, sending large streams of hot come into the air. Then I kept blasting away like there was no tomorrow. When I was finished, I sat back and pondered what a piece of work is man. We go about our daily chores, placing great importance on legal statutes and the like, but we are most happy when we can contribute a little bit of our seed to the cosmos. I mentioned this to my lovely wife, and she said I was crazy. She couldn't stop laughing.

One of the most erotic experiences we both had was at a party we had in our home for her birthday. We both had invited people we knew. She had invited this guy she knew from her office. I think they liked each other by the way they looked at each other. We all had a ball, dancing and getting high with a few joints. We also played some porno videotapes during the late evening, when I thought everybody was gone. I went upstairs to our bedroom and found my wife on her knees, and the guy standing up with his underwear down. All I could see was his back and his ass moving back and forth, fucking her face. The sight was too much for me. When I got close, he was shocked, but I told him it was okay and to let me get a piece too.

What I saw I couldn't believe. I was so hot that I pulled my hard cock out of my fly. The guy had already sprayed his load, and there was a little bit of semen dripping from my wife's mouth, but he had his big cock still in her mouth, fucking her face. She was still sucking and slurping and the lucky guy was still hard and slowly fucking her face. He had a huge set of balls. I couldn't stand it any longer and started to jack off and beat my swollen hard cock, just like Pee Wee Herman. The guy pulled out of her mouth and blasted into the air. I reached for the video camera and told her lucky friend to start shooting the fabulous porno scene. I gently cradled her head in my hands and put my cock into her mouth. After a few minutes, I pulled out and told her, "Open your mouth wide, flick your tongue a little, 'cause I'm gonna fill your mouth full of come like you've never seen it before!"

She stuck her tongue out and I sent large streams of sticky semen into her mouth. She started spitting come out of the corners of her mouth and I kept shooting come down her throat, giving her a good meal. She groaned and writhed in front of her friend and me. As we both rubbed and smeared the vast quantity of hot, sticky semen and saliva all over our glistening cocks, she must have really been enjoying it because she did exactly what we asked her to do. We kept taking turns putting our big cocks into her mouth and having her clean our cocks until we both got soft.

We grabbed a couple of beers and later sat in front of the TV and watched the greatest homemade porno movie I have ever seen! My wife couldn't believe her eyes when she saw herself on video being serviced by two gorgeous hunks like ourselves. But there she was. As we watched the most erotic porno experience we'd ever had, me and the guy got hard again and had my wife for dessert. The friend ate her cunt while she gave me good head, then he fucked her in the ass.

I love my Puerto Rican wife, but then, as I said before, who wouldn't?—*L.K., Los Angeles, California* ⚬┼▪

AMOROUS PAIR PERFORM FOR
IMPROMPTU GATHERING

*I*t was Valentine's Day, and I was with my girlfriend Minnie. We were on a Caribbean cruise, and one day we were offered the opportunity to go to a nude beach.

When we got there, there were only a few other people on the beach, but as the day went on, more people arrived, including some good-looking younger couples. I was completely naked, and my girlfriend was topless. I don't mean to sound egotistical, but we are both good-looking and were receiving quite a few appreciative glances.

We played around a little in the water and mostly just relaxed in the beautiful Caribbean sun. We started talking about sexual fantasies, and Minnie asked me what was one of mine. I told her I always wanted to make love in an exotic locale.

"Oh, you have, have you? What ever gave you that idea?"

I looked at her sheepishly and swore to her that this was not the first time I'd thought of it. We started kissing and gradually (and then suddenly) my dick started to get hard. Minnie reached down and started stroking my cock while I placed a finger or two inside her wet snatch. I looked around and saw a handful of people casually watching. What a turn-on.

All of a sudden, someone yelled, "Look at the size of that lizard!"

Well, I have a larger than average penis, but I have to admit that they were not referring to me or any part of my anatomy. There was a large iguana coming out of the hills. We laughed and decided we needed to cool off.

Standing up to walk into the water, there was no hiding my hard-on, but I didn't care. Once we were in the water, we kissed some more and decided to swim around the corner and look for a secluded cove or something.

We found a little cove, but there was a house and we were sure there were people in it. This started to turn me on more, and we started to make out in a little tidal basin. I lay down on my back and stuck my dick up in the air. The warm water felt good, and my girl-friend's mouth around my dick felt even better.

Presently a small motorboat rounded the point and immediately we heard a group of men yelling us on. Minnie pulled away from my dick and said, "Let's wait till they pass," but just then their engine stalled—yeah, right!

After a few minutes of a great blowjob, Minnie turned around into a 69 (to more cheers) and I ate the most beautiful pussy in the world while fucking her lovely face. When I couldn't take it any longer, I pushed Minnie away, put her on her knees and entered her from behind. Now I was fucking like a madman and watching our audience watching us. Now the guys in the boat had very somber looks on their faces, and I couldn't blame them. I, too, believe that sex is sacred and not to be entered into lightly.

We were both very excited about being watched and wanted our audience in the boat and in the house to enjoy the show. Minnie was howling and, soon, I was too as I unloaded a pint into her hole. Minnie was coming when I was, and when we were done, we splashed down into the shallow water and started kissing each other feverishly.

Miraculously, the guys got their boat restarted just then and roared away.

Now that we were finally alone (at least, if no one was in the house) we decided to finish things up in style. My girlfriend likes to have her asshole licked, and guess what? I like to lick her asshole. So she lay facedown in the shallow water with her head on the sand (kind of like a pillow) and I buried my head between her cheeks. Minnie started screaming and I knew I was giving her what she wanted. I love nature!—*M.M., Orlando, Florida*

SINGLE-HANDED AND BAREFOOTED, SHE TAKES ON THE CROWD

I have always been an avid reader of your magazine and have found both the pictures and the letters from your readers very stimulating. Recently I read two letters from fellow foot fetishists that made my prick hard to control.

My girlfriend Val likes to walk around the house barefoot when she comes to see me. She doesn't know it, but it drives me mad to see her sexy feet with her dainty painted toes. I've even seen her add a spritz of perfume to them as a finishing touch.

Last Sunday we dined out for the first time in months. Val decided to wear a semitransparent green chiffon dress, white panties, sheer pantyhose and a pair of gold high heels that I had never seen before. Her dress was fucking sexy. It had a bodice that lifted up her tits, which were somewhat visible through her extremely sheer bra.

We got into my car. Val looked stunning. Her blonde hair fell over her shoulders, and she crossed her ankles while we were traveling. "These shoes are a little tight, love," she reported. I hoped that meant she wouldn't have them on for too long.

When we arrived at the restaurant, we were seated at a quiet table in the corner. We sat gazing at each other over a glowing candle. It was all very romantic. I noticed a middle-aged chap at the bar casting a longing look in Val's direction.

"I love you," I whispered to Val.

"So do I, love," she smiled.

The chap I had noticed at the bar came over to our table and asked if he could join us. Men are always attracted to Val, and I know she loves the extra attention. I'm secure enough in our relationship that I don't mind sharing her sometimes. When I said he could join us, he sat down and introduced himself as Bill. He was well-dressed in a nice suit, and had his white hair combed back. His rugged face showed signs of his battle with the bottle.

Bill stared at Val, and I could tell he was thinking about fucking her. She seemed relaxed as she quietly sipped her bubbly. I excused myself and headed for the men's room. I saw that Val's feet were shyly tucked under her chair, her right foot bare, her shoe next to Bill's chair. I saw him reach down, pick up the shoe in his big hand and hold it in front of him.

When I returned to the dining room, the live band started playing. I noticed both Val's feet were now bare.

"I bet you won't, my sweet," Bill was saying to Val.

"Bet what?" I quizzed.

"I just bet Val that she wouldn't get up and dance barefoot on the bar," he replied.

I sat down and gazed at her shoes, which were now sitting on the table. When I picked them up I could smell the lingering perfume of her scented feet. Val blushed and looked at Bill.

"If I do, it'll cost you fifty bucks, Billy," she said.

"Okay, love, you're on!" was his retort.

A short while later, I went over to the bandleader and made a request. Val slipped her shoes back on to go to the ladies' room. She returned to the table just as the song I'd requested began. It was one of Val's favorite songs, and she asked Bill to join her on the dance floor.

She soon left him on the floor and headed toward the over-crowded bar. I was wanking myself, discreetly at the table. Billy slid back into his chair.

Val climbed awkwardly onto the bar, shoes and all, amid the deafening rock 'n' roll. The crowd cheered her. Her body was incredibly sexy. She gyrated her hips and played with her cunt through the sheer material of her dress.

My eyes were hazy with booze as I watched eager hands paw at her legs and feet. She lifted her feet to willing hands, and the straps of her shoes were quickly unbuckled. Then her shoes were gone! My dick was hard and red as Val dipped her right foot into a mug of beer. She lifted it out, dripping, and someone sucked on it.

She turned, squatted on the bar and pulled down the zipper in the back of her dress. She stood and slowly, very slowly, let her dress slide down her body until it puddled on the bar. Christ! Now her boobs were revealed, her big, brown nipples visible through her sheer bra.

Val's eyes were closed, her face was gleaming with perspiration and her hands were working on the waistband of her hose. "Take 'em off!" someone in the corner shouted. Val complied.

I couldn't believe it. My Val was standing on a bar clad in only a bra and panties. I staggered toward the bar, my prick still in my hand, trying to get to her through the crowd. I wanted to fuck her right there on the bar. Her shoes were drenched in a puddle of beer. Her nylons were on the floor in shreds. I picked them up and sniffed the crotch. I could detect the aroma of her cunt. The toes smelled sweaty and were sticky from beer.

The atmosphere was heavy with smoke, booze and the scent of sex. I looked up at her just in time to see her bra disappear into the crowd. Her beautiful boobs were bouncing around and her nipples were erect.

A guy next to me at the bar had poured sherry over her left foot and was licking it off her toes. Val reacted by putting her toes in his mouth. "Suck my toes, love. Come on!" she urged.

She seemed to be in a trance as her legs were caressed by many hands. Her white panties were still on when Val did the unexpected. She sat on the edge of the bar with her legs stretched out in front of her, her feet touching one guy on the nose and another on his hairy chest.

"You all want to fuck me, don't you?" she teased.

A resounding "Yes!" was the answer.

"Before I show you what I've got, you've got to make love to my legs and feet. Drive me wild," she instructed, "while the music lasts."

The crowd went mad. Val sat on the bar, visible from the waist up, leaning back on her arms, her legs stretching out into the crowd.

Her feet and toes were kissed and sucked, pricks were rubbed between her toes and come flew through the air. Her feet pressed against chests, pricks and faces.

When the music stopped, the action slowed. Val beckoned a young blond guy to her. "Drop 'em," she instructed, pointing to his pants with her foot. Hesitantly he did as she wanted. His tool was pink and large. She held it between her feet and started to masturbate him. The crowd hushed as the young guy squirmed and moaned. Val stopped and instructed. "Now take mine down." The crowd cheered as he obliged.

She took her panties and threw them at Bill, who put them in his pocket as a souvenir. "Come here," she said, pointing at him. "Get up here and fuck me!"

Bill's cock was bigger than I expected. When he sat on the bar, Val took his massive tool in her hands and began rubbing it enthusiastically. Then she lay down, her legs wide open, her cunt dripping wet.

Bill climbed atop her and entered her. He came within seconds.

I walked closer and stroked the soles of her feet. Bill was still inside her. He bent his head and began sucking her nipples. She wrapped her legs around him and crossed her ankles behind Bill's ass.

"Fuck me! Suck me! Harder, harder!" she urged. Her hands clutched at his back and her toes curled in intense passion as their bodies moved together.

When it was over, Val yelled and screamed with her climax. Bill sat up, his softening prick dripping with her juices. I helped her from the bar and we collected her clothes from the floor, except for her panties and her nylons, which were never found. For the rest of the night Val danced with me barefoot, which kept me horny all night long. And when we got home that night, we had a lovemaking session that lasted until the wee hours of the morning. I think we'll be going out for dinner more often now.—*T.K., London, England* ○╍▄

NEW GIRLFRIEND GIVES CRASH
COURSE IN CROSS-DRESSING

I just finished reading a letter about cross-dressing, and it was so good I had to sit down and write my own. I am male, age thirty-one. I have had the urge to wear women's clothing for years.

It wasn't until two years ago that this urge returned stronger than ever. I met a very understanding woman, with whom I now live. I told her of my fetish, adding that I could feel this desire to cross-dress building inside me once again. At first Lynn laughed, but after I convinced her I was serious, she started to help me out.

She told me the first thing I had to do was find out my sizes. Out came the measuring tape. First we measured my bra size, next my dress size and finally my shoe size. Then we headed out to do some shopping. I'd always hated shopping in women's clothing stores because I always thought the women were staring at me, but this time I felt totally different. Even so, I was still a little nervous.

The first stop was a large department store, as their selection is usually best. Upon arriving in the lingerie section, my girlfriend said, "Well, what do you need first, Bertha?" I just stared at her quizzically.

"If you're going to wear women's clothing, you should have a woman's name," Lynn pointed out. I didn't argue with her logic as she picked up a sexy underwire bra and held it up to me.

With a little smile on her face she led us over to the panties. Lynn asked, "How many pairs would you like?" as she held up a pair of pink ones trimmed in lace.

I replied, "I'll need a pair for each day of the week." Since I wear a white uniform at work, Lynn picked out five white panties and two pink ones for the weekend.

Then she said, "What else do you need, Bertha? How about a dress?"

I'd never bought a dress before. The first one we saw was a pink evening gown. It was very soft and sexy, and it was partially see-through. Lynn asked if I liked it and, when I said that I did, told me to take it to the fitting room to try it on.

I was flustered but I went nonetheless.

I put it on and it felt great against my skin. I could tell in the mirror that it was a perfect fit. Just then Lynn came in. She agreed I should buy it and said it was time to pick out a pair of pumps.

I quickly changed and we headed over to the shoe department. By this time I could hardly speak. Trying on a dress in the ladies' section of a huge department store, and now this—what could be next?

A saleslady came over and said, "Yes, ma'am?" to Lynn.

Lynn replied, "My friend here needs some help."

I stuttered and finally managed to say that I wanted high heels. The woman asked, "In what size, sir?"

I told her size ten wide, and she went off to see what they had.

While she was gone, Lynn said, "See, that wasn't too bad, was it?" I just looked at her. Then Lynn got up and said, "I'll be right back. I've got to get you a slip for your new dress and some pantyhose."

Now my heart was pounding. How was I going to talk to the sales-lady without Lynn there? Despite my trepidations, the lady was soon back with three boxes of heels. "Sorry to keep you waiting, sir, but I really had to look to find anything in your size. Take off your shoes and put these on," she said, holding out a pair of nylon knee-highs. "You can't wear socks with high heels." She opened the first box and took out a pair of black patent-leather pumps with four-inch heels. "Try these on first."

I was totally embarrassed. Once I had them on, she said, "Stand up and walk around in them."

"No, it's okay," I sputtered. "They fit. I'll take them."

But the woman insisted I walk around in them first. Just then, Lynn returned with an armful of bags.

"How are we doing?" Lynn asked the saleslady.

"Oh, I think these fit him very nicely," she answered.

Lynn said to me, "Well, let's see you walk around in them." With a sigh I got up. Clearly I was not to be spared. I staggered around, finding out that it wasn't easy to walk on stilts.

Lynn commented, "Well, it looks like you need a little practice." I had to agree.

When I sat back down to change into my own shoes, I couldn't find them. "Okay, Lynn," I said, "where are my shoes?"

"Bertha, since you need practice wearing your heels, I had the saleslady throw your old shoes away," she said with a grin. I realized I was going to have to wear the high heels home. I searched Lynn's bags while she was paying for the heels, hoping she had lied about throwing my shoes away. I didn't find them, but I did find a blonde wig, makeup, a pink slip, a dozen pairs of pantyhose and a razor.

I was still looking when Lynn returned and said, "Let's go." I just sat there. Gesturing toward a few women nearby, Lynn said, "If you want to stay, Bertha, I'll introduce you to my friends over there." I quickly stood up and staggered along behind her. Tripping along, I tried to get used to my new shoes. Lynn gave me the bags and said that since they were mine, I should carry them.

Once we got home Lynn asked me to join her in the bathroom. Once there, she asked me to take off all my clothes while she poured my bubble bath. Taking my clothing away, she returned with the razor. "Into the tub," she instructed as she handed the razor to me. "A woman must take care of her appearance, so when I come back I shouldn't see a single hair left on your body below the shoulders."

"I should shave off all my hair?"

"Well, I suppose you can keep the hair around your penis and balls," she relented.

When she returned, I'd finished. Now I had no underarm hair, chest hair or leg hair left on me. Lynn led me to the bedroom, where I saw all my new finery laid out for me. She told me to get dressed and call her when I was done. With my cock standing erect, I began with the pink panties. Then I put on my new bra, pantyhose and slip, and finally the dress. The feeling of all that smooth material against my shaven body was fantastic. As I stood admiring myself in the mirror, Lynn came in with the wig and makeup.

"Sit down, Bertha," she said. "Now we're really going to have you looking like a woman." She carefully applied my makeup, and then put on the wig. All I needed now were some tits for the look to be complete. Lynn left for a few minutes and came back with two soft foam balls, which she stuffed into my bra.

Instantly I had the shape of a woman. I admired myself in the mirror while Lynn snapped some Polaroids. I couldn't believe I looked so good.

After taking a dozen pictures of me, Lynn said, "Well, Bertha, are you ready to go out on the town?"

"No, Lynn, I can't do that," I protested.

"Why not?"

"After all I went through today, I just can't," I told her.

Lynn smiled and said, "You know, I didn't believe you when you told me you were a cross-dresser. I figured the best way to find out was to take you shopping. You didn't *have* to try that dress on, or the shoes. I thought it would be fun to test you. And now that I see you all dressed up, I approve very much."

Lynn went through my bureau and threw away all my underwear.

She told me that I should wear only panties and camisoles whenever I go out. She also requested that I shave my body regularly and wear pantyhose every day. She promised me that if I did as she asked, she would take me shopping with her and buy me all the nice things I needed. I quickly answered, "Yes, Lynn, that's a wonderful idea!"

From that day on Lynn has kept me supplied with all the lingerie a man like me could ask for.—*B.D., Dayton, Ohio*

THE ONLY THING BETTER THAN A NURSE IN UNIFORM IS WEARING IT YOURSELF

I've always had a thing for uniforms. Maybe that's why I married a nurse. Tracy's starched white uniform really turns me on, and her long legs in white stockings always get me hot and bothered. The only problem is that she works nights, and our schedules make it hard to find time together in bed.

The night shift does have its advantages though. There have been many mornings when I've been awakened by an angel in white standing alongside the bed.

One of the games we have developed over the years happens on mornings like these. She pretends I'm a patient, telling me it's time for my rubdown. Tracy reaches out, unbuttons my pajamas and starts to rub my body, slowly and sensually.

Just as if I were one of her patients, she explains just what she is about to do. "Good morning, Mr. Smith, it's time for you to get up," or, "Mr. Smith, it's time for your sponge bath." I'm always Mr. Smith on these occasions, and she is always Nurse Jones.

I look up at her beautiful tits encased in the virginal white of her uniform and watch them jiggle as she presses her hand into my body. She works her way down my body and snaps open my fly, revealing my semierect cock. With a smile she begins a massage of my member, and I am soon aroused and pointing skyward. Fumbling off her pantyhose, she leaves her uniform on as she climbs on the bed and impales herself on my rigid cock. Her long, lean legs flex, raising her delectable body up and down, and I watch her tits bounce each time she slides down my pole. I reach out and unbutton the front of her uniform but I'm frustrated by the heavy fabric of her bra, built for support and not for sex.

"Nurse Jones, there seems to be something covering your lovely tits this morning," I say.

"Of course, Mr. Smith. A professional must wear the proper clothing at all times," is her usual response.

Still, I locate her nipples and gently tweak them each time they come within reach. I can feel her juices dripping down on my balls as she continues to ride my peter, smiling down at me and asking if I approve of my therapy. I very much approve and tell her so, praising her medical abilities. I can feel the coolness of the air as she slides up off my cock and the incredible warmth each time her slippery slit engulfs me. Soon that familiar feeling starts to build, and I spray my white seed deep into her white-sheathed body, grunting and clenching my fists as I pound on the bed in orgasm. When I have finished, she sits still for a moment and then, rising gracefully, sits on my face for her reward. I greedily reach out with my tongue and lick her cunt, tasting her womanhood and my come mixed together. I explore the many folds of her vagina, sliding my tongue into the myriad nooks and crannies of her cunt lips. Each time I probe into her slit I can feel her shudder in pleasure, and I am rewarded with a little spurt of my own sperm. Clutching her magnificent ass, I press her clit to my hungry mouth and suck her until she comes, trying desperately to keep my lips fastened to her as she writhes in orgasm. As she calms down, I release her from my embrace and tell her how much I love her.

But while the mornings can be a pleasure, she needs her sleep and I have to get ready for work. The nights without her are long and lonely. I don't remember when it first happened, but one day, while thinking about her, I tried on my wife's silky white pantyhose. They're too small for me, of course, but seeing them on me when I looked in the mirror was a real kick, and somehow I felt closer to my missing wife. I suppose it was inevitable, but one night I fell asleep before I had taken them off. I awoke to feel her unbuttoning my pajamas and blearily realized I was still wearing her pantyhose. There was nothing I could do about it.

I could tell she was surprised. Her hands stopped as she went to free my cock for its therapy. Deeply embarrassed, I tried to sink into the bedclothes.

"Mr. Smith, there seems to be something covering your lovely cock this morning." Pulling down my pajama bottoms, she uncovered her white nurses pantyhose encasing my crotch. "Mr. Smith, I had no idea you wanted to be a nurse," she said. "You haven't told your wife about this, have you?"

I was dumbfounded. I didn't know what to say but stammered out something about taking them off right away.

To my complete surprise she replied, "Oh no, Mr. Smith. I think perhaps you need a new kind of therapy." With that, Tracy slid the elastic waistband of the pantyhose down past my cock and quickly sucked my flaccid member into her mouth. It didn't take long for her ministrations to overcome my embarrassment, and I felt myself growing in her mouth as she sucked on my cock with gusto. Soon she was sliding her lips up and down my prick while stroking my balls through the white nylon. I forgot everything except the circle of fire rising and falling on my rigid prick, and blasted a load of come into her as she sucked me dry. Removing her lips from my spent member, she lifted her skirt and tore out the crotch of her pantyhose. "Seeing as you like them so much, I won't take mine off either," she said. "It's my turn now, Mr. Smith!"

Pulling aside the skimpy panties she wore underneath her hose, I began to finger her cunt, playing with the hair that protruded through the jagged opening in her lovely white stockings. I slid my finger over her outer lips, outlining them and brushing lightly into the crack between them. I was really turned on by her impulsive actions and began to rub her clit through her pantyhose. Soon she was grinding her crotch against my hand as I rubbed her, pumping her hips and crying out, "Harder, Mr. Smith, harder!" I obliged, and she came with a roar. With a guilty look at the clock, I left her smiling in bed as I quickly removed her pantyhose, dressed and headed to work.

I was very nervous coming home that evening, but Tracy was not at all put off by my behavior that morning. I explained how much her nurse's uniform turned me on, which made her laugh. To her it was just what she had to wear for her job. A funny look crossed her face as she told me not to worry. She said if her uniform turned me on it was all right. Perhaps she could come up with a new therapy for me.

I was relieved, to say the least. The evening passed much as usual, and she left for work early that night. The following day was Saturday, so I puttered around the house as quietly as I could to keep from waking her. She arose about noon, which was unusual, and said she couldn't sleep anymore. To my surprise she had put on her uniform. She asked me to go out to her car and bring in the box in the trunk.

As I returned with the box, she greeted me with, "Good afternoon, Mr. Smith. I'm glad you arrived on time for your therapy session." So that was to be the game. "Please follow me, Mr. Smith."

She led me to the bathroom and said, "Please put the box on the sink and remove your clothes, Mr. Smith." I complied as she began to fill the tub. Following her instructions, delivered in a cool, professional voice, I climbed in the tub and was scrubbed quickly, impersonally and professionally. Tracy then shaved my face and drained the tub, but instead of telling me to get out she lathered my legs and started to shave them. By this time I had some idea of what she had in mind and enthusiastically cooperated with her. She rinsed me off, toweled me dry and opened the box.

Breaking her character as the cool, professional nurse, she said, "I borrowed a few things from my coworkers for your therapy. I hope you like them." She handed me a pair of plain white panties and told me to put them on. I did so. Next came a garter belt and white support stockings. "I thought these might be better than pantyhose, considering that you're built different than the average nurse. Do you know how hard it is to find stockings and garters these days? I hope you appreciate this," she said. I did, and told her so. I was taken aback as she handed me a utilitarian white bra. I hadn't figured on things going this far. With a look of exasperation she said, "Come on, Nurse Smith, you have to go on duty and you have no time to dilly-dally." Nurse Smith?

I held out my arms and she slipped on the bra, expertly fastening it around my chest. Out came two pliable bags of saline solution, which she inserted into the cups of my bra. Then she produced a slip and a nurse's uniform, one of her wigs and even a white nurse's cap. My own white sneakers completed the outfit. There in the bathroom mirror were two nurses, one taller and definitely scruffier than the other, but two nurses nonetheless.

I couldn't believe what was happening—my own wife had dressed me as a nurse. I had fantasized about this, but hadn't mentioned a word of it to her. I guess I should have had more faith in Tracy. She is always willing to try something new, and her years as a nurse have inured her to shock. She stepped back and scanned me from head to toe. "You'll do, Nurse Smith. At least for now. If you find it comfortable here at nursing school, I'll help you perfect your image in the future."

The day passed all too quickly. In my white uniform I helped with the housework, made the bed (with hospital corners, of course), played a game of cards and helped cook dinner. Tracy decided we should eat on the deck and, although I was nervous about leaving the sheltering walls of the house, I agreed. We live in the country with no close neighbors, but I was still a little apprehensive. After supper Tracy stood up and said, "It's time for my dessert."

To my astonishment she came over, knelt at my feet and lifted up my skirt. Drawing aside the white panties, she began to suck my cock. I was floored. What if someone came and saw us? What if . . . I soon forgot the "what ifs" as my prick grew under her attentions. There I was, a man in a nurse's uniform sitting out on my deck while being sucked off by another nurse. It was great. I loved every minute of it. I couldn't see my prick because of the jutting boobs on my chest, so I had to follow the action by touch. Not hard to do, as every little sensation was driving me wild. As my member stood straight out she began to tease it, just running her tongue lightly over my balls and cock, keeping me hard but not getting me off. She would concentrate on my balls, nibbling, licking and sucking, first one, then the other.

My pecker flagged with this attention to my balls, but before it could sag too much she latched onto the tip of my cock and slid her lips slowly and sensually down my pole, her tongue flicking at my manhood. As she slid her mouth back toward the tip, I felt the suction drawing my come from deep inside my body. With each breath I felt the tightness of the bra around my chest, and my eyes saw only the pure white of our uniforms. With exquisite slowness, she moved her mouth over my aching cock, sucking expertly, sending ripples of delight through my body. I felt the tightness in my balls that signals imminent release, but she must have felt it too: suddenly my pole was hanging all alone in the cool evening air.

Without a word she rose and seated herself on the edge of the deck and spread her legs. I know a hint when I see one, and I quickly descended the porch stairs. When she pulled back her skirt to reveal her bare cunt, I raised my own skirt and plunged my pecker deep into her. I held my position, crotch against crotch, and leaned over to kiss her. I withdrew my penis and, after a second of suspense, plunged back in and began to fuck her for all I was worth.

It was a strange and exciting feeling to be wearing a nurse's uniform, to feel the weight of the ersatz boobs on my chest as I rammed my manhood deep into her slit. I savored the subtle pull of the garters and stockings as I flexed my butt and drove my pecker home. Her warmth surrounded my cock over and over. I could hear the slight sucking sound as I pulled out, and her moans of lust as I pushed in again. Orgasm took her suddenly, her eyes wide open, staring at my white-clad body. "Fuck me! I want you to keep fucking me forever!" she yelled. "Don't stop! Oh God!"

After that nothing was intelligible, but I kept on fucking her. I felt as if I could keep this up for hours, driving my aching prick deeper and deeper into her cunt, savoring the rush of sensation as I penetrated her and the moment of coolness as I withdrew. Her moans rose in pitch and she again climaxed around my probing prick, clenching her muscles as the orgasm overcame her. With that I felt my balls tighten to propel my juices into her wet hole and I blew my own load, pumping spurt after spurt of sperm into her. As my sperm filled her, I kept pumping my pole until I was no longer able to keep it up.

I stood there, outdoors in the twilight, dressed in white, with my pecker inside my wife, holding her as much for support as for affection. She smiled up from the cedar planks of the deck and said, "Nurse Smith, you are one hell of a lover, but you look funny without your hair and cap!" I'd totally failed to notice that I'd lost my wig in my exertions, and it lay there at my feet.

"Nurse Jones," I replied, "I don't give a damn!"—*Name and address withheld*

Part Two

Letters to
Penthouse XIV

Three-for-All

**THEY TOOK A TRIP TO ATLANTIC CITY, AND HIS
WIFE TOOK A GAMBLE ON ANOTHER WOMAN**

*M*y wife Brenda and I have been married for fifteen years. Brenda is now forty years old, five-foot-four inches tall and one hundred fifteen pounds. She goes to the gym twice a day, and though she's not a body-builder, she has one of the best bodies around. She's also very good-looking, and has always been flirty, both with men her own age and with younger guys. She's a very hot lady, even though the only person she's had sex with is me! I started fucking her at a very early age, and have kept on fucking her and loving it.

Occasionally Brenda and I fantasize about her getting it on with another woman. It has always been something I wanted to see, and she always said that maybe someday it would happen. We recently went to Atlantic City, and weren't in our hotel room fifteen minutes when Brenda said, "Okay, let's do this right now!"

It only took about two seconds for me to get a phone book and call a local escort service. They told me the young lady would be there in an hour. Brenda was very excited. She came over to me and told me to stick my hand down her panties to see how wet she was. Her pussy was soaking wet, and her panties were soaked also. She was ready, and so was I!

The lady arrived on time and told us her name was Crystal. She was attractive, with long blonde hair and nice tits. Crystal also mentioned that she was a student fucking her way through college.

Brenda and Crystal both took their clothes off as I sat down in a chair to watch. When Brenda came over to me and started sticking her tongue down my throat, I knew she was very excited and ready to go. Crystal walked up to Brenda and started rubbing her tits from behind, grinding herself against her ass. Man, what a sight! Brenda then lay down on the bed and Crystal started sucking her pussy and rubbing her tits.

I picked up our videocamera and asked Crystal if she minded if I filmed her. She said it was okay as long as I didn't get her face on film. So there I was, filming this girl licking my wife's pussy, while Brenda pushed her hips up into her face. There was pussy juice all over Crystal's face. I knew I was one lucky fucker to be able to see this.

Brenda had said earlier that she didn't think she could do anything to the girl, but she did suck on Crystal's big tits and finger-fuck her pussy. She also let Crystal suck my dick while she did it.

It ended with Crystal filming Brenda and me, with Brenda on her hands and knees on the bed and me taking her doggie-style from behind. When I looked over at Crystal I saw that her hand was rubbing her pussy as she filmed us fucking. Then Brenda rolled over on her back and started playing with her vibrator, asking me to shoot my come on her pussy which I did with pleasure.

Afterwards Brenda said it had been fun and that she would gladly do it again. I found a swinging couple on the Internet who live not far from us, and we set up a date. I'm hoping that this time I will get to see Brenda eating pussy, and even sucking some strange cock!—*G.F., Hartford, Connecticut* ⊶▪

THE SILKY BLONDE IN THE BAR HAD EYES FOR THE WIFE, BUT TOOK ON THE HUSBAND TOO

*T*he silky blonde sitting across the room, with the brown eyes and swollen, pouty lips, had caught my husband's eye, but it wasn't him she was looking at with interest. It was me.

"You're a sexy, delicious man," I told him, "but she's giving me the eye."

"What?" He couldn't believe it. He looked at her again, shooting her his best you-know-you-want-me stare. No dice. She turned to me and gave me a shy but knowing chin-down, eyes-up gaze. "Damn!" Glen said.

I'd never been with a woman before, but was up for the experience, as long as Glen was there. I knew he would love it. I smiled at him, then picked up a cocktail napkin and put it between my lips, closing my mouth on it so that my lipstick left an imprint on the flimsy scrap of paper. Then I summoned the waitress over to us and asked her to bring the napkin, along with a fresh vodka martini, to the pouty seductress at the far table.

They say it's not so much how it's given, but how it's accepted that matters. Well, if that's the case, she did fine. She swiveled her chair to face us, sat up straight and spread her legs wide, her full black cotton dress riding up over her knees. She reached under the dress, pulled her panties aside and pressed my "kiss" to her bare pussy.

I stared for a moment, then, smiling slyly, looked over at Glen. He had sucked in his breath, his eyes wide. He turned to me in hopeful anticipation of what I might do. I looked back at the blonde and made a gesture with my thumb toward Glen, then turned it back toward me. The meaning was plain: both of us. The blonde hesitated for a second, and then nodded. We were in. With a red-nailed finger I beckoned her to come to us. She glided across the room until she stood only inches from me. "Lenore," she whispered.

"Rhonda," I replied. "And this is Glen." My hand slipped into hers, and we were on our way. As we walked out to our car, I couldn't help but wonder if the napkin with my lip-print on it was still up there next to her pussy.

We drove to a motel outside of town. As soon as we were inside the room Glen pressed us both against the door, one knee between Lenore's legs, the other between mine, and kissed us one at a time. As he stepped back we slid to the floor, tearing at our clothes. I tried to stand, but Lenore grabbed at my dress. As I fell to the floor, laughing, she tried to crawl past me to the bed. I grabbed her ankle and with one motion pulled her to me and slid her dress up, burying my face in her white-lace panties. She arched her back and I pulled the lace aside for my first taste of her. I gave her a gentle lick, then slid my tongue inside for a soft, sensual savoring of her sexual essence. My hands slid from her ass and up to her back and then to her hair, while I lost myself in the sensation of an unending pussy-kiss.

When I stopped for a breath I looked up to see Glen's face watching me in awe. He was naked and stroking himself. Damn, his cock looked so big! "Fuck me," I breathed. He knelt behind me, and I held my breath as he pushed himself in deep.

When Glen's cock was in me, I slid Lenore's panties off. Her face was scrunched up with pleasure. I began to lick her clit as my fingers explored her wet pussy. She sucked in her breath, pressing herself to my face. My chin pressed firmly against her crotch as I again dug my tongue deep inside. She was so tasty and slippery I couldn't stop. Oh God, I thought, was this what I felt like, tasted like, when I came in Glen's mouth? I wondered if I would feel it when she climaxed.

Yes! Her pussy started to contract and pulse. I dragged my tongue in a circle around her silky tunnel, then drew it out to flick her clit. I licked it broadly with the flat of my tongue as she spasmed, crying out her pleasure.

As her orgasm diminished I moved slowly upward, kissing her stomach, licking her navel, so lost in her sensuality that I barely noticed that Glen's cock was no longer inside me. I stopped to nuzzle at her warm breasts, then brought my lips to her mouth. Pressed together, we rolled across the carpet, kissing deliciously, eyes closed, clinging tightly, wrapping our legs around each other. Our hands never stopped searching, caressing and grabbing. I was drunk with these new sensations.

I ended up on my back, with Lenore on top of me. Now she slid down to taste me. Glen put a pillow under my head and, still holding his cock, knelt to kiss me passionately. Lenore was kneeling also, her ass in the air, her hands holding my hips as her red lips drew out my desire. Glen knelt behind her and licked her dripping pussy, reaching around her to cup her big, hanging tits in his hands. Her hips swayed and her back arched, her moan stifled against my wet pussy.

Glen slid his fingers inside her. At least one of them went into her ass, which seemed to drive her over the edge. The sensations he was giving her were being passed on to me. Her tongue, her lips, her sensuous mouth were working passionately on my crotch, enjoying me, tasting me, sending me into orbit. "Oh, God, I'm coming! I'm coming!" I yelled. And I did, all over her face.

Glen's fingers slid out of her and massaged her creamy ass. When she crawled up my body to kiss me with her glistening smile, he moved between my legs, his cock feeling bigger than ever before as he slipped it into me. His wild grunting told me that he was about to come.

"I want to see it," Lenore moaned, swinging herself off me. "Let me see it!" Pulling out just in time, he squirted his come across my stomach and breasts.

Lenore turned around to straddle my face. As my tongue circled her clit and delved into her pussy, she bent down, pressing herself against my come-dappled body to bring her mouth between my widespread thighs. Glen sat there on the floor, his hands caressing my legs as he watched us in this 69 position. With an intense interest, he watched her pleasure me, watched my pussy tighten around her pink tongue, watched her finger slide in and out of my clutching ass. His cock swelled up again, hard and throbbing. He knelt in front of her face and she raised her mouth from my crotch to take him deep into her throat. Then she slid her mouth off him, her hand moving his cock down toward my pussy. He began to fuck it again, and as he slid in and out of me Lenore's tongue laved his shaft, tasting the juices he was drawing out of me. Meanwhile her pussy was writhing against my outstretched tongue. My husband was fucking me, our sweet, silky blonde pickup was licking his dick, and I was lapping her pussy. All three of us were moaning loudly.

Under the double stimulation of my clutching pussy and Lenore's eager tongue, Glen was the first to come. I felt his hot juices squirting into me, a sensation that always excites me. I sucked frenziedly on the pussy in my mouth as I climaxed again and again, and I felt her shudders as she, too, spun into orgasm. It was utter bliss, total, time-stopping passion. Every sense was on fire. We finally collapsed into a tangled mass and slept hard.

When I woke up she was gone.—*R.G., Galena, Illinois* ⊶◾

WHEN HUBBY'S AWAY, THIS NAVY WIFE PIPES A COUPLE OF OTHER SAILORS ABOARD

*T*his experience took place some time back, but it's still as vivid in my mind today as when it first happened.

I was a naval officer, stationed at the base in San Diego. One evening my good friend and fellow officer Chuck and I decided to take a room at a hotel in the city to get away from the base. We checked into our room and proceeded to the dining room for dinner and a few drinks. The place was crowded, and we had to wait at the bar for a table.

As we sat there we looked over the crowd and noticed a very attractive blonde lady sitting by herself. At one point she glanced over at us and saw us watching her. To my surprise, she got up and started toward us.

I guessed that she was about twenty-five. She had on a sheer white silk blouse that accentuated her breasts, which must have been about 36D, and a tight skirt that melted into her luscious hips and stopped a few inches above the knee. She was about five feet nine, with a narrow waist and very shapely legs.

She came directly over to us and asked if we knew anything about the flights coming into the naval base that evening from overseas. It seemed she was supposed to meet her husband, who was flying in from Japan, but he hadn't arrived. I told her that all the overseas flights had already arrived, and the next flights wouldn't be coming in until around seven o'clock the next morning.

She seemed very disappointed as she thanked us. Then she asked if we were waiting for a table, and when we said yes she invited us to join her for dinner. We gladly accepted, and went to her table. She introduced herself as Jenna, and told us she had flown in from Chicago to meet her husband. As it happened, I was from Chicago also, and it turned out we had gone to the same school, although at different times.

That kind of broke the ice, and we settled in and ordered drinks. Jenna was very pleasant. She said she appreciated our company, as it would be a long night for her, waiting for tomorrow's flight. She told us she hadn't seen her husband in over seven months, since he had been deployed to Japan.

When dinner was over Jenna said she should be going back to her room, and thanked us for the dinner and the company. We offered to walk her to her room, which coincidentally turned out to be right next to ours. As we were saying good night a thought hit me. I told her that Chuck and I had planned to hit a few bars that night, and I wondered if she would like to join us. She said that would be fine, as it would help her to pass the time. She just needed a few minutes to freshen herself up.

We knocked on her door ten minutes later, and the three of us went out to a club, had a couple of drinks and watched the floor show, then went on to another bar. Jenna was very animated, a good listener and very pleasant to be around.

Finally, as it was getting late, we decided to go back to our rooms. As we unlocked our doors, she thanked us for being such good company, saying that she had really enjoyed herself, and offered her hand to say good night.

On impulse, I took her hand and pulled her up close to me, then planted a kiss on her mouth. She stiffened for a minute, and then kind of relaxed and melted into my arms. I felt her shudder and tremble. I asked her if she wanted to come into our room for a while. She hesitated a moment, breathing rapidly, and then said, "What the hell, sure. What he doesn't know won't hurt him."

As we went through the door she turned to meet me, putting one arm on my shoulder and giving me a long, slow French kiss. At the same time I felt her other hand on my crotch. She pulled down my zipper, reached in and got hold of my cock. She started to manipulate it, and it reacted immediately to her hot hand, becoming erect. Jenna said it had been seven months since she had held one of those, and she went down on it like a starved dog after a bone.

She was cooing and murmuring about how lovely it was as she rubbed her lips over it, then started licking it and stroking it with her hand at the same time. Next she fluttered her tongue over the glans and along the underside, all the time moaning and cooing. Then she put it in her mouth, deep-throating it and then withdrawing it very slowly, still holding it in her stroking fingers.

Chuck had been standing and watching with a stunned look on his face. Jenna looked over at him. "Don't just stand there," she said breathlessly. "Come over here and join us."

Chuck was out of his clothes in a flash, and his cock was at full attention. He approached her from behind as she crouched on her knees, working on my cock like there was no tomorrow. He raised her skirt, and I think we were both surprised to see that she had no panties on. (Later she told us that had been in anticipation of the meeting with her husband.) Chuck was going to plug into her, but she stopped him, saying, "Wait, it's not ready yet. Get on your back and let me straddle you so you can get me good and ready."

Chuck was only too glad to comply. She sat on his face and continued working my cock over big-time, until I knew it wouldn't be long before I would explode. Chuck was really lapping her twat, and she was twisting and turning and moaning, saying, "Yes, oh yes!" around my cock. I was ready to put my whole load down her throat. I started spurting and she took it all, gulping it down eagerly. When I was done she asked me to take her blouse off and play with her tits. As I did she went wild, squirming and throwing her head back, shaking it from side to side, rotating her hips and grinding her pussy into Chuck's face. "I'm coming!" she cried. "Rub my tits hard!" Then she shrieked as she had her first orgasm of the night. But it was far from the last.

As she recovered her breath I pulled off all my clothes, and then hers. Chuck was already naked. At Jenna's suggestion we shoved the two single beds togther. "I want to 69 with Chuck," she said, "and you can get ready to fuck me from behind." She was a take-charge person and knew exactly what she wanted, and we were more than willing to oblige.

Soon Chuck was lying on his back with Jenna's pussy draped over his mouth and his pole deep in her throat. Chuck was going wild, not having come yet this evening. I was sure he wouldn't last very long, the way she was throating him. I eased up behind her, spread her cheeks and put my now fully recovered cock at the entrance to her pussy. It was very slick with Chuck's saliva, and with her own orgasmic juices. As I started to slide into her, she shifted her hips to better accommodate me. Even with all the lubrication she was still tight. I had to ease it into her cunt slowly, inch by glorious inch. Then all of a sudden I felt Chuck's tongue lapping at the underside of my dick. It was something I had never experienced before, and I reacted by thrusting hard and driving my cock all the way home with one final plunge. I heard Jenna's gasp of pleasure as it hit bottom.

Chuck started coming then, yelling as he shot his jism into her gasping, gulping mouth. I was reaming her for all I was worth. Her cunt was like velvet. It felt like she had little fingers inside it that grasped and released my pumping shaft. She really knew how to fuck! I knew I wasn't going to last much longer the way things were going. Her ass was rotating and thrusting in time with my strokes. She was squirming and moaning and crying, "Yes! Yes! Yes, it's so good, don't stop!" I could feel her tightening and trembling, building up for a big one, and I wasn't going to be far behind. All of a sudden she squealed and shrieked, "Yes! Oh yes, right there! Fuck it harder! Fuck it harder! Fuck it harder!" And she exploded, and I spewed like a volcano inside her twisting, squirming cunt.

We lay in the afterglow for a few minutes. Then Chuck started to play with Jenna's tits, his erection coming back to full bloom. He rolled her onto her back and mounted her as I watched. He was soon fucking her wildly, thrusting long and deep, and she was responding, saying, "Yes, it's so good, oh it's so good, drive it in hard, do it faster, yes!" Then she was spasming and shaking, moaning, "Yes! Yes!" She clamped her legs around Chuck's waist, her heels drumming on his ass. With each thrust she pulled him into her with her legs, forcing him deeper. She was pumping her hips like a wild woman, their pelvic bones grinding together, and I could hear the slushing sound of her juices. Chuck's eyes were rolling as he started to come again, and Jenna was thrashing her head from side to side, almost howling as she joined him in orgasm.

Chuck rolled off her then, and we all cuddled up and went to sleep. It was about six-thirty in the morning when I felt something playing with my dick. It was Jenna. She was lapping on it, getting it hard and ready for another go-round.

All of a sudden there was a noise from next door. Jenna stopped licking me and said, "Oh my god, somebody just opened the door of my room."

Chuck got up and stuck his head out of our door. When he came back he reported that he'd seen a man coming out of her room and heading for the hotel office. "Oh god, it must be my husband!" Jenna said. His flight must have come in early. She grabbed one of our towels and wrapped it around herself, then picked up her shoes and clothes and ran out. The walls between the room were thin, and we could hear her shower running. It had just stopped when we heard her husband coming back. Not more than five minutes after that we heard the bed squeaking rhythmically.

Chuck and I turned to each other, grinning and said it in

unison, "What he doesn't know won't hurt him!"—*P.Y., Seattle, Washington* ⊙┰▪

SHE CALLS HER HUSBAND'S BLUFF AND LETS HIM WATCH HER WITH A YOUNG LOVER

I'm a thirty-five-year-old female executive with a large international corporation based in the southwest. Although I do not have huge tits, I do have a nice, firm ass which goes well with my five-foot-five, one-hundred-ten-pound frame.

One of my husband's fantasies has long been to see me go to bed with another man. I have always been resistant to this idea because I was afraid of the long-term consequences. But one night my husband and I had an argument, and in the heat of the moment I told him that a lot of men found me attractive and he should accept me for who I was, as they all did. Zach responded angrily that if I could do better than him, and find a guy that accepted me, then I should go to him. Well, little did he know that I already had one! His name was Brad, and he worked in my office. And now I decided to let Zach meet him.

About two weeks went by, and one Friday morning I was ready to set my plan in motion. I called Zach at his law office and told him to watch for a fax I was sending him. I said he should do what the fax said, and trust me. In the fax I informed him that I had arranged for the kids to spend the night at my parents, and that he should meet me at a certain local watering hole at seven o'clock that evening. I asked him not to approach me there, but to wait for further developments.

Brad and I left the office together, but not before I changed out of my conservative working outfit and into something a little more sexy. We got to the place around six-forty-five and took a seat at the bar. I spotted Zach almost immediately at the other end of the bar. When he saw me with Brad his jaw dropped, and his eyes showed his surprise and shock—and, yes, no small amount of excitement.

Brad and I ordered drinks and spent the first hour chatting and discussing the office and our work. Then Brad had to use the rest room. While he was gone I unbuttoned a couple of buttons on my blouse, revealing my cleavage and the top of my pink lace demi-bra. Immediately upon returning to his seat Brad commented on my boldness, and I replied, "You ain't seen nothing yet!"

Although Zach and Brad did not know one another, they were both watching my tits, along with some of the other men at the bar. One man even bought me a drink and expressed interest in me, which turned me on even more. After a few more drinks Brad wanted to go to a different bar, one that we often frequented together. I told him I had to use the rest room, and on the way there I grabbed a napkin and wrote the name of the place where we were going. As I came back I walked by Zach's stool and casually dropped the note beside him.

As we drove to the next spot I grabbed Brad's hand and placed it on my crotch, gently moving it back and forth against my cunt. While he was massaging my hole I could feel the juices flowing from my pussy and being absorbed into the crotch of my panties. By the time we got to the bar I was wet, excited and horny. Once inside, we ordered drinks and I awaited Zach's arrival. Within a few minutes, Zach walked in the door and took a seat at a table near the dance floor. After a minute I grabbed Brad's hand and said I wanted to dance. By that time I was feeling no pain and was becoming bolder and bolder. Soon I was grinding myself into Brad and rubbing against his dick until he became as hard as a telephone pole. I casually danced us over to where my husband was sitting, and then grabbed Brad's hands and placed them on my tight ass. He gently kneaded my buttocks and began to kiss my neck as our bodies glided to the music. My thong panties were dripping as I put on a show for my husband with my unknowing boyfriend.

We spent another hour at the bar before I told Brad that I had a surprise for him. I told him that my husband was on a golf trip with his buddies, and that I had rented a room at a local hotel for the two of us to enjoy for the night. What I didn't tell him was that I had also rented the room adjoining, and that my husband was going to be in it.

Before we left I again excused myself to go to the ladies' room, and upon my return I gave Zach a note that I had prepared earlier in the day, along with a key to the hotel room. In the note I told him that his fantasy about seeing me make it with another guy was about to come true. I also said that if he didn't want to see it, he should go home and that I would see him the next day. Would he or wouldn't he, I wondered, take me up on my offer?

On the drive to the hotel, I teased Brad by massaging his stiff cock through his pants. By the time we got to the hotel he was about to blow his wad. Once we were in the room, Brad went into the john to freshen up, and I unlocked the door to the adjoining room. Zach had not yet arrived, and I began to think that, despite what he had always said he wanted, the thought of me with another man was too much for him. Maybe I had called his bluff.

As soon as Brad came out of the bathroom we embraced and went into a long passionate kiss. He eagerly caressed my breasts and slowly began to unbutton my blouse the rest of the way. As I began to undress him in turn, I heard the door to the adjoining room creak open, and then I knew that Zach had shown up after all, and that my husband was now watching me seduce my lover. That fact alone made me become even wetter, and I moaned with anticipation. Soon I had all of Brad's clothes off except for his briefs, and I asked him to kiss my breasts, positioning myself so that Zach would have a clear view of the action.

As Brad worked his way down my neck to my tits, I looked over at the door to the adjoining room. It was only open a crack, but I knew that my husband's eye was close behind it. Looking directly at him, I smiled, looked over to him and mouthed the words, "Enjoy the show."

Brad attempted to unhook my bra, but I stopped him, saying that I felt sexier with it on. Zach was a lingerie freak, and I knew that he would enjoy it more if I kept my lace bra and thong panties on throughout the evening.

Soon Brad was gently licking my navel and begging me to let him eat my pussy. Who was I to deny the man his pleasure? I slowly eased out of my tight jeans and allowed him to pull them off me. As I mentioned earlier, one of my best attributes is my ripe ass, which was accentuated by my pink thong panties. I climbed onto the bed and Brad got between my legs and began to suck my pussy lips through the silk garment. By then my cunt was sloppy-wet and my musky scent was heavy in the air. I had shaved my pussy that morning, as I knew that both Brad and my husband loved a very trim snatch.

Up to that point I had been making sure that Zach could see and hear everything that was going on, but once Brad began to eat my pussy I was oblivious to everything but my own pleasure. I have had my snatch eaten by several men in my life, but Brad was the hands-down winner when it came to getting me off that way. Pushing my panties to the side, my lover spread my outer lips apart with one hand, and with that same hand pulled back my clitoral hood, exposing my pink little clit to the ministrations of his mouth. After several minutes of nibbling, sucking and licking, he slipped a finger into my cunt and began to stroke my G-spot with a slow yet forceful pressure which soon had me wailing. I came and came, screaming as the force of my orgasm overwhelmed me in its own beautiful way.

Panting heavily, I pulled Brad up to me and began to stroke his long, hard cock. My other hand went down to my wet cunt, and as I jacked off my lover I proceeded to caress myself to another orgasm.

After I came again I looked over at the door, which had drifted open a bit more, and I could tell that my husband was jacking himself off with vim and vigor. Obviously Zach was not disappointed with my activities on this wonderful night.

Soon I was licking my stud's eight-inch tool while keeping an eye on Zach's reaction to my cocksucking. This is one activity that I didn't do very often, but tonight I wanted to make sure that I put on a wild show to prove to him that I was desirable to other men. Slowly I relaxed my jaw muscles, and little by little I took all of Brad's manhood in my mouth. In order to heighten the experience for my lover, I began to massage his anus, then slowly inserted a finger in his butthole. After a few moments Brad shot his wad in my mouth, and I eagerly swallowed every bit of his come with delight and pleasure.

Soon Brad got up and went to the bathroom. I quickly jumped out of bed and went over to the slightly opened door and my lusting husband. The first words out of his mouth were, "You're so hot! I want you now!" I told him he'd have to wait, because this was not his night. And with that I smiled and went back to the bed to await the return of my lover.

Once Brad rejoined me in bed I quickly got him aroused again, then pleaded with him to stick his dick in my wet cunt. Soon I was on my knees, facing my husband, as Brad pulled my thong to one side and slowly entered my cunt with his eager cock. Within seconds I was moaning and urging him to fuck me harder than he had ever fucked me before. As he rammed his cock into my hole I was able to watch Zach pounding his meat in unison. After several minutes of fucking me like a porn star, Brad announced he was going to come, and soon we both climaxed at the same time as he shot his hot jism into my squirming cunt.

I still wasn't finished. Within minutes I got him hard again, and I began to gently suck and lick his cock and balls. After a while he moaned that he was going to come again, so I took his dick out of my mouth and finished the job by hand, letting him shoot his wad on my tits and body.

As we lay resting in each other's arms I heard the door close softly, and I knew that Zach had finally had all he could stand for that night, even if I hadn't.

Early the next morning, as I drove home, I wondered what kind of reception I would get from my husband. Upon my arrival, I found him still asleep in bed. So I removed my still wet panties and placed them over his face, then crawled into bed and snuggled up to him. He woke up instantly and fucked me more passionately than he had in months. Afterwards he swore that he would never take me for granted again—as long as I continued to prove to him how attractive I could be to another man!—*F.V., Lexington, Kentucky*

THE TWO GIRLS WANTED HIM TO GET INTO SOMETHING COMFORTABLE, NAMELY THEM

*A*bout fifteen years ago I met a Cuban-American couple named José and Anita, with whom I became really good friends. After a few years I moved to another state and lost contact with them. Last November I moved back to Florida and found out that they had divorced a few years ago. I looked up Anita, and we went out partying together a few times, as friends. One weekend we were out at the county fair when we met up with a girlfriend of Anita's named Roseanne. After a few hours of drinking beer and Jell-O shots, we decided to go to Anita's house and carry on the party.

Anita was wearing a tight-fitting miniskirt and a silk blouse that showed off her perky little braless tits. Roseanne had on tight blue jeans and a white T-shirt you could almost see through. Both of them were about the same height, around five feet four, petite, dark-haired and brown-eyed. Anita was in her thirties and Roseanne about twenty-two.

When we got to Anita's house the girls decided they wanted to change into something more comfortable. I said that they looked perfectly edible just the way they were, so why change? They just giggled and disappeared into the bedroom.

After about five minutes they called to me from the bedroom, asking me to come in and to help them out. When I walked in, Anita had removed her skirt. Her blouse barely covered her crotch and her pretty little ass. Roseanne was in just her T-shirt and panties.

I stopped just inside the door, looking at them and feeling my cock getting stiff. Anita came over to me and said she thought I had too much clothing on, and that maybe I should get more comfortable too. As she started undoing my pants Roseanne came over, and I started kissing her and rubbing her firm ass. I slipped my right hand inside the back of her panties and worked my way down to her sweet little pussy. Anita got my pants down and began giving me a blow-job, and my knees felt wobbly. We ended up on the floor, with Anita's beautiful mouth around my cock and Roseanne's crotch in my face. Roseanne's pussy was sweet and small and nicely shaved. When she started coming in my mouth, Anita reached up to play with her tits. This made Roseanne come even harder.

After she regained some of her composure, they both got on their hands and knees, shaking their asses at me, and told me to take my pick. I chose Anita first, since I had known her longer and had often fantasized about her pretty little body. I crouched behind her and eased my cock into her soaking-wet pussy. Oh God, it felt so good! Roseanne crawled up under us and started licking my balls while I fucked Anita. Then Anita began licking Roseanne's pussy. Thank God for mirrors, because I got to watch her eating that pretty little pussy while I fucked her.

After a while we changed positions, and Anita got to have a good tongue lashing while I got my cock into Roseanne's tight little pussy. When I said I was going to come they both moved around and started licking and sucking on my cock. Anita didn't like to swallow, but Roseanne did, and she deep-throated my cock while I came.

We all fell asleep on Anita's bed, with me in the middle. The next morning I woke up with my cock in Roseanne's mouth, and we started all over again.—*L.K., Tuscon, Arizona* ⚷▪

HER LOVER'S FRIEND IS A MASSEUR, BUT SHE GETS RUBBED BY BOTH OF THEM

*I*t was the first day of June, but it certainly was not going to be a typical day. Jason, my lover, had persuaded me to take part in a conditional threesome with his friend Stan, the masseur. The condition was that Stan's participation would be limited to giving me a full-body massage, and complementing Jason's efforts to bring me pleasure. Jason told me that Stan would not actually have sex with me, or even remove his clothes. I didn't quite understand why Stan would agree to this, but Jason assured me that he was perfectly happy with the arrangement.

Jason and I began to undress in my bedroom as Stan set up his massage table in another part of the house. As we did so we kissed passionately, confirming our love for one another. Then we walked slowly down the hallway and into the room where Stan was waiting.

I was still wearing my panties. Stan never took his eyes off of me as I slowly slipped them down and off. There I stood, totally nude in front of two men for the first time in my life. I was almost as nervous as I was aroused. My emotions were mixed as Stan asked me to mount the table and lie down on my stomach.

Jason stood at a distance of about five feet while Stan's hands roamed gently over my body. I began to feel uncomfortable, until Stan invited Jason to join us. Jason walked over to the side of the table and gently touched me. I raised my head immediately and looked into his eyes, recognizing the message of assurance he was sending.

So there I lay on the table, naked in the presence of two men, one fully clothed and one beautifully nude. Two sets of eyes were wandering over my body, and two sets of hands caressed me. Jason leaned over and gave me a kiss, which relaxed me, and I surrendered fully to the exploring hands. Stan placed his hands side by side on my body, palms down, then moved them smoothly upward. His fingers fanned out, molding to the contours of my body. Expertly he caressed my flesh, leaving a trail of heat wherever he went.

Jason was also generating heat, and his very touch was making me wet. As he trailed his fingertips down over my sensitive skin, I reached out for his throbbing erection. I held it tenderly, then stroked it lovingly. I love to give this man head. I am totally mesmerized by his engorged cock. I started feeding it into my mouth, wrapping my lips around the shaft, swirling my tongue against the underside. The taste of him made my body tingle. I felt him grow even harder as I took him deep, and then deeper, in my mouth. I grabbed his balls with one hand and began to squeeze them gently. His cockhead felt enormous in my throat as I hungrily engulfed it. In a matter of seconds my lips were rising and falling on his ruddy shaft. Shortly thereafter I came. I came just from the excitement of what I was doing to his beautiful cock, doing it under the eyes of another man who was playing with my body. I was satisfying one man and entertaining another. How absolutely exciting!

Stan's hands were on my legs now. After I came he ran his hands slowly up my thighs to my ass cheeks and began to knead them as if he were kneading dough. He placed the heel of his hand between my buttocks and pushed, first in one direction, then the other. I purred noisily beneath his touch. I felt the excitement gathering between my legs again. The more Stan massaged my ass cheeks, the wider I spread my legs. As Jason watched, his hand slid seductively over my body in a warm caress. Jason felt between my legs and fondled my wet pussy, igniting my passion further, while Stan watched in turn.

Stan now asked me to turn onto my back. As I did I made eye contact with him, and a jolting surge of lust almost made me reach out and touch him. My tits were now on display to the worshiping eyes of two men. Jason began to caress my right tit as Stan started on the left. For a minute they continued, each of them massaging a breast and a swollen nipple. Then Jason took charge, caressing both of them reverently, then sucking each of them into his mouth. He then proceeded to take first one nipple, then the other between his lips, sucking gently. Instantly I came, kissing him wildly.

I lay there panting hard, sprawled on the table, seeing their eyes traveling down my tanned body. Stan put his hand on my leg and confidently moved it upward. He rubbed my inner thigh while Jason put his hand on my crotch. My clit was hard and throbbing like a second heartbeat. Jason parted my labia with his fingers and barely touched my trigger, and off I went into another moaning orgasm. Once I recovered, I spread my legs wider so he could take my pussy lips between his fingers, pulling them apart to expose my wet interior. As he fingered me I started shaking uncontrollably, feeling another climax inexorably approaching. I could see that Stan was startled by the intensity of my reaction. Each time Jason touched my hard clit, my hips would buck. Each time he played with my pussy, I would go crazy.

Stan was staring into the open folds of my pussy. As Jason paused and withdrew his hand, Stan's fingers brushed against my soft inner thighs. I spread my legs wider, inviting him to explore further. His hand slid nearer to my crotch and touched my swollen cunt lips, but then moved away. Stan was an effective tease. He would periodically apply pressure to my pussy, then move elsewhere. This tantalizing form of massage left me aroused and eager for more.

Stan continued to slide his hands over my body. I spread my legs even wider, and my knee encountered the hardness in Stan's trousers as he stood at the side of the table. I looked up into his face and saw his eyes devouring my body like a piece of chocolate cake. I was very turned on by his obvious arousal. He slid his hand up my thigh again, just brushing my muff and caressing my cunt lips. My legs were as far apart as they could get, but I tried to spread them still further as I felt his fingers stroking and probing through my trimmed red bush. I held my lips apart with my fingertips, showing him the slippery pinkness inside. Now Stan didn't move away; he cupped my breast with his other hand as he slid two fingers directly into my juicy channel. After a minute he retracted them and ran them up and down my slit, looking me square in the eye. I began to moan as he tweaked the wet folds of my vaginal lips, and when he rubbed my clit I felt the tingle of approaching climax. I gasped as his fingers entered my pussy again, and my hips started to gyrate as I fucked his hand. Soon I was jamming my pussy down on his hot hand with spastic thrusts. I was completely out of my senses. Animal noises escaped my lips. My legs flew straight up and I started jerking and thrashing through another screaming orgasm. That one was for Stan.

*   *   *

Jason had watched with pleasure, but it was he who was my lover, and now he meant to show it. I reached to embrace him as he climbed onto the table. He slid his knees between my thighs and placed his shaft at my open pussy. My cunt lips puckered up and kissed the head of his dick. Moving forward, he eased the gentle giant of his masculinity into my hungry furnace. As he did so, Stan slipped his hand between our bodies, his fingers strongly massaging my pussy. The feeling of lust that rippled through me as he rubbed my hot wet cunt, while Jason's long cock worked in and out of my soupy snatch, was beyond words. Jason rose and fell on me with long powerful strokes, hard enough to rock my entire body. Chills ran through me as he filled my pussy with his wonderful cock. I thought of how excited it must make Stan to think of my wet pussy, wrapped around Jason's cock, and that thought excited me even more.

Suddenly Jason slowed his powerful movements, and I moaned with disappointment as he withdrew from me. My lover really knows how to drive me over the edge. After a moment he reentered me, slowly this time, but I wouldn't have any part of that. I wanted every inch of his glorious cock buried in my hungry cunt. I locked my ankles around his muscular back and pulled him to me hard, until that big monster was once again buried inside me.

I filled my hands with the warm flesh of his ass cheeks. Jason has amazing staying power, and now he sent me through half a dozen climaxes while remaining hard as steel, while Stan watched intently, his hand still between our bodies, stroking my pussy lips and presumably Jason's cock as that magnificent instrument continued to fuck me rhythmically.

After yet another orgasm, Jason and I changed places. I straddled his recumbent form as he ran his hands gently up and down my body, circling my breasts and teasing my nipples. Stan came around the table and put his hands on my ass, kneading it as I moved rhythmically up and down on Jason's mammoth cock. Again and again I rose high on his shaft and then sank down with tremendous force. Jason's stomach muscles tightened and his ass rose off the table, pumping up forcefully to meet me. His cock was pulsating madly, sending messages of pleasure through my body. The muscles inside my cunt began to contort. Jason grabbed my waist and pulled me down on his hardness. I wanted to—no, I needed to—feel his hot seed rushing into me. "Come with me, baby," I panted. "Come with me." I fucked him hard and I fucked him fast, ramming myself down on his cock, taking it deeper with every stroke. I started rocking my pelvis, totally lost in giving and receiving pleasure. "Now, baby!" I screamed. "Come with me now!"

Let me tell you, he came like a champion. He shot his load so hard I thought I'd go blind. Our bodies convulsed and collapsed on the table. Our mouths met in a heated embrace of abandoned passion. I told him I loved him then, and he said he loved me too.

That scene is still vivid in my mind. It was absolutely marvelous. I'll remember it forever, and so will Jason and Stan. I can't tell you how many times I've drifted off to sleep at night with my fingers in my twat, recalling that spectacular afternoon.

But I felt a twinge of sadness for Stan as he watched our passion. He had taken such good care of me, but no one had taken care of him. However, he left with a huge smile on his face, and a promise from us for further encounters. It may be that our next threesome will not be conditional.—*Name and address withheld* ⊶⬛

WHEN YOUR GIRLFRIEND MEETS YOUR EX-WIFE, IT'S EITHER HELL OR HEAVEN

I'm one of those guys who works twelve-hour days, so I don't have much downtime. What I do have is a great girlfriend named Lindsay, and a money-hungry ex-wife named Megan.

When I pulled up to my house one Friday night a while ago, I was not very happy to see Megan's little blue car parked next to Lindsay's Buick in our driveway. I knew there had to be a money-based battle going on inside. Megan always wants more, and Lindsay feels the need to defend me against her avarice.

But when I entered the house it was quiet, except for some slight muffled sounds from the upper bedroom. There were no lights on, and there was a scent of Patchouli in the air. I went up the stairs and peeked into the bedroom. There I found my beautiful girlfriend lying on the king-size bed, with her face buried between my ex-wife's thighs. A large dildo was on the bed table.

Megan is a slight woman, five feet tall, with naturally curly chestnut-brown hair reaching to the middle of her back. She has big brown eyes, full lips, small perky tits and a tight ass. She often uses sex as a weapon, and is more of a taker than a giver. Lindsay, on the other hand, is five feet six, with dark auburn hair reaching to her shoulders. She has these flecked hazel eyes that get greener when she is feeling horny. Her tits are very large and firm, and her ass is nice and round. She is a sensual person, and very giving in life and in bed. And she sucks a mean cock.

When I walked in Megan was moaning under the ministrations of Lindsay's tongue. She was rubbing her own tits, tweaking the hardening nipples between finger and thumb. Her eyes were closed, her legs wide open. Lindsay, propped on her elbows with her ass up in the air, looked up at me, her mouth and lips shiny and sticky with Megan's juices. Both women were buck naked.

"Wanna taste?" Lindsay asked. I leaned over and kissed her, tasting Megan's sweet pussy on her lips. The taste brought back memories of how tight and juicy that pussy could get in the throes of passion. I could only hope that this wasn't just a dream.

I then joined Lindsay between Megan's legs. Her clit was already enlarged and throbbing. The two of us double-tongued my ex as her ass came up off the bed. Our tongues interacted with Megan's clit, and with each other. Megan's hands came down, one on each of our heads. Lindsay gently held Megan's lips apart while I inserted my tongue and moved it around and in and out of her pussy. At one point Lindsay poured just a bit of chilled wine onto Megan's cunt, which made Megan thrust her pelvis upward. We lapped up the wine like kittens, our tongues whipping in and out of her hole and around her clit. When she came we both licked up her juices, sharing them with each other as Megan panted and moaned through her orgasm.

"Can we fuck you?" Lindsay asked, as Megan refocused after her hard come. "Let us fuck you, okay?" Megan nodded, still breathing hard.

Lindsay and I stood up now, and Lindsay deftly positioned my ex-wife at the edge of the bed. Her legs still spread wide, Megan lay there quietly playing with herself, inserting her finger into her cunt and using her thumb to stimulate her clit. Lindsay quickly undressed me and urged me into position, guiding my cock to Megan's opening. I slowly fed my dick into her hot pussy. As I did this, Lindsay came up behind me. I could feel her bush grinding against my back. She wrapped her arms around my waist like she was about to go on some sort of a bike ride. She then began to thrust her pelvis into my ass, ramming my cock farther into my ex. The two of us then began to fuck Megan rhythmically. To my surprise, Lindsay really started ramming her hips against me, which made me ram deeper into Megan, who twisted with pleasure and moaned louder the harder I fucked her. Her pussy was so wet and hot it was unbelievable as Lindsay and I pumped together back and forth.

Then Lindsay's grip around my waist loosened and her hands began running up and down my chest, stopping at my nipples. Before I knew it she was on her knees behind me, licking my ass, rimming my anus as I went on steadily fucking my ex. This went on for a few minutes, until Megan came again. I then turned around and began to fuck Lindsay's mouth. I wasn't ready to come yet, though. I really wanted to save that for her cunt. At this point I heard the buzz of the vibrator. Megan had picked it up and was using it on herself. I alternated between watching my ex-wife fucking herself and my girlfriend sucking on my big sticky cock. She slurped up and down on it, stopping at the head to work magic with her tongue. All this stimulation was overwhelming, and I had to pull out of Lindsay's mouth to keep from shooting my load then and there.

Now Lindsay lay down on the bed and demanded to be fucked. "You want this cock?" I asked her.

"Yeah, I want that cock," she said, and then, pointing to Megan, added, "and that pussy."

Megan climbed up and sat on Lindsay's face, and Lindsay's hands clutched at her ass, holding her there. I got between Lindsay's thighs and began to fuck her tight wet pussy. She hummed steadily as she lapped at Megan's cunt, and when I put in a good stroke she moaned and sucked harder, which made Megan arch her back and bite her lip, which turned me on even more. A heavenly domino effect if there ever was one.

* * *

Before Lindsay or I could come we switched again. Lindsay was feeling left out of the oral gratification game. I lay on my back as Megan straddled me and rode my cock with this sort of frog-like hopping motion, propelling herself up and down with her legs, her tits bobbing on her chest. While this was happening, Lindsay was sitting on my face and I was sucking and licking her sweet cunt and her sensitive clit. She was facing Megan, and she kept encouraging her to ride me harder. "Fuck that cock!" she moaned. "How does it feel, girl?"

"Yeah, he was always a good fuck," Megan replied breathlessly. "But you give better head, baby." With that the two of them leaned forward and kissed each other. To see them swapping spit while one was giving me pleasure and the other taking it made my cock throb even harder, if that was possible.

Finally, the two of them lay side by side over the edge of the bed, their asses sticking up, allowing me to stand behind them and fuck each of them in turn. They held hands as I switched my cock from one to the other. Megan came first, and Lindsay soon followed with a cry of pleasure as I shot my load into her steaming cunt.

After Megan left I asked Lindsay how this had all come about. She told me that Megan had come to the house, bitching about money, as usual, and in the throes of her fit she had looked so sexy that Lindsay had just leaned in and kissed her. Megan's hands had found their way under Lindsay's skirt, and next thing they knew they were upstairs. Apparently they'd gotten in about half an hour of sucking and dildo-fucking before I arrived.

Now I make two contributions a month to my ex-wife—one with my checkbook and one with my dick.—*D.F., Little Rock, Arkansas*

TWO HORNY LADIES IN A VAN ARE SPIED ON BY ONE VERY LUCKY PATROLMAN

*M*y friend Josie and I have been best friends since high school, and even though we are both married, we are still lovers when the mood strikes. We also work for the same company, and have to travel to Dallas on business every month or so. We usually go together in Josie's van, taking turns with the driving.

On our last trip we set out early in the morning and got to the city in good time. Our business meeting ended a lot earlier than usual, so we decided to go sightseeing.

We kept getting lost, and ended up on some back road in a kind of semi-rural area. It was kind of cool, and Josie was wearing this thin shirt and her nipples were sticking out. I started feeling horny, and I reached over and started rolling those big nipples in my fingers.

I have to tell you that Josie is a hottie! She's five feet seven, with really long sandy-blonde hair and a great set of tits. She has really big nipples, and when she's hot they get huge. She shaves her pussy, and we laugh about that because her husband thinks it's for him, but it's really for me. As for me, I'm part Native American. I have long dark hair and size 36C tits. I also shave my pussy because I love getting eaten out.

Josie started squirming in the seat as I played with her nipples, then reached over and gave me a little nipple rub in return. Pretty soon we decided we would pull over somewhere and have some fun. We found a secluded little side road that was surrounded by trees. We figured no one would even see our van, much less us.

Josie took off her shirt and then came and sat on top of me in the passenger seat. I took one big nipple in my mouth and slowly ran my tongue around it, sucking on her tittie. She started unbuttoning my shirt, and the rest of our clothes soon came off. Josie rubbed her titties against mine, nipple to nipple, because she knows how that drives me crazy. I put my finger in her pussy, feeling how wet she was as she ground her cunt against my finger.

We had bought a new double dildo before we left the city, and now we got it out. It was long and flexible. Josie put one end into her pussy and then put the other end in me. We started pumping that dick at the same time, but when Josie saw that I was close to coming she pulled it out of me. We reclined the seat back, and she started eating me out. No one is as good as Josie at eating pussy! She played with my clit till I thought I would scream, then ran her tongue along the edges of my pussy, slowly dipping it in and out.

I'm not sure what it was that made me turn my head, but when I did there was a state patrol officer standing at the window with his huge dick in his hand, stroking himself. I was a little startled but not panicked, and I calmly told Josie that we had an audience. When he realized that we had seen him, he opened the door and asked us what we were doing. Josie laughed and asked him what it looked like. He laughed too, then asked if we minded if he watched. "No," I told him. "But wouldn't it be more fun if you joined in?"

I thought he was going to come just at the thought of it. He went around to the side door of the van and we let him in. We told him our names, and he said his name was Phil. Josie and I started eating each other out while he took off all his clothes.

He seemed unsure of what to do then, so he just started stroking himself again as he watched us. We stopped sucking each other and asked him what he wanted to do. He didn't answer, but he started to caress our breasts. He seemed a little shy, so I climbed on top of him and took his dick inside me. He must have been at least eight inches long. I had never had a dick so big before, and it felt so good! But he was so excited that it only took a couple of pumps before he blew his wad.

We were kind of disappointed, but Phil said that he could get hard again and last longer the next time. We each stroked him, licking his dick and sucking on his balls, and after a few minutes he was ready again. I wanted to feel more of that dick, so I climbed on board again. He put his hands on my waist pulling me further and further down on his cock. When he saw that I was going to come, he stuck his finger in my ass, which made me start yelling for him to fuck me harder. He ground himself so hard into my pussy that his dick felt like a vibrator that couldn't turn off. I came like a wild woman.

Josie had gotten really hot from watching us, and now she bent over and begged Phil to fuck her doggie-style. As he did she asked me if I would lick her clit while he fucked her. She tasted so good, and she even managed to finger-fuck me at the same time. The two of them fucked in a couple more positions, and he finally came after she sucked him off.

I ate Josie's beautiful pussy until she came, then put one end of the dildo in her pussy and the other in her ass, and pumped her until she came again.

Phil was ready again, and he was just about to fuck me in the ass when his radio went off. It was his patrol station, asking where he was. We all started laughing. Phil told us he had to go, but that this had been the best day of his life. He gave us his phone number and said we could call him anytime, and then he left.

We headed back home, and now we are definitely looking forward to our next business trip.—*S.V., Austin, Texas*

HE MANAGES TO TURN A DISASTROUS DOUBLE DATE INTO A TORRID THREEWAY

*O*ne July night last summer I experienced a disastrous double date, which turned into a very enjoyable threeway. My friend Phil and I had arranged to meet our dates at a local country-western bar. When we got there it appeared that the girls had already consumed quite a few drinks before we arrived. As a matter of fact my date, Dotty, had become quite friendly with some other guy she had met earlier in the evening. Within half an hour of our arrival, she blew me off and left with her new male acquaintance.

Phil and his date, Julie, were having a great time, and I seemed to be out of luck. I tried unsuccessfully to get friendly with several unattached girls at the bar, but finally pretty much resigned myself to a lonely night. Julie started feeling sorry for me, and asked me if I wanted to dance. Phil didn't mind, so she and I hit the floor for a couple of fast dances, and then a slow one. I began to think that it would really be cool if Phil and I could double-team this girl, but I was reluctant to make any obvious overtures, because I didn't know how she or Phil would react.

Finally the three of us left for Phil's house, where I had left my car. During the ride Julie kept telling me what a great dancer I was, and how she couldn't believe that Dotty had jilted such a good-looking guy. She was pretty drunk, and I didn't know if she was just trying to make me feel better or if she was serious.

Taking a chance, I remarked that if she really felt that way, maybe she would let me join her and Phil for some three-way action. Julie said she didn't know about that, because she had never done it with two guys before. Phil offered no opinion at all. I brought up the possibility several other times during the ride, but she remained non-committal and Phil neither rejected nor supported the suggestion.

When we got to Phil's house, he asked me if I wanted to come in for a drink, and I accepted. Once inside the house, Phil asked me to help him fix the drinks in the kitchen while Julie waited in the living room. While we were fixing the drinks Phil told me that he would find an excuse to leave Julie and me alone for about ten minutes, so I could try to talk her into letting me join them in bed. If I couldn't, he said, I should take off and leave them alone so they could get down to some serious action.

Phil excused himself to go upstairs and straighten up the bedroom, and Julie and I enjoyed our drinks while I continued to try to convince her that she would really enjoy having sex with two guys. I told her that if she became uncomfortable at any time all she had to do was let me know, and I would leave. When Phil called down and told her to come on upstairs, she smiled at me and invited me to go up with her.

In the bedroom, things progressed rather quickly. When the three of us had removed all our clothing and got into bed, Julie took turns French-kissing us while Phil and I got busy squeezing her tits, playing with her nipples and fingering her pretty blonde pussy. When Phil started sucking one nipple while I sucked the other, her moans of pleasure let me know that I was not going to be asked to leave. Phil left me to enjoy her rather small tits with their perky little nipples, while he kissed his way down her body toward her pussy, which was covered with a nice little tuft of light blonde pubic hair. When her whole body suddenly jerked, I knew that his tongue had found her clit.

Before I knew it I was kneeling next to Julie's head, sliding my hard cock in and out of her wet, warm mouth while Phil continued to tongue-lash her pussy. Each time I slid my cock into her mouth she took a little more, until finally her nose was nesting in my pubic hair and the head of my dick was actually in her throat. She continued to take me into her throat until I knew that it would not be long before I let loose with a load of come. I could tell from the way she was hunching Phil's tongue that she was about to have an orgasm of her own. I told her that I was ready to come, and she deep-throated me one more time before I blasted a massive load of jism into her waiting mouth. She was still gulping it down when Phil's tongue took her over the edge, and she began to shake all over. My cock slid from her mouth, trailing a ribbon of come that she hadn't managed to swallow. It was a real turn-on, seeing my cock dangling in front of her face, with that small stream of come dripping into her mouth as she orgasmed.

After we had recovered somewhat, Phil asked if I would mind leaving them alone so they could get into some serious one-on-one fucking. Julie started sucking Phil's dick while I put on my clothes. As I was leaving the room, Phil was sliding a condom onto his cock as Julie spread her legs in anticipation of the fucking she was about to get.

Because of our work schedules, I was not able to talk to Phil about our adventure until almost two weeks later. When I did, he informed me that we were lucky to have had that experience when we did, because several days afterward, Julie had decided to get back together with her ex-husband, so the opportunity would never come again.
—*B.V., Allentown, Pennsylvania* ⚬┼▪

HER CHRISTMAS PRESENT WAS ANOTHER MAN, BUT SHE NEVER GOT TO SEE HIM

*R*ob, my husband of fourteen years, has always had a fantasy about sharing me with another man. I have to admit that since, until recently, he was the only man I'd have ever had, the idea turned me on as well. We had numerous sexual sessions during which we fantasized that four hands were caressing my body, or that another tongue was licking my pussy. All I had to do while he was fucking me was to whisper in his ear that I was sucking on another man's cock, and it would be enough to finish him off.

The problem is that every time we spoke about actually going through with it, we both got a little nervous and decided it was just a fantasy.

Last Christmas Rob booked us a romantic winter weekend at a luxury hotel. When we had checked in and gone up to our beautiful room, he said he had forgotten his cell phone in the car, and asked me to go down with him to get it. As we waited for the valet to get the phone, he suggested that I walk around the shops in the hotel and meet him in twenty minutes. I was a little puzzled, but it was obvious that he had some sort of plan, so I did as he asked. When I met him back in the lobby, he handed me an envelope and told me to take it up to the room and read it. I gave him a suspicious look, but played along.

I opened the envelope in the elevator. Inside was a piece of beautiful bond paper with a message neatly typed. It read:

"Welcome to the beginning of your dream weekend. The next few hours, I hope, will excite and thrill you beyond your wildest dreams. There will be a series of numbered packages inside the hotel room. Each of them will contain directions that are to be followed explicitly. Do not open anything without being directed to do so. When you are ready, open Number One and follow the directions inside."

I cautiously entered the room and saw a series of small numbered packages on the bed. I opened the first one. It contained some bath salts, and another message, which read:

"Take the enclosed bath salts, and your toiletries and makeup, and your wristwatch, into the bathroom. Make sure that one of the hotel bathrobes is inside the bathroom. Draw a hot bath and add the bath salts. When the bath is running, and you have completely disrobed, open Number Two."

The bath salts were my favorite fragrance. I started the bath and opened the second package. Inside was an aromatic candle and another note.

"By now the bath is running with the wonderful smell of your favorite fragrance in the air. Light this candle to help set the mood in the bathroom. Also, place your wristwatch nearby, and then open Number Four. Know that I will be dreaming of your soft skin soaking in the warm, scent-filled water, and that my longing to be with you will be growing by the minute."

I wondered why he had skipped Number Three. I found out later that it was only a test. Had I opened it I would have found a note rebuking me for not obeying instructions. However, I opened Number Four, in which was a copy of *Penthouse Letters*, along with the expected note.

"Take this magazine and enter the bath. Do not open any other packages until your bath is complete. Relax, enjoy your soak, read your magazine and dream of all the possibilities that might follow. After thirty minutes, wash your hair and get out of the tub. Once you have dried off and put on the robe, open Number Five."

I settled into the warm bath and opened the magazine. Rob had folded over a particular page, obviously to draw my attention. On it was a letter that described a threesome with two guys and a woman. It was really hot. I read it and stroked my pussy. I wanted desperately to come, but I also wanted to save it for Rob. Or whatever. I couldn't help wondering—he couldn't be planning an actual threesome, could he? My heart raced. I finished my bath, dried off and opened Number Five, to find a bottle of my favorite lotion. The note read:

"I am dreaming of how sweet your skin smells after your bath. Apply this lotion liberally to all those areas that I will want to explore. Then prepare yourself for the rest of your evening. Put on the robe, but do not leave the bathroom until you have applied your makeup and dried your hair. Then, when you are ready to get dressed, leave the bathroom and open Number Six."

When I was ready I sat on the bed and opened Number Six. A pair of sheer black stockings.

"You know what stockings do to me!" the note read. "I am dreaming of how hot you will look when they are on. I only wish I were there to slide them slowly up your thighs. Put them on and then open Number Seven."

Number Seven was a black lace garter belt. "The only thing that can make stockings hotter is a garter belt. I hope you like this new one. Put it on and attach the stockings. Know that wherever I am, my breath comes faster as I think of what you look like in this arrangement. Once you have the stockings fastened, open Number Eight."

Number Eight contained a push-up bra with holes for the nipples. "I love the appearance of your nipples. My heart still races when I glance at them. I long to caress them. I hate when you hide their existence. Please put on this bra so that I may look longingly at them when I see you next. Once you have it on, open Number Nine."

By now, I had assumed that I was getting dressed in this sexy manner to go out for an evening on the town. When I opened the next package and found a beautiful pearl necklace, that suspicion was reinforced. Until I read the note.

"If there could be any way to make your breasts more beautiful, it would be to highlight them with a new necklace. I hope you like this one. I look forward to seeing it against your soft skin.

"At this point, I hope your excitement has built to the highest levels of arousal and anticipation as to what may follow. But know that you can trust me not to let anything happen that you really don't want to happen. Now open Number Ten to set the evening in motion."

What did he mean by not allowing anything to happen that I didn't want? I wasn't sure, but I knew that if he meant to fulfill our fantasy, I did want it. I was more than ready for it. I held my breath as I opened Number Ten.

There was only a note. "If you wish to go further, phone my cell phone from the room. I will not answer the phone, so wait for the message request and then say only: 'I am ready to continue.' If you do not call, I will cancel the rest of the plan and we will go to dinner. If you do, once you have hung up you may open Number Eleven."

My heart was racing as I picked up the telephone. But I barely hesitated before dialing the cell phone. When I heard the message request, I whispered hoarsely, "I am ready to continue." I was breathing hard. With shaking hands I reached for the last package.

Inside were three flavored condoms and a blindfold. The note read:

"Move a chair into position near the bed, facing the door and visible from it. Once you are seated, put on the blindfold. Presently the door will open. Remain seated, with the blindfold firmly in place, and do not make a sound. There will be no speaking, and no peeking. The blindfold must remain on until I remove it. No matter what happens, you are not to reach out and touch. Just relax, and let your mind and imagination, as well as your body, respond freely and fully to anything and everything that may happen. Now sit down on the chair, put the condom with you favorite flavor on the chair between your legs, put on the blindfold and let your fantasy roam wild."

I put the chair in position, put a condom on the chair and placed the blindfold over my eyes. It was very effective; I couldn't even peek out the sides. I waited patiently as instructed, but my mind raced. A condom? Rob had a vasectomy. My heart pounded as I imagined the possibilities. After what seemed like hours, I heard the door slowly open.

I felt someone walking past me, and then there was music in the room. I held my breath. A moment later a hand stroked the inside of my thigh and touched my soaking pussy.

Then I heard three distinct knocks. I gasped, and for a moment I thought of ripping the blindfold off and running for the bathroom. I could feel my heart racing in my chest. I didn't move. I was relieved to find that the man touching me was Rob, for now he whispered in my ear to nod if I wanted him to answer the door. I hesitated, and then, very slowly, I moved my head up and down, nodding. Yes.

Rob left me, and I heard the door open and then close. I wondered if maybe Rob might be playing with my mind, that he had just knocked on the wall, that no one had actually entered the room. I had almost convinced myself of this until I felt two pairs of hands caressing my breasts, one from either side of the chair. One of them removed my bra, and the caressing continued. I caught my breath as shudders of passion ripped through my body. Who could the other hands belong to?

Now I felt a hand on my head, turning it to the left. I instinctively opened my mouth and a hard cock slipped in. I danced my tongue around the head. From the feel of it I was pretty sure it was Rob's. I sucked and licked it, tasting his pre-come. He pulled his cock from my mouth and turned my head to the right. Another cock brushed my lips. I hesitated momentarily, then opened my mouth again. My first taste of another cock! It was slightly bigger than Rob's, and hard as a rock. I could hear a hoarse moan over the music as I sucked the cock deep into my mouth. I couldn't tell if it came from the mystery guest or from Rob. The hard rod in my mouth started to stroke gently. Then it was yanked from my sucking lips, and I felt hot come shoot onto my breasts. Within a second, I felt Rob brush up against my left side as he spurted his own come onto my tits. To come so quickly, I thought, they must have been as excited as I was.

I sat there wondering what was next. Someone knelt at my legs and slowly spread my knees, stroking the inside of my thighs. Hot breath tickled my pussy as a tongue approached. I slid down on the seat and spread my legs further to give him access. I knew it was the mystery guest when Rob leaned over and kissed me, telling me how much he loved me. He also told me that every fantasy we had discussed was going to come true. I shuddered as I came on the stranger's tongue.

After a few glorious minutes, I was helped to my feet and led carefully to the bed. I was guided onto my hands and knees, and someone slid beneath me into a 69 position. Again I felt a tongue lick my slit as I leaned over to find the cock I knew would be there. My instincts told me that it was Rob below me. I felt the bed sag beneath my knees as our guest took up a position behind me. Rob stopped licking my pussy and spread my cunt lips with his fingers. I felt the stranger's cock nudge against my cunt. I was so wet from all the action that it easily slid in to the hilt—the first cock aside from my husband's that had ever been there. As the strange cock pumped into me, Rob stroked my clit. I moaned uncontrollably around his cock, which was still in my mouth. I love doggie-style sex, and knowing that my husband was seeing the action so close was bringing me to the edge again.

Just as I was sure I was going to be rewarded with a load of come in my mouth, the action stopped momentarily. Rob slid out from under me and repositioned himself, kneeling up in front of my face and sliding his hard cock back into my mouth. Again the stroking started. I was being bounced back and forth between the cock in my pussy and the one in my mouth. Rob reached over my back and spread my ass cheeks. I knew he was watching the stranger's hard cock thrusting in and out of my pussy. I sensed that Rob was about to come again, but again he pulled his cock from my mouth, saying that he had more fantasies he needed to fulfill before he came again.

The mystery man also pulled his cock out of me, and I knelt there, wondering what was next. A moment later I felt a lubricated finger probing my asshole. Then another finger started stroking my clit. The probing and stroking continued until I shuddered in orgasm.

Now someone slid underneath me, and someone's hands guided me down onto the waiting cock. I could tell it was Rob beneath me, and I rode him as I had many times before. He pulled me down onto him, and my come-covered tits pressed into his chest. I felt the bed sag again as the other man got into position behind me, and I raised my ass higher in anticipation. I moaned into Rob's ear as a hot-lubed cock touched my asshole. Rob started whispering in my ear, telling me how much he loved me, how beautiful I was and how I was making him so happy, as the other man's cock slipped past my sphincter and slowly entered my ass to the hilt.

A cock in my ass and one in my pussy at the same time! It was better than anything we had ever fantasized about. I had never felt so completely filled. They started to stroke in unison, and within a minute, I started to come. Even though I was supposed to remain silent, I moaned in Rob's ear, telling him again and again that I was coming, that I couldn't stop. I felt the cock in my asshole spasm as it shot a load deep into my bowels. Rob said he could feel it pumping its come deep into my ass through the thin wall separating their cocks. He stiffened and cried out as he shot his jism deep into my cunt. I collapsed in exhaustion on Rob's chest as the cocks slowly softened and slid from my ass and pussy.

Rob kissed me deeply and continued to caress my limp body. I was happy to just lie there on his chest, wondering what was next. After a minute, I heard the door to the room open and close again. Was another man entering? We had fantasized about a gang bang once... But then Rob removed my blindfold, and I realized that the mystery man had left. We were alone.

Rob asked me what I thought of his present, and I answered him with a deep kiss. He told me how thrilled he was that we had finally gone through with the fantasy. I begged him to tell me who the mystery man was. He just smiled and said that next time maybe we could do it without the blindfold, and then I would know. I only hope I don't have to wait for next Christmas.—*Name and address withheld* ⚬╾▪

CAN THERE BE NEW THRILLS AFTER EIGHTEEN YEARS OF MARRIAGE? ASK A FRIEND

*J*anet and I have been married for eighteen years, and our sex life is great. But like many couples we often make idle pillow talk about bringing another man into our bedroom. Janet's always been a quiet, reserved person and much too shy to make love to anyone but me, but that all changed after her recent birthday.

When Janet came home from work, I met her at the door with a

"Happy birthday!" and a bouquet of flowers, kissed her and told her that the kids were spending the night with friends so we could be alone. I ran a bath for her while she got undressed, then put some music on the stereo as she went into the bathroom.

After a few minutes I peeked in at her. She was in the tub with her head on a pillow and her eyes closed. Her entire body was underwater except for her legs, which rested on the sides of the tub. She had no idea I was standing in the doorway watching her.

The first movement I saw was her hands massaging her breasts just below the water. She gently rolled a nipple between each thumb and forefinger. I watched her pinch them and pull them upwards, moaning low in her throat. One hand moved to her cunt. I could see the water rippling, but as her crotch was lower in the water, I could only guess that she was giving her love button the same treatment as her nipples. Judging from the smile on her face, I'm sure I was right.

I was ready to come in my shorts, so I left her to her own devices. In the bedroom, I set out her sexiest black negligee, then returned to the living room just as her present arrived. It was my good friend Carl. He's a very muscular six-feet-two with a dark tan and sandy hair. From what I'd seen at the gym, I was sure he carried at least nine inches of prime rib.

I fixed us both a drink, and we sat down on the couch for a few minutes. I told him what Janet was doing in the bathtub, and explained my plans for the three of us. Then I told him to make himself at home while I went to talk to her.

Her eyes opened with a start when I entered the bathroom, but after she saw me she smiled. I kissed her passionately as she played with her pussy.

"What do you think about trying a threesome one night?" I asked.

"Okay," she replied. We'd gone through this before, and she probably thought I wasn't serious.

"When?" I asked her.

"I don't know. One night soon, I guess."

I moved my hand under the water until it was covering hers as it lay on her crotch. Slipping a finger between hers, I eased into her open pussy. She gasped when I wiggled it, and she continued to manipulate her clit. "Is tonight soon enough?" I asked her.

"What do you mean?"

That's when I told her that Carl was waiting on the couch. She was embarrassed at first, but the more I told her about my plans for the night, the faster her fingers moved over her cunt. Grabbing my hand, she plunged my finger deep into her pussy and said, "Okay! I can't wait to get started!"

I went out and changed into a bathrobe, then brought another one out to Carl. I watched in fascination as he changed. His cock hung down at least six inches, and he was still soft. It looked bigger that way than mine does when it's hard. I knew that Janet was going to enjoy the night.

When Janet came out of the bedroom she was wearing the sheer black negligee and nothing else. She sat next to me on the couch, and Carl flopped down in front of us on a beanbag chair. We began a casual conversation, passing a bong back and forth. I've always liked getting high with Janet, because it never fails to make her horny as hell.

Wanting to leave them alone for a moment, I excused myself to go into the kitchen to fix more drinks. I could still make out their conversation from there, and I heard Carl offer her another hit from the bong.

"Are you trying to get me wasted?" Janet asked him.

"Yes," he answered. "Why do you ask?"

"I was just wondering if you're trying to seduce me."

"Actually, we plan to fuck you all night," Carl said.

"Oh," my wife said. "Well, why didn't you say so?"

I didn't hear anything more after that. When I came back to the den with our drinks, I noticed that Carl had already started the party. His face was buried between Janet's thighs, her head was thrown back on the couch and her eyes were closed as Carl lapped at her pussy.

Carl raised his wet face and said, "Sorry, Glen, I was too hungry to wait."

"That's okay," I said. "She has plenty for both of us."

Her eyes opened at the sound of my voice. I looked into them deeply, then lowered my mouth to hers, parting her moistened lips with my tongue. As we shared this intimacy, I took a nipple in my fingers and rolled it between them. Janet lifted her hips, pressing her crotch against Carl's face while he pleasured her with his tongue and hand. Still kissing me passionately, she pulled his face even harder against her crotch. Moan after moan escaped her lips as she came with another man for the first time in eighteen years.

We broke our kiss, and Janet smiled and grabbed at my hard cock. Carl stood up and removed his robe. Janet's grip tightened on my dick and she let out a gasp. She watched as Carl's nine inches sprang free before her eyes. "God!" she breathed. "It's so big!"

She made no protest as I reached down and slipped her negligee off her shoulders, revealing all of her lovely body to Carl's hungry eyes. I lay her gently along the length of the couch. Without pausing she lifted a leg and placed it back, spreading her pussy open. I caressed her breasts with my palms and kissed her deeply as Carl moved his face back to her pussy.

I positioned myself on my knees beside her. Janet took my hard cock and rubbed it over her soft, wet lips. Carl's face was still in her muff, and she began to push back against his finger and tongue. Opening her mouth, she took my cockhead between her lips as another orgasm rippled through her body. When it passed, she began to suck my cock eagerly. She fucked Carl's finger and tongue faster as she moved along my shaft.

She trembled and moaned around my cock as yet another orgasm wracked her body. This was too much for me to take, and I blew my load down her throat. She continued to milk me dry as Carl licked her pussy. She released my cock from her lips, and Carl kissed his way up her body to her mouth. He lay on top of her, his thick cock pressing against her clit. Holding her face in his hands, he told her how beautiful and tasty she was. As he did so, she eagerly licked her juices off his face, something I rarely got her to do for me.

Carl moved away, pulling Janet to her feet as I moved up behind her, sandwiching her body between us. Carl's cock slid over her slit and pressed against her clit again, while mine was caught between her ass cheeks. This seemed to really light her fire. "I could really use a hard dick in me right now," she whimpered. "Will one of you boys please give it to me?"

I went over to the wet bar to fix us another cocktail, but noticed that the action had already started. Carl bent her over the pool table, rubbing his throbbing cock along her wetness, from her clit to her ass and back again. When his cockhead hit the entrance to her pussy, he paused for a second. He massaged her ass cheeks and shifted his weight forward. Then his dickhead spread her pussy open as it started to slowly penetrate her outer lips. Then he stopped briefly. "Are you ready to be fucked now?" he asked her.

Janet was panting and moaning, obviously dying for his cock. But what she said was, "Maybe we should wait for Glen..." Even as she said this her body reacted with a mind of its own. She pushed back against him, pressing her pussy harder against his cock. If she hadn't been so tight, his entire cock would've buried itself in her cunt right then.

She gasped loudly as his cockhead stretched her pussy open a little more, and an intense orgasm sent shivers through her body as her come gushed over his dick. She was still moaning as I came in with the drinks, and looked at me apprehensively. "Don't worry," I said. "I love a live show! I also heard you say you thought you should wait, and I love you even more for that!"

She threw both arms around my neck and hugged me tightly. "God I love you!" she said.

After that we got high again and started a game of pool. Each time Janet shot she leaned over the table as far as possible, giving us an excellent view of her ass and dripping cunt. We were both more than ready when she leaned back against the table and rubbed her hand up and down her wet slit. In a sultry voice she asked, "What's going on? Doesn't anyone want to fuck me?"

Carl backed up a step and said, "You should go first, Glen," and I stepped up to her. She was so wet that I buried my cock in her cunt on the first stroke, and she shrieked with joy. Her pussy gripped my dick tightly as I fucked her. Each time I pulled out, her pussy lips clung to my dick, and each time I pushed myself back in, a shrill yelp of pleasure escaped her mouth.

Carl climbed onto the pool table and lay on his side, moving his prick to within inches of Janet's face. She quickly stuck out her tongue and licked from base to tip. Then she wrapped her lips around the head. It barely fit in her mouth, and yet she dipped her head and took as much of it as she could. I stopped for a minute to watch Janet enjoy her newfound toy. But I was anxious to give her pussy the workout it needed, and soon I was driving into her.

Janet's head bobbed down on Carl's cock with every thrust. When

I pulled out, I brought her hips with me, and his dick slid out from between her lips. I began to fuck her faster, reaching around to play with her clit. I heard her moaning around Carl's fat cock and felt the pressure building in my balls as her cunt walls massaged my dick. I watched Carl's cock sliding in and out of her mouth. Then my wife reached up and pushed a finger into Carl's ass. His eyes closed and his buttocks tightened as he erupted, filling her mouth with scum.

We all went into the bedroom after that. Carl lay on the bed and Janet got on top of him in a 69, greedily sucking his cock as he licked my come from her pussy. I sat down in a chair to watch. I wouldn't have thought that seeing her with another man would make me so hard, but it did. The two of them were lying crossways in the bed, with Carl's feet and Janet's head pointing toward me, and I had a clear view of his cock sliding in and out between her lips. She looked up at me, gazing into my eyes as she licked the tip. She had both of her hands wrapped around his thick pole, slowly stroking it as she flicked her tongue back and forth across the head.

Drawing her mouth away from his prick, Janet sat up, pushing her pussy right down on top of Carl's face. With a look of determination I'd never seen before, she shimmed her ass back and forth across his lips as she tried to get herself off one more time. She looked up and motioned for me to come over to her side of the bed. When I got there she took one of my hands in hers and placed it around Carl's fat prick. She held it there, moving it up and down his slippery shaft as her other hand played with her nipples. She was grinding her pelvis against Carl's face, and she started telling me how he was almost as good as me with his tongue, and how great it felt buried in her pussy. I slid my mouth down to her breast, taking one of her tender nipples between my lips, nibbling it gently.

I continued to suck her breast as she moaned louder. Janet moans a lot when she comes; it's one of the many things about our love-making that turns me on. Then she gave a little shriek and her body rose into the air for a moment, before setting herself back on Carl's face. "Oh, babe, he's tongue-fucking my ass!" she panted, squirming wildly. Suddenly Carl groaned, and his come spurted over our hands. Janet was squealing while she rode his tongue, and her body tensed as she came again. She licked the come off our hands and Carl's dick.

Straightening up, she wrapped her arms around my neck and pulled my mouth to hers. Slipping her tongue between my lips, she pushed some of Carl's come into my mouth. After a moment of hesitation, I happily kissed her back.

Carl went out to the bathroom as we both fell back on the bed. She looked so sexy, lying there with her creamy white breasts exposed, her mound and thighs coated with pussy juice. I ran my hands gently over her face and through her hair. She nuzzled my throat, then lowered her head and took my nipple between her soft lips, flicking her tongue over it. She pulled my leg between hers, rubbing her thigh against my dick and balls.

"Have you enjoyed this evening so far?" she asked.

"Yes, I have," I replied.

"Did you like helping me jerk him off?"

I thought for a second, then said, "I like everything we do together."

Laying her head on my shoulder and playing with my nipples, she asked shyly, "Babe, is Carl going to fuck me tonight?"

I realized that, notwithstanding their close call earlier, Carl had not actually penetrated my wife. In spite of all that had happened up to now, this would obviously be a big step for her.

"I don't know," I said. "Do you want him to fuck you?"

"I need a hard dick in me soon or I'll go crazy! It might be nice to see what a nine-inch cock feels like."

Carl came back into the room. He crawled into the bed on her other side and snuggled up against her back. "Is it time for me to go now?" he asked.

"No, stay awhile," I said. Janet looked up at me, and I simply winked in return. She ground that great ass of hers back against Carl's growing cock. My own dick was rubbing her clit, and I pushed harder against her as Carl slid his cock over her buttocks. The increased pressure made her crazy with passion.

"Fuck me, Glen," she pleaded, before rolling me onto my back and climbing on top of me. She leaned forward to kiss me while she ground her pelvis on my hardness. Carl placed his hands on her ass and lifted her up, then grabbed my cock and guided it to her pussy. She was extremely wet, and she impaled herself on my pole with one smooth motion. Our pubic hair meshed together as she settled her weight down onto my stiffness. Her tits swung in my face as she rocked back and forth.

Carl moved up behind her, wedging his hard nine inches into the crack of her ass. He wrapped his arms around her and pulled her up until she was sitting, wedging her to take my cock even deeper inside her. He fondled her tender breasts, and she turned her head to meet his kiss. When the kiss ended, she crouched over me again, her breasts dangling as she bounced wildly up and down, ass sticking out toward Carl. His throbbing dick again stroked her butt and probed into her crack.

I felt like coming, but I pulled out before I did, and she moaned in protest. Carl placed his swollen cockhead between her legs and started rubbing it against her pussy.

"Come on, Glen," Janet pleaded. "Fuck me!"

"Do you want me to let Carl fuck you?" I asked. "Would you like to feel his nine inches?" Carl placed the head of his dick at Janet's pussy for the second time that night. She gasped as it throbbed against her. "Do you want Carl to fuck you?" I repeated.

Moaning into my ear, she begged, "Oh, yes, please, babe! Please let him fuck me! Let him put that big cock in my cunt and fuck me!"

I kissed her tenderly, then I lowered my hands to her breasts and gave Carl the go-ahead. He slowly pushed forward, spreading her pussy lips wide and sinking three inches of his thick meat into Janet's hungry, cloying cunt.

"Mmmm!" she moaned. She crushed her lips against mine and pushed her tongue deep into my mouth as her vagina was filled with the largest dick she had ever known. Then she broke our kiss and threw her head back, gasping with pleasure. Carl paused a moment, then slowly withdrew until only the head of his cock remained in her tight opening. Just this small movement had her juices running out around his dick and dripping onto mine. The look of ecstasy on my wife's face caused any incipient jealousy I might have felt to fade away. She was looking deep into my eyes as tears of satisfaction and joy rolled down her face.

Carl paused again to give her a moment to get used to his size, and like an addict she moved backward, trying to get more of him into her cunt. But Carl wanted to tease her a little first. Each time she moved back, he moved with her. Looking over her shoulder at him, Janet begged, "God damn, please fuck me, Carl! I need to be fucked hard!"

Carl finally gave in and set out to stick it to her. He placed a hand on each of her shoulders and plunged the rest of his nine inches into her cunt until his balls rested against her ass. Janet's eyes jerked wide open, and she screamed in wonder and ecstasy as she came, her twitching, writhing body suddenly collapsing on top of me.

When she could speak again, she whispered in my ear, "Glen, this feels so good! I've never been so full!" She was pinned against me as Carl went on banging her, pushing in and out of her tight little pussy. My cock rubbed against her clit with every lunge of Carl's body, stimulating her and me at the same time. Her hair spilled over my face, and her breasts mashed against my chest.

Soon she was gasping, "Oh! Oh! Oooh!" with each stroke of his dick. Her body quivered each time he sank his rod into her. Then she was off again, beginning another long, intense orgasm. As it built to a crest, she pushed back on Carl's cock as hard as she could, screaming out, "I'm coming! I'm coming!" With one hard final thrust Carl plunged his meat into her further than anyone ever had. His entire body convulsed as he emptied his balls into her cunt.

I was so turned on by all of this—the look of satisfaction on Janet's face, the sight of Carl's dick plunging in and out of her, the feeling of her body jerking and twisting against mine as she came—that I emptied my balls and shot my jism all over my wife's stomach and my own. Janet gave a final screech of pleasure as her body was shaken by spasms and her pussy gushed in the last throes of orgasm. A combination of pussy juice and come from all three of us was dripping onto my cock and balls and down the crack of my ass.

After a few minutes Carl got up and started to dress. By the time he was finished, Janet had recovered enough to get up and kiss him good-bye. As she kissed him she unzipped his pants and took out his soft cock. She leaned forward and took it into her mouth, swirling her tongue around like she was slurping an ice cream cone.

Carl gently but firmly pushed her away. "You are one hot piece of ass," he said. As he was going out the door, he turned to me. "Thanks," he said. "That's a terrific lady you have there. She's a great fuck! Call me again anytime you want!" And then he was gone.

I turned to my wife. She looked so beautiful with come drying on her body and more running out of her cunt. I cradled her in my arms and pulled her close. "I love you, Janet," I told her.

With a contented sigh she pressed her body against me. "Thanks for tonight, darling! You're the best husband and the greatest lover a woman could ever have!"

"I'm glad you enjoyed yourself," I said. "If you want, maybe Carl can come back another time."

She smiled. "We'll see," she murmured.

I held her lovingly in my arms. As we drifted off to sleep, the last thing she heard from me was, "Happy birthday, babe!"—*G.F., Fond du Lac, Wisconsin* ⊶■

WHEN THIS LADY CALLS ROOM SERVICE, SHE'S NOT THE ONLY ONE WHO GETS SERVICED

*M*y husband Dwight and I are both in our mid-thirties. I have brown eyes, brown hair and 38D breasts. I'm five-foot-eight and weigh one hundred seventy pounds. Dwight has black hair, a thick beard and moustache and dark brown eyes. He's five-feet-nine and weights two hundred thirty pounds.

Dwight used to tell me he had this fantasy about us having a three-some with another guy. Well, he finally saw it happen last weekend, when we decided to take a brief vacation. What was supposed to be a relaxing couple of days turned out to be much more than we had ever expected.

We drove to a casino hotel about one-hundred fifty miles from where we live. As we checked in, a bellman came over to take our luggage. I looked up at him and saw the most gorgeous black man I'd ever laid eyes on. He looked to be about twenty-five-years old, and he was very well-muscled. As he picked up our bags I noticed the bulge in his pants. We followed him to our room, and I whispered to Dwight that I'd love to try some of that. Dwight told me to get a grip on myself.

After we settled into our suite, Dwight went into the bathroom to take a shower and I decided to surprise the bellboy. I called down to the front desk and asked for someone to help me with the TV. (I'd only seen the one bellboy on duty, so I figured they would send him.) I stripped down to my white G-string panties, with nothing covering my sizeable tits. Was he going to get a surprise, or what? I'd never fucked a black guy before, but I figured there's always a first time for everything. And I could fulfill Dwight's threesome fantasy in the bargain.

Soon there was a knock on the door. I looked through the peephole to make sure it was the bellboy I wanted. When I saw that it was, I slowly opened the door and stood there in all my glory. The bellboy stood there starting at my shapely body, naked except for my panties.

I motioned him in, and as I shut the door behind him, I could tell he liked what he saw, though he was obviously trying not to stare too much. He asked me what I wanted, and I asked him to help me find the X-rated channel on the televsion. He found it for me, then asked me if I needed anything else. I looked down and saw that the bulge in his pants had grown considerably. I asked his name, and he said it was Clarence.

I said, "As a matter of fact, Clarence, there is something else you can do for me. Will you show me your black cock? I've never seen one before."

By then he was staring openly. But after a moment he shrugged and said, "Sure, what the hell?" When he unzipped his pants, I was in shock. I was looking at the biggest, thickest, blackest cock I'd ever seen. It had to be about seven inches long and at least three inches around. I knew I had to have it in my mouth and my hot horny pussy!

Without another word, I dropped to my knees and put the head to my lips. I licked up and down along the shaft and tongued at his balls. My pussy started getting wet as I heard him moan with pleasure.

When Dwight came out of the bathroom, naked from his shower I knew he was surprised to say the least. He said, "Jenny, what the fuck are you doing?"

Looking up from my sucking, I said, "Welcome to your fantasy, honey. Clarence here showed his dick to me, and I just had to have it." Then I returned to sucking Clarence's cock.

Dwight recovered from his shock pretty quickly! He knelt down behind me and began to finger my pussy, which was so fucking wet and hot! I got on all fours, still slurping a big, black cock as Dwight pulled my panties down and started sucking my clit until he had it as hard as I had the bellboy. Then he went for my inner pussy lips, sucking on one and then the other, until I was just about crazy with lust. He kept eating my pussy with vigor for anther five minutes, getting me off at least two more times before he stopped.

I told Dwight to lie down on the bed so I could suck his eight-incher while Clarence fucked me doggie-style. Neither of them had any objection to that! I got down on the bed on my hands and knees, and Clarence started fucking me really hard and fast as I went down on Dwight's cock. It only took a few minutes of getting rammed by them both before I screamed out that I was starting to come, and Clarence shot his load up my pussy at the same time that Dwight exploded in my mouth.

We all fell back on the bed, with me in the middle. As I lay there with a thick cock on each side of me, I couldn't help taking one in each hand and stroking them up and down. After a minute I turned to Clarence and started sucking his dick, which in its temporarily limp state could actually fit in my mouth. Then I turned and started blowing Dwight for awhile. I went back and forth between them, sucking each in turn until they were both stiff enough to bang me again.

Dwight laid me back on the bed so he could fuck me missionary style. And as he did, Clarence straddled my face so I could keep sucking on his big, black cock. He played with my tits and twiddled my nipples as I suckled his dick, and Dwight fucked me until I moaned with pleasure.

Clarence started fucking my mouth hard and fast, and Dwight followed his lead by screwing my pussy even harder. I had a whole series of intense orgasms as they double-fucked my squirming body. Finally Clarence cried out that he was coming and spewed his sperm down my throat, and soon Dwight shot all over my ass.

We all collapsed for a second time. Then Clarence jumped up and said he'd better get back to work. Dwight thanked him for letting him experience his threesome fantasy, and I thanked him for giving me my first black cock.

After that we expected that the rest of our vacation would be pretty anticlimactic, but as it turned out, that was only the beginning. I'll tell you more in my next letter.—*D.D., Lovelock, Nevada*

HE GETS HIS GREATEST KICKS FROM SHARING
HIS SEXPOT WIFE WITH HIS BEST BUDDY

*M*y pal Chuck and I have been best friends since grade school. We were inseparable while growing up, and we've shared just about everything. He was the best man at my wedding and had promised to be godfather to our fist child. As best buddies, we talk openly about everything. There wasn't a thing I hadn't talked about with Chuck, except maybe his desire to fuck my wife Marilyn.

It all started one summer when we all took a skin-diving trip to Aruba on Chuck's boat. We had stopped for lunch in a pretty secluded cove, and after we had some food—and a good deal of the local tropical beer—the conversation, as it often does, turned to the subject of sex. It was mostly just kidding and joking around, but there was an undercurrent of serious eroticism as we became more spontaneous and open.

Feeling a little turned on, and with the beer undoubtedly freeing up my inhibitions a bit, I found myself telling Marilyn what Chuck had said about her once. "Chuck thinks your mouth was made for giving blowjobs," I said bluntly. "He asked if you give good ones." And I grinned at my buddy like a cat who had swallowed the canary.

Chuck blushed and looked at the deck, but Marilyn glowered with an unusually horny smile. Surprised by her interest, I decided to follow up. "And I told him you suck great cock," I said boldly. When Marilyn kept smiling, Chuck began to get braver and asked if she liked sucking dick.

It seemed to me then that not only was Marilyn unoffended by this turn in the conversation, she was even a little turned on. She answered Chuck's question without hesitation. "Cocksucking is a skill," she said, still smiling. "An art that women have to develop through hard work and dedication." Then Marilyn surprised us both. Licking her lips seductively, she told Chuck that if he'd lie down on the engine cover she'd be happy to show him what she meant. Eagerly, he did as she suggested. Then, startling me even further, she knelt by him on the deckpad and worked his trunks down his legs, exposing his already rigid cock. Marilyn smiled down at my friend's erect penis, admiring its size and shape. She reached out and wrapped her hand securely around the taut, pink pole.

My heart pounded as I watched my bikini-clad wife on her knees next to my best friend, his trunks pulled down around his thighs. Bending over my buddy's well-muscled midsection, with his cock held delicately in her hand, Marilyn moistened her lips again, then looked over at me with hopeful eyes as if to say, "May I suck him off?"

My own cock was very hard by then. I suddenly realized how aroused I had become by the prospect of seeing my normally reserved wife sliding her lips around my best friend's cock, and how thrilled and delighted I was to see her so completely enjoying the idea. Here were the two people in the world I felt closest to, so why shouldn't they enjoy each other? And why shouldn't I enjoy watching them do it?

"You want his cock, don't you?" I said to Marilyn. "Suck it, my love. Show him what a great blowjob you give." I could see that she was dying to slide Chuck's cock into her mouth—as eager, perhaps, as I was to see her do it—and I didn't even have to check to see if Chuck wanted her to do it! My usually demure but suddenly sex-hungry wife beamed wantonly. She licked the tip of Chuck's cock and then slowly and methodically slid its length into her mouth, savoring the taste and feel of my friend's erection.

Like a street whore with a passion for her work, she playfully held the head between her lips, swirling her tongue around the fleshy knob, paying particular attention to the sensitive skin just under the head. Keeping her lips around his dick, she reached behind her back with both hands and undid the straps of her bathing suit top, letting it drop onto the hatch. Still working his pole expertly with her tongue, she began to slide her bikini bottoms over her hips and down her luscious ass. I moved in behind her to help, and she raised each knee in turn, allowing me to slide the garment down her legs and off, which left her completely, wonderfully naked, crouching on her knees with her fine ass in the air.

I watched with enthusiasm as my wife went on attentively, even lovingly, sucking and licking my buddy's rigid penis. I moved to the other side of the hatch and pulled Chuck's trunks over his legs and tossed them to the deck. Without removing her mouth from his cock, Marilyn lifted one leg and swung it over Chuck's head, offering him the sight of her naked pussy. Then she lowered her hips until that pussy was covering his mouth, and they were locked in an open-air 69. I was enraptured by the sight of the two of them in this ravenous sexual embrace. Marilyn savagely devoured Chuck's cock as he feasted on her soaking pussy with an enthusiasm that filled me with more pride and affection than you could imagine.

I was so intensely aroused by their passionate exchange that, though I didn't want to interfere in their lovemaking, I did want to add as much as I could to their pleasure. I knelt next to them on the deck and began to touch my wife's anus with my finger. "Go ahead and lick her ass," I whispered to Chuck. "Marilyn goes crazy for a tongue in her ass. See what she tastes like down there."

He took my recommendation and started licking her crinkled rosebud. Marilyn began to rotate her hips wildly and moan around his cock. She moved her head steadily, alternately sucking the tip of his dick and deep-throating its entire length, exhibiting a hungry passion which I had experienced but never before had the good fortune to be able to watch from such an exciting advantage point.

As Chuck's tongue disappeared into her asshole, my wife lifted her head long enough to cry out, "Yes! Yes, Chuck! Oh, yes!" Then she devoured his cock again, sucking it with a wild abandon. The two of them quivered with excitement as they came in tandem. Marilyn's body spasmed and shook, but she stayed crouched over Chuck, hungrily swallowing the semen he shot into her mouth, then devotedly licking the remaining come from his shriveling cock. She savored the taste, swiping her tongue back and forth across his penis.

Chuck's head dropped to the hatch pad in satisfied fatigue, and Marilyn swung her leg over him and sat up. "Well, Chuck, do I give a good blowjob or what?" she asked coyly when she had caught her breath.

"My God!" Chuck gasped. "Marilyn, you're sensational!" He turned to me, still breathless. "You are one lucky man."

I kissed my wife deeply, tasting his come on her lips. "I think we're both going to be lucky from now on," I told him. Then I looked into her eyes. "I love you," I said. "That was positively the most beautiful thing I've ever seen in my life. I never realized how much I wanted you to suck Chuck's cock. I never recognized how much you wanted to do it."

Marilyn kissed me again, then bent down and kissed Chuck gingerly, her tongue probing his mouth, tasting her own pussy on his lips. "I think we may have started something," she said playfully, putting an arm around each of us. "You know, I think I could get used to having two lovers."

Afterward the three of us cuddled together, kissed, caressed and celebrated our newly discovered sexual bond. I delighted in the afterglow of sex with my wife and my best friend.

But Marilyn wasn't finished with us yet. Her body trapped between us, she scooted down in the bed until her head was on a level with our cocks. Then she alternated between Chuck's flaccid dick and mine, putting one soft cock in her mouth and then the other. "I think I can work these little cocks back up to size, don't you think?" she said, shamelessly licking and sucking each of our organs in turn until we were both ready to fuck her again.

She took Chuck's cock into her mouth and gave him a slow sultry, erotic blowjob that surpassed even the one she had gifted him with before. She looked over at me from time to time as she sucked him, her eyes glittering with pleasure, both because of what she was doing and because she could see how much it excited me. When Chuck had come again, shouting out his ecstasy, Marilyn switched to me and gave me the same treatment. She swallowed everything I had to give her, then kissed Chuck and me, sharing the come in her mouth with each of us in turn.

We each fucked her twice more before that night was over. Now Chuck visits at least once a week, and occasionally, when I'm off at work, I call him to keep her company until I get home. We all love this, me perhaps most of all. Watching my buddy's dick disappear into my wife's pussy is more stimulating than any fuck film I've ever seen, and to see the love of my life with my best friend's dick in her throat is to know the depths of friendship and the boundaries of true love.—*L.K., Miami, Florida*

Stepping Out

A CASUAL JOKE LEADS TO A
LESS-THAN-CASUAL AFFAIR

*T*his story isn't about some gorgeous, big-titted blonde and a guy with a ten-inch dick. I'm a man in my early sixties and my friend Judy is in her late fifties. My wife has a problem: Sex is painful for her, so the most I get out of her is an occasional blowjob. Judy's husband had a stroke six years ago and can't perform sexually at all.

On New Year's Eve my wife and I went to a neighborhood party. After a few drinks she started feeling sorry for Judy and told me to dance with her. Judy and I danced very close. As we danced we began discussing our different sexual situations. I asked Judy half-kiddingly, "Would you like to go to a motel with me?"

She smiled and said, "I think we could work that out..."

At first I thought she was just pulling my leg, but after a couple more drinks we made a date for the following Monday, which was her day off from work. She was going to call me and ask me to come to her place to help her put some boxes of Christmas decorations in the attic, which was going to be a signal allowing us to talk and work out all the details of our upcoming tryst. When I didn't hear from her, I called and she said she'd changed her mind, explaining to me that in thirty-two years of marriage to her husband Ray she'd never cheated on him and didn't intend to start then. In fact, she told me, Ray was the only man she'd ever had sex with.

Later that day I drove by her house and noticed that she was at home and that Ray's car wasn't in the driveway. I thought that might just be a sign that something could happen between us, so I parked around the corner, walked back to her house and rang the doorbell. When Judy answered the door she gave me a look that said, "Oh my God, now what?"

Without another word she pulled me inside and quickly closed the door behind me. She was absolutely beside herself with anger and asked what I thought I was doing by stopping by her house unannounced. I shrugged my shoulders and told her that I just had to see her, and I asked if there was any way that we could get together. Then it happened: When I reached out to touch her she jumped in my arms and we started French-kissing and were soon undressing each other by the front door. In a few minutes we were in her bed and all I could think of was tasting her pussy.

I figured that we wouldn't have too much time to be with each other, and I knew I had to work fast. She had been wearing a pair of loose sweatpants, which I took off her quickly, before either of us could say a word. She removed her shirt herself and threw her arms back over her head and waited for me to make my move. I knew what I wanted and set out to get it.

I don't often get to give a woman head. My wife doesn't like it and only indulges me after she's taken a shower and is too clean down there. I spread Judy's legs apart, kissed her cunt and took a deep breath, taking in the smell of a pussy that had not been in the shower for several hours. I love that smell and don't get to experience it nearly as much as I'd like to. I kissed her pussy and started to lick her clit, probing her with tongue and finger. Judy came faster than I could imagine possible. I got so turned on that I got on top of her and we fucked like a couple of horny college kids on their first date. I couldn't believe it, but Judy came three times in about ten minutes. We actually came together on her third time. That was a first for me.

The following Sunday we met at a motel in a neighboring town and spent two incredible hours together. When she checked into the room she wanted to jump in the shower and wash herself but I convinced her to let me eat her cunt the way it was. She laid back on the bed and opened herself up to me and my waiting tongue. Suddenly I did something I never thought I would do. Taking in the strong smell from both pussy and asshole, I got so damn horny that I cleaned her bottom with my mouth. I had my tongue all the way up her asshole and she came while I was rimming her. Judy said she never heard of anyone licking an asshole but admitted it was very good. Since then I've asked her several times to leave her bottom unwashed for me, saying I would clean her body with my tongue. She didn't want to do that at first but after some convincing she agreed. I had meant the pussy only, but she left it all less than clean.

I've asked her to bring herself to me in the future without jumping into a shower and she agreed. I'd never have believed I could possibly enjoy eating an asshole with my tongue. I asked if she'd consider licking my asshole some day, she said she couldn't do that just yet, but that she'd think about doing it in the future. I'll be working on that in the weeks to come, even though it's definitely something a person needs to do willingly.

Unfortunately, Judy is starting to feel guilty about our affair. I've tried to help her get over it, but she says she'll be able to work it out on her own. I hope so. I would hate to have to give her up, because I think I've fallen in love with her. The sex we share is so wonderful and she's become a great friend to me. I hate to hurt my wife but I have to think of myself sometimes.—*F.B., Alamogorda, New Mexico* ⊶▪

TURNABOUT IS FAIR PLAY FOR A MAN WHOSE WIFE STEPPED OUT ON HIM

*M*y wife and I have been subscribers to *Penthouse Letters* for several years. She recently received a large envelope from your magazine, which I opened thinking it was our latest issue in a new kind of envelope. I'd thought for a while that she was cheating on me, and that issue's story about the nympho nurse confirmed my suspicions. When I confronted her about it she admitted to everything. It was quite a story, and for the first time I had all the details. We've been separated for several months as a result. Since we've split up, she's moved in with her friend Sharon.

I know this will sound unusual, but I became suspicious because our sex became more erotic after she had started her nursing job. She began to let me do things I was never allowed to do with her before. Ever since the first night she went out on the town without me, she let me butt-fuck her, and that was always taboo. I wasn't allowed anywhere near her asshole. But all of a sudden, she loved it. When she blew me, she let me come in her mouth, which I hadn't been able to do before.

I'm a bartender, and I work until one o'clock in the morning every day. When work is over I usually go out to other bars to unwind. About two months before Sharon and I separated, a guy named Bobby was becoming a regular at my bar, and we grew to be good friends. One night as he was hanging out in my bar and I was getting ready to leave, we decided to go to my unwinding sessions together. As we were talking he told me that before he left Europe he had married a Belgian girl named Sofia. She was coming to the United States soon, and he was looking for an apartment for them that would be in a good location and, most importantly, would have good security, because his wife would be alone for up to eighty hours a week while he was on duty at the fire station.

A couple of days after our conversation, I ran into the rental manager at my apartment complex. I asked her about the apartment next to mine, which I'd heard would be empty at the end of the month. She said it hadn't been rented yet, so I asked her to sit on it for a couple of days until I could tell Bobby about it. My building has very good front-door security and was in a good neighborhood, plus the apartment was right next door to mine. He made an appointment to see the apartment and wound up taking it. He said it was perfect, and since I would be living next door, his mind would be at ease about Sofia.

Bobby went to New York to meet Sofia and the two of them were all ready to move in when they returned. Bobby asked me if I wouldn't mind helping the two of them get their stuff into the apartment. I'd never seen Sofia, but after I heard how Bobby described her, I couldn't wait. When the day came, he pulled up in a rental van and out stepped an absolutely fantastic-looking girl with long blonde hair, a face of an angel and a beautiful figure. I thought my wife was a standout, but this girl had it all over her. She was wearing a cut-up T-shirt that just barely covered her tits (even though she was wearing a bra) but showed off most of her stomach. She also wore a tight pair of short shorts that started well below her belly button and showed off most of her ass cheeks. All I could do was gasp.

When I was carrying one of the boxes up to their apartment I made sure to follow her so I could check out her gorgeous ass when she put her box down on the floor. I just couldn't keep my eyes off her tits, which were standing at attention at all times and fighting to get out of her T-shirt. I could tell she knew that I was watching her, because when she looked my way, she'd smile and give me a long sexy look.

When they were all moved in, Bobby said that he and Sofia wanted to take me to dinner for helping them out. We went to a restaurant that had good food and a four-piece jazz band. The booths were set up in a horseshoe shape, so everyone could face the stage, and there was a dimly lit dance floor off to the side of the room. We had a great meal and quite a few drinks. Bobby and Sofia danced a few times. Bobby came back after one song and told me that Sofia wanted to dance with me, because she felt that they were neglecting me. I was afraid of what I would do if I got my arms around Sofia, so I declined, but Bobby insisted. We got up and (just my luck) the group played a slow song. We danced close, and she put her head on my shoulder. My God, she smelled fantastic. I couldn't believe how soft her skin felt as I rested my hand on her bare back. My cock got hard almost immediately.

Sofia lifted her head up and looked at me, saying, "What's that I feel?" She took her hand from my back and rubbed it slowly across my cock. She nuzzled her head back into my neck, pulled her hand away and pressed her mound against my erection. I had to follow her closely back to the table, because I didn't want Bobby to notice the bulge in my pants. When we sat down, she immediately put her hand on my thigh and rubbed my crotch. When Bobby excused himself to go to the rest room, Sofia's hand went straight for my cock. She unzipped my fly, stuck her hand in my shorts, squeezed and said, "I've got to see that tool one of these days."

"Anytime!" I said.

When she saw Bobby coming back from the bathroom, she released her grip on my cock. He said they had to leave, because he had to be at the firehouse at eight o'clock. I told him I was going to stay and finish my drink. I had a few more and I got bombed fantasizing about Sofia. I woke up the next day around noon, really hungover. I went directly to the refrigerator to find something cold to drink, but all I had was beer. I sat on the couch with just my shorts on, took a sip and put the cold can against my forehead.

There was a knock on the door, and before I could move, Sofia appeared (I must have forgot to lock it) carrying a plastic pitcher of lemonade she had made for me. All she was wearing was one of Bobby's long tank tops, which was so low-cut it barely hid her nipples but was long enough to just cover her ass. She told me to stay on the couch and she would get some glasses.

She sat very close next to me. Her bare leg touched mine and sent tingles in me. When she sat down, the shirt rode up above her crotch and I could see that she was a natural blonde. I got an instant hard-on. She looked and said, "What's that I see bulging up from your underwear?" I told her to take a look so she got up, took off her tank top, kneeled between my legs and pulled off my shorts, looked down at my cock and said, "I knew your prick would be a thing of beauty!"

She grabbed my rod and slowly started jerking me off, looking me straight in the eye. Then she kissed it, licked it down the shaft, sucked on my balls and went up the shaft again, tonguing the head of my cock. I was dying for her to put it in her mouth. Soon she started sucking my dick like a hungry animal. She sucked real deep, taking everything I had into her mouth. I got close to coming, so I pulled her head away and told her I wanted to fuck her beautiful body before I came in her mouth. She got up, bent over the arm of the sofa and stuck her ass in my face so I could fuck her doggie-style.

I kissed her butt and ran my tongue between her cheeks, circling her asshole with my tongue to get it real wet. I mounted her slowly, so I could enjoy feeling my thick cock pushing into her beautiful cunt. It didn't take me long to come but I enjoyed every second that I fucked her, because with each stroke I tried to go as deep inside her as I could. By the time I ejaculated, we were both covered in sweat. My orgasm felt like it would go on forever. Finally Sofia got up, put on her tank top, and told me to rest so I could be in her apartment by six o'clock. She was going to cook dinner for us. I was so worn out I fell asleep on the couch.

I woke up around five o'clock, took a hot shower and called to ask Sofia to leave her door unlocked, because I'd only be wearing shorts and didn't want anyone to see me in the hallway. When I went in to her apartment, she greeted me wearing thong panties and a see-through blouse with thin straps that just covered her tits. After dinner, we relaxed in the living room and started to kiss. Soon I started to lick her from her lips to her breasts. I licked, sucked and squeezed her beautiful tits and didn't want to stop, but I went down her stomach until I reached her thighs. I licked both sides and then started to kiss and lick her cunt. She smelled so good, I lost control and started sucking on her clit and poking my finger into her asshole. She started moaning and bucking back against me. I increased the speed I was finger-fucking her ass, and I kept on sucking her clit deeply. When she came, I could feel her ejaculate spurt into my mouth like a faucet had opened. She tasted delicious.

Sofia got up and led me to the bedroom. I mounted her missionary style, pressing my body against hers, fucking her slow and deep. In no time at all we both were ready to explode. She came first, making a sound that got me so excited I couldn't help spewing. After we took some time to catch our breath, we laid next to each other, kissing and exploring each other's body with our hands. She phoned her husband to say good night.

After she hung up the phone we went into the bathroom and showered together, with me pressing my cock against her ass. We went back to bed, wet. I turned her over and started to lick her asshole again. I drove my tongue in and around it, then I put my cock against the brown, puckered entrance. She spread her cheeks apart so I could enter her. I started out gently but with each pump I drove in deeper and deeper. She was gyrating, moving her hips from side to side and moaning with ecstasy whenever I sank it in. I was in heaven, and so was she.

I was having a hard time coming, and Sofia told me to take my cock out of her ass so she could suck it. She laid me down and took my cock in her mouth and gave me the most fantastic blowjob I ever had. When I finally blew my wad she took every drop in her mouth and swallowed it all down. The contentment on her face was clear. She laid next to me and I started to finger-fuck her cunt with my right hand and her asshole with my left hand. She was thrashing around like she was in convulsions, and she exploded all over my fingers. It spurted out of her cunt and I quickly sucked off my fingers. Then I went down on her and licked her clean.

She laid her head back on the pillow and asked, "You are staying the night, aren't you?" I told her that nothing on earth could move me off that bed.

The next morning I was awakened by the soft feeling of Sofia leaving a trail of kisses down the back of my neck. She licked all the way to my ass, where she settled inside my buttocks and gave my asshole a terrific tongue job. I turned to get in a 69 position and we licked each other's assholes for a long time. It felt so good, she had me trembling.

We spent the next two nights fucking, sucking, ass-fucking, ass-licking—you name it, we did it. We never left the apartment. Now I have three wonderful days a week with Sofia. I never had any trouble getting a girl at the bar, but now I don't even try to pick up women there, which should tell you exactly how satisfying Sofia is. This has been going on for over three months, and things with us are just as good as they were our first time together. The sex we have is absolutely fantastic and we both feel the same way about each other. Separating from my wife was the best thing that ever happened to me.—G.A., *Staten Island, New York* ⊶◼

SOMETIMES OUR GREATEST PLEASURES ARE THE MOST UNEXPECTED

I'm a happily married man and have never thought of cheating on my wife, until a few months ago.

I was in New Orleans for a three-day conference. I arrived a night early so I could get the registration out of the way and attend an orientation. I decided to go out on my own for dinner and went to a very popular, informal but crowded restaurant. I was waiting for my meal and watching all the customers when a very attractive woman asked to share my table. We spent the meal talking about our lives, the city and what brought us to town. It turned out that Josephine was attending the same conference, she was single and she was from out of town, too.

As we were finishing up with dinner and getting ready to leave, she asked me if I'd mind walking her back to her hotel. It was a few blocks away and she didn't feel comfortable walking back alone at night in this strange city. Having a small sense of chivalry, I agreed.

Up to that point, there had been no thoughts in my mind about anything developing between us. As we were walking back to her hotel, we came upon a doorway that opened into one of those beautiful old New Orleans courtyards. We stopped and peeked in and were caught off-guard by the sight of a young couple in the shadows making passionate love. They were fully clothed, but her dress was up over her hips and he was giving it to her doggie-style, and he was fucking her hard. They were so deeply into what they were doing, they didn't notice that we had been watching them. Josephine and I just stood there and watched in silence. I jumped slightly when I felt her hand softly entwine with mine. It seemed so natural that I just grasped hers back in response. She turned around, looked me in the eye and said, "We'd better go."

When we got to her hotel, she invited me in for a drink. There was a bar on her floor around the corner from her room. I felt a bit uncomfortable walking through a hotel with this pretty woman, but there was some kind of attraction between us that I couldn't deny. As we were making our way towards the bar, we passed a room and heard moaning and groaning. She stopped me and laughed, "Twice in one night? This must be a sign!" before showing me into her room just down the hall. I hesitated for a second when we reached the door, but she massaged my crotch and pulled me in. No matter how much I kept thinking about my wife, I couldn't resist.

My brain went completely blank when she fell to her knees, opened my fly and pulled out my cock. As I looked down, I was treated to the view of my cock completely disappearing and reappearing as Josephine deep-throated me. The events leading up to that moment as well as the thrill of the forbidden had me shooting into her mouth in no time. She moaned with pleasure as she swallowed my come. My wife rarely lets me come in her mouth, much less swallows it.

"Let me return the favor," I said as I pulled off her skirt and panties and laid her down on the bed. As I bent to eat her, it suddenly dawned on me that she was the first woman other than my wife that I would taste. Her scent and flavor were decidedly different from my wife's, and her aroma had me swooning. I was able to make her come much more quickly than I expected, and I had to hold on for dear life as she screamed her way through it.

After she calmed down, we decided to order some room service. I shared my fantasy of watching a couple make it, and I could tell she was intrigued by the idea of possibly screwing another complete stranger while I watched. When the delivery person showed up, it was a woman. Josephine cast her eyes down to the floor, blushing a bit, and said, "Sorry, I'm not ready for that." The delivery woman looked at us strangely and left. Josephine suggested we take a shower together. I ended up fucking her standing up under the pulsing stream of water, another first for me.

After cleaning up and drying off, I was overcome with an enormous feeling of guilt, so I dressed and left, apologizing to Josephine. She said she understood and gave me her business card, telling me to call her if I ever got the urge again.

When I got home, I tried my best to put this incident behind me so I could get on with my life. My wife seemed to notice that my lovemaking was a little more energetic, but she never said anything about it. A week later, I went into work and my boss introduced me to my new associate: a beautiful woman named Josephine!—*C.M., Chicago, Illinois* ○━▪

A HORNY WIFE USES THEIR COUNTRY GETAWAY TO GET SOME ON THE SIDE

*M*y thirty-eight-year-old wife Diane works as an auditor for an accounting firm and I have my own business consulting firm. We're both fairly well-off, so last year we bought a small country place about two hours from our home in the city. It's the very last house on a small road located by an old creek, without many other residences in sight (there's an undeveloped hillside above our property). Because of the way it's situated, we have roman shades on the windows but usually leave them fully open since no neighbors can directly see in and people rarely walk by. I often have to work on Saturday so Diane goes up almost every Friday for the weekend. I join her there on most Saturday nights, and our teenage children usually stay with relatives.

About five years ago, Diane started to exercise regularly, rising fairly early in the morning to work out at a local fitness center. As a result, she has toned her body into a very shapely 37-24-36 figure. She's five foot four and usually keeps her weight around one-hundred eighteen pounds. She's a natural auburn redhead with wide green eyes, a classic nose and a broad mouth with sensuous lips. She inevitably attracts attention when she walks into a room, but she has such grace that it's usually striking but not overly sexual.

Her audit assignments usually result in her traveling overnight at least once a month for a few days. While we've had a full, active sex life throughout our sixteen years of marriage. I've thought that she's probably had some affairs. When she drinks alcohol, she gets kind of flirtatious. At business parties, she always watches carefully not to drink too much, but on vacations, I've seen her get fairly friendly with some of the men whom we've met. To my knowledge nothing ever happened, but I could see the reaction she was getting.

Diane also cares about clothes and prefers outfits that are stylish and expensive. About six months ago, I noticed some changes in the way she was dressing. She always had some sensual lingerie, but now that seemed to be all she would put on. She was wearing low-cut bras and string bikinis or thong underwear. She stopped wearing pantyhose and started wearing garterbelts and stockings or just stand-up stockings. Her skirts and dresses were almost all above her knees or with fairly high slits. She was wearing tank tops and left her blouses open to show off her breasts more than before. At our place in the country, she would usually wear short shorts or tight jeans with halter tops in warm weather. She seemed to be going braless a good deal of the time, too. A few times when we were out in the country on a warm Sunday, I noticed that she would be wearing a skimpy sundress and nothing else. Her nipples frequently got stiff from brushing up against the dress's material. When we were in a local restaurant for lunch on one of those Sundays, I noticed several guys at a table near us looking our way. Diane smiled back. It even seemed at one point that she had crossed and uncrossed her legs so that they could see that she wasn't wearing undies. Diane didn't say anything about them.

A month ago, the kids and I were at our city home for the weekend. Diane had gone up to the country place on Friday morning. Diane said that she had to meet with a client whose office was in a town on the way to our country home. I planned to go up on Saturday afternoon. The kids had stuff to do in the city, and Diane's parents, who live down the street from us, were going to look after them. But on Friday afternoon, the appointment I had for that Saturday canceled out. I arranged with my parents to keep track of the kids on Friday night and decided I'd leave after rush hour and surprise Diane.

I approached our country home at about nine o'clock that night. To my surprise, I saw a number of other cars parked out in front. Instead of going up the driveway, I left my car about a hundred yards down the road. I had some binoculars in the trunk and went to the hillside overlooking our home. I got a clear view of the living-room window, a bedroom window and our hot tub.

When I looked through my binoculars, I saw Diane and the three guys whom I had noticed at the restaurant a few months before. Diane was dressed more provocatively than I'd ever seen. She had on a very short, tight black skirt that barely covered her ass, a pair of fishnet stockings, high-heel sandals and a sheer black blouse covering up a lacy black bra. The guys were wearing jeans and T-shirts and looked quite well-built. It seemed as if there might be music playing because Diane was swaying back and forth as she served hors d'oeuvres and drinks.

One of the guys got up and put his arms around her, grabbing her ass as they began to dance. He pressed tightly up against her as she gave him a deep kiss. I was shocked. I watched as Diane proceeded to dance with each of the guys. They didn't hesitate to squeeze her ass or touch her breasts. The dancing stopped for a moment until Diane started to strip for the guys. She undressed for them slowly, and she went up to each one to let him feel her breasts and rub her cunt. I noticed that she had trimmed her bush to a small, neat triangle. She then encouraged them to undress. They all had huge erections. She bent down and licked each prick but did nothing more. Instead, she led them to our hot tub. Once they were outside I could hear them as well as see them.

One guy was mentioning how much they missed Diane during the week. She said, "I don't think your wives feel the same way."

Another said, "But they don't know."

Diane looked over and said, "I'm not so sure about that..."

There was a lot of groping going on in that hot tub. Diane has sensitive breasts and really gets off when they are rubbed just the right way, and it looked to me as if that's what happened. They were in the tub for about fifteen minutes. After they toweled off, they wasted no time in moving to the bedroom.

From my perch I could see everything they were doing. I noticed that one of the guys had a videocamera. Diane started out giving one guy a blowjob while another guy ate her out. The third guy started filming them. They soon switched and let the video guy get a blowjob while the first guy started giving Diane head and the third guy took over handling the video. No one seemed to have gotten off yet.

Diane then motioned that she was ready to get fucked. The guy who was getting the blowjob got on top and began to move his prick slowly in and out of her. The guy with the videocamera kept filming, while the other guys sat off to the side watching with huge erections. After the first guy came, the one not filming immediately took his place. Diane seemed to be continually twitching and having orgasms. After about five minutes, he was replaced by the guy who had been working the videocamera. He lasted about ten minutes while the one not fucking her and not videotaping managed to get in the action with her licking his prick while he used his hand to increase her pleasure. It all ended with Diane apparently having a huge orgasm. The guys left at about eleven o'clock. I had been watching for nearly an hour and a half. I didn't know what to do or say.

After they were gone, Diane took a shower. She also changed the linens on the bed and put them in the washing machine. I then noticed that she turned on the television and inserted a videotape. It was the one they had just made. As she watched, she got out a huge black dildo and began to play with herself. When she was good and wet, she inserted the dildo and had another orgasm. She then stopped the video and turned off the lights.

I decided that I should stay somewhere else that night and found myself a motel room on the other side of town. When I returned in the morning, Diane expressed surprise at me getting there so early, but she also seemed delighted to see me. I said that I just missed her too much and canceled my Saturday meeting. I then took her in my arms and started to kiss her and feel her up, rubbing my hands where the hands of other men had been the night before.

Diane said, "My, you are horny, aren't you? But then, so am I." We proceeded to have one of the best fuck sessions ever. Diane was unbelievable. She did things to me with her mouth that I just couldn't believe. She used her cunt muscles to give me pleasure like she had never done before. I asked her to tell me a dirty story, and she started to tell me about what she did with the three men the night before, but as a story she was making up, not as something that really happened. I asked her if that was what she wanted. She looked up and said, "Maybe. If you wouldn't be jealous. Because no matter what my sexual fantasies are, you're the only man that I love."—*D.R., Boston, Massachusetts* ○––▪

SHE ASSUMES THE RIGHT TO FUCK OTHER MEN, AND HE SECRETLY APPROVES

*W*hen my wife Mandy turned forty, she announced that she intended to date and party with other men. Although I'm a sweet guy, a good father and generally supportive of what she does and wants to do, it turned out that I was deficient in one area. I wasn't satisfying her sexually. Before she got too old, she said, she wanted to see what it would be like to start fucking other men. Our daughter was off at college so she had much more free time than before. She didn't want to cheat behind my back and hoped that I would understand and stay with her.

Mandy is still a very striking woman. She is five-foot-eight-inches tall and weighs one hundred twenty pounds. She dyes her shoulder-length hair blonde. Recently she had plastic surgery to tighten her breasts—her measurements are now 36C-28-35.

The reality of the situation is that I've always fantasized about her sleeping around. In fact, I'm fairly certain that she had had some affairs before. Her libido has always been very strong. While we would fuck several times a week, Mandy would usually come every night, either by masturbating or by me fingering her or going down on her. But now it seemed like she was going to be more blatant than before.

I was correct. She began wearing sexually provocative clothes most of the time since she likes showing off her figure. She also began to attend sex clubs and often would stay the night. When she came home early in the morning, she smelled of sex and seemed sticky. All she would say was, "I made it with a bunch of guys again." Not infrequently, when I would call home during the day, she would say that she was busy, and I would hear male voices in the background. One time when she was out partying, I found a videotape in the VCR. When I played it, I saw that it was an amateur porn film that she had made. She was with two other women and six guys. They fucked and sucked in various positions for about an hour. I got so horny I masturbated.

The other weekend I went to a dance club with her. She was wearing a very short skirt and a low-cut blouse—and of course she didn't bother wearing underwear. While we were dancing, a tall black guy cut in on me. Before I knew it, they were dancing closely and he had his hands on her ass. After the dance, she left with him. I followed them to his car in the parking lot. Mandy looked around and didn't see me watching. She took off her clothes and jumped in the back seat with her new date. The car began to rock back and forth for about ten minutes. I went back into the dance hall. Mandy came in a few minutes later smiling and licking her lips. She told me she had made a new friend and was going to meet some friends of his and asked if I wouldn't mind going home alone. She came back home the next morning. All she would say is that she had the fuck of a lifetime.

It's been one year now. Mandy still can't seem to get enough sex. She's started doing it in public at sex parties, or at least that's what she tells me. Any man is fair game for her. She's even started to do some of our daughter's friends, almost always more than one at a time. Whenever I ask when will her affairs end, she says, "One day, honey, but not soon."—*L.H., Hartsville, South Carolina*

SOME INNOCENT KISSES LEAD TO A NOT-SO-INNOCENT NIGHT OF PASSION

*M*y name is Paula. My husband Wayne and I are avid bowlers. We are on a five-man team. Jimmy, Donna and Gene are the other three. Gene is the only one who is single. He's fifty-seven years old and weighs one-hundred forty pounds. He only stands about five foot three, but is one helluva good bowler.

Last season right after Christmas, Wayne got pulled off day work and put on the night shift. We had to hunt for a fifth man and found one. Our team has a special arrangement: If you get three strikes in a row you get a kiss. Naturally I mean that the guys kiss the girls and the girls kiss the guys.

One night Gene was bowling real well and getting his kisses. A few times he gave me some tongue. It took me by surprise, but it felt real good. It had been a long time since I had gotten a kiss like that.

After bowling, Gene and I went into the bowling alley bar and had a drink. Gene lifted his glass in greeting and said, "I hope I didn't shake you up kissing you like that before."

I assured him that it didn't bother me, and that in fact it felt good. Things went along about the same the rest of the month. Gene and I would have our after-game drink then I'd go home and play with myself. I wasn't getting much loving from my husband at that point. His only day off was Sunday and he was usually too tired to fuck.

As I was getting dressed, I realized it had been about three weeks since I'd had any cock. I thought to myself that if Gene gives me a tongue kiss that night I'd give him one in return.

When I got ready to go to the alley, my car wouldn't start. I called Donna but she and Jimmy had left already. I called Gene and he stopped by and drove me to the bowling alley.

It turned out to be a great night. I sucked on Gene's tongue more than once, as he did mine.

When Gene dropped me off at home I asked if he wanted to come up for a nightcap, and he accepted. I gave him a beer and made myself a nice strong cocktail. I told him to relax for a little while because I was going to take a quick shower.

I put on a silk robe and told myself, "Tonight, I'm going to get fucked."

When Gene saw me he said, "God, Paula, you look good enough to eat."

I laughed and asked, "Where do you want to start?" as I sat down next to him on the couch.

Gene said, "How about I start right here?" and put his hand on my tit.

Before I could say anything his lips were on mine and he started tongue-fucking my mouth. He pulled the sash from around my robe and moved his hand from my tit to my pussy. Gene sure knew how to use his fingers and soon he had my pussy wet.

I put my hand on his prick and felt it get stiff. I said, "Let's go into the bedroom so we can get more comfortable." I took off my robe and lay across the bed. Gene took off his boxer shorts and I got a good look at his cock. For a short guy, he was pretty well-hung. He was only semi-hard and his prick was three inches longer than Wayne's gets when he's completely erect.

I said to him, "Gene, you're really big. I don't know if I'll be able to take all that."

He said, "Paula, honey, by the time I get done, you'll be able to take it all." He told me to lay down on the bed with my ass hanging over the edge and my feet planted flat on the floor. He laid on top of me and we started kissing. His cock was resting right on the crack of my pussy. After kissing for some time he started sucking on my nipples. My juices were flowing. I knew he could feel the wetness on his cock and balls. I moaned for Gene to take me.

He licked down my belly. He knelt on the floor and spread my legs wide open. I felt his hot breath on my cunt before I felt his tongue. He licked up and down my crack, sucking on my clit when he found it. I moaned, "Don't stop, make me come."

He said, "You've got a beautiful clit. It's nice and big." He started sucking on it in hard, short bursts, stopping only to swirl his tongue over it. As I started coming he put a finger in my hole and fucked me quickly. He never stopped sucking on my clit and I could feel my juices running down my ass crack.

After he sucked me to a third orgasm, I said, "Jesus Christ, Gene fuck me. I have to feel that big cock inside me."

Gene knelt down between my legs. He scooped some of my juices in his hand and coated his cock with them. He put the head of his big prick at my hole and said, "Relax, Paula. Don't tighten up or I won't be able to fuck you." He put his hand around his cock and started easing it in my hole.

I could feel my cunt stretching to accommodate his fat cockhead. I moaned a few times before I felt my cunt muscles relax. Half of his cock slid in me with one strong push. I wailed, "Oh my God, I can feel every inch of your cock in me."

He said, "Get ready, because there's still more to go." He started fucking me and after a minute or so I could feel his balls smacking against my ass.

I said, "Gene, your cock is hitting spots no one's ever touched before!"

He told me, "Paula, you've got one tight pussy." In less than a minute I was coming again. God, I'd never been fucked like that before in my life. I was having one orgasm after another. It had to be about ten minutes before Gene told me he was getting ready to come. I could feel his cock swell up and felt the sperm spurting out of his piss hole. He kept fucking me hard. When I looked down at the base of his cock, I could see white frothy fluids collecting on it.

He finally stopped fucking me and pulled out, gasping, "Jesus, that was great!" My legs were still spread open. He put his finger in my cunt and I could feel our hot juices running between my lips and down my butt. I didn't want Gene to leave but I knew that Wayne would be home soon and I needed some time to get things cleaned up. Gene said, "Anytime you need some loving, I'm here."

I took his hand and said, "I'm sure I'll be seeing that big cock again."—*P.R., Akron, Ohio*

WHERE AN UNHAPPY MARRIAGE FAILS, A CLANDESTINE TRYST SUCCEEDS

You tap softly on my motel room door as I finish drying myself from my shower. I hasten to let you in and our third rendezvous begins. Your light business suit and briefcase identify you as a lady of the world, a businesswoman, petite and slender with a 34-21-33 figure that won't quit teasing me, although you never tease on purpose. Your body simply does it for you without fanfare or design! You completely look the part of what you are: a beautiful lady.

You stare at the tent forming in the towel wrapped around my waist then look up at my face. I give you a knowing smile and help you out of your suit as you reach to undress me. You leave your bra and panties on for me to remove. I unhook your bra, letting your breasts fall free. Then as I bend down to help you out of your suit pants, I remove your panties with my teeth. I start in the middle of your crotch and pull down each side of your hips. I nuzzle your crotch several times to reacquaint myself with your scent.

Soon your gorgeous, shaved cunt is exposed to me like an open rose. You bend down to my crotch and French-kiss my hard member. Then you take a step backwards, falling back onto the bed and I follow, pressing my lips lovingly to your tempting, beautiful vagina as I prepare myself for what's to come.

In a few moments you are very wet and moaning softly as I arouse you with my tongue and lips. I stay at my post for five minutes or so, then insert a vibrator in your cunt to massage your G-spot and grace you with an orgasm.

You writhe on the bed and I get caught up in your excitement. You reach for me and I move up your body to a more comfortable position, where I can kiss you on the lips and feel my hard shaft press against the entrance to your love cove. I kiss my way down from your forehead to your earlobes, your eyes, nose and mouth. Yes! I spend a great deal of time on your lips and mouth and then your neck, throat and onto your gorgeous breasts. I lick, nibble and suck them for several minutes, making the flesh hard and drawing it lovingly into my mouth.

It is almost time. I put a hand between your legs and pull out the vibrator. I relish the way you squirm against my fingers. You are almost ready. My kissing starts again at your beautiful cleavage and I keep going south, sucking your belly button and then your swollen, distended clitoris until it wants to jump out of its sheath! I go back up to caress your lips with my mouth, and once again my soldier stands at attention at the opening of your cunt. The head doesn't want to go in so you help him with your hand. Finally squeezed past the entrance, it is engulfed in your lubrication and slips easily into your wonderful opening.

I glance at my watch and see that we have spent nearly one full hour getting to this point. You moan and give this marine his marching orders. "Darling," you say, "stick yourself inside me and then come! Fuck me hard! Please! Make me come!"

My cock moves easily with you, and I settle into a steady motion, nearly withdrawing after each stroke only to plunge into you completely in the next second. I can feel the pressure growing in my testicles and know I will come soon. Your excitement intensifies and I know you desperately want to climax. You're thirty-two years old and have only been able to come with me!

I stroke faster and as deep as I can, my girth stretching your cunt walls more than anyone has ever done. Every muscle in your body seems to tense as you back against each of my thrusts, arching your back in harmony with my strokes. My foreskin slides in and out of your nether folds. I feel my knob slip past its edge and rub its sensitive head on your steamy cunt walls. It begins slowly and with each gasp for breath you fear you'll lose control, but my stroke is in perfect rhythm with your body. Finally you peak, your orgasm cresting until it crashes, subsides and you regain control.

We roll over together. Your climax is history, but you will never forget it as you tremble in my arms and tell me you want to lie there with me forever. We lie still and fall asleep for about a half hour, then awaken to prepare for the afterplay that might just turn out to be foreplay for the next round!

Whichever happens, we will take it in stride and ride the wind as though on horseback. You kneel astride me and feel my heat rise, engorging my cock with blood, making it hard almost instantly. You suddenly stare at me wide-eyed. "You haven't come yet! We have to make sure you have pleasure, also. Now you know how intense my climax was! Lover, I am so sorry!"

"That's okay, darling, that was your time!" I reply.

You begin to ride my rigid cock as it begins to swell to its fullness. You pump furiously and I know I can't take much more of your movements without coming! Then the sensations build to a peak. I can't believe I'm reaching my climax, then I'm soon coming! For at least a minute my convulsions feed white ropes out of my swollen penis into your soaked, satisfied pussy.

Nothing I can think of at this moment is more pleasing to the flesh than the feeling of your body against mine! You settle down on top of me once again, our bodies pressed together. I want to hold on to you forever!

"You fill me with your sperm like you fill me with love every moment we're together. I wish I could clone you."

"Clone me?" I ask, incredulous.

"Sure! So I could give one of you to every girl in America who's never had a climax! You could sure fill her bill!"

I smile and wisecrack, "It's just a natural talent, I guess, so most of my girlfriends tell me!" You throw a bed pillow at me and kiss me, then I chase you around the room, catching you just before you reach the safety of the bathroom where you could lock the door. I tickle you and we begin to play wrestle, finally falling backwards onto the bed. I straddle you as you lie face-up on the mattress. I bend down and try to kiss you but you turn your face away, giggling with the humor of the moment. I miss your lips but catch an earlobe as you try to get away. You turn your head back forcing me to let go of your ear. Then my lips are upon yours and we suddenly both stop for a second.

Our lips and tongues collide with great beauty and all you can hear is our frantic breathing as we kiss passionately. When we come up for air, you stare into my eyes and murmur, "Oh God, I want you again! Can we do it once more? Please? Can we?"

I smile down as you slowly open your legs and make room for me to mount you again. I move my knees over your legs and now I'm kneeling between them. We feast our eyes on both of our naked bodies and begin to merge them. I slide down to where my forearms lie on your upper thighs and my lips nearly touch your clit. I flick my tongue over your clit, then begin to suck it and lick it as softly as I can. You ask me to increase the pressure ever so slightly and I suck and lick your body for an incredible amount of time.

Soon you begin to gasp with the onset of another orgasm. I maintain a steady rhythm but increase the intensity with which I suck on your swollen, gorgeous love button. You stop writhing and settle down to enjoy the warm flood that is beginning to fill your pussy. I can feel my own climax rising slowly within my loins, then as yours fades out, I slip my sword to and fro in your sopping cunt and then come what seems to be a bucket of sperm.

We finish this tryst by lying side by side and sleeping until our wake-up call from the front desk. We then shower and get dressed quickly. You leave for home as though you were returning from a day of sales calls for your company. I kiss you a fond but reluctant farewell and we promise to call each other the next day.

I check out of the hotel and head home shortly after you have left, hoping that I don't look too clean for having been on a job site as an engineer for a contractor all day, and thus raising the suspicions of my wife.

"Well, how did it go today, dear?" your husband asks innocently as you meet him coming into your apartment building.

"Just great! In fact it reminds me of the great day I had last Wednesday!" you reply.

I reach for the doorknob just as my wife pulls it open. "Well, how did it go today, dear?" she asks smiling at me.

"Perfect! Just like last Wednesday. Not a piece of our equipment failed to perform, so I had no repairs to do!"

It was an honest answer! I can hardly wait until our rendezvous next Wednesday.—*H.T., Santa Fe, New Mexico* ⊶▪

A DISSATISFIED WOMAN FINDS PLEASURE IN SECRET LIFE AS A SLUT

*F*or the past six months, I've been leading a double life. To my family and friends I'm merely a wife, mother and part-time interior decorator. I have two children in high school and a husband who has been my faithful companion for more than twenty years. I have a nice house in the Southern California suburbs and am lucky enough to have a close circle of friends and neighbors. We belong to a mainstream church, and I participate in various charitable activities for a number of causes. That's been my life until last summer, when I began to feel very restless. Things were too normal and content.

Through exercise and some modest dieting, I had taken off ten pounds. One day when I looked at myself naked in the mirror, I realized that I still had a good body. My husband told me as much over the past few months, but as is often the case when someone close gives you a compliment, it didn't sink in. As I was checking out my body, I began to feel my breasts and was soon masturbating. After I had finished coming, it occurred to me that I really could use a few more summer outfits that might better show off my new figure. Because I was feeling so jazzed about myself, I wound up buying a number of very revealing outfits—a couple of skimpy sundresses, some halter tops, a few short skirts, and a low-cut, white party dress. I also got some sexy underwear. The salesperson at the store had been very helpful and confirmed that I really had toned my body. She measured me at 36C-25-35, which is almost the same as when I got married. I wasn't sure how my husband would like my new wardrobe, though, so I decided not to show it to him.

The next day I found myself masturbating again after my shower—not just once, but twice—but I still felt horny afterwards. It was then that I decided to call in to one of those casual sex lines that advertise in the free weekly newspapers. Before I knew it, I was talking to a man arranging to meet him at his hotel bar in Burbank a few hours later. Since it was a warm summer day, I wore one of my new sundresses, thong undies, sandals and no bra.

When I arrived at the hotel bar, the man on the telephone was already there, sitting at a table with a single red rose he told me he'd be carrying so I could identify him. As I walked toward him, he got a big smile on his face. He was certainly good-looking, appeared to be fairly trim, was dressed well but casually and appeared to be in his thirties, a few years younger than me.

He said he was in town on business but his meetings had fallen through. He had a good sense of humor. After two glasses of wine, I was feeling pretty relaxed. He then suggested that we go up to his room. I nodded and took his arm, rubbing my breast against it as we left the bar.

I couldn't believe how incredibly excited I was feeling. I was so horny that I initiated our first kiss the second we got inside his room. Acting as though I was an experienced hooker, I began to undress him by unbuttoning his shirt. He didn't resist my advances. His cock was already erect, and it was a real beauty: thick, circumcised and about seven inches long. Although I rarely give my husband head, I couldn't resist with this guy. I immediately began to lick his cock up and down. I was able to get it in my mouth and relax my throat enough to take him all the way. He was moaning with delight, and I surprised myself by how good I felt blowing him.

Before he came, I stopped and told him it was my turn to be eaten. He smiled at me and began kissing me all over, tonguing my clitoris while he slid his finger into my cunt. I was really getting wet. We moved to the bed, where I draped my legs over his shoulders so he could stick his cock as deep inside me as possible. I wanted him to penetrate me to the fullest. At first he moved slowly in and out. I began to twitch my vaginal muscles, grasping his cock hoping he would fuck me faster. We must have done this for about twenty minutes before he shot his load. I came almost immediately thereafter. I spent another hour with him, and we fucked and sucked each other until we both had come again.

That was the start of my new other life. Each week I arrange to meet a different lover whom I usually contact through some sex chat line. A few times I've just dressed in a sexy way and have gone to a hotel bar where there is likely to be a horny tourist or businessman. The sex has been unbelievable. Although I am feeling a bit guilty about my liaisons, I have said nothing to my husband about them, nor do my children have any reason to suspect that their mother has become a total slut.—*P.H., Los Angeles, California* ⦵⊷▪

INFIDELITY PROVIDES THE PERFECT ESCAPE FROM AN IMPERFECT MARRIAGE

*W*e rendezvous at the motel on the agreed upon date and time. I have already gotten the room and wait for you there. You slip in unnoticed, as usual. We are at least twenty miles from your home and sixty from mine. Meeting someone we know on the short walk from the car to the motel room door would be such a remote chance we don't even consider it. Then you are in my arms.

I push the door closed and it locks securely with the "Do Not Disturb" sign hanging on the outside knob. After several lingering kisses and the usual banter about heavy traffic or road construction, I begin by helping you out of your coat. Then we both shed our clothing and underwear. Soon enough we are both naked. More lingering kisses and soft, light caresses follow and we press our naked bodies together. Foreplay starts here—or maybe it actually started the moment you entered the motel room door.

I kiss and nibble up and down your gorgeous body as you lie on your back across the king-size bed. Your nipples stand at attention even before I begin to kiss them. The areolae stretch and pucker at my touch, the soft brown skin crinkling and contracting the way I love it. You moan and reach out to run your fingers through my hair and gently bring my face down and press it to your moist mound. I shudder in ecstasy as I feel your loins tighten in anticipation, as the quivers of your first of many clitoral climaxes begin. My tongue finds the tip of your newly released clitoris.

Since we rekindled an old affair several weeks ago, you and I have found intimacy and coital ecstasies, to say nothing of wondrous foreplay, that abounds only in the throes of one percent of all the sexual relationships in this world.

Your husband has given you two beautiful children but has never brought you to climax (or even close to one). He is a boorish, self-involved lover who thinks only of his own satisfaction. I am quite a bit older than you are and my wife has used the excuse that I'm "too big" for her vagina and that intercourse hurts. All of a sudden our lovemaking leaves her in pain? Come on! Spare me, please!

This is sometimes a common complaint among some older women, but a lot of them fake it to avoid the unwanted marital encounters and embrace the extramarital ones they yearned for but mistakenly abstained from in their wilder, younger days.

Needless to say there are remedies from their OB/GYN for those women with a genuine problem. But in reality there is nothing short of a miracle that will return the woman who fakes interest in sex to the arms of a loving husband.

You tell me again that the usual sexual episode with your husband lasts a lot less than ten minutes and is similar to the intercourse of rabbits. "Wham, bam, thank you ma'am!" is the way you describe your sex with him. Soon it's all over and you are left woefully unfulfilled, aching inside for some sort of release!

Sex is non-existent for me with my wife, but it is unbelievably, wondrously exciting with you.

We continue our foreplay often taking turns giving each other pleasure. After climaxing together you tell me that I am an artist at foreplay, often taking as much as two hours to complete our sexual union. When you have reached enough climaxes to nearly pass out from ecstasy, I join you in one of your spasms and we come down joyously together. We rouse some time later and do it all over again.

I could describe all this in much more vivid detail, but I'd lose sight of my point, which is that not all marriages are made in heaven. Far too many of us suffer through relationships that are plain hell for us, sexually! On the other hand, of course, there are an infinite number of reasons for maintaining a non-sexual, marital relationship such as I have with my wife and you have with your husband, while at the same time enjoying "forbidden fruit"!

Should it be called forbidden or just the natural release of emotion that often—if not released—destroys the best of otherwise "nice" people? I call it required love. It is a welcome release for both of us.

My wife is the belle of the ball! At a party we attended recently at our country club, she kissed more men, briefly but passionately on the lips, than she has kissed me in the last three months! This woman falls clearly in the "faking it" category! By the time the party was over, her little clit needed a life preserver to swim in the spring-fed atmosphere of her quim! I know her and I know she was soaking wet in her nether regions! She's one step away from a rip-roaring extramarital affair of her own, and guess what? I couldn't be more pleased for her! I hope she's involved in one such affair right now!

Then we will truly have an open marriage and both of us will be a lot happier! It sure isn't working for either of us as it is now! Sadly, though, this need not be the case! Sex therapy counseling could do wonders for her and for your husband, my dearest love! I would hate to lose you but we both know the only way we could part is if your husband could define and employ foreplay into his sexual vocabulary with you, and my wife could rebuild the great love we once shared.

Also, sadly, I know your relationship with your husband is more likely to return to a satisfactory state than is mine. Your husband is trainable! My wife, on the other hand, must play out the hand life has dealt her and grow tired of the "Wham, bam, thank you, ma'am!" style of lovemaking and find our kind of mutual pleasure, before she can ever be truly satisfied.

Foreplay is a key ingredient in a happy sexual union. Alas, I learned this too late to make a difference in my marriage, but now I'm making up for it!

I've found you, with the great needs that I can satisfy and you have found me with the great needs that you've wondrously fulfilled! All this may change one day, but in the meantime we must enjoy things the way they are! We must make the most of a great opportunity to give and receive satisfaction and true love to each other in the absence of such satisfaction from others! I will cherish you always!

You pause in our lovemaking to say, "I implore you to make love to me in all the wondrous ways I see written in your eyes." If our spouses did this, we probably wouldn't be here, and this letter wouldn't find its way to your great publication.

Thank you, *Penthouse Letters*! You've provided an outlet for our very special confessions! We hope other people find solace in the understanding we impart to all of you out there who live and love secretly, as we do!—*R.S., Canton, Ohio*

Swinging & Swapping

A PHOTOGRAPHER GETS A HELPER AND
LOOK WHAT DEVELOPS

When I was looking for a job as a junior in college, I answered an ad for a position as a photographer's assistant. It indicated a good salary for what sounded like pretty simple part-time work and free room and board on the premises. I was impressed when I met Colin, the photographer. He was obviously a bodybuilder, he was six feet tall, handsome and had dark eyes and dark wavy hair. He was impressed during my interview that I had some amount of experience behind the camera and wanted to know if I had any experience in front of it. He said he needed to photograph me because he could use my image or parts of it sometimes. He took a few shots then asked if I wouldn't mind stripping down to my shorts.

After a few more pictures, he asked me to drop the shorts. I hesitated at first but finally did so. Next he asked me to get an erection. I said I wasn't sure I could, so he said he'd help and started to stroke my penis, balls and nipples. My penis got hard, he got the shots he wanted and I got the job. He was pleased with my cock and the fact that I was a true redhead and that I kept myself in good shape.

Soon after I got the position, we were sharing our first assignment together. Colin had agreed to take pictures of a lady for her husband, who would be present at the session. After taking a couple of test shots, he asked the model—a pretty, well-built woman in her thirties named Petra—to put on lingerie. He then suggested that since the lighting in the studio was so soft, that her husband, himself and I strip to our briefs to make her comfortable. We all did.

The pictures Colin was taking got more and more provocative. He went up to Petra, reached around her back and unclasped her bra. Her nipples were hard, but he said that they weren't hard enough, so he asked her husband to suck one while he sucked the other. She started moaning and was obviously very aroused. I was snapping away, and he had a videotape camera running on a tripod. He removed her panties and, after some more shots, invited her husband to fuck her, which he did in the missionary position. The husband had a thin, five-inch cock. Colin took off his briefs and asked that I take mine off as well. Colin's penis was a little bit longer than mine but also a little bit thinner. The husband came quickly and Colin asked Petra and her husband if they wanted the two of us to fuck her. The wife said yes and the husband said yes, but only if he could suck us also. Colin said that was fine with him if it was fine with me. And it was.

They each sucked us and kept switching back and forth between us. Petra then said she wanted us to fuck her. Colin went first. Petra sucked my cock while Colin bent her over and fucked her doggie-style. Petra's husband was alternately licking my balls and Colin's balls and asshole. With the stimulation he was getting from both sides, Colin came quickly. The wife said since my cock was so thick, she wanted to be on top so she could control how deep I penetrated her. She rode me hard and when I got ready to blow my load, I flipped her over and drilled her till I came. Her husband then sucked both Colin's and my sperm out her cunt. All in all, it was a wonderful two hours.

At the time I was dating a freshman girl. I wanted to make love to her, but she wasn't ready. Considering everything we did together at work, of course I confided this in Colin. One night when I got to work he said I looked like I had blue balls again, and I admitted that Joanne left me high and dry. He seemed genuinely concerned about my lack of a love life and said he would teach me how to seduce a woman, but only if I would role-play the female part.

He slowly undressed himself and then turned his attentions to me, stripping me down, whispering in my ear and nibbling and nuzzling everywhere on my body. I was so incredibly excited that I opened myself to him completely. A hot bout of 69 ended with him blasting his come down my throat just before I came in his mouth.

Colin's lesson worked like a charm. I made it with Joanne on the next date, and we became more and more sophisticated lovers. I shouldn't have been too surprised, though, because Colin had on several occasions proved himself to be quite the experienced libertine. His own girlfriend was a married woman whose husband was rich, important and socially connected. The husband knew about

Colin and his wife and sometimes participated in their trysts. But Colin was free a lot of the time.

As Joanne hung around the studio more and more, she and Colin got better acquainted. I could tell he wanted her (she's a five-foot-ten blonde with a 35-24-34 figure). One Sunday afternoon after Colin had opened up his swimming pool, he suggested that the three of us go for a swim. Joanne didn't have a bathing suit, so Colin suggested that we all swim in our underwear. He told Joanne he knew that she wasn't wearing a bra, but it was okay because he saw breasts all the time at work. She looked at me and I nodded approvingly. I said I had to run upstairs and get some briefs since I wasn't wearing any. Colin said not to worry about it since Joanne and he had both seen me naked.

We started swimming with me nude, Joanne in her panties and Colin in a pair of Speedos. I got an erection. Colin told Joanne she should help me with that. When she didn't respond right away, he started sucking my cock. Joanne surprised me by pulling off his G-string and sucking him. We both came then started sucking her gorgeous breasts. I kissed her twat while Colin made love to her mouth. She had two or three orgasms that way. Then I fucked her cunt while Colin fucked her mouth. He and I wound up trading back and forth till we both came in her pussy. Colin took pictures of the three of us later on.

Joanne and I eventually married, moved to the suburbs and had three children. We always let Colin in on our sexual action whenever we visit him and he's kept up to date on his other threesomes. He's the godfather of our children, and all three of us believe he is the biological father of our dark-haired daughter. But he deserves it after everything he taught us.—*F.H., Seattle, Washington* o┼▧

HIS NEW YOUNG BRIDE WINDS UP HAVING
HER CAKE AND EATING IT TOO

I met Kathleen shortly after my first wife died of cancer. Our marriage had been a good one. We were deeply devoted to each other and very much in love, but our sex life was rather pedestrian. My wife was smart, nice and personable, but over the years her interest in sex had waned. We remained married and in love for thirty years, though, and I was in a deep depression over my loss.

Things picked up after I met Kathleen. I was fifty-five years old at the time and Kathleen was thirty-two. I was just casually talking to her in a restaurant at lunchtime, not looking for anything special, when she asked if I wanted to have a drink after work. I said I'd be delighted.

For the first time in months, I started to feel good about things, and my spirits really began to lift. She was dressed attractively in a skirt, white blouse and suit jacket. I was a little taken aback, and more than a little distracted, when I first met her because her skirt was a bit on the short side and rode fairly high up. When she sat down I got a good look at her long legs and especially her nicely toned thighs.

When we met for drinks later that night, she was wearing the same outfit as at lunchtime, but she had unbuttoned several buttons on her blouse, leaving her deep cleavage exposed in quite a seductive way. When I asked Kathleen why she'd asked me out for drinks, she said it was because I looked so sad. I told her my story, and she very sympathetically put her hand on my arm. We then decided to have dinner together that Friday night.

After supper she invited me back to her apartment to have an after-dinner drink. She served me some sherry and sat down next to me on the couch with a snifter of brandy. Her skirt had hiked way up, and I could see that she was wearing stockings with a garter. Her perfume was enticing. I put my arm around her and before I knew it, we were in a deep, passionate kiss. She began rubbing her hand on my crotch. Soon she stood up to put some music on and began to do a slow striptease for me. My cock was rock-hard.

When she was completely nude, she took me by the hand, led me into her bedroom and proceeded to undress me. She went down and started licking my cock, then turned her cunt to me. I moved my face close to her hole, taking in her wonderful scents, and proceeded to lick her. Before we could come off, she got on top of me and began to ride me. She had tremendous muscle control—I could feel her intentionally contracting her pussy on my cock as she bounced up and down. After a while we both exploded in orgasm. We spent the rest of that night and much of the weekend together. At my age, I wasn't able to fuck her as often as she wanted, but she taught me how to please her with the various vibrators and dildos she kept around the house.

I soon discovered that Kathleen was a smart, kind and outgoing woman. Her parents had been relatively poor, and she put herself through college and business school before landing her current position, a very responsible job at a well-known public relations firm. When I asked her during that first weekend why she wasn't married and didn't have a steady boyfriend, she laughed and said that it all had to do with her libido. She loved sex and needed constant variety. She didn't want to be tied down sexually to one man but wanted everything else that goes with a happy marriage.

Kathleen confessed that she had long been sexually active. She also said she was a bit of an exhibitionist. She became tremendously turned on when other people watched her in sexual situations. Since she liked to have men watch her, it was a natural decision for her to earn the money she needed by performing in strip clubs. She explained to me that the lap dancers at these strip clubs had different senses of the limits. A girl could make the real big money if she was willing to go all the way in some of the discrete private booths. Since she liked sex so much, she quickly (and deservedly) got the reputation of doing whatever a man wanted, as long as it didn't involve pain. While she was careful to dress and act very professionally at her day job, she liked picking up a succession of men in her free time. She said she even had a separate closet full of what she called her "slut clothes." She went out to clubs dressed to kill on the weekends and spent most of her vacations in places where she was likely to find multiple, good-looking male partners to play around with. I went with her on one of those trips. It was so comfortable and sexually gratifying that we agreed to spend even more time together. Our understanding, though, was that Kathleen was free to have sex whenever and with whomever she wanted, and I wouldn't ask any questions or try to change her.

I soon discovered the fact that Kathleen's intense sexuality was a real turn-on for me. In fact, on several occasions during our courtship, she let me hide in her closet and watch her having sex with other guys she'd picked up. I'd get incredibly horny, and we'd have great sex. After about six months, we decided to get married.

That was five years ago. My friends have come to accept Kathleen into our group, and Kathleen's close friends have done the same with me. But none of them are aware of Kathleen's and my sexual under-standing. Even at age thirty-seven, she still keeps in terrific shape. With her pretty face, auburn hair and 36-25-35 body, she has little trouble getting whomever she wants. She dresses attractively but not overly revealing when she's with them. Her slutty side only comes out when we make special arrangements or when she goes on vacations alone. On those occasions, I've watched Kathleen have sex with up to five men at once, most of whom are fairly young and all of whom are quite well-hung.

Since we're so comfortable with our arrangement, Kathleen has started performing at one of her old strip clubs again. Although most of the other girls are younger, she still manages to hold her own. I usually go with her, although we don't reveal to the customers (or the management) that I'm her husband. I watch her go off with other men. On a good evening, she makes close to a thousand dollars in cash. We don't need the money since we both have good-paying jobs, but it's nice to have some extra cash for our special vacations.

Those vacations have turned into absolute orgies for her. We often rent a large house at the end of an isolated road near a beach or on some island community. Kathleen brings only her most revealing clothes, like string bikinis, a few short, low-cut sundresses, tight skirts and skimpy haltertops and blouses. I get incredibly turned-on watching her and knowing that others watch her as well. While we spend most of the time entertaining Kathleen's men friends, we've also met a number of couples who like to swing. I'm always the gracious host. It always surprises me that no matter how many times Kathleen gets screwed in a day, she's always ready to fuck when I am. She seems to have gotten everything she's wanted: a secure, happy marriage and the freedom to do whatever she pleases sexually.—*P.B., Los Angeles, California*

AN AD IN A SWINGER'S MAGAZINE GETS A COUPLE MORE THAN THEY HOPED FOR

*T*he word "voluptuous" fits my wife Lynda to a tee. She's five foot six with natural 38DD tits and very sexy legs. I stand six foot four, weight two hundred fifteen pounds and am a well-endowed nine inches. We've been swinging in our local scene for a few years and decided to place an ad in a swinger's magazine to meet new people. We received lots of interesting responses but the one that really caught our eyes came from a couple who lived about an hour and a half from us. We wrote back and exchanged photos, and after corresponding for a while met at a quaint restaurant about midway between our houses.

Kim was very petite—only five foot two—but she was very sexy, with full breasts, long hair and a great personality. Her husband Ross was also very personable, and we all had a good time getting to know one another the first time we met. We got tickets to go see a professional baseball team and were planning on making a whole weekend out of it, obviously including some hot sensual fun.

The drive to Ross and Kim's hotel turned out to be an exercise in self-restraint, but unfortunately, the only self-restraint being practiced was mine! Lynda was dressed in a very tight pair of shorts and a halter top, it was obvious she wasn't wearing a bra. Her large-nippled 38DD's were sticking through the material, testing the limits of my restraint and my jeans! When we stopped at a rest area, Lynda got in the back seat with Ross and Kim came up front to sit with me. That just made things hotter as I had this short, very voluptuous and sensual woman sitting beside me.

While Lynda was sitting in the back, she started showing off a very nice pair of 38DD's to almost every trucker we passed and Kim started doing the same up front. I almost ran off the road a couple of times looking over my shoulder at my wife or watching the show that Kim was putting on! I wanted to skip the ball game right there and do something about my aching, hard cock. Matters weren't helped much by all the flirting and touching Kim and I were doing in the front seat!

After we checked in at the hotel, we had a quick bite to eat and headed for the stadium. The game was exciting but not as exciting as the continuous eye contact between Kim and myself. Lynda noticed what was going on and did her best to give me a severe case of blue balls, too! At one point we decided that if it wasn't too late we should go for a swim back to the hotel. The game was good but not great, so we agreed to split and take a dip. Once we were all in our rooms, we changed into our suits, but Ross didn't feel like swimming so it was just Lynda, Kim and me.

The three of us swam around for a while, with Lynda lounging at one end and Kim at the other. I was having the time of my life. I'd swim to one end and kiss and flirt with my wife then do the same with Kim. I even swam underwater to give Kim a momentary touch of my mouth on her pussy. A light rain started falling, making the whole evening even more erotic. After a while Lynda got out of the pool but Kim and I continued to fool around until we both looked up and saw a crowd of people on a second-floor balcony who were watching our erotic scene play out. Kim and myself were both quite embarrassed at that point and got out of the pool. We kissed good-night and went back to our respective spouses. I was so horny that night I could hardly sleep. And it didn't help matters any that my cock was as hard as a two by four when I got back to my room, but I didn't feel like waking Lynda up.

Ross called from his room the next morning and talked to Lynda. My wife got a sly smile on her face after she hung up the phone I was wondering what was going on. Suddenly she pulled my cock out and started giving me a great blowjob. Finally, some relief! I thought. But just when I was going to explode down her throat she stopped abruptly, jumped off the bed and got dressed. Then she told me that she and Ross were going out to get some breakfast and that Kim was waiting upstairs in their room. We kissed passionately, I told Lynda I loved her and as fast as I could stuffed my hard cock in my jeans, ran upstairs, knocked on Kim's motel room door and heard her sultry voice welcome me in.

I entered the room to find her laying on the bed wearing some really sexy lingerie. I was out of my clothes in a flash and practically tripped as I went to Kim and took her in my arms. I peeled off Kim's sexy outfit and I saw her beautiful nipples come to life. I just had to suck them and kiss them. I thought she'd come right then. Maybe she did come, because after quickly working my way down her body, I found her pussy very, very wet. As soon as my mouth and tongue touched her she was coming again, all over my face! I continued to eat her out until she couldn't take anymore and begged to feel my prick inside her.

She took my cock in her mouth just to tease me a little more, looking up into my eyes as my cock disappeared down her throat again and again! I couldn't take any more and finally made her stop so I didn't cream all over her face. I put my cock at the slippery entrance of her cunt. I tried to start out fucking her slowly, but Kim grabbed my ass and shoved her hips up so forcefully that I was in her completely with just a couple of small strokes. As I worked myself in and out of her hole I reached underneath and grabbed her ass so I could fuck her as deeply as possible. With all the noise, I thought for sure we'd get a call from the manager any minute!

It seemed like Kim was having one orgasm right after another. She sounded so exciting that it wasn't long until I lost control, jammed my cock in her to the hilt and just exploded. She was still coming, and we held on for dear life during the sensual explosion we were experiencing. Finally after the room stopped spinning we fell apart and lay beside each other, catching our breath. We had just finished fucking for the second time when we heard Lynda and Ross pull back into the parking lot from breakfast. We kissed and cuddled and exchanged a most heartfelt thank you for the incredible experience we'd just shared!

When the time came for us all to check out the next day, Ross walked with me to the main office to return our room keys. After some small talk he asked if I'd had as good a time with Kim as she'd said she had with me. All I could do was thank him for sharing his wife with me and give him a big smile. Nothing else had to be said!—*M.K., St. Louis, Missouri* ○┼▣

BEFORE THEY GOT HITCHED, THEY SOWED THEIR WILD OATS TOGETHER

*M*y fiancee's friend Antoinette came down to visit us at our apartment in Minneapolis. Antoinette is a tiny, sweet-looking twenty-year-old with a nice round ass and full tits. My fiancee Diana is hot, sexy and cute all rolled into one. She's a bit taller than Antoinette and sports a full, round ass, big, beautiful tits and a tight pussy.

Antoinette arrived on a Friday night, wearing a pair of skin-tight jeans and a skimpy T-shirt, and she had her blonde hair pulled back in a ponytail. She gave Diana a hug, then turned to me. As we hugged I playfully patted her ass. I felt my cock grow with lust.

The three of us spent that night lounging around talking, then we all got dressed for bed. Antoinette put on a pair of little pink shorts and a pink tank top. Diana had on gray shorts and a sleeveless T-shirt. I was wearing sweat pants and a shirt. We sat around in the spare bedroom, reminiscing about the old days, like school and such.

When Antoinette sat up to grab a photo album from her suitcase, her shorts slid open, exposing the slightest outline of her pink pussy. Needless to say, my cock started getting hard again. Diana noticed and, to my surprise, gave me a quick little smile.

Diana and I have talked about fucking other people before, and we were hoping this would be the weekend we'd finally get around to actually doing it. Antoinette was the object of my desire this weekend. For Diana it was Frank, whom I work with at an FM radio station. Frank's a pretty cool guy, about five foot nine, one hundred fifty pounds, and very good-looking. Nothing happened that Friday night, but Saturday was when it all went down.

I gave Frank a call and asked him to go with us to our local dance club. The place we went to is a real meat market for young horny people, and a great place to get cheap beer. We were all going for the dancing and drinking and flirting and who-knew-what-else.

By the time we arrived, the club was hopping, the drinks were flowing and the music was pounding. Diana and Antoinette grabbed a table near the dance floor and Frank and I went to the bar to grab us some drinks. After a bit we all hit the dance floor.

Diana and I started grinding up against each other and Antoinette and Frank danced together, just like we had planned. Frank doesn't dance much, but when it comes to bumping and grinding with a beautiful woman, he can more than hold his own. I noticed that Antoinette and Frank were getting hot for each other, and so could anyone who saw them. My cock was already hard from Diana grinding her sweet tight ass up against it. Little did I know that wouldn't be the only time that I'd be getting hard that night.

When the music changed we all decided to change partners. Antoinette immediately started rubbing up against me. My cock was rock-hard again. Antoinette rubbed her hand on my chest then moved it down, brushing against my manhood. A broad grin came over her face as she felt the hardness that had formed in my pants.

I looked across the way and saw that Frank was dancing close to Diana, and he had his hands on her ass. I saw him give her ass a squeeze, and Diana's face lit up with excitement. Then she turned around and began grinding her ass into Frank's crotch. I could only imagine how hard his cock was getting. We spent the rest of the night dancing, having some good sexy fun and occasionally switching partners.

After the club closed we took the party back to our apartment. On the way home things started getting better. Antoinette and Frank were getting hot and heavy in the back seat, kissing and petting, and pretty soon Frank had his hands in Antoinette's tight pants fingering her while Antoinette unzipped his shorts. She pulled out his hard, thick cock and began stroking it between her palms. I adjusted the rearview mirror so I could watch them go at it.

Diana looked at me and thought the same thing I did. "Why should those two have all the fun?"

With that Diana unzipped my pants and began sucking me off while I tried to concentrate on my driving. What with all the excitement, I started to push down on the accelerator every once in a while and before I knew it we were doing eighty-five in a forty-five-mile-per-hour zone. I stepped on the brakes to get down to the speed limit. I wasn't looking forward to getting a speeding ticket. I was just looking forward to Diana sucking my cock.

I looked into the mirror to see that Antoinette was on her back. Frank had pushed her pants down to reveal her pink pussy and was giving her face. She was in ecstasy.

Right when I was about to come we pulled into our apartment parking lot.

"We're home!" I exclaimed.

The festivities had stopped for the time being, until we returned to the apartment. We sat on the couch talking, listening to music while enjoying some more drinks.

"We should play a game," Antoinette said.

"What do you have in mind?" I asked, hoping for the best.

Antoinette thought for a moment. "How about Spin the Bottle?"

"Jesus, I thought you graduated high school," I joked.

"C'mon," she laughed. "It'll be fun."

We all agreed to play, using an empty beer bottle. Since the game was her idea, Antoinette spun first.

The bottle landed on Frank and they kissed. Then Frank spun. The bottle spun around quickly and finally rested on Diana. Frank looked at me for approval. I just smiled and waved at him to go ahead. Frank and Diana kissed for a brief moment, Diana adding a little tongue at the end.

A few spins later Antoinette and I kissed.

It wasn't too much later that the kissing gave way to some heavy petting. It started with Diana and Frank. They were kissing, but pretty soon Frank had her in his arms. He stuck his hand up Diana's shirt and started fondling her perfect tits. Frank quickly made his way into Diana's pants and went to work on her wet pussy. I couldn't help but get excited watching his hand doing a good job on my fiancee.

I glanced over at Antoinette. She was mesmerized by the show the two were putting on. She was rubbing herself through her pants and moaning softly.

Diana unzipped Frank's fly and his cock flopped into view. I've seen a few cocks in my day, but I have to admit that Frank's was the thickest I've seen, by far. Diana licked her hand and proceeded to give him the best handjob I'm sure he's ever had.

As I'm sure you know, I got pretty aroused by what I was watching. Diana sure was doing a fine job handling Frank's throbbing dick. Frank licked a finger then slid his other hand around behind Diana's back and started playing with her asshole.

Antoinette couldn't take it anymore. Her pussy needed some attention, so she crawled across the floor and stretched out in front of me. She leaned up until her lips touched mine. Soon after our tongues met, my hand went straight for her cunt. It was hot, wet and as tight as I hoped it would be. I used my other hand to lower her pants a bit more to make it easier to rub her clit. She moaned again as I rubbed.

She worked my pants open then dove down on her knees so she could start blowing me. As she swallowed my cock I looked over so I could watch Diana and Frank. Diana's hand was stroking his dick faster and faster, and Frank began breathing harder as he got closer to coming.

Suddenly, I heard Frank groan. I looked over just as Diana sucked Frank's cock all the way down her throat. Frank couldn't take it. He just exploded, spraying come into Diana's mouth. He seemed to come forever. Somehow Diana managed to take most of it in, and what she missed she licked off her tits.

That did it for me. I shot my load into Antoinette's mouth. Like a good girl she took it all, not missing a drop and making sure that I saw she swallowed it all by sticking her tongue out at me when it was gone.

Both Frank and I laid down on our backs, basking in the glow, with our cocks going back into their relaxed state. Diana looked at us.

"You guys are done already? I was just getting started," Diana said.

Antoinette moved over and wrapped her arm around Diana. "Maybe they need a little inspiration. Let's see if we can give them some."

With that Antoinette planted a kiss on Diana. Their hands instantly started exploring each other's beautiful bodies and they started rubbing each other's pussies while they continued kissing. Seeing that got Frank and me going again. Almost instantly my dick started coming back to life. Frank started stroking his cock, getting the mammoth ready for some more action.

Antoinette slid her hand up Diana's shirt, pulled her bra up over her big, firm tits, and proceeded to suck her nipples stiff. Diana showed her approval by reaching down and pulling Antoinette's head closer to her breasts. After a bit Antoinette pushed my fiancee down onto her back. Antoinette slid Diana's pants down and positioned herself between her legs. She then pushed aside Diana's black thong panties revealing a beautiful pink pussy.

"Lick my cunt, baby," Diana lustfully commanded.

Antoinette started out by licking circles around Diana's snatch, touching everywhere but her pussy. Antoinette ran her tongue around the lips and just around the hood. Diana was hot as hell and needed gratification. She held on to Antoinette's head and brought her face to her pussy.

"Lick it, you fucking tease!"

Antoinette obliged.

Diana started moaning even louder as Antoinette stuck her tongue deep inside her warm, wet folds, flicking it across the clit, teasing her.

By then I was whacking off, too.

Diana looked over at Frank and me with lustful eyes. "I need to have a cock in my mouth, and I need it now. Who's going to take care of me?"

I was more than happy to help. I positioned myself over her face and shoved my cock deep into her mouth. Diana went to work on my rod. Without missing a beat, Frank moved over to Antoinette. He pulled off her panties and then laid down with his head between her legs so he could lick her dripping pussy. Antoinette let out a soft moan as he moved his tongue across her lips. Seconds later he rubbed the rim of her asshole with a wet finger. He teased her by inserting just the tip of his finger inside her.

"Oh, my God! Give it all to me," she pleaded. "Stick it all in me now!"

By then Antoinette was fingering Diana as well while Diana sucked me off. Suddenly, Diana screamed out, "Yes! I'm going to come!"

Antoinette started to devour Diana's pussy to help bring her off. When Diana lifted her hips up, Frank slid his entire finger up into Antoinette's ass. Antoinette let out a muffled cry as she began to come, too.

Diana thrashed about as an orgasm rushed through her body. Antoinette had to do all she could to keep eating Diana out while she came. When they finished Frank and I moved out of the way and Diana and Antoinette lay side by side, kissing softly and stroking each other's hair as they regained their composure. They were far from done, though, as it seemed that their orgasms only made them hotter and hornier. They both got on their hands and knees, showing their asses to Frank and me. We looked over at each other and instantly jumped into action.

Diana's pussy was so wet I didn't even have to lube my cock to slide it in. Diana drew in a sharp breath. Antoinette groaned in ecstasy as Frank slid his thick prick in. Side by side Frank and I fucked our beauties.

I had to start slow, because Diana's pussy is naturally tight, like a virgin's. It took a little time to work it loose, but I was more than happy to do so.

Frank started off slow, too, but when Antoinette said, "Fuck me like you mean it," he really started fucking her madly. I watched his thick cock ram in and out of Antoinette's pussy and couldn't help but think that Diana would love some of the same treatment.

Diana must have seen Frank's cock at work, too, because she quickly got up and pulled Frank off of Antoinette and pushed him onto the ground. She then impaled herself onto his huge member. I could see his cock stretching her pussy further than ever, but Diana loved every second of it. As she bounced up and down Frank was licking and sucking her nipples and squeezing her ass.

I was so transfixed by what I was watching that Antoinette surprised me by shoving me to the ground, sliding herself onto my dick. She was turned around so she could watch Diana and show me her lovely ass. I saw her asshole begging for some action of its own, so I licked my finger and slid it on in. Antoinette threw her head back and squealed with appreciation.

Diana was close to coming again. She jumped off Frank's wet cock and got down on her hands and knees. Frank grabbed hold of her by the hips, fucking her from behind, his thighs slapping against her ass as he mounted her. Being my favorite position as well as Diana's, I pushed Antoinette down to the floor and fucked her the same way.

"Jesus, I'm gonna come," Antoinette said. "Fuck my asshole. Stick it in me and fuck it hard."

My cock, wet with pussy juice, slid easily into her asshole.

"Go deeper," she said. "Go deeper and harder, harder," Antoinette ordered.

I responded by pounding her ass as hard as I could.

Frank was doing the same to Diana's pussy. I couldn't understand how she could take it. She was wailing, it felt so good. "God, don't stop fucking me! I'm coming!" she cried.

Frank fucked her even harder. Diana cried out as she began to come. This finally took Frank to the point of no return. Grunts and groans came from him as he shot his load deep into Diana's pussy.

Two more strokes from me and Antoinette started to come herself. "Oh, yeah," she squealed. "Fuck me deeper! I'm coming!"

Hearing a woman's orgasm never fails to bring on my own orgasm.

My cock exploded as I pumped back and forth into her tight asshole. Antoinette started bucking against my cock with every one of my thrusts, practically daring me to fuck her harder. "I can feel your come filling me up," she said as I blew load after load in her ass.

Diana and Frank, exhausted, had fallen onto each other and were kissing passionately.

As I shot the last of my come into her, Antoinette's orgasms finally subsided, too. I pulled out and laid on top of her. We began making out. After a while we all fell asleep on the floor holding one another. We woke up the next morning bleary-eyed and fucked out and relived the previous night's events over coffee and Danish. That weekend Frank called in sick to work and we had ourselves a big, beautiful orgy.—*C.S., Minneapolis, Minnesota* ⊶▪

HER HUSBAND'S THREEWAY FANTASY COMES TRUE IN A MOST PLEASANT WAY

I'm a happily married woman named Annie. I'm five-feet-four-inches tall, newly blonde and I have luscious 36C breasts, a clean-shaved pussy, great legs and a firm, high-riding ass. Over the last few years I'd heard that a woman's hormones shift into overdrive when she hits her forties, and so far I'm not disappointed. I've become multi-orgasmic over the past couple of years. I've always enjoyed sex, but now it's my favorite form of recreation. I want to share with you my incredible experience of having two hot, sexy and attentive lovers who made my threesome fantasy a reality.

For years my husband Philip has been preparing me for a threesome. He carefully laid the groundwork by showing me porno videos, reading to me from *Penthouse Letters* and buying me sexy lingerie and erotic toys. He would write me hot, steamy love notes about how much he wanted to see another man's cock penetrating my mouth and filling my pussy. We had many passionate nights of wild sex while fantasizing about my mystery lover. I had reservations about bringing someone into our marriage even though we love and trust each other very much. We have a great relationship that all our friends are jealous of. I didn't want anything to mess it up, so I knew a threesome would have to be handled very carefully. Honestly, the idea of having a threesome really turned me on, but I couldn't imagine myself actually going through with it. The dawn of the new Millennium changed all that, though, as I adopted a sexy new attitude: Out with the old and in with the new!

Philip had made our New Year's Eve plans. I didn't know we were going to a swinger's dinner/dance at a local hotel until a few hours before we left home. I was angry and panicked at first, but I found myself getting very excited and aroused at the idea. I was surprised and delighted by the caliber of people at the party. I'm not sure what I thought they would be like, but they were all well-heeled and well-attired. Even though I was intrigued, we sat by a table near the door so I'd be able to make a quick getaway if I got uncomfortable.

We weren't there for very long when two other couples sat down and joined us. They were all friendly, engaging people. One of the couples, Kenneth and Phoebe, were very attractive, although a bit older than us. They're originally from overseas and have wonderful, charming European accents. They took pictures during the evening and asked for our address to send us copies when they got them developed. I was relaxed and enjoying myself, nearly forgetting where I was. I noticed as the evening went on that every time I looked across the table, Kenneth was looking at me. I liked having his attention. Nothing sexual happened that night, because I just wasn't ready for a real swinger's adventure.

Several days later, we received the pictures and a nice letter from Kenneth. About a week after that, Kenneth sent us another letter inviting Philip and I for dinner and a possible threesome afterward. He was very considerate and polite in the way he asked us to swing. I knew he'd be a good lover for our first time, because although he was obviously experienced, he was also a complete gentleman. Initially, I was panicked but each time I read his letter, I got more and more excited. My pussy was soaked. I couldn't think of anything else but making our threesome fantasy a reality. Philip and I had some long and hot sex after getting Kenneth's letter. I wrote back to Kenneth and accepted his gracious, exciting offer.

Kenneth called a few days later to say he was very excited about being part of our first threesome. Things really heated up over the next few days. All three of us were hot and horny as we made our plans to meet. Somehow I was able to get through two more days of work. What torture! Philip and Kenneth had several conversations about what I liked sexually and what they were going to do to me when we got together. Kenneth and I had several very hot phone calls ourselves.

Philip and I carefully put together my wardrobe. We finished getting ourselves ready and checked into the hotel about five o'clock that night. I jumped in the shower and prepared for our big evening. Kenneth met us at the hotel for dinner at about eight o'clock. He looked so sexy that I wanted to fuck him right then. I was ready for him, too, dressed in a black leather mini-skirt (without panties, of course), pantyhose, a garter-belt, a pair of high heel sandals with bright red toenails, and an open-nippled bra under a gold silk blouse.

Soon it was show time! The restaurant was empty except for two other tables. I don't remember much of dinner except that Kenneth's hands immediately began exploring between my legs. Like a naughty girl I spread my legs and let him in. The look on his face when he realized I wasn't wearing panties was priceless, but it didn't take him long to get used to the idea! He shoved his fingers in my bare, soaked pussy and then licked his fingers. Kenneth and Philip made me unbutton my blouse so their hands could stroke and tease my hard nipples through my bra. Before long Kenneth grabbed my hand and pushed it under the table and placed it around his big, hard prick. The waiter was having an especially good time watching us. I looked over at Philip and said, "I think that I'm going to be a very happy gal by the end of tonight." I knew I was in for a good time.

We went to our room and poured some champagne. While Philip went in the bathroom, Kenneth pulled his cock out of his pants and put my hand around it. I was so excited that I went over and sat on the sofa. Next thing I knew my leather mini-skirt was up around my waist, my legs were spread wide and Kenneth was tonguing my dripping wet pussy.

Philip came out from the bathroom to see the fun had started without him. He quickly dropped his pants and shoved his cock into my mouth. After I had several orgasms riding Kenneth's tongue, they switched places. As I became lost in the feelings that engulfed me, I began to think about how I was feeling. Was I scared? No. Shy? No. Hot and horny? Absolutely! In fact, I was enjoying myself more than

I imagined I would. It surprised me how easily I took to being with two men. We then went into the bedroom, where Philip had a video camera set up to capture our first threesome on tape. I couldn't wait. I was about to become a porn star!

Once we were in the bedroom, I changed into a slinky black negligee, leaving on only my black pantyhose, garterbelt and heels. I couldn't wait to get Kenneth's cock between my lips. I knew he would taste so delicious and feel so good once I had him in my mouth. I absolutely love to suck cock. After watching me eagerly suck Kenneth's cock, Philip went back to eating my pussy to several more orgasms. Kenneth got ready to fuck my shaved pussy with his eager prick. After fifteen years of fucking nobody but my husband, it felt so naughty having another man's cock in my mouth and in my pussy. "Kenneth, fuck me hard with that big, delicious cock," I told him between hurried breaths.

I was completely full of cock and loving every minute of it. My mouth was going to town on Philip's prick while Kenneth pumped himself in and out of my pussy. Kenneth flooded my already soaked cunt with his first load. Philip dived between my legs so he could eat my come-filled pussy while I sucked my juices off of Kenneth's cock. I was in heaven, it tasted so sweet.

Then Philip started licking me. He was so excited to be living out his fantasy of eating me after another man had filled me with scum. He stopped eating me to shoot his first load inside me, then went back to eat my cunt again. I'm a lucky gal to be with a man who loves me so much and is so willing to let me have so much fun while pleasing him.

After a short rest and a quick change of costume, I started sucking Kenneth hard again while Philip fucked my over heated pussy to another orgasm. I couldn't believe how much I was enjoying this. I knew that the guys were having a blast, too. Kenneth again fucked my pussy. His big cock felt incredible as it pounded its way in and out of my overworked twat. We had another wonderful orgasm together. Philip's tongue was ready for another load of come from my fucked-out pussy.

The fire burning inside me was very hot and it seemed like there was no extinguishing it. Philip started to fuck me in the ass, slowly at first but with increasing speed and depth while my seemingly insatiable mouth sucked on Kenneth's cock. It seemed like Philip was fucking my tight ass forever by the time he finally had his orgasm.

He came but he was still hard, and he continued fucking my asshole. I had another orgasm with my husband's cock in my ass and this stranger's cock in my mouth.

Philip jumped in the shower while I continued to suck Kenneth's cock until he came in my mouth. I couldn't believe it, but he was still hard and wanted to go a third round with my pussy. Philip came out of the bathroom to find me on my back with my legs spread wide and Kenneth wildly fucking away. Oh, yes, you better believe I had another orgasm. Philip again ate my pussy for me and then fucked it hard himself.

Finally it was my turn for a shower. Once I was cleaned off, I hung up my bathrobe and again changed into my lingerie, hose and heels. I climbed back into bed between my two studs with my feet at the head of the bed so I could look at them and stroke their penises while we relaxed. I was glowing from all my orgasms but I was still ready for more sex. I finally wore out my guys after three rounds of cock-sucking and fucking. It felt good to be such a dirty little whore, I couldn't believe it had taken me so long to finally do it.

Kenneth bid us both good-night and left. Once we were alone, Philip and I had some more incredible sex—once that night and twice again the next morning. We couldn't wait to get home and watch our new videotape, which got us even hornier and led to some more hot sex.

I hope that we can get together with Kenneth again. Maybe he can convince Phoebe to join us next time. Perhaps reading my letter might convince her and other women how much fun they can have with two men. Do I have any regrets? Just one: that I didn't have my first threesome years ago. I have some catching up to do!—*N.K., New Bedford, Massachusetts*

TWO GIRLFRIENDS LUSTING AFTER ONE GUY? WHY NOT A THREEWAY MARRIAGE?

*T*he summer after my junior year at college in the Pacific Northwest, I traveled with my friends Carol and Helen down to the Southern California home of Carol's boyfriend, George.

It was a Thursday evening when we arrived at George's huge sea-shore home. There we met his dad, Roger, a six-foot-five-inch muscular hunk, and Roger's equally knockout girlfriend, June. We were all tired from twelve hours of driving, so George showed Helen and me to our room, and he and Carol retired to his room down the hall.

I soon found out that our bedroom was directly above the master bedroom. I was awakened around midnight by loud moans and screams of pleasure coming from the room below. I heard June moaning and begging Roger to "put it in." When he did, she really started groaning and screaming, crying out, "You're so big! I'm coming! You're so big! Please come inside me!" After about forty minutes of this, he evidently *did* come inside her. She was moaning, "Thank you, thank you!"

The sounds were so exciting that I fingered myself to an orgasm before going back to sleep. But then I was awakened again by June's now-familiar moans. She was begging Roger to let her suck him. She kept saying, "I want you to come in my mouth!" Then there was muffled moaning for about twenty minutes. As I pictured him fucking her mouth, I got so hot, I finger-fucked my pussy almost to the point of another orgasm.

After that, he must have started eating her. She screamed and cried and begged for him to fuck her with his big cock. My trusty finger brought me to a convulsive orgasm when he came again. Then they finally went to sleep, and I did too, wondering just how big Roger's cock might be.

The next morning I was sitting on the pool deck reading the paper when Roger came back from a run. He was a huge man. I asked him his chest size, and he said it was fifty-eight inches; his waist was only thirty-eight. He also had the largest arms, the largest legs and the largest bulge in his crotch that I had ever seen. There was no fat on him, either, just one hundred percent man.

He sat down, and we started talking about all kinds of things. I found out that his brain was as large as the rest of him. I was so awestruck, I did not realize that my silk robe had fallen slightly open, exposing most of my breasts. To be honest, the fire in my cunt was so hot that I wanted to rip those running shorts off him and bury that bulge in my pussy. I stayed in a trance until the others showed up and joined us.

The rest of that Friday was fun. Helen, Carol, George and I played on the beach all day and were waited on by Roger's maid and butler. That night we all went out dancing till about two in the morning, when the bar closed. We arrived home the same time as Roger and June, and we all went to bed. Soon I was again awakened by the moans and screams from downstairs. My cunt was on fire, and I fingered myself to the queen of orgasms before I got to sleep.

On Saturday morning I was by the pool again when Roger came back from running. When he spoke to me I was trembling inside but somehow stayed calm. He soon left to work out down at the gym he owned.

Around noon Carol, Helen, George and I went swimming in the pool. June joined us for a while, then left to go to the beauty salon. She had a fine, sexy body, but even more than her body, I envied her her nights with Roger!

When Roger came back from his gym, he joined us by the pool, entering the water like an Olympic diver. He challenged George and Carol to a "chicken fight." He carried first Helen and then me on his shoulders while George carried Carol.

I nearly fainted when Roger put me on his shoulders. Just to feel those strong arms and to sit on those huge shoulders was almost orgasmic. George and Carol didn't have a chance against Roger, no matter who he was carrying.

That night we went out, and all Helen could talk about was what a hunk Roger was. When we got home and went to bed, I told Helen to stay up for a while and listen. Around three in the morning the moans and screams were coming up in full force. I had my hand under the covers rubbing my clit, and when I looked her way, I saw that Helen was rubbing hers too.

The next day June had to leave for her job as a flight attendant. Roger took her to the airport, and when he came back, we all went to his gym. Helen and I were awestruck at how much bigger Roger was than anyone else there. When he started lifting weights, I practically came in my pants.

That night George, Carol, Helen and I went out to the local college bar, and we all got smashed. We were so high that around one in the morning we had to call Roger to come pick us up. He took us home and put us all to bed. He put George in his own bed, but put Carol in mine. He said I could sleep in his room, and he would sleep on the sofa.

I got into his bed, but after a while I felt like I wanted company—specifically Roger's. So I put on a robe and went into the den, where he was sleeping in just a pair of thin running shorts. I went to him quietly and started to blow hot breath on his cock through his shorts. The shock of my life came when his cock kept growing and growing.

I had to see it, so I opened Roger's shorts and found myself staring at a prick at least ten inches long and maybe three inches wide. It was huge!

I couldn't stop myself. I had to suck on that cock. As I was struggling to get it in my mouth, Roger woke up. He looked at me in shock. I kept on sucking for all I was worth. He blew his load in about five minutes, and I swallowed as much come as I could. I kept right on sucking him, and in another five minutes he was hard again. Now I wanted him *inside* me.

I climbed up on his pole and started to work myself down on him. It took awhile, but I finally got all of him in me, and soon I was moaning and screaming just like June. When I reached orgasm, it was so powerful, I cried. Roger held me in his arms, and finally he came too. I was in love.

We woke up in each other's arms the next morning, and we had another session, with me riding him again. I haven't been so passionately aroused sexually for such a long time, and I got so loud, I was afraid I was waking everyone up. It was almost a relief when I finally came, after which Roger and I got up and showered together.

That afternoon I was lying by the pool when I felt Roger's huge hands putting lotion on me. He turned me over and put it all over the exposed areas of my body. Then he asked if I would like to go see a movie that night, and I said we should ask Helen to go too. I knew she wanted Roger, and I thought she should have a chance.

So that night when we got home, I told Roger I was tired and went up to my room. After a while I heard him and Helen laughing and when I looked out my window I saw the two of them skinny-dipping in the pool. Soon after that I heard Helen moaning like crazy, and I knew she was getting what she wanted.

The next day we decided that we both loved Roger, so the two of us went to him and proposed a threeway marriage. Roger was happy to accept, and we have been together now for five years. Roger and I were married in America, and he and Helen were married in Haiti. Helen and I have graduated from college.

By the way, George and Carol got married too, and live down the street from us. So we are really one big happy family.—*O.F., La Jolla, California* ⊶▣

A SMALL-TOWN COUPLE GOES TO THE BIG CITY AND SWINGS WITH "THE WELCOME CHAIN"

*I*n appearance, Rachel and I are your average small-town church-going couple. But appearances are deceiving.

Before we got married, I sensed that Rachel was passionate and adventurous. Although we both grew up in small towns, my four years in the military had given me a chance to experience a lot of wild nightlife. After our honeymoon, I knew I was one lucky man. Although my wife wasn't experienced at sex, she had a wild passion for it, in spite of her very conservative upbringing.

Rachel has red hair that looks almost bright orange, and green eyes that dance with mischievousness and laughter. She has a narrow waist and smooth, firm hips that I can't keep my hands away from. Her legs are long and as shapely as a dancer's. Her breasts are large and firm, with nipples that get hard as rocks when they are even the slightest bit excited.

Rachel took to sex like a duck to water. Her adventurous nature expressed itself fully in our sexual activities. Every time I introduced her to something new, she always found it exciting.

The first time I brought home *Penthouse Letters*, I wasn't sure how she was going to react. I left it out where she would see it. The next day when I came home from work, she was sitting naked in our easy chair. Her feet were on the seat, her legs spread apart, and her cunt was wide open, its lips wet and shiny.

She looked at me with her eyes full of lust and said, "Get naked and fuck my brains out!"

In a flash I stripped, laid her on her back on the floor and sank my dick in her pussy. When I hit bottom, she started coming. I pounded her for about five minutes, then exploded. She reached climax with me.

As we lay together in the afterglow, she looked in my eyes and said, "God, I love fucking you."

I really enjoy hearing her talk nasty, and she knows it. It also turns her on. I said, "Hmm, someone has been reading *Penthouse Letters*."

"Yes, but how did you know?" she said, and we both laughed.

After that, she became as creative with our sex as I had been. At home she was always a tease, but outside the house she was always the perfect lady.

I started buying her sexy lingerie, and she would strut around in it at home. She looked great in black half-bras that show her nipples, matching thong panties, nylons and garters. I realized that she was an exhibitionist when I saw the pleasure she got out of showing off for me. The more she flashed me, the hotter she would get.

One time, while I admired her strutting around teasingly in only a half-bra, stockings and garters as she set the table for dinner, I thought about how many guys would die to be in my shoes. Suddenly I had an image of some guy pounding his dick in my wife, with her legs wrapped around him as she squealed in an earth-shattering orgasm.

My dick turned to steel. Rachel bent over, teasing me as she put things on the table. I stepped up behind her and said not to move. She giggled, but stayed bent over. I dropped my pants and shorts, taking only enough time to rub my dickhead against her clitoris and start her juices flowing before I drove it home. That image flashed in my mind again as, three humps later, I blew my load like a cannon.

After that, every time I read in *Penthouse Letters* about some guy's wife screwing another man, I would imagine that it was my passionate wife screwing in sexual bliss. I was pretty sure that Rachel would also find this a compelling fantasy, but I also knew that we could never actually experience such a thing in our small town.

The corporate office of the company I work for is in a large metropolitan area, about a hundred and fifty miles from where we live. I make a trip there on business every other Friday. That's where I was buying *Penthouse Letters* and Rachel's naughty lingerie.

One of the guys I worked with in the main office was named Joe. He was single, and quite a ladies' man. He had been in the same branch of the service as me, so we had a lot in common and felt at ease talking about anything.

Joe knew how conservative small towns are, and he would kid me about how boring things must be at home. From time to time he told me stories about his activities with the ladies, and I would tell him how great a lover my wife was. One day over lunch, I told him that Rachel looked as great as any of the women in the men's magazines.

Joe just laughed, saying, "Man, you country boys sure have good imaginations." I kept insisting that I was telling the truth.

Later that afternoon, Joe asked me to come to his office. He closed the door and asked me to sit down.

"Okay, country boy," he said. "You have my curiosity aroused. I'll make a bet with you." He reached in his desk drawer and brought out a small shopping bag. "Have your wife put this on, and take some pictures of her. If she is anywhere near as good-looking as you claim, I'll buy you lunch anywhere you want. If not, you do the same for me. What do you say?"

I grabbed the bag and told him he had a deal. Then I looked inside, and both my heart and my dick started pounding. In the bag were three mint-green silk triangles with strings attached.

I said, "Joe, I can't have pictures of her wearing this developed in our town." He laughed and said he knew of a place that would develop them.

At home that night Rachel asked if I had picked up anything interesting. I retrieved the bag and dumped the contents on the bed.

She looked at it and asked, "What is that?"

I told her I thought it was a bathing suit, and asked her to model it for me. Then I went in the living room and waited for the show.

When Rachel came in wearing the suit, I thought to myself, Joe, my boy, you are not going to believe your eyes! She looked fantastically sexy as she started teasing me and strutting her stuff. I quickly got the camera out and started taking pictures. Her poses swiftly progressed from sexy-bathing-suit shots to wide-open-beaver masturbation shots. That night we wore each other out.

Two weeks later, in his office, Joe handed me an envelope containing the developed pictures. "This is some kind of joke, right?" he said to me. "That can't be your wife."

I assured him that it was. Although the pictures were not professional-quality, I was proud of how sexy and hot Rachel looked. I could not believe how excited I felt as Joe drooled over each picture. Finally he said, "Matt, I owe you a meal. Why don't I take you someplace where we can eat and get laid? Those pictures have me hornier than hell."

"No, thank you," I said. "I have more than I can handle at home."

"In that case, let's go to your house," Joe said.

Even though I knew it was meant humorously, the implied suggestion caused my dick to swell. On every trip I made to the main office after that, Joe would ask how my wife was doing, and I would tell him that she just kept getting better and better.

On one trip I mentioned that I needed to do something special for Rachel, since our third anniversary was coming up. Joe suggested I bring her to the city and let her see what wild and wicked things happen there. I told him that maybe the city needed to experience some wild country life.

Joe laughed, then said, "If you want Rachel to get the complete experience, why not let me take you two country bumpkins to a swingers' party? I could get you in as my guests. You could participate or just watch, it would be entirely up to you. They put red ribbons around the necks of first-timers, so everyone will keep that in mind if they want to approach you. What do you say?"

I was aroused by the idea, but when I got home I tried not to act overly excited when I asked Rachel if she would like to go. We discussed it for a few days, and she agreed. On my next trip to the main office, I told Joe it was a go. He acted like he had won the lottery. He had no idea that I was more excited than he was.

On our anniversary weekend, Rachel and I went into the city on Thursday. I gave her the names of several shops that carried sexy clothes and lingerie, so she would be able to do her own shopping while I was at work on Friday.

Both Joe and I had a hard time keeping our minds on work that day. When I got back to the hotel after work, my wife greeted me with a full-body hug and a passionate kiss, then showed me what she had bought. Each outfit was a voyeur's dream, but the last item she showed me was a killer.

It was a black silk dress that plunged all the way down in the back, to just below the curve of her hips. If you stood close behind her and looked down, you could see the crack of her ass. A thin string around her neck held up the front of the dress, which formed a deep vee that went halfway to her waist and barely covered her breasts. From the sides you could see almost all of her tits. With no lining, the thin silk showed the shape of each nipple in detail.

As Rachel walked, the silk caressed her nipples and caused them to stand firm and proud. The skirt flared slightly and reached only to mid-thigh. When she spun around, you could almost see her ass and her red-haired pussy.

Since the party didn't start until ten, Joe and I had decided to take Rachel out to eat and to a nice dance club. I asked her to wear her new black dress, which I called her "catch-me, fuck-me" outfit.

She said, "Honey, do you realize I can't wear any underthings with that dress?" I told her I knew that, and that I would love to see her give all those city slickers hard dicks. She called me a dirty old man, and I called her a wicked wench. But she wore the dress.

Although Joe tried to play it cool, both Rachel and I could tell that her dress blew his mind. The way he obviously lusted after her made us both proud. The sexual tension had all three of us hurrying through dinner. My wife wasn't much of a drinker, so when we ordered wine with our dinner, we explained that she should sip it very slowly. She had two glasses, and by the time we left, she was feeling playful and mellow.

Joe's car had a bench seat, so we all sat in front. Joe drove, and Rachel sat in the middle between us. At one point she leaned over and gave me a passionate kiss. Joe said he felt left out.

"She can't kiss you while you're driving," I said, "so you'll have to wait until the next traffic light."

At the first red light we came to, I rubbed her knee and held her hand while they kissed. When the light changed and they broke the kiss, I could see they were both breathless. I eased Rachel's hand over to my dick so she could feel how hard I was. There were only two more lights before we arrived at the dance club, but each time their kissing got steamier.

At the club, Joe and I took turns dancing with Rachel. She rubbed her body freely against both of us on the dance floor. It was the closest thing to fucking with clothes on that I have ever seen.

I was thrilled by the looks of envy all the guys were giving Joe and me. Their eyes followed every move Rachel made. Their stares of lust did not go unnoticed by her. She ate it up. We made sure she drank only enough to keep her feeling good without getting drunk.

We were having so much fun, it was hard to quit and leave for the party. But Joe knew what was in store and was determined to get there.

We started the kissing game again on the way. This time Joe had his right hand on my wife's bare knee and she rested her left hand on his thigh. While they kissed at a red light, I slid my hand up her thigh to within a few inches of her pussy. She fondled my dick with her free hand.

When the light changed and she turned to kiss me, I whispered in her ear that she should touch Joe's dick. She moaned, and as we kissed, I watched her slide her hand up his thigh. When she reached his dick she squeezed it. I heard him suck in his breath. Watching her touch another man's dick almost made me come.

When we broke our kiss, she whispered, "Honey, his thing is huge!"

At the next red light, I eased her legs open while they were kissing. As she opened up I slid my hand to her waist and took her skirt up with it. I worked my hand further up under her dress to caress her nipple. I saw Joe move his hand to her cunt, and she let out a soft moan as he made contact.

Someone behind us blew his horn, and Rachel and Joe broke their kiss with a start. When she turned to me, I could see Joe finger-fucking her. My hand was playing with her breast, gently squeezing her nipple.

Rachel whimpered and said, "I'm going to come." She raised her hips off the seat and started humping Joe's hand. She cried, "Oh, fuck!" and suddenly she jerked as wave after wave of climax rolled through her. She looked so beautiful sitting there with her legs spread wide, a look of total bliss on her face, and Joe's hand, wet with her juices, covering her pussy.

We tried to put ourselves together as Joe pulled up at the house where the party was being held. As we got out of the car, Rachel whispered in my ear, "Honey, Joe's dick is just plain *huge.*"

I whispered back that the way she had enjoyed playing with it, and her getting off so quickly, had almost caused me to come too.

She smiled and said, "Really?"

"I can't wait to see his big dick sliding in your sweet pussy," I replied. Rachel just hugged my arm against her breast and moaned.

We entered the house, and Joe introduced us to the hostess, an attractive blonde in her thirties, who gave us a bag and placed red ribbons around Rachel's neck and mine. The bag contained silk boxer shorts for Joe and me. Rachel stayed with the hostess while we changed. Joe explained to me that what Rachel was wearing was hot enough.

As we changed, I saw that my wife was right. Joe was hung like a horse. When we returned in our shorts, our erections were obvious, and my wife stared at Joe's hard-on with lust in her eyes.

Others were coming in, so the hostess asked Joe to show us around. Soft, sensuous music played on a speaker system throughout the house. I noticed that Rachel's dress had been shortened so it stopped only an inch or so below her butt. I found out later that she and the hostess had tacked it up with thread, so she could let it out later.

Joe took us in a large game room that could hold about thirty people. It had a full-size bar, with a bartender who was wearing only a pair of French-cut briefs. In the center of the room was a large round bed with a satin cover. Lounges, sofas, and chairs were arranged around the bed, and there was still plenty of space for dancing.

I don't know how much of the house Rachel saw as Joe showed us around the rest of it, her attention was so riveted on the bulge in his shorts. Every chance she got, she managed to rub her ass against it, and Joe obviously enjoyed what she was doing.

I whispered to her that her mouth was watering. She said she was sorry, but she couldn't help herself and she hoped it was okay with me. I told her I loved every minute of it.

When we returned to the game room, we each got a drink. More people came in as the evening went on.

Joe said to me, "Man, the way your wife has that dress fixed, everyone here can practically see her bare bottom. What do you think about that?"

I said, "I believe my wicked wife is thrilled by all the attention she's getting. Isn't that right, honey?"

Rachel smiled at Joe, and her voice dripped with lust as she said yes.

"In that case," Joe said, "why don't the two of you go dance, so I can sit down and enjoy the view?"

Joe took a front-row seat as we moved to the dance area. There were three other couples dancing there, in various stages of undress.

As we held each other close, Rachel said, "You know, the way things are going tonight, we could write our own story for *Penthouse Letters*. I could fuck you right here on the dance floor in front of all these strangers, I'm so turned on."

"I'll tell you what would be even better," I said. "If you were to screw Joe in front of everyone, that would really be something to write about. I'll bet he has never had as good a piece of ass as you before."

"Honey, are you sure you want him to put that big dick of his in your wife's pussy?" Rachel said.

"It would be one of my fantasies come to life," I said. "And I think that would fulfill one or two of your fantasies too."

She ground her pussy against my dick. "Okay, honey. Your sweet little wife is going to put on a show you won't soon forget."

"Good," I said. "Then let's show these city folks the prettiest ass in the world."

With that I reached down to her thighs and slid my hands upward, lifting her dress with them. We knew her bare butt was showing.

"Look what you're doing to Joe," I said, and I turned her so she could see him. About three inches of his dick was sticking out of the top of his boxer shorts. I felt Rachel press her body harder against me.

A minute later I noticed Joe talking to the hostess, although he kept his eyes on my wife's butt as he did. When they finished talking, he waved us over.

"You two are such a hot couple," Joe said, "that our hostess would like to introduce you to everyone in a special way. Can you handle seeing your spouse making love to someone else?"

Rachel and I looked at each other and smiled. "Yes," I said. "In fact, we were just talking about that."

"Okay, Rachel," the hostess said, smiling, "you're going to love this. It's called 'the welcome chain.'" She walked to the center of the room, near the bed, and said, "Ladies and gentlemen, I'm sure you've noticed that tonight we have a new couple. They're from the country, so we decided they deserve a welcome chain. Joe, come introduce them, then everyone can introduce themselves."

Everyone cheered as we moved forward. I counted ten guys and eleven women in the group.

"To be introduced properly, everyone must be naked," the hostess went on. "Joe's in charge of seeing that everything is done properly, so he'll go last. Okay, everyone, get naked!"

Although Rachel was a little nervous, she didn't hesitate. She took a deep breath and pulled her dress up over her head. I felt blood pulsing in my dick. As I stepped out of my boxers, I noticed that every guy there had a hard-on.

Joe said to rest my butt against the bed and asked Rachel to sit on the side of the bed, then lie back and spread her legs. The guys lined up in front of my wife, and the women lined up in front of me. Joe explained that each welcome would last a minute. When he gave the word to start, I watched the first man introduce himself, then step up and slide his dick in my wife. I was thrilled to realize that it was the first time in her life that anyone other than me was fucking her.

I was so focused on her that I didn't hear the first woman introduce herself to me. Suddenly I felt someone sucking my dick. When I heard my wife whimper with pleasure, I came. The woman kneeling before me never lost a drop. I was euphoric.

By the time the first minute was up, my dick was semihard again and my wife was on the verge of coming. The next man approached Rachel, and the next woman knelt and took me in her mouth. As the minutes went on, each eager "welcomer" took a turn. Even though I was getting great head, I couldn't take my eyes off my wanton wife.

Each guy managed to keep her on the brink of orgasm for his full minute without pushing her over. Each time one pulled out, I saw his dick shining with her juices and I saw her wide-open cunt and pulsating clit. She was almost out of her mind with the need to come.

I was surprised to see that the last person in my wife's line was a woman. Rachel was so far gone that she didn't even react when the woman introduced herself as Jill. Jill then bent down and rubbed her right breast against my wife's wide-open pussy.

I could tell Rachel knew *something* was different, but in her lust-crazed state she didn't want the sensations to stop. Jill rubbed her tit all over Rachel's cunt, then stroked her hard nipple over my wife's clit. She backed off briefly when Rachel showed signs of coming, then started in again.

By now there were no women left in my line. The hostess said it was time I had some real fucking. She bent over the back of a chair, and I entered her from behind. Happily, the chair was facing the bed, so I could still see what my sex-crazed wife was doing.

When Jill's minute was up, and there was no one left in Rachel's line, Joe stepped between my wife's legs. Laying his huge dick on her stomach, he asked how she thought he should conclude the welcome chain.

"Fuck me!" Rachel murmured. "Yes, fuck me with that big dick of yours!"

Joe said he'd waited all night to slide his dick in her red-haired pussy. "Reach down and feel how hard and big you've made it," he said.

Rachel reached down and took Joe's dick in both hands. She raised her head to look at it, and someone put a pillow under her head. I was still fucking the hostess, but I noticed that everyone else had gathered around to watch them.

"Hey, Matt, watch this," Joe said. "Your wife is fixing to get the fucking of her life."

Rachel was still holding Joe's dick as he pulled it back to position the head at the entrance to her pussy. He said to rub it up and down her wet slit, then put it in. She was breathing hard as she lined it up and eased forward. When he'd pushed in only about four inches, she went off like she'd been electrified, whimpering with sweet delight.

Joe waited until she was calmer, then said, "Wait, it gets better." He worked in all but about three inches.

"Oh, yes!" Rachel cried.

At that point Joe was in as deep as I'd ever been, but since he was a lot bigger around than I was, Rachel had to be feeling really full. She lifted her ass off the bed, frantically humping up to him. He moved in and out of her but held back about three inches of dick until she was on the verge of orgasm. Then he lunged, driving his dick all the way in. She cried out in ecstasy, her climax wracking her body.

At that moment I exploded in the hostess so hard, I thought my dick would explode. My shrinking dick slid out of her, but Joe stayed buried in Rachel. As she caught her breath, I crawled up on the bed and started sucking on her right tit. Then Jill came over and went to work on the other one.

"Oh, that feels so good!" Rachel cried out. She started raising and lowering her hips, humping Joe's cock. He responded, and this time really pounded it in her. A few minutes later, she pulled my head up and sucked my tongue down her throat.

She groaned, raised my face, looked me in the eyes and said, "Oh honey, it feels so fucking good!" Tears were rolling down her face.

Just then Joe let out a roar. My wife's eyes glazed over as he shot his load in her. She clutched at him and started coming again. While I didn't come with her, I felt she had let me be part of that exciting climax.

I moved back as Joe leaned forward and kissed my wife on the mouth. Then he rose with a satisfied smile and said she was the best fuck he had ever had, and he was quite sure all his friends would agree.

I watched in fascination as he slowly pulled his dick, wet with her juices, out of her pussy. I could not believe all the love and pride I was feeling, knowing my wife had totally abandoned herself in public to her sexual cravings. As I stared at her wide-open pussy, I saw Joe's spunk drip down the crack of her ass to form a wet spot on the sheet.

As she lay there recovering, with her eyes closed and her legs spread wide, a nice-looking brunette stepped up to her and said, "Let me clean you up for my husband, sweetheart." She bent down and started sucking Rachel clean. When she finished, her husband turned my wife over on her stomach and fucked her doggie-style.

The more she got, the more she seemed to want. I'm not sure how many men fucked her that night, but I loved every minute of it.

Daylight had broken by the time we drove back to our hotel. We invited Joe to sleep with us instead of driving on home. Of course he accepted. We dragged ourselves to the room, stripped off our clothes and crashed on the bed. With Rachel between Joe and me, we were asleep in seconds.

I was dreaming about a procession of dicks going in and out of Rachel's pussy while my cock felt like it was covered with hundreds of butterflies. As I floated from sleep to consciousness, I realized my wife was sucking my now-hard penis.

Seeing that I was awake, she slid up my body and whispered, "Want to watch me fuck Joe some more?"

I smiled and said, "Who are you, wicked wench, and what have you done with my sweet, innocent wife?"

"I think she got screwed up so her brain's in her pussy now," she said, rubbing her crotch on my leg.

Joe was on his back, with one leg stretched out at an angle. Rachel crawled between his legs and used her mouth on his limp dick. She didn't just suck it, she made love to it. It soon stood tall and proud. I wasn't sure whether he was awake when she moved up and crouched over his towering pole. Again I was amazed by the size of it—not to mention the fact that Rachel was able to take the entire thing up her pussy.

She held his dick with both hands and rubbed the head all over her cunt. She soon had it shining with her juices. She looked right at me as she slid herself halfway down over the huge rod. Her eyes glazed over, and her body twitched from the thrill of his entry. But she kept her eyes on mine as she paused for a few seconds. The pleasure in them was almost tangible.

In a soft voice she said, "Honey, you like seeing his big dick in my cunt, don't you? Can you see how full and wet my pussy is?" She began to move up and down on his pylon, taking in a bit more each time and emitting a cry of joy with each downstroke.

Joe was awake for sure now, and his hands moved up Rachel's body to her tits. "Damn," he said, "I must be dead, because this has got to be heaven!" He tweaked her nipples while she drove down on his dick until she had it all in. When she hit bottom, her body exploded.

After she caught her breath, she started screwing again. I lay there watching them fuck in all kinds of positions for about forty-five minutes. I guess Joe could last so long because of all the screwing he'd done the night before. I know my wife loved it, and so did I.

Rachel and I agreed that we really enjoyed living out our fantasies, and we have nothing but good feelings about our experience. Now she often accompanies me when I make my trips to the main office, and we spend a night or two with Joe. We haven't gone back to the swingers' club yet, but we probably will soon.

Yes, small-town life has its advantages, but for certain things, there's nothing like the big city!—*M.H., Lancaster, Pennsylvania*

HE FANTASIZES ABOUT A HOT WIFE FIT FOR
SHARING WITH HIS FRIENDS

*I*n this fantasy I was married to an Italian beauty with dark brown eyes and chestnut hair, who had matured remarkably from the innocent teenager I first knew.

In our ten years together, Luisa had filled out so well, at five-five, one hundred thirty pounds, that I was the envy of friends and associates. I didn't mind when she wore clothes that showed off her body. I even encouraged her. I was pretty sure she wasn't quite aware of the feelings she could stir in a man, and we were never short of neighborly men stopping by, or of pool-party invitations.

Once she wore a pair of shorts I'd requested that almost caused an incident at a party. Of course she didn't know I'd run them through the dryer twice as long, and they'd shrunk to the point that they showed the bottom of her ass and the soft stretch material was form-fitting around her crotch. A fellow who'd had too much to drink cornered her in the kitchen. His wife didn't appreciate it, but we bailed him out, saying he'd had too much. Luisa was no worse for the wear, and it was a turn-on for both of us.

At times I'd ask her about fantasies. I shared mine, but she wouldn't admit to having them. She was afraid, I think, that by speaking them, she'd give them a life of their own, losing control of them and of herself. This made her that much more special and mysterious. I often wondered what went on in her fantasy world. All women have one, right?

One night at our "guys' night out," the fantasy life of the housewife came up, as sex usually did in *some* form. Things get looser after enough smoke and alcohol, and guys gave up bits and pieces about themselves and their wives.

Sherm asked me, "Art, how about Luisa? She's one hot piece. I bet she's got fantasies about doing another guy, no?"

That got a lot of attention, and I didn't know what to say. I didn't know!

"Or another woman, covered with suntan lotion?" Gil ventured.

After some prompting, I finally said I thought it was only standard married sex stuff. That got a chorus of boos. My anger caused me to blurt out that I'd bet Sherm and Gil a thousand dollars I was right, and that all we had to do to confirm it was call Sherm's wife Maria on the speakerphone. Maria is Luisa's best friend—besides me—and would simply agree. That would be the end of it.

When we got Maria on the phone, she said that Luisa had admitted an orgy fantasy among others. My jaw dropped. Luisa hadn't told me a thing about it, and now eight of my friends found out simultaneously. Plus now Sherm and Gil were expecting me to cough up the five hundred each I'd promised them. Well, I drowned my sorrow in a few more beers and said I'd get back to the guys on the money, which I didn't really have.

The next few days I tried to figure out how to pay the debt and fretted that Luisa hadn't confided in me. I took comfort in at least knowing she *had* fantasies.

On Friday, Gil called me at work to suggest we have lunch. When we were done eating, he said he'd been talking to Sherm. They felt bad about our "bet" and had come up with a "solution."

"Since Luisa has that orgy thing—" he began, but I protested. He went on, "Why don't we forget about the bet? You can just set us up with Luisa."

I was a little flustered—first, that my friends wanted to fuck my wife, but second, that part of my mind was already beginning to plan it out! However, I wasn't going to tell Gil that.

He continued, "You know, just us. The others don't have to know. Hey, it might even be her dream come true! She's one hot piece of ass, Art. All of the guys would kill to get some of that."

In a hushed tone I said, "Look, this is my wife we're talking about, not some hooker. What if it was *your* wife?"

"Shit, pal, Sherm's already *done* Connie, just like I've fucked Maria. Besides, you've got it wrong. We're not talking about sex for money, just a little swapping. Most of the guys do—except you and Luisa, and maybe another couple."

I was incredulous. "You guys swap?"

"Not formally. It's spur-of-the-moment, like over a joint. All good, clean fun."

"Marriages all intact?" I asked. "No problems? No pettiness?"

"Better than the seventies," he said.

"Even if I said yes, Luisa would never go for it," I said. "She doesn't even *like* Sherm. Look, I'll get you the money."

"Forget the money," Gil said. "That was just a joke. Talk to Luisa. Maybe this is the chance she's been waiting for."

That's where we left it. Throughout the day, and into the commute home, I pictured myself saying, "Look, I want you to sleep with not one but two friends of mine, including one you hate, because while they say I don't owe them, I did make a drunken bet about fantasies you have that you won't admit to me, but only to your friend Maria."

No, it wasn't fair to blame her for that. She could confide in who she wanted.

I could say, "They think maybe you'll *like* having them do God-knows-what to you." That gave me a tingle. What would they do to her, if they could? The images roaring through my mind like an unstoppable freight train left me glad I didn't have to walk right away. I never realized how kinky my imagination could be.

That mood stayed with me through dinner and the ensuing evening, except during sex, when somehow the freight trains roaring in my mind led to mind-blowing orgasms. Luisa asked what had changed my mood so abruptly, and I confided in her—up to a point. Her eyes widened, her lips parted in surprise, as she heard about the bet, then Gil's suggestion of what we could do, not as a bet, but as friends, and then his claim that we were the only ones who *weren't* swapping.

Not wanting to raise the subject of fantasies, I didn't say what the "bet" was about. While I explained Gil's idea, my boner sprang up. Luisa must have felt it as it throbbed against her inner thigh.

"You want to know, do I want to fuck Gil and Sherm? *Sherm,* of all people?" Her hand slipped to my hard-on, massaging as she talked. "And apparently this is a turn-on for you?" She pushed the covers off and straddled me, still holding my pole. "You want me to do it, huh?" It was more a statement than a question. She rubbed my cockhead against her wet cunt lips. As she worked my cock back in her cunt she said, "Tell me you want me to fuck them. Tell me."

As she rode me like a bucking bronco, I lost it. I said yes, and we both rode a huge orgasm to its climax. Afterward, we lay there in bliss, holding each other.

Luisa said, "Sunday night we'll say they're coming over to watch football."

"Will it make it easier for you if I'm not here?" I asked.

"No, no," she said, "if I'm fucking your friends for you, I want you here to see what they do. All I ask is that you don't say anything. I might lose my nerve."

I was glad she said that. I didn't want to miss seeing it either.

When I called Gil to convey the invitation for Sunday, he was in full agreement and said he'd pass the word to Sherm. That set, we waited for the main event.

Sunday was steeped in preparation and anticipation. Luisa seemed nervous yet relaxed, in that the burden was all on Gil and Sherm. If nothing else, it would be different from the familiar sex we shared. She seemed absolutely radiant.

Seven o'clock finally arrived, and so did the guys, carrying a couple of bottles of champagne and flowers and a pouch. We exchanged nervous pleasantries. As Gil uncorked a bottle of bubbly, Luisa came down the stairs in a French maid's outfit she'd worn at Halloween, complete with thigh-high black stockings and high heels.

She said, "I'll get that," took the bottle and handed glasses of champagne all around. When she bent over to give the guests theirs, she flashed me, and I saw she had no panties on under that short skirt. As she bent to fill my glass, I knew the guys were getting a first hard look at the delights they were soon to enjoy. She paused at my glass for quite a time, legs slightly askew. She was basking in the embarrassed look on my face as her happy cunt smiled at Gil and Sherm.

Her perfume, my favorite, filled the air with her every movement. I was lost in its fragrance—she wore it the first time we had sex. She proceeded to down the rest of the bottle and handed me the next one to open. Champagne is her drink of choice, and just a little makes her horny, so I was surprised at how much she was drinking. Nerves? Or abandon? I popped the cork and prepared to refill her glass, but she took the bottle and sat on Gil's lap, sipping away.

She kissed Gil and said to Sherm and him, "What did you boys have in mind?"

Gil's hand massaged her stockinged thigh while he whispered—something nasty, I'm sure. Luisa giggled. "What do you think my husband would say?"

The men stood, and Luisa undressed them. They kissed her and explored her supple body through the thin fabric. My nervousness and a growing erection made me change positions, watching my friends seduce my wife—or was it vice versa? Sherm's hand slid under her skirt, cupping her pussy and making her shudder and moan between kisses.

With that she led us upstairs, smiling at me. Her sweet ass glided ever so gracefully. In the bedroom, she led me to the chair by the bed and said, "Sit." I sat.

"Tell me again what you want to do to me," she cooed to the others, and they did as they finished undressing.

Sherm sprawled out across our king-size bed. His cock dwarfed Gil's—and mine, for that matter. Gil stood French-kissing Luisa deeply and undid the last few buttons on her outfit. It slipped to the floor. She stood massaging Gil's cock in her hands. Her body was hotter than ever. The light danced off her milk-white tits, nipples fully erect. She backed onto the bed and knelt between the men.

Sherm came up behind Luisa and kissed the back of her neck and shoulders. Both men poured massage oil on their fingers, which danced around her tits, cupping and kneading. She loved oil massages, and especially loved this four-handed one. I enjoyed watching it too. Gil waved his cock at Luisa, and she ran her tongue up and down it, lingering to suck the head. From his pouch Sherm drew a ten-inch cock-shaped vibrator. He lubed it with K-Y jelly. I started to protest, but Luisa stopped me.

"You promised not to say anything."

I slumped back in the chair as Sherm, now smiling, rubbed the vibrating slick stick against my wife's pussy lips, finding her clit occasionally, as evidenced by the gurgles that came from her cock-filled mouth. Gil was saying how good she sucked and how good it felt. In a matter of moments, she stopped sucking. Rocking on the vibrator shaft, she had her first orgasm of the night.

They turned her on her side so Sherm could enjoy her tongue. Gil knelt between her thighs and nibbled at her pussy and clit, driving her wild. Sherm's fully engorged cock looked enormous. I saw some apprehension in Luisa's eyes.

"I'm not sure it'll fit," she whispered.

But it was Gil who worked his cockhead in her pussy, then plunged in.

"It's everything I thought it would be," Gil said. "Your pussy is like silk." He plowed her rhythmically, and with the head of Sherm's pole in her mouth, she just moaned and grunted. I couldn't believe I was seeing my wife lying between my friends, with one fucking her and the other stuffing his giant dick in her face. What a turn-on! I wanted her but couldn't have her—just a foot away.

Gil pulled out, and Sherm moved toward Luisa's sweet pussy.

"I'm not sure—" she started.

"Don't worry," Sherm said. He rubbed a lot of K-Y on the vibrator and went at her pussy lips again, while Gil wiped off his cock and she downed more champagne. The buzzing of the vibrator soon brought her back to a rhythmic frenzy.

"Oh, that's so good!" she exclaimed.

Her body was already in convulsions when Sherm slid the vibrator between her pussy lips. With a back-and-forth, in-and-out motion, he soon had it three-quarters of the way in her box, stretching her cunt wall. She thrust her hips up to receive the probe, loosening up hitherto-unreached areas of her pussy. Sherm worked the vibrator deeper, all the way in to the nub. On the final thrust of the dildo, Gil again waved his cock at Luisa from above. He spread oil on her tits, then greased her body generously all over till she shimmered in the light.

Sherm pulled out the vibrator slowly. Luisa, still whimpering, now worked his bulbous head in her gaping hole.

"Ooh, it feels bigger," she squealed.

"I've always wanted to fuck your wife, Art," said Sherm, working into a faster rhythm. "Look how she likes my cock."

To her he said, "Baby, you like my cock, huh? Say it!"

"I like it," she squealed. "Fuck me! Oh yeah, hard, like that! Come on my tits."

Sherm's huge cock was buried to the hilt, and my wife was lost in lust, her pussy lips straining to take it all in. They held her leg up and rolled her on her side, and Gil got in behind her greased body, making a sandwich.

"Hey, what are you—" Luisa started to say, but never got a chance to finish. Gil's well-lubed cock worked in her virgin ass, and both men pumped in and out of her orifices. To this point she'd been a virgin to all but me. Now she'd lost her cherry to the world *both* ways. All three of them grunted and groaned, on the verge of a major orgasm. Sherm and Gil prepared to pull out.

Luisa yelled, "Come in me, come in me! Don't stop, it's so good!"

They all rocked until they came, all three tired, Luisa exhausted. The guys kissed her again and again in appreciation of what she'd shared with them, thanked me, got dressed and left.

The sight of Luisa lying spread-eagle on the bed, her cunt dotted with come, was too much! I crawled between her legs and ate her pussy till she mewled. I followed that up by fucking her till I loaded her cunt up again. Afterward, we lay in each other's arms for quite some time, basking in the afterglow, then showered together and went to bed exhausted, happy and in love.

The next morning I took the day off from work, and we enjoyed a leisurely breakfast together. In the course of conversation, the subject of sexual fantasies came up. I asked how Maria would know about her orgy fantasies.

She laughed. "Orgy fantasies?" she said. "That's *her* fantasy. She's been teasing me like that for years. I would never tell her something like that."

It had been a gimmick set up by the guys to finally get in her hot box! But neither of us was complaining. In fact, we were planning an encore performance. I got to see my wife do things I never would've thought she'd do. Now we set up and acted out our fantasies together, opening up our marriage to more erotic excitement than ever, secure in our mutual love.

How many marriages are secure enough for a man to ask his wife to fuck another guy, or for a woman to ask her husband if she could? Just wondering.—*A.N., Cleveland, Ohio* ⊶▪

HIS WIFE'S OLD FRIEND KNEW SECRETS THAT DROVE HER WILD WITH PLEASURE

I met my future wife while stationed overseas in the service. Years later, when I got out of the Army, I chose to stay here in Denmark and marry Tina, a gorgeous green-eyed blonde, five feet, a hundred and five pounds.

Not long ago we were at a disco club when we ran into an old friend of Tina's named Rikke, a tall blonde with green eyes and a sexy body. They hadn't seen each other in ten years, so they had a lot to catch up on. Rikke loves sex and likes to talk about it. At one point she began talking about the time she picked up two guys, and went from detail to detail. Eventually I excused myself and went to the bar to get a drink.

When I returned to our table, Rikke was alone. Tina had gone to the ladies' room. Rikke asked if she could ask a personal question. I said sure. She asked if Tina was still so crazy about threesomes, because she would really like to have sex with us. Before I could answer, she had an idea. We could go to her place, and later her boyfriend would be coming by. Carl happens to be black. Rikke said Tina always had a fantasy of fucking a black guy.

All this talk about fucking was making me horny. Tina and I had never discussed this fantasy of hers. We *have* had threesomes before, but it was always two girls and one guy, me. Still, the thought of seeing my wife get fucked by a black dick and at the same time me fucking Rikke—well, that was an opportunity I couldn't pass up.

Rikke told me not to say anything to Tina. She got out a cellular phone from her purse and called Carl. As she told him about her plan, I got the idea. He was supposed to walk in while the three of us were engaged in hot sex.

The three of us arrived in Rikke's apartment and had drinks to loosen up. Minutes later we were on the bed seriously exploring each other's bodies. The women had gotten themselves in the 69 position when Carl walked in. At first Tina didn't notice him. Rikke sure did, though. She went straight for his dick, which was extremely large. Tina watched her sucking him off while I fingered her. Rikke asked Tina if she wanted some. Tina didn't answer.

Carl kissed my wife and laid her gently on her back. She closed her eyes while he positioned himself between her legs. Seeing this, I slid over toward Rikke and sucked on her pussy. I glanced over at my wife and saw Carl fucking her with his giant dick. By now my own was hard, and soon I began to fuck Rikke.

The four of us continued fucking the whole night, until we fell asleep from exhaustion. When I woke up, it was still dark. My three bedmates were not only awake, but at it again! Carl was fucking Tina hard and fast. She moaned and twisted and gave a squeal as she exploded in orgasm.

Tina and I are looking forward to other adventures. You can bet we plan to share them with *Penthouse Letters* readers.—*L.J., Copenhagen, Denmark*

AT A NUDIST RESORT, GETTING NAKED IS JUST THE START OF THE FUN TIMES

*I*t was a humid day, a great day to be at a nudist resort. We found lounge chairs facing the sun, the pool and the poolside bar. It's fun to sit around the pool at a nudist resort, because that's where all the nudists are.

We were on our second round of drinks when we saw a couple scanning the pool area from their balcony above the poolside bar. They had evidently just arrived, for they were still clothed. The man was taking off his shirt, and as he did, he saw my wife, Beverly. She saw him too but nonchalantly went on reading her book as she slowly spread her legs, giving him a view of her trimmed pussy. I wasn't paying that much attention to them, because I had a great view of his wife removing her dress in the full-length window. All she had on now was a lace G-string and half-cup bra that held her very full breasts up and out, fully exposing her hardened nipples.

She slid her G-string slowly down her legs, displaying her nearly completely shaved treasure box. Then she joined her husband on the balcony, wearing only her bra. I noticed that Beverly had put her book down and was coating her legs with suntan oil. As her hands spread oil over her spread thighs, she continued to offer an intimate view. The man's focus never left her. He reached down, unfastened his pants and removed them, exposing a large cock more than halfway to being hard. He pointed us out to his wife, who looked at us and smiled, then gave her husband a long, sensual kiss. He patted her ass as they went in their room, his nearly hard cock swaying as they walked.

Beverly looked at me and said, "That was a lot of fun. What a sexy couple!" And we both thought that was that. But a few minutes later a couple of drinks arrived, with a note inviting us up to the couple's room. With very little discussion, we decided to accept. I should tell you, if you haven't figured it out, that Beverly and I are exhibitionists and love to be naked. The thought of being in close quarters with such an attractive couple, our bodies totally bared to each other, had us shivering with excitement.

The man greeted us naked at the door and introduced himself as Drew. He was the warm and friendly type, shaking my hand and kissing Beverly's. He seated us at a small glass table just big enough to hold our drinks. As he introduced us to his wife Anna, he stood next to the seated Beverly with his cock only inches from her face. Anna sat across from me, still wearing that sexy bra. As we chatted, she stared openly at my cock. Drew, still next to Beverly, rested his hand on her shoulder.

At one point Anna told a funny joke, and as we all laughed I noticed Beverly's hand on Drew's leg. She leaned forward as she laughed, and his cock brushed her cheek. It filled out to impressive proportions. Anna put her hand on my thigh and invited me to join her in the kitchen to make more drinks. I looked back as we left the room. Beverly was smiling broadly as she listened to Drew and watched his hard-on bobbing an inch from her lips.

As much as I wanted to watch this rapidly developing situation, I was distracted by Anna's teasing. She led me in the small kitchen, talking away, with her arm around my back, her hand resting on my hip just above my buns. As she talked, she moved closer, pressing her breasts against me. Her hand slipped down to caress my ass crack. I had no idea what she was talking about, but when she licked her lips, I couldn't stand it anymore. I pulled her to me and kissed that soft, sensual mouth. Wow! I was hard in a split second. When we broke apart, Anna gave me a sexy smile and started making drinks. I moved in behind her and stroked her tits and pulled on her nipples while my cock slipped between her legs.

As I expected, when we returned with the drinks, Beverly was giving Drew head, which she loves to do. She stopped reluctantly as we came in but continued stroking his cock as she sipped her drink. Drew and

I remained standing, with our cocks looking as if they might burst any second. The women kept their eyes on our love-muscles while teasingly displaying their tempting assets.

Every so often as we talked and drank, one or another of the ladies gave Drew or me a stroke or two, a quick lick or a lingering suck, keeping us on edge for what seemed like forever. Anna started talking about the differences between our cocks—in width, length and taste. I saw my opportunity and wondered about the differences in their pussies. In no time at all, Drew and I were tasting, licking and sucking on their treasures, as Beverly and Anna sat side-by-side on the sofa, legs spread wide, moaning uncontrollably.

I couldn't wait. I moved forward and slid the head of my dick up and down over Beverly's moist love-lips. Drew and Anna leaned over for a closer look. Drew took hold of my cock and pushed it in Beverly. As I pumped her, he sucked on her nipples and played with her clit. Anna moved around behind me, licking my balls and the underside of my cock as I slid in and out of Beverly. Drew stood up and placed his cock in front of my wife's face. She didn't need to be asked twice, or even once. She was slurping and sucking in no time.

As Beverly went down on Drew, Anna moved around to my side so I could lick her pussy while continuing to drill Beverly for all I was worth. Before long we all erupted in orgasmic bliss. Anna trembled as I licked her, watching Drew pump his load in Beverly's mouth. With a howl, I came inside my wife. After we had all calmed down, we made arrangements for later, and Beverly and I headed back to our room. We were so worked up, we made love once more as we relived the evening. When we kissed good night, Beverly still tasted Anna's pussy nectar on my mustache and I tasted Drew's come in my wife's mouth.

I love making new friends!—*K.G., Phoenix, Arizona*

Serendipity

WHAT'S MORE FUN THAN POKER? YOUR POKER PAL'S WIFE NAKED IN A HOT TUB

*T*his all happened to me some time ago, on a Saturday afternoon when I went over to my friend Kenneth's house for our monthly poker game. I thought your readers would enjoy hearing about the "fix" I got myself into.

There were six guys playing, and of course Kenneth's wife Annabel was there. My wife and I had known Kenneth and Annabel for many years, and they were good friends. After playing for a couple of hours, I was losing my ass and decided I needed a break. I folded my hand and got up to get some beer for everybody. I went in the recreation room, where there was a bar and also a hot tub. Annabel was there, and she helped me hand out the beer.

Annabel and I watched the game for a while, then went back to the recreation room to watch some TV. I asked her if it would be all right if I got in the hot tub to relax for a while. She said she would join me. I didn't take this as any big deal, because we were old familiar friends and I figured a little nakedness wouldn't bother anybody. I stripped down quickly while she went in the bathroom. She came out with just a towel around her. I grabbed a couple of fresh beers and handed her one of them. She took hold of my hand and dropped the towel as we stepped in the tub.

As we talked, I couldn't help looking at Annabel's tits. They were just under the water, but the jets were on and I couldn't really see them. She saw me looking and asked if I thought they were too big. I said I couldn't see them with all the bubbles. So she sat up straight, bringing into view a pair of the biggest tits I'd ever seen. The only bigger ones I'd seen were in magazine photos.

Trying not to stare, I asked how big they were, and Annabel said 42DD. They didn't sag much, but maybe that was because of the water and the bubbles. Most big tits don't have nipples to match, but these were an exception, big and long and hard. I fell in love with them. I'm not a big tit lover, but those nipples gave me a hard-on. I still dream about what they looked like.

Annabel told me that her nipples were really sensitive. She said she liked her husband to spend a lot of time playing with them and sucking on them. I said I thought they looked great on her. She smiled and reached over to give me a hug. She said she really liked me. Then she leaned her head back and closed her eyes, spreading her arms along the rim of the tub. Her nipples were just above the water. I couldn't help myself. I reached over and twirled one lightly between my finger and thumb. She opened her eyes then and looked at me, but she didn't move. She just said if I didn't stop, I'd make her come. But I *couldn't* stop!

I lifted one of her huge tits and sucked on the nipple. With my other hand I played with her other nipple. They seemed to grow even longer and harder. I loved them. As I sucked and nibbled, she grabbed my hand and put it on her pussy. She said she wanted me to make her come quickly.

I whispered, "No problem," and found her hard clit. It was like a small dick. I rolled it between my thumb and finger, and in almost no time she climaxed. I stopped sucking on her nipple and looked up at her.

"God, that was great!" she said. "I loved it."

I played with her clit some more, and she was on her way again. She was moaning and squirming, and it didn't take long for her to come a second time.

I grabbed my beer and took a long swig. I was still holding the bottle when I felt her hand moving down my stomach. She reached my dick, which was hard and ready to burst. When she touched it, it jumped. Then she started to rub it. She found my nuts and spent some time stroking them. I told her she should stop before I came in the tub. Instead she grabbed my cock and started to jack me off. She stroked and rubbed me like an expert, varying her touch and tempo. Finally I just leaned back, closed my eyes and enjoyed it.

After a while Annabel told me to stand up. She said she wanted to suck all the come out of me. I stood up in the water and she deep-throated me instantly. It wasn't long before I came right down her throat. That was one fast blowjob! After she milked me dry, I told her that I had dreamed of her sucking me off. I also told her that I was in love with her tits, and she smiled and said she would flash them at me every chance she got. She said she would turn herself on for her husband by thinking about my cock down her throat.

That was the last time we were together, but I'll always remember that hot tub. And who knows what might happen in the future? —*F.V., Stratford, Connecticut* ⌕▪

IT WAS THE FIRST TIME FOR THEM BOTH, BUT THESE YOUNG LOVERS LEARNED FAST

*A*ngela and I were eighteen and had been dating for two years before we had sex. She was, as the old song goes, "five feet two, eyes of blue." She was very affectionate, but she would get upset if I tried to put my hands on her breasts or any other private place.

Like most males, I was intensely curious about the female body. The only naked women I had seen were in the pages of magazines. I would often try to imagine what a naked woman would look like in real life. When I saw a woman, I would try to envision her pubic hair and the crack between her legs. But I didn't think I would ever see Angela's pubic hair or her incredible rear end or any other secret female parts of her until we were married.

One Saturday night I took her home after a date during which we'd done some heavy necking. We were kissing good night at her front door when she whispered to me that she was having her period. That startled me, because she had never shared that kind of information with me before.

She went on to say, "I started on the pill after my last period, so when this one's over I'll be safe and we can *do it*."

I drew her to me and kissed her passionately, sliding my hand down over those sweet little buttocks, which she had never let me touch before. I took great pleasure in just running my hand across those marvelous round cheeks. Angela gave a wicked little giggle and moved her hips back and forth slightly, to show me that she was enjoying it also. Then she said good night, spun around and went in the house, leaving me standing there stunned.

As you can imagine, I had a hard time going to sleep that night. All I could think about was my sweet, amazing Angela. She and I were actually going to do it! My hands were really going to be on her breasts, and on that superb butt. Not only that, but I would actually be fingering her pussy! This was almost more than I could imagine. With my hand on my erection, I reached for a tissue. I knew I was going to be squirting into it in a minute. As I tried to imagine sliding my hard-on in Angela's sweet young body, it wasn't long before I soaked the tissue with my semen.

When I saw Angela at school on Monday she gave me a knowing smile. We sat together during lunch, and she told me that her period was over. She said I should come to her house after school; her mother wouldn't be home until six, and her father was out of town till Thursday.

I couldn't believe it. In just a little while I was going to have sexual intercourse. Angela and I were actually going to fuck. After school I hurried to her back door so no one would see me, or the lump in my pants. She was waiting for me with a sweet and loving smile. She had taken off the blouse she'd been wearing and put on a sweatshirt. I put my arms around her, and we kissed as though we were pledging our lives to each other.

Sliding my hand up under my sweetheart's sweatshirt, I felt her bare back. A little thrill ran through me as I realized that she wasn't wearing a bra, and that her breasts were naked under the sweatshirt. I could have devoured that sweet, marvelous young woman right then and there. Looking in her pretty blue eyes, I had a sense that she was reacting to my hand being on her back as strongly as I was—except that she didn't have an erection to deal with.

Angela took my hand and led me up to her bedroom. Here I was, in my sweet love's own room, where she spent a lot of her life, much of it naked. She'd probably had sexual fantasies right there on that bed, and perhaps even masturbated while lying there. I'd heard that many women masturbated almost as much as men.

Angela sat on the bed and pulled me down next to her. We kissed, and I ran my hand up the back of her shirt again. She sank down on her back, and my hand slid around her body, going instinctively to her breast, her marvelous breast. The sensation was so fantastic that my other hand soon joined in, and I was holding Angela's naked tits at last, my palms stroking her nipples.

Emotions went roaring through my body. I knew absolutely that I was the only guy that had ever touched those breasts. The nipples were getting stiff, telling me that she was also enjoying what my hands were doing. Her blue eyes were smiling up at me as if to ask, "Do you like my tits?"

Now Angela took hold of her sweatshirt, pulled it over her head and tossed it on the floor. I pulled her to me, so that her perfect bare breasts squashed against my chest.

We kissed, and then she pushed me back and said, "Let's do it with your chest bare also!" She unbuttoned my shirt and we took it off, while I filled my eyes with the most perfect breasts ever created. She put her arms around me, and our bodies pressed together. Oh, how marvelous to feel those hard little points pushing into my chest!

Drawing back again, Angela began playing with her own tits, cupping them in her hands and making her nipples touch mine. Lord, I loved this woman! As she cupped her tits, I bent down to kiss and lick her precious buttons, drawing each of them in my mouth in turn.

"Oh, I love what you're doing," Angela whispered. "It feels so *good.*"

So I continued, running my tongue all over her breasts and nipples for quite a while. We were soon rolling around on the bed, with her tits in my mouth as she emitted satisfied little humming sounds. All this activity made her skirt ride up, and I couldn't help sliding my hand up her leg to her buttocks. I felt those marvelous round cheeks through her silk panties. They did not disappoint me in any way. They felt just like I had imagined they would.

Slipping my hand under her waistband, I moved it to her bare buttocks. The thrill that flooded my nervous system was almost indescribable. This sweet wonderful girl was letting me play with her naked rear end. My fingers went in her crack and slid over her anus. Again, I knew that I was the only guy in the world who had ever done this—or, I hoped, ever would.

My fingers traveled on between her legs, and I felt that special crack with the hair around it. Angela parted her legs so I could reach all the way to her pubic bone and that intriguing triangle of hair. There I was with a breast in my mouth and a hand on a naked ass, my finger exploring a real live woman's cunt, and that woman the most wonderful one in the world. It was almost more than I could take in.

Pulling my mouth off Angela's nipple, I looked in those beautiful eyes. Again she gazed at me as if to see if I liked the feel of her secret parts. I think she saw in my eyes that I did. A second later she pulled away and hopped off the bed. Then, facing me, she pulled off her skirt and panties and laid them on a chair. Stark naked, she walked toward me, smiling at me to show me I was special. I saw that she was a natural blonde—not that I'd had any doubts.

Climbing back on the bed, Angela took my hand and slid my index finger between the lips of her cunt. I was overwhelmed by a desire to hold her close and kiss her, which I did while I ran my finger around in her vagina. She nestled against me and emitted soft purring sounds as I continued to finger her.

At one point Angela told me to push my finger toward the front wall of her cunt. She said that that was her G-spot, and that it gave her immense pleasure. She sucked in air as I ran my finger around it. Then she rolled on her back, gasping, "Oh! Oh! Oh!" over and over.

Finally she pushed my hand away, saying, "Let's get the rest of your clothes off." As I stood up, she unbuckled and unzipped my pants and anxiously helped me push down my pants and undershorts. There I was, completely naked, with my penis standing straight up in a salute to her. She took hold of my erection as I stood in front of her, and started rubbing it between her palms. Looking in that lovely face, with the beautiful blue eyes, I was again overwhelmed by the knowledge that I was about to enter into coitus with this wonderful young woman.

We lay on the bed again, Angela on her back, I on one elbow, looking down at her. Gently, she pulled me closer, until I was lying on top of her, with the tip of my penis bumping against her crotch.

Remembering that this was her first time, I took it slow and easy. I took my penis in my hand and slid it up and down in that fantastic valley of pink flesh. Finally I slid the tip of it in her funnel, planning to ease in slowly. But she wasn't going to wait. She thrust her hips up toward me, taking almost the entire length of my tool in her sweet body.

It would be impossible to describe how incredible it felt, being buried in that sweet, wet, tight, warm hole. Looking down, I saw my erection sliding in and out of that marvelous fur-covered crack. Angela, with her eyes half closed, locked her heels behind my butt and pulled me more tightly against her.

I was trying not to move too quickly at first, letting Angela get used to me. But she had different ideas and bucked her hips strongly up and down, setting up a rigorous rhythm. Each time I plunged in her, our pubic hair intermingled. My mind reeled. I was fucking a woman for the first time, and she happened to be my most favorite human being in the world, and she was turning out to be eager and passionate as well as beautiful. I had to be the luckiest person in the universe.

"I want more than one orgasm," Angela panted. "So the longer you can last, the more pleasure you'll give me."

"Oh, you sweet, sweet woman!" I said. "I want to give you as much pleasure as I possibly can. But remember, I don't have any experience with this."

Suddenly she said, "God, I'm coming!" Her body was already tensing, her eyes were closed, and she was panting. Then I felt her vagina pulsing and contracting tightly around my penis.

Through some miracle I was able to hold off my own climax. Angela asked me to stop a minute to let her catch her breath. We spent the time hugging and kissing, and cooing at each other.

Finally she said, "I'll get on my hands and knees. You enter me from behind."

Suddenly, right there in front of me was the cutest butt in the whole world, with Angela's little brown bud of an anus winking up at me. Her vagina looked so nice and inviting from that angle, with her pink labia all swollen and ready. I entered her with my cock, and we soon established a more vigorous rhythm than before. I also had a better view of my cock sliding in and out of her hairy slit, just below her asshole.

As I thrust in her, I ran my hands over her back and around to her tummy, finally grasping her breasts and playing with her nipples. She begged me to go for broke this time, so she could feel my semen squirting in her. With my hips bouncing off her nice round cheeks with each stroke, I knew it wouldn't be long before I blew my load in her body. Soon I was blasting away full-force in this fabulous woman's inner sanctum.

"Oh, I feel it squirting!" gasped Angela. "It's making me come again!" She gave a series of deep guttural grunts, and I felt the now-familiar contractions. I wanted to stay in that satisfying hole of hers forever, but my depleted cock shrank down and plopped out unceremoniously. We sank down on the bed, and caressed each other again in the beautiful afterglow.

After ten minutes or so, Angela gently picked up my soft organ and examined it. She lifted my scrotum with care, and looked between my legs to see how everything fit together. Then she laid my penis back on my tummy and ran her fingers lightly over it as she said, "My, what a marvelous thing you have there." She leaned down and kissed it on the back side. It twitched. She lifted it up again, slid the foreskin back a little and kissed it right on the tip. "Do you like it when I do that?" she inquired.

"Yes! It feels awfully good," I said.

"I taste myself on you," Angela said.

"Do you like that taste?"

"God, yes!" she gasped. "It's a real turn-on."

I desperately wanted her to do more. Which was apparently her plan as well, for she continued to kiss my cock up and down, and finally slid the tip of it in her mouth. Soon she was taking as much cock in her mouth as she could, and I was rapidly getting hard again.

Now Angela turned and swung one leg over me, putting her vagina and her anus right in front of my face. There they were, the most marvelous little cunt and asshole in the world. Then it suddenly occurred to me that she wanted me to do her also. And I was surprised to realize that I was looking forward to it.

I put my hands on her hips and drew her closer to me. I could smell the soap she used, and the muskier odor of her cunt. I wanted to study her thoroughly. I parted her pussy lips and looked into this most fascinating hair-encircled female hole. Angela started rocking her hips back and forth, and I guessed she was getting impatient.

I obligingly brought my lips to that sweet opening and kissed her on the labia. Then I pushed my tongue past the hairy lips and slid it deep into her slit. After probing as deeply as I could, I licked my way up toward her clitoris, and stroked and nibbled that tiny erection with tongue and lips. Then I licked my way down over her slit again to her asshole, in which I stuck my tongue as far as it would go. Angela was in a rapture as I went from one end of her cunt to the other. I felt her moans reverberating against my cock, which was still in her mouth.

Suddenly Angela raised her head and gasped, "Here I go again!" She tensed up, and I felt her juices coursing onto my tongue. She sank back down on the bed, and after catching her breath she said, "Let's do a long slow one now." With her on her side in a fetal position, I entered her from behind, and we made love that way for a long sensuous time, completely wrapped up in each other's pleasure, until we burst into an utterly satisfying mutual orgasm.

We lay together peacefully for a long time. Finally, looking in those beautiful eyes of hers, I said, "I'm so in love with you, I can't stand it."

"We're going to have a fantastic life together," Angela said softly. "Starting with this afternoon."

"Darling, we started two years ago," I said. "Sex is just icing on the cake."

Angela smiled. "Now do you understand why I wouldn't let you touch me before?" she said. "I knew I would love it, and go nuts, and lose control. We sure know how to fuck, don't we?"

I laughed, because I had never expected to hear her use that word. "We were sure good at it for the first time," I replied. "And it can only get better!"

Well, Angela and I have been married for ten years now, and I was right. It's only gotten better.—*V.P., Tulsa, Oklahoma*

HE DOES THREE WOMEN AT A BIRTHDAY PARTY—AND IT ISN'T EVEN HIS BIRTHDAY

I have always enjoyed reading *Penthouse Letters,* but never expected to be sending in a contribution. However, I just have to tell you about something that happened to me last Friday night.

It was Randi's twenty-first birthday, and she was having a party at her house. She and I had hooked up briefly last year, and we were still quite friendly. Her hard, athletic body and very aggressive nipples were among the major reasons for our continuing relationship.

At the party, Randi told me that she had slept with the boyfriend of a coworker of hers named Dina, and now she wanted to fuck Dina herself. Randi was an equal-opportunity fucker. She said she was going to try to fuck Dina that very night. She had gotten it in her head that this would make a great birthday present to herself.

Dina was a hot blonde with beautiful tits and a perfect ass. Randi's intentions became obvious when she and Dina danced together at the party, their bodies grinding together as Randi fondled the blonde beauty openly. Dina seemed to be as ready and willing as she was. As the night progressed and more alcohol was consumed, the twosome got hotter and hotter.

Dina had brought along her roommate, Audrey, a slim brunette who was less well endowed than either Randi or Dina, but whose tight dress outlined a pair of perky nipples that drove me crazy. I ended up dancing with Audrey for most of the evening. Finally almost everyone had left the party, and Audrey and I were still dancing. At this point I turned and saw Randi and Dina kissing on the couch, with their hands down each other's pants.

When Audrey noticed what I was looking at, she said to me, "Do you want to join them?"

At first I thought she was kidding. I replied, "Sure."

But she *wasn't* kidding!

She took my hand and led me over to the couch, where she immediately joined the other two women in their making-out session. Soon there were hands exploring everywhere, and clothes were being slowly removed, including my shirt. After a few minutes Randi gaspingly suggested that we all move to her room. To my astonishment the three of them hurried off to her bedroom—with me close at their heels.

In the bedroom the women swiftly ripped off the rest of their clothes. Three naked chicks now dragged me to the bed, with only my pants on. I found the closest pussy and began gnawing away as the other two women munched each other. Soon there was just a blur of legs, breasts and pussies around me, and I seriously could not believe that this was actually happening.

Then, between moans, Dina spoke up. "Someone still has his pants on," she said.

I remedied that by removing my remaining clothes posthaste. My erect dick jumped out, eager for a piece of the action. The women all gathered around me and began helping themselves to my cock, balls and ass.

Then Randi said, "Come on, Bill, I want to see you fuck Dina."

I was more than willing to comply, and obviously so was Dina. I eased slowly in her moist twat and began to screw her. Fortunately I'd had enough Jack Daniel's to keep me relatively calm and prevent me from prematurely ending this once-in-a-lifetime experience. As I pounded into Dina, I saw Randi mounting Audrey with a large dildo and humping the shit out of her.

After bringing Dina to orgasm, I next took on Randi, pumping her hard body for a while. The other women lay down on either side of her so I could finger them at the same time. After Randi was spent, I moved on to Audrey, and I finished her off too.

All this time the women kept shouting encouragement. "Fuck her harder, Bill! Make her scream! Fuck that pussy!"

By now I was more than ready to blow my load. I got behind Randi and did her doggie-style, while she ate Dina out at the same time. Audrey reached beneath us and diddled Randi's clit with one hand while stroking her own with the other. I held out until I heard both Audrey and Dina cry out in climax, and then my throbbing cock exploded deep inside Randi's body. She too orgasmed as I finished shooting in her, and we all collapsed with exhaustion.

The party was finally over. Randi said it had been a great birthday. We all got dressed and said good night, but not before I thanked all three women for making me the happiest man alive.—W.S., *London, Ontario*

HE STARTED OUT STUDYING FOR FINALS AND WOUND UP STUDYING A SEXY COED

It was final-exams week at the university, and throughout the dorm students were frantically cramming in those last bits of knowledge before the dreaded exams. I was alone in my room, absorbing as much calculus and physics as possible, when I heard a tapping on my door.

Not particularly wanting to be bothered with visitors, I was tempted to ignore the intruder and go back to my painstaking academic pursuits. But when the knocking persisted, I reluctantly gave in. Maybe a break wouldn't be a bad idea after all. I had no idea who the visitor might be, and when I opened the door I was more than a little surprised, and very pleased indeed, to see Georgette's sweet face.

Georgette was majoring in psychology. Her room was two floors above mine in the dorm, and we had known each other for almost the whole semester. I had always found her personality extremely appealing—not to mention her slim, petite body, perfect breasts and gorgeous face.

"Hey, sexy, thought you could use a break," she said with a warm smile.

I felt a tingle in my midsection. I invited her in, and we sat on the couch. We started talking about all sorts of things—school, parents, philosophies of life and so on. At one point she started talking about women and the various things they wanted and needed in life. Seeing a possible opportunity here, I responded by asking her in a half-serious, half-joking manner if she would like me to satisfy one of those needs for her.

Georgette gave me a slightly puzzled look, as though wondering exactly what I had in mind—although she probably had a pretty good idea. At that point I got up and took a bottle of scented oil from a shelf. Her eyes lit up, and a smile flourished on her sweet lips. I knew that she was a sucker for a good massage. She had asked me to rub oil on her back once before, when we were swimming with a group of friends. The silky feel of her flesh and her soft moans of pleasure as she squirmed under my hands had made my cock stand up and salute under my bathing suit.

Now Georgette lay down on her stomach, closing her eyes in anticipation. I lifted up her shirt and rubbed the oil softly into the skin of her back. In no time at all I had her in a trance. As before, she began to moan with appreciation. She wasn't wearing a bra, so there were no straps to get in my way as my hands roamed over her back.

I knew that if I was ever going to indulge myself in her sweetness, this was going to be the night. Still massaging her back, I leaned over and kissed her neck. Her only response was another moan, but I assumed that was a good sign. But it was an even better sign when, in one smooth motion, she turned around on her back, wrapped her arms around me and pulled my body close to hers. She kissed me slowly and passionately, her tongue sweetly probing my mouth.

When the kiss ended, she purred in my ear, "You satisfied one of my needs. Now let me satisfy one of yours." And with that she slid her mouth slowly down my body, kissing my chest and stomach. She unbuttoned my pants and let my throbbing cock out of hiding. Then she hungrily let the whole thing slide in her mouth and proceeded to work some unbelievable magic on me with her wonderful lips and tongue.

I was in another world, and I couldn't get enough. But I didn't want this to be a one-sided affair. After a few minutes, heroically restraining myself from coming in her mouth, I pulled away and began to remove the tight black sweatpants she was wearing. When they were off, along with her panties, I buried my face in her sweet pussy and lapped hungrily at her love juices.

I concentrated hard on what I was doing, and Georgette had a powerful orgasm before I became aware that she was saying something in a quivering voice. I raised my head to listen. What she was saying was, "Fuck me."

I was not about to argue. I eased my manhood slowly in Georgette's love-pocket. She moaned loudly and bucked up against me. We moved together strongly, and too soon I spewed my massive load inside her. But I only needed a moment's rest before coming back to action, thrusting in her even harder than before, until she screamed in ecstasy and erupted in the most explosive orgasm I had ever seen, her entire body gyrating with incredible climactic joy.

Exhausted, we lay there in each other's arms, in a sweaty, oily mass. It wasn't doing my couch any good, but I couldn't have cared less about that.

"So," Georgette said finally, smiling at me, "aren't you glad you took a break from studying?"

"Hell, yes!" I replied truthfully. "And please feel free to interrupt me at any time!"—*L.H., Berkeley, California*

HER HUSBAND PREFERRED DRINKING TO LOVING, BUT SHE CRAVED BLACK MEN ANYWAY

I would like to share with you an unexpected sexual experience I had not long ago. I had a coworker named Ralph who had a very bad drinking habit. I didn't particularly care for him—not because he was white and I am black, but because he could be very obnoxious at times. Nevertheless, when he was ticketed for drunken driving and lost his license, I felt sorry for him, and I agreed to drive him to and from work until he could make other arrangements.

I was a little early the first morning I stopped by his house to pick him up. His wife answered my knock. She was a strikingly attractive blonde, wearing a transparent negligee over a pair of see-through thong panties. Her tits, with their long pink nipples, were plainly visible, and I must say they were twin beauties.

Her husband was just getting up, so she invited me in and offered me a cup of coffee. As she preceded me inside I could see she had a beautiful ass, nice and round. The strap of her thong was buried deep in the crack of her ass, and from the back it looked like she was completely naked. When she poured me a cup of coffee I could see the luxuriant mound of her blonde pussy hair and the thick lips of her cunt. Needless to say, my big black cock was standing at attention.

She told me her name was Megan, and we made pleasant conversation while her husband got dressed. She made no attempt to change into something less revealing. I had never actually seen a naked white woman before, except in pictures, and I really liked it. I badly wanted to stick my dick up her cunt. All during the day at work I could not get that beautiful woman off my mind. It was too bad, I thought, that she was married to a loser like Ralph.

The next morning Megan was wearing the negligee again, but this time without the thong panties. It gaped open slightly, and I could tell that she was aroused; her nipples were erect and her clit was swollen and red. Maybe I had a chance at that pussy after all. As she stood close to me I took a chance and put my arm around her. She responded by pressing her body against mine. Our lips met in a deep tongue-searching kiss. My hand groped for her pussy. I thumbed her clit and slipped a finger inside her. She moaned and pressed closer to me. Then we heard Ralph approaching, and broke apart.

After that I made a habit of getting there early each morning. While Ralph got ready, Megan and I did some heavy petting. We got bolder and bolder, until one morning I took out my dick and pushed the head of it against the opening of her cunt. She begged me to put it all in, and with one thrust I was balls-deep inside her pussy. I fucked her furiously, but before either of us could come we heard her husband's footsteps. I quickly pulled out, and just got my dick back in my pants before he came in. "Another time," Megan mouthed at me, and I smiled and nodded yes.

The right time came sooner than I had anticipated. One night Ralph and I stopped at a bar on our way home from work, and Ralph started drinking heavily. Soon he was falling-down drunk. He was nearly passed out by the time I got him home, and Megan helped me get him laid out on a couch. In a minute he was unconscious, and Megan and I were in each other's arms.

We kissed long and passionately, her lips sucking at my tongue. She slipped out of her dress, and she had nothing beneath it. Her beautiful tits were bare and inviting, and the lips of her cunt looked like rose petals. I kissed and tongued every inch of her fabulous body. Megan sucked and licked my cock and balls. Finally I couldn't hold back any more; I had to put my cock into that sweet juicy pussy. Man, that woman could rotate her ass! We finally climaxed together, and I shot a large load of come deep inside her cunt.

As we lay resting, Megan told me that when Ralph had first told her that a black colleague would be picking him up for work, she had been interested even before she saw me. She had planned to show me her pussy and tits, and she was hoping I would want her. It had been too long since a black man had fucked her. A black boyfriend had taken her cherry, and she really loved black dick. I pounded her hot tight blonde pussy twice more before I left that night, and her husband slept through it all.

Every night after that we would go to a bar, and Ralph would get drunk and pass out. I'd take him home and Megan and I would fuck.

One time a friend of mine was getting married and I gave a bachelor party for him. I invited Ralph and Megan, who were the only white people there. Some of the guys kept giving Ralph free drinks, and when he passed out Megan fucked eleven of my black friends. Her blonde pussy could take a licking and just kept on dicking!

Am I still fucking Megan? You bet I am. The woman just can't get enough black dick.—*Name and address withheld* ○┼▪

HE STOPPED TO HELP HER CHANGE A FLAT TIRE, AND GOT A REWARD HE DIDN'T EXPECT

I am a twenty-eight-year-old single man, and I work as a salesman for a lumberyard. As part of my work I travel around the area to call on various builders and construction sites.

One late summer day last month, after making several calls with some success, I was driving between towns when I noticed a van pulled off the road with a flat tire, and a nicely dressed woman next to it. I pulled over and offered to change the tire for her. She was glad for the help. As I got out the spare tire I noticed some grocery bags in her car. While I was changing the tire I checked out the lady. She had a nice figure, sparkling green eyes and long auburn hair that cascaded around her pleasantly attractive face.

When I finished changing the tire she offered me some money. I told her I couldn't take her money, but I would settle for one of the apples I had seen in her grocery bag. I said I often stopped to help people, and just hoped that if I was ever in trouble, someone would do the same for me.

The lady smiled and opened the door of her van, saying, "I have something for you." I thought she was going to give me an apple, but instead she turned and sat on the floor of the van. Then she reached out and grabbed my belt, pulling me closer. To my amazement, she then unzipped my jeans and pulled out my stiffening cock. She looked up at me with a twinkle in her eye and wrapped her lips around the head of my dick, which became rock hard in a matter of seconds. She ran her tongue around the rim of my cockhead, and then sucked on it, making it bigger. She slowly ran her tongue up and down the sensitive underside of the shaft as she caressed my balls through my pants. Soon she was sucking in my whole cock, right to the base. By now I was running my hands through her beautiful hair. Periodically, she would glance up at me. She really seemed to be enjoying what she was doing, and I was just loving it!

My hips were moving, pumping my cock in and out of her mouth. Now she undid my pants and pulled them down, along with my shorts. Her hands grasped my butt as she went on sucking and licking, her tongue tickling the sensitive underside of my cock. I felt a wet finger circling my asshole, and then it was worming into my ass. I was going crazy; this woman was incredible!

My breathing was getting coarse, and I broke the silence to say I was going to come. "Hmmm," she moaned appreciatively, and intensified her motions. I had an amazingly intense orgasm. I just kept coming until I thought my balls were going to shoot out of my cock.

"That was good," she said, smiling at me. "I love to suck cock, and that was quite tasty." She looked at her watch and said, "Twelve minutes, not bad." I pulled up my pants and she headed around to the driver's seat. She said, "Thanks again for everything," and then started up the motor and pulled away.

I went back to my car and sat there for a few minutes, stunned but happy. When I got back to the yard, and my coworkers asked how my day had gone, I told them it was the best ever!—*H.E., Joplin, Missouri* ⊶▪

WHO WAS THE SEXY NUDE NIGHTTIME VISITOR? IT WAS HIS FRIEND'S WIFE, OF COURSE

*M*y wife and I love reading your magazine, and I would like to tell you the true story of what happened to me a few years ago. I lived in Pennsylvania at the time, and traveled all over the western two-thirds of the state as a representative for my company. One particular stop on my route was in a small town, and the people I worked with there, a couple named Josie and Craig, became very dear friends. They often invited me to spend the night at their home, since the nearest motel was about thirty miles away from where they lived.

Craig was a fun-loving person with a ready smile and a collection of wild stories that he would share at the drop of a hat. His wife Josie was a beautiful woman, with the kind of figure one dreams about, but usually sees only in magazines. She could cook up wonderful meals and was always fun to be around. But there was never a hint that she was interested in me in any way.

One night, after eating a well-prepared meal at their house, I was planning to get back on the road; but because of the lateness of the hour, and the fact that a blizzard was being predicted for the area, I was persuaded to stay the night.

After spending what remained of the evening in pleasant conversation, we bade each other good night and I headed for the spare bedroom. A light from the yard outside illuminated the room, but I was so tired it didn't take long for me to fall asleep.

Around two in the morning I was awakened by a soft touch on my shoulder. I opened my eyes, and there beside me stood the most beautiful nude woman I had ever seen. It was Josie, of course, and she was even more attractive than I had imagined. Her tits were huge and perfectly shaped, her legs were curvy and sensuous and her pussy was full and inviting, just the way I like them. Without a word she lay down beside me, and then she took my rapidly growing cock into her eager mouth.

There was no way I could keep my hands off her. I touched every inch of her beautiful body, kissing, sucking, licking and enjoying. She stopped her sucking and gently guided my face to her love nest. My tongue went to work excitedly. I have been told I have the most talented tongue around, and fortunately it seemed to impress Josie. Soon her whole body was quaking with one powerful orgasm after another. While my tongue worked its magic I gently pinched her nipples and massaged her wonderful tits.

I don't know how many times Josie erupted in pleasure, but after a while she pulled me up over her, and I could tell she wanted all eight and a half inches of my cock inside her as deeply as possible. Soon we were fucking like there was no tomorrow. In beautiful harmony we feasted on each other. I could sense her holding back her cries of ecstasy as she built slowly to the most intense orgasm of all, and soon I felt her whole body tense and quake. I couldn't hold back any longer; I stifled my own shouts as I fired my hot come deep inside her spasming pussy. It was the most powerful climax I had ever experienced, and it felt like I had unloaded the largest load in the history of sex.

We held each other tightly for some time, allowing our hands to caress each other freely. After some moments Josie moved her pussy to my face and I eagerly drank our love juices and cleaned her love nest with my tongue. She began to stiffen again, and soon reached another beautiful climax. Getting off me then, she leaned down and kissed me deeply before disappearing into the night. Not one word had been spoken during the entire time.

I soon fell asleep again and slept soundly till morning. Craig and Josie greeted me in their usual friendly way, and we enjoyed a pleasant breakfast together. Josie never gave the slightest hint that anything unusual had happened.

I often spent the night there after that, and each time my nocturnal visitor would come to my room. Each of our lovemaking sessions seemed more intense and exciting than the last. But we never said one word to each other about it, even when we were alone.

Unfortunately, Craig was transferred to California about six months later, and shortly afterward our office moved to New England. Though Craig and I have talked by telephone many times about business, I have never heard a word from Josie. Oh well, it was wonderful while it lasted, and it makes for a great memory.—*L.F., Providence, Rhode Island* ⊶■

HOW TO LIVEN UP A DULL CHRISTMAS PARTY: HAVE SEX WITH SOMEONE ELSE'S WIFE

I was at a cocktail party at my brother's house last December, about two weeks before Christmas. Among the guests was a beautiful young woman in her mid-twenties, who showed up unaccompanied. I struck up a conversation with her, and soon we were seated on a couch next to a tall Christmas tree covered with about a thousand mini-lights and streams of tinsel.

The lady's name was Felicia. She had beautiful long dark brown hair, for which I have an undeniable fetish. She had a wedding band on her finger, and I soon learned that her husband was expected to join her in about an hour. She wore a lavender dress with a hemline that came to mid-thigh. It proved to be a terrible distraction, as my eyes kept drifting down to her legs during our conversation.

I was instantly captivated by her. When she spoke her eyes sparkled, and her voice had a smoky bedroom quality. She was intoxicating, and I felt my testosterone level markedly rising. There was a raw sensual energy pulsing between us, and I could tell that she sensed it as much as I did.

At one point I went to get her another drink. When I returned and handed her the cocktail, I let my fingertips brush the back of her hand. The mere touch of her skin was a turn-on.

A few moments later I was telling her how much she excited me, and that I would very much like to go someplace with her where we could be alone. Felicia looked at me with wide eyes. Until then she had been flirting openly with me; now she must have realized that I was ready to take to the next level what she may have intended as a mere flirtation.

She reminded me that she was married. "So am I," I shrugged. After another hesitation, she bluntly asked if sex was what I had in mind. I confessed that the idea had indeed occurred to me.

I could see her struggling with herself. She said that her husband was supposed to be there about nine o'clock. I told her that we wouldn't need to be gone long. She asked me where we could go. I said my brother had a guest bedroom upstairs where we would not be disturbed. She took a deep breath, and then, almost imperceptibly, she nodded.

I proposed that we leave the room separately and meet upstairs, so our departures would be less conspicuous. She agreed, and after a moment I stood up, strolled out of the room and headed upstairs.

A minute or so later I heard her coming up the steps. She reached the top of the stairway and looked around for me. I called to her from the far end of the hallway, and she moved toward me, her expression a mixture of anxiety and anticipation.

I led her into the bedroom. Once inside I locked the door, and we began hurriedly undressing. The moment we were both naked I was all over her, caressing her breasts and letting my hands rove down to her rump. She leaned her head against my shoulder and her soft-scented hair brushed my cheek. I kissed her all over her face, her neck and her shoulders, and gently licked the rubbery nubs of her nipples.

Felicia sank to her knees to perform fellatio on me. "You don't have to that unless you want to," I told her.

"I do want to," she said. She put her mouth on my cock and coated the head with her saliva. Tingles shot through me. She took the whole thing into her mouth then, and to my delight she demonstrated an uncommon knack for just the right kind of touch, the right kind of movement by which she could pleasure a man with her lips and tongue. I clasped her shoulders and stroked her neck with my thumbs on either side. She dug her fingers into my buns as she sucked me. Her long hair brushed across my legs as her head bobbed up and down, and her nose nestled into my pubic hair at each downstroke.

I found myself wondering if she swallowed, titillated by the erotic image of my semen running down her throat into her digestive tract. I was tempted to let her continue working her oral magic until I blasted off inside her mouth. But her skill at this foreplay seemed so promising that I feared I'd shortchange myself if I settled for a blow-job. Besides, I didn't want to be selfish; I wanted to give her as much pleasure as she was giving me.

I pulled my dick out of her mouth and pulled her to her feet, then gently pushed her onto the bed and lay down next to her. We curled into the 69 position, my mouth fastening onto her pussy as hers went back to my cock.

I fancied myself a fairly accomplished cunnilinguist, and I began lapping at the pink folds of her vaginal lips, dabbing at her clitoris with gentle swabs. A quiver rippled through her body. She was wet. The scent of her pussy filled my nostrils and her brown patch of pubic hair tickled my chin.

Meanwhile Felicia was kissing the base of my shaft while the tip of my penis bobbed under her chin, pushing into the fleshy underside of her jaw. She nibbled at my testicle sac, sucking the skin with her mouth, pulling and stretching the skin of the scrotum outward and then releasing it. Suddenly I felt her take my balls into her mouth, wrapping her lips around the scrotum. Her tongue rolled the twin orbs around in her mouth like two balls of candy she was trying to melt on her tongue.

I was devotedly slithering my tongue into her slit when Felicia abruptly broke off this intensely erotic play. She sat up and rolled me over onto my back, then climbed on top of me and straddled me, guiding my cock into her pussy. I groped at her tits, craning my neck to bring my lips up to her nipples, which were just beyond reach. She rode me back and forth, becoming progressively more bold and violent. Loose strands of her tossing mane of brown hair swept across my face and chest as she bent over me, her jouncing pussy sheathing my rod completely each time her torso sank down on me.

She had me in a fever. I'd never before been balled as aggressively as this, and it really lit my erotic fuse. I heaved up, tumbling her off me. I grabbed a pillow from the head of the bed and placed it under her spine as I pushed her onto her back and spread her legs.

Her hands grabbed my head as I lowered my face to her crotch. Her fingers combed through my hair, raking my scalp. The sight of her snatch in front of my face mesmerized me, and the rich distinctive aroma of her cunt brought an adrenal rush to my brain.

Moistening my tongue and lips, I began ravishing her little garden, licking and massaging the pink folds unhurriedly with savoring laps and gentle caresses up and down, back and forth over the full length and breadth of her crotch, from the crown of her pubic mound down to her anus. I rubbed one hand over her smooth flat tummy while the other slipped under her butt, fondling each cheek before pushing down into the crack separating the fleshy buns, spreading them apart to expose her anus. Finding the mark, I attempted to insert my middle finger into that passage. It was closed up tight, but with a little coaxing the muscles began to relax, and my finger wormed its way through the anus and into her colon. I kept it there as I continued to stimulate her entire vaginal region with my lips and tongue until I brought her to orgasm.

After that I moved up from her pubic area and began to cover her lower body with soft kisses. I zeroed in on her belly button, and soon discovered that she was hypersensitive in that spot. Licking her navel set her off. Consequently I devoted more attention to this hot spot, and listened to her purrs of approval as I slowly caressed that belly button with the tip of my tongue.

Finally I moved up and positioned myself over her body, my legs between hers. We gazed into each other's dilated pupils, savoring that moment of wild anticipation before the final feverish ride to climax.

Her boobs pushed against my chest, the nipples hard and sensitive to the touch. I reached down to her groin and spread the lips of her labia. With my dick I plowed the pink furrows, probing for her opening. Finally I found the mark and wedged in until I pegged her hole dead center, and then I slid into her firmly and steadily, penetrating deep into the inner sanctum of her canal.

Her twat was moist with secretions, and I moved in and out of her with ease. Felicia's arms and legs wrapped around me. Her breath blew sharp warm gusts on my neck. Her fingers dug into my shoulder blades. Her thighs hugged my loins and her knees dug into my ribcage. The backs of her calves rested on my lower back. With each thrust of my penis into her tight slippery pussy her heels bounced on my rump, and my testicles slapped against her buttocks.

Our tempo picked up as we both felt the rapid approach of orgasm. I bore in with powerful, penetrating jabs, pounding her butt into the bedspread. She clutched me frantically with arms and legs as her climax washed over her. "Splash me," she gasped into my ear, over and over again. "Splash me, splash me!"

It was pointless to try to prolong my explosion further. She was in a fever for me to cream her, and I simply could not hold back my orgasm any longer. Grabbing her waist, I sank my penis as deeply into her as it could penetrate, then went rigid as I erupted.

A torrent of semen burst loose, flooding the depths of her canal in swift spurts. Each pulsing jet of ejaculated fluid sent waves of sensation coursing up to my brain, paralyzing me with ecstasy. The contractions went on and on until it seemed that they would never stop.

Finally I collapsed on top of her, gasping as I pulled air into my lungs. We lay in a heap, two panting bodies drenched in sweat and secretions. But when I attempted to caress her after recovering my breath, she pulled away, fretting that her husband might at this moment be downstairs, wondering where his wife had disappeared to. I withdrew my penis from her vagina, but I couldn't help telling her what a marvelous, wild fuck she had been. She kissed me and returned the compliment, then sat up on the edge of the bed and began to get dressed.

We kissed at the doorway before going out, then went downstairs separately to rejoin the party. No one appeared to have even noticed our absence.

Sometime between nine-thirty and ten, Felicia's husband finally arrived. He walked up to his voluptuous wife, slipped his arm around her waist and kissed her affectionately on the cheek. They looked like a perfect couple. He seemed like an amiable, jovial fellow who I might like to go have a beer with. Yet I felt no tinge of remorse at the fact that I had fucked his wife in an upstairs bedroom less than an hour earlier. He would be none the poorer for it, and she and I would take away from this party a very pleasant memory.—*R.V., Tuscaloosa, Alabama* ⊙┼▩

HIS BUS GETS BOGGED DOWN IN THE RAIN, BUT A COLLEGE GIRL MAKES HIM EVEN WETTER

*T*he clock on the LCD told me it was nearly eleven. Only an hour to go before the weekend. The night air was brisk and full of promise. I yawned briefly as the light changed from green to red. The CB cued in with an inaudible protest from a coworker. The light changed and I made a right. There was an elderly man waiting at the bus stop with a plastic bag in his hand. He swung it back and forth impatiently.

I stopped and opened the door. Off in the distance a lightning bolt danced across the sky. The old guy and I eyed each other surreptitiously as he got on, but neither of us spoke a word.

Six blocks later I glanced in the rear-view. The terminal was just around the corner, and there were only six people left on the bus. A young couple was doing some deep kissing and heavy petting—the guy's hand was up her skirt, for Pete's sake. My new friend with the plastic bag stared out the window. A young mother was doing her best to calm her fretful child. Seated close to me was what looked like some long-haired oddball in a trench coat, leaning forward in his seat and focusing on the floor.

The elderly man stood and pressed the buzzer. It was music to my ears. I stopped and he stepped off. "Rear!" a voice from the back called, and I reached for the lever to open the side doors. More people got off.

As I started up I glanced in the rear-view again. Everyone had left except for the long-haired freak. As I looked closer I realized that that mass of hair covered the face of a young girl, no more than twenty, possibly a college student, judging by the sweater and pants she wore. She was dozing on the seat. Then the bus lurched and she jerked awake. She stared at me through her silky, overly permed hair. "I'm sorry," she said, giving me a sudden smile. "I must have fallen asleep."

Suddenly lightning flashed again, and a sudden rainstorm descended on the city. I turned on the windshield wipers, but they were about as effective as pieces of paper trying to scoop up a puddle of water. As I concentrated on propelling the bus through the deluge, I became aware that the college girl had gotten up and come over to me. Now she knelt down beside me.

"What…" I said.

She unzipped my pants and began slobbering over my dick. It seemed like she couldn't get enough; she was trying to swallow it all. I turned off the avenue onto the street that would lead to the terminal, and plowed into a hell of a flash flood. The sound of the engine stalling made me drive my fists against the steering wheel. She stopped sucking and said again, "I'm sorry."

"For what, for God's sake?" I said, and ran my fingers through her hair. She pulled my pants to the floor. Then she got up, removed her slacks and panties, leaned back over the steering wheel and raised her pelvis to my face. Her blonde pubic hair pointed straight to her snatch. "Now that's the ticket!" I cried, and tongued her fiercely, savoring her juices in my mouth. Then I stood, turned her around and bent her over the seat. I slipped on a condom and took her from behind, feeling the tightness of her juicy cunt as it hungrily devoured my cock.

After some time she pulled away, exclaiming, "Now, I'm ready for a real ride!" She backed me down into the driver's seat and jumped on my lap. With her back toward me, she moaned and squealed with pleasure as she slid down my shaft. I stuck my hands under her sweater and grabbed both of her firm supple breasts from behind, bouncing her up and down. I was starting to peak. "No don't stop!" she screamed, clutching the steering wheel and twisting wildly around my dick. I tried to hold back, but I knew it wouldn't be long. Then she brought one hand to her breasts, and the other went down to massage her clit. "Oh God, yes!" she shrieked. "Ride up inside me!" Drowning in her perfume, I unloaded inside her with such force that it drove her over the edge, and she cried out with an unearthly shriek before slumping back into my arms.

"They're coming," she whispered. I looked up and saw the headlights of a tow truck. I knew my supervisor would be coming too, ready to bust my ass for not completing my route. I chuckled nervously and raised her sticky thighs off mine. She quickly slipped on her slacks and slipped out the side door. She left her panties behind.

Later, as the tow truck hauled the bus away, my supervisor sighed as he wrote me up. "You ought to have your license revoked, you know that? But you got lucky this time, buddy."

He was talking about the accident, but he didn't know the half of it. "Hey, it was an act of nature," I answered.

"I know, that's why I don't fire you," he bellowed. "But you still fucked up. Again!"

"Right," I said. I turned away and dropped her panties on the ground as I braved the rain back to the station.—*F.G., Dover, Delaware*

Pursuit & Capture

SHE LOVED IT WHEN THIS UPTIGHT BUSINESS MAN TURNED INTO A SEX-CRAZED ANIMAL

*M*y first date with Roger started out more like a business meeting than a romantic encounter. After we had ordered our dinner, and as we were drinking our first cocktail, he started his pitch.

Roger was a bachelor in his forties and not bad looking, although he had always seemed to me to be somewhat formal. He was an executive vice president of a fairly large company, and it appeared that to him the bottom line was everything. I was about ten years younger and unattached at that point. I was looking for a relationship, but I wasn't at all sure that Roger was the one.

Roger told me frankly that he wanted a relationship built on sex. There were to be no commitments, other than that neither of us would see anyone else as long as the relationship lasted.

This totally blew my mind. I had not been prepared for anything like this. I told him that I didn't know if I wanted a relationship like that, and I would have to consider it for a while.

After dinner and more cocktails, he invited me to his house to see some pictures he'd taken on a recent trip to Africa. I was surprised to hear about this journey, and I accepted his offer.

His house was one of those homes that could be pictured in *House Beautiful,* with marble-tiled floors, lavish surroundings, and lots of crystal, brass and coral.

I sat on a luxurious couch that seemed to cradle my whole body. Roger sat next to me and opened a huge picture album that rested on the glass table in front of the couch.

The pictures really surprised me. There was Roger, dressed in rugged clothes and sporting a week's worth of beard from not shaving while in the wilderness. I saw him going on a rafting trip, and hunting animals on safari. In short, I saw a totally different person from the uptight businessman who was sitting next to me on the couch.

Not that I don't adore businessmen in suits, but there is something about a rugged-looking, adventurous, bearded man that sets my blood boiling!

Roger began to tell me about how it felt to be away from civilization. How you live and breathe differently when you have to depend on Mother Nature and her moods for your very life sometimes. The more he talked about being in these uncivilized situations, the hotter he was making me.

At one point I reached across him to get my drink from the table, and suddenly we were in a hot and heavy embrace. I didn't know what had come over me. I was uncontrollable! I was out of my mind with lust! I was acting uncivilized, and loving it.

My mouth covered his. My tongue was everywhere. I pulled his suit jacket off, as well as his starched white shirt. The sight of his hairy chest increased my lustful desire. My tongue wanted to taste every part of his manly body. Protocol, manners and good taste all went out the window as I sucked and nibbled, my tongue darting here, there and everywhere.

After I had tasted every part of his body, he laid me on my side. He was as lust-crazed as I was. He licked and sucked at my body, front and back, pulling off my clothes in a frenzy. When I was naked, he pulled me up onto my knees with my ass up in the air. I heard his breathless voice saying that since we were acting like animals, we might as well fuck like them, and I moaned in agreement.

As I reached between my legs to guide his dick inside me, he reached around to put his hands on my breasts, holding on to them like handles as he began to fuck me wildly. Soon I was bucking like a bronco as he rode me, plunging his hard dick so far inside me that I thought it was going to come out of my throat.

My orgasm was so violent that I fell off the couch. Roger came with me, still inside me, his dick spewing come. I was still twitching after I landed on the carpet. Roger finally stopped coming and pulled out of me, panting heavily. I was, incredibly, still not satisfied, even after my orgasm; I wanted more. I wanted Roger's animal cock. With a cry of lust I dove after it and took the now limp hose in my mouth, practically swallowing it whole. Roger made a sound of surprise as I slurped and licked the rubbery pole, moaning as I labored to make it hard again. I couldn't believe my own actions, but I couldn't stop myself either. I reached around to slide a finger into his asshole, worming it deep as I tongued and suctioned his dick.

"God, you sweet thing!" Roger panted. "You're so fucking hot!" It was working; his dick was hardening again. I swirled my tongue around it, then raised my head and looked wildly into his eyes.

"Stick it up my ass," I heard myself say. "I'm a fucking animal, Roger, and I want it up my ass. Please."

"I knew you would be this way," Roger rasped as he turned me onto my hands and knees. "I saw it in you from the first. I knew it would be this good."

I started to answer him, but instead a shout of pure pleasure came from my mouth as his slippery cock-head breached the portal of my asshole. I pushed back at him, cursing the tightness of my anus for preventing me from taking that hard gorgeous tool all the way immediately. Roger grabbed my breasts and kneaded them, licking at my back, taking little short strokes as my sphincter relaxed little by little, moving into me slowly, slowly. I lowered myself from my hands to my elbows, resting my head on the carpet, sticking my ass up as high as I could, still pushing it back at him. I was panting and groaning as I took his glorious pole deeper and deeper up my narrow back passage.

I whimpered with joy as I finally felt the front of his thighs against my buttocks, telling me he was in all the way. My whimpers turned to full-throated cries when he started to fuck my ass. Within a minute I started coming, violently and repeatedly. Then, when Roger gasped out that he was about to shoot, I pulled away and turned over onto my back so I could take his sperm on my body, stroking his throbbing cock as that beautiful come splashed onto my tits again and again.

We fucked in every position possible that night. Roger was the wildest, most uncivilized, most sex-crazed lover I had ever known.

Needless to say, I finally took him up on his offer. It's kind of strange in a way, having a love affair based strictly on fucking. Sometimes I wonder if we could have a more meaningful relationship, but he seems to be really sincere about not wanting anything but sex. So if I want to continue having this wild animal in my bed, I have to accept him on his terms.

In another way, though, it is really liberating. Roger and I have no sexual hangups and no inhibitions. We know we are with each other strictly for the fun of it, and there are no holds barred. We do everything we can think of, and fulfill each other's fantasies in every way possible.

So who's complaining?—*J.B., Des Moines, Iowa* ○⊢▪

HE LUSTED AFTER THE SEXY UNDERGRAD, BUT SHE WAS STILL A VIRGIN—OR WAS SHE?

I met Annabel while I was studying for my law degree at a large university. Although I was almost thirty years old, I was still rather shy and inexperienced. I would gaze longingly at the adorable female undergraduates walking around campus, but I rarely spoke to them, although their fresh beauty all but brought tears to my eyes.

One day I was sitting alone in a popular coffeehouse, reading, when Annabel asked if she could sit at my table, since there were no free ones left. I vividly remember my first glance at her face. She looked gorgeous, very young and innocent, but friendly. She had big green eyes, black hair and small, even teeth. I later found out that she had been a part-time model.

Of course I said it was fine with me for her to sit there. She smiled and sat down, and we started to talk.

Annabel had a captivating habit of looking straight into my eyes as she chatted. I found out that she had just started at the honors college a month ago. Much to my surprise and delight, she seemed to value my opinion, and freely asked my advice about classes, extracurricular activities and so on. I managed to appear nonchalant when she talked happily about her boyfriend. Of course she has a boyfriend, I thought: She's too beautiful and smart not to be taken.

Nevertheless, she did seem to be flirting with me a little, and as the afternoon went on she admitted that her boyfriend went to another school, and that they had agreed to see other people while they were apart.

When it was time to leave I offered to walk her back to her dorm, and she accepted. At the entrance to her building, she smiled and asked, "Can I call you sometime?" Of course I didn't really think she ever would.

But within a week I heard her soft voice on my answering machine, and a few days later we had a wonderful, casual date. I couldn't understand why she seemed impressed with me. She even seemed truly excited to ride in my sports car. (I had long ago resigned myself to the fact that guys usually expressed a hell of a lot more interest in that car than women did.)

I liked her too, but what primarily impressed me was her face and her compact, delicious body. I craved her. When she gave me one paltry good-night kiss, I grinned continually for days.

On our third date she wore tight black jeans and a little green sweater that accentuated her flat stomach by ending right above her navel. At the end of the evening I finally got her back to my room. She seemed a little nervous, which gave me confidence, although I was sure I was more nervous than she was. We started to kiss on my couch. At first, she just poked her tongue into my mouth in a tentative manner. She was definitely holding back a little, and I began to wonder if she was still a virgin. But in a little while she asked me if I wanted to give her a "massage." She pulled off her sweater and quickly rolled onto her stomach.

I couldn't believe my luck at the prospect of getting this pretty eighteen-year-old in the sack. There was no clasp on the back of her bra, so I just slid my hands beneath the thin green band as I caressed her shoulders and back. I could see the outline of her bikini underpants through her very tight jeans, and I attempted to slide my fingers beneath them. But the jeans were so tight my hand got stuck, and I had to take it out.

I was so horny now. I flipped her over and, without much pretense at massage, tackled the front clasp of the bra that obscured her cute little breasts. When I opened it, Annabel immediately sat up and climbed onto my knee. I leaned forward and kissed her nipple, then softly sucked on it. As it got hard, she let out a little sigh and started to rock back and forth on my leg. I went on sucking for all I was worth, and she got more and more aroused, grinding her crotch into my knee. I held her by the hips as she obviously enjoyed the friction and sucking. "Keep going," she whispered. "Just like this." So I continued to lick and suck and nibble on her breasts as she humped away, her eyes now closed. Soon she let out a few gasps, then whispered something unintelligible and moaned. Then she shuddered as she came in her jeans.

After a few moments, she smiled and, to my chagrin, said that she thought it was time to go. She had a test the next day and she had to study. Or something.

I realized that she was an incredible cocktease, but what could I do? I was just bedazzled by her, and let her dress and go without a word of protest or reproof. At least I'd gotten to second base.

I was frenziedly anxious to arrange another date, and when I did I vowed to go further. After all, I had learned to open a front-clasp bra on my first try. This time, however, I had still more stuff to learn.

We were back in my room, on my bed and slightly drunk. This time I pulled off Annabel's shirt to find a Calvin Klein sports bra, with no clasp at all! I didn't really know if I could easily yank it over her head, so I just lifted it over her tits, and concentrated on sucking them again. As before, she perched on my knee. I watched as she gyrated, gasped, murmured something and came.

Now was my chance. I wanted to show her just how much I wanted her. My hands went to her waist, and I undid the top button of her tight jeans while rolling her onto her back. Much to my chagrin, there were buttons all down the fly. I had never owned a pair of button-fly jeans, nor stripped them off any girl, so I didn't realize that you could just pull down and free all the buttons at once. Instead, I fumbled at the first damn brass rivet.

After what seemed like an eternity, I managed to guide it through the buttonhole. As I forged ahead to the next metal button, my fingers brushed against the waistband of Annabel's bikini panties. Annabel must have thought I was going so slowly in order to tease her, and she began to squirm with lust. "Hurry up!" she whispered urgently. "Make me come!" Well, sap that I was, instead of taking the opportunity to sweetly torture her a little, I immediately accommodated her by plunging my hand down between the partially opened denim jeans and her thin cotton briefs.

I really had to push a little to get my hand down to her crotch. Her panties were already very wet from her first orgasm, and I rubbed her pussy through them as well as I could in the constricted space. It was a little uncomfortable for me, but it seemed to be working out great for Annabel. The pleasure made her bounce around, but my trapped hand was securely in place and never lost contact with her vagina. She was thrashing and moaning with excitement. Soon she was convulsing again, and my fingers were moistened further by the increased wetness of her panties.

Now, as she relaxed and caught her breath, I had ample time to undo the rest of her fly and pull her jeans down her legs. It was then that she smiled shyly at me and said that she wasn't ready to go all the way, and she wanted us to leave our underpants on.

Once again I complied with her wishes. In a frenzy of lust I went down on the beautiful freshman, vigorously licking and nibbling at her crotch through her panties. Occasionally, I would push the panties in and out of her slit. I concentrated on licking her clit through the thin material, until she shoved her crotch at my face and pounded her little fists against the bed as she treated herself to a third orgasm.

I so much wanted to fuck her now! But Annabel explained that she was still a virgin (though I wondered now how true that was). She told me that she had even prevented her boyfriend (I'd forgotten about that jackass!) from getting too carried away, by making sure they always left some clothes on. She also confided that his penis was so long that it sometimes poked over the top of his shorts. Well, that didn't make me feel so great, especially since mine is about average; but it didn't cool off my desire for her either.

She didn't object when I started kissing and stroking her in an attempt to get her heated up again. It seemed to work, and this time as I caressed her vagina I managed to slip a finger under her panties and work it inside her. She seemed a little startled at first, but then her face became contorted with ecstasy. I couldn't believe that this was a first for her, but she squirmed and panted with the joy of fucking my finger. More juices poured out of her, and a moment later she whispered: "Oh yes! I'm almost there!" She was shivering and tense, at the brink of climax.

At that moment I abruptly stopped, bringing a wail of disappointment from her. Taking advantage of her passion, I quickly got on top of her slender body and started to dry-hump her. Annabel went wild with lust and wrapped her legs around me. We mashed our underpants together. I concentrated on trying to rub my cock against her most sensitive spots. I felt her wetness seep through our briefs and onto my penis. I couldn't hold back any more after all these weeks of dreaming and fantasizing about Annabel, as well as fooling around with her. I cried out as I came, and I ejaculated all over her panties and her flat little stomach. As I did so, my young bedmate pushed demonically up against my spewing cock, setting off her own climax. Because I'd kept her waiting, this orgasm, her fourth of the night, was her most intense. Annabel squealed loudly and rolled her head from side to side as she once again came in her panties.

The pretty freshman, now all tuckered out, fell asleep next to me. I was elated. Deep down, though, I probably realized that I could never keep a girl like that for very long.

Even so, it was a shock when I called her the next week to arrange a date and found her cold and distant. She brushed me off by telling me that she had an appointment with her teaching assistant. Well, good luck to him, the bastard!—*G.V., Sacramento, California*

BOTH SHE AND HER RECORDS WERE GOLDEN OLDIES, BUT THEY STILL MADE GREAT MUSIC

I'm a thirty-five-year-old man, and my girlfriend and I have been going together for three years. Rachel and I have always had a good sex life and to this day I have no complaints. Rachel is tall and sleek and has lots of long dark hair. She also has a very large, very close Jewish family that meets all the time for parties, holidays and just for the hell of it.

One of the key figures in this family is Rachel's aunt Sybil. I often got paired with Sybil at holiday dinners, because we share an interest in old records, and we hit it off in spite of the vast difference in our ages. Sybil is in her early sixties, and is the antithesis of Rachel; she's on the short side, and still has a fleshy kind of sexiness, with big breasts and powerful hips. She has dyed red hair, and she likes to show herself off in classic open-toed high heels and old-fashioned dresses that show off her bosom. Though she never married, she has a reputation in the family for having led a pretty wild life when she was young.

The last time the family got together for Passover, I was seated next to Sybil as usual, and we sat talking and laughing together for a long time after everybody else had moved to the other room. As we talked I couldn't help being very aware of Sybil's still highly attractive body. The dress she was wearing gave me a constant view down her capacious cleavage, where I could see the tops of her lacy bra cups, which just barely contained those great breasts. In addition, the hem of her dress had ridden up a bit, showing off a lot of stocking top, and her still firm and solid thighs. Hard as I tried not to stare, I couldn't help myself, and I knew that Sybil was aware of it. To my surprise, all this flamboyant fleshiness, plus her closeness and the way she had of constantly touching the person she as speaking to, was getting me very turned on, and I had to make an attempt to hide the growing bulge in my trousers.

Sybil is too sharp not to notice such a thing. I saw her eyes flick over my crotch, just before she smiled at me knowingly and asked, "So how's your sex life with Rachel these days?"

A little embarrassed, I replied that it was fine. "That's good," Sybil said, still smiling. "Life without good sex—" She shrugged. "What's the point? But then, you're a good-looking man, you know that. And I have always loved the company of a good-looking man. So listen, you want to come over some afternoon and listen to those old Patti Page records I've got?"

I couldn't believe it. I was being openly propositioned by my girlfriend's sixty-two-year-old aunt! I said I would like to very much.

Later on, feeling pangs of guilt, I mentioned to Rachel that Sybil and I had made a date to listen to some old records. Rachel couldn't care less about old records. "Good," she said. "Do it. She needs the entertainment." Little did my sweet lady know just what she was approving.

So I went over to Sybil's place one afternoon, and she opened the door to me in one of her great old dresses, which still fit her as though it had been poured on. She could have been a famous movie goddess, a bit on in years but still sexy as hell. She poured me a drink, put Patti Page on the turntable, sat herself down next to me on the couch, put her lips to mine and slid her tongue into my mouth. It was all over for me right there. I was hard in an instant, and now I found myself making out with a woman almost thirty years my senior.

Sybil was an expert at making out. She knew how to move against me as we kissed so that it drove me crazy, and within minutes I was running my hand inside her low-cut dress and feeling a long, hard nipple inside the bursting bra cup. She let out a little purr, and I can't tell you how sexy it was to hear it, while my fingers kneaded that delicious nipple. The way her thighs worked against mine I could tell she was getting very turned on indeed.

I slid the top of her dress down then, and undid the front of her black lacy brassiere. A pair of the most beautiful breasts I'd ever seen dropped into view, and I sucked one large hardening nipple like a man possessed, while she writhed beneath me.

While I sucked her nipple I moved my hand down to the hem of her dress and slid it up the inside of her warm, full thigh. My fingers moved up, encountered the garter straps at the top of her stockings, and moved on to her hot, moist cunt. She was wearing garters but no panties. I gasped again as her hand adroitly undid my trousers and slid them down so that my cock popped up into view. Her fingers caressed it lightly. "Just beautiful," she breathed into my ear. "Would you like me to suck it, darling?"

"God," I said breathlessly. "Would I!"

And in a moment this sixty-year-old sexpot was kneeling between my thighs and giving me the blowjob of my life while I caressed those massive breasts. Sybil knew how to bring me right to the point of coming, then make me wait. When I thought I couldn't take it any more, she said in a low voice, "So what do you say we fuck now?"

She led me into her bedroom, with its king-size bed, and I undressed her, piece by piece, unzipping her dress and letting it fall to the floor, dropping her slip and bra, till she was standing in her pearl necklace, her garter belt and stockings and high heels.

"What would you like?" she smiled.

"I want to lick you," I said.

So Sybil sat on the edge of the bed and spread those beautiful thighs, and I dove between them and lapped up her delicious juices. Sybil wrapped her legs agilely around my head while I did that, locking her stockinged ankles behind it. Then she started to come, letting out deeper and deeper moans, her hips twisting and spasming convulsively.

"Fuck me now," she whispered harshly. "Fuck me with that beautiful cock of yours."

We slid together onto the bed like practiced lovers. She braced her high heels against the sheet and spread her stockinged thighs wide as I eased my cock into that fabulous, experienced cunt. Sybil had a gift that I'd never encountered in any other woman: her cunt could suck you like a full, thick-lipped mouth, while swallowing you down more easily than the most talented throat. But just as with her blow-jobs, she knew when to slack off, and how to keep you going and going and going. Licking her lips, her eyes misting and her cheeks deeply flushed from her orgasms, she must have come a dozen times as I reamed her with powerful strokes. One of her hands was down between my legs, caressing my balls and my ass and the base of my cock as it moved in and out of her. I'd never felt anything like it in twenty years of fucking.

At one point she flipped herself over and had me give it to her from behind. After a few minutes of that she effortlessly rolled back. "Come now, come," she breathed, drawing me down to her and enfolding me in her arms. I let out a yell as I plunged deep into that bottomless wet cunt and poured out an endless, hot river of come. Sybil cried out and convulsed beneath me, her suctioning cunt squeezing every last drop out of my spasming cock.

"Well," Sybil panted, "wasn't that a nice way to spend a pleasant afternoon?" If I'd had the strength to talk, I would have agreed with her.

Patti Page had long since sung herself out on the turntable when Sybil took my now limp dick into her mouth and got me hard again, and I shot a load of come down her eager throat. Later still, as she was letting me out at the door, she said, "Maybe we'll do Theresa Brewer next time, yes, darling? It's so nice to share the old music with you."—*Name and address withheld* ⚬━▪

IF THIS IS HOW WAITRESSES SERVE THEIR CUSTOMERS IN PORTUGAL, WE'RE ON OUR WAY

*W*hile on my way home from a long European business trip, I stopped for a few days in Lisbon, treating myself to a boutique hotel with a bar on the roof terrace, overlooking the ancient Portuguese city and harbor. On my first night at the bar I noticed the waitress right away. She seemed Portuguese, but not as conservative as most of the women of that country. She had long, very black hair pulled back in a bun, and dark mischievous eyes in her exotic face.

Because of my traveling and the cares of business, it had been two months since I'd had sex, and after a couple of drinks I was feeling ready for something more than cocktails.

The more I looked at the woman, the more inviting her glances became. When she brought over my last drink, I noticed she had turned the lights out and closed the door to the bar. I was the only customer left.

"You're closing up—do I have to leave?" I asked.

She shook her head and put a sexy CD on the sound system, the music spilling into the warm night air.

I could hardly believe it when she walked over to me and started unbuttoning her oversize blouse. The high, full breasts that had been hidden under the big shirt now gleamed in the moonlight. I pushed my chair back as she reached me, and ran my hands under her long flowing skirt, my fingers exploring her long muscular legs. As I slid my hands upward, her skirt gathered around her waist, and the higher I reached, the more skin my fingers discovered. She wore nothing underneath—no underwear, no barrier to her tight round bottom.

She moved closer and swung her leg over mine. Nearly panting, I looked up at her, never releasing my gentle hold on her ass as it came into contact with my jeans and growing hard-on. When she straddled me her breasts landed right at mouth level. I took one rosy nipple into my mouth and suckled, pulling at it with my lips and twirling my tongue around the hardened bud.

Her head fell to my shoulder and she moaned softly in my ear, gently grabbing my lobe with her lips.

I lifted her up and shifted her mound onto my erection. She grabbed my jeans and worked the fly open. My cock sprang free, and the naked flesh brushed against her vagina. It was hot and wet.

I stood up quickly and sat her in the chair. She gasped and smiled. I kissed the smile as I slid one finger into her inviting opening. It was juicy and tight. I pulled her to the edge of the chair and put my head between her smooth tan legs. They tightened around my ears when my tongue found her clit. She groaned and arched her back, throwing her head back and pulling the remaining pins from her hair. I could sense she was close to climaxing, and she called out in Portuguese, "Please...please..."

"Please what?" I lifted my head to ask.

"Please, now," she begged. Her eyes were wide and her face flushed. The trace of cockiness she had displayed when coming on to me had disappeared. She was a woman needing to be fucked.

I pushed my jeans down and grabbed the arms of the chair on either side of her. I wanted to slam into her juicy core, but held back, rhythmically bumping the head of my rocket against her slick portal.

Frenzied with lust, my Portuguese delight grabbed my ass in her hands and pulled me inside her, thrusting her cunt up as her fingers grabbed onto the swell of my cheeks.

I was beyond holding back, pumping hard and long, stroking her as she rose up to meet each thrust. With the sweat pouring off both of us, I ground into her, and she came over and over.

Suddenly she looked up and cried, "Wait—not inside me. I want your cream here." She brought her hands up to her tits and circled them with her fingers, rubbing her tight nipples with her thumbs.

"If that's the way you want it, sweetheart," I said as I picked her up and laid her on the tile floor, never breaking contact between our wet, hot bodies. As I resumed fucking her I accelerated my motions, pumping in and out of her like a piston, watching her face contorting with ecstasy as she matched me thrust for thrust, moaning and begging me to come on her breasts. Harder and harder I rammed into her, getting closer and closer to the edge, until at the moment of release I pulled out and shifted up, grabbing my cock and spurting my seed over her dusky heaving breasts.

She sighed and shuddered as I pulled back to catch my breath, looking at the picture she made, her shirt still on, but unbuttoned, her gorgeous chest rising and falling as she caught her breath, her skirt wrapped around her waist, legs spread and twitching every now and then as she came down gradually from her orgasm. Finally she turned her head to meet my eyes.

"Thank you," she smiled, with the sparkle back in those big brown eyes. "Would you like me to clean you off now?"

I could tell she didn't mean with a napkin. My too-long-deprived cock, even moments after being drained, had already begun to twitch slightly, just from the sight of her in that sexy position. Now, hearing her invitation and looking at her full, sensuous mouth, it showed definite signs of bestirring itself.

I moved up, straddling her body, until my still half-flaccid hose hung over her mouth. That mouth opened sexily, her tongue reaching out as if beckoning to my tool, which I slowly lowered between those waiting lips. The touch of her tongue made me groan, and when that mouth closed around me and the tongue went to work, the process of revitalization was completed in less than a minute.

True to her promise, she cleaned me off, using her tongue like a washrag and her lips like a vacuum cleaner. I couldn't hold still, and she gave a moan of pleasure around my dick as I began to fuck her face. I did it slowly at first, going gradually deeper, and soon found that she could take as much as I could give her. Her hands came up to clutch at my ass, encouraging me to speed up the rhythm of my mouth-fucking. Then one of them slid down to my balls, stroking them and squeezing them gently, driving me absolutely wild. I wasn't sure how much longer I could hold out.

I wondered if she wanted me to come on her tits again, but if so she gave no sign of it, continuing to pull me into that siphoning mouth. And then I felt that familiar surge before I spurted into her throat, and she gulped down each spurt as it came.

She smiled at me again as I fell back, panting. "Thank you," she said softly. "And there will be no need to tip for the drinks, sir."
—*B.D., New York, New York*

FOR HIS FIRST TASTE OF FREEDOM, HE PLUCKS A RIPE GEORGIA PEACH

*A*fter more than two years of stress, fighting, wet dreams, jerking off and flirting with damn near any woman who'd allow me to, I'm finally being released from one of California's many correctional facilities, and being paroled to a foreign land, Georgia.

I admit that when I first got here I was scared as hell to go outside. Can you imagine yourself in a secure and controlled environment, where people no better than you boss you around all day long and night, where fights occur more commonly than the sun rises and where the only women you encounter are off-limits female officers? Imagine going through this, which isn't half of what a person experiences as a prisoner, every day for more than two years. Nothing ever changes except the tension in the air, which only increases as the days go by.

So you see what I faced, going from an atmosphere where things always moved at a slow pace and I could predict the happenings, because they never changed, to a place where I was out of step with the times. I didn't know anyone, even though I had lots of family there, and everything and everyone seemed to be moving at the speed of light, while I was moving at twenty miles an hour. Boy, how time flies!

Two things compelled me, little fish that I'd become, to step out into this storming ocean of a world. First was my will to survive as best I could without risking my freedom. Second was pussy!

Not long after I was home, I started hanging with my cousin Herman, who's a few years younger than me but mature for his age. I've never been the type to ask another person to help me meet women, but this time I made an exception.

"My girlfriend Shirley has an older cousin you might like," Herman said when I asked him the question.

"What does she look like?" I asked.

"Well, Shirley's about—"

"No, you dope," I broke in. "Not *Shirley*, her *cousin*! What's her name? Just tell me whatever you know about her."

Herman proceeded to give me the lowdown on her to the best of his ability. Wylene was my age, and lived in a town about fifteen or twenty minutes from where I was living at the time. Before I went home that night, I told my cousin to try to persuade her to call me. I didn't want her to get the wrong impression of me by having a total stranger call her.

That call came sooner than expected. Four days later I was at home, bored out of my mind, when the phone rang. I wasn't expecting any calls, so I let my grandmother answer it. I was shocked when she said it was for me. After I regained my composure I put the phone to my ear and said hello.

"William?" It was Herman.

"What's up, bro?" I said.

"I got somebody wants to talk to you."

"Who?" I asked.

Then, like the first intake of fresh air upon my release, that was so pleasing, I heard a voice so sweet and feminine, I knew I had to have her. Now I've heard the stories about chance meetings over the phone, and the woman sounds so lovely in your ear that you know she has a body to match, only to find the opposite. Too bad for them, this is me.

"Wylene," she answered enticingly.

"How are you, Wylene?" I inquired.

"I'm fine," she said. She was forcing me to say more.

"Wylene," I said, "would you mind calling me back when you're alone, so we can get acquainted privately? You have the number, don't you? Good. I'll be waiting for you." Then I hung up.

Wylene called back, and we spoke until four in the morning. She was an intelligent person. We discussed our families, backgrounds, aspirations (she wanted to be a nurse, while I just wanted to remain free and work from there), life experiences and numerous other topics. We set a date for the Sunday after next to go to church together.

When Sunday arrived, I had my uncle pick her up for service. When they got back to my house, I went out to open the door for her—and to get my first look at her. When I opened the passenger door, I had to step back for lack of breath. What took my breath away, the center of my attention, was one of the most gorgeous women I've ever seen.

I held my hand out to her and introduced myself. When she placed her hand in mine, I noticed how smooth and delicate hers was—small, with slim fingers and maintained nails, telling me she was a woman who took care of herself. I helped her out of the car and received another surprise. She was almost a foot shorter than me, five feet two or maybe three inches, with long, straight black shoulder-length hair that she let hang down and frame her attractive face, with its almond-shape eyes, succulent lips and smooth, unblemished skin, free of makeup except for a light coating of red lipstick.

She was neither slim nor chubby, but what some would call thick, with a flat stomach. She had more than enough ass and tits for a woman of her size. I couldn't wait to get my mouth on those generous-size tits while uncovering the rest of what she had to offer.

After church we returned to my house to relax and get something to eat. Once we finished eating, I changed clothes and asked Wylene if she would like to go for a walk. We ended up at a nearby park, where we sat on a set of bleachers and talked for a while. There was a tension all around us that I'm sure she noticed, and if I'm not mistaken, the source of that tension was purely sexual, for which there was only one possible form of relief—sex!

"Wylene," I said, placing my arm around her waist. I couldn't get enough of saying her name. Like calling a rose a rose, to address it any other way would be unacceptable.

"Yes," she answered, looking up at me seductively. I'm not sure she was aware of how lovely she looked, or the effect she was having on me, and not just physically.

I placed my other hand underneath her chin and gently tilted her head back to where I could kiss her comfortably. At first I was only going to kiss her lightly on her lips, but once I placed my lips on her and felt her lips part, I slid my tongue in her sweet mouth, feeling her tongue gently caress my own. I felt the vibration of a moan and the pressure of her breast as she leaned into me, pressing her chest against mine. I don't know how long we stayed locked in this passionate kiss, but when we finally parted, we were both winded.

After I caught my breath, I took hold of Wylene's hands, those hands that I ached to feel roaming over my body, and led her to the entrance to the swimming pool for the little cover it provided. The pool was closed on Sunday, but it wasn't water I was interested in diving in. I was interested in diving my tongue as deep as I could between the legs of this beautiful woman.

I placed Wylene's back against the wall and leaned down to give her another kiss. Those voluptuous lips parted readily to admit my tongue into her mouth, and I couldn't help but wonder if those lips would part just as willingly to admit my dick. I let my hands slide down Wylene's backside until I had her round ass in my hands. I kneaded the moons of her ass gently but firmly.

She pushed off of the wall and then wrapped her arms around my neck. When she leaned into me this time, she felt the giant bulge in my pants. I heard and felt another moan escape Wylene's throat, and

I wanted so badly to fuck her then and there. But I restrained myself. I broke our embrace and dropped to my knees. I started pushing her dress up around her waist, until I caught the scent of her aroused pussy and the sight of her flower-print panties.

Wylene held her dress up while I pulled her moist panties off, uncovering her hairy crotch with its honey-coated pussy lips. I kissed the inside of those luscious thighs while sliding my hands up her curvaceous legs until I reached her musky mound. As I ran my fingers over her pussy lips, her juices spilled forth. I slid two fingers in her boiling cunt, and she gave a low moan.

"Mmm, William," she said, placing one of her hands behind my head, inviting me to taste of her love. I raised one of my knees off the ground and felt Wylene place her foot on my mid-thigh, giving me easier access to her and allowing me to thrust my fingers deeper into her conflagrant cunt. I started sucking on Wylene's clitoris, sending further waves of pleasure through her body while she gasped and moaned steadily above my head.

After a while her breath quickened and her movements became more pronounced, telling me her orgasm was building up. I started licking and swirling my tongue inside her honeypot, savoring the taste of her juices while stroking her clit with my thumb.

"Yes! Yes!" Wylene yelled as her come flowed into my mouth. I swallowed as much of her narcotic nectar as I dared, further intoxicating myself with her love while longing to get her in my bed. She took her foot off my thigh to lean down and lick her come off my chin, then further blessed me with a passionate French kiss. After I helped her straighten her clothes, we started back toward my house. On the way we discussed getting together again soon, which we agreed to do the next day—my house at eight in the morning.

When Wylene arrived, I greeted her with a deep, tongue-probing kiss. I hadn't bothered to get dressed that day, and she looked a little surprised when she saw me with only my robe on. But she accepted my kiss readily enough. She was wearing a pair of tight-fitting stone-washed blue jeans that showed off more than they covered, a white blouse that she let show a little cleavage, and a pair of brown heels that left her toes exposed and that matched her belt. She looked stunning, and I felt my dick start to harden.

Not to seem overexcited, I asked Wylene if she would like anything to drink. She declined. So much for formality. I went and sat on the couch, then beckoned for her to come over. When she came over, she sat on my lap and felt my semierect prick. She gave a short gasp but leaned down to kiss me. I started undoing the buttons of her blouse, eager to suck on the nipples of her huge tits while her hands slid inside my robe and caressed my chest.

Once I had her blouse undone, I reached around and unclasped her bra, freeing those ripe melons with their hardened nipples, which were quickly recaptured inside my waiting mouth. I flicked around the nipple and halo of each of her tits before sucking as much as I could in my mouth.

"Oooh," Wylene moaned as I tugged on her nipples. After a while she slid off my lap and knelt between my legs. She undid the belt of my robe, uncovering my now fully erect dick. Then she started stroking me slowly while she lovingly flicked and licked circles around the head of my cock. When she finally sucked me into the sweet warmth of her mouth, I thought I was going to come then and there. I watched my cock slide in and out of this gorgeous woman's mouth and listened to the slurps and moans she made while her head continued bobbing up and down, up and down. Her jaws were concave with the pressure she was applying to my throbbing cock. The feeling of her mouth was exquisite, and the pressure so intense, I knew I wouldn't last much longer.

When Wylene sensed I was about to come, she pulled her mouth away with a loud pop. "No, not yet," she said, smiling. She started taking her clothes off. "Now I'm ready," she said, straddling me. Reaching behind her, she guided my cock to her dripping twat. When she started sliding down my pole, I couldn't believe how tight and hot she was, and couldn't stop myself from thrusting upward, driving my cock deep inside her.

"Ah!" she cried out, rising slightly. I grabbed her round ass and thrust as hard and buried as much of my cock in her as I could. "Yes, baby, yes!" she groaned, now bouncing on my rod. "Harder, baby! Give me more!" she panted in my ear, pushing her ass down as hard as she could to engulf my dick.

I rolled Wylene onto the couch, laying her on her back. I repositioned myself with her legs on my shoulders, then drove as powerfully into her as I could, feeling my dick stretch her to new dimensions.

"William, I love you! I love you, William!" she repeated as I continued to pile-drive in and out of her gripping snatch. After some time I felt her body start trembling and her fingers clutch my back. "Oh, I'm coming! I'm coming!" she yelled, and I felt her cunt convulsing around my dick. Her release soaked both my hardened member and my balls. When I announced that I was on the verge of orgasm, she said, "Come in me, baby. Come in my pussy."

With her legs still on my shoulders, I kept thrusting in her, hard and fast, until I exploded, my seed spilling out between her thighs. "Mmmm yes, baby," she moaned, pulling me down for a passionate kiss as I enjoyed the feeling of our two bodies being made one.—*W.R., Atlanta, Georgia*

THIS TWOSOME'S MATING DANCE MUST SET SOME KIND OF RECORD

*T*he philosopher Schopenhauer said that men spend their lives either reflecting on the past or anticipating the future. They therefore miss the moment. They live in a state he called "ad interim," in-between. That is what I am living now. All I do is reflect and anticipate. The moment means nothing to me. Having said that, here is a sexcapade for your titillation, reflected from the fun-house mirror of my past.

A decade or so ago, a future codefendant of mine and I were at a famous swinging club in the Latin Quarter of New Orleans. We had moved there a year earlier from Los Angeles, and had finally figured out that there were some bars much more "tie-friendly" than others. Although the superhip semi-goth clubs we'd been in were full of ultracute, stitched-tight, languid, insolent, sassy girls in their early twenties, they wouldn't give us a sniff. I'm sure it didn't help that the two of us were the only men in the place with suits and ties. We must have looked like government agents—or, worse yet, their fathers, even though we were only in our late thirties.

But our new hangout was known as a "tie bar." We had finally found a trough we could consistently feed from. My black Armani, black BMW and black-faced Rolex were just what these women in their short, tight black miniskirts had in mind. We lost most of the nubile lasses in their early to mid-twenties, but struck it rich with the red-hot late-twenties-to-early-thirties demographic. Not as tight, but twice as wet.

So one night these two blonde Russian girls are sitting at the bar, one looking extra-fine in a micro-mini and the other a bit of a slob. Both girls are late twenties. I get no action from the micro-mini, but Paul arranges a luncheon date with the other one for the following day. The "luncheon date" amounts to him getting sucked off in his dented 1984 Caddie at high noon on a main thoroughfare as gaping pedestrians pass by like it's a fucking peep show.

"It was kind of embarrassing," Paul said, and I imagine it was.

So we see these White Russian (as opposed to Asiatic or Arab Russian) girls on and off over the next few months. I still can't get a glance from the micro-mini, and Paul doesn't want any more action from the performance artist.

A year or so passes by, and I turn into pretty much a solo, lone-wolf act, the way I like it. The micro-mini dumps the slob, and we keep bumping into each other at this new, chi-chi bar. She shows up with various female Russian émigrées and introduces them to me. I get lucky and take home two or three of them—and believe me, that Russian pussy is hot.

About two more years pass. The micro-mini is no longer quite as good-looking as she was, and guess what. Now she wants me! And guess what else. I no longer want her.

Finally one night she actually asks *me* out. "Tim," she says, "will you take me to the Dockside to eat oysters?" I take her to the Dockside, we eat oysters, and I take her home. She can't believe I just drop her off. No kissing, no groping, no finger-fucking, no nothing.

I have been through this "when I wanted you, you didn't want me; now you want me and I don't want you" routine before, and know just how it works. It's my turn now to tease, to reject, and I can't wait! I continue to see her as usual over the next few months, hit on her friends and am cordial but aloof and unavailable toward her. She can't figure it out. But I do slow-dance with her once or twice during the evenings when I run into her—part of the tease.

The black guys I grew up with taught me all about slow dancing. They called it "grinding." I am grinding my cock against that wet

Russian pussy (I don't *know* it's wet, I'm just *assuming* it is) while cupping her exquisite butt cheeks and pulling her as close as possible. I can almost see it going in and out.

I damn near pop off in my pants. I come off the dance floor with my dick sticking straight out. She thinks it's funny. And it is. It's also sort of embarrassing for me. I put my hand in my pocket and try to push it down. I adjust it parallel to my leg, but it's still rock-hard. You may wonder who's really teasing who. Trust me, I am teasing her.

This happens many nights. She asks me to take her home many times, but I always say no. I tell her, "I could never satisfy you." This is probably true.

She begs. One night I relent and say, "I won't take you home, but you can suck my dick out in the car."

She won't go for that. I'm somewhat surprised. She coos, "I want you to eat my pussy too."

Now I can understand that, and am tempted, but I shake my head no, replying, "Sorry, not tonight." Truly, it is much better to reject than to be rejected.

Another night she suddenly asks, "Do you want to fuck me in the ass?"

Somewhat taken aback, I answer, "I'll pass." But I'm thinking, "Goddamn, this girl is fucking nasty."

Excuse this break in the story, but I have to jack off. I *am* in prison, you know. There, that's better.

Every story has its climax (I just had mine), and so does this one. So it's mid-November, and I'm at the bar where we first met the Russian girls over five celibate, seed-squandering masturbatory years earlier, and sure enough, she is also there, as usual. The ritualistic slow-dance tease begins. We come off the dance floor and go to the bar. I am more drunk and more stiff than usual tonight. Who says alcohol causes impotence?

I decide to take the tease to a new level. I am facing the bar, and so is she. I say, "Give me your hand." She hesitates but presents the hand. I put it on the stiffest drink in the house. She pulls the zipper down. My dick pops out like a jack-in-the-box. It is a good thing I do not wear underwear. Although the bar is crowded, nobody can see what is going on. Remember, we are facing the bar.

She is squeezing the engorged shaft and tip. She says quietly, "My God, Tim, it must be seven inches."

I smiled. You would have smiled too if you had that dick. Okay, so it was an exceptional night. She works her way down (or is it up?) to the balls. She is lightly cradling them, kind of squeezing, but not really. She then begins to softly touch around the moist perimeter of the ball sac. She withdraws her hand and, get this, gives her hand a big sniff. No, no, it's not a sniff. "Sniff" is too crass a word. It's a slow, hypnotic inhalation, as though she is taking in a thick cloud of the finest masculine musk. Her eyes glaze and begin to roll back. I think she is going to pass out. By the way, my dick is still out.

Next, as though by an act of pure will power, she refocuses, turns around and disappears into the crowd.

About an hour later I am sitting in the shadows at a table somewhat adjacent to the dance floor. My dick is no longer out. A couple of couples are conversing nearby. I pick her up with my peripheral vision. She is homing toward me like a cruise missile. Smiling, she stands in front of me. She straddles me. Straddles my crotch. She slips her tit out.

"Suck it, Tim," she says, and I do. It's a real nice tit.

One of the couples see what is going on and pretend not to look. They look.

"Do you like that?" she asks. I nod and start licking. She pushes my head back and covers the breast.

"Give me your hand," she says, and again I do as she asks. She inserts my hand down the top of her skirt. It descends, of its own accord, to the panty line. I draw the panty back. She rises up slightly to make it easier for me. Both couples at the tables are now staring. I don't give a shit. I pass the pubes like they're not there (maybe they aren't) and go straight for the honey hole with my middle finger. It's real wet. I dab the clit. It's hard like a small ball bearing.

I linger. She jerks my hand out and says, "Taste it, Tim." Again, I do as I'm told. I suck my middle finger. Sweet. Now my eyes roll back like I'm a bull moose in full rut. I am in a trance. And then she hops off, giggles and once again blends into the crowd.

I am now determined to take her home with me the next time I see her. But forty-eight hours later I am bum-rushed, handcuffed and dragged into the elevator of my high-rise apartment by a half dozen rabid DEA agents.

I'm sure that that Russian minx often wonders whatever happened to me. So do I.—*T.L., Shreveport, Louisiana* ○┼▪

E-PENPALS MAKE EROTIC USE OF WHAT
THEY'VE LEARNED ABOUT EACH OTHER

*L*auren and I had worked in the same department for about two years. She's a highly intelligent, attractive, sexy woman in her late twenties, with these great legs and highly kissable lips. She's also a great dresser. She would wear suits with nice short skirts that showed off those great legs. Every time we had a department meeting, I would try to sit in front of her or beside her to get a better view of them. She also has a fine ass, which I would take a peek at every time she walked past my office.

I always wondered what it would be like to be with her, but I never acted on that impulse. Over time we became pretty good friends, and began communicating by e-mail. We asked each other pretty reasonable questions. The agreement was that if a question was too personal, you didn't have to answer.

One day I pushed the envelope and began to ask sexual questions, such as did she like to suck cock, or did she like to have her pussy licked, or had she ever masturbated? To my surprise, she answered all my questions, and in some detail. She said that she liked sucking cock more than having her pussy eaten, which was a huge turn-on for me. She also said that she had a vibrator at home that got regular use when she was in the mood.

Then one day I decided to take it a step further and started asking questions related to us. I told her that since we had been e-mailing each other, I was getting very turned on and wanted very badly to kiss her. I asked her to come to my office after everyone had left. Her first reply indicated that she was hesitant, but an e-mail or two later, she thought that it might be fun to do.

When the time came Lauren knocked on my door. I said to come in and shut the door behind her. I was a bit nervous because we *were* at work, but at the same time I was very excited by that fact. I had always fantasized about fucking a coworker in my office. Once Lauren was in, with the door closed, we kissed for about twenty seconds. I have to say, she is a *very* good kisser. Her lips were incredible.

That happened on a Friday afternoon, and I had to wait till Monday to try and take it further. All that weekend I thought I was going to bust. All I could think about was kissing Lauren and having those gorgeous lips on my cock, and eating her pussy. Monday came, and the first thing I did was e-mail Lauren. I said how nice the kiss was, and said I wanted more with her. I think she wanted more also, because she agreed to meet me at lunch for some real fun.

We met at a storage house our company has. I got there first and waited for her to show. When she did, she had on this very sexy short skirt with white stockings. She decided that she wanted to take her stockings off. At this point my dick was really hard. She came out of the bathroom, and we locked lips. As we kissed, long and passionately, I unbuttoned her blouse to get at her nice breasts. The nipples were really hard and pointy. I made my way down to them and began to suck on them.

She was rubbing my cock through my pants. She unzipped my pants and took out my cock. She seemed to approve of what she found, because she said "Damn!" under her breath. She took my hard-on in her mouth and sucked away, driving me crazy. She had written in one of her e-mails that she was good at sucking cock. I certainly couldn't disagree!

I couldn't take it anymore, I wanted to lick her pussy. I sat her on a desk and spread the legs. She was wearing these white lace bikini panties, and I saw the hairs of her pussy through them. I pulled her panty lining to the side and began to lick her pussy lips. I nibbled on her clit, then stuck my tongue in her. Her pussy was so wet, and tasted so sweet! She moaned as I tongue-fucked her, but it was getting late and we both knew that we had to get back to our desks.

Back at work, Lauren and I e-mailed each other, saying how much we had enjoyed our lunchtime snack. I told her how sweet her pussy tasted, and said that I wanted to fuck her. She said that my tongue in her pussy was all she could think about, and that she wanted me to fuck her with my big dick. She said that just thinking about it made her pussy wet. We decided to have round two the next day, this time making sure we got there early enough to fuck.

The next day I couldn't wait till lunch. When noon finally came, I hit the door and headed straight to the storage house. Lauren showed up soon after, wearing another short skirt, this time with black stockings and black high heels. I find black on a beautiful woman an incredibly erotic color, so you better believe I was horny as hell.

Lauren took off her stockings again, and we kissed. She grabbed my ass with both hands and pulled me close. Then she rubbed my chest and began to stroke my cock through my pants. I took off her blouse and began nibbling on her beautiful tits. She pushed me back so she could unzip my pants, which she pulled down along with my boxers. My dick sprang out, and she jerked me off for a while, as she kissed my chest and then my stomach.

Her mouth reached my cock and engulfed it. I was going crazy. She deep-throated it a couple of times, and I thought I was going to shoot down her throat right there. To keep from coming too soon, I stopped her and sat her on a small table and spread her legs. This time she had on a pair of black lace bikini panties. They were very sexy. I pulled them off.

Her pussy was soaking wet. I dove right in, licking and sucking on her clit. I stuck a finger in and finger-fucked her while I ate her pussy. She moaned as I continued eating her pussy and finger-fucking her. She set her hands on my head and eased my face deeper in her pussy, then pushed me back.

I figured there was something wrong, but Lauren looked me right in the eye and said, "I want you to fuck me." She didn't have to ask twice.

I bent her over the desk and began to fuck her from behind. I got a close look at the ass I wanted so much to touch. I fucked her pussy hard as she moaned. I fondled her fine ass while I fucked her, which seemed to turn her on more, and the more she got turned on, the more I got turned on. I pulled my dick out of her pussy and spread her legs a little more. I squatted down and ate her pussy again, only this time from behind. I kissed her ass cheeks and squeezed them, loving how they felt in my hands. Her pussy tasted even better this time. She pushed her ass in my face, and I fucked her from behind with my tongue. I slid two fingers in her pussy and finger-fucked her while I ate her out.

I wanted to fuck Lauren some more. She had mentioned once that she liked to be on top, so I lay down and pulled her on top of me. She fucked me hard, bouncing up and down on my dick. I couldn't believe this mild-mannered woman could fuck so well. I parted her cheeks and thrust my cock inside her. I felt the juices from her pussy running down the shaft of my cock.

She whispered, "Fuck me! Fuck me!"

I asked if she liked being fucked like this, and she moaned, "Ye-e-es."

I rolled her over so that I was on top of her and began to bang the hell out of her pussy. I spread her legs as wide as I could get them. Her pussy was so wet, my cock slid right in. I slowed my motion and stroked deeper inside her. She put her hands on my ass, pulled me closer to her and moaned, "Fuck me harder."

I picked up the pace and soon was fucking her uncontrollably, fucking harder and faster with each thrust. I had one leg on my shoulder and the other wrapped around my arm so I could reach deeper and deeper in her.

I felt myself coming and wanted to spray my hot come in Lauren's mouth. She had mentioned in one of her e-mails that she didn't mind having a guy come in her mouth. I pulled my dick out and positioned myself closer to her mouth. As the head slid between her lips, I exploded. I think it was the most come I've ever shot. She swallowed spurt after spurt, with only occasional drops dribbling down her chin.

Lauren and I were drained, but we got ourselves together, gave each other one last kiss and went back to work. That afternoon we ran into each other several times, and she must have noticed the big smile on my face. We haven't been together since, but we have stayed good friends. I think we have gotten closer.

I would love to fuck her again, but the opportunity hasn't presented itself. If it does, I will definitely take advantage.—*M.N., Pittsburgh, Pennsylvania* ○┼▪

THIS SUMMER DAY TURNS INTO A SCORCHER
OF MORE THAN ONE KIND

*T*he sun beams through the curtains of my bedroom window, waking me up. I glance at my bedside clock and realize that it's eleven o'clock. I'm peeved at myself for sleeping most of the morning away. I grab my housecoat and make my way downstairs to start the coffee maker. Nothing like a fresh cup of java to start a girl's day off.

I open the patio door blinds to look out at the beautiful scenery. The sun shines warm and invitingly upon my deck. Not wanting to waste any of its beautiful rays, I make my way to the bathroom and slip my housecoat off. As the hot water from the showerhead beads and pounds against my soft skin, I realize that it has been weeks since my body has been touched by the loving hands of a man.

My pussy becomes excited. Was it the sight of the beaming sun, or the warmth of the streaming water? I start to lather and caress my body with the soapy puff pad. Tilting my head back, I allow the shower flow to hit my face. I let out a slight sigh. My pussy becomes more and more excited as the pressure of the water hits my breasts and clit simultaneously.

I become greedy for the sensation and turn my body so the shower pulses directly against my hot pussy. I begin to finger myself. Groping at my breasts and fondling my clit, I feel myself getting hotter and wetter. As the water continues to pulse against my clit and my fingers move faster and faster in and out of my pussy, I find myself building to an orgasm. I let out a roar as I come. If only that were a cock instead of my fingers working my cunt so feverishly!

I lean my head against the cool wall of the shower stall. I close my eyes and let my body succumb to the sensations. I know that it won't be long before I will find myself in a state of ecstasy once again. With that thought in mind, I quickly rinse myself off and start thinking about my daily tasks, which have yet to be performed.

Once I turn off the shower, I shiver from the burst of cold air that hits my tingling body. With my nipples still erect and sensitive from my orgasm, I towel myself off carefully. I send chills through my body when I reach my pussy.

I slip my housecoat back on and make my way back downstairs. The coffee is ready, and I pour myself a cup. I open the patio doors and take my cup out onto the deck. A warm wind is blowing briskly. I tilt my head upward to allow the sunshine to beat down on my face. I slide into my lounge chair and let the housecoat fall open. I lie back and allow the warmth of the sun to soothe my bare flesh. The heat unexpectedly stimulates me. I take in a deep breath, and as my chest swells, my bare breasts luxuriate in the warmth of the sun. Mmm, it feels so good!

I close my eyes and begin to fantasize about a man sucking and licking my clit. My hand reaches down, and once again I find myself fondling my pussy. I am overcome by thoughts of sexual encounters.

I am so horny that it doesn't take much to start the juices flowing again. My hips gyrate quickly against my own hand. My clit and pussy long for release. I finger-fuck myself feverishly into oblivion. With the exhilaration of the fresh air and the warmth of the sun, I am soon nearing another orgasm.

I let out a loud scream that causes the birds to fly away. With every part of my body tingling, I lie there relaxed and exhausted, yet still wishing I enjoyed the company of a man. I decide that I will make this my number-one priority for the day.

After finishing my coffee, with some reluctance I get dressed. Since it's so warm out, I throw on just a short T-shirt (no bra) and a tight miniskirt (no panties). Now I'm ready to venture out and strut my stuff.

It really is hot. I put the top down on my convertible. Then I carefully adjust my seat belt so it enhances my bust. I feel the sun beating down on my head, and crank up the stereo. With the tunes rocking and the wind flying through my hair, I cruise to a nearby pool hall, where I am surprised by the number of cars I find parked in the parking lot. I don't pay much attention to the cars. I just think of the men they have brought here. I hope that inside I will find one who can perhaps satisfy the sexual hunger that is consuming me.

I put up the convertible roof and strut lewdly toward the entrance. I fling the outer doors open and pass from the bright sunshine to the relative darkness of the room inside. It takes a while for my eyes to adjust. The smell of beer and stale cigarette smoke soothes my senses. I look for my first hopeful.

Walking over to the nearest table, I feel every man's gaze burning into me. I walk to the wall and grab a cue. I chalk the tip as suggestively as I can. You twirl the cue in my fingers as you approach the table.

"Care to play?" you ask.

"Why, certainly," I reply.

I walk behind you while you rack the balls up. I enjoy the view of your ass, and even give it a squeeze before proceeding to the other end of the table. I bend over, giving you a good view of my breasts down the front of my shirt as I prepare to break. I give you a devilish smile as I smack the balls in motion.

I now walk toward you to prepare for my next shot. As I bend over the table again, you can see the bottom of my ass cheeks. You find this stimulating, and can't resist slipping your hand under my skirt and giving a manly squeeze. I let out a squeal of delight.

Feeling frisky, I purposely back my ass into your crotch and wiggle my ass as I continue shooting, sinking ball after ball. I feel your cock growing through your skintight jeans. What a delicious feeling! I take my cue and stroke it lovingly, hoping to leave no doubt of my passion for big hard shafts. I miss my next shot and make a gesture with my hand that it's your play.

As you bend over the table, I walk up behind you, reach my hand between your legs and gently squeeze your balls. You find this invigorating. You back your ass up against my arm, allowing me to reach your cock. I obligingly give it a friendly squeeze. I let out a breathy "Hmm." I am no longer interested in the game—at least not the game of pool!—and neither are you.

You stand up and look around the room to see if anyone is looking. Then you cup my breast with one hand and reach under my skirt with the other. I'm very hot and wet. My nipples are fully erect from the touch of your hand. You give me a strong kiss on the lips, and squeeze my breast at the same time. I let out a groan of passion. I am so-o-o horny! As we are intertwined with the kiss, I reach down and grope your cock. I start to unbutton your fly. But you stop me.

Shocked, I step away and look you in the eyes. Could I have been wrong? Did you not want the same thing as I did? I am overwhelmed with feelings of rejection. You take my hand and lead me to a secluded corner of the room. It is there that the passion begins.

You place me up against the wall facing you and lower yourself to your knees. Lifting my skirt, you begin to lavishly nibble and suck on my clit. I groan with desire. I throw my head back and enjoy every sensation while lifting one of my legs and placing it on your shoulder. You then reach around and place your hands on my ass and squeeze firmly. I press my pussy harder against your face. I feel myself building fast to an ultimate climax.

Just as I begin to reach my peak, you stop. I take a deep breath. Your face is dotted with my love juices. I moan and plead with you to finish me. You smile. We kiss again passionately. I lick the drops of my juices from your face.

I reach down and unbutton your pants, freeing your throbbing cock. I take it in my hand. It's so hard, so eager to be loved. I gently pull myself away, never letting go. We turn, and now you are leaning against the wall. Eager to receive the benefit of my talents.

I go to my knees. I lick the tip of your cock, while still stroking your shaft with my hand. I give it a squeeze, allowing droplets of your come to escape. I lap these up greedily. Now I wrap my lips around the end and take you deep in the back of my throat. My mouth feels hot around your cock. You place your hands on my head for the ride, as I bob up and down your shaft, slowly at first, then picking up speed. I rub your balls with my hand in perfect synchronization with the strokes I make with my mouth, giving you extreme pleasure. I feel your manhood swelling and stiffening as I receive it deep in my throat.

Finally I suck you so hard that you explode. I swallow every drop. You become weak, but I don't stop. I continue the rhythm of my mouth on your cock and my hands on your balls, until you become hard once again. You are amazed that this can be done!

But I still need release. You stand me up and kiss my neck and face while fingering me. I am soaking wet from my arousal. I whisper in your ear that I need to be fucked. You oblige by bending me over the pool table, which is only inches away. I hike up my skirt and spread my legs wide, allowing you to have full access to my pussy. You enter me, and I let out a moan. You pull out and tease me with the tip of your cock. I dig my nails into the fabric of the table while begging you to penetrate me fully. I need to be fucked, I tell you, and fucked *hard*.

You are making me crazy. Finally you pound your cock deep in me.

I start to breathe heavily and moan. You grab my hips and pump me faster and faster. I feel myself ready to explode. Wanting the release, I encourage you to quicken the pace. I bounce against your groin, making sure that you hit every area of my inner pussy. I spread my legs as far as I can, so you can go deeper with each stroke. Eventually I explode. You keep pounding me and reach around and fondle my clit, increasing the intensity of my orgasm. We continue this motion until you fill me once again. Finally drained, we separate.

Every nerve in my body tingles. My legs shake from exhaustion. You help me to a booth and sit me down. As we wait for the waitress, we look around the room and notice that no one was even watching us while we had sex. We both giggle at the thought of what a fine pair of sexual exhibitionists we are—apparently we couldn't even manage to get caught in the act! It certainly wasn't for want of trying.

You reach down and stroke my pussy lightly, and it's like electric-shock treatment. You barely brush my clit, and that sends total shivers through me. I in turn reach down and give your satisfied cock a gentle squeeze. We kiss passionately again. I feel myself getting wet again. You pull your head away and smile. We both know that we will be doing it again soon. *Real* soon.

The waitress comes with the drinks. As we take time to allow our bodies to luxuriate in the exhaustion from our lovemaking, we watch the other people in the pool hall. There must be something in the air that arouses us. You lean over and nibble on my ear. I let out a slight moan. I'm amazed at how horny I am. I tilt my head back, exposing my neck. You suck gently on it. I am getting wetter and wetter by the second, and suggest that we leave so we can be alone. You agree.

As we step out into the parking lot, you grab my ass and give it a squeeze. As if I needed to be excited more! We race to my car. I start it up and put the roof down. I want desperately to be naked, and tell you so. You hike up my skirt. As we pull out of the lot, you lean down and give my wet pussy a kiss.

"More!" I scream. "I want more!"

You bury your tongue in my opening. We approach a stoplight, and I tell you that you should really lift your head up—not really wanting you to. You decide that it would be better if you continue, and you start to flick my clit with your tongue. I giggle from sheer pleasure. My giggle attracts the attention of the occupants of the car beside us. I don't care. I just want you to continue. You make a mumbling sound I can't understand, but I feel the vibration, which excites me even more.

I know that I must pull off and have you continue with what you are doing. I want us to be alone. Once the light turns green, I step heavily on the gas, which causes the tires to squeal. I throw my head back and laugh as we quickly pull away from the other cars. The whole time, you continue to fondle my clit and pussy with your loving tongue. I speed through town to a secluded spot by the lake. It is only when we are there that you stop.

We climb out of the car. You reach in the back seat and grab the blanket that is conveniently there for such an occasion. You follow me as I venture toward the water. You lay the blanket out and suggest that I join you. I'm too frisky to stay still. I start to perform a striptease for you. I begin by lifting my T-shirt slowly to expose my breasts. You lie on your side, hold your head in your bent arm and watch the show. I now remove my shirt completely and rub it against my erect nipples. I toss you the shirt. You catch it and smell the sweet perfume it holds.

As I continue to dance, I fondle my breasts, then slide my hands down toward my crotch. I reach under my skirt and rub the inside of my thighs while bending my knees to a right angle. You bend your head down to take a peek at my dripping pussy. I stand up so as not to ruin the show and turn my back toward you and lift my skirt, exposing my beautiful ass. I bend over so you get a good view of my ass and pussy. In this position, I insert a finger in my pussy, moving it slowly in and out. I am getting wetter and breathing harder. The sun keeps my half-naked body warm.

I remove my finger so I can release myself from my skirt. As it falls to my ankles, I step out of it gracefully, without missing a beat of the music that is playing in my head. I casually kick the skirt aside and now stand fully naked in front of you, stroking myself with my hands in what I believe is a very erotic way. It must be working. You become extremely hard and have to undo your pants to be comfortable.

I take that as an invitation to join you on the blanket. Once I lie down, there is no stopping us from exploring each other with our hands and mouths. You roll me on my back and bury your face in my clean-shaven pussy. I squirm as your tongue burrows deep in my waiting hole. You blow gently, almost bringing me to orgasm. I want to suck you while you nibble on my clit. I turn my body to gain access to your wonderful cock. I take it deep in my mouth and suck it passionately.

With my lips stroking your cock, I squeeze your balls gently, and drops of come escape from it. Never before have I tasted anything so salty yet so sweet. I want more. Suddenly you stop and turn yourself so you're lying on your back. I take this opportunity to straddle you. I tease your cock by allowing only your tip to enter my dripping cunt. You grab my hips and try to have me impale myself totally on you. Not being able to resist, I allow you to fully enter me.

We begin those beautiful rhythmical strokes. I reach down and lovingly squeeze your balls in synchronization. I feel myself building to an overwhelming orgasm, and when you insert your cock, I feel you getting harder and harder. We both quicken the pace and break into a sweet sweat. I start to explode, and you splash wildly inside me as your cock releases. We both moan and grunt wildly.

The outdoor quiet is broken by our sounds of pleasure. I collapse on your chest, still breathing heavily. You wrap your arms around me. I feel fully satisfied now, as do you. We lie exhausted on the blanket, letting the sun dry us off. We've accomplished what others only dream out in fantasies.

I lay my head on your chest and become mesmerized by the beating of your heart. You stroke my hair away from my face, lean over and give me a passionate kiss. After what seems like only a brief moment in time, we dress and head back to the bar, where I drop you off at your car.

We look deep in each other's eyes, both of us knowing that our paths may never cross again and yet neither of us will ever forget our rendezvous today. We kiss one last time and go our separate ways.—*L.R., Montreal, Quebec* ⟳

HE CAMPAIGNS TO PUT SOME "GIVE" BACK IN THE GIVE-AND-TAKE OF SEX

I met Melissa while I was studying law at a large university. I always gazed at the adorable undergraduates walking around campus. Although I was almost thirty years old, I remained shy and rather inexperienced, and rarely spoke to these girls. Yet their beauty brought tears to my eyes.

Then one day I was sitting alone in a popular coffeehouse reading when Melissa asked if she might sit at my table, since there were no free ones left. I vividly remember my first glance at her face: She had the "Brooke look." I mean that she reminded me of Brooke Shields as a teenager. She looked gorgeous—very young and innocent, but friendly. She had big green eyes, black hair and small, even teeth. Honest to God, I found out later that she had been a part-time model.

Under the circumstances, I was barely able to stammer out a "Sure." She sat, and we talked. She had a captivating habit of looking straight in my eyes as she chatted. I found out that she had just started at the honors college a month ago. I discovered, much to my delight, that she seemed to feast off of my opinions, and I advised her freely about classes, extracurriculars, you name it. I managed to stay nonchalant when she talked happily about her boyfriend.

Of course she had a boyfriend, I thought. She's beautiful and smart. Nevertheless, I flirted as much as I could, and as we got to know each other better, she admitted that her boyfriend went to another school and they had "agreed to see other people."

I offered to walk her back to her dorm. She let me and then, at the dorm entrance, smiled and said, "Can I call you sometime?"

Impossible, I mused. There's no way she'll ever call. But within a week, I heard her soft voice on my answering machine.

Next we had a wonderful casual date. God knows why, she seemed impressed with me. She even seemed truly excited to ride in my sports car. I had resigned myself to the fact that guys expressed a hell of a lot more interest in it than women did. I definitely hadn't bought it to lure models! I liked Melissa too, but what primarily impressed me was her face and her compact, delicious body. I craved her. At the end of that casual first date she gave me one paltry good-night kiss, but it left me grinning for days.

On casual date number three, she wore tight black jeans and a little sweater that highlighted her flat stomach by ending right above her navel. I finally got her back to my room. Fortunately, she was a little nervous too. She was breathing quickly—although still looking right at me—and that gave me confidence.

We started to kiss on the couch. At first, she just tentatively poked her tongue in my mouth. I was thinking already, I wonder if she's still a virgin. She was definitely holding back a little. Nevertheless, as if she had planned everything and wanted to stay in command, she asked if I wanted to give her a massage! She pulled off her sweater and quickly rolled on her stomach.

I couldn't believe my luck at getting this pretty eighteen-year-old in the sack. But I had a couple of problems, since I had never screwed such a slim, small-breasted girl before.

To begin with, I couldn't find a clasp on the back of her sports bra, so I just caressed along the thin band of it, along with her shoulders and back.

Then I figured that I'd reach my hands slightly inside the back of her jeans. I could see the outline of her bikini underpants through them, and I wanted to stroke her just down to that line. But her jeans were so damned tight, I couldn't do it. My hand got stuck, and I had to take it out!

I was so horny now, I turned her over and, without much pretense at massage, started to touch her cute little breasts through the sports bra, marveling at how the Calvin Klein insignia circled her taut pale skin. But I still didn't know how to deal with the bra. I wondered if I could casually hoist it up over her head. Unsure, I just lifted it over her tits.

She immediately sat up and climbed on my knee. I leaned forward and kissed her nipple, then sucked softly on it. As it got hard, she let out a little sigh and started to rock back and forth on my leg. I sucked for all I was worth, and as she got more and more aroused, she ground her crotch into my knee. I held her by the hips, and she enjoyed the friction and sucking.

As always, though, she wanted to orchestrate things, whispering, "Keep going, just like this."

So I did, and she humped away, eyes now closed. Soon she let out a few gasps, whispered something unintelligible and moaned. She shuddered as she came in her jeans. After a few moments, she smiled and said, remarkably, that she thought it was time to go—she had to study or something!

She was an incredible cocktease, I realized, but what could I do? I was already under her spell. I let her dress and go without a word of surprise or disagreement. At least I'd gotten to second base. I became frenzied to arrange another date, and this time I vowed to go further.

On that next date, though, I had still more delicious stuff to learn. We were back in my room, on my bed. Both of us were slightly drunk. This time I pulled off Melissa's shirt to find a green satin bra with a front clasp. I had never tackled one of these front-openers before, but after taking a deep breath, I moved my slightly trembling hands to her chest and unsnapped the bra on the first try!

As before, I concentrated on her delight. Once again she perched on my knee, and I watched as she gyrated, gasped, murmured something and came. Now was my chance.

Before she could leap off the bed, my hands were at her waist and I undid the top button of her tight CK blue jeans while rolling her on her back. Much to my chagrin, the jeans were button-fly. I had never owned a pair of button-fly jeans or had occasion to strip them off any girl, so I didn't realize that you could just pull down and unbutton all the buttons at once.

I fumbled with the first damn brass rivet until, after what seemed like eternity, I managed to guide it through the buttonhole. As I forged ahead to the next metal button, my fingers brushed against the waistband of Melissa's bikini, which matched her bra.

She thought I was going so slowly in order to tease her, and she started to squirm with lust. "Hurry up!" she whispered urgently. "Make me come!"

She was eager for more sex, and like a sap, I accommodated her immediately rather than taking this opportunity to sweetly "torture" her a little. Instead, I plunged my hand down between her denim and her briefs. I really had to push a little to get my hand down to her vagina. Her panties were already very wet from her first orgasm, and I just rubbed up against them with the little room my hand had in the confined space of her clothing.

I had now managed to get my hand trapped down both the back and the front of Melissa's pants! Still, it worked out great for her. The pleasure made her bounce around, and my trapped hand was securely in place and never lost contact with her clitoris. She thrashed and moaned with excitement. Soon she was convulsing again, and my fingers felt her genitals suddenly get even more juicy.

Now, as she relaxed and caught her breath, I had ample time to undo the rest of her fly and pull her jeans down her legs. It was then that she smiled shyly at me and said she wasn't ready to go all the way and we should leave our underpants on. Once again I obliged the beautiful freshman. I went down on her, licking vigorously, then nibbling at her satin panties. Occasionally I would push the panties in and out of her slit, then lick her clit again. She shoved her crotch at my face, pounded her little fists against the bed and treated herself to a third orgasm.

I so wanted to fuck her now, but she explained that she was still a virgin. Was she really? She appeared at the same time to be kind of innocent, and yet selfish and slutty. She said she even prevented her boyfriend—I'd forgotten about that jackass!—from getting too carried away by making sure that they always left some clothes on. She confided, though, that his "thing" was so long that it sometimes poked its way over the top of his shorts.

Well, that didn't make me feel so great, especially since, so far, she had only indifferently rubbed my dick. As you will imagine, I wanted to prove myself and take control for a change.

She seemed a little tired, but I kissed and stroked her some more to get her heated up again. It worked, and this time as I caressed her vagina I worked a finger in her. She seemed a little startled at first, but then her face became contorted with ecstasy. I guessed that this wasn't a first for her, no matter how innocent she acted. Still, she was hungry for experience, and could hardly stand the joy of flicking my finger.

More juices poured out of Melissa. This time she whispered, "Hurry! I'm almost there!"

She was shivering and tense, poised at the brink of climax. At that moment I stopped abruptly, giving her a taste of her own medicine. I quickly got on top of her light body, helped her wrap her legs around me and started to hump. She went wild with lust. We mashed our underpants together. I concentrated on keeping my cock pushed against her most sensitive spots. I felt her wetness seep onto my penis.

As I began to ejaculate, I reached down and made sure that my cockhead was free. It felt much better that way, and I creamed all over. I had an amazing orgasm—after waiting so long!—while my young bedmate pushed demonically against me, setting her off as well. Because I'd kept her waiting too, her fourth orgasm of the night was the most intense. She cried out and rolled her head from side to side as she came in her panties. The pretty freshman was all tuckered out from sex and fell asleep next to me. I was elated.

Although I'm sure I realized that I could never keep a girl like that for long, I couldn't hide my shock when I called her the next week to arrange a date. She was cold and gave me some excuse about an appointment that evening with her teaching assistant. I thought, good luck to him, the bastard!—*N.O., Springfield, Massachusetts* ○┼▣

SHE GETS HIM BY WINNING A BET, THEN WAITS EIGHT YEARS TO WIN ANOTHER ONE

*A*ll through high school I'd had a big crush on this guy named Mickey. I was totally infatuated with his all-American good looks, tan skin, athletic build and gorgeous brown eyes. I had made it very clear on several occasions that I wanted him. He was very shy and quiet, but there were occasional playful glances and a few instances of mild flirting—just games, really—so I kind of knew that the feeling was mutual. Unfortunately, the timing was never quite right for us to get together, and we never did.

It wasn't until a few years after high school graduation that we finally did manage to hook up. One night I was hanging out with a few of my male friends, one of whom was Mickey. We were driving around downtown in my car, trying to find somewhere that we could just hang out and drink a few beers (in this particular town places like that are few and far between).

I finally told the gang that I knew about a secluded place on a quiet boulevard where we could all go for a while. With a disbelieving smirk on his face, Mickey, who was sitting beside me, said, "Yeah, right. If you can find a secluded place on the boulevard, I'll do anything you want!"

The guys in the back seat laughed and rolled their eyes, but my pussy was telling me that this was the night! I did know a spot, a dark parking lot behind some buildings that was deserted at night. I put the pedal to the floor, and we were there in a jiffy. "Is this secluded enough?" I asked as we got out of the car.

Without any hesitation, Mickey grabbed the beer and handed it to our friends. "Go take a walk. A long walk..." he said.

I tried to act cool, but it was difficult. My heart was racing, my nipples were hard and I was well past the point of being ready. Without another word, Mickey grabbed my waist and pulled me close to him. I could feel his cock pressing through his pants. My heart raced when he kissed me for the first time. It was without a doubt the most loving and passionate kiss I'd ever experienced.

Shivers ran down my spine as Mickey picked me up and set me down on the trunk of my car. He lifted up my skirt and pulled my panties aside, exposing me to him fully as I just closed my eyes and let him do what he wanted. He bent down and his tongue immediately penetrated my cunt. Strangely, it felt both cool and warm as he moved it up and down, licking my pussy and clit with his thick, fat tongue. I moaned and giggled at the same time, and that's when I came.

I sat up immediately and kissed him so that I could taste my cunt juice. I think he liked that. Knowing that our time was limited before our drunken idiot friends would be back to interrupt us, Mickey wasted no time sticking his cock inside me. It was larger than I was used to, but I was so wet that it went in with no problem. I moaned with pleasure and looked deep into his dark, sexy eyes. We both released years of built-up sexual tension as we came simultaneously. Our time together was short, but it was oh so sweet—and it was definitely worth the wait!

Mickey quickly buttoned up his pants as I pulled down my short brown skirt. "My God, you felt so good," he said quietly.

"I wish I won bets more often," I said, straightening my clothes out with a huge smile on my face. I was on cloud nine, knowing I would remember that night for years to come.

And it was indeed years to come. Though we kept in touch and saw each other occasionally, it wasn't until eight years later that Mickey and I got together again, when the two of us and some other old acquaintances spent the day with a mutual friend who was in town for a visit.

The day we spent together was really fun. We all joked and laughed about old times, and eventually the topic of our "boulevard bet" came up. We spoke of it casually at first, but then I looked over and noticed Mickey watching me intently. "You know, I really enjoyed that night," he said finally, his gaze not quite meeting mine.

My heart raced. But that had happened such a long time ago, I figured, and I didn't have any reason to think that it would ever happen again. But that night I just couldn't think of anything else. I was so incredibly horny that I even got off on my pillow—twice. Even that didn't help, though. I wanted him again, and I thought that he wanted me, too. The next day I finally gave in and called him. I knew he was out on a camping trip with some of his friends that day, but I eventually managed to reach him on his cell phone.

"I was hoping you would call me," he told me quietly. "You'll never believe it. The guys and I have a bet going."

"Oh, no, not another bet," I laughed. "What's it about this time?"

"The guys said you'd call me and want to get together again. If we do, then I lose and I have to fetch beer for them for the next twenty-four hours."

"Well, I guess we probably shouldn't get together then," I said, teasing him as well as myself.

"Oh, but that's okay with me, because I win either way!" Mickey said.

"What do you mean?" I asked.

"If we don't, they have to get me a beer any time I want one," he explained. "But if we do, then I get to spend the night with you, and I really win!"

It was obvious to me that was what he genuinely wanted, and I had a really good feeling about it. He invited me to come out and meet him at the campsite.

When I got to the campground we took a walk around. It was dark and quiet, though there were still a few people around. We went down to the river hand in hand. The air was warm and the water was extremely cold. We waded in a little way, and then Mickey grabbed me by the hips and lifted me up onto a large rock. It was the perfect spot, and I suspected he had scoped it out well ahead of time.

He pulled my sweatpants off. As he set them down beside me, one of the legs fell into the water. He pulled it out and touched it to my left breast through my sweatshirt, which sent shivers down my spine and made my nipples stiffen and swell. We kissed, gently at first, and then gradually harder and more intensely. I was getting moister by the minute—and not from the water! My pussy actually felt hot, and the touch of his fingers on it intensified the sensation. I reached down to grab his bulging cock. I had forgotten how big and perfect it was. I had dreamed about this very moment so often and for so long—ever since that encounter years earlier—that I couldn't wait to have him inside me again.

It was starting to rain slightly. I took off my sweatshirt and Mickey began sucking on my nipples. He kept teasing them with his tongue and with his cold, wet hands, then nibbled at them tenderly as I ran my fingers along the length of his hard penis. I noticed a small amount of pre-come on the tip and bent down to lick it off. His head went back in ecstasy. I can't begin to describe how sweet-tasting he was!

My passion was intensifying until it became almost unbearable. I lay back down on the rock as Mickey stood in the river. He pulled my legs up to his shoulders and put his cock deep inside me, steadying himself with his hands on my ass. That triggered an instant orgasm, which had me moaning and gasping for air.

It began to rain harder by then, and lightning flashed and thunder clapped in the distance. The storm was moving closer, which only increased the intensity of our lovemaking. Mickey pumped his cock in and out of me, faster and faster, and the feeling of the hard rock against my back and the cold, fresh air hitting my face and breasts only added to my pleasure.

Mickey stood between my legs and continued pushing himself into my cunt. The droplets of rain mixed with the sweat he was working up as he fucked me, grabbing his cock and pulling out until only the thick, round head was still lodged inside me. The faster he fucked me the closer I got to having another orgasm, and the closer I got to coming again the more loudly I started to moan.

By that time Mickey was moaning, too, and his face showed his total satisfaction. I couldn't hold back any longer and let go, coming again and again, until finally he pulled out, had his orgasm and squirted a huge load all over my heaving stomach.

The lightning was getting a little too close for comfort by then, so we ran up the riverbank and got into the tent for shelter. My hair was dripping wet and I knew I looked a mess, but it didn't matter. We dried off and got together for at least three more hours of intense probing, licking and fucking. It was another memorable night. And for all I know, that memory might have to keep me entertained for another eight years—unless I can come up with another good bet. It's a good thing I like to gamble!—*Name and address withheld* ○━▣

HE PICKED HER UP IN A BAR AND FOUND THAT SHE LIKED IT QUICK, NASTY AND PUBLIC

One Saturday night I was driving around aimlessly, and finally ended up at a club called Diamond Jim's. I decided to check it out, thinking it was a titty bar which, the bartender later told me it had been a few years before.

I went in and sat at the bar. About three drinks later a woman walked in who immediately stoked my fire. She was a Latin-looking lady with long black hair, a short black skirt and matching high-heeled shoes. She sat at a table halfway across the room, her slender body turned a little bit toward the bar.

I got a feeling she wanted company, and following my instinct I got up and approached her. With her permission, I sat down at her table and we made small talk. She told me her name was Elena. I told her I was single, and she said she was legally separated. She told me she usually went to bed early, but had come to the bar that night because she couldn't get to sleep. She was visiting a friend who, like me, lived on the other side of town.

When I asked her what she liked to do she gave me a sly grin and replied, "Do you mean what would I like to do right now?"

I didn't take this bait, explaining that I was asking about her hobbies and so forth. I don't remember what she said they were. A few minutes later she broke off the conversation by looking me in the eye and asking, "Can I be blunt with you for a second?"

I said she could, then braced myself. She paused and then said, "I want to know why you sat with me."

"Because I find you attractive," I replied.

"Do you think I'm attractive because I'm wearing a short skirt?" she inquired.

"No," I said. "I just think you're cute. You're a very pretty woman."

"Hmmm," she responded with a gleam in her eyes. Then she said, "Would you like to go outside with me and fuck?"

Of course my instinct was to say yes immediately, but I hesitated. I couldn't believe I was so lucky, but Elena assured me that there were no strings attached. We left the bar right then.

Outside, we walked to a dark corner behind the building, but we were still visible from the adjacent street and from any vehicles leaving the parking lot. I suggested we go somewhere more private, but Elena said, "No. Right here is fine," adding that our visibility turned her on. "Let's see what you have," she murmured. "Do you think you can satisfy me?"

As I pulled out my dick she made a sound of approval. I lifted her skirt and was thrilled—but not too surprised—to see that she wasn't wearing panties. I tried to enter her but wasn't quite ready. I explained that I needed some foreplay to get things going.

I usually like a lot of foreplay, including sexual teasing. I also like a lot of sexy talk, hugging, kissing and stroking when I have sex. As I see it, a sexual encounter is to be savored, not rushed. But that wasn't the time or place for a marathon fuck, and Elena seemed like she was only interested in the basics, anyway. She bent down and sucked my dick until it was up and ready. When I was more relaxed, I turned her around and nailed her from the rear.

While fucking her, I stroked her hair and every inch of her body. Her hot pussy engulfed my dick as her mouth had a few minutes before. I moved faster, squeezing her ass and watching her sweet pussy lips gripping my cock as it moved in and out of her.

I whispered in her ear, "You're so damn sexy. Your pussy feels so good. So nice and tight."

Aside from everything else she had going for her, Elena was very vocal. "Yes, fuck me," she panted. "I'm so wet. I want to feel you come inside me. I love the way it feels. It's all warm and sticky. Oooh, fuck me!"

That I did, until I came. Her pussy full of come, she said, "Yes, now I can get to sleep."

We walked back to the bar entrance. She asked whether I wanted to go back inside with her, but I declined. We'd both gotten what we came for, so we exchanged good-byes.

I stood alone in the parking lot for a minute, and then I reconsidered and went back inside and took a look for her. I was thinking with my dick, wondering if there might not be an opportunity for an intense sexual relationship there. But when I looked around the bar, she was nowhere in sight. I assumed she'd already gone home to sleep.

Since that encounter, I've imagined us meeting again by chance, but it hasn't happened. I've imagined her fantasizing about our encounter, playing with her pussy while replaying the scene in her head. I've imagined her masturbating later that morning, and then licking our come from her fingertips.

I wonder if Elena had public sex before, or whether she's had it since, or whether it's something that she does all the time. I wonder if she's told anybody about our encounter. And I wonder if she'll ever read this letter.—*R.F., Chillicothe, Ohio* ⊶▪

ONCE THEY DECIDED TO GO BEYOND FRIENDSHIP, THEY REALLY WENT ALL THE WAY

I'd been after Minnie for years—sort of. It had become something of a joke between us, and I think we lost track of whether or not we were serious about it a long time ago. We're both happily married, and we have been for years. There's never been any joking around about us running away together or anything. Everything basically started because we talked together a lot about this and that, and we finally came to the conclusion that we were probably the last two people in the world who would ever cheat on our spouses.

"We're just too boring," I remember saying to Minnie once. "But if you ever decide to do it, promise you'll cheat with me." She promised she would, and we both laughed. That's how it all started. I guess we had to establish that we were safe from that kind of thing before we could really begin to discuss our deepest feelings together. Minnie always confided in me when she was getting fed up with her husband

Al, and I would go to her if I was having trouble with my wife Anne. We'd blow off a little steam, complain about our spouses for a while and then we'd both go home and make up with them.

Before we parted, though, we always made our standard running joke about how we ought to go to bed with each other and just get it over with once and for all. "If I were as compatible with Al as I am with you," Minnie once told me, "we wouldn't have these little discussions."

I understood how she felt. I love my wife dearly, but once in a while I wondered how things might have been different if we had never gotten married. But then my boring side came back to the surface, and I realized that it was very important to me to be faithful to my wife, who I love very deeply.

Even so, my discussions with Minnie became more graphic as the years went on. We talked often about what we'd do together if we finally gave in to our wilder impulses and had that affair. Don't be fooled by my saying we've been talking like this for years. We're not a couple of elderly frumps. At thirty-eight, Minnie is sexier than most girls in their early twenties. Her tits are very full, and the fact that they're not riding quite as high as they once did makes them that much more voluptuous. They're like fruit that's almost too juicy to eat, but you know you have to finish it once you've started.

That's how Minnie finally turned out to be, just like wonderfully ripe fruit. The two of us had resisted the temptation to have sex with each other for a long time, but at last she was bursting with juice. And once I had that juice running down my chin, I had to keep swallowing until I'd had it all.

One day we were talking, as we had so many times before, about her problems with her husband. It sounded to me as if they had reached that point that all married couples seem to get to, where they were hardly having sex at all, and when they finally did have sex it was more out of obligation than because they wanted to. Millie looked me square in the eye and claimed that she hadn't had an orgasm in six months she hadn't given herself with her own fingers.

"Even so," I told her, kidding around as usual (or so I thought) "I'd like to see that for myself. That may not be the way you like to get an orgasm, but it would sure do the trick for me. Actually," I continued, not really thinking about what I was saying, "you should just let me do it. It wouldn't be cheating if you just let me rub you a little. You don't think you're cheating when you rub yourself. What's the difference? It's only cheating if we fuck."

Like I said, I was basically joking, but I could tell from the look on Minnie's face that she was seriously weighing what I'd just said. "I don't know if that would hold up in court," she finally said with a bit of a laugh. "But I'll tell you this: I'm so desperate to get off with someone else that I could almost think about it."

This was turning out to be less lighthearted than most of our flirtations, and I started wondering if we were finally crossing the border into the serious consideration of adultery.

We joked about it a bit, but the joking got more and more serious. "So tell me how it would be if we slept together," she said finally.

We were sitting in the lounge at a small bowling alley just outside of our hometown, where we met sometimes when we didn't have anywhere else to go. Her hand was lying on the table, so I put my hand lightly on hers and began to stroke it as I talked.

"Well, you know that I'd be gentle with you," I assured her in a soft voice. "There wouldn't be any of that quick, insensitive stuff that Al is into. I like to go slow and soft when I'm making love with a woman. I wouldn't go for a lot of kissing and stuff to warm up, though. We've been waiting for this a long time, and I don't think we're going to need a lot of foreplay to get us in the mood. I know you wonder about me, and I wonder about you. So I'd just start right in by unsnapping those jeans you're wearing."

As my fingers continued to caress the back of her hand, Minnie drew in a sudden breath. I looked at her and realized that she'd closed her eyes in order to imagine it better. It wasn't the most romantic setting, but I decided to give her my best shot.

"I'd pull your zipper down, but I wouldn't take your pants off," I continued. "I'd ease my hand into your panties and work it around until I had enough room to get at your pussy. There's something so sexy about putting your hand on a woman without undressing her first."

The more I said to her, the more I could tell that my words were beginning to have some sort of an effect on her. Minnie moved her fingers apart, just as though she were spreading her legs. I picked up on the hint and worked my own finger into the V that formed there and applied some gentle pressure. She sighed and her lips parted slightly. "I can't believe that you understand what I need so well," she murmured. "But, please, tell me some more about how you'd do me."

"Well, I'd put just the tip of my index finger right on your button. After you come, I know I'll want to play all around, touch you everywhere, probe inside you as far as I can. But first I want to get you off, make you come, make you relax and accept me. So I'd go right to your clit and get to work.

"But I wouldn't do it too fast. At first I'd just press against your clit, to see how hard it is and how much pressure you like. I'd move it from side to side and up and down. Then I'd go in circles, and I'd listen to how you responded to each motion, trying to find out which one was just right for you at that moment.

"Once I knew what it was that you wanted, I'd concentrate on giving it to you, except I'd go just a little slower than you wanted me to. And as you got closer to coming, I'd go slower still, but I'd press down a little harder until you finally just slip right over into a slow, pounding orgasm."

Minnie groaned slightly, and then she snapped her eyes open, the way you do sometimes when you wake up and realize you weren't supposed to be sleeping. She stared at me, looking perturbed, and then stood up. I got up, too.

"No, you sit here and finish your drink," she told me, hastily pulling out her lipstick and applying it with a slightly shaky hand. "I just remembered that I was supposed to be home early tonight. I'll see you same time next week?"

She leaned over and gave me a peck on the cheek before she ran out, but I knew I'd upset her. I'd really gone too far, and I kicked myself for doing it. After all these years, I was afraid that I'd finally ruined things for good. Things were never going to be the same between us. That much was obvious, and I was really sorry about it.

The next time I saw Minnie I was all set to apologize. I'd been thinking about it and was pretty sure I knew how she'd approach it. She was going to pretend that it had never happened, and when I brought it up she would laugh it off. I wasn't really comfortable with that, but it was better than ruining our friendship.

That wasn't the way it turned out at all, though. We met at a much quieter place the next time, and we got a table where no one else would hear what we were talking about.

I tried to talk first when we sat down, but she cut me off. "Look, I know what you're going to say, but it's just not going to happen. We can't go back to the way we've been. We slipped over the line."

"I know," I admitted, "but we're both adults. We can control our feelings."

"Well, I'm getting tired of controlling my feelings," Minnie informed me. "The way I see it, there are two things we can do. We can either stop seeing each other completely..." She took a deep breath. "Or you can go ahead and do what you told me you would."

She looked me right in the eye, not at all the embarrassed housewife she'd been the last time we met.

"I'm wearing the same jeans," she pointed out.

"So you are," I said, trying to smile with a confidence I wasn't feeling. "But where would we go? Let's get serious here for a minute."

Minnie held up her hand. There was a ring wrapped around her index finger, attached to a single key on a big plastic tag. She twirled it a little. Suddenly she was the brave one.

"Well?" she asked.

I swallowed and smiled. "Let's go," I said.

Just as I'd promised, I didn't waste any time once we were in the motel room. We had barely spoken on the drive over in her car. We'd both been trying to make our peace with what we were about to do. I, for one, failed completely, but I wasn't about to back out. So when the room door shut behind us I had my hands on her belt before she was able to get her lips on mine.

As a result, our first kiss missed, and I had trouble seeing what I was doing with her zipper. We were fumbling and stumbling all around the room, trying to kiss and get her pants unfastened. Soon we were laughing together again.

That was what had been missing between us since I'd first brought up the subject of rubbing her pussy. Everything had been so serious that we were in danger of losing the original impulse. But we were suddenly having fun again, and just like that I wanted her more than I'd ever wanted a woman before.

Minnie took the problem of the jeans into her own hands, practically ripping them off and throwing them and her panties into the corner of the room. "I know you said you were going to do it to me with my pants on," she hissed between giggles, "but I was beginning to think I'd die of old age before you got there. So come on, tiger."

With that, she flung herself on her back on the bed. The sight of her lying there with her pussy exposed and her shirt and bra still on was so lewd and erotic that I got an erection instantly. In another second my hands were all over her, trying to remember that I'd vowed to go slowly and make her masturbation session last. At the time I'd told her that, though, I didn't realize that I would be just as excited as she was. Still, I was determined to go slow and make it an exciting experience for both of us but it wasn't going to be easy.

Her slit was every bit as wet as I'd described it as being. It felt hot against my fingertips as I quickly moved around between her puffy labia, finding her clit and getting a general feel for the shape and size of her pussy. Her clit was bigger than I'd imagined, and it was as hard as a tiny cock. I gave it a gentle, tentative flick of my finger to see how responsive it was.

Minnie let out a gasp and dug her chin into my shoulder as I lay there beside her. "Rub me," she said. That was exactly what I intended to do, and I proceeded to go around her clit in little circles, every once in a while crossing that tender bud of flesh with my fingers and drawing a gasp or a moan from her. Even though I moved slowly, she was obviously already climbing the ladder of orgasm. But then she stopped moving and groaned in a way that wasn't the least bit sexual.

"It's not enough," she finally sputtered between gritted teeth.

"What do you want?" I asked, sorry to disappoint her and a little hurt that she hadn't given me more of a chance. "Faster?"

"No, silly," she responded with a quick, sexy laugh. "I want you to lie on top of me and stick that cock of yours into me. I thought it would be enough just to feel you touching me, just to come like a woman again. But it isn't enough. I want to be fucked."

If I'd stopped to think about it, even for an instant, I probably would have backed out of the whole thing. After all, I was the one who had joked that it wouldn't be adultery if we didn't have intercourse. Somewhere deep inside I kind of believed that. By masturbating Minnie, I felt like I was helping out an old friend. If I took my own pants off, I knew that I'd really be betraying my marriage vows.

But I didn't stop and think about it. Not even for a second. Lying next to me was a voluptuous woman who was also my best friend, and I suddenly admitted what I'd always known. All that flirtation all those years was completely serious, and every word of it, every joke, every gesture, had been leading up to this.

In a second my clothes were slapping the wall in the corner and falling on top of hers. She had pulled off her shirt, but left her bra on. Somehow, keeping that one item of clothing on made her much sexier than if she'd been naked. It was a white, lacy bra, and as I slipped my hard dick into the place where it had wanted to be all these years, my whole attention was on her heavy tits in that little lacy contraption.

Our bodies had minds of their own, and knew just what they wanted to do, so we let them go at it. They fell into a perfect rhythm at once. Meanwhile we just stared into each other's eyes with deep, abiding affection as our genitals did their thing. I held myself up with one arm, and with my other hand I began to caress her beautiful breasts through the lace that almost hid them from me. Her nipples were straining to get through the flimsy fabric, but they were trapped inside, as we had been trapped: able to see and feel each other, but unable to come together.

All that had changed now, and it was changed forever. I stared into her eyes and felt her breasts, and I suddenly realized that I was spraying a jet of come into her sweet pussy, which drank it up just as fast as I could deliver it.

We have no idea where this affair is going to go from here. I don't think I want to leave my wife, or that Minnie would want me to. We've agreed not to discuss it for a while, until we know a little more about how we feel about each other. For the moment, though, I'm just glad that we've admitted the depth of our passion.—*K.G., Duluth, Minnesota* ○─■

THE LADY GUARDED HIS COCK, AND TOGETHER THEY MADE THE JAILHOUSE ROCK

I'm a prisoner incarcerated at a southern penitentiary. I'm a big fan of *Penthouse Letters*, and I really enjoy reading about the sexual adventures your other readers have, so I had to write and share the story of a short fuck session that happened between a female corrections officer and myself last year.

This officer, who I'll call Ms. Flame (which obviously isn't her real name but is a good way to describe her personality), worked in the prison unit I was housed in, a unit of one-man cells. Female officers are a big deal in prison, because when you don't have access to pussy it's something you can only dream about. The only way something like that can become reality is if you get lucky enough to catch the eye of a female guard. As fate would have it, I caught the eye of the beautiful Ms. Flame.

One day as she was on the tier passing out mail, I decided to see how she would react if she saw me jacking my dick. Just the thought of having those sweet lips wrapped around my pole or being able to lie between those fine legs while I was pumping my meat into her was enough to give me a hard-on. So there I was with my dick in my hand when she made it to my cell. The way she looked at my rigid pole told me all I needed to know.

I decided to put on a show for her every time she came on the block for her tour. This went on for a few weeks until I couldn't take it anymore and decided to take the next step. I would risk asking her to make it possible for me to give her some dick for real.

I knew that I would get myself into some deep shit with the prison administrators if she reported that I was making sexual advances to her, but at that point I was really thinking with my cock, not my brain. I figured that the pay-off would be worth the risk involved, so I wrote Ms. Flame a note telling her how I would love to lick her sweet pussy and have her suck my dick.

Because my job is cleaning floors and washing windows, I knew that we could find a way to have a quick but meaningful fuck session in one of the storage rooms, if she was willing. After I gave her the note, I sat back and waited to see what she would do. The next day when I saw her, her reaction blew me away. She gave me a big smile when she walked past my cell. I knew then that somehow, some way, she was going to make it possible for us to get together.

The time came one Saturday morning a few weeks later while I was on the job, scrubbing the windows and mopping the floor in another part of the unit. I was told by another inmate, a friend of mine, that

Ms. Flame wanted me to help her get some supplies from one of the storage rooms. I knew then that it was on.

When I walked into the storage room, there she was, the woman that I had spent many nights fucking in my mind. There was no time for talking—we both knew why we were there. After locking the door I walked up to her and started kissing her and touching her big, soft tits. I knew we didn't have much time, but I had to suck her big pink nipples, if only for a minute or two. Her skin felt so soft. I took her tits out of her bra, sucking on one while I played with the other.

Finally I left off sucking her tits, eager to get to her pussy. When she undid her pants I saw to my delight that she wore thong panties and, better yet, didn't have any hair on her pussy. I have never seen such a beautiful sight. I guess she saw the admiration in my eyes, because she lay back on a stack of boxes and invited me to have a taste.

"My pleasure," I said as I began to tongue her. She was really hot, and in no time at all she pulled me harder into her sweet cunt and came all over my face. Her pussy juice tasted sweeter than honey.

When I got up, with my dick sticking straight out, she said she wanted me to fuck her from behind. I had no problem with that. I got behind her and slowly stuck my dick in her pussy. It had been a while since I'd fucked some real cunt, and I knew I wouldn't be able to last too long. As I balled her I played with her clit. She was really fucking herself on my dick, matching my strokes and banging my prick hard. I was fucking her like a madman, and the small sounds she was making told me that she loved every second of it. In a few minutes she screamed and came again, and I shot off, filling her hole with so much come that the shit ran down her legs.

After getting some paper towels to wipe off with, she planted a big kiss on my lips then pulled her pants back on and left the storage room. We were able to get together a few more times after that, but then she was moved to another unit. I still see her around the prison from time to time, but I know I'll never get another chance to have that sweet pussy again. I'm trying real hard, but so far I haven't caught the eye of another female officer. I guess it's back to reading *Penthouse Letters.—Name and address withheld* ⊶▪

TWO COWORKERS USE THE CONFERENCE
ROOM FOR A SPECIAL KIND OF MEETING

I'd had my eye on Chet ever since he was transferred to my office. He's big and blond and incredibly sexy, plus he's very nice and a complete pleasure to be around. As fellow workers, we naturally struck up a friendship, which gradually became more and more intimate—and more and more flirtatious. With each encounter our conversations became increasingly daring, and I knew it was only a matter of time before our relationship would eventually become physical.

One day, coincidentally, we both found ourselves at work early. There were only a few other people in the office, so I went over to his desk to get in a little flirting before the workday began. After a few minutes of sexy banter, Chet came right out and said that he would love to reach out and put his hands on my big, beautiful breasts. I was a little bit startled, but I played along, saying that maybe we should go into the conference room and discuss it in more detail. To my surprise, he jumped up from his desk and led the way!

We stepped into the conference room and he locked the door behind us. The shades were still drawn over the windows, but he didn't turn on the lights. He reached out and his hands found my body in the dimness. He began to shower me with kisses, and as he thrust his tongue into my mouth, my nipples became thick and erect. I felt my pussy begin to pulse as his kisses became more intense and his hands roamed over my body, caressing my shoulders and tickling me along my rib cage. It was almost too much to bear. Oh god, I thought to myself, I have to feel this man's mouth on my cunt!

Almost as if reading my mind, Chet lifted me onto the conference table. He gently removed my nylons and began massaging my inner thighs. The feel of his fingers trailing up my legs and the way he clenched my calves when he spread my legs apart were so distracting that I almost forgot we were in a (semi) public place where we could be seen at almost any moment. But that only helped to make the experience more exciting for me.

By the time he turned his attention back to my breasts, my snatch was absolutely dripping with anticipation. I wanted to cry out, but I knew that others would be arriving for work and I didn't want to be heard. I wanted him to hurry, but at the same time I also loved the way he was gliding his hands slowly over my legs and stomach.

I could hear his breathing becoming more rapid as he drew my panties down and off, and soon I felt his warm breath between my legs. And then his tongue was on my clit, licking slowly, teasing me. I began to moan as his mouth engulfed my flesh, unable to keep quiet as his talented tongue brought me to an amazing orgasm. He then lifted me up to my feet and kissed me so we could share the wonderful taste of my come together.

Chet then turned me around and told me to bend over. I placed my hands on the table and spread my legs for him. He slipped his dick into me and began a slow, rhythmic pumping. Oh, how I wanted to scream out! His big cock was almost more than I could handle. He held onto my waist and picked up speed, slamming his prick into my cunt over and over again with a determination that I'd never experienced before. He reached around and grabbed my nipples, kneading them as I rocked back and forth on his massive rod. I was ready to feel his come burst into me. I felt another orgasm coming on and was thrilled when we came at the same time, our juices mingling and spilling out of my pussy and onto the edge of the table.

We both composed ourselves as best we could, rearranged our clothes and quickly went back to our desks like nothing happened. I tried hard to concentrate on my job, but thoughts of work took a back seat to thoughts of pleasure! I can't wait to get Chet into the conference room again, but with no one else around, so I can make as much noise as I want to!—*L.Q., Phoenix, Arizona*

Open Season

THEY TOOK THEIR NEW VAN TO THE DRIVE-IN, BUT THEY DIDN'T SEE MUCH OF THE MOVIE

*L*ast spring I finally bought a new van at the behest of my wife Ginny. Complete with curtains, a cooler and a full-size air mattress, it became our own private box at one of the few remaining drive-ins in the area. We would go every Saturday night. It really didn't matter what was playing, as the movie was secondary to the fun we had in the back of the van. It took us back to our days of courtship, and the anticipation that built up during the week was really exciting.

Usually Ginny dressed in tight terrycloth shorts or a slip dress, or some other sexy thing, for these evenings. One night she looked so sexy that I suddenly thought it was a hell of a waste to keep her all to myself. So I arranged to have Wally, a friend of ours who works with Ginny, meet us at the show later that evening.

You should have seen her that night. She wore a cut-off T-shirt that exposed the bottoms of her large breasts, and a pair of those form-fitting terrycloth shorts. Ginny is on the short side at five feet three, and most of her hundred and twenty pounds are topside. She has long brown hair and big brown eyes, and her perfume drives me crazy.

We arrived at the drive-in, got into the back of the van, arranged our refreshments and commenced to have our little party. Half an hour later Wally showed up, right where I told him we'd be.

By that time Ginny and I had had a couple of beers each, and Wally brought more. Ginny and I were lying on the air mattress, and after a while I suggested that Wally crawl in on the other side of her for the remainder of the show.

Although she hadn't planned for this, Ginny was very congenial, not to mention buzzed, and more than a little horny. Still, she did her best to try to keep her shorts from riding up. Not easy, considering that we were all lying on our stomachs and elbows, watching the movie out of the back of the van.

After a while I put my hand on her back and lightly massaged it, working my hand under her shirt. I leaned over to kiss her left ear, and heard her swallow hard when my tongue touched her earlobe. By this time my hand had gone down onto her ass.

I heard her gasp quietly when she realized that Wally's hand had found its way onto her leg, and was working into her shorts. She looked at me with dreamy, lust-filled eyes, and I smiled and nodded at her.

Wally was on his side now, his hand inside her shorts, and from her reactions I guessed he had one or two fingers in her cunt. After a series of soft, slow moans, she rolled onto her side facing me, and pressed her ass against him.

I pulled her shirt up, then sucked at her milky-white tits and sweet nipples as Wally's hand continued playing deep inside her shorts. He removed it briefly as I reached down and pulled those shorts off her. As I'd suspected, she wore no panties. Wally's hand quickly returned to cover her pussy mound, and she moaned deeply.

I lay back now, not wanting to miss anything, taking in the incredibly hot vision before me. Ginny was looking at me with half-closed eyes, moaning more loudly and twisting her body, squirming her gorgeous ass against Wally's loins as he sucked on her ear and neck while his fingers probed her wet pussy. She turned to face him now, scrabbling at his zipper and pulling out his big cock. As she massaged it he put a hand under her leg and spread her cunt wide. Their crotches pressed together and I could see her rubbing her slit along the shaft of his prick.

Finally, the head of his cock disappeared between her tight pussy lips. With that Ginny's eyes opened wide, and she grunted, "Oh yeah! Deeper!" Her body pushed forward to accept the massive tool that invaded her, filling her lusty cunt as Wally began to thrust. Moans and grunts escaped from my wife's parted lips, his cock stretching her pussy walls as he went deeper than any man had gone before.

Ginny rolled over onto her back, spreading her legs wide to take even more of him. His movements were harder now, more forceful. Ginny was panting hard, and moaning, "Yes, fuck me, oh yeah!" Her large breasts bounced and shuddered with each stroke.

Then Wally cried out that he was coming and attempted to pull out, but Ginny wrapped her arms and legs about him and held him there, and in a moment they reached orgasm simultaneously, Wally filling my wife's stretched cunt with his come.

As he rolled off, I took his place, inserting my cock into what felt like a subway tunnel, big and wet. It didn't matter though, because in only moments I shot inside her, adding my come to his.

I sure am glad my wife talked me into getting a van!—*F.P., Asheville, North Carolina* ⚭

HIS WIFE GETS WORKED UP WHEN SHE WORKS OUT, ESPECIALLY WITH HIS FRIEND

*M*y wife Rebecca and I have been married for eighteen years. We have had a great marriage and a good sex life. But in any marriage, after a long time the sex tends to become routine, and for several years I had been trying to spice it up somewhat, but to little avail. Rebecca allowed me to buy her a few dildos, including a big thick one ten inches long, which she can take all the way. She enjoyed these, but on the whole her attitude toward sex was pretty traditional and straightforward.

I enjoy reading *Penthouse Letters*, especially the stories about a husband watching his wife seduce another man. I have a fantasy that I have told Rebecca about. It involves us going to a bar, but pretending not to know each other. Rebecca would dress very sexily, and at the bar she would find a good-looking man, dance with him and get them both excited with some belly-rubbing, hip-grinding slow dances. Then I would pretend to pick her up, and we would go home and have wild passionate sex. The good-looking stranger would stir up her emotions and I would reap the benefits. I tried to get her to act out this scenario, but she nixed the idea, saying that it was a fantasy and should remain just that.

Let me tell you a little about Rebecca. She is about five feet five inches, one hundred twenty-three pounds, and has a beautiful body, with small but firm breasts, and legs that are indescribable. She always gets second and third looks from guys, especially when showing off her body in something revealing—which I always urge her to do. She has bought lots of short skirts and shorts to display her assets. She says she does it for me, but I believe she enjoys it also. I am proud to be seen with her.

I work at a supply house, and had been there for many years when a guy named George came along and was given a cushy outside sales job, with a high-dollar income and lots of other perks. He was about thirty, and he hadn't worked his way up the ladder of success as I had, but was given the job because of politics and family ties. He was good-looking and a smooth talker, with a lot of charisma about him. I resented him at first, but after a while we became friends, and because of him my life became more interesting.

After we got to know each other, our families began spending time together. George's wife's name was Gracie, and they had two children. Our wives enjoyed each other and our children played well together.

Shortly after coming to work with us George joined a local gym and started working out with weights and taking a karate class. Evidently he had done this before, because he was in tip-top shape already, lean and muscular, with very little body fat.

I had piddled around with weights before, but not seriously. George kept encouraging me to be his workout partner, and finally I decided to give it a try. George encouraged me to work hard at it, and after a few months the results began to show. My wife noticed this, and decided she wanted to work out with us, if we would help her. I discussed it with George, and he said to bring her along. By this time George had a part-time job as a trainer and overseer at the gym, and he said he would help bring Rebecca along slowly.

At first Rebecca dressed very conservatively for our workout sessions, wearing long loose shorts and one of my T-shirts that was about three sizes too big for her. The three of us worked out together, and George gave her some tips about proper diet and toning up.

As fine as Rebecca already looked, she soon started looking even better. In fact, she looked terrific. Working out seemed to agree with her, not only physically but mentally also. She began to dress more sexily, in tights and low-cut tops, and even in skimpy shorts. Needless to say, she had everyone's attention. She had that sensuous, sultry look, and she loved it.

*   *   *

I soon noticed that George seemed to be paying extra-close attention to my pretty wife. Sometimes he would "accidentally" touch her
breasts while helping her on or off an exercise machine, or brush her
pussy through her tights while helping with leg extensions. When
he spotted her as she did bench presses, he would stand directly over
her, his cock just inches away from her luscious mouth.

When I mentioned this to Rebecca she just brushed it off as no
big deal. She never tried to avoid his touch, and in fact she always
asked him to spot her when she did the bench presses. She wouldn't
admit that having his cock that close to her was a turn-on for her,
but I wasn't fooled. They were playing a little game with each other,
but I felt that I was the winner, because after every work-out Rebecca
would be very horny, and would screw my brains out.

One day it became obvious to me that the stakes in the game were
getting higher. Rebecca was doing squats, with the bar behind her
neck. On her final set George jumped over to help her.

In doing squats the spotter stands behind the lifter and helps him
or her come up if necessary. George pressed his crotch into my wife's
ass and helped her with each up and down motion. This definitely
wasn't accidental contact; I could see him pressing his pelvis into the
cheeks of her ass. Rebecca seemed to enjoy it as much as he did, if
not more. She did fifteen reps instead of the usual ten. All the time
George kept his arms around my wife's waist to keep her from stumbling forward as he helped her.

When he stepped away as Rebecca racked the weights, I could see
the bulge in his shorts. Instead of being angry, I was actually turned
on, and I had to walk away to hide my own bulge. Mine was not as
big as George's, however, and I remember thinking that he must be
much longer and thicker in the cock than I was. As for Rebecca, her
breathing was heavier than usual, her chest was heaving and her
tights were wet—especially between her legs.

That night I suggested to Rebecca that maybe we should take a
break for a while. It had been a turn-on for me to watch my wife get
excited, but I knew they were getting close to the point of no return,
and I didn't want to lose both a wife and a friend. Rebecca admitted that George had been getting bolder, and to her surprise she was
enjoying it. She said he had really gotten to her that day. She even

said that the feeling of his firm masculinity pressing against her ass made her so wet and horny that she hadn't wanted to stop.

Finally my wife confessed that she had thought about screwing George, wondering what it would be like. As she talked about it she got so excited that when I knelt between her legs and tongued her dripping cunt, she came almost immediately.

On New Year's day the gym was closed, but none of us felt like foregoing our workout, and since George had a key we agreed to meet there in the afternoon. I had to go to the office that day to complete a little paperwork, so I told Rebecca to go ahead and I would meet them there when I got finished.

Upon leaving the office I headed straight for the gym. It was locked, but I had a key which George had given me some time earlier— a fact which both he and my wife had evidently forgotten. As I came through the side door, which was partially hidden by some bleachers, I saw Rebecca warming up. She was wearing silk running shorts and a tight tank top. I had never seen her in such a getup, and she looked extremely seductive. George was at the other end of the gym, also loosening up. I was about to announce myself when I heard Rebecca call to George. When he went over to her, she told him that her knee had been bothering her. She said she wanted to do some knee bends, and wanted him to spot her in case the knee went out. I hadn't been aware of any knee problem, but George quickly got into position to spot her. I stepped back behind the bleachers and peeked through them to see what would happen.

I couldn't believe what I heard Rebecca say next. She told George to stand really close to her, as he had the other day, because her legs were wobbly. Obligingly, George stood so close behind her that his cock once again pressed against her buttocks. The only thing separating them was the cloth of their shorts. He wrapped his arms around her waist and the two of them did a few reps. I could tell by the way her breasts moved that Rebecca wasn't wearing a bra, and I had a strong suspicion that she had no panties on either.

After a few knee bends, Rebecca took George's arms from around her waist and slowly put one of his hands on her breast and the other over her crotch. I couldn't believe it! My traditional straight-laced wife was turning into a vamp right before my eyes.

George slipped the straps of her tank top off her shoulders with one hand, while the other slid up under the leg of her shorts. As he pushed the shorts up, I could definitely see that I had been right about the panties.

As they stood there with George firmly pressed against my wife's back, he slowly but methodically worked his finger in and out of her moist slit. My homemaker wife laid her head back against him and began to moan, doing a different kind of knee bend now as she rode up and down on his probing finger. Both of them were getting hot and sweaty. Every now and then George would remove his finger from her soaking-wet pussy, lick it, run it across her lips and reinsert it. As he finger-fucked her he kissed and licked her neck and ears, which she loves. In a short while Rebecca exploded into orgasm, panting and hollering in a way I hadn't heard before. Her legs got weak and she almost collapsed to the floor, but George caught her.

My dick was throbbing, and I had to struggle to control my breathing as I shot a load of jism into my shorts.

But Rebecca wasn't through with George yet. As soon as she recovered her breath she reached down and opened his shorts. They fell down, and his swollen dick stood almost straight out. It was a good two to three inches longer than mine. Rebecca gasped and smiled when she saw it. Then she kissed him, ramming her tongue down his throat while she embraced his muscular body.

Then, grabbing his erection, she gently led him to the bench, where she lay down as though she were going to do some bench presses, asking George to stand behind her as if to spot her. As he leaned forward slightly, his cock pointed at her face. Grinning up at him, Rebecca told him she had thought of this many times. Then she took his huge shaft into her mouth and began to suck on it. She alternated between licking his balls and sucking his dick. When George started to come, she didn't remove his dick from her mouth, as she does with me, but swallowed his whole load, then licked the last drops off the tip of his dick. She was actually moaning as she did this.

Then she went on licking him and stroking him until his cock got hard again. "Oh god, fuck me!" my hot wife said.

George moved around the bench, then bent down and pulled off Rebecca's shorts. He parted her thighs and got down on top of her, and then became only the second man ever to enter my wife's pussy. Her body arching off the bench, Rebecca told George breathlessly that he was the only man she'd ever had besides me, and that he was bigger, and she wanted it all. As she grabbed his buttocks to pull him deeper, George began ramming vigorously into her. Rebecca was displaying a passion such as I had never seen before. It was obvious that she was in pure ecstasy. She kept moaning, "Oh, you feel so good, fuck me harder." She was bucking and grinding her hips into his. Sweating heavily, both of them exploded together wildly in what looked like an orgasm to top all orgasms.

And still it wasn't over. George picked her up and carried her to the chin-up bar. She held onto it while he draped her legs over his shoulders and began to tongue her wet, squirming pussy. Hanging on to the bar for dear life, my wife writhed and twisted until she had climaxed again.

Now George was rigid again, so they screwed one more time on the gym floor before calling it a day. Afterward my wife told him that it had been the most pleasurable workout she had ever had.

Still trying not to make any noise, I eased out the gym door and returned home. When Rebecca arrived I told her I'd had to work a little later than I'd expected, so I hadn't gone to the gym.

Rebbecca just smiled at me. "Really?" she said. "Did you think I forgot about George giving you that key? I knew you would be there, and when I saw you come in I figured you would enjoy what happened as much as I did. Only I didn't expect to enjoy it quite as much as all that!"

"Neither did I," I said. We grinned at each other. We were both so turned on that we fucked right there in the living room, and I came into her freshly screwed pussy after only a few strokes. But that was just the beginning. From there we moved to the bedroom, where we fucked and sucked each other all night long.

George has now moved away, and we're looking for a new workout partner. Rebecca is much freer in her attitude now, and she says she wouldn't rule out having sex with him, if he's attractive. I tell her I will make sure that he is.

Also, Rebecca went to the mall the other day and came home with a very sexy dress and some new high heels, saying that she thought we might now act out my fantasy about going out dancing. Kind of anticlimactic now though, don't you think?—*K.A., Columbus, Ohio*

WHEN HIS WIFE FINALLY FULFILLED
HIS FANTASY, SHE REALLY WENT ALL THE WAY

*M*y wife Sylvia and I are professional people in our thirties. Sylvia is five feet two and about a hundred and five pounds, with dark hair, a big beautiful set of breasts, a small waist and an ass that just begs to be fucked. I always took pretty good care of that.

I guess there are a lot of guys who fantasize about watching their wives get a big cock stuffed in their tight little pussies, and I'm no exception. Sylvia works in public relations, and I have a good management job in aerospace, and both careers require that we do a lot of entertaining and some traveling. I'm on trips about ten days a month, Sylvia a little less. At times I have said to her that I knew guys must hit on her sometimes during her trips, and kidded her about trying a little strange cock. At first she was kind of pissed that I would even kid about it. Then, one night while we were making love, she told me something that had happened on her most recent trip.

It had been one of those times when nothing had gone right, and the customer she'd been dealing with had been a real jerk. One of the customer's assistants happened to run into her the first evening, when she was nursing her misery over a drink at the bar. His name was Gil, and he was a good-looking guy about her age, with a great body. Sylvia said they hit it off pretty well. He apologized for the hard time his boss had given her, but explained that he treated all females that way at first. If they didn't back down, he generally ended up signing the contract. Gil gave her some suggestions as to how to handle him the next day. They had a couple more drinks together, and he took her to dinner at an upscale restaurant. They had some good wine with the meal, and after dinner he said he knew a nice place that played great music, if she would like to dance a little. He promised he would get her back to her hotel early.

Sylvia was really feeling the booze, and she figured what the hell, go for it. Gil seemed like a nice guy, and he was looking better as the night went on. They drove in his car, a little sports model built for two. She had a little trouble getting into the small car, and her dress slid up around her ass, giving Gil a good look at her little white panties before she was able to get herself arranged in the seat. She noticed a large bulge in his pants as he stood looking down at her. When she embarrassingly mumbled something about small cars, he just smiled and said they did have some advantages.

All the way to the club Sylvia was thinking about the bulge in his pants, wondering what his cock looked like and what kind of lover he would be. Once they got to the place they found a small table and ordered more drinks. She said she knew she was getting a little drunk, but by then she didn't really care.

After a couple of close dances and a couple more drinks, Gil was openly running his hands up and down her back as they danced, moving them lower and lower until he was playing with the cheeks of her ass, and pushing his rock-hard cock into her belly as he held her close. Her panties were sopping wet and she was getting horny as hell. Gil suddenly bent down and kissed her, a long wet tongue-sucking kiss that took her by surprise. At the same time he took one of her breasts in his hand and tweaked the hard nipple between his thumb and forefinger.

At that point Sylvia reluctantly broke away from him. With an effort, she reminded him that she was a married woman, and did not have sex with other men. She said she was sorry if she had misled him, but she wanted to go back to her hotel.

I guess Gil must have been a real gentleman. He said he was sorry if he had done anything to offend her. He was also married, but had been so attracted to her that he'd gotten carried away.

The next day her meeting was a success, due to the instructions Gil had given her on how to handle his boss. She got the contract and headed home.

After Sylvia told me that story she apologized, saying she was sorry she had let things go as far as she had. I'm sure she expected me to be pissed; but instead I found it very exciting. Just thinking about my wife with this strange man gave me a raging hard-on. Unable to hide my arousal, I told her that this was one of my favorite fantasies.

Sylvia looked at me for a long time, and finally said, "You mean you *want* me to fuck another man?" She was almost in shock. She said I didn't love her any more, and carried on like that for a few minutes. I told her I loved more than ever, and that all I wanted was for her to get as much pleasure as she could from sex. I told her that thinking about her taking another man's cock in her mouth or pussy excited me very much, but that if she decided to do it, she had to promise me that she would tell me all the details, and not keep any secrets.

Sylvia said she didn't want to talk about it any more, and the subject didn't come up again until a few weeks later, when we were invited to a dinner party hosted by a guy named Ray, who worked for another company. Ray and I had run into each other on business trips from time to time, and had become good friends. We would generally get together whenever he was in town. Ray was a horny bastard and never missed a chance to get some strange pussy. He had females in damn near every town he had ever visited.

On this particular night, Ray and one of his partners had just closed a big sale and were planning to celebrate. Ray called me at my office and invited Sylvia and me to join them.

Ray had never made any bones about how sexy he thought my wife was, and he had told me a number of times, more or less kiddingly, that if he ever got the chance he was going to fuck her. I generally didn't pay much attention to that, because I knew Sylvia was not very impressed with him; she said he bragged about his conquests too much.

When I called Sylvia to let her know we were invited out, she said she had to come into town for some shopping and would meet me at the restaurant around five. I was just getting ready to leave my office when a problem developed, and by the time I was finally able to leave it was almost six. I hurried to the restaurant. It was "happy hour" and the parking lot was full, so I had to park way out in the back. I knew the layout of the place pretty well, and I decided to go in through the employees' door, which would lead me into the bar area.

I stood at the far end of the bar, my eyes adjusting to the dimness as I looked around for Sylvia and the others. I finally spotted them in a corner booth. My wife was sitting between Ray and another guy, and it looked like they hadn't waited for me before starting the party. Sylvia had worn a dress that I always liked. It was cut low in front and showed a lot of cleavage, and none of that was lost on these guys. I stood and watched for a couple of minutes. Ray had his hand on her shoulder and was leaning close, saying something to her, and at the same time looking down at her boobs. She tilted her head back and laughed at whatever he said. I could tell that she was a little high. The guy on her other side leaned over to her also, and his hand disappeared under the table. I was sure that that hand was on her bare leg, probably testing to see how far she would let him go.

Then Ray pulled her to him and planted a big kiss on her mouth. That got her a little off-balance, and her legs parted enough so that the other guy's hand slipped all the way up to her crotch, and I was sure he was getting a good feel of her panty-clad pussy.

My reaction to all this was complicated. First of all, I was really pissed at Ray and his buddy for taking advantage of my wife. Second, I was pissed at my wife for not objecting to all their groping. And third, I was astounded at myself, because I had the biggest hard-on of my life! I realized that I was turned on by watching my wife get hit on by two guys, especially since she seemed to like it so much.

I figured I'd better make my appearance before they got arrested or asked to leave. I went out the back and walked around to the front door, making a big entrance. I slid in next to my wife, gave her a big sloppy kiss and told her she looked fantastic. I said it was probably a good thing I wasn't much later, or these guys would probably be attacking her. That got a big laugh from all of them.

Ray introduced me to his partner, whose name was Vincent. He had made a reservation for dinner, and now we were informed that our table was ready.

Dinner was great, with good food and good wine, and we were all pretty relaxed. Shortly after we finished, a small combo started playing, and Vincent asked Sylvia to dance. They danced about three dances, and I noticed he was holding her closer with each number, and running his hands up and down her back, finally sliding them onto her ass. They came back to the table with Vincent sporting a large bulge in his pants. Then Ray danced with her, and it was pretty much the same thing. He was openly feeling her up whenever he thought I wasn't looking.

At about ten-thirty Vincent announced he was booked on a midnight flight and had to leave. He gave Sylvia a big kiss and told her he'd really enjoyed the evening, and that she was a beautiful woman, and with that he was gone. Sylvia then asked Ray where he was staying that night. He replied that he had planned to go home on

Vincent's flight, but a last-minute meeting had come up, and he had to stay over till the next day. He said he hadn't yet booked a place for the night. Sylvia looked at me and said, "Why doesn't Ray stay at our place? We have plenty of room, and we can all have a nightcap at home."

I had a hunch that something had been discussed between them while they were dancing, but I just played along. When we got to the parking lot I told them to go on home, as my car was almost out of gas. I would try to find a station and fill up, then follow them home. So off they went, Ray following behind my wife.

Actually I had plenty of gas; I just wanted to give them some time alone, to see how far they would go. I knew Sylvia was feeling no pain, and all the groping she'd gotten was bound to have her pretty horny. I went back to the bar, had another drink, chatted with the bartender for about an hour, then headed for home.

When I got to our street I parked in front of a neighbor's house, then walked around our house and into our backyard. It was pitch black and I had to be careful not to trip, but I arrived at the back of the house, where there was a big picture window that let me see into our family room. I kept back in the darkness so they couldn't see me, and peeked in.

What I saw almost floored me. My wife was wearing the sheerest black negligee I have ever seen. It clung to every curve of her body. Her big firm breasts with their large nipples were just barely contained by the gown; her neat little triangle of dark pubic hair was faintly visible, as was the entire outline of her sexy body.

They had evidently had at least one drink, and now Sylvia said they needed another. She moved in the direction of the bar, but Ray stepped in front of her, pulling her into his arms and kissing her on the neck and shoulder. Her head fell back and I heard her gasp. Then he drew her face to his and kissed her, his tongue playing tonsil tennis in her mouth. In another moment she was responding, putting her arms around his neck and returning the open-mouthed kiss. In no time they were moaning and groaning and exploring each other's bodies.

My cock was throbbing like a drum as I watched Ray strip off the black negligee, and then tear out of his own clothes. Sylvia took one look at his cock, pointing straight at her, and immediately went down on her knees. With complete abandon she began licking and kissing his prick. She sucked both his balls into her mouth and slowly started jacking him off. After alternating between his cock and his balls, she surprised me by suddenly taking his stiff pole all the way down her throat. She pushed him onto his back and got on top of him in a 69 position. I stood there looking at my wife's up-thrust ass while she blew my old friend, who at the same time was munching on her hot pussy. I knew if I stayed there I was going to come in my pants. Instead, I decided to join the fun.

I didn't know how they would react when I walked into the family room, but I should have realized that they knew I would be coming home at any time. Sylvia had decided to act on my fantasy, and Ray had been only too happy to go along. They barely paused in what they were doing as I came in. That was fine with me. I tore off my clothes and applied myself to my wife's beautiful squirming ass, first loosening it up with my finger and then sliding my eager cock slowly but surely into her tight narrow tunnel. She pushed back against me and moaned a little, still sucking on Ray's shaft. I knew I couldn't last long, so I concentrated on watching her and Ray go at each other. They were both obviously close to coming, so I started pumping my wife's ass faster and faster. Finally we all exploded at about the same time, in a mind-blowing three-way climax that left all of us limp, exhausted and happy.

We rested for a few minutes, then had another drink and talked about what had just happened. The talk just made us horny again, and soon Ray and I were both hard and ready for more action. My lovely wife was treated to the best fucking of her life that night, and when Ray left the next morning, we both agreed that it had been a great experience, and that it made our love for each other all the stronger.

We are looking forward to Ray's next visit. He says he has a friend he wants us to meet—a black man. Sylvia is as eager as I am to give it a try, and I'll let you know how it turns out in my next letter.—*S.C., Charleston, South Carolina* ⚬━▪

A HAWAIIAN VACATION GOT HIS WIFE PERMANENTLY HOOKED ON WELL-HUNG YOUNG STUDS

*F*or the last year, my wife Irma has been having a series of affairs with men in their late teens and early twenties. She is forty-two, but still has a terrific figure. At five feet four, with her long auburn hair, green eyes, wide mouth and slightly upturned nose, she is a real sight for hungry young eyes; and since she dresses to emphasize her sexuality, she comes across as inviting and accessible in every way.

Previously, during the course of our twenty-year marriage, Irma had had a few discreet affairs. She was always quite flirtatious, mainly because it turned her on sexually, but also because she knew it excited me. I always liked the fact that other men would swarm about her, and always totally supported her in her exhibitionism. Though she liked to turn on men by exposing herself, there were only a few occasions when she let someone else get truly intimate with her. But all that changed last summer.

We had decided to take our vacation in Hawaii. I asked Irma to bring along her most revealing and sexy clothing, and she was more than happy to comply. She took several skimpy sundresses, some short skirts, very short shorts, a few halter tops, a see-through blouse, thong bikinis, skimpy underwear and high-heeled sandals. She also painted her fingernails and toenails bright red for the trip, and at night she made up her face to accent her lips and eyes. Needless to say, everywhere she went she drew long stares. It was hard for me to walk along with her, since just looking at her would get me sexually aroused.

One afternoon I came back early from a golf game. I knew Irma had gone to sunbathe on the beach, and given the skimpiness of her bathing suit, I thought she was unlikely to be alone for long. But I didn't expect what happened.

When I got to the door of our room, I heard a commotion inside. There seemed to a couple of male voices, and above them I could hear Irma shouting, "Fuck me deeper! Harder!"

I didn't know what to do. Rather than go inside, I just listened at the door for what seemed like an hour or so. The men kept saying things like "Unbelievable!" and, "This is what dreams are made of!" and, "No one will ever believe this!"

Irma, for her part, kept shouting in ecstasy, saying things like, "Let me suck you deeper!" and, "Do it to me again!" and, "Your staying power is fantastic!"

Finally the door opened and two guys came out of the room. They looked about eighteen or nineteen. I watched them leave, and then I went in. Irma was still on the bed, totally naked and spread-eagled. There was come all over the sheets and her body. All she said when she saw me was, "Nirvana!"

She then told me to take off my clothes and fuck her. I had an incredible erection. She took it in her mouth and sucked it for a minute before I flung myself on her open body. Although her cunt was stretched and slushy, I had a quick, intense orgasm.

Irma then told me that she thought she would never be the same. She said those young boys had been fantastic. They would come and still say hard. She said that in about two hours with them she must have had more than a dozen orgasms. The pure sexual ecstasy of what she had just gone through was unbelievable, and it was something she thought she would want again and again. Dressing like a slut was no longer enough for her, she told me. She wanted to *be* and *feel like* a slut, to express her sexuality no matter what, and to be available for young studs whenever she could.

All I could do was nod and say, "I love you, and I want you to do anything at all that makes you happy."

We had another week in Hawaii, and Irma arranged to get together with her young hunks every day. On the next to last day, she had them bring two other friends to our room, where she proceeded to service all of them fully. This time she let me watch, and I can't tell you what a thrill it was to see my gorgeous wife tossing about on the bed with four guys, moaning and gasping with ecstatic pleasure as they used every part of her body. She let them fuck her two and three at a time, and she came and came, until she wore them all out. I could barely keep myself from jerking off as I watched, and when they left I again jumped on her and fucked her wet cunt for about ten seconds before I shot off.

While Irma is more discreet at home, she still regularly picks up young guys. Rather than risk what the neighbors will say, she usually gets them to go with her to some cheap motel. She tells me everything, and we always have great sex when she does. She now wants me to film her fucking a bunch of young, well-hung guys, so she can have something to look at in the future. Oddly, the more wanton she becomes the more I hunger for her, and I just know that we will be together always.—*M.D., Tucson, Arizona* ○┼▪

HIS WIFE IS HOOKED ON COCK, AND HE'S HOOKED ON HER CREAM-FILLED TWINKIE

I'm married to a beautiful woman named Daisy who could easily pass for a high-fashion model. Her long, sleek legs, beautiful ass and perfect C-cup tits always draw stares from the men she passes, and her lush lips and deep blue eyes are made for stirring up sexual thoughts. But what I love most is her silky-haired, always-wet pussy, which is the sweetest I've ever tasted. I can't keep my tongue out of it. Recently, I found out why her pussy is always so wet. It caught me by surprise to learn that my wife is hooked on hard cock, and not just mine!

One night I bumped into Liz, an old friend of Daisy's from years back, at a bar after work. We started talking about old times, and the more we talked the more I found out about my wife. I could never get Daisy to talk about what kind of sex life she had before we got married, but the fact that she was great in bed led me to believe she was quite experienced. Liz said that Daisy was always getting hit on and had lots of men at her beck-and-call. It seemed that all the guys she dated got into her pants, and she thought nothing of fucking three or four guys a week. Liz even thought that Daisy was a nympho because of all the fucking she did. Liz was surprised when we got married, and thought I must be pretty damn good in the sack to keep Daisy faithful. Still, I had a raging hard-on thinking about Daisy fucking all those guys.

I work nights, and sometimes when I'd get home and climb in bed with Daisy, I'd slide my hand to her pussy and find it hot and creamy. I always thought she'd been masturbating because she's constantly horny, but after talking to Liz I began to wonder. When I saw two used rubbers in the trash, I *knew* she was fucking other men.

Surprisingly, the thought of my woman being hooked on cock didn't upset me. I know she could have had any man she wanted, but she married me, so I was confident that she loved me. We have a great relationship and I didn't want to do anything to spoil it, so I just kept quiet. Then I started fantasizing about seeing her getting fucked.

I started looking forward to the nights I came home and found her pussy filled with come. I got hooked on the smell and taste of her freshly fucked twat. At first she tried to keep me from going down on her. She'd stiffen up as I removed her wet panties and spread her legs, obviously worried that I would notice the come matting her pubic hair. I made it a point of telling her how sweet she tasted and how much I loved her creamy pussy. Then one night as I was going down on her, Daisy grabbed my head, pulled me hard against her cunt and had three orgasms in a row, her body shaking as she begged me to keep sucking her.

Eventually she got more and more turned on by the fact that I was licking her come-filled pussy and not suspecting a thing—or so she thought. Some nights she'd take my hand as soon as I was in bed and put it between her legs so I could feel how wet she was, knowing I would go down on her. I was getting sloppy seconds four or five nights a week, and I was loving it. Our sex life was never better!

But what I really wanted was to watch her with one of her lovers. I started leaving work early, and soon enough I got lucky. I saw a strange car in the driveway, so I parked down the road and sneaked into our backyard. It was just after dusk, and with the lights on in the house I could see through the living room window perfectly.

There was a man sitting on our sofa, but all I could see was the back of his head. There was no sign of my wife. Then the guy let out a groan and his head fell back. Daisy stood up with a sly smile and licked her lips. She was wearing a black silk robe, but it was hanging open and she was totally naked underneath it. When she slipped the robe off her shoulders and let it fall to the floor, the man stood and grabbed her breasts, tweaking her nipples. My stomach churned and my dick throbbed as the pair began to kiss.

When she led him down the hall to our bedroom, I noticed that the only thing he had on was his shirt. When I saw the bedside lamp come on, I moved over to the bedroom window. The curtains had a two-inch gap, and the window was cracked open just the way I'd left it that morning.

I recognized the guy. His name was Chuck, and he was one of the trainers at Daisy's health club. I'd met him before and found him as friendly as he was handsome and muscular. "What's the matter, baby?" I heard him ask. "Isn't your husband taking care of you?"

"He tries, God bless him," Daisy told him, "but you know I need more than he's able to give me." Her hand was stroking his prick as they stood next to the bed, groping each other. His manhood hardened in her grasp.

Daisy turned around and lay back on the bed. "Fuck me now!" she pleaded. Chuck wasted no time mounting her, and she was moaning as soon as he filled her pussy. He kept asking her questions while he fucked her, and her replies seemed to turn both of them on even more.

"Does your husband fuck you this good?" he demanded.

"No," she panted in reply.

"Is my cock bigger than his?"

"Oh, yes!"

"Whose cock do you like more?"

"Yours!"

"Will you think about me the next time he fucks you?"

"Yes!"

"What do you want?"

"Oh, please don't stop! Fuck me!"

"Where should I come?"

"Oh, God, come in my cunt, please!"

Then she came, her arms and legs wrapped around him, twisting underneath him as a monstrous orgasm consumed her. All throughout her climax, my wife's lover didn't let up his assault. He buried his cock inside her, his ass flexing and his balls contracting as he emptied his load in her twat. I came all over my hand as I watched this erotic scene play itself out.

Chuck got dressed and left shortly afterward. Daisy pulled on a pair of panties and crawled into bed, looking completely spent.

I went back to my car and waited for half an hour, then pulled into the driveway at my usual time. Daisy pretended to be sleeping as I slid into bed. The smell of sex was still strong as I cuddled against her. She grabbed my hand and guided it to her panties, making sure I felt how wet they were. I put my hand inside to feel her box, and she lifted her hips and shed her underwear so I would have an open invitation to give her head. I sucked her nipples until they were hard, then kissed my way down her sweaty belly to her cunt. After my tongue finally penetrated her pussy, she grabbed me by the head and moaned, "Oh, yes, lick it good, honey! Lick it good!"

It wasn't long before I was positive that my wife got off on the idea of me sucking another man's come from her pussy. She came three times in ten minutes as I ate her out. Then I slid my cock into the hottest cunt I'd ever felt and started fucking her passionately, wondering if she was thinking about her lover's big cock while mine was inside her. We came together in a great climax, and she told me she loved me before we fell asleep.

Things have only gotten better since then. Over the last month or so I've watched my wife fuck four different guys, three of them more than once. I'm planning a romantic vacation for us soon, and I hope to get her seduced and fucked by more than one guy at our resort. I'm one husband who just loves sharing his wife's pussy!
—A.R., Mason City, Iowa ○—▪

A NIGHT OF CELEBRATION AND A WILD WAGER MAKE WINNERS OF THEM ALL

*A*bout a year ago, my wife Meryl and I had a small party to celebrate a promotion I'd gotten. As the night wore on and the drinks took effect, everyone began feeling pretty good. Meryl was dancing with most of the guys there and put on quite a show, because she becomes kind of an exhibitionist when she's had too much to drink. She was wearing a black mini-dress and black stockings. The guys really liked it and more than a few times I saw the guys rubbing and squeezing my wife's ass as she did a bump-and-grind with them.

The party started thinning out around midnight and soon the only people left were my wife, myself and two of my friends. One of my friends suggested we play darts. We began making some friendly bets until my wife suggested that we up the ante. She suggested that my friend Bud bet five hundred dollars on the next game if I bet her. I thought she was kidding, but she got a big grin on her face and said she wouldn't have suggested it if she didn't hope I'd lose!

I figured that my wife must have gotten really turned on by all her flirting! Bud must have, too, because he took me up on it even though I'd won the first three games. Meryl smiled again and went back to cleaning the night's mess. As she cleaned everyone was getting distracted by the sight of her stocking tops and the brief glimpses of her little ass we got when she leaned over.

As fate would have it, I actually lost that game. My wife laughed when she heard Bud's cheer. Even I was secretly thrilled about paying up when Bud said he wanted to collect. My wife got very excited as Bud walked over to her and put his arm around her waist and led her to the recliner. Meryl looked over at me. I couldn't move.

Bud stood in front of the chair and spun Meryl around to face me. By the faraway look in her eyes, it became obvious that she suddenly realized how much she was going to enjoy herself. Bud ran his hands down from her shoulders over her breasts and down her stomach all the way to mid-thigh. Meryl shivered as he tickled her flesh with his nails. Then he caressed her body back upwards. His hands brought the hem of her skirt with them and soon he began rubbing my wife's panty-covered pussy. Meryl began to moan and sway as Bud kissed her neck and ground his crotch against her ass. My other friend Dave came over to watch the events unfold, obviously hoping he would be getting some of the action. Soon Bud's fingers were inside my wife's panties, sliding in and out of her pussy.

As Bud began to frig my wife faster, she leaned her head back and urged him on, grabbing his hand and holding on fast. Meryl guided Bud's fingers along the outside of her cunt lips when she needed time to breathe and made sure that he worked his way back to her clit as she got closer to coming. The faster he fingered her the more out of control she went, until it was clear she would soon come.

The pace picked up until I saw my wife have a long, shattering orgasm. Bud held her up as her legs started to give out. Meryl would have cried out but Bud had been kissing her deeply and his tongue was down her throat. After she came back down to earth, Meryl became even more excited about what was happening.

Meryl turned to look at me for a second but Bud spun her back around and rested his hands on her shoulders. Meryl slowly went down to her knees. Bud sat on the chair with Meryl on the floor looking up at him. He unzipped his pants, pulled out his cock and stroked it. He told Meryl to touch it but she hesitated briefly. I knew she wanted to blow him, but she was afraid of my reaction. Finally Bud looked deep in her eyes, pulled her close and put his cock to her lips. He rubbed his cockhead all around her face and then told her to suck it. She opened her mouth and then began blowing him. Meryl was worried about sucking a cock other than mine—especially right in front of me—but I let her know it was okay.

She got into it quickly and soon Bud came in her mouth. Meryl was caught off-guard but managed to swallow all his sperm. When he was done, Meryl licked Bud's cock clean. She thought her fun was over, but it was just beginning. Bud told her to crawl over to Dave and suck him off, too. Meryl looked so sexy on her hands and knees that I almost came in my pants. She crawled up to Dave and licked her lips as she pulled out his cock. Less than a minute later Dave came in her mouth too, and she wiggled her ass sexily back and forth as she wiped the come from her lips. When Meryl was done swallowing Dave's sperm, Bud walked over, stood her up, took her by the hand and led her upstairs to our bedroom.

He motioned Dave to follow but told me to stay out of it, saying this was between the three of them. For the next several hours I listened to the bed banging against the wall, springs creaking and Meryl's moans, howls and screams as my two friends took turns fucking the living hell out of her.

After Bud and Dave left the next morning I went to check on her. Meryl was on the bed, exhausted and limp. There were several huge wet spots and stains on the sheets. When I walked up to her I noticed that her pussy was gaping open and so filled with come that it practically flowed out of her. I noticed something else: her asshole was stretched as wide as a half-dollar and she had a couple of hickeys speckling her butt. I rolled her over and saw dried come stains on her bush and her tits. But the real kicker was seeing a couple more hickeys covering her thighs, stomach, neck and breasts.

Meryl stayed in bed all day after that and didn't mention what had happened. The strangest part of all was that later on she actually thanked me for it and told me that she'd fantasized that something like that would happen, although she never thought it would. She was pleasantly surprised and said she had a great time. I gently kissed her and for the next week waited on her hand and foot. Since then Meryl has gotten very uninhibited and isn't afraid to do anything sexually anymore.—*F.D., Englishtown, New Jersey* ⊶▪

A LONG WEEKEND AND A SEXY STRANGER HELP THEM RENEW THEIR LOVE

*M*y wife and I have been married for over twenty years. While we're not kids anymore—I'm forty-three and she's forty—we're in pretty good shape and still enjoy our sex life together.

We recently had the rare opportunity to get away for a four-day weekend without our two pre-teen kids. After dropping them off at my mother's house, we headed to the airport, looking forward to our extended weekend of sun, surf and sex. Thanks to my wife's successful career and our booming stock portfolio, we had spared little expense in booking reservations at a very posh Caribbean resort.

We arrived late in the afternoon and checked into our suite. My wife suggested we go down and check out the beach and quickly started changing into her bathing suit. I for one was more interested in going down and checking out my wife's still-plentiful charms. The sight of her naked, voluptuous body, big breasts and ample fanny still gets me horny after all our years together. But I figured there would be plenty of time for lovemaking over the next few days, so I stuffed my hard-on into my bathing suit and off we went.

The beach and the water were beautiful, so we enjoyed what was left of the afternoon relaxing on the beach and sipping a few drinks. While we were there, I noticed a guy lying on a lounge chair about thirty feet from us, apparently engrossed in a novel. He looked to be in his mid-thirties and was quite fit and somewhat handsome. Although he seemed distracted by his book, he did glance up and take a good look at my wife a couple of times. I mentioned it to her and she just smirked, saying that she had checked him out too, and he wasn't bad at all. When we got up to leave, we made eye contact with the stranger and said hello.

Back in our suite, the sun and the drinks had made us a little too relaxed to have sex but I figured the next morning we would have one hell of a time. My sexy wife even gave me a great cock-teasing when we showered together, fondling my dick and balls and telling me how she'd fuck the hell out of me before breakfast the next morning.

After dinner we decided to go to one of the lounges that featured dancing to a soft-rock band. I'm not big on dancing but my wife likes it and since we were on vacation, I thought, What the hell? When we sat down and ordered a drink, who should be sitting at the next table but our novel-reading beach friend? When he noticed us, he nodded and held up his glass in greeting. I'm not quite sure what possessed me at the moment, but I went over, we introduced ourselves and I asked him if he wanted to join us. He said that since he was alone he'd love some company.

He came over to our table and I introduced Paul to my wife. He was quite talkative, probably from being by himself for the last couple of days. Apparently Paul, who like my wife had a busy career in sales and marketing, had been divorced in the last six months and decided to take a much-needed vacation by himself. He told us his work kept him busy so he didn't date much, but he had hoped to meet some people on this vacation. So far, he said, almost everyone he met was with somebody or, as he put it, just not very interesting.

Paul turned out to be a lot of fun and we all had a great time partying together. We took turns dancing with my wife, who loved the opportunity to hold the attention of two men. She was unusually outgoing toward our new friend, too, and seemed taken by him. I noticed during one slow song that Paul took my wife to the far corner of the dance floor, where they seemed to be doing a slow grind against one another. It occurred to me that maybe all this male attention and being on vacation in this exotic locale would make my wife hornier than ever. At least I hoped it would.

When we bid good-night to Paul and returned to our suite, we had a nightcap and recounted what had been a great day. I teased my wife that I thought Paul had the hots for her and asked her what she thought of him. She would only acknowledge that she thought he was nice but downplayed any sexual attraction between them (at least on her part) and quickly changed the subject.

I awoke the next morning thinking that I had died and gone to heaven. My wife was kneeling over me, sucking my tremendously horny cock to full life. I had always fantasized about my wife waking me up that way, but in all our years together she had never done so. When she noticed I was awake, she told me to go freshen up and come back to bed fast because she needed a good fucking. I couldn't believe my ears—or the sudden change in my usually straight-laced wife—but I was excited as hell and not about to complain.

While brushing my teeth it occurred to me that my wife's unusual behavior might have been fueled by Paul's attention to her the previous evening. Since I had always fantasized about my conservative wife being naughty and unfaithful—at least once—I decide to test the waters. My wife sometimes played into my fantasy to get me excited by saying that yes, she would like a different lover, but never agreed to do it for real. Something was different this time, though. We were far from home and I knew she had a real candidate.

When I got back to bed, my wife was anxious to resume sucking my cock, but I stopped her and shyly asked what had come over her. She said she just had a serious case of the hots for me, but I said I thought that the previous night out dancing with Paul had made her that randy. She said to shut up, what difference did it make and repeated her desire for a hot fucking. As she tried to grab my cock, I pulled back and told her that I thought she should go to Paul's room and give all three of us a thrill we'd never forget.

Before she could tell me I was out of my mind, I stressed that we were in another world far from home and knew an attractive single guy who was undoubtedly horny as hell. The opportunity would never be better. At that point she asked me if I had lost my desire for her and was I trying to push her off on a stranger. I responded that since we were out to enjoy ourselves for a few days maybe we should indulge some fantasies, and I admitted that the thought of her having sex with Paul was a tremendous turn-on. I spent the next several minutes explaining my desire for her to be with another man, admitting that I didn't know why but that it aroused me to unbelievable heights. Finally a devilish grin appeared across her face and she agreed to do it.

Since she'd already showered, all she had to do was put on some makeup and pick out a sexy outfit. As she was preparing herself and babbling about how she couldn't believe she was doing this, she suddenly had a panic attack wondering how she would approach him. She asked what to do if he wasn't interested. I assured her that there was no doubt he would want her. All she had to do was knock on his door and tell him that she found him very attractive and nature would take care of the rest. If he had the least bit of interest in my whereabouts, I told her to tell him I was taking a walk along the beach.

That seemed to settle my wife down, and she was actually brimming with confidence when she slipped on a wicked black teddy and matching black heels. In order to conceal her wear from the other guests, she put on a white terrycloth robe just as she was ready to leave. I told her to have a good time and said I'd be waiting to hear all the naughty details and have some fun myself. We kissed and off she went.

I have to admit that the two hours my wife was gone were exhilarating. I was practically climbing the walls, imagining what must be taking place in Paul's suite as I sat alone in our room with a raging hard-on. Were they going down on each other? Was Paul licking and sucking on my wife's big, sexy breasts? Were the sight and feel of another man's hard cock thrilling my wife? Was Paul's cock bigger than mine? Was Paul, with great self-control and the ability to last long, driving my wife to one orgasm after another? The thoughts going through my mind were thrilling.

Finally, after what seemed like an eternity, my wife entered our room. Her quiet demeanor—combined with a shit-eating grin on her face—told me all had gone as hoped for. She laid down next to me on the bed and slowly recounted all the lusty details. It turned out that what I had imagined might have taken place did, and then some. She admitted that the sex had been incredible, partly due to Paul's prowess and partly due to the naughtiness of being with another man. She anxiously asked if I still loved her and I assured her that I did, more than ever. In fact I told her that at that moment I had more desire than I had ever had for her. With that we began making love, although my wife was merely accommodating me, as she was clearly satiated. In spite of that, I was filled with lust as I visualized their tryst. I came almost immediately.

The rest of the vacation went along in a similar pattern, with my wife getting together with Paul two other times. He always thought I was walking the beach totally unaware of what was going on, but that didn't matter to me.—*L.F., New York, New York*

A CHANCE MEETING HELPS COLLEGE BUDDIES
TEACH EACH OTHER A LESSON

*I*n college my frat brother Nat was one of those men that women just couldn't resist. His ability to seduce the opposite sex was legendary, and he usually wound up bedding two or three new coeds every week.

I always thought his exploits were great, because he fucked most of these women in his room, where I could watch by sneaking through our adjoining bathroom and peeking around his door. I can't tell you how many times I beat off watching him pile driving some sexy young thing. Giving credit where it's due, Nat really was a stud. He was tall, trim and handsome, and he definitely knew his way around a woman's body. Then there was the matter of his sexual prowess: being hung like and having the stamina of the proverbial horse.

After graduation we parted ways and fell out of touch. That could have been the end of the story, except that after three years my new bride, Sandy, and I ran into him at a telemarketing seminar we were attending.

When I introduced them I couldn't help but notice that familiar old look of lust in Nat's eyes as he checked out Sandy's luscious body. She stands just over five-foot-six and has a 36C-24-35 figure. Just like I'd seen him do hundreds of times before, Nat turned on the charm and started flirting with her. He wormed his way into joining us for dinner, where he continued to work on Sandy during the entire meal.

Seeing him in action again reminded me of watching him fucking all those coeds. I couldn't help but wonder about him seducing her. After dinner I asked her what she had thought of him, and she replied, "He's sweet, and so good-looking, too."

The next morning Nat walked with me to the opening session, but he left right after the first speaker got up to talk. I had a sneaking suspicion that my wife was going to be his agenda for the morning, but since I was sitting there with my boss, I couldn't follow him. I also couldn't get the image of him fucking Sandy out of my head.

She and I had made arrangements to meet for lunch. When Sandy arrived Nat was with her. They had been together the entire morning. Sandy's nervous energy and Nat's typically cocky demeanor made me suspect that he had indeed gotten into her panties.

There was no session that afternoon, so Sandy and I played some miniature golf then went swimming. She was being more like her old self again until Nat showed up. Her reaction to him was very apprehensive, like she was afraid of what he might say or do.

She seemed in a hurry to get away from him, and she asked if we could go to a concert that one of her favorite groups was giving. I said sure, so she took a shower while I went to buy the tickets. Unfortunately, when I asked the desk clerk where to purchase them, he told me that the concert had been sold out for weeks.

After I returned to the pool area I noticed Nat hanging around outside the sliding glass patio door to our room. My heart skipped a beat when he slowly opened the door and stepped inside. With mixed emotions clouding my brain, I ran to the patio and peeked in. I could hear the shower running and saw Nat standing at the open bathroom door. He was casually undressing while watching Sandy take a shower.

That was my moment of truth, and the voyeuristic part of me won out. I just stood there anxiously waiting for Nat's next move. When he joined Sandy, I quickly took his place outside the bathroom door.

He had waited for her to lather up her hair and face, then slipped into the shower with her. Since she and I frequently shower together, I'm sure she thought that I was the one standing behind her. While she continued washing her hair, I got an instant hard-on watching Nat's hands roaming freely over all my wife's feminine charms.

It wasn't until he snuggled up against her and pushed his big horse dick into the crack of her ass that Sandy became suspicious. Nat's erection is a good three inches longer and considerably thicker than mine. When Sandy noticed the obvious difference, she froze and reached back to feel the invading appendage in an inquisitive way. She then hastily rinsed the soap from her face and swung around trying to cover her breasts and pussy. But even as she was saying, "Nat, what are you doing? You've got to get out of here!" he was nudging his pole between her legs.

Sandy reached for his head, but he took hold of her hands and guided them down to his cock. She tried to maintain control, saying, "Please Nat, I can't believe I'm doing this. I love my husband." But I knew Sandy was his when Nat released her hands and she kept rubbing up and down his manhood. She was almost pleading when she said, "What happened this morning was beautiful."

Nat smiled back at her and replied, "Yes, I know. It was three hours of unbelievably incredible sex." Knowing Nat, I could tell that they would soon pick up where they had left off, but I didn't mind. I can't describe what a turn-on it was watching the master at work again. The forbidden fruit of my old friend working on my beautiful bride only made it more exciting. My confined dick was so hard that it throbbed.

Sandy's resolve evaporated as she said, "It was the best, but I don't know how you can top it." With that she raised one foot onto the edge of the tub and drew Nat's tremendous totem toward her love tunnel.

Nat put his hands around Sandy's waist and slowly pulled her forward, sinking his dick into her as the space between them closed. He then lifted her and pressed her against the shower wall, driving his cock all the way inside her wet, yearning pussy. Sandy wrapped her arms and legs around him, squeezing him close, surrendering her body to him completely.

Nat wasted no time pounding her hard and fast. He was slamming it to her with such force that her entire body jerked each time he thrust in. It definitely was not lovemaking, it was pure, unadulterated, animal lust. It didn't take long for him to get his rocks off, but as he erupted deep into her, blasting her full of his seed, Sandy shuddered, literally shaken by a much stronger orgasm than I had ever given her.

They finished showering in silence. I went back onto the patio when the water was off, but I knew old Nat well enough to realize he wasn't finished pleasuring my wife's body yet.

They came out of the bathroom together, both wrapped in towels. Sandy was visibly turned on, and it was obvious that she couldn't keep her hands off him. Nat had his arm around her, chatting her up, saying, "All right baby, I'm ready for another round any time you are. I could spend all day fucking you. What do you want to do?"

He steered her in front of the dresser mirror then nuzzled and kissed her neck and ears from behind. Sandy loves that, so when she started to relax Nat reached around, loosened her towel and let it fall to the floor, saying, "Look at you. You're the epitome of femininity, of womanhood itself. The most beautiful of all creation." He then cupped and squeezed her breasts, tweaking and rolling her ultra-sensitive nipples. As a hand slowly drifted down her body and slipped between her legs, he continued, "Look at how she reacted to intimacy, to being touched. See how her nipples are erect and proud, and how wet and wanton her pussy is. Give in to your needs and desires, babe. Let yourself go. Let yourself go completely. You'll be glad you did."

I thought Nat was being corny as hell, but Sandy absolutely melted. Almost in a trance, she closed her eyes and laid her head back onto his shoulder, then opened her stance, giving him easy access to her pussy. Nat swirled two fingers around inside her vagina and rubbed his thumb across her clit while Sandy reached back and wormed her hand inside his towel to stroke his cock. In an instant she had him erect and ready to go again. I watched with amazement as my bride bent forward and again guided Nat's pole into her steamy pussy.

Sandy gasped loudly as Nat flexed his hips and thrust his tool all the way inside her in one smooth motion. It was then that I realized why Nat always did so well with the ladies. As he began plunging in and out of her with long, powerful strokes, he grinned and said, "Yeah, babe, you've loosened up nicely. I told you your pussy would stretch out after having me a few times. Let's see, if I haven't lost count, this is number seven, isn't it? But there's going to be many, many more times between the two of us, aren't there?"

I could tell that the effect of watching herself in the mirror getting fucked by Nat's super shlong was turning Sandy on beyond belief. She was being rocked by orgasm after orgasm as Nat's cock probed way up inside her, stimulating places I had never been able to reach. Sandy was so out of control with passion and excitement that she could only answer Nat's question by blurting out between moans and sighs, "Oh, God. Yes, anything...."

Because he had just come, Nat was able to hold out a lot longer that time. He pounded into her from behind for a while, then turned her around and continued with her sitting on the dresser. After about fifteen minutes he moved her to the bed. When Sandy sprawled out on her back, flinging her lean legs wide open, I was shocked by the unbelievably aroused state of her pussy. The lips were swollen open and bright red and her vagina was literally stretched out forming a wide, wet cavern. God, Nat's cock really was huge, and my sweet, beautiful bride couldn't get enough of it as she eagerly steered its length into her cunt.

In the missionary position Nat really plowed into Sandy's furrow, the two of them becoming quite vocal as time went on. After a while they were making so much noise that they started attracting the attention of the other guests around the pool. I had two choices: either walk in and confront them, or leave before I was accused of being a Peeping Tom. I really didn't want to stop watching, but I also didn't want to put Sandy in an embarrassing position, so I chose the latter and went to take a seat out by the pool for a while.

I went back an hour later and watched when Nat finally emerged through the door. I tried to make sure he wouldn't see me, but even though I had hidden myself well, something or other gave me away and I caught his eye. When he spotted me he stuck his head back in the room and made sure I saw my wife wrapping her arms around his neck and giving him a long, passionate, open-mouthed kiss.

I could tell that Nat was feeling pretty full of himself as he strutted away, but I couldn't have cared less. My only concern was for Sandy. I ran to the room and found her still naked sitting on the bed. The room reeked of sex, and she was a gooey mess with gobs of sperm matted in her pubes and running down her thighs.

When she saw me she broke down, thinking I'd "caught her in the act." "Oh, my God," she cried. "What have I done?" We had a long talk and I put all her worries to rest by telling her the whole sordid history of old Nat and me, including how turned on I got watching the two of them. At first Sandy felt understandably perturbed with me, but I finally convinced her that what just happened had nothing to do with love or with our relationship. It amounted to no more than recreational sex, and that made her feel a whole lot better.

To show Sandy that I really wasn't upset with what had gone on between them and that I really meant what I had said, I told her that

I loved her just like always and that I trusted her completely. Since we both enjoyed her having sex with Nat so much, I said that I wanted her to continue seeing him for the remainder of the seminar.

Taking me for my word, Sandy spent every morning and every afternoon fucking him for hours on end. She even spent the entire last night we were there in his room.

I felt slighted because I didn't get to watch any of that, but I had one consolation. In the morning when I went to pick her up, Sandy was all bubbly and happy and looked as satisfied and content as any woman could be. That alone made the experience worthwhile.

On our way back home we reaffirmed our love for one another and agreed that, at least for now, we both wanted Sandy to continue having liaisons with other men. Basking in the glow of her newfound sexual freedom, Sandy teased me about wanting to watch, saying, "I don't know what to think about a husband who would rather see his wife getting fucked by other men instead of doing it himself." I proved her wrong by pulling over and showing her that I wanted to do both with her.—*H.F., Marietta, Georgia*

WANT TO PLEASE YOUR GIRL? GIVE HER A HOT LATIN LOVER IN AN OLD SPANISH CASTLE

I'm a well-off, healthy, middle-aged businessman who loves water sports and sex. I have a beautiful Puerto Rican girlfriend named Teresa, who's about half my age. She's quite tall and has brunette hair, big eyes, a marvelous, charming smile, a perfect body and (best of all) big, hard tits that make her very, very sexy. She knows what she has, and loves showing it off. Her whole wardrobe is designed to display her sexy body as much as possible. We're never bored with each other, and we're always planning new ways to enhance our already terrific sex life. Among our diversions, Teresa and I love to travel.

Last year we were in Spain, and for a while we stayed on a mountain overlooking the sea at a luxurious hotel that used to be part of a medieval castle. It was a very romantic spot. On our first day there, as we were having a couple of drinks before dinner, we were attended by a very handsome Spanish waiter named Carlito, who spoke both English and Spanish. He served us with a charming smile, and gave us some useful tips about the local beaches, restaurants and so on. "What a handsome man this is!" Teresa said to me at one point, leaning closely toward me. "Darling, I wouldn't mind fucking him at all."

We returned for drinks the next afternoon. Teresa was wearing a very sexy and daring outfit, as usual. After chatting with us a while, Carlito asked if we'd be interested in visiting the older, unreconstructed part of the castle. Of course we were!

The walking was not always easy, and our new friend helped Teresa along by holding her hand, even putting his arm around her waist from time to time. I soon noticed that they were holding hands continuously. "You know," Teresa whispered to me, "he's rubbing my hand on his cock, and he has a really big one." I knew full well that this wasn't a complaint, so I said nothing in response.

Near the end of the tour Carlito said he had one more room to show us. Wanting to give Teresa an opportunity to be alone with him, I said I was tired and would wait for them as they went on. When they returned, both of them were smiling from ear to ear.

Back in our room, Teresa told me that the waiter had practically undressed her. He had kissed her tits and pussy, and both of them had gotten extremely hot. "He wants me to go back and fuck him someplace in the bar storage room," she told me. "May I go there and fuck him, please?"

"No," I said, seriously. When she looked disappointed, I smiled and said, "I'm going to town for an hour, so you can fuck him comfortably in our room."

When I came back, she had an even greater smile of satisfaction. "It was marvelous!" she enthused. "Incredible! He has the most beautiful, enormous cock I have ever seen. It must be over eleven inches! When I ate his cock, which of course I had to do, I could hold it with both hands and still suck on the head!"

We were supposed to leave the next morning, but Teresa asked if we could stay one more night. "Under one condition," I said. "You have to let me watch."

"Of course," Teresa replied, smiling. "I'll get even more horny, knowing you'll be seeing us."

Our hotel room was small but up very high in the building. There was a kind of balcony halfway up, running along one side. That time, when Teresa invited the waiter to the room again, I remained hidden on the second floor, where I could stay in the dark but still had an excellent view of the bed.

I couldn't believe the size of his cock and how Teresa could stroke him with both hands and suck him at the same time. That made him moan with joy. Then he went to work on her pussy and tits with his tongue, and finally they fucked marvelously. When he entered her, his penis looked so big I expected it to come out of her mouth! But she took it all, and she loved it.

When he left, she took a bath and said, "Now it's your turn. I'm horny from knowing you were watching, so fuck me even better than he did." And that's how we ended our adventure.—*Name and address withheld* O—▪

IF HIS WIFE DOESN'T KNOW HE SAW HER CHEATING, HOW CAN HE MAKE IT HAPPEN AGAIN?

I recently watched my wife Sandra have sex in our home at my urging. Her partner's name was Jake, and he never knew I was there. Even though we'd never met, I had to tip my hat to him. The two of them had hot, steamy sex, and he got her off more than once before he lined her pussy with come. When he left, my pretty, sexy, thirty-five-year-old wife was satisfied and sleeping soundly, with his sperm oozing out of her cunt, making sticky spots on our sheets.

I stepped out of the closet where I'd been hiding, undressed and crawled into bed beside Sandra, holding her close as we both fell off to sleep. I had jacked off twice watching their wild carnal coupling, so I was nearly as spent as she was.

Although my wife didn't know it, that wasn't the first time I watched her fuck another man. The last time was twelve years ago, when we had been married for just under three years. Sandra and I were at my annual company picnic. I knew that she could be very flirtatious at times, but it wasn't until that day that I really thought my gorgeous redheaded wife would ever really cheat on me.

Sandra had been flirting with a coworker of mine named Sam. I was chatting with a group of guys when I noticed the two of them wander off alone. I didn't think too much of it until I saw them enter an enclosed picnic shelter on the far side of the park. When I didn't see them come out for a while, I went over, wondering what was going on.

When I got close to the shelter, it was obvious what they were doing. I heard voices, mostly my wife moaning and crying out, "Yes, yes, yes! Fuck me! Just like that! Yes!"

Feeling numb with shock and surprise, I went closer and peered through a screened window. Standing between her legs, his shorts and undershorts down around his ankles, was my coworker Sam.

Very shortly I heard Sandra cry out, "Oh, yes, I'm coming, coming! God, you're making me come!"

Not only had I never seen my wife experience an orgasm, I hadn't even seen her show much reaction at all during sex. My macho coworker was making her squeal in ways I'd never heard before, and his cock was getting her off in ways mine never had.

As she climaxed, her splayed legs flapping wildly before locking around his, Sam went over the top. He rammed that log inside her slowly and with great determination, then leaned forward and ground his body against hers. Their mouths met in a feverish, open-mouthed kiss. I saw his butt muscles clenching and releasing as he started to come. He broke off their kiss, arching his back and letting out a deep groan as he planted his seed deep inside my wife.

When he finally stood up, pulling his dick out of my wife's slippery hole, I could actually see some of his cream oozing out of her freshly fucked, sperm-filled snatch.

Sandra sat up and asked if she could borrow a bandana and then wiped her crotch, cleaning off his sperm and as much of her juices as she could. She glanced up at him with a concerned look on her face, saying, "I really hope my husband screws me tonight, in case I get pregnant from this."

He frowned at her. "You're not on the pill?"

"I use a diaphragm," Sandra told him, "but I don't have it in. I mean, I certainly didn't plan on us doing this. It just happened. You're just so damn sexy! You turn me on and all, but I don't want to fuck up my marriage. And believe me, I don't want to ruin yours, either. I'm never telling anybody about this, and promise me you won't tell anyone, either!"

He assured her that he wouldn't, and she went on. "That's why I hope my husband screws me when we get home," she said. "Hopefully I can fuck him and conveniently forget to put my diaphragm in. Then if I get pregnant, he'll never know."

"You'd do that?" Sam asked. "You'd deceive your husband that way?"

Sandra nodded and said, "Well, I did this to him. If I had your baby and he thought it was his, it would be a lot better than if he knew about this."

At that point I turned and hurried away, quietly heading back to the other side of the park. Along the way, I stopped at a restroom. I had to pull my shorts and underpants off and wash off my crotch, because in spite of my shock at seeing my wife cheat on me—and even telling my coworker how she was willing to deceive me into believing I had fathered another man's baby—the truth was that I had come in my pants!

Whether or not I was ready to acknowledge it, the sight of my wife passionately fucking another man had excited me beyond belief. But that wasn't all. I knew that my wife had taken my coworker's sperm in her body. I'd seen it leak back out, and I'd seen her try to clean it up. She'd been full to overflowing with his semen, and I loved it.

For reasons I do not understand to this day, the knowledge that my wife was full of another man's sperm turned me on! You must think that sounds insane, but it's the truth! I was probably more scared that she'd been knocked up than she was. But something about it was incredibly arousing. I couldn't understand it then, and I still don't, but when Sandra finally came back and told me some bullshit about having gone for a walk, I got so horny thinking about it—and looking at my wife's tummy and crotch—that I actually slipped off to the men's room again and jerked off two more times.

The next morning I had to leave for a week-long business trip. It wasn't until I got back the next Friday that we finally made love.

It was about three months after that Friday night that Sandra gave me the news: She was pregnant! I knew that Friday could have done it, but I had to be suspicious. I managed to hide my suspicion from her like she hid her tryst—and what I knew were very strong questions about the paternity of her baby—from me. I even managed to keep quiet about my knowledge when the answer became obvious, because it turned out that our son looked just like Sam. By the time he was two years old the resemblance was uncanny. There wasn't a doubt in my mind.

But paternal questions or not, I loved that tyke from the moment he was born. As far as he was concerned, I was his father, and he was daddy's boy all the way. We're still very close as father and son, and I couldn't possibly love him more if he had come from my loins.

When our son was about two and a half years old, I again suspected that my wife was having an adulterous liaison with someone. We were back in Sandra's hometown, staying with her parents for two weeks over the Christmas holidays. One night we attended a party hosted by a very good friend of hers from high school. Sandra spent a good part of the evening talking with a guy named Peter. I learned from Sandra's girlfriend Judy that Peter and my wife had gone steady during their senior year in high school.

When I asked Sandra about him afterwards, she just said he was an old friend and that they had dated at one time. I didn't think too much about it until the next day, when Sandra asked me to look after our son because she was going to visit Judy. She was gone for nearly three hours, and while she was out Judy called the house asking for her. I didn't know what to say, so I just told her Sandra was out.

When I hung up the phone I began to get suspicious. I thought about Sandra's diaphragm, which I knew she kept in her toiletry bag. I couldn't help myself. I had to check it out. I got out the bag and looked inside. The diaphragm wasn't there.

When Sandra got back, she immediately headed for the bathroom, where she showered and changed her clothes. When she finished I sneaked into the bathroom and pulled the panties she'd been wearing out of the hamper. They were wet and sticky in the crotch, and I could smell the musky aroma of her cunt and the strong odor of male semen.

It was pretty obvious that she'd had sex while she was out, and most likely she'd fucked Peter. But at least this time she'd taken some precaution and brought birth control with her.

Again, even though I was stunned by the knowledge that my wife had cheated on me once more, every time I looked at her that evening I found myself thinking about Peter's sperm inside her. The thought kept my dick hard all evening long, and that night Sandra and I had some of the hottest, wildest sex of our married lives.

Sandra went out alone a few more times during our stay, and each time her diaphragm was missing from her toiletry bag. I had no doubt that my wife was having a fling with her one-time boyfriend during that visit.

The following May, Sandra took our son and again flew home to visit her parents for two weeks, this time alone. As I was helping her pack on the day she left, I sneaked a look into her toiletry bag. Sure enough, her diaphragm was there, in its case. Obviously she was planning to continue her affair with Peter. A wave of jealousy (or something) came over me, and while Sandra was out of the room I took the diaphragm out of the bag and put it back in her dresser drawer. I figured that by denying her contraception, I'd nip her affair in the bud. At least that's what I told myself, but maybe what I really wanted was what actually happened.

Sandra had a baby girl that February, exactly nine months after that trip to see her parents. The fact is that I'm not sure whether the real father is Peter or myself. Our oldest daughter looks more like Sandra than anybody else. Sandra and I made love on the day of her return, so I just can't say for sure. But, as with our son, our daughter is loved as much as a human being can possibly be.

A couple of times after that I became aware that Sandra was cheating on me again. We had another girl when our oldest daughter was two and a half. The new baby, like our son, didn't look like either of us. She looked like a man with whom I am virtually certain that Sandra had an affair. He was a younger guy, a college kid who worked as a lifeguard at our local swimming pool one summer. He and my wife started talking one day at the pool, and as I played with the kids I noticed their furtively exchanged looks, their incidental touching and their sly, knowing smiles. Then one day when I came home a little early, I saw him sneaking out of our house. Sandra was in our bed asleep, with nothing on. The covers were a mess, and wet spots speckled the sheets. Before she woke up I checked her dresser drawer. Her diaphragm was there in its case. She hadn't used it.

I never told Sandra what I'd seen, but I beat off that afternoon thinking of my wife, her abdomen filled with her young lover's sperm. When our third child was born late the following spring, she looked, as I say, just like him.

Even though Sandra always used the diaphragm when she and I had sex, we both pretended to believe that it had failed when she became pregnant. But after our third child was born, I finally had a vasectomy. Maybe the danger of getting pregnant without being able to explain it kept Sandra faithful for a few years. But recently I began to suspect her of seeing somebody else again. When she began to seem unusually worried and distracted, I knew that something was wrong.

My suspicion was confirmed when I found a discarded home pregnancy test kit in the trash can as I was taking it to the curb for pickup. That alone told me that my thoughts had been correct. But that wasn't all. I found the indicator and saw that it showed positive. Sandra was pregnant again.

Now I knew why she had been acting so worried. There was nothing to do except confess her pregnancy and her affair, because I knew that she'd never have an abortion. But she was probably afraid to risk our marriage by telling the truth. In spite of her affairs, I knew she loved me and that she didn't want our marriage to break up.

What she should have realized was that I felt the same way. There was nothing that would ever make me leave her. Even so, I was also afraid of the strain that uncovering the truth might put on our relationship at this time, so I came up with a scheme.

The fact was I had often recalled that long-ago day when I saw my wife getting fucked by Sam during the company picnic. The memory never failed to excite me, and a part of me had always wished I could actually see Sandra in another man's arms again. Now I finally saw a way to fulfill that desire and to solve Sandra's problem—our problem—at the same time.

One night after we had made love and Sandra was feeling mellow, I "confessed" to her that I had long had a fantasy of watching her with another man, and I wondered if she would ever consider it. Of course, I knew that ordinarily she wouldn't have, but I was giving her a chance to create an excuse for her latest pregnancy: the diaphragm must have failed when she was fucking this strange guy. Sandra wavered a little, but I knew in the end she would have to agree, and she did.

So that's how I came to hide in the closet and watch my wife fuck some guy she had picked up at the grocery store. Afterward we both agreed that it had been very erotic, and Sandra wondered if we might do it again sometime. Obviously that won't be until after she's had the baby.

I know that secrets usually aren't good for a marriage, but because Sandra and I have kept ours, our marriage is safe and secure and very good. Of course, Sandra doesn't have as many secrets as she thinks she does. My secrets are that I watched her with another man long before this recent session, I know she's cheated on me, our children aren't mine and I get turned on knowing she has another man's sperm swimming around inside her womb, looking for an egg of hers to fertilize. So as it turns out, my biggest secret is that I know her secrets, but she doesn't know mine!—*C.Z., Boise, Idaho*

ELEGANT LADY OR SEX-CRAZED SLUT? HIS WIFE WAS BOTH, AND HE WASN'T COMPLAINING

*B*eneath her normally sophisticated and elegant facade, my wife Julia is a come-loving slut. Let me share a recent experience to explain what I mean.

Julia is a thirty-four-year-old, auburn-haired, white-skinned beauty. She has incredible, perfectly shaped legs, a small tight waist, breasts the size of grapefruits and great feet. She enhances her immense natural beauty by applying enough makeup to her face and eyes to cause people to wonder if she is a high-priced call girl. She turns heads wherever she goes, and she's so used to the attention that she often doesn't notice—but I always do. My dick gets hard whenever I see people's eyes following her across a room.

Julia usually dresses in a sophisticated yet sensual manner, and her wardrobe is full of sleek, elegant designer clothes. She also has a large collection of slutwear, including tight micro-minis, tops with plunging necklines, see-through dresses, many pairs of shoes with five- and six-inch heels and every imaginable type of ankle bracelet to draw even more attention to her legs and feet. She never wears panties or a bra, and in warm weather she's always naked beneath her dresses, skirts and blouses. In cold weather she wears sheer pantyhose, but her dark pussy and prominent cunt lips are always uncovered for those lucky enough to get a peek. And when she's in the mood, she loves being an exhibitionist and showing off her body.

During the ten years we've been married, we've had an active and adventurous sex life. In addition to our normal sexual relations and exhibitionist experiences, we've shared fantasies with each other and occasionally acted them out, but no experience was more exhilarating than the one we had last weekend.

Julia's all-time favorite fantasy is to make love to a muscular black stud with a huge cock. During the past year, she developed a relationship that allowed her dream to become a reality. Michael is a personal trainer at the health club that Julia belongs to. Last year he caught her eye, and when her female trainer moved away, Julia decided to hire Michael to help keep her in shape. After working out with him, she would often come home and tell me how wet she got staring at the bulge in his shorts and watching his eyes devour her face, breasts and pussy. Within minutes we'd jump into bed and fuck the night away like animals while she fantasized that it was Michael's fat black cock that was bringing her to ecstasy instead of mine.

A couple of weeks ago, after one of our Michael-induced lovemaking sessions, I told Julia that watching her seduce him would be the greatest sexual experience of my life, and that I wanted her to make it happen. Apparently that was all the encouragement she needed, because later she told me that she had arranged a "sex date" with Michael the following Saturday night. We were going to meet him for dinner, go to a nearby nightclub to dance for a while and then come home for a little "nightcap."

We couldn't wait for Saturday to arrive, and the sexual excitement built throughout the week. On Saturday, Julia spent an extra-long time getting ready. She sent me out of the bedroom and told me that my patience would be well-rewarded. And was she ever right! When she walked into the living room, I got an instant hard-on. Her face and hair were beautifully made up, and she was wearing a semi-transparent, low-cut brown mini-dress that showed off her tits and legs. As usual, she wasn't wearing any underwear. The hem of her dress covered her cunt and ass with maybe an inch to spare. If you looked closely enough (and you sure couldn't help but do that), you could see her large brown nipples and dark, perfectly trimmed pussy through the thin material of her dress.

Julia was also wearing an attention-getting gold charm ankle bracelet, a pair of clear plastic platform slides with six-inch heels and a pair of sexy gold-hoop earrings. As she sat down across from me, her short dress gave me a perfectly unobstructed view of her glistening pink cunt lips. I knew it would definitely be a night to remember!

After drinking a cocktail at home we drove to the restaurant, took our seats and waited for Michael to arrive. Everybody in the restaurant noticed Julia's entrance, and it was clear that she was the main topic of conversation. A few minutes later a tall, handsome, muscular black man walked in the door, and I knew it must be Michael. His eyes met Julia's, and they both smiled as he quickly approached our table. Julia stood up, hugged him, gave him a kiss on the lips and introduced him to me. We shook hands and we sat down to begin our adventure. Every eye in the place was on us, and the room was filled with an air of sexual tension and speculation as to what the three of us were up to.

We had a few drinks, ate our dinner and then decided to go to the nightclub to dance. Michael followed us in his car as we drove to the club. On the way Julia asked how I was feeling. I told her that I was very turned on and put her hand on my bulging crotch to prove it. I then asked her how she felt. She responded by reaching between her legs, fingering her dripping cunt and slowly licking her honey-coated finger clean. She asked me if I wanted a taste, and of course I said yes. She reached down again and brought up a scoop of the sweetest dessert I ever had.

When we arrived at the dance club, Michael hurried over to our car and opened Julia's door. She rewarded his courtesy by sliding out slowly, spreading her legs and giving him a long look at her oozing cunt. They smiled at each other, and we walked inside.

The club was crowded, noisy and dark. We made our way to our reserved table next to the dance floor. After ordering a round of drinks, Julia and I got up and danced to a slow romantic song, during which she rubbed her body against mine. After that she switched her attention to her willing prey. For the next hour, Julia and Michael danced every dance, fast and slow, and with each song their moves became increasingly suggestive and erotic. During the fast dances they gyrated in sexual harmony, their faces conveying their escalating desire. During the slow dances they pressed against each other, humped each other's legs and explored each other's body with their eager hands.

When Michael began massaging her tits and ass, Julia responded by giving him a long French kiss and reaching down to feel the bulge between his legs. She whispered something in his ear, and he immediately reached between her legs and began to finger her. Within a couple of minutes Julia had a shuddering orgasm on the dance floor in front of me and a multitude of mesmerized onlookers. After a few more minutes, during which she had started to regain her composure, Julia grabbed hold of Michael's hand, walked over to our table and announced that it was time for us all to go home.

On the way out to the car, Julia told me that she was going to ride with Michael to make sure he didn't get lost. I followed them, and as I watched them in the car ahead I saw Julia rest her head on Michael's shoulder, then start to kiss her way down his neck and cheek. A minute later her head had disappeared from sight as she got her first taste of what lay in store for us.

When we came to a stoplight I pulled up beside them. Looking down from my vehicle into Michael's sports car, I saw my sexy wife sucking on the biggest cock I'd ever seen. We got home a few minutes later, and luckily Michael hadn't yet blown his wad. I was relieved, because I wanted to witness that for myself.

As I unlocked the front door, Julia embraced Michael, telling him that she wanted to be his whore, and that she was going to give him his greatest sexual experience ever. They kissed as I opened the door, and we walked in.

Once inside, Julia excused herself to freshen up. Michael asked her not to wash her sweet cunt, and she promised to keep it nice and wet for him. As I mixed our drinks, Michael asked me if I minded him fucking my wife. I told him that I was enjoying myself, and that he should go ahead and do whatever he wanted, but that I intended to watch the action and join in if asked. He smiled and toasted me, and then he and I sipped our drinks as we waited for Julia to return.

A little while later Julia walked into the living room. She had reapplied her makeup and put on sexy black crotchless panties and a half-bra that completely exposed her nipples and pushed her magnificent tits up and out. Her glistening cunt lips were swollen and begging for attention. Sheer, seamed stockings, a diamond ankle bracelet and six-inch black slides completed the outfit.

She sat down across from us and began to slowly rub her clit, explaining that she wanted to start things off by masturbating for us. She told us to watch carefully but not to play with ourselves during the show. She then proceeded to finger-fuck herself to a beautiful orgasm. Afterwards she stood up and motioned for Michael to come over to her. They kissed and rubbed each other, then Julia dropped to her knees and began what just had to be the most memorable blowjob of his life. I began stroking myself as I watched my beautiful, wicked wife on her knees before her black stud.

Julia lowered Michael's zipper slowly, unbuckled his belt, pulled down his pants and slipped off his briefs to free his ebony hard-on. After staring at it for a long moment, she looked up at him and said breathlessly, "I love it!" She kissed the head, licked the entire length of the shaft and finally opened her mouth as wide as she could and began to suck it. She could only get half of it down her throat, so she began to stroke the rest, her mouth and hands moving in unison. As the pace increased, she told Michael not to worry about coming in her mouth if he wanted to.

A few moments later, Michael told Julia to stroke him faster and to open her mouth wide. He then proceeded to shoot stream after stream of thick white come into her mouth and onto her tits. By the time he had finished, my wife had swallowed what seemed like a quart of his jism. Julia slowly licked his cock clean, swallowing every drop of their juices.

Watching my wife behave like such a whore was the most thrilling thing I'd ever done. And then she topped it off by standing up, walking over to me with the come shining on her body and giving me a long, deep kiss. The taste of Michael's come in her mouth was so exciting that I began to lick the remaining globs of ejaculate off her breasts until I had devoured it all.

Julia suggested we go into the bedroom. She lay down and asked me to sit in the chair and watch her make love to Michael, but not to jerk off. She then asked Michael to kneel beside her face and lower his dick into her mouth. She told him how much she craved his cock and started to suck him to another full erection. When he was hard she opened her legs wide, spread apart her drenched, swollen cunt lips and begged him to fuck her with his black rod.

I watched in disbelief as my wife's cunt completely engulfed his penis. They started fucking slowly, and Julia met each of Michael's thrusts with her own. Gradually the rhythm increased and Julia started moaning louder and louder. Finally she yelled, "I'm coming, I'm coming!" as she reached what she later told me was the best and longest orgasm of her life. Michael hadn't come yet, and he began to fuck harder and faster until Julia asked him to pull out and lie down on the bed. He rolled over and lay on his back, his dong pointing straight up toward the ceiling. Julia then proceeded to straddle him and lower herself onto his prick. I was enjoying the show immensely, but I was also aching with desire and frustration. Fortunately, Julia was about to ease my pain and give herself another first-time sexual experience.

Firmly perched on Michael's black baton, Julia beckoned me to the bed, then asked me to coat my prick with baby oil and fuck her ass. I gladly did as she requested, slowly pushing my prick into her small, tight asshole. She moaned as I slid it inside, and when I had shoved it in all the way, Julia yelled "Fuck my ass! Ram it in hard! Fuck my ass, fuck my cunt, fuck me, fuck me! Shove both of your cocks into me. I want to get double-fucked!"

Michael and I humped Julia like a two-piston fucking machine. The sensation of this double-penetration fuckfest was absolutely incredible for all of us. Julia started coming first. Then I went off, shooting wad after wad into her tight ass. And before either of us had finished, Michael emptied his load into her cunt. We collapsed in a heap and tried to catch our breath.

Michael and I were ready to call it a night, but Julia said she wanted us to get it up one more time for her. She told us to kneel next to her face, me on one side and Michael on the other, then asked us to stroke ourselves and let her lick and suck our cocks. Julia began to finger herself while she licked and sucked our dicks, moving from one to the other and back again. She told us how much she loved tasting her cunt and ass on our cocks. Michael and I both had raging hard-ons. Julia then knelt on the bed and asked Michael to fuck her doggie-style while she sucked my dick. After a few minutes of perfectly choreographed fucking and sucking, she asked her new lover to take his cock out of her cunt and shove it up her ass. He cheerfully complied, and soon his prick was buried deep inside her asshole. Julia reached down and fingered her clit as we synchronized our movements. Soon she was moaning and whimpering around my cock, the contortions of her mouth driving me crazy. The sensations, added to the sight of my wife getting fucked up her ass by this big black stud, were too much for me. I had never seen her act like such a fucking slut before.

Just as I was about to explode, Julia raised her head and yelled, "I'm coming, I'm coming! Oh, please make it last for me! I'm coming!" Then she swallowed my cock again, and I shot my load into her eager mouth. A minute later Michael started moaning as he filled her ass with another load of come.

After she had once more recovered her breath, Julia said that she wanted to give us a taste how great the entire night had been for her. She then told me to lie down on my back, and she lowered her dripping cunt and ass over my face, saying, "Open your mouth and taste my ecstasy." Huge wads of come began to pour out of her cunt and ass into my mouth. The taste of Michael's come and mine, mixed with my wife's juices, was incredible. I eagerly licked up all of the liquid and swallowed every drop. Now Julia pulled Michael toward her and gave him a deep, wet kiss. She asked him if he liked the taste of my come. He nodded and stuck his tongue in her mouth, swabbing up as much as he could get.

Finally the three of us lay down, with Julia in the middle. We hugged and kissed, and Julia told us how much she enjoyed being fondled by her black and white studs. We sucked her tits and fingered her to a few more orgasms before we all drifted off to sleep.

When Julia and I woke up in the morning, Michael was gone, but he had left us a thank-you note and some of the greatest sexual memories of our lives.—*B.W., Tuscaloosa, Alabama* ⊶▣

HIS BOSS SENT HIM OFF ON BUSINESS TRIPS, THEN GAVE THE BUSINESS TO HIS WIFE

I've always enjoyed traveling on work-related assignments, so when my boss began sending me on an increased number of business trips,

I considered myself fortunate. I didn't know why he was doing it all of a sudden, but I was getting to travel all over the country and stay in (reasonably) nice hotels on someone's else's tab, so I didn't even bother to give it a second thought.

One day I left the office to go to the airport, but on the way I realized that I had left an important file at home, so I had the cab turn around and take me back to my house. When I walked in the door I noticed that the answering machine was on. I was surprised to hear my boss's voice—and I was even more surprised to hear what he was saying.

"Hi, kitten," I heard. "Your husband has just taken a cab to the airport, so we've got two nights to howl. I thought I might come by around lunchtime so we could have ourselves a little matinee roll in the hay. I'm horny as hell for your pussy, kitten. Give me a call when you get in. Bye bye."

When I heard this I suddenly realized why I'd been so generously assigned all those overnight business trips recently. My boss Steve was fucking my wife Maggie, and he probably had been for months. It also explained why Maggie had never complained about me being away from home so much. Strangely enough, when I realized exactly what was happening, I got an immediate hard-on.

Just as I was about to get back in the cab, my wife drove up. She had just gone to the store for a few things and was surprised to see me home. I explained to her that I'd come to pick up a file I'd forgotten and that I had to hurry if I wanted to make my plane. We kissed, and then I was off. I kept thinking about my boss and my wife, and I had a hard-on for the whole flight.

That night I phoned home about ten o'clock. Maggie sounded out of breath, and I told her so. She said she'd been doing some exercise. Yeah, I thought, I knew exactly what kind of exercise she was doing and who she was doing it with.

I decided to let things continue as they were, at least for a while. I had to admit to myself that I was increasingly turned on by the fact that my wife was screwing my boss on a regular basis. Then one night I decided to tell Maggie that I had always fantasized about her getting fucked by another man. I told her that the idea really turned me on, and that I wouldn't object if she ever felt she'd like to have some strange cock. I said it would probably be thrilling for both of us if she would share her experiences with me, or even let me watch.

Maggie was astounded when I said that. She stared at me for a long time, really taken aback and basically speechless until she looked me right in the eye and said, "You know about Steve and me, don't you?"

I put my hand on hers and told her that I'd known for some time. I assured her that I wasn't upset about their affair, and I asked her to tell me about it. She took a deep breath and started to explain how everything had happened, and she saw how hot and hard I was getting as she told me the whole story.

She said that Steve had come on to her several times in the past and she hadn't responded, although she found him very sexy. Then at a company party one night he had gotten her outside in the dark. She had allowed him to back her up against a wall as he faced her, leaning toward her with his hands braced on either side of her head. Occasionally he would let a hand drop and "accidentally" rub against her tits. She thought it was accidental the first time, until it happened again and again. Finally he bent his elbows, moving forward to kiss her.

Perhaps a little carried away because of the drinks she had consumed, she returned his passionate kiss. He took her hand and placed it on his cock, saying, "Look how much you affect me!" His size and thickness really turned her on, and she finally agreed to his suggestion that he come by the house the next day.

Maggie told me that he had turned out to be a fantastically good fuck. He could hold off for the longest time before coming, and she had several orgasms.

I have to admit that I'm not a great lover. I tend to go off too fast, and I'm seldom able to bring my wife to orgasm before I come. Maggie said she'd never known how wonderful fucking could be until she started having her affair with Steve. He opened her up to all kinds of sexual fun. She even became an expert at sucking cock, which was something I could never get her to do for me in all the time we've been married.

We agreed not to tell Steve right away that I knew the two of them were carrying on. I was afraid that Steve might overreact and break it off with her, he might fire me, or both. I didn't want either of those things to happen, and neither did she.

We started seeing more and more of Steve as a couple, while

Maggie continued to meet with him on the side. Eventually Steve began to get the idea that I knew what was going on, and that I was okay with it. He became more open showing his interest in my wife, and eventually it was accepted among the three of us that he's her lover. It's been that way for six months now, and none of us has any complaints.

I soon realized that it turned Steve on to display his obvious lust for my wife right in front of me, and we both realized that it turned me on to be openly cuckolded, as it were. For instance, when the three of us go to a restaurant, Steve sits next to Maggie and I sit across from them. Soon I'll see his hand going under the table, and I'll watch her face as it goes up her dress.

Steve often comes by the house now to fuck Maggie. We'll have a few drinks, and then the two of them will go upstairs and he'll screw her in our bed. I listen to their sounds of passion then I often jerk off, coming hard when I hear her scream with the orgasms she gets from another man.

I still go out of town on business trips, and sometimes I'll call her up and she puts the phone on the bed so I can listen while they have sex. When Steve goes on trips now, he sometimes takes my wife with him as his "personal assistant." On their last business trip, an old friend of his was attending the same convention, and the three of them had a wild time together, with my wife satisfying both men at once, taking them on in every position they knew and making them come several times over. When she finally got home and told me about it, I came without even touching myself. It may seem peculiar to some people, but we have come to enjoy our lifestyle, and none of us would change it for anything.—*R.G., New Orleans, Louisiana*

Clusterfucks II

HER SEX-HAPPY PAST CATCHES UP WITH HER, TO HER HUBBY'S GREAT DELIGHT

Gina and I were in college together, but at that time I never dreamed she would one day become my wife. She came from a small town and a very protective environment. Let loose in a big college, she wanted very much to fit in, and in her naive way she let this desire carry her far beyond what most girls would consider the realm of acceptable behavior. Gina was only about five feet five, but well proportioned, with blonde hair, a beautiful face and a warm and loving personality.

In her freshman year she started dating an upperclassman named Kyle, a soccer and swimming jock and a very charming ladies' man. Kyle taught her about sex, including how to suck cock, and she loved it all. Kyle had the reputation of being exceptionally well hung, so she was able to learn from the best.

I heard about these events at the time through the stories and rumors that went around the school, but they have since been confirmed by Gina herself, now my wife.

Kyle had a friend named Avery, whose father was a real estate agent. He would sometimes let Avery use an empty house for a weekend party before putting it on the market. On this particular weekend Avery invited eight or ten guys, along with their girlfriends, and of course Kyle and Gina were included. The guys hauled mattresses from their dorms, and stored up a huge supply of beer, alcohol, snacks and pot. They spread the mattresses out around the huge living room, and though it was warm they built a fire for light, as the electricity was turned off. They also made sure they had plenty of candles.

The party was a great success from the beginning. At about two in the morning Kyle declared that he wanted to get some sleep, so he dragged his mattress upstairs to one of the bedrooms. He came back to get Gina, and some beer. Several of the other guys also moved their mattresses to private rooms, where they retired with their girl-friends. Some of them probably had sex, and some of them simply passed out from drinking too much.

Kyle had made sure that neither he nor Gina drank enough to inca-pacitate them, but Gina was not used to alcohol and was feeling no pain. Kyle didn't bother to close the door to their room. It was fairly dark, with only a few candles burning, and the moonlight entering the room through the curtainless windows. At one point Avery and another guy named Dino happened to pass their room. They had gone downstairs for more beer, and on their way back they saw Kyle's open door. Looking in, they saw Gina sucking Kyle's cock while he finger-fucked her pussy. Kyle saw them standing in the moonlight and motioned for them to come in, which they did. Avery started playing with Gina's tits, rolling her nipples between his fingers, and Dino took over for Kyle at her pussy, playing with her clit and prob-ing her cunt, while Kyle enjoyed the blowjob he was getting.

Gina was so hot she had lost all her inhibitions. She didn't pro-test as they rolled her on her back. Dino eagerly took to eating her pussy while simultaneously fucking her with his finger. Avery still concentrated on her nipples, holding her breasts with both hands as he moved his mouth from one to the other, sucking the nipples, add-ing to the frenzied pleasure she was feeling from Dino's tongue. Kyle was kissing her, plunging his tongue deep in her mouth while she sucked on it avidly. Between kisses he whispered encouragement to her, telling her to let herself go and experience the utmost pleasure. Gina went wild.

"Yes, yes, oh, I love it!" she cried. "I've never felt anything like this! Oh, do it, do it!"

They soon had her on her hands and knees, getting fucked by Kyle while she sucked on Dino's cock. Avery lay beneath her, tantaliz-ing her tits and clit as she took care of the other guys' cocks. They switched places several times, so that each of them had access to both her mouth and her pussy. Kyle warned them not to come in her pussy so they wouldn't make her pregnant, but they each pumped two big loads of come into her mouth before leaving her with Kyle.

The next day Kyle assured Gina that she'd done nothing wrong, but had simply made it possible for all of them to enjoy themselves in the most wonderful manner. In his charming way, he convinced her that she was the best woman he'd ever known. In this way he got all the blowjobs and pussy he wanted. Gina loved giving him pleasure, and didn't mind doing it for his friends as well. They had threesomes with Avery or Dino a couple of times, but did not do it with both of them again until several months later.

Avery's father had told him about a secluded empty farm that he had not yet sold. Avery suggested that he, Kyle and Dino get together a picnic lunch and some beer, and take Gina on a quiet picnic in the country.

They took along some blankets and a mattress. At the farm they played some Frisbee until they were all hot and sweaty, after which they all stripped and jumped naked into the pond. After that they took Gina up to the barn, where they had left the mattress. Kyle started things off by asking her to enlarge his shrunken cock, which had been shriveled by the cold water. Of course Avery and Dino soon joined in, and Gina sucked all three guys off. Then they took turns fucking her again.

Kyle graduated that spring, and all of them drifted apart. It was only after that that I really got to know Gina well. I knew about her past, and was fascinated by it, and by her. She responded to my interest, and eventually we were married.

Two years after that, Gina and I attended a wedding, where we happened to run into Kyle. He'd had a lot to drink, and just before we left he took me aside and said that he hoped I was enjoying all the things he had taught my wife. Then he laughed and said, "You must know about us, right?" I told him I did, and that I didn't mind one bit. "Well," he said, "I bet Gina would like a refresher course."

"That's fine with me," I said. "Whatever Gina wants she can have."

Kyle just laughed at that and strode away. I went looking for Gina, but by the time I saw her Kyle had gotten to her first. It looked like he was coming on to her. I stood and waited. Finally Gina came over to me. She told me that Kyle was in no condition to drive, and suggested that we take him to our house.

By the time we got him home he had passed out. We got him

stripped down to his undershorts and put him to bed in the spare bedroom.

About four in the morning we heard him stumbling around looking for the john. Gina got up to guide him to the bathroom. I must have fallen asleep again, because the next thing I knew it was about six, and I heard Kyle saying. "Don't leave yet, baby, I've got more for you."

A few minutes later Gina came back to our bed. I pretended I was asleep. I knew he'd fucked her again. But I was not jealous. Actually, I was turned on!

Later that morning we were in the kitchen when Kyle came down in his undershorts. He acted like he was king of the walk. He patted Gina on the ass, then bent forward and planted a kiss on her breast. He looked at me and said, "You're a lucky SOB to have such a fantastic wife. I never got married because I couldn't find another woman like her."

After he had eaten he got up, threw his arms around Gina, and French-kissed her right in front of me. He winked at me as he went upstairs to take a shower. When he called for a towel, Gina took one up to him. She didn't come back right away. Finally I went upstairs to see what she was doing. Through the open bathroom door I saw her on her knees, sucking Kyle's cock. Kyle just grinned at me.

After that Kyle began coming over on weekends, and I was often left alone in bed, or working around the house, while he and Gina fucked. Gina and I talked it through, and I assured her it was okay with me. She told me she would call it off anytime I wanted, but I explained that it really turned me on to think of her with Kyle, and it made our sex life better when he wasn't there. Gina and I still love each other, so all of us are happy.—*J.H., Grand Rapids, Michigan* ⚲

THIS BAKERY MANAGER LOVES BLACK MEN, AND THEY CALL HER THE DONUT HO

A few months ago you published my letter telling about how I had spied on my sexy young wife Molly as she snuck off to a motel with two black guys who were doing some carpentry work at the bakery she manages. She was supposed to be working late, and I was supposed to be playing golf, but instead I watched through the motel window while she had all kinds of wild sex with her two black studs. This is what happened later that night.

I went back home, very turned on. I decided not to tell her what I'd seen, leaving open the possibility of seeing more of it in the future. Molly came home around ten o'clock, looking fairly fresh for someone who had just participated in an all-out fuckathon, I offered to make her a drink, asking how her work had gone.

"It's a good thing I went back to the store," Molly replied. "That new girl had everything screwed up!"

As she took a big sip from her drink I stepped behind her, reaching around and massaging her lovely tits while kissing her neck. Her boobs were still swollen with excitement. As I tried to slip my hand down her jeans she suddenly stopped me, setting her drink on the counter and turning around. In two seconds flat she had my pants and underwear down around my ankles. Dropping to her knees, she stroked my hard cock.

"Ummm! What got you so hard?" Molly asked.

"I missed you," I said.

"It looks like my husband needs some special attention from his favorite bakery lady," Molly said.

"Do blowjobs fall under that category?" I asked.

"They do tonight," Molly said as she proceeded to deep-throat my swollen member. All I could think about while she sucked my cock was watching her earlier that evening with those two black studs, fucking them like an out-of-control nympho who couldn't get enough dick. Finally I couldn't take it any longer. "I'm going to come!" I announced.

Molly pulled my cock from her lips, stroking it rapidly. "Want to come in my mouth?" she asked.

I answered by shoving my cock back into her mouth and shooting my hot come down her eager throat.

Molly excused herself and went to the bathroom to clean up while I got ready for bed. As I watched TV in our bedroom the phone rang. It was Al, the night manager at Molly's store, asking if she was home. She was out in the living room, so I hollered down the hallway that she had a phone call.

"I'll take it in the kitchen," Molly replied.

I told Al she'd be on in a minute. When Molly picked up on the other extension, I hung up, then got out of bed and slipped down the hallway, stopping just outside the kitchen. I heard her say, "By all means, put Biff on the phone." There was a short pause. Then she said, "Hi!" By the sound of her voice I strongly suspected that Biff was one of the carpenters she had been fucking earlier that night.

When she spoke again it was in a lower tone. "What? What do you mean you're not done with me yet?...Right now? That's crazy!...Listen, how about tomorrow afternoon, while my husband's at work?... Well yes, you know I want it! Oh god, I want it as much as you do!... Well, can you help me come up with something to tell my husband, so I can get out of the house?...Well okay, I'll give it a try."

I continued listening long enough to learn that she was to meet him down at her store before going back to their motel room.

Before Molly hung up the phone I hurried back to bed. She came into our room and told me that Al was unhappy with the carpenters' work, and wanted her to come back to the store to help him supervise the rest of the remodeling, which just had to be done before opening time the next day.

"That's okay," I told her. "I have an early day tomorrow, and I need to get some sleep."

She disappeared into the bathroom to touch up her makeup, then made a hasty exit out the door.

In no time at all I was up and dressed. I hopped into my van and headed back to their motel. I figured they would have kept the same room. I backed the van into the same spot I had occupied earlier, outside the window of their room. As before, I could see through the back windows of the van right into the room, without being seen myself.

Ten minutes later Molly's car pulled up and parked close by. She got out, accompanied by Carl, the other carpenter she had been with earlier. As they approached the door to the room I heard him say, "Have any trouble getting out of the house?"

"No," Molly replied. "Biff's story worked great. But I almost got caught when I got home before."

"How?" Carl asked.

"My husband wanted to have sex with me as soon as I walked in the door. My pussy was still full of your come, and Biff's, and I had no idea how to explain that, so I pulled out his cock and have him a quick blowjob, right in the middle of our kitchen."

With that they disappeared into the room. From my vantage point I could see the bed, but not much more, so the first thing I saw was Carl lying back on the bed, totally naked. Molly climbed on top of him for some 69 action. I saw that she had put on a garter belt, nylons and high heels for her late date. Carl began eating away at her tasty little bakery tart, while she proceeded to deep-throat his chocolate fuck-stick.

At that point I saw Biff, the other carpenter, pulling up in his truck. Evidently he had decided to put a few more men on the job, for he had brought two new black guys with him. He took a cooler from the truck and the three of them approached the room, pausing as they looked in the window.

"Check this out!" Biff said. "Carl's warming her up for us." He put the cooler down and opened it up, saying, "How 'bout we all have a beer and watch for a while, and I'll finish giving you the lowdown on this girl."

"I'm cool with that," one of the guys replied. From their later conversation I learned that his name was Harry, and the other guy was Sam.

"How'd you meet up with her?" Sam asked.

"She's the bakery manager at a store we've been doing a job at," Biff replied. "And she started coming on to us right from the start. Giving us free donuts and telling us how she really appreciated black guys, and that she'd love to party with us sometime. When we started working tonight, she told me that her husband was off playing golf or something, and she'd love to go someplace and have a drink with us before we got started. She said she'd show us both a good time."

Just then Carl said something to Molly and she got on top of him, positioning herself to ride his big cock.

"Look at that!" Biff said. "Carl's pleasing her, she loves to have his big black dick in her tight little pussy." Evidently she was having a wonderful time for she now lowered her eager pussy onto his towering black shaft.

"No condoms," Sam remarked.

"Nope," Biff said. "She's been broke in right! The Donut Ho just loves riding bareback."

"Finish telling us what happened when she came on to you," Harry said.

"Well, we went out to a bar to have a drink," Biff said. "I still wasn't sure if this girl was for real, or just a dick tease. But then she put my hand on her thigh and pulled up her skirt, showing me those nylons and that sexy garter belt. I knew right then we were about to score big-time.

"She's got this real sexy voice and she actually talked our dicks hard, telling us how she'd go all out to please a couple of big black guys like us. Letting us play with those nice titties while she stroked our dicks under the table, right there at the bar. I slipped my hand up her skirt and said it was too bad she was wearing panties, and she said she'd gladly take them off if we'd just take her to a motel. Shit! She even offered to pay for the room.

"Well, before we left she went to the ladies' room, and when she met us outside the bar she shoved her panties in my pocket. She gave me something else too."

"What was it?" Sam asked.

"Bakery lube," Biff replied, pulling a small bottle from his pocket. "I'm pleased to report that me and Carl both enjoyed a little back-door action with the Donut Ho earlier this evening."

"No way!" Harry said. "She gave you an invite to fuck her up the ass?"

"She sure did," Biff replied. "And she loved taking every inch of our big black dicks up that tight little asshole."

By now Carl had moved Molly around and was fucking her doggie-style.

"Take a good look," Biff said. "This girl loves taking black dick any way she can get it."

"She won't mind that you invited us along for a gang bang then?" Harry asked.

"Hell no!" Biff replied. "She'll be happy to pull some extra booty duty."

"Damn, all I can say is, you the man, Biff!" Sam said.

"You two wait here," Biff said. "I'm going inside. I'll let you know when it's cool to come on in."

Biff grabbed the cooler and knocked on the door. Carl stopped fucking Molly just long enough to let him inside. Then he went to the foot of the bed and motioned to Molly. She slid her ass toward him and raised her legs straight up into the air. He wrapped a hand around each of her ankles as she guided his giant cock into her waiting pussy.

When I saw Biff again he was totally naked. He came up to the window and cracked it open, so his buddies could listen in. Now we could all hear Molly begging Carl to fuck her deeper and harder, moaning loudly as he began to piston his mighty black shaft rapidly in and out of her cock-hungry cunt.

A few moments later Carl announced, "I'm ready to come!" He withdrew his cock, and Molly scrambled to sit on the edge of the bed so she could take it in her mouth as he delivered his load of hot come down her throat.

"Damn!" Sam exclaimed. "She swallows too!"

"I can't wait to do that to her," Harry added. "But I'm going to fuck her up the ass first!"

As Carl moved away, Biff sat down on the edge of the bed. Molly got off the bed and knelt down in front of him, her head dropping to his lap, her mouth devouring his huge dick.

"That's it baby," Biff said as she sucked on his hard cock. "Take it deep. Sorry I was late," he went on, "but I had to stop and pick up a couple of things for you."

Molly pulled his dick from her mouth. "Like what?" she asked.

"I brought along a couple of friends," Biff said. "They're both big bakery fans. Come on in and join the party, boys!" he called out.

Once the guys were inside I got out of the van and quickly assumed their post outside the window. Now that they were in the light, I could see that Harry and Sam were both younger, probably in their early twenties, and had extremely muscular bodies. Biff was standing up now, while Molly remained on her knees, stroking his cock.

"I was telling these boys how you run a real full-service bakery for your black clientele," Biff said. "Offering up everything from bagels to blowjobs."

"And let me guess," Molly said, starting to giggle. "These two aren't interested in bagels tonight."

"We'll let you be the judge of that," Biff said. "C'mon boys, show our sexy bakery lady just what you got for her."

Harry and Sam whipped out their dicks for Molly's inspection. "Whoa!" she exclaimed. "You're both huge!" She stroked their solid black shafts.

Molly was right—their cocks were fucking humongous! Harry's was the biggest of all, well over ten inches, while Sam's looked to be about nine inches long and was super-thick.

Harry reached down, touching Molly's wedding ring. "Does your husband know you like wrapping that mouth around fat black dicks?" he asked.

"I sure hope not," Molly replied. "I usually take care of guys like you in the afternoon while he's at work, or when he's out playing golf, like earlier this evening."

"Ever had four black dicks at once?" Harry asked.

"I love being shared," Molly replied. "I've done two at a time a lot, and three guys a few times, but you guys will be my first foursome."

Two at a time, a lot! I thought. It was obvious that my supposedly faithful wife had been a slut for black cock for some time. My dick was so hard I thought I might come in my pants if I as much as touched it.

Molly climbed onto the bed, getting on all fours as Biff mounted her and started fucking her doggie-style. Harry and Sam stripped away their clothes. Harry then stuck his solid black shaft into her waiting mouth, while Sam played with her lovely tits.

The guys proceeded to work my wife through a variety of sexual positions as they all enjoyed her lovely body. At one point, as Molly was lustfully riding Sam's thick black shaft, Biff pulled out his bottle of bakery lube. I watched as he stood at the foot of the bed, lubricating his massive tool before climbing aboard, then nudging the tip of his huge dick into her anal passage. "This is what I meant when I said we weren't done with you yet," Biff grinned. He slowly snaked his shiny black monster up her tight ass while Sam continued fucking her pussy.

Harry grabbed the bottle and lubed his magnificent cock in anticipation of getting his turn at her butt. When Biff finally exploded in

Molly's ass, the two of them hardly missed a beat as he pulled out and Harry quickly replaced him.

I watched in amazement as this woman, who had often told me that I was more than enough man to keep her satisfied, eagerly took a royal reaming up her ass and pussy by two black dicks that were nearly twice the size of mine. She moaned louder and louder as the two of them double-fucked her with their super-sized pricks, eventually making her come so hard I thought she might pass out. Sam pulled his cock out of her grasping, moaning, whimpering mouth, evidently saving himself for her ass.

Sure enough, as soon as Harry exploded into my wife's anus, Sam took his place. He turned Molly onto her side and lay behind her, inserting his thick black shaft up her anal passage, reaching around her to play with her hard-nippled tits. Meanwhile Carl and Biff started to get dressed, telling Sam to hurry up. They had to get back to the bakery and finish up their job, and Sam was supposed to help them. "I'm coming!" Sam exclaimed as he shot his last load of come into my horny cock-loving little wife. "I'm coming. I'm coming now!"

"There's only room for three in the truck," Biff said. "So you need to catch a ride home with the bakery lady, Harry."

"That's cool," Harry replied. "Cause I'm not done with her yet."

I quickly got back into the van so the guys wouldn't see me as they came out. When they were gone I went back to my post at the window. Harry was lying on the bed with Molly sitting on his cock. He played with her tits while they talked.

"This turned out to be my lucky night," Molly said. "Getting shared by four black studs, and now I get to go one-on-one with my favorite."

"How come I'm your favorite?" Harry asked.

"You're the best looking, you have the best body, and most important, you've got the biggest black dick!" Molly said. "It's so nice and hard, and I love the way you fuck me with it!"

Then she started moaning softly as Harry began pumping her pussy with his big cock. For the next half-hour the two of them proceeded to fuck like a couple of sex-crazed animals who couldn't get enough of each other. Eventually their pace eased a bit, and they resumed talking.

"Are you ready to fuck me up the ass again?" Molly asked.

"Would you like that, baby?" Harry asked back.

"Umm-hmm!" Molly replied.

"I'm always willing to help a woman in need," Harry said, rolling her onto her side and slipping his huge dick up her ass. "Ain't nothing I like better than fucking a sexy married lady up her tight white ass!"

"I can tell you like it," Molly panted, "You do it so fucking well!"

Harry began rubbing her clit as he fucked her harder, eventually bringing her to another intense orgasm and delivering another load of come deep inside her ass.

When she had recovered her breath, Molly said, "Listen, I'm getting my hair done after work tomorrow, but what are you doing Friday afternoon?"

"You!" Harry replied in a firm voice. "On your husband's bed. With some of my friends. And taping it! What do you think of that, baby?" Molly moaned softly and started rubbing against him again, as I made a mental note to stay home from work on Friday and hide in the closet.

And I'll tell you all about it in my next letter.—*B. G., Salt Lake City, Utah*

THEY WERE THREE VISITING FIREMEN, BUT HIS GIRL PUT OUT THEIR FLAMES

A few years ago my girlfriend Jeanette and I were on a ski vacation at a major resort, staying at a condo we co-owned at the time. Jeanette is a gorgeous blonde with a knockout body. One night, after returning from a great dinner that included plenty of drinks, we grabbed some more booze and mix and headed for the huge outdoor hot tub. It was fairly late and there was no one else around, so we stripped down and jumped in naked. It was a beautiful night, clear and starlit, and it was great being in the warm tub with two feet of snow all around us.

We fixed a couple of drinks, then started kissing and fooling around. I lifted Jeanette up so that her fabulous tits were out of the water, and her nipples hardened in the cold winter air. I started sucking her tits while she stroked my throbbing hard-on under the water. Then she pulled away from me and told me to sit up on the edge of the tub. As soon as I did she engulfed my cock with her eager mouth. Jeanette is a world-class cocksucker, and she soon had me ready to explode. I held off as long as I could while her head bobbed wildly up and down. Finally I couldn't hold back any longer, and I shot a huge load of come down her throat. She kept stroking and sucking me to get every drop.

As I began to regain my senses, I looked up and saw a man approaching the hot tub. I said, "We've got company." Jeanette quickly whipped my cock out of her mouth, grabbed my legs and yanked me off the edge of the tub and into the water.

The man came up to the tub and asked if it would be all right if he and his friends joined us. I looked at Jeanette. She just smiled at the man and said. "Sure, as long as you don't wear suits, because we don't have any."

His eyebrows shot up in surprise, but he said, "Sure, no problem." He went back to get his friends, and a few minutes later he and two other men approached the tub. They were all well built, attractive young guys, wearing towels.

Jeanette watched them approach, then turned to me and said in a low voice, "You'd better hurry up and decide how far you want this to go."

"As far as you can take it," I told her.

When they reached us we all quickly introduced ourselves. Their names were Greg, Lou and Stan. Then the three guys dropped their towels and stepped into the tub. We offered them drinks, and we all started talking. It seemed they were all firemen from the same town in Ohio, here on a ski vacation, just like us.

As the drinking continued the conversation gradually became freer and more insinuating, until at one point Stan commented on Jeanette's tits. She was sitting between me and Lou, the first guy we'd met, with her legs draped over one of mine. I slowly raised my leg, lifting her body in the buoyant water until her tits were completely exposed. Lou reached out and started fondling her left tit, and I stroked the right one. Jeanette moaned softly and leaned back, sliding off my leg as she did so. I grabbed her hand under the water and guided it to my now throbbing cock, and she slowly stroked it as we fondled her gorgeous tits while the other two guys looked on. I leaned over and kissed her, then gently nudged her, trying to turn her toward me so I could get at her pussy. Jeanette shook her head. "I can't move," she whispered.

"Why not?" I whispered back.

"Because he's got his finger in my ass," Jeanette said.

I eased back from her a bit. Jeanette pulled Lou's face to hers and they kissed passionately. She pulled away from him, then turned around and pushed him back against the wall of the tub, moving in against him. Reaching down, she grabbed his hard cock and lowered herself slowly onto it. She started to ride him with long, steady strokes. Soon she increased her pace and kept going faster and faster, until water was flying everywhere and she was grunting and squealing. After a minute she came violently, gasping and panting.

Now Jeanette lifted herself off Lou's cock and urged him up onto the edge of the tub, as she'd done earlier with me. His rather large cock stood straight up, pulsing and throbbing from the wild fuck she'd just given him. Jeanette lowered her mouth to him and took him in all the way to the balls with one deep suck that took his breath away. She then went into a wild, hair-flouncing blowjob.

The guy named Greg now moved in behind Jeanette and started to push his cock against her. She didn't pause or slow down her cocksucking, but she spread her legs apart invitingly. But because of the angle and the water, Greg had some trouble getting into her. I reached down between her legs and spread her cunt lips open, then grabbed his cock with my other hand and guided it into her. "Oh God, he's putting me in her cunt!" Greg moaned. He was so turned on that he started coming after about six hard, fast strokes in Jeanette's pussy.

He slumped back into the water as Jeanette went on sucking on the cock in her mouth as if she was starved for come. In another minute Lou let out a groan, grabbed her head in both hands and came so massively that she couldn't swallow it all. Some of it ran back down over his cock and balls, and after she had gulped down all she could, Jeanette carefully licked every remaining drop off his softening cock and his scrotum, until they were clean.

Jeanette turned to me now, pushing me against the tub wall and immediately mounting me. Her face was flushed, her nostrils flaring, and there was a fire in her eyes I'd never seen. At that moment she was pure sexual animal, and I had never been so turned on in my life. The water hadn't yet washed Lou's come out of her cunt, and I could feel it bathing my cock as she pumped up and down. She rode me slowly, but the excitement that had built up in me at seeing her with the other guys, combined with the feeling of my cock sliding in and out of her slick, come-filled cunt, had me blasting a load up inside her in no time.

Jeanette eased off me, kissed me and moved over to Stan, the one guy she hadn't done yet. He tilted himself up to sit on the edge of the tub, and Jeanette said, "Oh my God!" I looked over and saw her reach out to grab a cock that was longer than any I'd ever seen, and nearly as thick as her wrist. She put both hands around it and started to stroke it, then lowered her head to it and got as much of it in her mouth as she could manage. Apparently, watching her had had its effect on him too, because in no time he was coming. Jeanette seemed surprised at the suddenness of his orgasm; she pulled away just in time to take a huge glob of his come squarely on her tits. She quickly got him back in her mouth and swallowed the rest of his load.

When he was done Jeanette eased back into the water between Lou and me. Immediately we each started sucking on one of her tits. Greg now came over and put his hands under her ass, pulling her toward him until she was floating on her back, supported by the three of us, two of us sucking her tits and Greg eating her cunt. She gave a long, low moan and said, "Oh fuck, I don't believe this!" And then she was coming, thrashing and squirming so hard we had trouble holding on to her.

Finally we all settled back and had another drink. It was close to dawn when we all thanked each other and went back to our condos. The next day Jeanette couldn't believe what we'd done, but we agreed it had been fantastic. We even thought of having a repeat performance, but the firemen must have gone back home, because we never saw them again.—*D.R., Boise, Idaho* ⚭▬

THREE UNSEEN LOVERS SEND HER INTO AN UNPRECEDENTED STATE OF UNDILUTED ECSTASY

I lay on the bed, naked except for the red satin blindfold that covered my eyes. The room was warm, yet I felt cool, quivering with anticipation, my nipples hardened by the gentle sweep of air from the ceiling fan.

The three of them had slowly and deliberately removed all my clothes after slipping the blindfold on me. The touch of their hands, lingering teasingly on my gradually bared body as each garment was removed, was thrilling. The last thing to go was my satin panties, but only after each one of them had taken their turn stroking my moist folds through the thin material. I was already aroused, even though they hadn't yet begun to truly please me.

I could hear soft sounds as they shed their own clothing. I restrained myself from reaching out to touch them, because this was their time to pleasure me. Suddenly I felt the soft, gentle pressure of fingertips, first on my tummy, then on my thighs, then on my face. I realized then that all three of them were teasing me, first with gentle flutters, then with full, sensual caresses. I tried to distinguish the two men from the lady who was with them, but I could not. They were all so gentle.

The hands continued moving over my skin, driving me totally crazy with anticipation. No one was stroking my intimate parts yet, the ones that were by that time screaming with desire to be touched. Then a fingertip lightly brushed a nipple. I felt my pussy clench with the shock, as the red-hot bursts of excitement coursed through my breasts. A fingertip then flicked my other nipple, and again my pussy clenched. I began moaning softly, begging for more. The fingers lingered awhile on my breasts, kneading and rolling my nipples. But then there were new sensations, and I realized that it was no longer the caress of fingers I was feeling, but that of lips.

I cried out with joy as I pushed my breasts upward to be captured and suckled. I was not disappointed. A soft pair of lips surrounded each of my nipples, pulling at them gently and massaging them lovingly with the aid of tongues and teeth. I felt my arousal begin to build as my body responded to the stimulation they were lavishing on me.

Then I felt something new: a very soft and gentle pressure on my pussy. It was a tongue, giving me the beginning of a gentle bathing, teasing my erect clit and softly lapping my juices. I raised my hips, striving for greater pressure, and felt the face of my lover pressed against my mound. The skin I felt was soft and smooth, and I knew that it had to be Carolyn, my dearest friend in all the world. She knew exactly how to please me.

Excitement continued to build from deep within me. I felt my clit being engulfed by her soft lips and gently massaged by her warm, wet tongue. The lips suckling my breasts had not let up for an instant, and I came to realize there were three pairs of hands stroking all over my body. The stroking, caressing, licking and nibbling gradually became more insistent. I felt beautiful sensations everywhere. It seemed as if there were a dozen people pleasing me instead of just three.

I felt Carolyn's tongue enter my hot, flowing center as the stimulation of my nipples became even more intense. A mouth covered mine, and a warm wet tongue sought my own. I felt my legs being raised up onto a man's shoulders, followed by the feel of a hot, hard cock being guided to my pussy, burying itself deeply and sliding in and out slowly. My cunt throbbed with pleasure, and although part of me wondered which of the men it was, I didn't care. I just wanted it to go on forever.

I could feel a delicious orgasm beginning to well up inside me. Just then the tongue in my mouth was replaced by a second cock. I sucked greedily, losing myself in the soft feel of the head against my tongue. I could no longer refrain from touching him, whoever it was. I placed my hands on his muscular ass, drawing his body closer and swallowing him whole. I knew that familiar taste and feel: This cock belonged to my husband. I whimpered with pleasure knowing it was Frank who was pumping into my pussy.

Soon enough I felt the brush of long hair across my belly as Carolyn's lips traced a wet trail down to my clit. She began licking my sensitive cunt rapidly while her husband's cock continued to slide in and out of me. As I was being triple-fucked Carolyn leaned over the length of my body. I could feel her breasts gently brushing my skin.

That did it! The wave rose inside me and crested like a magnificent fountain. It seemed to freeze at its peak, and time stopped as my body arched, rigid with exquisite anticipation. Then, with a heady explosion that started deep in my pussy and spread throughout my body, the wave crashed and I finally came, my orgasm sweeping over me in a rush, blocking out all other sounds and sensations in the room.

I would have loved to scream out my joy, but the cock thrusting into my mouth muffled my cries. The wave rolled on for what seemed like forever, then subsided. My heart pounding, I felt a flush of heat on my face, neck and heaving breasts. Slowly I became aware of three pairs of lips gently kissing me all over, on my face, my breasts, my soaking wet pussy. Each kiss brought with it another small shudder of pleasure.

Finally I felt the blindfold being removed from my eyes, mercifully allowing me to see. Adjusting myself to the light that had until then been denied me, I gazed up and saw the smiling faces of my three exquisite lovers. I hadn't wanted the feeling to end, but I had something to do. I sighed with pleasure and, smiling into the adoring face of my husband, I breathed softly, "Your turn!"—*F.D., Savannah, Georgia*

THE GROOM AT THIS BACHELOR PARTY ENJOYS THE BACHELORS AS MUCH AS THE STRIPPER

I'm getting married on Saturday to the girl I've loved since high school and I'm really worried that she'll find out about the shit that happened at my stag party. I barely remember most of it, frankly, but my best man videotaped the whole thing. He set up his camera on a tripod as the stripper started her performance, and let it roll all night.

Chelsea, the girl who my friends had hired to strip for us, was much better-looking than I had imagined a stag-party stripper would be. We'd all had too much to drink by the time she started her show, but we were all ready to go, since we'd warmed up by watching hard-core movies on the hotel's television set.

After Chelsea stripped, she started to give me a lap dance. She straddled me and rubbed her pussy all over my crotch for several minutes, all the while letting me handle her tits and nipples to my heart's content. Still, maybe because of the booze, or because I'd never done anything like that before, or because I knew I had an audience, I wasn't getting the hard-on you'd think I would.

Everybody else was, though. You can see on the video how one guy after another shucked off his trousers and began fondling himself.

By the time Chelsea gave up on me, she had five other erections bobbing around the immediate vicinity of her face.

Sam took the first blowjob from her. He led her over to the sofa and sat down while she knelt in front of him. The girl was a natural redhead, her copper-tinged pubes peeping out from between her thighs as she knelt, begging to be plugged. A couple of minutes after Sam hit the sofa, Otto, my college roommate, was banging her doggie-style.

I was relieved to no longer be the center of attention, but I was also disappointed that my limp dick had dealt me out of the game so far. Besides being embarrassed about my inability to get it up, I was also really ashamed that my equipment was the smallest in the room. There wasn't a cock in sight that wasn't at least two or three inches bigger than my own, and the dick Sam was feeding Chelsea was really rocking her world. Otto had a big rod too, but he didn't win any prizes for performance. Within a couple of minutes he groaned out a climax and fell away from Chelsea's face. That was the first time I'd ever watched people fuck, and I stared in awe at her gaping cunt.

Otto's spunk was glistening on Chelsea's pussy lips and starting to run down her upper thighs. But that view vanished as Zach moved behind her and slid every inch of his thick black cock into places I'd surely never reach. Chelsea moaned loudly in pleasure and forgot all about Sam, who hadn't come by then. His penis was glistening with Chelsea's saliva, pulsing and throbbing as it stood up from his lap.

After giving Zach her full attention, Chelsea looked over and motioned for me to come sit on the couch with her. When I did, she put her face in my lap and started to give me head. Zach wasn't too happy with that situation, and he suggested that I lie down on the floor so Chelsea could blow me with her head down and her tail up in the air where he wanted it. I was pretty plastered by then, so I didn't have any trouble getting horizontal. Chelsea moved over me so that we were in a 69 position, and in a second or two I felt her delicious mouth on my peter. She gobbled my joint like a madwoman, while right over my head she and Zach continued fucking up a storm. It was actually pretty fascinating to have such a close-up view of two people fucking, but either the embarrassment or the alcohol was still getting between me and a decent erection.

* * *

Zach's climax was approaching, and he was really slamming his shlong in and out of Chelsea's pussy. That was definitely better than any porno movie I'd ever seen, and I stared in wide-eyed fascination as his black shaft rolled her cunt lips in and out of her snatch, inches from my face.

But the view of Zach fucking Chelsea was nothing compared to watching her come. She went into a series of incredible spasms as her cunt squeezed and clamped on Zach's dick. He bellowed out his own orgasm and slammed into Chelsea really hard. I couldn't see it, of course, but I knew he was unloading sperm deep inside Chelsea's cunt.

I wasn't ready for what happened next. After Zach slowly withdrew his shiny dick, Chelsea planted her juicy crotch firmly over my face, saying that I'd better learn to eat pussy if I hoped to please one woman for the rest of my life. It was a good thing my friends couldn't see me blush.

I didn't know what else to do but to try to get her off like she said, so I started tongue-fucking her pussy while grabbing onto her ass cheeks to hold her in place. I'd never performed oral sex before, and I couldn't believe how hot her pussy lips felt against my mouth. It was like her cunt was on fire. She tasted much better than I thought, too, sweet and slick and creamy. What I didn't realize was that the taste I was reveling in was my buddy Zach's thick dick-droppings.

Chelsea told one of the guys to go get her purse. She took out a tube of lubricant, slathering some of it all over my joint for a few minutes. Then, with Sam still plowing the back forty and her left hand fisting my cock, she reached behind me with her right hand and started rimming my ass with her well-lubed fingers.

"Try this, Harry," she whispered hoarsely as she slid one finger into my bottom while still pumping my penis. She must have touched my prostate because after a few minutes of her talented fingerwork my dick was finally standing up, almost fully erect for the first time that night.

"See, Harry, you can do it," she said softly, sliding a second finger between my cheeks. The way Chelsea's fingertips delicately tickled their way around my asshole felt very sexy. I pumped my hips to keep my dick moving between the fingers of one hand while she squeezed my buttocks with the other and ran her fingers an inch or two into my sphincter.

Between being carried away with what Chelsea was doing and being kind of drunk, I didn't even notice everything else that was happening around me. But when I watched the videotape later on, I saw that my friends Benny and Cary had been standing off to the side, slathering some of Chelsea's lube all over each other's cocks. I guess they were getting tired of waiting for their turns to come up and their dicks were just about ready to explode. They started off by stroking themselves, but soon they switched and were doing each other!

I saw something else on the tape that I didn't notice at the time. At one point Chelsea motioned to Cary that he should get behind me and then communicated to him with some quiet gestures that he should take over fingering my bunghole. Still kneeling in front of me, she put both hands on my ass cheeks and pulled me towards her mouth as Cary, grinning conspiratorially at Benny, slid two of his fingers gently into my sphincter. At the time I had no idea that one of my friends had taken over from Chelsea, and I continued to enjoy the stimulation of my anus, which finally had me hard enough to enjoy Chelsea's blowjob. You can see Cary and Chelsea exchange glances as she pulled more firmly on my buttocks, opening me wide as Cary withdrew his fingers and quickly slid his long, thin cock into my dilated asshole.

Believe it or not, at that point I really had no idea of what was going on. I swayed on my feet and closed my eyes as what had felt good in my ass began to feel even better. But I still thought that Chelsea was the one who was fingering me. Her face was buried in my crotch, her hands stroking my ass cheeks, and Cary was sliding a boner and a half gently up my rectum. On the third or fourth stroke he brought his arms up and wrapped them tightly around my waist. That's when my eyes finally popped open and I knew exactly what it was that I was feeling.

Sam had never stopped screwing Chelsea while watching me lose my anal cherry to Cary, and by then he dumped his come into her gash. He reached up to pinch my nipples lightly as Cary went on pumping me from behind. Then Zach began to stroke my pecker as Chelsea released it from her mouth.

I was a little bewildered at this turn of events, but at the same time I was more sexually excited than I could remember. A few seconds later my cock exploded its pent-up come all over Chelsea's shoulders.

Cary had a tremendous orgasm just a few seconds after that and gave my bowels a tremendous squirt of sperm. Benny finally got to screw Chelsea, too. After he filled her twat, she squatted over my face, and I ate her out eagerly, again savoring the taste of my buddies' salty sperm. We all laughed when Chelsea said that I was the first bridegroom she'd ever known who drank more sperm at his bachelor party than she did.—*Name and address withheld* ○┼▪

THEY SET OUT TO FULFILL THEIR SWINGING FANTASIES, AND THAT'S JUST WHAT THEY DID

*S*oon after my boyfriend Gerald and I started dating we realized that we both had fantasies about having sex with strangers. We talked about going to a swingers' club and finally found a place that looked like what we had in mind. It was out of town, so we took a weekend vacation and set out to fulfill our fantasies.

We were both a little apprehensive about doing anything at first. We looked around, then had a couple of drinks. That loosened us up to the point where we finally had the nerve to go into one of the theme rooms, where you could watch the scene through a small window. The first we came to was the bisexual room. There were two women in there—a blonde and a redhead—lying on a large round bed. The blonde was licking the other's red pussy, and they were both enjoying the hell out of it.

I was beginning to get excited myself and decided that I wanted to participate, but I was too scared to walk into the room. When the blonde strapped on a dildo and started fucking the girl she'd been licking, I glanced to the side and saw that Gerald had gotten a bulge in his pants as he watched them.

The redhead looked over at the window and saw us watching. She smiled at me and motioned for me to come join them. What the hell, I thought, and before Gerald could say anything I stood up, made my way into the room and stripped my clothes off. Not surprisingly, Gerald was right behind me, and we found that there were two men in there as well, sitting and watching everything that was going on. On a table off to the side of the bed were some oils, dildos and other equipment we could play with.

I was welcomed by the blonde, who without any preliminaries took me in her arms and kissed me. A little nervously, I looked over at Gerald, who just smiled and nodded his encouragement. He soon came into the room and kissed me, reassuring me that whatever I wanted to do that night was okay. He then went and sat down in the corner, leaving me to get busy with the two beautiful women. The blonde laid me down on the bed and started to kiss my nipples, and the redhead quickly joined her. She then moved down to my already wet and anxious pussy and started licking and sucking. I came almost immediately, having one orgasm after another as much from the excitement of being watched by a crowd as from what my new-found partners were doing to me physically.

The blonde decided to test out my pussy-eating skills, so she spread her legs and squatted over my face. That's when I learned how to lick pussy.

Out of the corner of my eye I saw one of the men walk over to Gerald, kneel down in front of him and start sucking his cock. Gerald not only allowed this, but he was soon tangling his fingers in the strange man's hair, eagerly fucking his mouth while he watched the three of us women eating and sucking each other. Then the other man in the room approached him and held out his dick for Gerald to suck, which he did willingly. I watched as my lover shoved his cock deep into the first man's mouth and dumped his come down his throat. The second man pulled out of Gerald's mouth and shot a load of jism all over his chest.

The blonde girl leaped off the bed and started licking the come off Gerald's chest, sharing it with the second man, who turned out to be her husband. Gerald walked over and kissed me deeply. I could taste the dick he'd been sucking, and he could taste the blonde's pussy on my tongue. We gave each other a reassuring and loving smile at the turn our love-making had taken.

After having a couple more drinks, we found an empty room and started kissing and groping each other. In a few minutes a couple walked in and asked if they could watch. The idea of strangers watching *us* fuck made me so hot! It must have excited Gerald too, because we really went at each other. He was already fucking my ass when the man walked up to us and pulled out his cock for me to suck. I turned around to look at Gerald, and he was smiling. "Go ahead, suck him," he said.

Like a good little whore, I took the stranger's cock in my mouth and started to blow him. This turned Gerald on so much that he quickly came up my ass. The man asked Gerald if he could taste his come in my ass. Gerald smiled and said, "By all means, go ahead."

As the man moved behind me, Gerald went over to the woman, who was busily fingerfucking herself. My lover helped her out by kissing her breasts and fingering her pussy along with her. I watched them, more turned on than ever. Meanwhile the strange man knelt behind me and started eating my cunt and my asshole, pushing his tongue deep inside each of them in turn, sucking the sperm out of me as I came over and over and over.

The man then asked Gerald if he could fuck me, but Gerald was so busy eating the woman's cunt that I didn't know whether he heard the question or not. "Yes, go ahead and do it!" I said to the stranger. "Do it! Fuck me good and hard!" He then thrust his cock inside me and plowed me hard and fast, bringing me to orgasm several more times as he commented on how good it felt to be fucking it.

Gerald was soon fucking the stranger's wife. She yelled as she came, and then told him she needed a break. But Gerald was just getting started. He came over and asked me to get on top of the stranger. When I did, he got behind me and worked his prick into my ass. They were both fucking me so good! I could feel their cocks going in and out of me, and it drove me wild.

At that point another couple came in and decided to join us. The woman went over and started licking the stranger's wife's pussy, while the man stood in front of me and gave me his cock to suck. I had three cocks in me at once, filling all my holes, and it was the hottest and most erotic thing I had ever experienced. The three of them came almost at the same time, and I found myself with a smile on my face and my pussy, ass and mouth full of come.

We spent the rest of the weekend doing even more. We're really looking forward to our next trip.—*V.S., Lansing, Michigan* ⊶▪

HE SETS UP A BASKETBALL GAME WITH A SPECIAL TROPHY FOR THE WINNER: HIS WIFE

*M*y wife Stephanie is a beautiful, petite thirty-year-old brunette, and we've been married for ten years. About five years ago we started talking about Stephanie's fantasy of being gang-banged by a group of young studs. I always enjoyed the effect these discussions had on her, so I agreed that for our tenth wedding anniversary, which would also be the weekend of her thirtieth birthday, I would arrange for her fantasy to come true.

I work part-time at the gym on a military base, where every Friday night there was a pickup basketball game between five black Marines and five white sailors. I began to put my plan into action by asking the ten studs to schedule their game for after closing time one Friday and telling them that I'd provide a very special and interesting trophy for the winners. They must have had some idea of what I had in mind, because they agreed willingly.

I then told Stephanie to show up that night in her sexy tennis outfit: a short skirt with white-cotton panties and a cotton shirt that, when worn with no bra, shows off her large nipples.

When Friday night came, I closed the weight room early and set up a video-camera. Stephanie and I had agreed that this was to be a one-time event, and we wanted to be able to enjoy it over and over again.

The guys were just warming up in the gym when Stephanie walked in. She looked a little nervous but fantastically sexy. I wasn't sure how she would feel when she saw the ten guys who would soon be filling her with come. She had never slept with a black man, but just by watching the Marines taking their practice shots, I could tell that was about to change real soon.

The guys were thrilled to find out that the trophy I'd promised them was my wife. I explained that the contest was to be a simple game of twenty-one points, with the winners getting to fuck her pussy while the losers (if you could call them that) would have to settle for blowjobs. For an added twist, the winners and losers would pair off, each pair taking her in her mouth and pussy at the same time. The guy in each pair who could refrain from coming the longest could fuck her ass as a bonus.

I could see that Stephanie was going crazy watching ten sweating studs with erections trying to win her favors as a sex trophy. Finally the Marines won the right to her pussy by a score of twenty-one to fifteen.

I moved behind her and whispered, "Enjoy," as I pulled her shirt over her head, exposing her breasts. She smiled at the gasps and moans that came as they looked at her. I took her hand and led her into the weight room, the others following to claim their prize.

I had the five black Marines line up on one side of a weight bench, with the five white sailors on the other side. Then I bent my wife over it, crouching on all fours by the side of the bench for support. I gently kissed her as she looked into my eyes and told me she loved me. I then prepared her to be gang-fucked by ten horny studs.

I lifted her skirt and pulled down her panties, exposing her wet, shaved pussy and the first Marine and the first sailor in line pulled down their shorts. Stephanie moaned in anticipation as she got a look at two of the cocks that were about to invade her body.

I watched with mixed emotions as the Marine positioned the purple head of his tool at my wife's pussy and slowly pushed it in. A low moan escaped her lips, but her open mouth was quickly filled with the sailor's erection. With encouragement from their teammates, they began to fuck her really hard. Her body moved in rhythm with the Marine's thrusts, but from the way her lips and tongue were working on the cock in her mouth, I knew she'd be having mostly black cock up her ass, because her oral talents would make short work of the sailors.

Sure enough, within five minutes she was drinking her first load of come. The still-hard Marine pulled out of her pussy reluctantly, although he was willing to wait for the tight little ass that he had been looking at while he was fucking her.

The second pair moved into place and started to work her over. I stroked her hair and played with her nipples as I watched her dream come true. She soon began to shake with her first orgasm of the evening. Once again the sailor in her mouth was the first to come.

Stephanie continued to experience a strong orgasm with each new set of cocks. The third Marine's cock was larger than anything she had ever taken. As she cried out in ecstasy under his hard, steady strokes, she kept letting the cock in her mouth fall out. The Marine finally shot into her pussy and the sailors cheered, happy to know that at least one of them would have her ass.

The fourth team fucked her steadily, both guys trying to hold out for her ass, but as with the first and second teams, the sailor fucking her mouth lost out to her cocksucking talents.

As I was watching the last Marine push himself into my wife's pussy, I heard her give a gasp. I looked up to see that she was staring at the last sailor's cock, which was a real monster. She was hardly able to get her mouth around it, let alone suck it off. I wondered if she could take that thing up her ass if, as seemed likely, he was the winner of this round. Sure enough, the Marine in her pussy didn't last ten strokes.

The five winners, hard-ons in hand, lined up at the foot of the weight bench as I put my wife on her back with her legs spread wide. Using the come dripping from her pussy to lubricate her, I started worked my fingers into her asshole. She thrust her ass back against me as she told them to come and claim their prize.

The first guy lined up his cock and slowly pushed it into her back tunnel. She made a hissing sound as he moved inside her. I bent down to kiss her, and then I played with her breasts as the Marine shot into her ass.

Stephanie climaxed as the second guy fucked her, and she came again with the third. I enjoyed watching her and hearing her gasps and moans of ecstasy. The fourth guy didn't take very long, and then it was the fifth sailor's turn.

Even though the come from the four previous cocks had left her stretched-out ass pretty well-lubed, I still wasn't sure she could take that monster cock and asked her if she wanted to call it off. But Stephanie said no. She was panting with anticipation as she gazed at his tool. She was so hot for it that she went further. She told him that if he could bury his cock inside her to the balls, she'd let the five losers have her ass also.

I could only watch as the sailor's giant dick began to push her asshole open. Just as the massive head pushed past her anus, she had the most violent orgasm I had ever seen. Everyone in the room watched in awe as, inch by inch, she took his cock up her ass until his balls slapped against her cheeks with every thrust. As he continued to plow into her, she started to suck the five cocks that would also have their turn in her ass.

When the sailor finally shot his load up her backside and pulled his spent cock out of her dripping asshole, she crawled over to me and pushed me down onto a mat on the floor. "Now it's your turn," she said as she lowered her pussy onto my aching cock.

I finished the night enjoying the feeling of my wife lying on me with my cock in her pussy as five more cocks filled her ass with come. With each new climax Stephanie looked into my eyes and said, "Thank you."

We often look back at that night and enjoy watching the tape of her taking on those ten young studs. The guys often ask me when they can have another such contest, and when I mention that to Stephanie it gets so hot that I can't help thinking it's got to happen again.—*B.R., San Diego, California*

www.ingramcontent.com/pod-product-compliance
Lightning Source LLC
Chambersburg PA
CBHW010646100726
47901CB00009B/2451